I0612067

The Time Dragons Trilogy

A Time for Dragons
Dragons Past
No Future for Dragons

by

GARY GENTILE

Chimaera Bookworks
P.O. Box 57137
Philadelphia, PA 19111

Additional copies of this book may be purchased from the same address by sending a check or money order in the amount of $25 U.S. for each copy (plus $4 for domestic shipping per order, not per book). For a list of available titles that can be ordered online and paid by credit card, visit the author's website:

http://www.ggentile.com

Cover art by Charles R. Knight

Contents:

International Standard Book Numbers (ISBN)
1-883056-36-5
978-1-883056-36-0

Original copyrights - 1985, 1989, 1989

Printed in the U.S.A.

A Time
for Dragons

CHAPTER 1

"Rusty, I'm going to need a hand pulling this motor." Scott raised a greasy hand to his broad forehead and, with the back of his wrist, rubbed an itch below his blond crewcut. He laid down the worn socket wrench and spun free the last nut holding the motor mount in place. When he finished scratching, he used both brawny hands to crank the motor out from under the cowling. An overhead vent pushed air gently across his face and evaporated tiny beads of perspiration. He picked up a rag and wiped his sticky palms on it, then unscrewed the shiny metal end cap.

Rusty sat at a computer console, typing with frenzied concentration. "Okay, I'm almost done with the exercise. I'm having a little trouble with the velocity-matching equations. The computer keeps throwing in variables." Scott could see that his mousy features were piqued. Pale skin reflected the cool fluorescent light.

"I got a little bit of that last week." Scott used a screwdriver to pry the shims apart and slide them along the steel shaft. "But I only had to worry about fuel consumption on the attitude controls—not vector analysis. It was enough to make me glad I'm taking missile maintenance rather than flight programming. Hey, while you're there, key in the work order and find out whether we're supposed to change the armature or just clean it."

"Will do. I'm tired of this anyway. I'll pick it up later down in my room. Maybe I can get Dad to help me." His fingers flicked over the keyboard with unerring speed.

Scott knew his job and did it efficiently. The four big air compressors and attendant ventilator and filter systems were rigidly maintained. They were the mechanical hearts that pumped the lifeblood into Maccam City, and kept its two thousand underground inhabitants alive. With each compressor in a separate quadrant, the city

could function without difficulty on any three, and squeeze by on two for a while: there were always bottled reserves. But it paid to never let them go too long without a complete checkup.

Rusty read the video screen. "It says here that it should be inspected, and replaced or repaired at technician's discretion."

"Good. That means me, and I don't think it looks too bad. We'll just sand the commutator, file the grooves, and shove it back in place. And I'll be home in time for Mom's apple pie—while it's still hot. I can smell it now." He raised his nostrils into the airflow.

Scott was glad to take the easy way out. The ten-horsepower motor weighed easily a ton, so that temporary replacement required setting up a block and tackle, as well as maneuvering hoisting dollies. But the carbon traces could be filed off with a sanding block while one of them rotated the armature manually. He could change the brushes by himself in a few minutes.

"Nice try, Scott. But I happen to know that you have a date with Becky tonight. Faron told me."

Scott blushed. "Sometimes I don't think that kid sister of yours has enough to keep her occupied. She spends too much time snooping." Under such confined living conditions, where everyone was physically close, Scott sometimes found it galling that everyone knew his business, his habits, his likes and dislikes. He was reminded of the differences of opinion between his father and Rusty's: between expansionism and continued incest, as his father stated it in his blacker moods. It just was not right for people to live in one another's laps.

"She doesn't snoop—she just listens."

"I wouldn't mind her plastering her ear to everyone's cubicle so much if she didn't blab everything she hears."

Rusty smiled. "Oh, she doesn't tell *all* she hears—not to everyone, that is."

"Just tell me what else is on the maintenance agenda."

Rusty stared at the monitor. "Oil the louvers and check the linkage, recalibrate the dampers, clean all the relay contacts—wow, what a bore—and vacuum the breaker panels. Then, we have to—"

Rusty stopped reading. For a moment the only sound Scott could hear was the whirring of auxiliary machinery and the clacking of contactors and relay switches. He looked up from his work. "What's the matter?"

Red eyebrows pinched over Rusty's freckled face. "I don't know. The computer just went off line." Long, delicate fingers ran over control buttons lining the side of the console.

"What?" Scott put down his screwdriver, wiped his hands on the rag, and walked to the user terminal. Over Rusty's shoulder he stared at the blank screen.

"I've reset the power switch and tested the input channels, but they're all dead. And I'm getting no response from any of the mode switches. It doesn't make sense."

Scott stuffed the rag into a baggy patch pocket, next to the flashlight. "That's strange. I've never seen that happen before. What do you think it is?"

Rusty pushed the chair back on its slider. "I don't know, but I'm going to check the terminal blocks."

Sitting on .his knees in front of the console, he turned the thumbscrews that held the front access panel in place. Just as he pulled off the metal cover, the lights in the room dimmed.

"Nice going, Rusty. I don't know what you did, but you'd better undo it fast."

"I haven't touched anything yet." Rusty leaned the panel against the console pedestal. "What the heck is going on?"

Scott looked up at the flickering fluorescent lights, caught in the voltage drop. "Whatever it is, it's weird."

No sooner had he spoken than the lights went off altogether. Scott felt a tingling sensation run the length of his spine. For a moment the darkness was absolute. Then battery power took over and the emergency lights kindled on. The room was a contrast of black shadows and narrow white beams of light. Rusty was silhouetted with one hand in the act of reaching into the control panel.

"Listen!" Scott tried to shout but it came out

a whisper. He heard no machinery whirring, no contactors clacking, not even the minute buzz of arcing switches. And the whooshing of forced air that was subliminal to him was still. He dashed across the room to the workbench near the partly disconnected main drive motor. He thrust his hand below the vent. "It's stopped. Rusty, the air has stopped."

A three-dimensional picture of the city's ventilation system flashed through Scott's mind with tortured ease. Air drawn in from the surface, by means of great compressors, was pumped down hundreds of feet to the maze of underground passageways and the warren of cramped cubicles. It had to pump continuously or the inhabitants would soon suffocate.

"Let's check the power leads!" Rusty let the access panel slip to the floor, and vaulted past Scott. "There must be something wrong with this sector."

Squeezing through the crowded mechanical room, winding around auxiliary motors, exposed belts, and miscellaneous machinery, all of which was now still, Scott followed Rusty to the darkened corner where the main power distribution panels were crammed. A bank of tall metal cabinets housed circuit breakers, contactors, relays, control switches, and manual bypasses. The annunciator panel, which should have been lit up like a Christmas tree with red and green indicating lights, was blank.

Scott pulled the flashlight out of his pocket and bent over the instrument board. "The ammeter's dead. The voltmeter's dead. Nothing's coming through."

"There's got to be *something*." Rusty touched the gauges as if that would actuate them. "What'll we do?"

Scott took two steps to a nearby intercom station. He flipped a toggle and spoke into an acoustic diaphragm. "Compressor room three to central processing, come in please." After five seconds that seemed like an eternity, he repeated the command. "Compressor room three to central processing, come in please."

Rusty's eyes were as big as saucers. "The whole sector must be blocked off!"

"Yes, but they must know it by now. They'd have to. It would register on their monitors right away."

"But they might not know how bad it is until they run a check. Let's get down below and make a verbal report."

Scott could see the sense in that. "We'll probably bump into a contingency crew on their way up. And they'll need every hand they can get."

"Then we'll turn around and come back up with them. But if the problem is down there, that's where they'll need us."

"You're right." From early childhood Scott had been drilled against every possible emergency, had been trained to think clearly and act decisively. "Let's go."

Scott led the way through a nearby doorway, ducking under the low lintel. He ran along a corridor that was only slightly wider than his broad shoulders. Fifty feet away, he slammed into the door at the end of the passageway and practically flung it off its hinges.

Beyond was a closet-sized room that was packed with exposed conduits and electrical panels, one dim emergency light, and two steel doors that sealed off the elevator shaft and the stairwell. Scott's stocky finger gouged the recessed button. When nothing happened, he punched the button again.

Rusty opened the door of a small distribution panel. He reset the breakers by flipping them off, then on again. "The power's out here, too. The elevator's out of commission."

Scott wrenched open the adjacent door and charged into the stairwell. He barely reached the first step when he coughed and stopped abruptly. A vile, stinging vapor rose up the shaft, glowing green in the weak beam of the lone emergency light, and curled around his soft-soled slippers.

He inhaled only a whiff of it, but that was enough to send him staggering backward through the door, blinded and gagging. He tripped and fell headlong on the concrete floor. As he rolled out of the way, Rusty shoved the steel door shut: a momentary respite against the noxious fumes.

Rusty knelt by his friend and grasped his shoulders with both hands. "Scott, are you all right?" Rusty had breathed only from the periphery of the acidic gas, but it had felt like swallowing nettles. "Wha—what is that stuff?"

Scott sucked in great lungfuls of fresh air. Slowly, the prickly pain subsided. "I don't know, but we've got to warn them. It's coming up the—"

Rusty finished for him. "If it's coming up the shaft, the whole city must be inundated with it."

"But what could cause—" Scott had no time

to finish his thought. The strange green vapor started seeping around the edges of both doors, eating through the rubber gaskets that kept the city hermetically sealed. As Scott watched, gray paint flecked off the sills and iron turned orange with rust. The doors became pockmarked with pinholes where the gaseous acid was eating through metal and dissolving steel.

An instant later the green gas flowed out the pipe shafts. Electrical panels foamed, plastic breakers melted. With a crash the elevator door fell in as its hinges were consumed. It hit Scott a terrible blow on the head and shoulder, and scraped Rusty's cheek. The virulent vapor boiled into the tiny room.

A blast of pungent gas hit him in the face. Rusty howled with pain and fell back, rubbing his eyes. Scott, still under the hissing metal, felt tears rolling down his cheeks. He threw aside the heavy door. "Come on, let's get out of here." He grabbed Rusty by the arm, pulled him out of the room, and dragged him along the paneled corridor.

The gas curled wraithlike along the floor, green fingers that destroyed everything that lingered in its path. Terminal blocks and copper wires were eaten away. The emergency light winked out.

Stumbling with his burden, Scott pushed Rusty into the mechanical room. The redhead slipped to the floor, retching violently. Scott slammed the door and leaned hard against it, as if that would hold back the noxious gas. For the moment he gathered his strength, thankful for the air that gave him life. But the reprieve was short-lived.

At his back, the door started making crackling sounds. Rusty looked up from the floor with tear-filled eyes. Scott moved away from the noisy barrier, staring in the dim, gray light as the green vapor seeped through the metal trim. The steel door groaned and warped. BB-sized holes burst through the metal. Gas hissed out like steam through a broken radiator.

"Let's go." Scott grabbed Rusty's arm as he raced by and jerked him to his feet. In the middle of the machine-filled room, Scott stopped. He stared at the still blank computer screen. The dead console represented the city, the people. *His* people.

He turned and looked at Rusty. Rusty's words echoed his own thoughts. "There's nowhere to go but—outside."

CHAPTER 2

To Rusty's knowledge, the emergency exit to the outside had never been opened. It had been practically forgotten for over a century—ever since the great plague, the result of human folly and biological warfare, had wiped out mankind. The barrier that had protected them all these years was now working against them.

Rusty jiggled the massive handle to no avail. "There must be a key here somewhere."

At the other end of the room, the corridor door fell off dissolving hinges and crashed in smoldering ruins. White smoke boiled off the linoleum; the floor buckled as the underpinnings crumbled.

Scott bent to inspect the timeworn lock. "If there is, I never heard of it. Grab some tools." Then, amid the sizzling sounds of disintegrating electrical parts, collapsing stanchions, and the sagging of heavy machinery, he ran and got them himself.

At Rusty's feet he flung down a metal box full of sockets and wrenches. "Try these." There were no exposed nuts or bolts; the latch itself folded back and covered them. Rusty scrounged a plastic-handled screwdriver and tried ineffectually to bend the latch out far enough to get at the screws underneath.

The deadly, green vapor crept across the floor, enveloping everything like a hungry demon. The hissing and breaking-up noises sounded like the gnashing of giant teeth.

Rusty shook his head. "Socket tools are useless. We need something heavy. A chisel, or something."

Scott stared at him for a moment, then darted back to the workbench. He returned with a box full of hammers, chisels, and pry bars, and dumped them on the floor. "Let's try the bruiser tools."

Rusty jammed a three-foot crowbar behind the latch, but the thick metal would not bend. "It's no use. It's tempered steel. Try the hinges."

He glanced over his shoulder at the advancing green menace. Sheet metal disappeared as if it were paper going up in flames; massive pipe racks broke away as their supports melted. The gas reached the computer console and attacked its delicate electronic components. Plastic parts softened, contacts fused, resistors and diodes broke down, chips became unstable. Insulation dripped off to leave copper wires gleaming, then the copper itself began to pit and corrode.

Scott picked up a long chisel and a heavy mallet. There were no screws on the hinges; the large pistons were welded to the framework the same as a vault door. He banged away along the tempered bead.

Rusty coughed. The first tendrils of pungent vapor reached him. He ignored the irritation in his eyes, continuing to look for another way out. He picked up the crowbar. "Scott, the intake shaft. It's our only chance."

The room was practically eclipsed as the green, poisonous gas rose to the ceiling and hovered thickly around the self-contained battery packs. One by one the emergency lights fizzled and went out.

Sneaking around the main compressor, Rusty led the way to where only a sheet-metal plenum separated them from the great air shaft that fed the city. Huge removable filters were taken out periodically and cleaned. The slit opening that was left when they were withdrawn doubled as an access trunk to the air ducts; accumulated dust was vacuumed out on a regular basis.

Rusty slipped the crowbar through the handle. The retaining clip that kept the filters from vibrating out was held in place by six hefty sheet-metal screws. Already the screwdriver was rusting away as the green gas billowed past the emergency exit.

Icy hands pushed him out of the way. Scott placed the point of the chisel against the first screw head. One mighty whack of the sledgehammer sheared it right off. In a few seconds he broke all six of them. Together they pulled the hundred-pound filter out on its track and sent it crashing to the floor.

With corrosive gas literally nipping at his heels, Rusty plunged into the darkness of the air duct. He started coughing right away, but this time it was because of the fine dust that he had stirred. Now he wished that he had done a better job of vacuuming the month before.

Scott stepped in beside him and thumbed on the flashlight. "This way." He used the beam as a pointer. A green mist was slowly dispersing through the compressor vanes, where the vertical shaft plunged into the depths of the city.

The horizontal connector extended fifty feet to the outside riser. An oily residue offered unsure footing. Static dust clung to the walls. At the far end of the plenum, a series of rungs that were bolted to the wall led upward. Rusty heard loud crashes from the crumbling machine room, and saw a trace of deadly gas explore the filter opening.

With only the weak light to see by, Scott started climbing. The wrought-iron rungs were dust laden with an underpinning of aerated grease, making them slippery. He went only a few feet when the yellow glow disclosed a screen mesh blocking the shaft. The hinged gate was barely visible under a century of accumulated dirt and rust. Looping his arm through a metal rung for support, he wiped the barrier clean with his rag. "Oh, no. It's locked."

Rusty saw the glint of the brass mechanism, and handed up the crowbar. "Use this."

Scott took the tool, slipped it through the arched shackle, and pried against the antique casing. But the years had not affected the brass workings—it was still as solid as the day it was manufactured.

The acrid odor of gas stung Rusty's nostrils. He climbed up behind Scott, shaking. His rail-like arms were not built for strength, and he was weakening fast. "Hurry it up."

Scott strained against the lock. "I'm working as fast as I can." He leaned hard against the crowbar. He pulled not only with his free arm but with his whole body weight. The lock snapped with an abruptness that caused him to topple backward. He caught himself with one hand, tucked the crowbar under the arm that was hanging onto the ladder rung, and worked the shackle out of the hasp. He pushed hard. The gate moved an inch on rusted hinges, and stopped.

Using the crowbar again, he pounded the gate open by degrees. When it swung partway out from the wall, he slipped through the gap. Then, with both feet planted on the grid, he lifted his friend through the opening.

Rusty rolled onto the grillwork and lay gasping. Gobs of dust stuck to his mop of red hair. "I need to rest. My lungs are stinging, and my arms can't take it."

"Don't give up now." Scott shone the flashlight down through the grating. The thin sheet-metal walls were melting away like butter, revealing rough-hewn rock.

Rusty rolled over, and nursed his aching arms. His shallow cheeks were twisted in pain. "You'd better get going."

* * *

Scott shone the light up the riser. Fifty feet above, a dim light filtered through another grating. "All right." With the crowbar in one hand and the flashlight in the other, he jumped onto the ladder and started climbing by hooking his wrists over the rungs. He stopped after ten feet. "Come on."

Rusty rose weakly to his feet and started up. "I'm right behind you."

Scott ascended rapidly. From the bottom of the shaft, the metal grating hissed as it dissolved in the acidic gas. "Are you all right?"

Rusty saw nothing below in the darkness. Above, Scott was a smudge clinging to the wall. "Just keep going."

Scott surged ahead. Rusty rested, and watched him stop just below the next landing. There was another gate, and another lock. He inserted the crowbar under the slider, and wrenched hard. The brass lock did not give, but the hasp ripped completely off and fell away, crashing on the disintegrating grillwork fifty feet below.

"The gate's still stuck." The metal was twisted as if some minor earth movement had jammed it in place. Scott smashed at the barrier with great upward swings of the crowbar. Loud clangs reverberated off the metal walls of the riser. The hinges remained stuck, but the screen mesh sprung out of its holding bracket. He pushed through to the landing, heedless of the sharp points that tore his clothing. "Hurry," he shouted. His voice echoed tinnily.

In the dim light that shone down, Rusty saw the green gas surging after him. He clung to the rungs with aching arms. Scott was only ten feet above him, yet he seemed so far away. Rusty scaled the ladder slowly, laboriously, reaching out for a rung, pulling himself up, and reaching out again. He thought he would never make it when suddenly Scott pulled him through the twisted grill.

He leaned back against the wall, and felt the metallic coolness through his thin suit. "I need a rest."

"There's no time." Scott shone the flashlight through the grating at his feet. There was no bottom anymore, only a green, swirling mist that beckoned menacingly. "We have to go on."

"On to what?" They had nothing to go on *to*. They were merely running away. Except for what he had seen on disk, Rusty knew no world other than the narrow confines of corridors, closets, nooks, and pigeonholes. All available living space was filled with essential computers, machinery, and life-support equipment. Walls were lined with shelving for hydroponics. All his life had been spent in a subterranean dwelling surrounded by people and imbued with constant clamor. He felt secure in cramped quarters.

Outside, space existed on a different scale. It was a cold, quiet, inhospitable world. Through history disks he had seen the endless expanse of desert, the limitless sky, the unimaginable emptiness. Outside there was nothing but barren land, torturous rocks, rugged mountains and wild rivers, burning heat and unfathomable cold. Outside was so—*uncontrolled.*

"I don't know. The unknown, I guess." Rusty could see the uncertainty on Scott's face, his bland features. Fifty more rungs led to another landing. And beyond that—what? More grates? More ladders? Rusty did not fear just the unknown; what he feared was the sheer openness. Scott put a helping hand under his arm. "But I'm not giving up. And I won't let you give up, either."

Rusty groaned, and stretched his sore muscles. "Yes, you're right. But you'd better let me go first, in case I—slip."

Scott grinned and punched him lightly on the shoulder. "You're doing fine." He helped Rusty to his feet and pushed him toward the ladder.

With the first faint tendrils of green gas rising through the grating, Rusty grabbed the lowest rung and pulled himself up. He had already climbed more than fifty feet, and there was no telling how much farther the riser went beyond the next grate. After ten rungs he stopped and rested. Then, through sheer will of mind, he climbed ten more.

Scott bumped his feet. "You're doing great." He had put away the flashlight, for now there was sufficient light filtering down from above to show the way. "But don't stop now. I can smell gas."

Rusty, too, could smell it: a few wayward molecules wafted ahead of the main body. He could also hear the dissolving metal, and pieces of the lower grate giving way and crashing down to the bottom of the riser. He climbed ten more rungs, counting each one to himself so that he could rest on the tenth. He looked up; there were only twenty more to go.

"My arms—" Something pungent entered his lungs. Sweat beaded on his forehead, and ran in rivulets under his arms. His eyes began to sting. But it had to be worse for Scott.

"Don't stop now."

Rusty climbed five more rungs. "I can't—" But when he heard Scott cough, he did. He was only ten rungs from the top before his strength waned to nearly nothing. "I'll never get the gate open."

Scott coughed again, uncontrollably. "Let—me—get—past—you."

"How?" Now Rusty went into a spasm of coughing. Oh, how his arms arched.

"Pull in close—and I'll—climb over you."

Rusty had no choice but to comply. His arms were so weak that he was afraid that he might fall at any moment. Was a quick, merciful death preferable to a choking, lingering one? Scott scrambled over him like a spider, stepping on the sides of the rungs. He climbed right up to the gate and started beating on the lock with the crowbar.

Instead of corrosion-resistant brass, this lock was case-hardened steel—and rusted solid. He inserted the crowbar under the shackle and pried. The lock remained immobile, the hasp secure. He applied a twisting motion, with more leverage, and pulled down with his whole body weight. Then he used the crowbar like a maul and beat against the lock, the hasp, and finally the gate.

A few feet below, the green gas thickened. Rusty's meager strength paled. Breathing in starts, he watched Scott's mighty efforts. The grating that covered the rest of the shaft was oddly bent, the reinforced seams separated in places. Peering through the mesh, he saw in the half-light that great sheets of rock had dropped off the natural cave roof onto the protective grating, stressing the metal to the breaking point.

"Scott, the frame—" Scott looked around, and noticed the crumbling condition of the entire gate assembly. He jammed the crowbar into a tear in the mesh, and pulled. Although the gate was independently fastened and remained unmovable, the entire framework shook around it.

"I can't—hold on—much longer." Rusty's voice was a harsh whisper. With his eyes tightly shut, he breathed through the upper fabric of his jumper, and watched helplessly as Scott worked.

"Hang in there, Rusty. I'll get through this thing yet." Holding the rung with one hand, he leaned out and pulled down on the snagged crowbar with the other. A ribbon of green gas curled up the riser. Fresh air hovered only a few feet away, but it might as well have been a mile. He took a deep breath and held it. Pulling hard, the gap opened an inch, then another. Metal screeched on metal as the welded framework slipped farther apart.

Rusty was beginning to tremble from the strain of clinging to the cast-iron supports. He was weakening from the deficiency of oxygen in the air. He stood close to the wall, so that most of his weight was on his legs. "Scott." His voice was a feeble gasp.

The shriek of tearing metal made Rusty's spine quiver. He jerked to attention and saw the crowbar ripped out of Scott's hand, saw one foot slip off the rung, saw him dangling by one sweat-covered hand. He gasped involuntarily, and took in a great lungful of fiery air. Then the entire grating, along with several tons of rock, thundered down the shaft, passing by him because of the notch left by the still standing gate. The plummeting mass took the partially dissolved remains of the next grating with it, then piled up on the floor of the riser in a great cloud of dust.

Scott regained his grip on the ladder. The green gas had been sucked down with the debris, offering a temporary respite as fresh air from outside poured in. Partially revitalized, Rusty coughed the dregs of poison from his lungs.

The only barrier in the way now was the gate that had just saved them from being torn off the ladder. Reaching out, Scott grabbed hold of the torn edge and swung out into the air. He dangled freely for a moment, then pulled himself up onto the narrow lip to which the grating had been attached. He took only a moment to catch his breath. "Come on."

Rusty clung to his perch, ten feet below. His eyes were glazed, and his grip was loosening. He could breathe, but his strength was gone. "I—can't—make—it."

"Sure you can." The green gas was already streaming back up the shaft. "It's only a few feet. You can do it."

Rusty closed his eyes, reached up, grabbed another rung. He hesitated, then pulled himself up. Scott yelled encouragement. Rusty coughed. His knees were shaking like reeds in the wind. But he reached out for another rung, pulled himself up, then reached out for another.

Rusty was no longer looking up. His head hung limply, resting on his clenched fist. His other hand groped blindly for the next rung.

"I can almost reach you." Scott leaned out over the edge and dangled his right arm. "Just a couple more steps to go."

Rusty climbed up another rung, and rested. Then he climbed another, and rested longer. The gas was getting thicker. His coughing sapped his strength. When he was within reach of the grate, he stopped.

"I'll never—get around."

"Reach for my hand," Scott ordered. Slowly, Rusty let go with one hand, and reached out. Scott caught it and guided it to the ledge where he could get a grip. "Now the other."

"I—can't—" Rusty's muscles were beyond aching—they were going numb. He was afraid to let go.

"You have to. It's the only way."

Now Rusty went into spasms, caught with one hand on the ledge and one on the ladder. His jerking weight proved too much for the ancient bolts. With a sudden wrench the rung tore out of the wall and went spinning down the deep shaft.

Rusty screamed as sweaty palms slipped off the ledge, and his body swung outward into the void. Scott's face and shoulder were slammed against the metal, but he did not let go. Instead, he clamped down harder on Rusty's wrist until the pendulum effect brought him swinging back into the wall.

Rusty grappled instinctively with his free hand and found the ledge. Fear gave him uncommon strength, and he hauled himself halfway up while Scott rolled back and added leverage to his contortions. With legs flailing against empty air, Rusty kicked hard and hooked his heel on the metal shelf. Scott grabbed the back of his collar, and Rusty squirmed right over on top of him.

As soon as they stopped flopping, two more bolts gave way and the metal ledge sagged dangerously in the middle. Rusty kept scrambling, felt solid rock under his hand, and rolled into a cold, granite floor. Scott landed beside him, breathing hard.

They were inside a low, rock-strewn cave that was flooded with bright, yellow light.

Rusty breathed deeply. He started to take stock of his surroundings when he felt a stinging sensation on his feet. The corrosive gas was still rising up the airshaft. With a gasp that gave

Scott warning, he crawled away on all fours.

His body was bruised and bleeding, his stamina was at an end. Yet somehow he inched over the sharp rocks until he reached the base of the scree below the entrance. His fingers were scraped, his nails torn. He lay there quivering like a fish out of water. Scott, he noticed, lying next to him, looked the worse for wear.

Scott glowed triumphantly. "Well, we made it."

Sucking in the hot air, Rusty was not sure what they had made. Behind him was his home, his family, his friends, the only life he had ever known. Tears welled in his eyes, this time not from the pungent gas. The awful dread of loneliness swept over him. In a matter of minutes his life had become meaningless.

Still, he was urged on toward survival. The back of the cave was filling with acrid fumes. Like an insect pursued by a relentless spider, he did not have the time to grieve. Scott got up silently and moved on. Painfully, Rusty followed him. On hands and knees he climbed up the rubble of loose rock. From the top of the pile he had his first real view of the outside.

He saw waste and desolation, craggy rocks and dry ravines, hot sand, and a frightening, infinite blue sky. And somewhere in that great beyond was the rubble of once great cities, the ruin and destruction of a once mighty civilization. It was a vast unknown. Yet, behind was certain death. Forward there was a chance of life. Rusty steeled himself to take that chance.

"Our folks—"

Scott stood tall, and faced the outer reaches. "I know." Without looking back he took a step forward, and became the first of his people in over four generations to feel the burning rays of the sun upon his tender skin.

CHAPTER 3

Scott sat on a smooth boulder whose cool surface lay close by the shadowed cliff face. "How about a short rest? I feel like a wet noodle." He pulled his arms out of the sleeves of his jumper, pushed the material down to his waist, and let the air dry his chest.

The ravines cut deep into the rocky terrain, with sheer walls that sometimes blocked the sun. Even though he knew nothing of shade, it did not take long to discover that the air was cooler

there. Aimless wandering soon pushed Rusty to despair. He would long since have given up hope for survival had it not been for Scott's dogged persistence.

"I thought you'd never ask." Rusty squatted on the uneven ground and pressed his back against the rock. The bright sun beat down unmercifully. Thirty minutes in its withering heat and he was thirsty, an hour and he was parched. Walking was easy exercise for him, but dehydration was sapping his energy. Where was there water in this barren desert?

Scott flexed muscles cramped by years of tight city living. The thin material of his one-piece uniform was pockmarked with holes where the acidic gas had eaten through it. His back was covered with red, round pustules. Yet he gave no sign of discomfort.

The sun distorted into an orange ball as it neared the horizon. Rusty was thankful that it would soon be night and the inexorable heat would be gone. The short exposure to the sun's radiation enhanced the freckles on his face, and changed his color to a glowing red. Silent and brooding, he was drifting into a shell of loneliness when he was snapped from his reverie by a sharp, loud clap.

From history disks he remembered the sound of thunder. He also remembered that it was associated with atmospheric electrical discharge. But there were no clouds in the sky, or signs of a storm approaching. Then there was another thunderclap, followed by a piercing scream.

Rusty's hackles rose and he became instantly alert. "That sounded like a man."

Scott jumped off his perch and shoved arms into his sleeves in one easy motion. "Let's go."

They ran toward the south, urged on by some deep-seated instinct. The narrow ravine curved slightly, and the high walls sloped downward until they merged with the ground. The gully emptied into a flat, boulder-strewn arena that stretched hundreds of feet across.

Again there was a loud retort, and a cry of pain. Several other ravines terminated in this natural amphitheater, and from one of them someone stumbled out, with hands thrust forward, and collapsed onto the ground. When Scott and Rusty reached him they found a small, wizened man with a blackened face and singed hair. He was wearing a tattered uniform like their own. The soles of his slippers were worn through, and the sidewalls hung ludicrously around his ankles.

The man gasped, one arm clutching spasmodically at his side. His jumper was partially burned off. His thinning hair was covered with dust, his lips dry and cracked. Scott knelt down and cradled the man's head in his lap. Rusty pulled the protective hand away from his rib cage; he gasped when he saw the horrible wound under the charred cloth. The skin was still smoldering, and the putrid scent of burnt flesh permeated the air. Rusty gagged.

The man's mouth worked futilely, but no words emerged. He coughed, and a clod of blood hit the ground and soaked into the sand. With his last remaining strength he gestured behind him. Then he slumped over and went limp. As he did so, Rusty saw another, smaller, hole in his back, as if an electrical arc had gone right through his body.

Rocks crunched up the ravine from which the man had approached. A searing beam of intense light, pencil thin, burned through the air with the smell of ozone, and exploded against the rock wall above Rusty's head. Molten droplets splattered outward like tiny brands of fire, spraying his clothing and leaving black scorch marks on material and skin.

A long shadow appeared; above it was a creature that was something out of a nightmare. Eight feet tall it stood, on two stout, slightly bent legs that thinned below the knees to raised heels with dewclaws and three-toed, splayed feet. A fat tail dragged on the ground, balancing the forward-leaning body. The bulging abdomen tapered upward to a narrow chest from which sprouted two scrawny arms which ended in taloned paws.

There was no telling where the chest ended and the neck began, but the head was supported by a long, snakelike trunk that arched upward in a slow curve. Two red, beady eyes glared out above tiny, birdlike nostrils. The mouth was a grisly, horizontal slit filled with gleaming white teeth honed to sharp points. The creature was covered with a patchwork quilt of brown and tan scales.

A flash of light sprouted from a gold-colored packet that was clutched in the right paw. A hot beam sizzled through the air between Scott and Rusty, and hit the ground with enough energy to fuse sand into glass.

Scott lurched out from under the dead man and rolled to his feet. Rusty jumped the other way with catlike agility. Together they ran across the open arena as light beams crackled from behind and licked fire at their heels.

Rusty reached the head of the ravine first, running with a fleetness that Scott could not match. Another blast of energy singed a rounded boulder, and ricocheted into the cliff face to Scott's right. He darted to the opposite wall and charged after Rusty.

The ravine twined through the desolate wasteland. The lizardlike creature dogged them relentlessly with the long reach of its flaming weapon. Rusty ran like a deer, but Scott was soon gasping for air. Before long the twists and turns took them out of the line of fire.

"I can't catch my breath." Scott sprawled across a large boulder, dripping sweat.

Rusty stopped and ran back. "We can't stop now."

"How much—of a lead—do you think—we have?"

Rusty looked down the ravine. "Not enough for me."

"Well, I can't run—forever. Let's find a place—to hide."

Rusty nodded silently. While Scott trotted along as best he could, Rusty flitted from side to side, checking rock outcrops and boulder groups. Finally, he stopped in front of an overhanging ledge that stood barely a foot in height. He dropped to his belly and scurried into what appeared to be a small cave.

He poked out his head. "Scott. In here."

Scott lay flat and worked his body into the crevice. His chest scraped dirt off, the top. "I think we're in the clear."

Rusty sat against the back wall where the ceiling was high enough for him to crouch. He felt much more comfortable in the cave, surrounded by close, solid walls. The agoraphobia was telling on him. He drew his knees up to his chin, and listened. Several minutes passed in silence. Just as the tension was beginning to wear off, he heard a scraping sound outside. He got down low so he could see out the opening.

The reptilian creature slithered past on its two bulky legs, the long tail making a track in the dirt. The periscopelike head veered from side to side, but the bumpy lidded eyes did not see their hideaway.

The gold packet in its paw was attached by a shiny metallic cord that passed under the right arm to a square, contoured box that it wore on its humped back. Stout straps arched over the narrow shoulders, crisscrossed the chest, and went around the bulbous waist, holding the box firmly in place. A moment later the beast passed out of view.

Scott rolled up on his side, facing Rusty. "What was that thing?"

Rusty slid to the back of the cave and curled into a fetal position. "I don't know. I've never seen anything like it."

"Let's hope we don't see it again." Scott pulled out the flashlight and sat up. He thumbed the switch, and slashed the beam through the dank air. The shelter was twenty feet long and ten feet deep, but the way the ceiling sloped near the back, some of the space was inaccessible.

"Where there's one there's bound to be more." Rusty felt secure in the cave, as if he were back in his cubicle and the lights had been dimmed for sleep. In fact, it was getting dark now that the sun stood almost below the distant ridges. The coolness of the cave was a welcome relief. He kept a wary eye on the low entrance.

Scott explored a far crevice. "That was Roger, you know."

"*Who* was Roger?"

Scott worked his way back until he was crouched next to Rusty. He picked up some withered strings that looked like dried stems, or perhaps roots. "That man back there."

Very quickly, coolness was giving way to chill. "You mean, Roger the motor mechanic?"

Scott continued to study the curled strings. "He must have been working in one of the other ventilator rooms."

"Then—others might have escaped?"

Scott picked up more of the curious strings, some still green. "Maybe."

"We've got to look. We've got to find them. Alone out here—"

"Ah-*ha*." Leaning on his haunches, Scott shone the light at the low ceiling. Between Rusty and him, a patch of moss clung tenaciously to the gritty sandstone, a colony of tiny tendrils with white spore caps growing down. "Well look at this." As he flashed the beam around, it became evident that there was not just one cluster, but many.

Rusty ignored the discovery. He was close to hysteria. "Scott, we've got to go look for the others."

"We've got to survive first."

"But we need them." Rusty's skin was like ice

under the remnants of his jumper. The unbearable heat of the day was escaping rapidly in the dry, nighttime air. "We need them."

"Snap out of it, Rusty. We're no good to anyone dead." He pulled Rusty close and pointed the flashlight beam at the ceiling. Glistening drops of water, condensed in the cool air of the cave, collected on the stems and ran down to the enlarged tips. Each clump of moss was a miniature sponge. "We need water, and food. We need to stay out of the way of—whatever that thing is out there. And we're not going to do anything until morning. So take it easy. Let's just wait and see what happens."

Rusty wanted to wake up from this terrible dream. "Sure, Scott. I'm—I'm sorry. I'm just not—well, I'm just frightened."

Scott put a reassuring hand on Rusty's shoulder. "Don't worry about it. We're both a little spooked. I'm just as scared as you are. But we've got to face up to it. We have no choice. Maybe tomorrow—"

Rusty felt momentary solace. "Thanks, Scott. Thanks. I'm just glad I'm not alone."

"Don't worry about it. Now, what do you say we take a drink and get some sleep?" He pressed his lips to a patch of moss and sucked loudly.

Rusty followed his example. The water was bitter, tainted with iron, but it was wet. He slurped greedily. The pangs of hunger still gnawed at his stomach, but at least his thirst was quenched.

After they sucked the moss dry, Rusty said, "You know, I'm actually freezing?"

"And I thought it was only me." Scott wrapped his arms about his chest. He turned off the flashlight and lay it down.

In the darkness, Rusty could imagine that he was back in his cubicle—that none of this was happening. But the illusion fled when he stretched out on the cold, hard floor. Sore muscles ached, cuts and bruises throbbed, his skin was on fire. And outside, as stones cooled and contracted, they snapped in the stillness in a way that reminded him of those terrible lightning bolts. He slid down next to Scott and, side by side, they lay on the dirt-covered stone, touching for warmth.

He had no idea of where they would go, what they would eat, or how they would find water. Throughout his youth, the simple amenities of life had always been provided. Like everyone else, he had had to tend the hydroponic gardens, maintain well pumps and air compressors, help manufacture goods, make repairs, and learn a multitude of occupations. Each individual was a functioning unit of the whole, with a basic understanding of the complex and delicate balance of life in Maccam City.

Never had Rusty had to fend for himself. There had always been those more knowledgeable to be questioned, or more experienced to look up to. There had been father and mother to comfort him, brothers and sisters to confide in, aunts and uncles and nephews and nieces and cousins to provide different degrees of love and a sense of belonging. Now he was on his own, full of fears and self-doubts. He was glad that he had Scott's strength to rely upon.

Rusty did not fall asleep for many hours. For the first time in his life he felt heat, cold, hunger, and thirst. For the first time he experienced fear and loneliness. And for the first time, he did not know what tomorrow might bring.

CHAPTER 4

"Ooooh. Rusty, I sure hope you feel better than I do."

Rusty stirred, but emitted only a groan.

Scott sat up, shivering and racked with pain. His back felt like ice from lying on the cold ground. He reached for the light switch, but jerked back his hand when it smashed against the jagged rock wall. For a moment he sat still in the darkness: staring, feeling, remembering. Gradually, he rolled onto his hands and knees and crawled out of the cave. The sun already flooded the ravine with delicious warmth.

"Rusty, come on out." He chafed his stiffened limbs and managed to work out some of the chill. A couple minutes of calisthenics left him breathing hard, but feeling good. Then he crawled back into the cave and shone his light into Rusty's face.

Rusty's eyes were half closed and his hair was twisted into knots that shot out at odd angles. "I feel awful."

"You look awful. But a little exercise will make you feel better."

"I'm too sore to exercise. And my face stings like the devil."

Scott sat cross-legged on the ground. "Sunburn. I had a taste of it once when I fell asleep under an infrared lamp."

"So what do we do about it?" Rusty curled tighter into a ball.

"I plucked some moss off the ceiling during the night, and held it against my face. Here. It's soft and cool."

Rusty took the patch of moss and dabbed it on his reddened skin. "Any sign of that thing?"

"I forgot all about it, but I'll check." He squeezed back out and scanned the length and breadth of the ravine. He studied the ground, but was not able to discern any tracks that the beast might have left. "I don't see anything. Come on, it's nice and warm out here."

Rusty peeked out warily, squinting in the bright sunlight. "Where do you think it went?"

"I don't know. I don't even know where it came from."

Rusty slowly eased out of the opening. He got to his feet and walked in a slow circle, hunched over like a gnome. "I want to go back."

"Back where?"

"Back to where we found—Roger. There may be others wandering around."

"But that's suicide. I don't want to bump into that thing again. I think we should keep going."

Rusty stood straighter now, but still grimaced. "Keep going where? This way, the way that lizard went? What makes you think it isn't still up there, waiting for us?"

"Well—"

"Maybe it was on its way home. We don't know that. We don't know anything about it. And we can't assume anything. It's just as likely to be behind us as in front of us. Or maybe they're all around us. No, I say we go back and look around. We have to be careful, and keep our eyes open. But we have to see if there are any others."

Scott ran his hand through his short hair. "I guess it doesn't make any difference which way we go. All right—but I'm going to carry a couple of rocks just in case."

What he would do with the rocks, if they came across another creature, he was not certain. He had never attacked anyone—or anything—in his life. Yet, in a different sense, he had spent his whole life preparing to attack.

They stayed long enough to drink whatever water had accumulated in the moss overnight. Then they cautiously picked their way along the ravine. After thirty minutes, with the converging of ravines nowhere in sight, they sat down to reason it out.

"This doesn't seem familiar to me," Rusty said.

Scott looked around, shaking his head slowly. "These ravines have so many twists and turns and offshoots—and they all look alike. We might be walking in circles."

"I don't suppose there's a food dispenser anywhere around?"

Scott placed a hand on his own grumbling stomach. The mention of food reminded him of apple pie; apple pie reminded him of his mother; his mother reminded him of . . . Those kinds of thoughts would lead to madness, he thought. "I'd settle for a raw leaf and a drink of water." He wiped sweat off his brow. "Or just a drink of water."

Rusty indicated the rock wall to his left. "Why don't we climb to the top of this hill and see where we are?"

"Good idea." Scott led the way, climbing slowly so as not to get too far ahead of Rusty, and so he could point out handholds and footholds. Despite the aches and pains, thirst and hunger pangs, he felt strong. He had a strange sense of going somewhere.

The view from the top revealed in one direction an almost infinite plateau, and in the other a land broken by draws and gullies. The sky was a deep blue studded with white clouds that hugged the flat horizon. The land was a light brown with rock outcrops that were a dark shade of gray.

"Doesn't it look green over that way?" Scott pointed across the plateau.

"I can't tell. My eyes are a little blurry."

Scott surveyed the sparse flora: tiny shoots only inches high, and patches of wiregrass. "Well, where there's vegetation there's wa—" Suddenly the air vibrated with a curious, deep thrumming. Scott looked around, shading his eyes with his hand.

"Look! Over there!" Rusty pointed over the canyon land from which they had just walked. "What's that?"

In the sky, a golden dot reflected the sun. It panned above the craggy desert on a shimmering heat wave, approaching closer and looming larger, but still too far away to be distinct.

"I'm not sure, but I'll bet it's—alien." For a moment, Scott thought that this was why Maccam City had existed for all these years, and he longed to be arming a missile to shoot down the invader. But the word foreign did not seem to fit this particular menace, not since they had run into that monster yesterday. The world was not the way he had been taught—it was much, much worse. "Let's take cover!"

Scott found a crevice in which they could both fit. It provided shade as well as protection while they watched the flying perambulations of the alien machine.

"Do you think it's looking for us?" Rusty said.

Scott shrugged. "Or other survivors—if there were any." He lapsed into silence. He did not want to say too much for fear of getting up Rusty's hopes. They had escaped by the sheerest coincidence of being on maintenance duty at the time of the attack. Roger must have been repairing a motor in one of the other compressor rooms. The lizards had tracked him down with little effort, and Scott did not intend to fall into the same trap.

The golden dot flitted back and forth across the sky for an hour before the thrumming muted with distance and the object receded from view. When they emerged from concealment, Scott turned away from the direction in which the machine had flown off, and headed toward the plateau where he thought he could see a touch of green.

"Well, I guess we know where we're going."

"No we don't. We just know where we're going away from."

"Have it your own way."

"But what if there are others? How are we going to find them if we don't stay and look for them?"

"Rusty, we don't even know where we are. We can't find anything in this wilderness. We can't live without food and water, and that's what we have to look for. We have to keep going. I don't know where, I just know that we won't find anything by sitting still."

By mid afternoon, Scott did not think that walking would solve their problems, either. There was no shade at all in the rough, rocky terrain, and the sun poured down unrelenting heat. His tongue felt like a ball of cotton in his mouth. His sores stung as sweat deposited salt into the wounds. His sunburned face and hands were a bright cherry red, and the skin was blistered. His feet were constantly tormented by pebbles and sharp rocks; the soft soles of his slippers were almost worn through. And the knees and elbows of his jumper were torn from scrambling over rocks: the material was delicate and was not designed for rough outdoor life.

Still, because there was nothing else to do, they kept going. Then Scott spotted something on the ground besides the dry, twisted sprigs. "Look. A flower." He stooped low and inspected the yellow blossom. As did everyone in Maccam City, Scott had a good knowledge of botany and horticulture.

"It doesn't look like anything I've ever seen before." Rusty fingered a pointed leaf. "Ouch!" He drew his hand back sharply. "It bit me."

"Plants don't bite." Scott got down on hands and knees and examined the leaf closely. "It's covered with little hairs, probably razor sharp."

Rusty plucked the tiny filaments from his fingertip. "I don't think it's edible."

"I agree. But maybe that is." Scott pointed to a twelve-inch bulbous tube that grew next to a boulder. As he approached it, he reached through his memory for identification. "It must be a baby cactus."

"Yeah, don't these things grow twenty feet tall?"

"Hey, there's another one. Rusty, let's get up this hill where we can see."

A moment later they were surrounded by sparse, crinkly vegetation and gnarled, stunted trees. More of the cactuses were here, as well as some larger ones. Several were in bloom, their yellow petals unfolded to catch the rays of the sun. And the ground was covered with a variety of grass.

"It's a forest," Rusty said.

"Yes, and if we only had a processor we could grind it into extract." Scott plucked some flowers and shoved them into his mouth. He chewed thoughtfully for a moment. "Well, it's not great, but—"

"Forget the flowers. Let's see if we can find some water."

"Good idea." Scott plucked another flower anyway. He plodded over the soft sand after Rusty. "There must be a stream around somewhere."

They walked quickly, going deeper into the woods where the trees grew thicker and the vegetation taller. Forgotten now were the aches and pains, the cuts and bruises. They jogged along through the stunted forest until they bounded into a cliffside clearing—

—and ran right into an eight-foot-tall, scaled lizard!

The monster was walking parallel to the rock face, looking upward, when it swung its snake-like head in their direction. It made a creepy, sibilant sound, reached behind its back, and brought its huge paw around clutching a gold firing capsule.

Scott and Rusty jumped away from each other at the same time that there came a crackle of thunder and a blast of fire. Where they had been standing was now a molten puddle, slowly solidifying, while droplets of searing sand were spewed up into the air.

Rusty, in his eagerness to get out of the way, struck his foot against a protruding root. He went down hard, air whooshing out of his lungs. The reptile swerved the gun in his direction.

Scott was momentarily paralyzed, the rocks hanging limply in his hands. Then he leaped into action and hurled one straight at the scaled creature. The granite projectile bounced off the tough hide and, while it did no discernible damage, it unsettled the reptile enough so that Rusty had time to clamber out of the way of the lightning bolt.

Now the creature swung back to Scott. A beam of light shot out of the gold-colored gun. Scott rolled to the side and avoided the blast, but was showered with molten debris as the heat ray plowed into the ground.

The sound of the lightning bolt no sooner died out than something else clove the air with a whoosh. The creature struck forward, its head jerking as if pulled by an unseen string at its feet. It tried to hiss, but a thin, wooden shaft had pierced its throat.

The gun fired another blast, but it was harmlessly spent into the ground. The monster wavered on its powerful hind legs for a moment, then crashed sideways where it lay with its left hind foot clawing futilely at the blue sky.

A loud whoop-whoop-whoop rent the air from the rock ledge. Scott looked up and saw a nearly naked savage, wearing only a loincloth and moccasins, standing with legs spread wide, and holding a carved wooden bow in one hand. Even as he watched, the savage reached over his head, past black, shoulder-length hair, and tugged another arrow out of a quiver on his back. He notched it to the string, drew it back, and let it fly past Scott and into the trees.

A bolt of lightning crackled out of the woods and singed the rock at the savage's feet. This was followed by a loud hissing sound, and the crash of a body as another lizard fell into the clearing eyeball to eyeball with Scott. A fat tongue licked sharpened teeth, and the jaw worked reflexively. Thick, viscous blood drained out of the wound in the throat. The dying gasp of air that exhaled in Scott's face was fetid and nauseating. Yet, the legs and paws continued to move mechanically, as if animated by an unseen puppeteer.

Revulsion made Scott sick. He rolled over just as the savage leaped off his perch and landed with a thud on tautly muscled legs. "Come quick. Follow me." He gestured with his free hand, then turned and fled without looking back.

No more invitation was necessary. Scott scrambled to his feet and, picking up Rusty on the way, pursued the scantily clad man across the clearing. Another reptile plodded out of the woods next to a fallen comrade, and chased them with a beam of light. There were two more behind it. But by the time they drew a bead, their targets had vanished into the trees.

Once out of sight of the conflict area, the savage wove a circuitous course around the trees and brush. He was so fleet of foot that twice he had to stop and wait. Even so, they soon outdistanced the slow, bipedal lizards.

They entered the shadow of a line of hundred-foot-high cliffs. Dragging Rusty by the hand, Scott did his best to keep the savage in sight. He watched in awe as the man danced over a field of loose boulders as if they were pebbles on the beach. He and Rusty had to negotiate each rock at a snail's pace, either by walking around or climbing over. Day-old wounds were aggravated by the acrobatics.

The savage waited patiently whenever he got too far ahead, and stared back with dark, watchful eyes. It was not until they reached an area where great sheets of rock sheared off the cliff face offered concealment that he waited for Scott and Rusty to catch up.

Scott eased his worn and weary body to the ground. "Thanks. . . . Thanks—a—lot."

Rusty pressed one hand to his side. "Yeah. You—really saved—our necks."

The bronzed savage studied them without expression. His chest was deep and muscular, his abdomen flat and strongly delineated. Blue veins coursed over the muscles of arms and legs, and protruded from the sides of his thick neck.

"Men stick together. It is code."

There was an odd enunciation to his words,

as if each syllable was supremely important. He stood stoically, with hands hanging by his sides. Then he untied a smooth, bulging pouch from his waistband, removed the corded line that snugged the top, and offered it to Scott. Still catching his breath, Scott only stared at it and wondered what it was. He was at the point of asking when the savage took it back, put the tip near his lips, and squeezed the soft, rounded base. A stream of clear liquid shot into his mouth.

When the pouch was handed to him the second time, Scott took it eagerly. He wrapped his cracked lips around the opening and sucked out the life-giving water—and would have drunk it all had not the savage pulled it away from him with the ease one would use in taking a toy from a child. He handed the pouch to Rusty, who greedily drained the rest of it. When the empty flask was handed back, the savage meticulously wound the cord around the top and retied it to his waistband.

Rusty lay back on a slab of rock. "Thanks again."

"Yes, I'm sure glad you happened along. They would have gotten us for sure."

The savage looked at them blankly.

"You really know how to shoot that thing." Rusty indicated the bow which was still clasped tightly in one brawny hand.

Suddenly the impossibility of the situation exploded in Scott's brain like a rampant warhead. There were not supposed to be any people living on the surface of the Earth. "Hey, who are you anyway? And where did you come from?"

The savage, still standing tall, stabbed a thumb at his chest. "I am called—Death Wind." Then he extended his arm and pointed. "I live south." His pronouncement stated, he folded his arms across his chest.

"Uh, yes, well, it's nice to meet you, uh, Death Wind. My name's Scott."

"And I'm Rusty."

"Where from?"

"Maccam City," Scott replied.

"City?"

"Yes, an underground city. Back there." Rusty made a sweeping gesture with his arm. "Somewhere."

"Underground?"

"Yes, we've always lived underground. Ever since the plague."

Scott got up from the ground, and approached

Death Wind. "In fact, we didn't know there were people living on the surface anymore. I always thought that nothing could live out here—not even animals."

"Nomads live here. My people are Nomads."

"You mean, there are others?" Rusty stepped forward and stood by Scott's side.

"Many people. Many tribes. All Nomads."

"And you live around here?"

"Live here in summer. We hunt. In winter, we go south. Plant crops. Soon, we go south."

"You hunt? You mean, like—animals?" Scott licked his lips. "Do you have—food?"

"And more water?" Rusty added.

Death Wind nodded imperceptibly. "You need." It was not a question, but a statement of fact. "You friend." He thrust out his hand, fingers outstretched. Scott stared at it, wondering what it meant. When he did not react, the savage grabbed the inside of his arm, just below the elbow, and held it firmly. With the other hand, still holding the bow, he took Scott's fingers and wrapped them around his own dark arm in the same manner. His touch had a gentleness that seemed odd for one who appeared so coarse.

"Men stick together. It is code." This time it sounded like a chant.

At last, Scott understood that this was a bond of friendship. He clamped down on Death Wind's arm, and repeated the formula. Then Death Wind and Rusty exchanged the same greeting.

"You come with me." Death Wind turned and continued the march. Scott and Rusty traipsed along behind.

"Say, where did you get the bow and arrows?" Scott asked.

Death Wind handed the bow to Scott. "I make."

Scott ran his hands over the carved wood, and marveled at the balance. He plucked the taut string. "How about the arrows? Do you make them on a lathe, too?"

Death Wind plucked an arrow from the quiver and let Scott have it. "Lathe?"

"Yes, lathe." He nocked the arrow and pulled the string. It hardly moved at all, and he wondered how the savage had bent the bow almost in half as he had. "I've never worked with wood but this is obviously machine made."

"Machine?"

"Yes, don't you make this on a machine?" Scott released the arrow and inspected the tip. It

was triangle-shaped, and appeared to be some kind of stone.

The savage touched a sheathed knife at his waist. "I make with this."

Rusty took the arrow when Scott was through examining it. "What are these purple things sticking out the end?"

"Feathers."

"*Feathers!* You mean, like from birds?"

Death Wind remained silent.

"You mean there are birds still alive?"

"You never see?"

"I've seen them on disk. But I thought they had all died out—along with everything else."

"Disk?"

"Yes. You know, a computer disk."

"Computer?"

Rusty shoved the arrow back into the quiver. "Don't you know what a computer is?"

"Animal?"

Rusty stared at Scott, and burst out laughing. "No, it's a—well, a—kind of machine." Rusty launched into an explanation of what a computer was, and all the things it could do. Death Wind listened, but made no comment. His face remained impassive, so Scott could not tell whether he understood or not.

By that time Death Wind had led them up a nearly vertical climb to the base of an immense overhang. It was high above the surrounding plateau, offering an overview of the desert and the faraway ravines from which Scott and Rusty had recently escaped. The cave was large enough to fit a fair-sized house. It was Death Wind's solitary campsite, consisting of a fire pit, a collection of pine needles, a pile of wood, and a pack with carrying straps.

"Sit." Death Wind pointed to the pine needles. Rusty collapsed on the makeshift bed, obviously worn out. Scott removed his slippers—or, what was left of them. The soft sole had worn right through, and his feet were cut and scraped. He kneaded them tenderly.

From the pack, Death Wind produced what appeared to be a loaf of bread, except that it was too solid. When he took out his steel-bladed knife, Scott saw that the blade was almost as long as his forearm. He sliced off a chunk of spongy matter, cut it in two, and handed it to them. "Eat."

Scott had no idea what the stuff was, but he was too hungry to ask. He tore off a bite and knew right away that he had never tasted anything like it before. It was chewy, and required quite a bit of effort to swallow, but it was not unpleasant.

Between mouthfuls, Scott said, "This is good. What is it?"

"Meat."

"Meat? You eat meat?" Death Wind did not answer. By this time Scott figured out that he never answered questions that were either rhetorical or self-evident. "Yes, I guess if you hunt animals you must eat them."

"Stands to reason," Rusty said.

"What do you eat?"

Scott talked and chewed at the same time. "Vegetables. Plant food. Anything that grows, really. All our food is cultivated in hydroponic gardens."

"Hydro—ponic?"

Without stopping his intake, Scott explained. "Yes, you see, it's like farming, but more scientific. We live—lived—in a closed environment. Everything has to be recycled. Human organic waste material is used for fertilizer for plants grown in trays, in nutrient solutions, under artificial sunlamps. We grow—grew—mostly things like roots, tubers, and nuts; things that could be plucked from underneath. Any part of a plant we couldn't eat raw was converted into meal in processors. We made bread out of it. Nothing went to waste."

"You have rain?"

Scott laughed. "No, it never rains underground. We recycle our water, too. Or, at least, most of it. When water was thought to be unusable it was sprayed outside to be carried away by the wind—atmospheric dispersion, we call it. But we had wells drilled below the water table, and pumps that ran constantly."

Scott found it impossible to tell from Death Wind's expression how much he understood—or believed. His dark eyes carried no emotion. He sat unmoving, like a rock. He breathed slowly and deeply; even his chest did not move. Scott had the impression that the savage's body was a well-trained machine; trained, perhaps, for survival. And Scott found himself admiring that trait.

Death Wind rummaged through his pack and pulled out another smooth-skinned pouch. He took a small drink, then handed the pouch to Scott. This time he was careful to leave some for Rusty. Death Wind stood up when Rusty returned the empty pouch. "I get more water."

Scott watched the graceful motion of the savage's body as he climbed down the rocks. He flexed his own muscles. He thought of himself as strong, and in good physical condition. But compared to Death Wind he was badly out of shape, and incredibly weak.

When he turned to address a question to Rusty, he found him dozing peacefully on the bed of needles. It made Scott realize how sleepy he was himself, how sore he was, how woefully exhausted he was. He wanted to wait for Death Wind, to talk some more, to find out about this strange and wonderful, and awful, world into which he had been thrust. But he was gone so long that Scott found himself drowsing off. He lay back for just a moment to rest his eyes, and fell instantly asleep.

When Scott woke up the lighting was somehow different. He could not place it because his mind was fogged, as if in a drugged stupor. He lay for a long time staring at the roof of the cave, seeing nothing more, hearing nothing stir. When he finally rolled up to a sitting position, he saw Death Wind hunched over a sheet of brown material, working quietly.

"What are you doing?"

The savage looked up expressionlessly, then pointed to his feet. "Moccasin."

Scott inspected his own, practically nonexistent, footgear. "I guess I could use a new pair of shoes. And some more food, if you don't mind my asking." Death Wind stopped his work long enough to slice off two portions of meat. Scott chomped into the food ravenously. He poked Rusty in the ribs. "Hey, wake up before I eat your breakfast, too."

Rusty groaned and rolled over. "Is it time to get up?"

"It's morning already." He handed the other slice of meat to Rusty, then cocked an eye toward the low-lying clouds. "And judging by the light, it's not early either."

"I don't need food. What I need is a cool shower and something for this headache."

"We're lucky to have enough water to drink, much less bathe in." When Scott stood up to claim the water container, he found a new ecstasy in pain. He sat back down with a moan.

Death Wind quit his project, and brought water to the two invalids. "You sick. You need rest. I take care until you are better."

"Thanks." Scott accepted the water with a grimace. "But why are you doing this for us? You don't have any idea who we are."

"No matter. You are men."

"Sure, but you almost got yourself killed by taking on those big lizards."

Death Wind seemed neither proud nor embarrassed. Scott took this as a measure of his confidence. The savage had not made any decision on the matter; he had acted only as gravity acts when an object was let go and it fell to the ground.

Rusty cleared his sore throat. "Uh, Death Wind, I know this is asking a lot, especially after you've done so much for us already, but—could you help us look for our—for other survivors?"

The savage poured gray powder from a small sack into a hollowed-out log, then added water from his smooth-skinned canteen. He stirred the concoction with a stick. "No others."

Rusty stopped chewing. "But, there must have been. We couldn't have been the only ones to get out of there alive. Yesterday we found another man who had escaped, so there should be others."

Death Wind kneaded the mixture until it had the consistency of thick glue. "He wore clothes like you. Your tribe?" Rusty nodded eagerly. "You saw him?"

"Dead. I follow trail. See track of many dragons. No others."

"But, there must have been—"

"Rusty!" Scott found himself irritated by his friend's insistence. "Face the facts, will you? We were the only ones to get away. The rest are all dead. I know it isn't nice, but that's the way it is. And the sooner we accept it the better off we'll be."

Rusty lapsed into silence, glaring at Scott. Death Wind looked from one to the other. He took a handful of paste and rubbed it first on Scott's hands, then on his feet.

"That feels cool. What is it?"

"Medicine from plant. Help heal. Soon you be better." He applied it to Rusty's wounds next, smearing generous portions wherever he found cuts, scrapes, or blisters. He also laid a thin layer on his face, where the sun had burned his skin to a painful cherry red. When he was done, he went back to his task of making moccasins.

Scott realized that the material from which he had cut the triangular pattern was animal hide. He watched in fascination as Death Wind, using his own broad foot as a last, converted the flat, tanned skin into footgear. With his foot in the middle of each sheet he wrapped the hide in such a way that one pointed end became the tongue and the flat end became the heel. With the point of his knife he punched holes along the other two sides of the triangle, folded them over the top of his foot, and laced them with thin strips of previously prepared hide. When he was done, he had a moccasin that wrapped tightly around the foot as high as the anklebone.

Scott was trying his on for size when the air started to vibrate. There was an all-too-familiar thrumming sound in the near distance. Immediately, Death Wind dragged them to the back of the cave. Soon a gold-colored disk floated into view. It hovered at a thousand feet and was close enough so that he could make out details.

The aircraft was shaped like two curved bowls, one inverted over the other. Square cutouts along the rim appeared to be ports. Underneath, in the middle, was a tubular protrusion about a quarter the diameter of the disk. Surrounding this, hundreds of needlelike projections spouted purple beams downward, which, after a while, merged into one shimmering heat wave.

As it cruised out of sight, and the thrumming sound was swallowed by the intervening cliff face, Death Wind said, "You bring."

Scott said, "What do you mean by that?"

"You bring dragon. You bring airboat. They never come here before. Three days ago I see boat in air, dragon in woods, in desert. They search. I hide. Then I follow, watch. Strange smoke fill air in desert. I find dead man, killed by dragon. I follow your trail, bring you here. I think dragon seek you."

"But, who are they? And how did they find our city?"

Tears rolled down Rusty's cheeks. "And why did they kill our people? What did we ever do to them?"

"Dragon bad. They kill men." That seemed to sum it up as far as Death Wind was concerned. "Tomorrow I go to my people. You come and live. We take care. Men stick together. It is code."

Scott realized that for him and Rusty there was no other choice. Thrust into a hostile world about which they knew nothing, they could never survive alone. Their future was irrevocably tied to this man of the wilderness.

Death Wind offered them more than security: he offered them life.

CHAPTER 5

For Rusty it was another miserable night. Asleep long before sunset, and wakening long after dawn, he still felt exhausted even though he did nothing but lie around eating, talking, and healing. His sunburned skin was peeling in layers which he picked at constantly. And the bed of pine needles was not exactly like the linen-covered foam rubber that he was used to.

Death Wind twice again refilled the canteens. He gathered leaves for bedding. He kept a constant vigil for dragons. And he collected a supply of plant sap for medicinal purposes, to help soothe Rusty's painful skin and to prevent Scott's acid-burned pustules from getting infected. The savage worked constantly for their benefit.

With his huge knife, Death Wind cut off another portion of meat. "You eat much."

Scott licked his lips before taking a bite. "After a lifetime diet of vegetables and ground greens, this is quite a change."

Rusty lay snug at the back of the cave, nibbling. "Meat doesn't have the concentration of protein or vitamins that our processed food has, nor is it as easy to eat. All this chewing is a waste of energy. And besides, the high fat content is unhealthy in the long run."

"Where did you hear all that?"

"Oh, I've read a lot of disks on nutrition. Our diet is a lot better than what it used to be."

"You read much. You smart." Somewhere in this world of scrub brush and twisted piñon pine, Death Wind had found two long, slender tree trunks. He shaved the bark off them with his knife, then indicated Scott with his chin. "You strong."

Scott blushed. "He's spent as much time at computer terminals as you have in the woods. There's nothing he doesn't know about them, or can't figure out. Just like you know all this stuff you've been telling us about plants and animals."

"What I don't understand is why you move around so much. Instead of migrating back and forth, wouldn't you be better off staying in one place?"

After he shaved off the bark, Death Wind started whittling one of the trunks into a pole. "Stay still, dragon find us. We move, they not know where we are."

Rusty wrestled with the tough meat. "But you're out in the open all the time. Do you really like it?"

"You like living in cave, like groundhog?"

"He's got you there, Rusty."

"Yes, well, it was the only kind of life I ever knew."

"You should have watched more movies instead of text disks. You always thought I was wasting my time, but I was looking for something like this. The only way I could get it was on a computer screen."

"But this"—Rusty swept his arm toward the arid desert—"is not what I saw on disk. Life was different in the old days, before the plague. I don't think I can get used to this kind of life."

"Well, as Death Wind says, you don't have much choice."

Death Wind worked on the end of the pole, shaping it to a nasty-looking point. "I teach. You learn. Work hard, you become warrior."

Rusty pouted. "I don't think I like the sound of that."

Scott leaned forward, eyebrows knitted. "What's involved in becoming a—warrior?"

"Child stay with family: cook, sew, mend. Learn to fight: bow, arrow, spear. When ready, go on trial. Alone. Many days. When he kills, he becomes warrior. Two day ago, I was child. Today, warrior."

"You mean, you have to kill one of those dragons to become a warrior?"

"No, kill beast of field."

"What kind of beast?"

"Sometimes small." Death Wind held the palm of his hand two feet above the rocky floor. "Sometimes big." He made a great circle with both arms. "But he who kill dragon be chief someday. My time come. I go on trial, look for beast. Many day, travel far. See airboat. See dragon. I hide. I stalk. I kill. Now I am warrior, someday chief."

"Well, you're a warrior in my disk." Scott finished eating, and wiped his mouth on his tattered sleeve. "And you certainly lived up to your name."

"I choose name. All children named by mother, father. But when kill, become warrior, choose own name. I kill dragon. From now on I am called Death Wind."

Rusty decided that it was less dangerous to take an examination in guidance control or trajectory computations. "And how do we go about becoming warriors? We don't know anything about killing."

Death Wind passed the sharpened pole to Rusty. "You take spear. I teach. Soon you kill, become warriors."

Rusty viewed the spear askance. It was carved so that the pointed end was thicker, and heavier, and the tip needle sharp. He passed the device to Scott. "Suppose I don't want—to kill." For some reason, he found the act of shoving this wood into flesh appalling.

"Must kill to survive."

Rusty swallowed hard. If he disliked the outside world before, he was beginning to detest it now.

Scott's eyes were aglow. He hefted the spear over his head, and made short, thrusting motions. "You show me how to use it, Death Wind. I don't care about becoming a warrior—I just want to get even."

* * *

They did not leave that day—or the next. Scott and Rusty were simply not well enough to travel.

"Skin like baby." Death Wind applied more paste to Rusty's sunburn, to Scott's back. He also made them sit in the sun an hour at a time, in order to accustom them to the searing effects of solar radiation. At the same time, by converting a hide blanket into clothing, he taught them to sew. With a large cactus spine for a needle he fashioned tunics that were loose enough to allow circulation, but which kept the hot sun from bearing down on tender skin.

Rusty did not like the exposure of the breechcloth. The purpose of the unconnected front and rear panels was one of sanitation—it never had to be removed. "If you don't mind, I'll sew the flaps together and make a pair of shorts."

"Civilization dies hard." Scott laughed. He seemed to soak up everything Death Wind had to say. Already he could throw the eight-foot spear with a fair amount of accuracy. And Death Wind allowed him to carve the second pole. It was less than perfect, but good for a first try.

At the end of a week they were dressed, armed, and ready to depart.

"We not wait any longer. Need food."

In all that time there had been no more sightings of the dragon flying machines. But Death Wind led them through the piñon pine forest with his usual stealth, instructing them on the importance of always being alert, of being at one with the environment. He also interpreted the

plant life they encountered along the way, naming flowers and edible herbs. By afternoon they passed out of the arid desert terrain and entered a forest of spruce and fir, and juniper with its dull blue berries. The world was transformed into a land of green, from the soft grass to the low-lying bushes and the tall treetops.

"Legend say dragon bring plague, clear the land for their seed."

Rusty dragged the tail end of his spear, for his spindly arms were not used to holding such weights. When Death Wind indicated a halt in a shallow ravine, he was more than relieved. "What did they seed?"

"Eggs." The savage dropped his pack on the sandy soil, and started to scrape a hole with his bare hands. "Not like mammal kind, so bring egg of lizard. After mammal dead, lizard grow and take over land."

Scott leaned against his spear, using it as a third leg. "But where did the dragons come from? How did they get here?"

In a purely human fashion, Death Wind shrugged. "Not know."

"But your legends must say something."

Death Wind gathered leaves from the ground and stuffed them in the hole. "Legends speak only of fact, not make-believe. Anyway, it not matter. They are here, they are in control, and we must live in their world."

"Isn't there some way of fighting them?"

"Too many. Too strong. Mighty weapons." The leaves absorbed moisture like a sponge. Death Wind held them over the opening of a canteen and squeezed out the water.

"Ouch!" Rusty jumped, and slapped at his foot. A small creature, about the size of his thumb, fell to the ground and scrambled away. "What's that?"

The savage pounced on it. When he held it up Rusty could see the six madly moving legs, the brown, chitinous body. "Bug." Death Wind plopped the still living insect into his mouth, chomped down once, and swallowed. Rusty promptly threw up.

"We certainly seem to have different eating habits," Scott said. "And I'm not sure I care for all the things on your menu."

"When hungry, you eat."

"Not me." Rusty wiped his mouth on a large green leaf. "I'll never be that hungry." When Death Wind scavenged under a rotting log and found half a dozen slimy, mucus-covered white grubs that he promptly threw down his throat, Rusty got sick again.

"Take it easy, Rusty. You're losing all that valuable breakfast."

"Go ahead and laugh, Scott. I don't see you sticking your hand out for any grubs."

Death Wind continued to wring out the wet leaves. It took two hours of tedious work to fill both water pouches. Rusty was astonished at his perseverance. And the water that he collected, the three of them drank in minutes.

"Is that how you got the water you gave us in the cave?"

"Desert dry. Water scarce. Later, we find stream."

But before they found water again, they found food. Death Wind froze in the thick of the dense forest. He held up his hand for silence. Rusty heard movement. At first it sounded like something crashing through the underbrush; then it was tearing bushes out of the ground, ripping them asunder. Whatever it was, sounded big.

"Stay. Keep spear ready. I circle."

Death Wind slipped away soundlessly, like a ghost fading into mist. Rusty clutched his spear with nervous fingers, half hidden behind a fir tree. Ten minutes passed, then twenty. Still, he heard only the rutting of a wild animal.

Then there was a squeal like that of a fire alarm that went on and on, punctuated now and then by louder war whoops. Scott took off at the first sound, spear at the ready. Rusty chased after him. By the time he got to the action, it was all but over.

The animal that Death Wind was calmly watching in its death throes was a giant chameleon. Its strangely frilled head was fully a third of its five-foot-long body. An equally long tail writhed wildly. The arrow in its breast was snapped off close to the smooth, bright green skin, and blood was pouring out as if from an open faucet. It sucked air in labored gasps, like a fish out of water.

Scott approached close, held his spear over his head with both hands, and stabbed down with all his might. The thrust carried the spear through the neck and pinned it to the ground. There was a momentary resurgence of activity as the creature leaped about with newfound energy, but it quickly faded. Scott held the spear in place until all movement ceased and the blood stopped flowing.

He pressed his foot to the ugly head, and worked the spear back out. "I thought you were going after food."

Death Wind nodded imperceptibly. "Food."

Rusty pointed a trembling finger. "But that thing's a lizard. You can't eat it."

The savage picked up the broken, feathered end of the arrow, and stuck it in his pack. "Lizard is beast. Beast is meat. You ate. You liked."

"You mean we've been eating lizard meat all this time?" Rusty's question went unanswered. "But, I thought we were looking for pigs, or cows. Livestock animals. That's what the computer disks say."

"No pig. No cow. No big mammal since plague. Only man and small mammal hide— live."

Scott wiped the blood off the end of his spear by rotating it on the ground. "Is this what the dragons brought? Are these the kind of creatures that hatch out of their eggs?"

"Are—are there many—beasts like this?"

"Many." Death Wind drew out his knife and started dissecting the chameleon. One thrust from chin to crotch disemboweled the animal. As the still warm viscera poured onto the ground, he cut one organ out of the bloody mess and tossed it aside. "This one small."

Scott touched the organ with the tip of his spear. "What's that for?"

Death Wind tapped the water pouch on his belt. "Bladder." Rusty put a hand to his mouth. "You mean, we've been drinking out of some lizard's urine sac?"

As was his way, Death Wind did not answer. He peeled back the skin and cut away great chunks of meat.

Scott followed the savage's example. With his hands he waded into the mass of flesh and blood and took the steaks as they were cut. "Are we going to eat it raw?"

"Raw meat go bad quick. We cook tonight. Last many days."

The skin made good carrying sacks. Before long, all three marched off under a new load. Rusty's scrawny arms had all they could bear. He switched his load from one shoulder to the other, each time taking a new grip on the folded skin. The smell of blood was nauseatingly close.

The sky was turning from pale blue to light purple by the time they reached Death Wind's objective. The stream was barely two feet wide, and only several inches deep, but in seconds it carried more water past them than they had seen in a week. Weapons and supplies were dropped unceremoniously. All three lay flat on their bellies, placed their lips on the surface of the cool liquid, and sucked in great quantities of water.

"I never thought I'd have enough to drink again." Rusty cupped the water in his hands and washed the grime from his face and neck. "It feels so good to be clean."

"Your hair could use a shampoo, too. And a comb wouldn't hurt." Scott sat by the stream, splashing water in Rusty's direction.

While Scott and Rusty played and bathed, Death Wind cleaned out the chameleon bladder. He opened it wide at each end, put a rock inside, and sank it in the creek.

Scott started unpacking the meat. "Death Wind, when do we eat? I'm starved."

"Make camp first. Then gather wood for fire." The savage cleared a circular area of brush and grass until only bare earth remained. He lined it with large stones from the creek, and filled it with leaves, dry needles, and wood shavings. He took a flint from his pack and struck it against the back of his knife. Sparks flew into the tinder and, after several tries, ignited it. Then he blew on the tiny flame until he had a small blaze burning. Gradually he added more needles and shavings, then small sticks, and eventually round logs with peeling bark.

Rusty laid chunks of meat by the fire. "Death Wind, don't we have to worry about the dragons seeing all this smoke?"

"Dragon not travel at night." He lashed together two sets of sticks into A-frames, skewered several pieces of meat, and laid them over the hottest part of the flame. "They cold."

Rusty was cold, too. He moved closer to the fire, exhilarated not only by its physical warmth but by the quieting effect it had on his mood. "Don't they have clothes?"

"Blood cold." He tapped himself on the chest with his fist, and said, "Blood warm." Then he pointed to the meat on the stick. "Blood warm."

"You mean, the dragons are cold-blooded animals, but the lizards are warm-blooded?"

Scott shoved a small piece of meat on a spit and held it over the fire. "That isn't the way I remember my biology."

Death Wind cut off a thin slice of meat, and tasted it. "Good." He cut more and passed it around. "Eat while hot."

Rusty passed the meat from hand to hand be-

cause it was burning his fingers. The freshly cooked meat had a fragrance that whetted his appetite; he suddenly found himself famished. "I take back all I said about meat before. This is delicious."

It tasted so good that Rusty ate more than he thought possible for his stomach to hold. With darkness all about them, he stared into the red blazing logs, hypnotized by the flickering flames and coruscating embers. In his mind he was catapulted back to a time when men gathered around fires for protection from the elements and wild animals. And for a moment this horrible world was not so bad after all.

When all the meat was cooked, the fire was allowed to die out. Finally, with eyelids drooping, Rusty could stay awake no more. He lay back on the bed of leaves, staring up at the nighttime sky. What he saw made his eyes spring open, and sent a chill down his spine. "Look!"

Death Wind bolted for his bow and arrow. Scott stared upward, blinking sleep from his eyes. "I don't believe it."

The savage had his first arrow nocked. He looked up and all around, half crouched and waiting for the attack. "What you see?"

"Why, they're all over. It's beautiful," Rusty said. "I never thought it would be like this."

In the disks they had always been cold and uninspiring, but when seen through atmospheric heat waves they danced about like living entities. Rusty glanced at Death Wind. In the partial darkness he could see a sign of expression in the savage's face. Confusion? Disbelief? Disorientation? It was nice to know that he had emotions. Rusty laughed right out loud. "The stars!"

CHAPTER 6

"Up! Up! Up!"

Before Rusty could do more than open his eyes, the savage picked him up and pushed him into the cover of a nearby bush. A moment later Scott landed on top of him. After the rustling of the leaves stopped, he heard the thrumming that meant that a dragon flying machine was in the area.

Scott pushed branches out of his face. "What's he doing out there?"

Death Wind stood right out in the open, and

stared up at the sky. The sun sat on the horizon like a dull, orange globe, pinking the heavens. The hum grew louder for a moment, and the savage's dark eyes locked in intense concentration. When the sound of motors reversed pitch, and the machine started receding, he motioned them to come out.

"It is safe."

Scott brushed himself off. "Why did you stay out in the open like that?"

"See airboat, avoid danger. Take weapon, come with me. I show you."

Rusty squinted his eyes. The dragon machine was only a golden speck, moving directly away. With his spear over his shoulder like a rifle, he followed Scott and Death Wind through the woods. The tall trees offered faint comfort, but they dispelled the feeling of openness. The air was filled with the same odor of burnt wood he had smelled the night before while they cooked the meat, except that this was thick and sickening. They stopped at the edge of a blackened swath of destruction, a hundred feet wide, as if a giant blowtorch had been played across the ground incinerating everything in its path. "Airboat pass high, safe. Pass low, death. Sound is different. Be ready to run."

While there was the sign of a great conflagration, there was no flame or smoke. Trees were scattered everywhere like a field of fallen monarchs, denuded of leaves or needles. Patches of cinder were all that showed where bushes had stood. There was dry, blackened earth where once had been fields of verdant, green grass.

Rusty remembered the shimmering that emanated from underneath the machine. "Scott, can rocket propellant do this?"

"No, the ground isn't scorched. This is no chemical reaction." He scraped a fingernail full of soot off a charred trunk. "This is some kind of molecular vibration."

"Whatever force they use to power their aircraft must discharge an awful lot of energy."

"They've got a kind of science that we know nothing about." Scott turned to the savage. "Death Wind, how long does it take to learn all the dangers of this world?"

"Whole life of child is learning. Once learned, go on trial." Death Wind led the way back to camp.

"But you just became a warrior the other day. How long did it take you? How old are you?"

"Two hundred fifteen."

"What?" Rusty tripped over a lichen-covered log and hit the mossy forest floor with a thud. Scott helped him up. "Two hundred and fifteen years?"

"Moons," the savage said.

Scott pushed vines out of the way. "How old does that make him?"

Rusty calculated quickly. "Why, he's younger than we are. He's only seventeen."

"Believe it or not, Death Wind, we're adults in our world. We've learned most of the necessary material and passed our tests."

"Sure, we're just taking postgraduate courses now."

"That not make you warrior."

Rusty rubbed a sore elbow. "I'm not saying it does. I'm only saying that we're equal in our knowledge with respect to our own societies."

"All men equal."

They reached the campsite, and Scott immediately unwrapped a helping of meat and cut portions with Death Wind's knife.

"All Rusty's saying is that you'd have as much trouble adjusting to our way of life as we are adjusting to yours. The difference is that here a simple mistake can mean death. You don't have makeup tests."

Instead of eating right away, Death Wind took the bladder out of the creek. The overnight immersion had purged it of residue. He looped and knotted one end, filled it with water, and tied off the other end. Then he presented it to Scott. While Scott and Rusty ate, he went about the task of making packs out of the giant chameleon skin, stitching with cactus spine and strips of skin. "You say you always live underground. How you know about stars and constellations? How you know about the moon? How you know about the North Star?"

Rusty laughed. "We have science courses along with everything else. It's like I told you before, everything is on computer disk."

"I do not understand this—computer disk."

"And Rusty's too smart to be able to explain it to you. Let me just put it simply. The computer is a device full of knowledge, and the disk is a way of retrieving that knowledge. A disk is like a book."

Death Wind's face brightened. "Book?" He stopped working for a moment and rummaged through his pack. He brought out a musty, moldy object and held it out. "Book."

Scott reached out for the slender volume.

"That's it. That's it. Disks are like this, only the print is so small you can't read it. The computer enlarges it so you can."

Death Wind nodded. "I like books. Read pictures all the time."

"Do you understand the words?" When Death Wind did not answer, Scott opened the picture book to the middle and pointed to the large typeface. "Do you know what these mean?" The savage shook his head. "Then maybe we can bring you some knowledge from our world by teaching you how to read."

Rusty took the book from Scott, and opened it to the faded title page. It read, *The Song of Hiawatha*, by Henry Wadsworth Longfellow. "Death Wind, where did you get this book?"

"City. South. Much broken."

"By broken, do you mean it's in ruins?"

Death Wind nodded.

"Will we be passing this city on our way to your village?"

"Way south. Maybe pass later."

"Can we stop there, do you think? I'd like you to take us to where you found this book. If we can find a library, we may be able to learn what happened after the plague. Our history disks stop when the input terminals went blank."

Scott said, "You see, we're still waiting for a counterattack."

Death Wind looked from one to the other.

Rusty handed the book back to Death Wind. "Our city was originally built as a missile coordination center with intercontinental capability. We integrated high orbital command modules and military telecommunications—"

Scott put a hand on Rusty's shoulder. "Rusty, you're talking way over his head. Let me try it." Facing Death Wind, he continued, "In the old days people fought with missiles, not bows and arrows. These missiles are like, well, like giant spears, only much more deadly. They could be launched at targets thousands of miles away. But the missiles aren't kept all in one—quiver. They were scattered all over the country. Maccam City is a control center—we directed the throwing of these spears, so to speak."

"I have heard of these weapons that kill at a distance. Called—guns?"

"Not exactly. Guns are small weapons, hand held."

"Like dragon lightning thrower?"

"Exactly, except that the guns we had threw pieces of steel. But missiles are much bigger, as big as—" Scott looked around for a moment, then pointed upward. "As big as those trees." Death Wind looked up at the fifty-foot ponderosa pine. "And one of them could level an entire city."

"What you mean? Weapon for animal or dragon, not city."

"Not in the old days. There were no dragons then. But there were great wars, nations fighting other nations, in which millions of people were killed."

Death Wind's expression contorted into a mixture of horror and disbelief. "You lie. Men not fight men. Men need men—for food, for protection, for family. Why you make up this story?"

"It's not a story. That's the way it was."

"Men need men. To live."

Rusty said, "Maybe now, but not a hundred years ago. Then, man's worst enemy was man. There were always other nations—"

"Tribes," Scott interrupted.

"—trying to take over weaker na—tribes."

"You come from these men who kill men?"

"Yes. And all these years we've been waiting. We never knew which side started the plague, but in case they started throwing missiles at us we wanted to be ready for them."

"I not like this. You speak maybe truth, maybe lie." Death Wind's eyes narrowed. "You still—kill men?"

Rusty saw they were treading on dangerous water. "No, you don't understand. Our ancestors were trying to prevent this from happening. These aggressors had missiles, too, to throw at us. We never intended to use ours except in self-defense."

"And besides, the world is different now. There may not even *be* any others. The plague may have backfired and gotten them, too. I don't know. But what Rusty is saying is that we would like to find out."

"And if you could take us to this city, we may be able to determine who won the war."

Death Wind had not moved in many minutes. "My heart is troubled over your words. When we get to tribe, we talk with chief. He is warrior for many moons. He will understand. Let him decide."

CHAPTER 7

By the time the sun reached its zenith, the trio was on the trail. Each was now carrying a well-stocked pack, and had his own canteen. Death Wind carried his bow over his shoulder. Scott and Rusty practiced spear throwing as they walked through the green, fertile forest. Rock outcrops and rolling hills provided relief in the terrain.

Death Wind picked up a rock chip. "Flint. You save. Start fire, make arrow tip." Later, when he found mushrooms growing on a log, he broke one off, sniffed it, snapped it in half and inspected for infestation, then ate it. "Never take from ground, get sick. From log, okay."

Scott plopped a mushroom into his mouth. "Tastes kind of musky." He handed a piece to Rusty.

"No thanks. I'll pass."

"Come on, Rusty. You've been eating mushrooms all your life."

"But they were grown under sterile conditions, then purified and processed."

"And we don't live like that anymore. From now on we're men of the forest, and we have to start thinking that way. We can't cling to our old values. Instead of striving for good grades we have to find food and water, make clothing and shelter, live each day at a time."

"But I don't like it. I don't like being outside, I don't like all this moving around, and I don't like killing animals and eating food off the ground."

"Well, whether you like it or not, you'd better get used to it. Because we're going to live this way for a long time."

Death Wind picked up a long stick. "Nomad have no village, have no home. He wander forever, escape dragon. No choice. We do what we must."

A tear hung on Rusty's cheek. "That's easy for you to say. You were brought up that way."

Death Wind held his stick out sideways, halting Scott and Rusty in their tracks. He put a finger to his lips. Soundlessly he tiptoed toward a hollowed tree stump. Scott detected movement, as if something were flashing in and out of sight, at the upper end of the rotten wood.

Suddenly the stump exploded with living creatures. They leaped out in all directions and hit the ground with all four legs clawing for traction. Death Wind swung his stick with unerring accuracy, catching several of the lizards in the air and batting them left and right, and clubbing others on the ground.

Scott leaped after one, but when he tried to grab the creature it stood up on its hind legs and was gone in an instant. The rest that made it to the ground and got out of Death Wind's reach scattered through the underbrush. Rusty stood rooted to the spot as several raced right past him.

"Those things sure are fast." Scott stood up and brushed himself off. He picked up one that Death Wind had killed, and noticed that the skin was smooth, that the animal felt warm in his hand. "Are these things warm-blooded, too?"

"All warm, except dragon." He dismembered the lizards with his knife and discarded the bodies. "Legs good. We eat."

That night, Scott took a turn at starting the fire. He scratched his flint across the steel blade and tried to aim the tiny sparks into the tinder. Time and again the sparks either missed, or were swallowed up without igniting the leaves and dried moss.

"It looks so easy when you do it." Eventually, by blowing gently into the tinder, he coaxed the fire to life.

Death Wind pushed a sharpened stick through the fat legs and roasted them over the hot flames. After they had been cooked, the skin peeled off readily and the meat underneath was soft and tender.

Rusty grudgingly nibbled on a leg, held delicately with a leaf so he would not get his fingers greasy. "It's not bad, but it could use a little salt."

Scott smiled. "Do you have to complain about everything?"

"I can't help it. I'm tired. Trying to keep up with Death Wind is like running a race."

Scott turned to the savage. "How far is it to where your people are camped?"

"Me, two days. You, four days. All, three days."

"There, you see. He's going slow for our benefit."

Rusty put a small piece of mushroom cap on his tongue. "Great."

Scott scooped some water out of the stream. It was cool in his throat. "And how long does it take your people to move to their winter location?"

"One moon. Maybe two." He chewed heartily on his sixth lizard leg. "No hurry."

By late next morning the dense pine forest gave way to fields of open grass dotted with rock piles and hillocks, and populated by deciduous trees such as quaking aspen, cottonwood, and birch. The land was much brighter, and the ground was covered with flowers of delightful colors.

Scott continued to practice with his spear. He had carved a comfortable grip that was just the right size for his hand. The balance point was one-third of the way back from the tip. He liked the feel of it, for it gave him a sense of power.

"Hey, what's that?" Rusty pointed to something that fluttered by with random, jerky movements. It pierced the air on saffron wings, which folded delicately over its tiny body when it landed on sun-seeking blossoms.

"Butterfly."

Rusty chased after it in the open field, dragging his spear. He tried to catch it with his hand, but could not anticipate its quick, darting motions. "They're all over the place."

Scott turned cheerfully to Death Wind, but saw the Nomad standing stock still, staring off in the distance. His nostrils flared as he twisted his head, catching a scent. "What is it? What do you smell?"

"Lizard." Death Wind cocked his head, listening. "Big lizard."

Scott tightened his grip on the spear. He looked across the idyllic glade, full of colorful flowers and flitting insects. Then he heard a crash, followed by something that was a cross between a snort and a bark. "Can we eat—"

Before he could finish, he saw an animal step out of the cover of tall brush from beyond a hillock. It was a dark gray mass the size of a tank. The massive head was at least five feet long. Two spearlike horns reached out from above the eyes, while another, shorter and stubbier, pointed upward from the nose. A flared shell stretched backward, protecting the beast's thick neck. It moved on four trunklike legs.

Rusty froze in the middle of a living bouquet of flowers. A gasp escaped his throat. "That's a triceratops."

The ten-ton beast grazed noisily, uplifting roots and bushes and small trees. It crunched limbs and leaves in its powerful jaws and swallowed indiscriminately whatever passed its smooth-skinned lips.

Death Wind motioned for caution. Loud enough for Rusty to hear, he said, "Beast have

dim eyes. Maybe not see."

Even as he said it, Scott felt the wind shift. The triceratops stopped in midstride. It raised its mighty head and craned its neck. Large, round eyes peered myopically from under bony brow ridges. The three sharp prongs triangulated on Rusty.

"Run!"

Scott chased after Death Wind as he ran a zigzag course through the woods, dodging trees and leaping over bushes and broken logs. Rusty was on his heels one moment, then soaring past the next. Scott cast a glance over his shoulder and saw the ungainly looking creature catching up with him. Thundering hooves propelled the triceratops closer every second.

He broke out into another clearing and saw Death Wind waving him on toward a large rock mass that stood several hundred feet away. The moss-covered rock, topped with shrubs and saplings, stuck sharply up out of the ground to a height of twenty feet. The sides were broken with jagged edges that were draped with vines.

As Death Wind neared the outcrop, he made a tremendous leap that carried him halfway to the top. He grabbed onto a narrow ledge and with the strength of his arms he pulled himself onto the rock.

Following the savage's example, Rusty dropped his spear and vaulted as high as he could, but fell a foot short of the ledge and slid back down to the soft earth.

"Spear!"

Rusty picked up his weapon and thrust the blunt end up the rock face. Death Wind took the spear and pulled it hand over hand, with Rusty hanging on. Sinew strained and veins protruded until Rusty's hand found the ledge. A dark brown hand clamped down on his wrist and hoisted him up.

Without letting go of his spear, Scott hit the rock at full speed and tried to run right up the side. His momentum carried him just to the level of the ledge, where Death Wind's hand reached out for him. They missed by inches, and Scott slipped back down the rock face, scraping skin off knees and knuckles.

The spear imbedded in the ground and could not be dislodged. Without wasting an instant, he climbed the eight-foot pole like a monkey, and was almost at the top again when the triceratops crashed into the base of the rock pile. With a single thrust of its powerful head, the spear snapped in two like a toothpick.

Scott fell right onto the head of the triceratops, between the bony plate and the base of the two long upper horns. The beast thrust its great head up in a stabbing reflex and flung him over its tanklike body as one would fling off a fly. Scott landed on his side and back, the pack taking the brunt of the fall, and rolled over dazed. He saw the short, pointed tail flicking across a broad rump, and expected to be trampled any moment. But the triceratops, despite its great size and its massive head, was too stupid to turn around to see what happened to its quarry. It continued to make spear thrusts with its horned snout, gouging deep furrows in the rock face.

Death Wind shouted war whoops to distract the beast. This kept the triceratops so enraged that it continued its senseless attack on the wall.

Scott crawled out of the way of the swishing, whiplike tail. He stood behind the creature, wondering what to do next. Death Wind sidled along the ledge, drawing the animal to the side. As the triceratops changed its angle of attack, Scott slipped around behind it until he reached the rocks and found a place where he could, with some difficulty, climb up to safety.

As soon as Scott was out of danger Death Wind lapsed into silence. Now the beast snorted aimlessly, its imaginary enemy gone. Its head was showered with dirt and debris, its large eyes blinked away dust. Within moments it forgot why it was pounding its head against the rocks. It ambled on its way, snorting and gouging bushes out of the ground with its stubby central horn.

When he recovered his breath, Scott said, "I'm beginning to think this outdoor life is not all it's cracked up to be."

CHAPTER 8

"Where did that—dinosaur—come from?" Scott blew on his knuckles where the skin had been torn off.

Death Wind mixed a salve from his meager supply. "Dragon bring."

From the top of the outcrop Rusty watched the dull-witted beast trundle off into the woods. "But you don't understand. Dinosaurs lived on the Earth a hundred million years ago. I've seen them on disk, and that horned monstrosity is a dead ringer for a triceratops. It's inconceivable

they could have evolved on another planet in exactly the same form. It just doesn't make sense."

Death Wind concentrated on applying the healing goo to Scott's wounds.

"How about the smaller ones, Rusty—the ones we've been eating? Did you recognize any of them?"

"No, there were thousands of different dinosaurs—tens of thousands, I guess. In their heyday they were as plentiful as mammals were before the plague. The paleontology disks I've seen were just overviews. A lot of the dinosaurs we know about were reconstructed from a few bone fragments, sometimes only one, so there are bound to be differences in their real appearance. But something like a triceratops is well known, from many intact specimens."

Scott grimaced as Death Wind smeared his concoction on his skinned knees. "And you have no idea where they came from, other than they appeared on Earth the same time the dragons did?"

"Many moons ago, men plentiful. Cover earth like grass in field. Live everywhere, without fear. Together. Then disease come, kill all: mammal on ground, bird in air, fish in river. Some hide, live. Then dragon come, hunt down men. More than that I do not know. Must move always, stay away from dragon, find food, take care of little ones."

With the danger past, they climbed down to the grassy field.

Scott picked up the broken pieces of his spear, picked at the splinters, then discarded the tail end. "Yes, I guess it doesn't leave much time for study."

Rusty combed leaves from his hair with a short-needled pine branch. "First dragons, now dinosaurs. This world gets crazier all the time."

The world got crazier the next day when another dragon flying machine passed by. Death Wind cupped his ear. "Listen to sound."

At first, Rusty heard nothing. But as the gold saucer got closer, riding on its shimmering beam of purple radiance, the high-pitched thrumming sent irrational chills of fear down his spine. He wanted to reach out with his spear and strike the hated enemy craft out of the sky.

As if the dragons were cooperating with Death Wind's lessons, the machine descended. Then Rusty could distinguish the lowering of pitch that meant its deadly beam was reflecting off the ground, and that molecular destruction was occurring.

Just before dark it passed by again. "Many airboat, not good."

Scott carried the stub of his spear over his shoulder. "Do you think your tribe will move away or take cover before we get there?"

Death Wind scanned the forest. "If so, we find. We camp here tonight. But be on watch for dragon. Be ready to run, or fight."

"I think I'd rather run," Rusty said.

"Run if possible. But if you fight, move quick. Dragon think slow, move slow. You get out of way easy, like butterfly."

Rusty slept restlessly. His dreams were full of dragon airboats that flew by and incinerated them in the propulsion blast. He tried sleeping close to a birch tree, using an exposed root for a pillow. But ants and other nocturnal insects crawled over his body without any regard for his terror, and after several rude awakenings he was forced to move out into the open where he had nothing but stars for a ceiling.

Death Wind roused him early in the morning. Groggily he accepted the piece of cold meat that Scott handed to him, and chewed it absently while he stumbled through the forest in the half light. The pace was telling, and it seemed to him that the Nomad was showing some anxiety about his tribe. Three times in the morning they heard airboats, but always too far away to be seen.

"What's that low rumbling noise?" Rusty said.

Now Death Wind broke into a trot. "River. We close."

Rusty, who found he could run fast in short spurts, was not so fast in the long haul, especially carrying a spear and a pack full of food. Periodically, Death Wind called out in his stylistic war whoop. But the only answer came from aspen leaves quaking in the gentle breeze. Still, he ran toward his brethren. Rusty was exhausted when he caught up with Scott and Death Wind.

They stared at a blackened clearing, a smoldering circle of destruction, as if a dragon airboat had dropped close to the earth at this one spot and had taken off again. All around it was green and beautiful and untouched.

"Watch for dragon," Death Wind whispered. He led the way around the ugly scar, moving as gracefully and as silently as only one who was born and bred in the forest could move. His bow

was held in front, an arrow notched. Despite its weight, Rusty cocked his throwing arm and prepared to launch his missile—or run.

Rusty could detect no discernible footprints around the burn zone, and if Death Wind saw any signs he made no mention of it. They veered close to the river, slinking through the thick vegetation that grew upon the banks. The roar of rushing water became thunderous, and Rusty caught a glimpse of the raging torrent as it cascaded down a large cataract, tossing spume high into the air. The spray landing on Rusty's shoulders brought with it a sharp coolness.

Suddenly the once thick vegetation ended. A blackened swath of fallen trunks and shriveled limbs lay rotting on the ground. The path of destruction went right into the river, where the tumbling water obliterated any further traces.

The forest continued beyond the dead zone, and Death Wind wasted no time leading Scott and Rusty through the debris. Rusty's spear kept hanging up and he fell far behind the others. His moccasins filled with mud as he waded through the sooty swampland. When he reached the trees on the other side he saw that the woods extended only a few feet before opening up to another patch of charred destruction. And beyond that, there was more black death.

They came to a great clearing, crisscrossed by so many burnt tracts that hardly a tree stood within a mile. Huge boles, shorn of bark, were flung like giant matchsticks lying pell-mell on the ground. The wood was blackened, the earth glazed, and the land pockmarked as if hundreds of explosions had torn it apart. Nothing was alive; nothing was intact. Nothing even remotely resembled any form in nature except the whitely gleaming remnants of human bones that were partially melted into a gray ash. Disembodied fragments like broken pipe stems attested to what they had once been. The dragon airboat, held aloft on its deadly, purple beams, must have traversed this area again and again with ruthless abandon.

Death Wind stood like a statue, uttering not a word. A wayward breeze tossed his long hair off his shoulders, revealing muscles that now sagged with despair.

Then the stoic statue that was Death Wind, killer of dragons, began to wilt. Great, gleaming tears streaked down his dusty cheeks, rolled off his quivering jaw, and dropped onto his outflung, heaving breast. The muscles in his neck bunched into knotted cords. And still the silent tears flowed.

After many minutes, Death Wind strode into the ruin and desolation that had once been his people's camp. He kicked violently at anything that got in his path. Scott kept at a respectable distance. Rusty lagged behind, struck with fascination and horror.

For an hour they roamed the former encampment, seeking signs that some of the Nomads had gotten away. But of the many footprints that Death Wind pointed out, none had been made in the act of escape. It appeared as if the dragon airboat had made increasingly smaller circles, herding the people to their deaths.

Rusty's spirits sagged. In the span of a week he had lost not only one family, but the promise of another.

Death Wind stooped down and picked up a clod of clay that had been fired into brick by the sudden, intense field of force from the dragon machine. In his strong, brown hand he squeezed it until it crumbled into dust. He let the particles sift through his splayed fingers.

"I feel now—what you feel. Your grief is my grief. I share your sorrow." He paused for a moment and looked up at the sky. "From this day on, till death take my spirit, I vow vengeance against the dragon and their ilk. I, Death Wind, killer of dragon, have spoken."

Later that night, while the stars plastered the velvet sky like scintillating diamonds, and embers burned brightly in the fire, the three orphans ate in disconsolate silence. Scott carefully arranged three felled trees so that their ends met in the flames. As the logs burned down, he snapped off the cinders and pushed them in farther.

"What about the other tribes?"

Death Wind stood on the rocks above the falls, listening to the rumble of cascading water. He stared listlessly over the churning foam. "All south."

Rusty knapped a piece of flint, as Death Wind had shown him, and made his first arrowhead. "Well, can't we find them? Can't we join them?" When the savage did not answer, Rusty persisted. "After all, they're your people, too. You said all Nomads are the same."

The quiet that followed was ominous. After many minutes Death Wind spoke sibilantly. "I vow vengeance. No seek Nomad. Seek dragon."

"But what about us?" Rusty said.

"Tomorrow we part. I go my way, you go yours."

Scott jumped up, his eyes burning red like the fire. "Go? Go where?"

"You follow river. Find Nomad."

Rusty ran to Death Wind's side. "But, we can't do that. I mean, you can't just leave us. We don't know this world. We'll die out here."

"You smart, you strong. You live."

"No!" Scott screamed. "You're not leaving me here. If you're going after dragons, I'm going with you."

"Now, wait a minute, Scott. We don't have a chance against the dragons. There's no sense getting killed for nothing."

"Was your father nothing? Was your mother nothing? Your brothers and sisters? Are you going to just write them off? Well, I'm not. I'm going with Death Wind to get even with them—or die trying."

"No." Death Wind folded his arms across his chest. "I go alone. I take my sorrow. You take your sorrow. May our sorrows never meet again."

"What are you talking about? Why can't I go with you?"

Death Wind faced the crackling fire. His face was as impassive as ever. "Dragon seek underground city. They find. They destroy. But you escape. They track, and find my tribe. Kill my people. Because of you, they are dead."

"Hey, don't think you can blame us for that." Scott stood between Death Wind and the fire. He forced the savage to look at him. "How do you know they weren't looking for your people and just happened to stumble across our city?"

Death Wind would not be prodded into an answer. "You know not the way of fighting. I must go alone. I go fast, you not catch. I have spoken." Death Wind calmly sat down and lay by the fire. He closed his eyes, but Scott would not leave him alone.

"You just try to get away. I'll follow you. I'll track you down. Maybe I can't keep up, but I'm sure going to try. I'll keep going till I drop. And if I lose you, I'll fight them alone. You hear me, Death Wind? You hear me. I'm going with you."

Rusty curled up on the scorched earth. There was a hollow pang in his chest, as if his heart were pounding to get out. And there was no solace in his dreams.

CHAPTER 9

Scott looked up at Death Wind at the first hint of dawn, when the brighter stars were still visible and the black sky was fading to purple. "Up. Eat. Soon we go."

Wary eyes pinched at the savage. "You mean, you're going to take us with you?"

Death Wind nodded slowly.

"How come the change of heart?"

The savage was silent for a long time, his face twitching. "Maybe you right. Maybe I right. I not know. All—confusion. But this I do know: according to code men help each other—always."

A smile broke out on Scott's face. "That's the way to go." He reach over and punched Rusty on the shoulder. "Wake up, sleepyhead. Death Wind says we're going with him." He gathered his legs under him and stood straight and tall. He grasped Death Wind's extended arm in the Nomad greeting, then he threw his arms around the savage's shoulders and hugged him like a long-lost brother. "Now you're talking. And you won't be sorry, either. We won't let you down, will we, Rusty?"

"Huhn?" Rusty jammed a fist into his eyes, and rubbed away cobwebs. "Uh, well, no. I guess not."

"We go east. Through abandoned city. Over tall mountain. Across Great Desert. Into Dark Swamp. Where dragon live. There we die—for our people."

"I'm not too crazy about dying, but I'll give it my best shot." Scott's voice was full of enthusiasm. "Won't we, Rusty?"

Now Rusty was awake, or almost. "Yes, sure we will." The uncertainty in his voice gave way to sincerity. "We'll launch a tirade against those dragons that they won't forget for a long time."

They veered away from the river, heading east. On the trail, Death Wind marched like a living machine: his legs pumped like pistons and his lungs moved air like a bellows. His long hair streamed back in itinerant breezes, sometimes entangling in the quiver full of feather-studded arrows.

Scott soon found that his determination did not make up for his still-soft muscles. He was in a constant state of fatigue. He worried about Rusty, but if his friend had any trouble keeping up the pace, he did not complain about it. His long skinny legs stretched out two steps to Scott's three.

All that day, and the next, and half the following, they trudged inexorably toward the abandoned city where Death Wind had found the chronicles of another, and earlier, wandering soul. When they reached the outskirts of the ancient, once-thriving town, Scott was sorely disappointed.

"It isn't exactly what I expected."

What he saw was a hundred years of decay and deterioration in which wooden houses had long since collapsed, brick facades had fallen in, and multiple-story buildings had toppled. Sand and dirt and dust had swept over the whole, leaving an amorphous mass that hardly resembled anything with pattern and meaning.

"Dragon airboat fly low over city, roads, houses. Always destroy. First kill man, then kill memory." After a wistful moment, Death Wind added, "Book this way."

He stalked off through crumbling walls and uncertain foundations. The one-time residential district was now nothing but rotted wood and disjointed cinder blocks, and a morass of broken blacktop that had once been a busy street. Weeds and small shrubs grew wherever they could find enough dirt to hold a root.

"But why? Why do they want to obliterate us?"

"It doesn't matter why," Scott said.

Closer to the heart of town, in the former commercial district, rusting steel frameworks, like twisted, garish skeletons, were all that was left of the sharp clean lines of skyscrapers. Mounds of detritus completely smothered the streets under many feet of brick, marble, and slivers of glass. The trio climbed and scrambled over the broken tumulus.

An eerie silence hung over the abandoned city. Since the time of man's defeat, the only sounds made here were made by the wind, or by the gradual collapse of his construction.

Death Wind raised his hand and tilted his head with great concentration. He notched his bow.

"What is it?" Scott whispered. "What do you hear?" In the pale quiet he heard the hissing of steam, and something heavy scratching across the stone debris. He fingered the splintered end of his spear where the shaft had been broken.

A leering lizard head rose above the mound of rubble in front. The head was mottled gray and tan, and swayed on the long stalk of a neck.

As it stood up straight on thick hind legs, the unwieldy paw swung around, gripping the firing apparatus of its lightninglike gun.

An arrow sliced the air and pierced the soft part of the upper neck. The beast let out a hiss of pain. It was hurt, but not to the point of death. An instant later the gun was brought to bear and a shaft of fire spat from the nozzle.

Where the beam struck, Death Wind stood no more. Dodging to the right, he loosed another arrow on the fly. This one sank into the broad breast between the short, gnarled arms. Lightning flashed unaimed, its energy spent uselessly in the air.

Rusty launched his spear. The finely honed point clove the broad abdomen with such force that the animal spun partly around from the momentum. Another arrow glanced off the forearm and penetrated the chest. The creature hissed horribly and drew back its injured limb. The gun dangled by the cord from the power pack.

Scott rushed from the left. As he leaped over the rubble embankment he delivered the coup de grâce by ramming his stubby spear into the unprotected underbelly. The creature twisted away, ripping the spear out of his hand. But the two-chambered heart had been pierced, and the dragon died on its clawed feet while its jaw still worked silently from side to side. After several seconds, the autonomic reflexes stopped and, levered sideways by the thick tail, the dragon crashed to the ground.

Death Wind ran to Scott's side. He cast furtive glances all around, then looked down at the drooling mouth. "Dead."

He placed one foot on the dragon's coarse scaled neck and pulled out his precious arrows. After wiping off the blood on the leathery skin, he returned the arrows to his quiver. Then he pulled out the two spears, held them high over his head, one in each hand, and faced his companions.

In a voice that was triumphant without being loud, he proclaimed, "Hail, warriors, killers of dragon."

Rusty was too stunned for words. Scott threw his arms around him and lifted him off his feet, dancing with him in a small circle. He tried to make a war whoop like Death Wind's, but as soon as he made a sound the Nomad squeezed them both together with his muscular arms.

"Where one—more. Always quiet."

Scott curbed his tongue but could not stop grinning foolishly. Meanwhile, Death Wind lost no time in unsheathing his knife. He knelt by the fallen foe and started hacking away at a scaled leg.

"Hey, what are you doing?" Rusty asked.

Death Wind kept cutting. "Meat almost gone."

"But that's—that's a dragon. You can't eat it. It's—it's an intelligent—being."

"If you can call that intelligent." Scott tried to hide the revulsion in his voice, even though he felt the same sense of impropriety at eating one's enemy. But, after all, Death Wind was the teacher. . . . "Hey—the gun."

He leaped forward and picked up the hand-held unit of the weapon. The gun assembly consisted of a molded plastic box with a power lead extending from one end; an eight-inch nozzle extended from the other end of the power lead. The hand unit was too large to fit comfortably in his hand, but when he held the unit awkwardly, he found that he could reach the firing stud with his index finger. He aimed the nozzle away from him, and pressed the trigger. A bolt of lightning shot out and incinerated a nearby stone wall.

"This—beamer—still works." He fumbled with the unfamiliar buckles, and released the straps from the dead owner. The power pack and holster came free. The pack was contoured for the curved, humped back of the dragon, but with a little restructuring it could be worn by a man.

Scott started adjusting the straps when an ear-piercing shriek echoed off the ancient crumbling walls, and sent shivers down his spine. A loud, sharp bark was followed by the release of energy from a beamer. Three more barks rang out in rapid succession.

Scott swung around to see Death Wind off and running. He hefted the power pack by the straps and dragged it along with one hand. Rusty hesitated long enough to retrieve his spear and Scott's stub.

They dashed through the rubble between two buildings that still stood as high as three stories. Splashes of light could be seen through the city ruins some two hundred yards away. They came to a low stone wall: all that was left of a building front. Scott looked over it to see a squad of dragons moving ponderously past them only a few feet away.

Six of them marched in staggered formation. With beamers in their clawed hands, they were firing rapidly after a lone retreating figure that was dressed in a smooth, light brown burnoose that billowed in the breeze.

Momentarily exposed, the lone human turned and spat fire from a tubular weapon that was cradled in one arm. Holes appeared in the chest of the leading dragon, and it fell to the ground hissing. The lone defender drew fire from five beamers, but ducked out of sight before the air was riddled with lightning bolts.

Scott aimed his newfound beamer at the nearest reptilian body and pressed the firing stud. Instantly a beam of light shot out and sizzled through flesh. It left a black, burning hole from which blood poured like water through a hole in a dike. As ponderous heads turned to see what was nipping at them from the side, Death Wind pierced one in the eye with his deadly, flint-tipped arrow.

Temporarily out of tie line of fire, the cloaked figure jumped up and made more barking sounds with the rifle. Crack, crack, crack, and down went another dragon. Scott fired again, and there were only two pursuers left. A squad of reinforcements came into view, shooting their beamers as they approached.

In the heat of first battle, Scott stayed too long in one spot. A bolt of lightning stabbed between his legs and hit a steel supporting beam behind him. The flash singed hair off both calves, and the backs of his legs were scorched by bits of molten metal. Then he leaped to the side, and remembered to keep in motion.

Rusty launched his good spear into the stomach of a dragon. It hissed and writhed and, while not dead, was at least knocked out of the action. With glacial speed the dragons of the second squad redirected their fire, but by the time the lightning bolts were let loose, Rusty was long gone.

Ducking beamer blasts, Death Wind shot another arrow with less precision than usual—it missed completely. Fist-sized holes burned through the crumbling wall that he hid behind.

While Scott scurried for protection, an intense staccato of rifle fire sprayed the dragon platoon, taking the heat off of him. In the confusion, Rusty jumped up and threw the half spear. It wobbled in its wild flight, and glanced off the hamstring of the nearest dragon. As it spun around, Death Wind took careful aim and pierced its cold-blooded heart with an arrow.

The air blazed with beamer charges. Scott flitted from brick pile to brick pile with the agility of a cat, and while the dragons concentrated their fire on him, the stranger's weapon continued to take its toll. As Scott's protection melted down in front of him, he ran back and dived over a wall, crashing right on top of Rusty.

Death Wind joined them a moment later. He led the way toward the lone defender. Scott stuck his head out long enough to make several more shots, but most of the damage to the dragon squad was coming from the continuous barking of the automatic rifle.

Cupping his mouth, Scott shouted, "Run for cover."

If the stranger heard him there was no time to answer, for the surviving dragons now drew a bead on the shooter who stayed too long in one spot.

The broken wall offered some defense until the trio gained the safety of a doorway to a brick-strewn ruin that had once been the lobby of a building. The rifle barked out of the adjacent window.

The cloaked figure stepped back behind the safety of the pitted marble slabs, and threw aside the shawl. "Nice shooting, fellas, but this is no time to duck your tails. We got 'em on the run."

Under the cloak she was dressed in a coarse skin blouse and matching skirt. The loose-fitting clothes tied about her slender waist in a way that did nothing to hide her curvaceous body. Bandoliers carrying ammunition pouches were draped over both shoulders, crisscrossing between two bulging breasts. Long black hair hung loose past her waist.

"Hey, you gonna give up now, or what? We got a battle to win."

Without waiting for an answer she discarded the empty clip from her rifle, snapped in a full one from her bandolier, and stepped back outside and started shooting. Scott and Death Wind exchanged shrugs, then went back out to help her fight.

Two more squads of dragons moved into position, firing with precision now that their quarry was pinned down in one place. So many beamer blasts hit around them that the air seemed to crackle with live electricity, and the dust from blasted stone walls was getting too thick to see through.

The trio spread out and formed a line behind a mound of rubble. The dragons kept coming. The girl mowed them down: she was deadly accurate with her automatic rifle.

Scott was quickly getting used to the awkward firing mechanism and returning fire at a prodigious rate with growing success. Death Wind stayed calm, shooting his arrows slowly and deliberately.

Suddenly Rusty clawed at Scott's back. "Look out behind."

Over the din of battle he heard the peculiar thrumming in the sky. Turning to where Rusty was pointing, he saw the golden airboat, glinting sun off its smooth back, moving directly toward them. It flew low, purple beams thrusting down like neon stilts. Like a hungry demon, the excess energy ate up the streets, the rubble, and the remaining parts of buildings. Wreaths of black smoke rose from the ground as stone and steel structures were pummeled into unrecognizable slag.

"Hide," Death Wind shouted. Scott wasted no time ducking into the doorway after Rusty. He stopped there to cover the others' retreat. Death Wind punched the girl hard on the shoulder and stabbed a finger at the approaching machine. "Hide."

But the girl kept firing. As soon as she sprayed the dragon soldiers with a clip of bullets, she dropped the metal magazine and replaced it with another. She kept up such a rapid rate of fire that her pouches were quickly being emptied.

"Run, you cowards," she taunted as Death Wind ducked into the doorway next to Scott. "I'll do the fighting."

Beamer bolts came so thick by now that the wall in front of her was quickly disintegrating, and the ambient temperature rose by many degrees. With sweat streaming down her stolid face, the girl remained steadfast and continued to shoot into the advancing horde. She seemed determined to engage the enemy until her own life was forfeit. She swung around and, with a full clip, fired fiercely up at the bottom of the hovering aircraft.

"She's crazy," Scott uttered.

Steel-jacketed bullets laced into the glowing purple cones, dousing the pillars of light and sending out shrapnel that damaged others. The machine was only a hundred feet high, and a mere fifty feet away. The air smelled of heat and ozone. The thrumming sound rose in pitch as it soared upward to get out of range. But it was still moving forward.

"Down here," Rusty shouted from the bottom of a debris-filled stairway.

Scott stood riveted in place. Pride would not let him leave his post. Following the girl's example, he fired the beamer at the energy thrusters. The cones shattered like glass.

Death Wind slung his bow over his shoulder, grabbed the girl around the middle, and lifted her off her feet. She screamed obscenities and kicked futilely as the Nomad dragged her into the building. Then all sound was drowned out by the thrumming of the fantastic motors.

The savage carried her down the stairs to where Rusty waited. Scott leaped without a moment to spare, reaching the concrete floor without touching a single step. He barely got under cover when the building overhead burst apart, and a blast of heat rained down with all the fury of an active volcano. Scott tumbled forward on top of Death Wind and the girl as wooden beams and a cloud of plaster showered down from the floor above.

The heat was insufferable as the multistory building settled down. Bricks and stonework fell like raindrops, filling the cellar with tons of dust and debris and smoldering wood, threatening to bury them.

But the worst enemy was the heat. The air was as hot as boiling oil, and clung as tightly. It seared Scott's lungs as he tried to breathe, turned his clothing to furnace lining. He pulled the loose skin of his shirt over his mouth and sucked air through it. He screamed when hot air flowed like molten lava into his lungs.

As suddenly as it came, it was over—except for the occasional dropping of loose bricks and splintered chunks of wood. Outside, all was silent as the machine swooped away to lick its wounds.

Brushing debris aside, bleeding from a dozen wounds, Scott found himself miraculously alive—but sealed inside a dark, dusty tomb. For long moments he coughed and gagged, and tried to find clean, fresh air to breathe.

The girl cleared her throat. "We really brought the house down, didn't we?"

Scott groaned as he disentangled himself from her and Death Wind. "Rusty, are you all right?"

From somewhere in the darkness came a weak voice. "I guess I'll live."

Scott heard the Nomad crawling over the rubble. Death Wind found him, and practiced hands ran over his body and limbs. "Hurt?"

Scott grimaced. "Nothing that a few weeks

convalescing wouldn't cure." He had no broken bones or severed arteries, just cuts and bruises. But he was beginning to view such wounds as an accepted norm.

Death Wind checked out Rusty, then moved to where he had left the girl.

"Hey, keep your hands off me."

"Hurt?"

"Not as much as you'll be if you touch me again."

There was a scuffle in the blackness, and Scott felt a board come loose and land in his lap. He pushed it aside.

"Hey, anybody here got a name? I'm Sandra."

"I'm Scott, and that board you just threw landed on top of me."

"Sorry. Who's the stringbean with the red hair?"

"Rusty."

"How original. And Mr. Hands?"

There was a moment of silence before the Nomad pronounced his name. "Death Wind."

"You must be joking. Where'd you pick up a moniker like that?"

After another silence, Death Wind said, "You hurt?"

"Just a coupla scratches, if it's anything to ya."

Scott started moving around, to test the size of their prison. Fallen beams prevented most of the debris from hitting anyone with full force. In absolute darkness, they worked together to clear out some of the boards and bricks until there was room to move around.

"Hey, anybody got any water? I sure would like to wet my whistle."

Scott dug around in his pack and brought out his water pouch. "Drink sparingly. We don't have much."

"It might be all we need unless we get some air in this coffin." Sandra slurped noisily from the bladder, then slapped it against Scott's chest, still half full. "Thanks. You know, you guys came along at the right time. Whatcha doing in this burg, anyhow?"

Scott seemed to be the only one who was willing to hold a conversation with her. He let some water clear the dust from his throat. "Looking for the library."

"Nothin' better to do, huhn?"

It had been a hard day. It looked as if it was going to be a harder night. He handed the bladder to Rusty. Death Wind moved debris out of the way, passing bricks, stone, chunks of mortar, and broken beams to Scott, who passed them on to Rusty.

"We were looking for information—about the dragons."

Sandra moved out of her corner and helped in the digging. "The only thing you need to know about them is that they're vermin to be shot on sight." She huffed and puffed as she lifted large sections of masonry and pushed them behind her. "Listen, now that we all know who we are, how about if I start the biographies?"

After a moment of silence, she went on. "Okay, I can see the curiosity's killing ya, so here goes. I come from a long line of administrators. They're the people who tell others what to do, 'cause they don't know how to do it themselves—or because they don't have the guts to do it. My folks have been running from the dragons ever since they were born, moving all over the country instead of staying in one place and fighting them. For a hundred years they've run us ragged, picking us off one by one. About fifteen or twenty years ago, our big cheese decided the gang was getting too big, so they split up and spread out. They figured that small units could move faster and hide better. And that's what I've been doing all my life, running and hiding."

"Where's the rest of your, uh, gang, now?" Rusty asked.

"They smoked us out about a month ago. There were about a hundred of us living in a subway in an old burg north of here. We—"

"Excuse me, but, what's a subway?"

"Don'tchu know nothin'? It's a bunch of tunnels—part of an underground railway. You know—trains? Anyway, we been living there about eight years. Ran into a small group that had built quite a complex down there, so we merged with 'em. Been there ever since.

Scott hoisted a heavy beam out of the way. "I thought you said your bands moved around all the time? Eight years in one spot isn't what I call traveling. We've lived in Maccam City all our lives—"

"Hey, who's telling this story, anyway?"

"Sorry." Scott concentrated on his work. They reached the base of the stairs and started making a pathway up to the surface.

"Now, where was I? Oh, yeah. Well, it was all right, I guess, living there. The place had a lot of advantages, and we spent a lot of time out in the open, shooting dinosaurs for food. That's the part I liked best, even in the winter. I always liked the snow."

"You mean, there were dinosaurs living where it was cold?"

There was a long silence following Rusty's outburst. "You gonna let me tell this story, or not?" The work went on. "Okay. So we went out on hunting trips, we worked the fields for grain and vegetables, we picked wild fruits. And every once in a while we'd—lose a few people. We'd see a flyer in the air, then we'd scatter, run and hide like rabbits, crawl into a hole and pull it in after us. But they would never fight back. Said it would give us away, and we didn't want to attract any attention."

Sandra stopped working and got quiet. "Anyway, about a year ago we started seeing a lot more activity: flyers, war parties, dragons, were turning up all over the place. Before that, it was always chance encounters. Then, they started going after us actively. They seemed to be—searching. That's when I lost—my father."

Scott felt a pang in his chest. He was glad no one could see his face in the dark cellar. His hands were suddenly clammy.

"He was out hunting with three other men. Flyer musta come down right on top of 'em. Never found more than a puddle of slag an' some liquefied bones." Sandra sniffled faintly. "Anyway, that was a year ago. Then, last month, the dragons found our hideout. I was in the fields with my mother, so we were lucky—if you can call staying alive lucky. When we got back to the tunnel that night, after they'd gone, we couldn't even get in. The place was filled with some green, poisonous gas that ate through metal like acid—"

Scott found himself gasping. He managed to keep quiet until he heard the end of her story.

"Well, we ran into Tom and Ned that night. They'd been out hunting, an' we were the only ones left alive. We hightailed it out o' there, but as soon as the sun came up they were onto us again. We played hide-and-seek for a week before they caught us at the edge of town. Tom was gunned down before we knew what hit us. I blew two of 'em away before my gun jammed. Then we started to run. When it looked like we were circled, Ned an' my mother shoved me into a dumpster—a stinkin' dumpster—an' took off. They didn't get far—"

Sandra's bravado faltered. She whimpered for a moment, managing only to utter, "They were picked up and taken away—" Then she burst into tears, sobbing hysterically.

Scott froze with a brick in his hands. The pathos of the story was too vibrant for him to hear without a strange feeling of déjà vu.

Death Wind said, "What you mean, take away?"

Scott heard the scuffle as blows landed on the savage's body. "I told you to keep your hands off me." The rifle clattered in the confined space. "You touch me again an' I'll fill you full of holes."

In his deadpan voice, Death Wind repeated his question. "Dragon take?"

"Something wrong with your English, fella?"

"What mean, take?"

"I mean what I said. They were carried off, up in the air, in one of those golden spaceships from over the rainbow."

Scott could hardly contain himself. "You mean, they were kidnapped?"

"Hey, am I talking funny, or what? I said they were taken away, captured. They didn't leave no ransom note, or nothin'."

"Death Wind, is this possible?"

A shaft of light shone through the hole, and the way to the surface was almost open. The Nomad stopped working for a moment. "Dragon always kill. Always."

"You guys must be thick-headed or dull-witted. I'm telling you I saw them. And if you're calling me a liar, I'm gonna pull your tongues out by the roots."

Scott could see light glinting off beads of perspiration on Death Wind's face. Cheek muscles bulged as he clenched his jaw. But it was Rusty who broke the charged silence.

"Sandra, listen, we're just trying to understand something that is very—foreign—to previous dragon activity. So, please don't get angry. But, are you sure your mother was alive when they took her aboard the—flyer?"

"She walked."

"Ned, too?"

"Ned, too."

Scott watched dust particles glimmering in the light as they were siphoned upward in the exchange of air. "This is something new. What do we do now?"

Death Wind stared at Sandra with dark, fathomless eyes. "Wait till dark," was all he said, until dark.

CHAPTER 10

Under the cover of darkness Death Wind went out on his own. He was gone for more than an hour, and when he returned he brought back full canteens and a chunk of meat. "Still warm."

Scott coaxed a small fire to life in the artificial cave. He took the water gratefully, drank a conservative amount, and passed around the rest. A warm glow suffused through the close confines, reflecting off four dirt-smeared faces.

"Gee, thanks." Sandra took a slice of meat and sank her teeth into it. She chewed and swallowed the first bite. "You may talk funny, but you're a pretty good scrounger."

Death Wind did not answer. Scott looked askance at the meat. It had an unfamiliar taste, and he was fairly sure where it came from—but he refrained from asking. It was something he would rather suspect strongly than know for certain.

"So you guys are gonna conquer the world, huhn?" Sandra garbled with her mouth full. "What makes you think I wanna go along?"

"You alone," Death Wind said.

"Yeah, an' what makes you think I'd be any better off hanging around with you guys?"

"Men stick together. It is code."

"Gee, where'd you pick up that corny line? An' look here, buster, I'm not a man, see."

"You man."

"Yeah? An' you been in the woods too long. I'm a girl, you know, like in woman, female, opposite sex. Or hadn't you noticed." She settled her arms in her lap and unnecessarily thrust out her chest.

Scott almost choked. "I noticed."

Sandra's eyes twinkled in the flickering light. She seemed to take pleasure in Scott's admiration.

Scott smiled at her.

Death Wind gestured with his hands. "I man. You man. All man." He pointed dramatically at her upper chest. "You warrior. You very brave."

"I must be, to sit here next to you wearin' nothing but a codpiece." Sandra pointed to the loincloths and tunics that Scott and Rusty were wearing. "And you two aren't exactly over-dressed."

Rusty drew his legs under him, as if to hide his nakedness. "This isn't my normal attire."

"What Death Wind means is you killed a dragon today," Scott explained. "In the Nomad culture that makes you an adult."

A smile touched her lips. "No kidding? Then that must make me an old woman, 'cause I blew about ten o' them suckers away."

Scott sighed heavily. This girl just did not seem to have any respect for convention. "Look, all Death Wind's trying to say is that we can't just go off and leave you—alone. It's too dangerous."

"And you're gonna take care of me, is that it?"

Scott tried to be patient. "No, but there is safety in numbers."

Sandra finished eating, and wiped her mouth on her sleeve. "Well, I'll think about it. Ask me in the morning. Right now I wanna get some shut-eye."

Scott still wanted to talk more with this outspoken girl, but once she made up her mind to go to sleep, she did just that. He cradled his head in his arms, and watched the dancing phantoms in the fire until he drifted off into dreamland.

In the morning, it was a cautious crew that climbed out of the hole and listened for dragons. A careful survey revealed none that were still alive. Scott looked at the dead bodies that were lying where they had fallen, burnt to a crisp by the escaping flyer. The dragons had little of what in human terms would be called reverence. The only thing they had done for their dead was to strip them of their weapons.

Death Wind collected water from a puddle that writhed with mosquito larvae. Sandra viewed it with disapproval, taking instead a drink from Scott's canteen. "If you think I'm drinking from that cesspool, you're crazy."

"You drink last night. No complain."

She spit out what she had not swallowed. "You idiot! What's the idea of giving me that rotten water?"

"You thirsty."

"Of course I was thirsty. That doesn't mean you have to poison me."

"You look very much alive to me," Scott said.

"A corpse would look alive to you. You know, I'm beginning to hate the bunch of you. You didn't look too eager to fight yesterday, an' yet you're talking about attacking the dragon capital. I think you'll all get killed before you even get there."

"At least we're going to try."

Rusty shuffled along behind. "Maybe if we could find this library we could learn something about our past, or discover a weakness in the dragons."

"They ain't got no weaknesses, an' the sooner you learn that, the better. They got technology, transportation, and superiority in numbers."

Scott said, "So what are you going to do? Pick them off one by one?"

"Ever hear of guerrilla warfare?"

"Sure. I guess that's what this is."

"Oh, you're gorillas, all right. But that isn't what I meant. I'm thinking about heading back up north an' hanging around the subway till I can get captured. Maybe they'll take me to my mother."

"Assuming they don't kill you instead, what good will that do you?"

"I figure on carrying some concealed weapons and escaping after I find her."

"We go south," Death Wind said.

"Well, wait a minute. Why don't you stick with us until we find the library? We can talk about it then."

"Library gone. I check last night. Airboat smash."

Rusty slammed a rock on the ground. "Oh, that's just great!"

"Watch your temper there, skinny. You almost hit me."

"Sorry."

They paused at the top of a huge pile of rubble. They could see many miles in all directions, and everywhere there was ruin and desolation. There were no flyers in the sky.

"You come with us."

"Let's get one thing straight right now, buster. You don't give me orders. No one does."

"It is safer to be together."

"I'm not so sure I'd be safe with you." Sandra dimpled her blouse with her thumb. "Besides, I've got my own way of doing things."

"Mind made up?"

"That's right. My mind's made up."

Death Wind stared at her hard. Then he stuck out his hand and grasped her forearm. "Then, we part here. May your path be safe and healthy. May you find what you seek. Maybe we meet again." The Nomad turned and started to walk away.

"You're leaving? Just like that?" Sandra turned pleadingly to Scott. "What is this, a one-night stand?"

Scott was aghast. "Hey, Death Wind, you're not really going to leave her here on her own,

are you?"

"Yes, what about the code?" Rusty added.

"Code of honor, not force." To Sandra he said, "You want, you come. You want, you go."

"Yeah, well, maybe I'll just go my own way. I got along fine without you before. An' you don't need me anyway, so go on an' get outa here."

Death Wind checked the straps on his pack, and realigned his bow and quiver. He raised his hand in the universal gesture "Peace." Then he walked calmly away.

Scott was torn with indecision. Here was a girl, alone, and in need of company. And there went the savage, possibly his only salvation in this world. Something had to be done to bring the two opponents together. Rusty broke after Death Wind, pleading, and Scott soon followed.

"Hey, Death Wind, we just can't go off and leave her. It's not right."

"Maybe we can talk it over some more, come to an agreement."

"She'll get killed out here."

"How about if we just sit down for a pow-wow, or something."

By the time they were a hundred yards away, Scott heard a yelp from behind. "Hey, wait up." Sandra ran after them, with long hair flying and bandoliers slapping. Her petite moccasins beat a dusty path over the loose debris.

Scott stopped, holding onto Death Wind's muscular arm so he could go no farther.

Sandra caught up with them and stood leaning on one leg, swinging her rifle casually. With forced nonchalance, she said, "You know, two's company and three's a crowd, but four's got the making of a good little army. An' I think you can use a good gal with a gun. So maybe I'll tag along—for a while. But don't think you're gonna give me any orders, see?"

Scott smiled. "Glad to have you along."

"Yeah, well, your long-haired buddy don't seem too happy about it. But I like you guys. You got spunk."

Rusty slapped the savage on the back. "Aw, Death Wind just keeps things in. He'll get to like you, too. Won't you?"

Death Wind stared at Sandra with unspeaking eyes. He turned and led the war party out of the ruins.

* * *

By the campfire that night, Sandra toasted meat on a spit. "Where'd you get the name

Death Wind?"

The Nomad stirred the coals with the tip of a new spear that he was fire-hardening for Rusty. "As small boy I hear of legendary man known as Death Wind: traveler of great distances, chief among his people, killer of dragons. When growing up I think that I want to be great traveler, chief of my people, killer of dragons. I go on trial many time, always come back empty-handed. Always I wait—not kill lizard. I wait for the day when I kill dragon. When I killed, I chose name. Not because of what I am, but because of what I want to be."

"You know, my father used to talk about the Nomads. I don't think he ever met any, but he knew about them. He used to say my mother was just like them. Do you know what he meant by that?" When Death Wind did not answer, she went on. "My mother isn't like most women—she's a tough cookie. What kind of women are Nomad women?"

"All Nomads warriors. Men, women, all the same."

"An' what about this trial of manhood you're so proud of? Is there a trial of womanhood, too?"

Death Wind inspected the spear tip.

"Well, what do the women have to do to—prove themselves?"

Death Wind let the spear cool a bit, then handed it to Rusty. "Women kill lizard."

"Oh, is that all? Well, I guess that does make me a woman by your standards. Maybe I should choose a new name for myself. Whaddaya think?"

Death Wind chewed a slice of warmed meat. With a flat sandstone, Rusty honed the soot off the spear and sharpened the blade.

Scott eased his feet out of his slippers and scraped ground-sand from the bottom of his feet. He wriggled his toes with newfound freedom. Then he fluffed up the leaves and branches that he had collected for his bed. "I think Foot-In-Mouth would fitting."

Fire leaped into Sandra's eyes. "You shut up, you, or I'll—I'll—"

"Talk me to death." Scott rolled over and stared up at stars.

Sandra hit him with a stick. "You know what's the matter with you guys? You just ain't got any fun in your life."

"Is there something wrong with your English?" Scott said.

This time Sandra got up and kicked him—but not too hard. "You know, if I had a brother, I'd want him to be just like you.

* * *

The solitude of the thick green forest was suddenly broken when a raucous scream bellowed down from the treetops. Death Wind yanked an arrow from his quiver, staring skyward. But when Scott pulled the blaster from its holster, the savage stayed his hand.

"I want to kill, not destroy."

Scott had no idea what he meant by that, but he put the gun away anyhow. He could see nothing in the air besides green flicking leaves and a blue sky. Slowly Death Wind stalked through the woods, gazing upward and listening for a repetition of the strange caw. Whenever he heard it he stopped and stared. Finally, his right arm drew back on the string, the arrow flew, and an animal fell out of the trees.

"What kind of lizard is that?" Scott stared at the still living beast. It weighed perhaps five pounds, and was as long as his forearm. Four taloned paws fluttered in the air; loose folds of flesh stretched from the forearms to the scrawny body. The pointed, toothless beak jabbed at the arrow protruding from its furred breast. The tail fanned out like a horizontal rudder.

"Bird."

"That ain't no bird, it's a flying lizard."

The animal expired as Scott scooped it up. What he at first thought was fur was really a network of horny shafts, from each of which sprouted a closely woven mesh of soft, silky barbs.

Death Wind took the animal and pushed the arrow through the flimsy body. "All same."

"Rusty, what do you make of this?"

Rusty did not touch the bird, but looked at it closely. "I've seen pictures of early birdlike reptiles. This—this is probably some progenitor in the beginning of the evolutionary scale."

"In plain English it's still a lizard, feathers or not. Besides, I've seen real feathers and they're a lot finer than these." Sandra plucked out one of the slender tubes. It proved to be hollow.

Death Wind held the bird carelessly by the neck, and looked forward to where a small brook sliced through the forest. "We camp here. Climb mountain tomorrow."

"Mountain? Where's the mountain?" Scott looked around and saw nothing but trees.

"Come here." Death Wind walked a few steps

into an open glade and pointed up.

From under the cover of the forest the mountains were not visible, but in the open the tall peaks stood out in stark relief against the heavenly blue: dark mounds of craggy granite that were streaked with white near the top. The tall peaks stood so close that Scott felt as if a strong wind could topple them right on top of him.

"Wow," Scott said, his jaw dropping. "I never realized they were so—grand."

"You seen one you seen 'em all. Let's get a fire going."

That night Death Wind carefully plucked the precious feathers from the prehistoric bird, then cooked it along with the rest of the day's catch of small lizards. And early in the morning, long before dawn, he roused them all for the climb.

Scott flexed his arms and legs, eager to put them to use. But he soon found that climbing brought new muscles into play. As they got higher and higher, his thighs and calves ached at every step. At times they went straight up, searching for handholds and footholds and resting occasionally on narrow ledges with a spectacular view of the forest. Even the ruins of the city could be seen as a brown smudge in the middle of the vast greenery.

"Can we rest a moment?" Scott sat down on an outcrop, but Death Wind kept on with his tireless, machinelike gait.

As Sandra walked by, she said, "What's the matter, can't you take it?"

Scott grimaced, and forced his legs to respond. He trudged along last in line. The air became thin, causing headache and fatigue. The pack grew heavier, especially since he was further burdened with the dragon beamer. Finally, he was forced to pause every few steps to catch his breath and regain his strength.

Hours passed, and still they toiled upward. Scott at least had the satisfaction of knowing he was not alone in being out of breath, for hardly a word was spoken during the climb. For the hundredth time he stopped to gather in a few lungfuls of air before continuing, when something smashed him on the top of the head.

He had the beamer in his hand even before he looked up. But all he saw were three backs, and nothing else around. "Hey. Something hit me." Then Sandra turned around and threw a rock straight at him. It came so fast he could not dodge it, and it slammed into his chest and broke into a thousand pieces of cold crystal.

"What is this?" he said when he realized he was not hurt. He wiped a smear off his tunic; it was like ice.

"It's snow, silly. Don't you moles know anything?"

Scott climbed up to their level. Rusty scraped a handful of white fluff off a rock and molded it into a ball. "Scott, this is really snow. It's wet, and cold." He tossed it to Scott.

"So this is what snow is. But what's it doing out here, in the summer?"

"It's the altitude. It stays colder up here, especially at night. So there's snow all year long in the shade."

"So that's why we're trying to make this climb in one day. Death Wind, why don't you tell us these things?"

"Everyone know this. I forget that you live in ground."

"Well, it's nice to know you're not perfect."

"Come. Soon we be at top."

Soon turned out to be a way of reckoning that was not Scott's. By the time they reached a pass below one of the lower summits it was late afternoon. They stood on a vast field of snow.

"Isn't it gorgeous?" Sandra faced the wind coming from the east, her hair flying back in a wild torrent.

Scott chilled quickly as the sweat evaporated from his skin. "I'm not sure I'm in any condition to appreciate it."

Many thousands of feet below stretched a green and verdant pine forest fed by clear, cold mountain streams visible only by the jagged stands of cottonwoods that lined their banks. Unlike the western forest, this one ended a few miles away. From there, and for over a hundred miles, Scott could see nothing but a flat, endless desert.

"Look at that." Rusty pointed to darkened streaks that marked the sand at irregular intervals. They all pointed east.

Scott shivered now, and was anxious to get going. "Flyer tracks. It looks like we can follow them right to the dragon city."

"How long will it take to cross the desert?" Sandra asked.

"Half moon. Maybe more."

Rusty said, "Two weeks in the open? Without shelter?"

Scott did not balk at it for an instant. "Then let's get going. I'm freezing already, and I don't want to get caught up here after dark." He took the lead for a while, eager to keep moving in order to build up some warmth.

Scott soon discovered that climbing down, while easier physically, was more difficult technically. He often found himself searching with his feet for a ledge he could not see, or hanging onto a handhold afraid to let go. It was not until they got to a point where the slope was not so steep that he found a comfortable gait. Then he made up for lost time by running, and leaping from boulder to boulder, as he had seen Death Wind do the first time they met. Sore muscles were forgotten for the moment as he exhilarated in the unbounded freedom.

Nightfall found them camped beside a meandering brook, on soft grass, and totally exhausted by the day's strenuous activity. It was almost too much of an effort for Scott to even gather wood for the fire. But once it was done he collapsed by the burning coals, thankful that the mountain had been climbed, that one more barrier between him and revenge had been crossed.

"I don't know about you, but I'm taking a bath." Sandra showed no shame as she shed her dirty clothes and waded into the water where it pooled chest deep. She plunged completely out of sight and came up with her long hair plastered against her head. "Boy, is this water cold. But it sure feels good. Come on in."

Rusty was already on his way. "It sounds good to me." However, he doffed only his tunic, and splashed into the stream wearing his shorts.

Death Wind and Scott watched them gambol in the water, playing and swimming. When the Nomad handed the slender book to him, Scott said, "Sorry, but I'm too tired for tonight's reading lesson."

Scott sat comfortably by the fire. Even if he felt like taking a bath he would not have gotten in the water with a nude girl.

Rusty was out of the water within a couple minutes. He raced barefoot to the fire and stood there shivering, great goose bumps covering his freckled skin. He picked dirt out from under his nails. "I don't know how she can stand it in there. That water is freezing."

Sandra washed all her clothes before she came back to the fire with her shawl only loosely wrapped around her. Scott tried his best to look away. If she had strong inhibitions about having her body touched, she did not seem to mind it being seen—and admired.

"You know, I'm getting attached to you guys,

even if you are a little stuck-up." After wringing out her tresses, Sandra tilted her head and rotated her neck so that her hair stroked the fine skin of her back. She sat cross-legged by the fire. Scott noticed that her tan spread over her entire body, without any lines of discretion.

"What is that?" Death Wind pointed to Sandra's earlobe.

"That? Oh, that's an earring. I have two, see?" She bared the other ear. The jewels caught the sparkle of the fire, each facet glittering.

"Why?"

"Why what?"

"Why do you wear it? What is the use?"

"Well, it doesn't really have a use. It's just ornamental—and sentimental."

"What this mean?" Death Wind looked at Scott, and repeated, "What does this mean?"

Sandra pouted. "Scott, you better stretch your English lessons to include vocabulary."

"He's doing fine, soaking everything up like a sponge."

"What is sentimental?"

Sandra sighed heavily, and covered her ears with her black tresses. "You see, my mother gave them to me. Besides making me look pretty, they remind me—that is, they make me feel—I mean, they give me a feeling of—oh, forget it. I'll explain it later."

"Maybe you can explain something to me." Scott laid his weary bones down before he fell down. With his head resting a log, he went on. "Did you have computers where you lived? In the subway, that is."

"Whaddaya think, we were savages, or something? Of we had computers. That's why we moved in with those people. And we had all kinds of gadgets, too. I'm quite a repairman, used to tinker with the machines all winter long, when it was too cold to go outside."

"And did you have movie disks?"

"Oh, yes. I used to watch them all the time."

"Hmmnn." Scott was thoughtful for a moment. "How old were you when you moved in there? You've picked up quite a bit of old colloquialisms, so I figured it must have made an early impression on you."

"Well, I guess I was about eight. My mother and father had already started tutoring me, and when we found the subway people they showed me how to use their computers."

"Oh, so you're sixteen years old." Sandra looked stunned for a moment. Then Scott started laughing, and could not stop.

"You tricked me," Sandra screamed. She looked from face to face, but found no sympathy anywhere. "Oh, you men are despicable. And just when I was beginning to like you." She got up and walked off in a huff.

Scott winked at Rusty. The latter smiled back. Then Death Wind leaned over and said in a secretive voice, "Strange woman."

CHAPTER 11

Scott studied the dragon gun with the intensity of a mechanic. "It's definitely a laser beam. I can hear the capacitor recycling after each shot." He took his ear off the power pack. It was one piece of molded plastic with no visible means of access.

Rusty looked at the funneling nozzle. "I don't know what kind of battery can store that much power, and there's no telling how long the charge will last. What does the nozzle do?"

"It focuses the beam, like the ones we used to use for cutting metal. Only this is a lot more powerful. I can burn a hole through one of these lizards at a hundred feet. At two hundred feet—"

"If you can hit anything at that distance," Sandra interrupted.

"At two hundred feet it will singe, but the beam is spread too wide to be deadly."

Sandra patted the rifle butt. "I can hit a bull's-eye at a thousand feet with this."

"Yes, but I'm afraid to practice too much because I don't know when this thing will die out on me."

"But you don't hafta allow for droppage—it shoots exactly where you aim it."

"Listen, do you have to show off all the time?" Scott's face clouded with anger. "If you want me to admit that you're better than I am, all right. You're better. Now get off my back."

"Well, sor-ree. I didn't think you were so sensitive about it. Come on, Death Wind, let's go for a walk and leave the two brains alone."

She dragged the Nomad off by the hand. Once they were out of hearing, she said, "Which do you think is better?"

Death Wind kicked over a rotten log and picked up a handful of grubs. One by one he popped them into his mouth. "Bow is best. Always make arrow."

"Yeeck, how can you do that? Those slimy

things make me sick just to look at 'em."

"No taste. Throw past tongue. Swallow."

"But why do you do it? Don't we have enough meat?"

"Habit." Then, remembering Scott's schooling, he said, "It is habit. Always take opportunity. If stomach is always full, there is no hunger."

"Yeah? Well, let me show you something."

The forest was green and fertile and full of all that was wonderful in the world. Tall grasses wisped in gentle breezes, colorful flowers adorned the ground, and wildlife abounded. Insects added a melodic drone that was a lure into serenity. Feathered lizards flitted in the treetops, gliding from one branch to another rather than actually flapping their forearms and flying. This was the kind of life that Death Wind knew and appreciated.

Sandra bent down and picked a spiderwort. Its purple blossoms were taking in the sun. She stuck it in Death Wind's face. "Smells good, right?"

The Nomad wrinkled his nose. He shrugged.

"Don't give me that. If we're going to be friends you have to be honest with me. Now, does it smell good, or doesn't it?"

Death Wind gave in reluctantly. "Smell goo— yes, it smells good."

"That's better." Under some bushes Sandra found a cluster of wallflowers, whose golden petals rivaled the warmth and color of the sun. She snapped off several of the foot-long stems and held them together like a bouquet. With a long, deep inhale she sniffed the freshness. "Well, they don't smell all that great—but they're beautiful. Right?"

"They—are pretty."

"Right. And if I take this purple one and place it over my ear, like so, it makes me look pretty, too. Don't you think so?"

For the first time Death Wind took a long, deep look at her. She was from a different culture, but she had many of the same qualities of the women of his tribe. And, in some ways he could not yet identify, she had more.

"Yes. You are pretty."

"Why, thank you." Sandra pirouetted daintily, hugging the wallflowers close to her breast.

He did not even notice the incongruousness of the rifle slung over her shoulder. He saw only her gay eyes, her flowing hair, the shape of her body, the softness of her skin.

"And I would like you to have these." Sandra

handed the bouquet to Death Wind.

He took them, not quite knowing what to do with them.

"You see, these are like the earrings my mother gave me. I give you the flowers because I want you to have them, because I want you to think of me when you look at them. And because I hope you'll remember me in some special way. That's kind of what sentiment is all about. It's a way of feeling."

Death Wind was not sure he understood it any more than he understood the strange churnings going on inside his body. He knew only that this girl brought with her a new kind of friendship.

Death Wind and Sandra returned to camp bearing three dead lizards, as well as fruit and berries, for the larder. Rusty separated strands of lizard gut that could be used as threads, while Scott stitched a new pair of moccasins.

Scott held up his latest creation. "Hey, what do you think of these?"

Death Wind inspected the dried skin. "Good. You make more?"

"Will you make more," Scott corrected. "And we already have. Rusty and I have ours, and this pair's for you. Now, if the lady will supply her foot for measuring I'll see if she's really Cinderella."

"Don't you think I can make moccasins?"

"Oh, I have no doubt about your ability to do anything you set your mind to. But I had to do something while you were out, uh, bringing home the bacon."

"All right, wise guy. If you're trying to shame me into making my own, forget it." Sandra put her best foot forward. "I never look a gift horse in the mouth."

Scott removed her badly worn slipper and placed her foot flat on the dried sheet of lizard skin. He said "Hmmnn" several times, marking places by making creases. "Any particular style you'd like? Left folding? Right folding? Double folding? Get them while they're cheap."

Sandra's face softened into a smile. "Come on, silly. Are you done?"

"Not quite. Would you like to see our line of shawls? Yours is lovely, but not very practical."

"Oh, yeah? Says who?"

Scott smiled broadly. "Says Death Wind. He says we're all going to need hats in case we're out during the day, so we don't go batty. I figure we can attach a hood to your shawl, like a burnoose."

Sandra thought about it. "Well, if you say so." She removed her outer layer and allowed Scott to affix a makeshift hood to it.

Death Wind ignored the banter and rechecked the packs to make sure they had everything they would need for the crossing: freshly cooked meat, sheets of skin for tarps, and plenty of bladders filled with fresh water.

As the strongest of the group he carried the largest pack, loaded down with meat and water. Rusty carried a smaller one, suitable to his weight and leanness, filled mostly with fruits and tubers the savage had collected. Scott, besides the heavy power pack for the beamer, had slung underneath a small pack with odds and ends. Sandra was weighted down with her two bandoliers and a small pack of essentials. All carried water, as much as they were able, as well as a tarp for shelter.

That night, in the cool cloak of darkness, they set out upon the Great Desert.

* * *

Close up, the desert was not as flat and unbroken as it had appeared from miles away and thousands of feet up. It was rough and cragged in places, and sometimes split apart by arroyos whose steep walls and dry bottoms were crossed only with difficulty.

At first light the desert was already warm. By the time the sun came into view the heat was unbearable. It reflected off the sand as it would off glazed oven brick. Death Wind directed them to scrape stones and sand into a knee-high platform.

"Most heat, low. We stay above."

Then he took out a dried lizard-skin tarp and showed the others how to erect it. Stones weighted on the end facing the prevailing wind kept out most of the sand, while short sticks propped up the sides and the other end. The only shade available was that which they carried with them.

"Lie flat, stay cool. Move only when you must."

All day long they waited out the heat, sweating, and sleeping fitfully. Within hours Death Wind felt dreadful thirst, and knew that the others, although uncomplaining, must also be feeling it. He passed around a canteen.

"Take only mouthful, hold on tongue, then swallow."

The hours of discomfort stretched on interminably. When the sun was at the zenith each tarp became a furnace. By late afternoon the heat reached its peak. Finally, when the sun dipped below the tall mountains to the west, Death Wind got up and folded his tarp. The heat lingered on for hours while they marched ever eastward. The first day passed uneventfully.

Under a rising star field, the desert was cast in bright relief. Life abounded in this rocky desert, from great fields of scrub to many varieties of cactus, agave, ocotilla, yucca, and the strangely gnarled joshua trees. Warm-blooded lizards that lived underground or in the floral shade dashed about with energy to spare. When the moon rose, the land was nearly as bright as day.

Along the way they passed more than one trail of glazed sand and burnt smudges. "These very old. See how sand start to cover. Another moon and the desert will swallow them."

On the third night they came to a river. It was not as large as the one by their last campsite, but it was too wide and deep to swim or wade.

"Gather driftwood. We build raft."

Twisted timber was lashed together with vine, and made large enough for the packs. Then it was launched into the slow-moving water and pushed across to the opposite bank. There Death Wind called a halt.

"Whenever we find water, we rest."

They spent the remainder of the night and all that day by the river, drinking water like camels, replenishing food supplies from what they could scrounge. Death Wind collected salamanders and crayfish from under rocks, and roasted them whole in the fire.

"This is good. You eat, make you strong." He tossed an unskinned salamander into his mouth, then broke open the shells of the crayfish and sucked out the innards. Rusty had clubbed an unnamed lizard with his spear, and after it was cooked he shared it with Scott and Sandra.

"Good," Death Wind said. "More for me."

Days later, Death Wind called a halt at a dry streambed. "We dig hole, find water in ground."

They had to dig three feet down, but the water was there just as the Nomad said it would be. He put his mouth to the sand, sucked through his lips until his mouth was full, and spit it into the pouch. They all took turns at the task.

Then they lay under their tarps, constantly harassed by ants and other biting insects. Death Wind had a unique solution to marauding bugs—he ate them.

"Listen!" cried Rusty.

The muted thrumming sound of a flyer vibrated the air. But the golden ship was a long way off, paralleling their course.

"Do not worry. Our tarps cannot be seen from the air."

Scott shaded his eyes and watched the flyer disappear to the east. "Well, it looks like the slimy lizards are going to lead us right to the gate."

"I sure would like to fly in one of those things," Sandra said. "It beats walking in this heat."

"Can't say much for the company, though," Scott said.

Death Wind concentrated on finding water. With his long knife he lopped the top off a large barrel cactus, then beat the pith with the blunt end of Rusty's spear until it was a mass of juicy pulp. This could be sucked out with a hollowed stem, or the whole plant could be chopped down and the precious liquid poured out into a tarp and funneled into the canteens.

After that, Death Wind indicated a fracture line in the rock. "Shade make water. It roll down hard surface into small pool. There you drink with tongue." The amount was small, but in the desert no source of water was overlooked.

When they had started their journey across the Great Desert the moon was nearly full, a white beacon in the sky. Each night it appeared later, and smaller, until now the thin crescent disappeared altogether. And still there was no end of the desert in sight.

The food ran out. The oddly horned chameleons that scampered across the sand were fast and hard to catch. Vegetation grew sparse, and the cactus smaller and harder to find. The few streambeds they crossed had not carried water in years, possibly decades.

"I—I'm feeling so weak." Sandra paused for a rest, and Death Wind relieved her of the bandoliers. He stuffed them in his now empty pack.

Scott licked lips that were dry and cracked. "How much farther?" But there was no way of knowing, and no answer was forthcoming.

"I'll take your small pack." Rusty shrugged off the straps, and helped Scott get rid of the fanny pack. He tucked it inside his own, so Scott would have to carry only the beamer and its power pack. Rusty used his spear as a staff, to pole him across the wasteland.

Death Wind too felt the terrible toll the desert was taking. His shoulders sagged; his steps grew shorter. He struggled to observe through filmy eyes. "Over there. You see?"

They all looked up at a lizard the size of a small chicken. Scott aimed and fired. The laser beam was on target, but its energy had fanned out in the distance. The creature leaped up on hind legs and darted off with little more than a hot foot.

Sandra dropped immediately to one knee, led the lizard with the sights, and brought it down with a bullet through the head.

"Way to go," Scott shouted.

Death Wind ran and picked it up before the precious blood dripped out of the severed neck. Then he closed his lips over the still pumping artery and drew out a mouthful of warm, red, life-giving liquid. He handed the prize to the others. Now there was no squeamishness as they partook of the sacrificial bloodletting.

They ate the lizard on the spot—raw.

The blood provided much needed salt, but it also made them thirsty for more. Death Wind spent hours digging a deep hole. The result was a layer of slightly damp sand. He covered it with a shred of material torn from Sandra's burnoose. When it became moist he sucked on the upper side. It did little more than wet his tongue, but it assuaged the craving that was driving him mad. He shared his technique with the others.

The desert was too dry for grubs, but insects crawled in the cracks and crevices. Death Wind ate them with glee, unmindful of the still-working mandibles and the flailing, tickling legs. First Scott, then Sandra, and finally Rusty followed his example.

Death Wind handed out round pebbles. "Put in mouth, roll over tongue. It make you feel better." The pebbles gave them no water, but the false sense of comfort kept them going—for a while.

Sandra collapsed, and three pairs of arms helped her to her feet.

"We rest now."

"No." Sandra shrugged off the men. "Just point me in the right direction, and let's keep going."

When she succumbed the second time Death Wind let her lie where she fell. "We rest."

Scott and Rusty dropped their weary bodies to the ground and fell asleep, while Death Wind stood watch.

As far as he could see there was nothing but flat, rolling desert. He barely had the energy to suck in the air to fill his lungs. Every breath was pain—but pain, at least, was life. And because of his own weakness he feared for the others to whom this was more than torture.

After an hour he roused them. "Five-minute rest do us good. Sandra, you lead."

With the weakest in front, Death Wind concentrated on his own footsteps, putting one foot in front of the other, over and over, again, and again, and again, and . . .

Sandra he half carried: one slender arm hung limply over his broad shoulder, and her long hair mingled with his. Rusty could no longer hold onto his spear, so he tied it to his pack and let it drag behind him. Scott kept walking off on a tangent, apparently unaware of where he was going. Only Death Wind's constant shouting kept him oriented.

Rusty swooned, and sank to the ground. He opened his eyes and stared up at Death Wind. "Go on without me. I can't make it."

"We go together—or not at all." The savage lifted Rusty to his feet, let him lean on his other shoulder. Scott held onto the straps of Rusty's pack, so that he was half led, half dragged in the right direction. Sandra's eyes rolled loosely in their sockets, and she mumbled deliriously.

"Keep walking. We find water soon." Death Wind was the nucleus of an eight-legged creature that slithered across the rocky desert, supporting two people and towing one.

A tiny cactus offered relief from thirst. A snake caught unawares lent its body. A cache of lizard eggs gave them all some liquid and a small amount of energy. They walked, and still nothing was before them but more desert. They moved ever slower, but they moved.

A foot-long lizard scuttled out from under Death Wind's foot, but so befuddled was his brain that by the time he drew his bow it climbed up on two legs and ran away. He notched his bow anyway, and held it ready for the next time. When it came, he was ready for it, and a two-foot-long specimen fell writhing to the ground.

Death Wind skinned it, and the blood and meat brought them out of the depths of despair. He ate none himself.

With this extra bit of energy Sandra unlimbered her rifle. The next lizard that popped up in front of them went down severely wounded. Death Wind crushed its skull with his foot. They ate again, and rested among some loose boulders, looking like a group of desiccated mummies.

Only Death Wind had the volition to go on. He hoisted Scott up and left him standing with his eyes closed. Then he pulled up Rusty and Sandra. The four walked abreast. Scott supported Rusty who leaned against Death Wind who held up Sandra.

A lizard appeared, but so entangled were the four warriors that it escaped by the time Death Wind freed an arm and pulled an arrow from his quiver. It was hours before they saw the next one. Death Wind stepped aside to shoot and, without his support, all three of his companions fell to the ground. He only nicked his target, but then Scott got out his beamer and, from the prone position, fired at the retreating animal. By that time it was so far away that instead of burning a hole in the beast it was only cooked. But it did not get away, and the hot meal helped to revive them from their lethargy.

Death Wind saw a lone shrub planted incongruously where there was nothing else but sand and rock. He pulled it up out of the ground, shook off the clinging dirt, and handed out the roots to his companions. They sucked off the slender shoots and got minute portions of moisture.

Then there were desert wildflowers, and they ate the blossoms and sucked the roots. A small cactus fell to Death Wind's knife, and nurtured them all. He wrenched it free of the earth and pulled squirmy blobs out of the tangle of dirt around the roots. Rusty and Sandra fought over the slimy grubs.

The sun appeared, and on the horizon there was a blur. Death Wind's weakened eyes could not tell if it was an hallucination, or a line of cliffs. He hoped it was a rock wall where they could spend the day, for the saving of a few degrees of temperature could mean the difference between life and death.

The blur was not a cliff face—it was a stand of stunted trees. There was also grass, and cactus, and insects by the hundreds. Death Wind broke off stems from an ephedra shrub, which had hollowed tubes, and showed the others how to suck up ants as they crawled over the ground. They feasted on grubs and roots, and were happy to have them.

Scott managed a grin. "I never thought I'd be so happy to see a grub." He plopped another one into his mouth.

Rusty turned over a log and gathered wood lice. "I'll trade you a louse for a grub."

Sandra pushed Rusty out of the way. "You idiot, you almost let that earthworm get away." She clawed the dirt until she was able to pinch the end and pull it out. She swallowed it without even thinking.

Despite the growing heat Death Wind urged them on. Now the wide hat brims brought some comfort. The grass grew thicker, the shrubs more plentiful. Small lizards abounded. They were fast, but the warriors were desperate. Death Wind showed them how to kill their prey instantly by biting the neck.

A trickle of water an inch wide and scant fractions deep carved a muddy path through thin underbrush. Groveling on their bellies, they slurped greedily until Death Wind pushed them away.

"No need to hurry when food and water plentiful. Drink now, drink later. We build our strength slowly. When strong, we fight."

CHAPTER 12

"This is a fine pickle you've gotten us into."

Death Wind was unperturbed by Sandra's words. He parted the branches in front of him and thrust out his head. From the top of the giant willow tree he looked down at the fifteen-foot-tall iguanodon as it pulled leaves off the lower branches and stuffed them into its cavernous mouth. The harmless vegetarian was interested only in browse, but any dinosaur had instinctive defense mechanisms and it was best to stay out of its way.

"Why didn't you let me shoot it?"

"Kill for food, run for life."

"Next time, you run. I'm not gonna let an old fossil that shoulda been dead for a million years chase me around like a rabbit."

Rusty balanced on the limb next to her. "More like a hundred million years."

Sandra glared at him. The iguanodon wandered off on business of its own, and Scott climbed down from his retreat. "Come on, Sandra. That thing's too big to kill with our puny weapons."

"That's no reason to give up." She alighted on soil that was soft and loamy, and squished underfoot.

Death Wind hit the ground with a thud, his

eyes ever on the alert and following the direction of the animal's departure.

Scott took the packs that Rusty lowered to him. "Why can't you live and let live? Is there some reason you need to slaughter everything that gets in your way?"

"You shut up, you, or I'll feed you to the dinosaurs." She pulled back the bolt and made sure a round was chambered.

"Does that mean you don't like me anymore?"

"It means I'm gonna bump off anything that resembles a dragon until I get my mother back."

Death Wind started off toward a grove of magnolias. "Lizard not dragon."

When Rusty retrieved his spear from a thick patch of laurel and sassafras he fell behind. He ran to catch up, his packs only half on. "Besides, you'd be wasting ammunition we'll need against the dragons."

Scott plucked a white blossom from a dogwood, and sniffed it. "Sandra, you just don't like Death Wind telling you to go climb a tree."

"I told you to shut up or I'll—Oh, forget it. But the next time I'm not running. I came here to fight."

"We fight when the time come. For now, save strength."

Scott lagged back for a moment and broke off a sprig full of dogwood flowers. "Yes, save your urge to kill for the dragons."

"I'm not listening to you."

His hand reached out. "I bet you'd listen if I—"

The cracking sound that interrupted him could have been a tree splitting, or two rocks crashing together sharply. A moment later two more cracks were followed by a muted shout that was unmistakably human.

"Let's go." Scott was off and running even before Death Wind. He plowed through dense foliage, then over a field of tall grass toward a grove of stately palm trees. The spreading leaves blocked out much of the sun, and some of the heat. A faint breeze cooled the air. He saw what he was getting into long before he reached the area of conflict. A lone man in a loose tunic of olive drab cloth was being pursued by a hulking monstrosity that was cousin to the triceratops.

Rusty matched his pace and uttered a groan. "A styracosaurus."

The splayed shield that protected the neck was ringed with tiny, daggerlike projections that could stab at the face of any predator that tried to bite its leathery nape. The two horns above the eye ridges were short and stubby while the one on the nose stuck out like a long, squat sword. And that sword was being wielded by ten tons of flesh and bone.

With hair and beard as white as snow streaming over hunched shoulders, the lone man limped for the sanctuary of a group of head-high boulders. As he squeezed among them the wily styracosaurus felt no hesitation in climbing right over the top and taking swipes at the old man. For something that size, it moved with an amazing fawnlike grace.

A long, rapierlike tongue darted out, reaching into a crevice where the clawed forelimbs could not fit. One bullet skipped past the nose and spun off the curved shield into the air; another was swallowed by the raging mouth. The beast subsided, licking its wounds. But the tiny pistol bullets were little more than bee stings.

Death Wind charged past and loosed a flint-tipped arrow. It hit the dinosaur in the rump, in the sensitive area under the swishing tail. The thick appendage swept from side to side. The shaft snapped off like a reed, but the point was still deeply imbedded. The styracosaurus pivoted in rage. It caught another arrow full in the face, but it was harmlessly absorbed by the horny material of the neck shield.

Before he could draw another arrow, Death Wind was almost caught in a crossfire as a lightning bolt seared past him on one side and a burst of rifle bullets sang dangerously close by on the other. Neither seemed to show any immediate effect other than to further provoke the beast. The beamer blackened the thick hide, and the bullets spanged uselessly off the ornamented skull.

The styracosaurus charged, and the trio scattered like frightened doves. Momentum carried the dinosaur far past where they were standing before it comprehended that there was nothing in its path but a palm tree. It gored the sloping trunk, shredding bark as if it had gone through a sawmill. Its red, beady eyes fell on Rusty.

Armed with only a spear, Rusty hung back. Now, as he turned to run, his feet twisted around the shaft and he toppled over in the waving grass. The dinosaur lunged at this new two-legged foe.

Death Wind broke the beast's concentration with a well-placed arrow right behind the neck shield. Sandra's bullets pricked the coarse hide like so much rock salt. Scott kept firing the beamer. If there was enough time he might be able to erode the beast away.

The bright blasts of light attracted the dinosaur's attention. The small brain could not hold more than one thought at a time, so it swung toward Scott. But as the animal swept through the grass, Rusty sprang up from the ground and lunged with his spear. The hand-hewn weapon, molded so far away and carried with so much travail, now earned its worth. Rusty was almost bowled over as he embedded the fire-hardened tip just behind the foreleg in such a position that when the blunt end gouged into the soft earth, the beast's own momentum forced it straight into its vital organs.

The styracosaurus blundered to a stop. Rusty, now defenseless, ran toward the boulders where even now the old man was emerging from cover. Scott let go a couple of beamer blasts that befuddled the dinosaur enough to keep it tracking in circles.

"Get outa my way! You're in my line of fire." Sandra danced for a new position.

Scott pivoted as the girl put the rifle to her shoulder, and fired. Rusty and the old man met in the knee-high grass. Blue eyes peered out from under bushy white eyebrows as he spoke with throaty precision. "I think we've met our match."

Scott scuttled by them, yelling, "Run for cover. We'll hold him off."

Death Wind ran around the styracosaurus whooping and waving his arms. Sandra merged with Rusty and the old man, and ripped out the spent magazine. The dinosaur narrowed its gaze on the threesome; this was something on which its puny brain could concentrate. With arrows nipping at its heels and beamer blasts tanning its hide, it snorted and charged with the determination of a speeding freight train.

"Aim for the eyes." The old man held his gun out at arm's length and fired his last two cartridges.

Sandra crouched professionally on one knee. She slammed a full clip into the breech and pulled back the bolt, chambering a round. The styracosaurus came on like ten tons of locomotive destruction. With cool deliberation she aimed for the horned, shielded face and the two gleaming eyes.

"The eyes," the old man breathed, with religious fervor.

Sandra squeezed the trigger, and kept squeezing. A stream of bullets only split seconds apart stitched a zigzag line across the armored face, splintering horn and pinging off bone.

The beast was twenty feet away and closing fast. Sandra looked over the sights, then put the rifle across her bent knee. The thundering forelegs crumpled suddenly and the styracosaurus hit the ground like a bulldozer, plowing up great rows of dirt and grass. The furrow made by the long front horn stopped at Sandra's feet. With a single convulsive gasp it sank to the ground with its legs spread-eagled, and expired.

Sandra brushed loose hair from her face. "It was dead as soon as my first bullet went through the eye and into the brain. But it takes 'em a little while to figure it out."

CHAPTER 13

The old man looked at Sandra with a mixture of awe, respect, and surprise. "Oh, my," he uttered in a voice that was somewhat creaky but full of intonation. "This comes as quite a shock."

Scott helped steady the old man while he dusted himself off. "Are you all right?"

He shoved the rusted pistol into a brown leather holster that was cracked and faded with age. Casting his steel-gray eyes around the group of warriors, he studied their odd attire and anachronistic assortment of weaponry. His bushy eyebrows arched sharply. "Yes, I'm quite unscathed thanks to you and your arsenal. I'm glad you happened along."

"Men stick together. It is code."

"Ah, a member of the Nomads." The old man's smile slowly turned into a frown. "But tell me, what are you doing so far east? You people travel along the Rio Grande."

"Come kill dragon."

"I see." The old man pursed his thin lips. "An admirable goal, if only it were practical. I admire the courage of your venture if only for its audacity. How close is the rest of the tribe?"

Death Wind hesitated. "People all dead. Killed by dragon."

The old man's features contorted wryly, caught between pain and disbelief. His gray eyes veered off and stared sightlessly into the forest. "Oh. Oh, my. That is a pity. This unexpected increase in dragon activity must be to blame. What was your tribe?"

"Sintu."

Now the old man was horror-struck. "I—I can't tell you how—sorry I am to hear that. And the other tribes?"

Death Wind shrugged. "They are south. We come alone. We fight to the death."

"And have you forgotten the Nomad ethic to kill only when necessary—and practical? Rabbits live long because they hide."

Silence was Death Wind's only reply. Now the old man swept the motley crew with eyes that had lost their sparkle. "And you four are all that's left of a once noble tribe?" There was sadness in his voice.

"Oh, we're not Nomads," Scott said, pointing. "Rusty, and Sandra, and me. I'm Scott. We just sort of met on the way, and tagged along."

"I see. And what's your name?"

The Nomad folded his arms across his chest. "I am called Death Wind."

The old man was quite taken aback. "That's—that's quite different. And why did you choose that particular name?"

"To become a warrior, I killed a dragon."

"Ah, then the name is well deserved. Anyone who manages to kill a dragon is quite a warrior in my book. I honor your choice."

Death Wind gestured to the others. "These are warriors, too."

"Even my little girl, here?"

Sandra recoiled like a viper. "I'm not your little girl. I'm not anyone's little girl. I don't belong to anyone." She slung the rifle onto her shoulder, pulled the shawl tight, and pushed out her chest. "And I'm not little, either."

"Yes, I can see that. But you are a feisty one, though."

Rusty said, "She knocked out a whole squad of dragons—single-handed."

"I'm impressed." The snowy eyebrows launched high into the deeply etched forehead. To Sandra, he said, "But let me point out, my dear, that the possessive pronoun may be used to denote relationship or connection, not just ownership. Now, what say we repair to my humble abode and celebrate this fortuitous meeting? The drinks, such as they are, are on the house."

So saying, the old man turned and hobbled toward the pile of boulders, where he searched until he found a carved stick that served him as a cane. He leaned heavily on it, and waited while the others retrieved their packs from where they had left them before the fight. Already flies and numerous insects were gathering around the body of the styracosaurus, for in this jungle terrain and steamy atmosphere, flying bugs abounded.

"Excuse me, sir," Rusty said, when they began walking after the old man. "But, you haven't told us your name."

The old man smiled. "Well, I've gone under quite a few titles and appellations in my day, but most of the time I'm just called Doc. I am, you know. A doctor, that is." He tapped his bent left leg with the cane. "The last doctoring I did was to set this bone. Didn't do a very good job of it, I'm afraid. But then, there were mitigating circumstances."

"I set an arm once," Sandra said. "It wasn't so hard."

Doc was unperturbed. "Yes, the trick is to do it as soon as possible, before healing begins. In my case, I was buried under a rockslide for two days, nearly delirious with fever. By the time I dug myself out it was too late. It needed to be broken and reset, and I couldn't do it myself. I've always hated pain, you know."

Scott was awed. "Didn't you have any—friends?"

"All killed by the dragons. The only reason they botched the job in my case was because they didn't know I was under that pile of rocks they had beamed down on us. You see, I was in charge of a spying party that kept an eye on the dragons, and their city. Now, instead of seeking them out, I am forced to hide from them—an exigency of which I'm not exceptionally proud. I'm afraid my spying days are pretty much at an end. Now, I can barely manage to get around enough to shoot some fresh meat."

"You mean, you go out after dinosaurs with that thing?" Rusty pointed to the holstered pistol.

Doc laughed heartily. "No, I stay away from the big ones. Rabbit-sized dinosaurs are about all I can handle with this peashooter. Mostly, I live out of cans, but the diet gets so humdrum after a while. I assure you, I'm not senile enough yet to think I can attack a styracosaurus and get away with it. No, I stumbled on that one quite by accident. Or, should I say, it stumbled on me? It must have broken out of the pens."

"Pens?"

"You don't seem to know much about your

enemy. Knowledge of one's foe is important in any war. You see, those beasts are cattle to the dragons. They're herd animals, and they graze them out here in the reclaimed jungle. Of course, it wouldn't do to have them wandering all over the place, so they have them fenced in. The one you killed is what you might call a stray cow."

Sandra whistled. "That's some cow. I'd hate to meet the cowboy who lassoes it."

Doc laughed. "The dragons don't use lassoes, naturally—they use slaves. And they don't seem to mind much if they lose a few. They can always hatch more. On the other hand, all the dinosaurs relocated here are vegetarians—plant eaters, that is—and fight only defensively."

"You mean, we don't have to worry about running into an allosaurus?" Rusty said.

"You wouldn't be likely to find an allosaurus in any event. Besides the fact that the dragons wouldn't bring any carnivorous competitors with them, the allosaurs are from the wrong period. They lived in the Jurassic. All the dinosaurs you find nowadays came from the Cretaceous."

Scott scratched his head. "I don't understand. No matter what period the dinosaurs are from, how did the dragons get them all here in their spaceships?"

Sandra said, "Because, stupid, the dragons didn't come out of space. They came out of time.

Doc looked startled. "Oh, my, we do have a strange group here: two who are ignorant, one who knows all, and a silent Nomad who keeps his own council. And all traveling together."

The forest opened into a field, acres in size, with the ruins of a one-story concrete building in the center. Waist-high grass wafted silently in the breeze, while a wood slat nailed diagonally across the splintered opening in the cement wall clattered haphazardly.

"Well, here's home."

Doc followed a narrow path beaten through the grass. It passed over a couple of six-foot-diameter clearings where nothing grew. The thin layer of dirt was tinged red at the edges.

"Rusty!" Scott stopped in his tracks, staring down at the ground.

"I—I see it."

Scott dropped to his knees and quickly wiped the dirt away with his hands. In seconds he revealed an ancient iron surface. He scrubbed more. The rusting iron plate had six straight

cracks radiating outward from the center, like pie wedges. "It can't be."

"But, it is. These are missile silos."

Doc stared at Scott and Rusty as if they were ghosts from the past. "Oh, my. I think perhaps we'd better have a *long* talk."

CHAPTER 14

The copper kettle whistled on the makeshift metal stove. Doc removed the boiling water from the heat and blew out the flame in the dish of dinosaur fat. He spread an odd assortment of cups on the slab of wood that served as a table. Into each he dropped a handful of finely chopped leaves and stems, then added the water. He passed out the cups of steaming brew.

"I'm not used to having company, as you can see." He reserved the only chair in the room for himself, as well as the crate parked next to it on which he propped his aching leg. "So you must excuse my housekeeping. By the way, this is my own special blend, collected fresh every week. I hope you like it."

The concrete building was surprisingly cool, and drinking the hot, flavored water had a soothing effect that plain, cold water did not possess. Death Wind sliced meat from a slab in his pack.

Doc spread out a hand-drawn map on the tottering table. "Now, Death Wind, can you tell me approximately where you picked up these two itinerants?" He traced a line along the brown parchment with his index finger. "This is the Rio Grande, what your people call the River of Life. Here is your southern camp, and up here is the northern extremity of your summer migration. The other tribes are farther west and south."

Doc held an oil lamp over the middle of the map. Four others sat in the corners, casting weird, yellow, flickering shadows across the messy room. Wooden boxes and cans of rations had been hastily pushed aside to allow space for the guests.

A dark finger stabbed the paper. "Here."

"Hmmnn. That would seem to put them in the western quadrant. Yes, I can see how that would happen. And Sandra?"

"Here."

"Yes, that makes sense. It's along one of the old highway routes—probably covered with sand for quite some time.

"Hmmnn." Doc moved the lamp over the

map, and studied the surrounding areas. "I find it remarkable that your people have been living in complete isolation for more than a century. But considering the circumstances I guess it was the only viable option. You're lucky that your ancestors were trained to operate a command center instead of a missile base, otherwise you probably would not be here."

Doc sat back in his chair and propped up his leg. "You see, my predecessors were also opportunely stationed in an underground installation, near a place called the District of Columbia."

"The Capital," Rusty said.

Doc nodded in an aside to Death Wind. "Yes, it's what you would call the chief hogan of this once great country. It seems that in the old days men had some very queer notions. They believed in something called specialization. Everyone studied a particular branch of knowledge and strived to learn as much as possible about as little as possible. Now, there was really nothing drastically wrong with this because technology had become so complicated that it was the only way one could learn a sufficient quantity about certain complex jobs—although it did leave one ignorant of other facets of contemporary disciplines. Compartmentalization of the vast store of human knowledge was necessary in order to carry civilization onward, and upward—so to speak.

"Unfortunately, due to certain carryovers from prehistoric times, when mankind lived as an animal instead of as a society, not everyone had the choice of where he stood in this great maze of aristocracy. There were restrictions placed upon people because of artificial and wholly imaginary boundaries such as race, creed, political persuasion—and sex.

"To make a long story short, very few women were allowed to reach high enough stations in the military hierarchy to be assigned to the highly classified missile sites. So even though many underground installations survived the coming of the dragons, the survivors died out through attrition. In an old manner of speaking, it takes two to tango."

Rusty was enthusiastic. "Boy, you really know your history."

"It's all boring to me," Sandra said. "Get to the point."

"Yes. Well, from what you've told me of Maccam City, my guess is that your home was at one time the main control center for the entire

United States. In military parlance that would be Missile Control Center—Main. Appropriately abbreviated to MCCM, this would have come down as the acronym Maccam."

"Wow, I never came across that in any of the history disks." Scott nodded slowly. "It seems logical."

Doc sipped his tea. "And, I would also guess that because of the many functions required for coordination and administration, and the inherent clerical work involved, a proportionately large secretarial contingent must have been necessary for efficient operation. Thus, in addition to individual survival, Maccam City was granted racial continuance as well."

Sandra was still skeptical. "So how come you know so much—or think you do?"

Doc sighed patiently. Answering the question instead of the implication, he said, "I grew up in the main political structure situated under the now defunct city of Washington. It managed to survive under the same set of circumstances which I've just described. I had access to many disks, as well as a direct, word-of-mouth link to the past."

"But you lived on the surface," Rusty said. "Why didn't our ancestors ever come out of the ground?"

"Because they were scared," Sandra said.

Scott jumped to his feet. "That's a lie. My father wanted to leave the city years ago, but the council wouldn't let him."

"Whoa, please. Can we act a little more civilized. We really can't afford to fight among ourselves."

"But she said—"

"I heard what she said, and if you'll take my advice, young man, you'll ignore her vituperations. And you"—Doc pointed a gnarled finger at Sandra—"will stop trying to foment trouble. Do you want to fight dragons, or comrades?"

Sandra pouted, but remained silent. Scott sat down, glaring at her.

"Now, as I was about to say, from what you've told me my guess is that Maccam City was conceived as a self-contained emplacement designed to carry out a nuclear retaliatory war. Its personnel must have been instructed to remain hidden in such an event, and thereby remain safe from bombs and their resultant radiation. According to your own testimony, and in light of your presence, Maccam City was capable of functioning for many generations without external support. You were, in a manner of speaking, an ace in the hole."

Death Wind shuffled to his feet and looked down on the doctor. "You speak lies. Men do not fight men."

"Ah, my good friend, I can understand that to a Nomad the concept of internecine strife is repulsive as well as unbelievable. But a look at our two warring associates disagreeing because of differing beliefs is proof enough that men did not always, I'm ashamed to say, stick together."

Death Wind slowly sat down. After an uncomfortable silence Rusty said, "Well, let me ask you something else, Doc. Are you trying to say that for a hundred years we've been trained to counterstrike a nuclear attack that never took place?"

"Quite simply, yes."

"What a waste of time. You guys have sure been played for a coupla fools."

"Sandra, please dispense with the antagonism. To elucidate, Rusty, the best guess I can hazard is communications failure. Remember that the dragons' victory was as complete as it was instantaneous. Practically the entire human race was liquidated overnight. Without human guidance the electrical power systems failed. And while places like Maccam City were in a state of perpetual preparedness, trained and maintained like a well-oiled machine, the rest of the world came to a dead stop. Those who lived through the catastrophe had their hands full trying to survive. And no one, not even those in Washington, knew what had caused the plague."

Scott ignored his tea. "And all these years we've been waiting . . . waiting . . . "

"From generation to generation," Rusty finished.

"You guys are worse than fools, you're grade A, number one suckers."

"My dear, where did you learn such poor manners?"

"It wasn't from a namby-pamby like you."

"I'm glad to hear that." Doc stood and gazed at the map. "I was in that area ten or fifteen years ago, and I never knew . . .

"Never knew what?" Rusty had to repeat his question, louder, before Doc snapped out of the imaginary world of his mind.

"Oh, I was just thinking." He leaned back into his seat, propped up his leg. "You see, the Washington complex retained a semblance of the civilization and technology of the bygone era. We

had all the modern conveniences: generators that still worked, when we could find the fuel; operable computers; a storehouse of disks. As a youth I studied medicine, among other things. I was really quite a scholar, with a wide range of interests. But as I got older I realized that if mankind was going to reclaim his kingdom he had to expand. I went on many expeditions in search of other pockets of mankind that had survived the calamity. Inevitably, we found some. They were living in caves, in subways, even in sewers. And from each group of survivors I picked up stories, rumors, threads of information. First I heard about spaceships that flew on beams of destruction. Then I heard about a race of dragons that inhabited the bayou country. Then I saw my first dinosaur.

"The Washington shelter had been isolated for over fifty years, and we never knew, never even suspected, what had befallen mankind. What we had thought was a worldwide epidemic disease perpetrated by enemy biological warfare, we discovered to be a pogrom instituted by a race of lizardlike demons. More than that was conjecture.

"In order to ensure man's survival we spread out, so that all our eggs were not in the same basket. Runners maintained contact between groups, scouts explored new territory in search of hidden conclaves. Families and friends split up, perhaps never to see one another again.

"I did quite a bit of traveling in those days. I came across the tribes of the Nomads, learned their customs and ways of life. And possibly I helped impart in them the true knowledge of man's heritage. The Sintu, by the way, are descended from guides and concessionaires, perhaps even tourists, who happened to be in Carlsbad Caverns during the critical phase of the epidemic—something which might account for the American Indian influence on their descendants: their rituals, their habits, their closeness to the earth. Anyway, I'm straying from the point."

Doc brushed a leathery hand through his long, white hair, then ran it over his mouth to dry his lips. "Separated from my family, I joined a group of younger men. Our purpose was to keep an eye on the dragon city, learn what we could about them, follow their movements, discover their weaknesses. One day we were caught by dragon soldiers and wiped out. Only I survived. I had to crawl for miles to reach the safety of this silo. It was six months before I could get about, during which time I almost died of a fever that lasted for weeks. I lived on canned stores, some of it rotting. But I had no choice. Since then, I've lived here as a recluse, unable to observe the dragon city, unable to return to my people."

Doc's voice trailed off. He stared sightlessly at the darkened ceiling, lost for the moment in the failures of his past. Visibly, he shrugged off nostalgic thoughts. "I've always hoped that one day mankind would win back this beautiful planet. And that he would take better care of it than he did before. But it's only a dream. Only a dream."

"That's what we're going to do," Scott said.

Doc snickered affably. "Four youths, against the whole dragon race?"

"Four warriors," Death Wind said.

"It's not exactly what you would call an army, is it?"

"But we can try," Scott said, with determination.

"Yes, and you can die trying. Ah, in my youth I had the same delusions of grandeur. Now it all seems so futile."

"You're just a has-been who doesn't have the guts to go out and fight."

Doc looked at Sandra sharply. "Sandra, I'll forgive you your harsh remarks on the assumption that the exuberance of your youth has overtaken the dictates of your humanity. You're sadly misunderstanding the severity of the situation if you think a spear, an arrow, a rifle, and a stolen beamer are going to topple the superior technology and the sheer mass of numbers that the dragons have at their control. It's like attacking a stone wall with a toothpick."

"If you had done something years ago we wouldn't be in this mess now."

Doc's voice went up a note. "If we could have done something years ago we would have. But remember that it was over sixty years after the plague before we recognized our enemy. And by that time they had gained such a foothold that no weapons at our command could fight them off. We had lost the tools and the knowledge of our civilization. We were a primitive people struggling to survive, and ill equipped to fight."

"So you're just gonna sit here an' die?"

"Ah, if all decisions were that simple." Doc stroked his bushy beard, recovering his composure. "As things are, we are powerless. The dragons have started a new expansion program;

they have increased their numbers, augmented their food supplies, and expanded their grazing area. Their city is spreading, their dominance is growing ever farther. Your own stories attest to that. Dinosaurs now roam most of the country, and soon the jungles will catch up with them. Even my poor observation post is on the verge of being overtaken by encroaching ranch land. There is more aerial traffic than ever—six flyers if my observations are correct, each capable of carrying a hundred soldiers. And they are systematically seeking out man's last strongholds, destroying the vestiges of his architectural creations.

"I'm afraid, my young friends, that the time for stopping the dragons is already past. We are the dinosaurs of this new age, doomed to extinction while a stronger and more viable breed takes over. Man was once a great and noble race, and he was endowed with even greater potential. Now he is vermin only slightly tolerated by a mightier race. You see, in real life it is not the good and the righteous who survive, but the most ruthless."

Doc dropped his leg to the floor and pushed himself up out of the chair. He picked up his cane and an oil lamp, and hobbled for the doorway.

"Your hostility is well deserved, my dear, but I'm afraid it's misplaced and just a little too late. Now, if you will excuse an old man, I must rest these weary bones."

The stooped and disillusioned patriarch retreated through the door to an adjacent room, and left the four youths with their thoughts.

CHAPTER 15

The oil lamps were out, the concrete bunker was clothed in darkness, and the old man lay serenely asleep on a silver disc covered with palm fronds. He snored smoothly until his dim world burst into brightness and his dreams recoiled into the fantasyland from which they had come.

He lurched upright in his jury-rigged bed, with rusting metal vanes snapping loudly beneath the fronds. He was blinded by the intruding light, and for several moments groped around shielding his eyes against the glare. Then, as he adjusted to the brightness, he began to comprehend what had happened.

"Oh, my." He squinted up at the ceiling of the cubicle, unwilling to accept what he saw.

He clambered down from his circular bed and rushed out into the narrow, concrete hallway. Here, too, where there should have been utter darkness, the corridor was alive with a yellow, unflickering light. It was as if the roof had suddenly been peeled off and the sun shone down.

He heard a yell, and instinctively ran in that direction. He turned a corner just in time to see Death Wind swinging his hand wildly, as if shaking off a cloud of bees. Sandra, standing by his side, laughed at his antics.

Scott stepped out of a doorway wearing a tool pouch full of wrenches, pliers, and screwdrivers. "What's the trouble?"

"Our mighty warrior has never seen a light bulb before, and he just got stung when he touched it."

Death Wind blew on his fingers. "Hot."

"Hey, Scott," came a shout from inside the room. "The breakers are holding fine. All we have to do is check the switches and—oh. Hi, Doc. Did we wake you?"

Doc quickly regained control of himself. "You certainly did. Pray, tell me, what is going on?"

Scott said, "We just turned on the juice."

"But—how? I've searched every corner of this place, and there's no fuel for the generators."

Rusty wiped grease off his forehead. "Oh, we didn't bother with the generators. We turned on the reactor."

"The *nuclear* reactor?"

"You know of any other kind, gramps?"

"But, it takes uranium—and the proper know-how."

"You forget, we're specialists. Scott and I have spent our whole lives in a place like this. Of course, this place could use a little maintenance to bring it up to snuff, but . . . "

"But how did you get the reactor going?"

"We pulled out the control rods," Scott said. "Of course, the damping motors won't run without the generators, so we switched to manual override and raised the rods by hand. But now that the reactor's supplying electricity we can run the dampers on reactor mode."

Doc put his jaw back in place. "Oh, my. I really must sit down. Would you boys help me back to my room? I seem to have forgotten my cane."

With Sandra and Death Wind leading the way, Scott and Rusty each grabbed an arm and escorted the limping man to his bed. They helped him onto the edge where he remained sitting with one leg dangling and one propped up. Doc looked around at the smiling faces.

"Perhaps you'd better explain."

Rusty took the initiative. "According to standard operating procedure, shut-down missile bases are left in Code Two condition: that is, with warheads on safe and primers removed. We did a little checking and found that everything was in order. The missile pods had been sealed, the control room had been locked, and the reactor plant had been evacuated and fully damped. We found the restarting checklist and turned everything back on. Of course, we still have to clean out the electrical cabinets and dust the contacts and check the circuitry, but so far everything works."

"Not only that," Scott added, "but I inspected the missiles. The warheads are still in place, with the fuses out. All we have to do is rearm them. They're ready to fly."

"But—how can that be after all these years?"

"The rockets run on solid propellant so it can't leak away. Remember, that was necessary in the old days because they were never really intended to be launched except in case of emergency. They were mostly a deterrent, a bluff against enemy attack."

Rusty took the ball. "We activated the computers, too, and plugged in a few disks. It's still operational, although there are a few bugs."

"And there aren't any old movie disks," Sandra complained.

"I'm pretty sure that with some routine maintenance we can have the whole installation back on line. Scott's the best there is in missile repair—"

"And nobody can beat Rusty when it comes to plotting trajectories. We're going to show those dragons a thing or two. We'll knock those flyers right out of the sky."

Doc ran crooked fingers through unkempt, snowy hair. "It seems that while I was asleep the whole world has changed. Uh, you wouldn't josh an old man, would you?"

"Not if that old man's willing to put his money where his mouth is. We're gonna fight those dragons with whatever we have, right down to the fingernails. I'll scratch their eyes out if I have to. I want my mother back."

"Child, revenge is sweet, but you can't bring back that which no longer exists."

"You shut up, you, or I'll—" Sandra flung her long hair over her shoulder. Her eyes narrowed. "My mother's not dead."

"I know what you said, but—"

"I'm telling you she was still kicking when those slimy beasts dragged her into the flyer." She stared defiantly at her companions' blank faces. "All right, I know you think I have an obsession about my mother. Well, maybe I do. But you guys all lost your families to the dragons, so don't try to kid yourselves that your motives are all that noble. You're as selfish as I am, only I'm willing to admit it."

"That sounds like an astute observation, one with which I would not care to argue."

"Good. Then let's go all the way and assume that, since I'm not crazy, there's a chance that my mother's still alive—and that we can rescue her."

Doc sighed. "Just don't get your hopes up." After a moment's silence, he went on, "Well, now that that's settled, let's get back to the business at hand. How about if I rustle up some chow?"

Scott removed his tool pouch. "I'm ready to eat."

"You're always ready to eat," Sandra said.

Doc found his cane and led the group to the other room. He had difficulty locating the light switches, but when he did and the bulbs glowed with yellow brilliance, he realized how easy life would be if he did not have to constantly refine dinosaur oil for the lamps.

He gestured with his hand. "Please excuse this. In the dark I had no idea I was such a messy housekeeper."

Sandra blew dust off a pile of plates. "Don't worry about it, as long as you can cook on an electric range."

"It's something I haven't done in quite a while, but I don't think I've lost the touch. You can be the judge of that."

Scott found a rag and started wiping out bowls. "Anything would be better than raw grubs."

Sandra laughed. "For once, you and I agree on something."

Doc opened cans of meat and vegetables and mixed them in a saucepan with a quart of water. After more than a century they were slow to rehydrate.

Rusty set the table with silverware. "We've got practically all the lights on in the lower levels, and we found some nice rooms. You can move into deeper quarters if you want."

Doc stirred the mixture as it heated. "I almost hate to leave this squalor." The soup boiled rapidly on the red-hot elements, and soon Doc ladled out steaming portions to everyone. "Well, what do you think of it?"

Death Wind fumbled with the unfamiliar utensil. "Food," was his only comment.

"Ah, a man after my own heart. He understands the simple essentials of life."

"Definitely better than earthworms. And this tea of yours ain't too bad, either."

"I accept that as a compliment of the highest order." And in his mind, he could not help but add: considering the source. "Now that your bodies are being taken care of, I have some food for thought."

Doc sat in his chair and propped up his bad leg. "As I see it, now I've got no choice but to help you. Your skills need to be wedded with my knowledge, and your rashness needs to be tempered by my sagacity. With that combination I think there is a better chance of success. Besides, if I don't help you, you'll go ahead and do it on your own. And I'd like to be there at the finish line."

Scott and Rusty cheered. Sandra snorted. Death Wind, as usual, was silent.

Scott stopped slurping his soup for a moment. "That's great, Doc. But could you give us some background information? Rusty and I are still pretty much in the dark about the dragon invasion. And every time I ask Sandra she gives me a dirty look and says ask the old—well, she's pretty tight-lipped."

Doc played with his beard for a moment before speaking. With his leg up on the crate he appeared to be lounging, but it was only way he could stop the constant throbbing. "Most of what I know about the dragons is a careful blend of observation, word of mouth, and deduction, with a good bit of supposition thrown in to fill in the gaps. But I think it conforms fairly closely to the truth.

"The dragons came here from the past, the late Cretaceous I suspect, about sixty million years ago, through an artificial window they created in the space-time continuum and kept open by a power of unimaginable magnitude. To herald their coming they released into the atmosphere a bomb which disseminated a viral nerve gas that killed all breathing animals with a highly evolved central nervous system: mammals, birds, reptiles, amphibians, and fish, although most ocean dwellers escaped because the plague-producing virus could not exist for long in water. One bomb was dropped over each continent, and the virus spread by the wind. Within a week it was all over. When their hosts ceased to exist, the virus died out, and the dragons had virtually a virgin planet all to themselves.

"Naturally, there were survivors. Burrowing animals, bats, possibly bears in hibernation. Anything that had not breathed in the deadly virus during its short virulent stage, were spared, although many of them must have died anyway because of the changes brought about.

"Into this world empty of dominant life forms the dragons brought eggs from their own time, and began raising the saurian livestock on which they feed. Now they are spreading their influence even wider, even faster, although there is opinion that every ten years or so the dragons drop bombs on the other continents of the world, presumably to keep them sterile until they are prepared to expand from North America."

Rusty toyed with his food, finally pushing the bowl away. "But, Doc, if there was a civilization of intelligent—well—lizards in the past, why hadn't fossil evidence been dug up?"

"Who says it hasn't? Naturally, you wouldn't expect to find traces of cities, or machines, or artifacts. They would not survive in recognizable form throughout the millennia. But there are many examples of bird-hipped dinosaurs, such as the struthiomimes, which the dragons resemble. There must have been hundreds of skeletons in museums all over the world similar in form and size. But even an experienced paleontologist could not tell from bone fragments what kind of brain the bearer had."

"Yes, I can see that. But another point: didn't the dinosaurs die out around the end of the Cretaceous?"

"Right you are, my lad. Your profound knowledge never ceases to amaze me. At that time there was only one massive protocontinent, known as Pangaea. For some unknown geological reason Pangaea broke up into the individual land masses we recognize today. At the same time the little mammals, our very ancestors, took over the Earth, and the age of the 'thunder lizards' came to a rather abrupt end. The theory

has been advanced that it was the appearance of these early mammals which spelled the end of the dinosaurs' reign, perhaps because they were smarter than their predecessors, or ate their eggs, or were more adaptable to changing climatic conditions. No one knows for sure. My guess is that in their own epoch the dragons are on the verge of dying out, and the discovery of the time transporter has offered them a way to a less troubled era: a place-time where they can expand their cold-blooded rule."

"That reminds me of something, Doc," Scott said. "Death Wind has told us that the dragons are cold-blooded, while the dinosaurs are warm-blooded. I don't quite remember it that way from the history disks."

"Yes, before the coming of the dragons it had only recently been theorized that the dinosaurs might in fact be warm-blooded animals, and that the mammals and birds are actually offshoots which then split and developed along different evolutionary lines. There was convincing experimental data that animals of such bulk could not have heated their bodies solely through the warmth of the sun, as true lizards do, and that they must therefore have had internal regulators.

"The dragons, on the other hand, are related to the true lizards. They can't stand the cold, and never go out at night. Instead, they huddle in enclaves for warmth. They are not only cold-blooded, but ruthless. They are completely without feeling, without sentiment, without love or affection. Their eggs are hatched in great nurseries, their wounded are dispatched, their dead left to rot. They are cold and calculating not just in body, but in mind. They have an urge to conquer which knows no bounds of humanity, if I may use the word in its broadest sense. We just happen to live in a territory which they wish to occupy, so they must exterminate us like pests—or parasites."

"Then we have to make sure they don't succeed," Scott said.

To which Death Wind added, "We will fight to the death."

"For revenge."

"For my mother."

"For our folks."

In the silence that followed Doc examined his newfound, friends. He sensed a dedication among them that reminded him of times past. Working together, these four seemed to have become a unit that was far greater than the simple addition of four talents. His heart reached out for them, and for their goals. He felt a longing he had not felt in years.

"Your devotion to duty overwhelms me."

Scott said, "We didn't come all this way for nothing."

"And we ain't about to give up."

"I see that."

"And if the dragons are expanding their sphere of influence, as you said, this may be our last chance," Rusty said. "But why have they waited so long?"

"Another astute observation, my friend. For that you must understand how the dragons arrived here. Some thirty years ago a certain restless and wayward, and I must say bold, scout sneaked into the city and spent many days exploring, making maps, and learning dragon ways. From him we learned that the temporal opening through which the dragons and all their belongings must pass is extremely small: hardly larger, in fact, than a closet. Besides this, another limiting factor is the energy requirement for each transfer. The receiving end of the transporter, in our time, is powered by a huge capacitor bank which is constantly being recharged. But I think that the energy level here is insignificant when compared to the amount of power required at the transmitting end, where the actual warp machine is located. They can transmit, of course, without a receiving apparatus, but not as often or as efficiently, and not, I suspect, as accurately. The machinery at this end is a fine tuner, an anchor which designates the exact place and time to which objects are sent.

"Lately, I believe, they have stepped up their power production in order to allow more transfers. With the aid of a spyglass I have watched the movements of their flyers. Recently, in addition to riding over man's ancient cities with their disruptor beams and dropping bombs which have unbelievable destructive power, they have been seeking out the last pockets of human resistance and stamping them out."

"My people?"

"My friend, the Sintu relied too much on stealth and movement, and did not impart enough variation into their migration route. The dragon warship may even have followed the path of your people to the vicinity of Maccam City, although they may have found it in any event.

"Now the dragons are expanding exponential-ly. With a larger base camp, with more supplies, with more personnel, they are burgeoning forth like a plague of locusts. As their influence increases, mankind's will lessen. At this moment we may represent one of the last vestiges of *Homo sapiens*, the hangers-on of the few who have escaped the dragons' clutches and have refused to give up."

"I thought you gave up a long time ago," Sandra said.

"Ah, that spiteful tongue again." Doc spoke without resentment. "My dear, before I met you I think I had given up. I was an old man, crippled and alone. But your spunk has inspired me. Your otherwise quixotic quest is doomed to failure without my assistance. Indeed, if you are going to attack the great city of the dragons as you intend, you will need my guidance. You will need to know the layout of the streets and buildings, how to get about without being seen, what to be wary of."

"Then you'll help us!" Scott shouted. "And do you still have the map that scout made?"

"That I have, young man. That I have." Tapping his gray temple with a crooked finger, Doc said with pride, "I keep that map right here where I can't lose it. For, you see, *I* was that scout. And I intend to go with you."

CHAPTER 16

"This is just an auxiliary testing station, with the mainframe computer acting as our fault detector," Rusty explained to Doc one afternoon. He flipped switches and showed how the gauges took readings on each circuit. "Since the lower levels were hermetically sealed, problems with moisture and oxygenation were eliminated. And with solid-state components time and nonuse is not a factor—by design, these printed circuit boards will last forever. Malfunctions occur only during use. But we're experiencing a lot of insulation breakdown on the high voltage lines. There's also been some drying and cracking of dielectric material in transformer and motor windings: we've got shorts all over the place."

Doc gazed reverently at the vast array of dials and switches, and the blinking lights of the annunciator panel. "What about that roomful of spare parts on the launch deck level?"

"We'll use them if we need them, but with triple redundancy we've been able to reroute all the circuits we need. Remember, we're not fixing this for a standby emergency. This is a one-shot deal, so what we want is immediate firing capability. Most of the equipment we're not even trying to repair, such as the air conditioning, telecommunications, and remote control servo motors. We're going to open the silo lids by hand and leave them open."

Doc leaned on his cane and tugged at his beard. "But won't you have the same percentage of electrical failures in the missiles themselves? How can you know in advance that they'll perform satisfactorily?"

Rusty smiled. "Let's go down to the control room and see how Scott's making out. After all, he's the missile man. All I do is set trajectories and push the firing button."

They found Scott sitting at a console surrounded by video screens, flush-mounted gages, and seemingly endless rows of toggles, each of which was tagged and numbered. When he heard Doc's question he leaned back in the chair and arched his back. Then he rubbed his eyes.

"Thanks, I can use a break to answer questions. Well, missiles have very few moving parts. With a solid rocket propellant there's no motor and no fuel feed: once it's ignited it keeps on burning until it either reaches its target or runs out of fuel. All the sensing devices and telemetering equipment are made with silicon chips and solid-state circuitry. The only real maintenance problem is from auxiliary engines that control guidance and attitude. Each missile has four, and these have to be in perfect working order or it won't track. So far, I've condemned two missiles as irreparable, but I'm going to cannibalize them for spare parts. That still gives us eight working missiles that we can count on functioning."

Doc shook his head in admiration. "And you have the knowledge of all this? Why, you're mere children."

Scott laughed. "You're showing your age. But, to answer your question, I don't have all this knowledge—but the computer does. Here, let me show you."

Leaning forward in his seat, he keyed the input panel and began typing instructions into the computer. The display screen lit up with an intricate pattern of interconnected dots and lines.

"Each missile has a computer access terminal. Once the cable's plugged into it, any malfunctions are automatically registered. Most of them can be corrected from right here, by computer rerouting. If it can't, then I have to perform a physical check. But the computer still guides my work, like an electronic overseer. Of course, I have to be familiar with the circuitry, but mostly I have to be able to read computer lingo."

"I see." Doc studied the diagram on the display screen. It showed enlargements of circuit diagrams, and highlighted in red those areas where trouble existed. Then, to show that he did understand, he said, "And those yellow lines indicate probabilities where failures might be."

"Exactly. Of course, the computer can do only so much. When it comes to nuts and bolts, or screwdrivers and wrenches, then it's up to me. But the computer also monitors my work so if I goof up it'll tell me I did something wrong."

"This is completely different from the computer we had back in Washington. That was really only a very complicated storage bank. It could do calculations and repeat stored material, but this—this computer actually does something creative."

"It's not as creative as you think," Rusty said. "It's just making calculations according to its program. It has limited applicability, since it's designed to do one particular job. Outside of that, it's useless."

Doc snorted. "And you boys feel certain that you can activate these missiles and knock down those flyers?"

"Once we entered the codes we gained unlimited access to the command and ballistic channels," Rusty said.

"It's simple mathematics. Six flyers, eight missiles. We can't lose." Scott leaned back again. "And it's unlikely they'll have any antimissile systems, or forms of electronic evasion. They've never needed any defense mechanisms. No, we've got them cold, Doc. We've got a weapon they're not prepared for. They've been fighting vegetables for a hundred years. Now those vegetables have suddenly grown teeth, and they're going to bite."

"Don't let your contention get the better of you. Revenge is an awful monster. It can make you take chances you would not otherwise consider."

"And win against odds you wouldn't otherwise bet against," Rusty said.

"Yes, that too."

"Besides, we've got nothing to live for but revenge," Scott said. "And if what you say about the dragons expanding their territory is true, we've got nothing to lose. They want to wipe us out, and unless we fight back, they're going to do it."

Doc nodded his gray head. "You speak with logic."

"However, we're missing one essential piece of equipment—we need a radar antenna. Without it all this fancy electronic apparatus is useless."

"Oh, my, that could prove to be a problem. The hills around here are so overgrown with Cretaceous fern that I don't suppose the original is still standing. At least, I've never come across it."

"The original didn't stand," Rusty said. "It flew. It was part of a network of orbiting satellites. But every station was equipped with emergency low-range antennas for close order surveillance. For what we need we could wire through those, if they still existed. There should be spares in stores, but we haven't been able to find any. Do you have any idea where one might be?"

Doc scratched his head. "I did some rummaging when I first moved in here—that's how I found these clothes. But that was a long time ago . . . I saw so many unfamiliar items." He pursed his lips. His cane clattered up the corridor, but he said over his shoulder, "I'll have to sleep on it for a while."

*   *   *

Work was going well until several days later when Scott divulged a serious problem during dinner, when the whole company was together.

"As you know, these are conventional ground-to-air missiles. That is, they're non-nuclear warheads intended for anti-insurgence from the Gulf of Mexico quadrant. They have a range of about five hundred miles—assuming we have radar pickup with that range—" His voice trailed off as he cast a glance at Doc.

"I'm—uh—still sleeping on it."

"Right. The attack computer can't lock onto a target without a dish antenna. Rusty and I have talked it over and we may be able to build one. But what I'm getting at is this. The proximity fuses are filled with a highly sensitive explosive. In accordance with shutdown procedures, they've been removed and put into storage. We've found them, but after a hundred years they could be unstable. It's going to be touch

and go resetting them on the warheads."

There was a moment of silence before Doc intervened with a question. "I know this must be overtly obvious to you, but tell me: what happens if this primer goes off when it's being set?"

Scott explained, "The missile explodes on the launch pad—along with the rocket propellant. We won't lose the whole base, just the one silo—and the person who sets it. Rusty and I have already discussed it and, well, my work will be done at that point. Setting the fuses will be the last thing I'll do. If anything goes wrong . . . "

There was a collective gasp that lasted for no more than two seconds before Death Wind jumped up and said, "I set."

A general hubbub ensued, which Doc did his best to quell. "Very commendable of you to volunteer, but in light of the fact that I'm the oldest and therefore the most expendable, I think I should be the one to take the task to hand."

Now there was more jabbering and disorder. Scott had to shout to be heard. "You can't, Doc. We need your experience when we attack the city. Once I get the missiles in working order, Rusty can handle the programming."

"Now, wait a minute, Scott. If you had to you could work out the computations."

"Oh, sure, I can fumble through and maybe get it right, but can we afford to take that chance? You're the one who tutored me, remember? We can count on you to get it right the first time. And we can't let Death Wind try it because we need him to get us to the city—through that jungle."

"All of a sudden everybody's a hero." Sandra banged her spoon on her plate. "You'd think they were giving away gold stars, or something, the way you guys are jumping at the chance to get yourselves blown to smithereens. Why don't we decide this democratically?"

"What do you have in mind, my dear?"

"Obviously, you'll have to let me do it. I'm the only one who's not indispensable. I can't do anything but shoot a gun and run my mouth. And nobody likes me anyway, so there won't be any bad feelings if I go sky-high."

"There is no doubt about your querulousness," Doc said dryly, "but that is no reason to say that we don't love you, each in our own way. I, myself, am quite fond of you—in a grandfatherly fashion. And I'm sure these young men all feel a certain, shall we say, attachment, toward you. Am I right?" But he went on quickly before either of them could agree—or object. "Besides, the ultimate success of our venture rests more with you than with any one of us. There is one task that only you can perform, one that will require a great amount of courage on your part."

"Oh, yeah? And what's that?"

"You can have children."

For the first time since he had known her, Sandra was struck dumb. Red with embarrassment, she spit and sputtered and gesticulated wildly—but not a word would come out. Finally, all dignity fled, she ran out of the room in a rage.

Then the four men laughed uproariously. There was room for humor no matter how serious the situation.

Eventually, Death Wind had the most winning argument. It was not because he was any less valuable, but because no one could find any fault in his reasoning. He merely pulled his long-bladed knife out of its sheath, held it threateningly before their faces, and said, "I set."

He got the job.

CHAPTER 17

"Doc, don't move."

Doc opened his eyes and saw Rusty creeping slowly toward him. He had grown so used to his two ground-floor rooms that he disdained against moving to another sleeping cubicle in the lower levels.

"I think I've found it."

"Found what?" Doc sat bolt upright and shook himself free of his lethargy.

"The spare radar antenna." Rusty put his hand on Doc's shoulder and prevented him from moving.

"I knew it would turn up. Where was it?"

Rusty brushed away some of the palm fronds that comprised Doc's mattress and exposed the gleaming metal underneath. "You've been sleeping on it."

"Oh, my." He looked down between his legs and saw the overlapping vanes, the edges tinged with rust.

Rusty helped him out of bed. "Careful. We don't want to bend the metal."

"I knew I was close to the solution, but . . . "

"It's all right." Rusty lifted it up and shook the dried matting to the concrete floor. "It's not damaged—you had it padded pretty well. I found the receiver down below in an open crate, so I knew you had been in it."

"It must have been when I first found this haven." By that time Rusty was already out the door with his prize. Since he no longer had a bed. Doc decided it was time to get up and help.

Later, while Doc supervised the setting up of the antenna, Death Wind and Sandra did the actual labor. Several hundred yards from the missile complex, Death Wind climbed the highest tree on the highest hill and sheared away the upper branches. To this he lashed a metal conduit, like stepping a mast, on which was mounted an electric motor with a coupling.

On the ground, the receiving horn was attached to the parabolic reflector, where Sandra spliced the electrical leads. Ropes were strung from the antenna to the tops of the adjacent trees. Then Scott and Rusty turned out to help hoist it into position. Death Wind climbed up the tree that was to be the tower, and with the others pulling on the ropes from the side, the whole affair, including a short spar and the trailing wires, was lifted to the uppermost point. With three guide wires maintaining its vertical attitude, Death Wind wrapped his legs around the peeling trunk and with well-toned arm and shoulder muscles he pushed it straight overhead and let the spar down into the rotor aperture. Once the power leads were connected, the antenna could be rotated 360 degrees to give full coverage.

While the control work was being attended to by the electronic wizards, Doc, Death Wind, and Sandra concentrated on the silo doors. With lubricating oil and elbow grease, they worked open the rusted glide plates. After pounding and prying with hammers and chisels, crowbars and come-alongs, all eight missiles were eventually laid open to the sky. Now it remained only to attach the proximity fuses.

"Do you want to do this again?" Under Scott's direction, Death Wind performed the practice maneuver faultlessly for the fifth time in a row. "I just want you to be sure."

The savage shook his head and handed the mock-up fuse to Scott. "I am sure." He took a real fuse from its wooden storage crate and cradled it in the sling around his neck.

Scott slapped him on the shoulder. "Okay. Good luck."

Death Wind put his foot on the upper rung of the maintenance ladder inside the silo. Sandra ran up and knelt in front of him. "Please be careful." She kissed him lightly on the forehead, then joined the others and went below to watch the delicate operation from the control room. The video camera was angled so in case something went wrong they could learn from Death Wind's mistakes.

"I'm praying for you, lad." Doc felt his own tension mounting, as if he were right in there with the Nomad, setting the fuse. He looked incongruous wearing a tool pouch over his loincloth, and working on a sophisticated device that might be the cause of his immolation, when until recently he had never seen any weapon more advanced than a bow and arrow.

From the staging platform Death Wind manipulated the various nuts, bolts, springs, and cotter pins with a deftness learned in the wilds. He was a natural mechanic; tools seemed to fit into his hand as an extension of his body.

Doc practically jumped out of his seat when he heard the savage's war whoops echoing from the chamber. He disappeared from the video screen in a way that made Doc catch his breath. Then a door burst open down the corridor, and a moment later Death Wind was standing among them.

Sandra was the first to throw her arms around him, followed by Scott and Rusty, laughing and cheering.

Death Wind grinned from ear to ear. He cast a wry face at Sandra. "It was—piece of cake."

After that, the other seven were easy.

*   *   *

"Are you sure this thing works?" Sandra asked in a bored tone.

After six days of monitoring the radar screen, Doc was beginning to wonder too if it was functioning. "It must be doing something, or we wouldn't have seen that storm that got Scott so upset."

"Yes, they didn't have those in the training manuals. I didn't know what was going on with all that snow on the screen, and we never had hurricanes in Maccam City." Scott fingered a mode switch for computer verification. "Everything checks out okay. Doc, you've been watching these flyers for years. Is there any pattern to their schedule?"

"None that I've ever been able to determine. Like I said, the average is one or two passages per week. The only thing I know for certain is that they always use the Mississippi River. They either go south to the Gulf, then west to Mexico and north from there; or they go north until they come to a prominent landmark. I suspect they have no navigational aids, so rivers and mountains must be quite useful to them."

Rusty squinted at the dials. "Well, assuming we knock down one of their machines, how soon would they be able to replace it?"

"I would guess at least a year. You see, the temporal transporter has very a small scope. It's not a—box, or anything you would recognize. It's a focal point where a vast amount of energy is discharged in such a way as to rip open the fabric of time. The field of influence is some eight feet in diameter and, from what I've seen, one simply walks into this focal point where the presence of matter causes an instantaneous discharge in the capacitor bank. The capacitors need to be recharged before it can be used again."

"Did you say walked?" Sandra said.

"Once, I saw what I believe was a delegation from the home world—er, time. These were very fat dragons, four of them, wearing capes inlaid with braid and jewels, and they appeared out of nothing in the middle of the warp field. All the capacitors instantly discharged, and it was more than a day before it was used again. I followed these characters around all that time while they made their inspection of the city. Then, they simply walked into the transporter field and vanished—gone back to their own time, to report to their superiors. Although, while I think of it, the terms backward and forward may have no real meaning in the Einsteinian sense of space-time."

"So what you're saying," Rusty said, "is that anything bigger than eight feet across has to be sent here piecemeal and reassembled."

"And in addition to all the other necessities that are already scheduled for transport. In order to maintain the status quo—"

"The screen," Death Wind said calmly.

All eyes were instantly riveted to the radar screen. With each sweep of the electronic hand there was a splash of blurry patterns. But now there was one very solid image moving slowly near the perimeter.

Rusty grabbed a chair and threw some switches. "That's no storm front—it's a real target."

"Take it away, Rusty." Scott let him slide his chair in front of the console where he could reach all the controls. The computer viewscreen spewed out distances, altitudes, speeds, course projections, time delays, and coordinates. Rusty's fingers flashed across the keyboard. Scott threw one massive hand switch. "Missile Number One is ready for launch."

"Eat 'em up," Sandra said.

Only Doc groaned.

While Rusty was making computations, Scott explained, "In the past all this would have been done automatically. Satellite scanners would compute a continuous intercept program that could be fed into the missile guidance systems with only a thousandth of a second delay. But we have to—"

"It's ready, Scott."

Scott wiped his hands on his tunic. "Well, here goes." He flipped up the protector cap on the red firing button, paused to look once more at Rusty, received a grim nod, and pressed the button home.

The annunciator panel came alive with green lights—the go ahead. Almost immediately a red light blinked on, flashing a warning for mechanical override. There was a grinding sound as of the clashing of gears while the computer waited the programmed ten-second delay for cancellation of the order. When it did not come, it was forced to carry out its instructions. The concrete foundations began to vibrate. Ancient plaster dropped off the walls and ceiling. A roaring explosion reverberated throughout the complex.

Then there was a strange, preternatural silence.

Scott threw up his hands. "It's off. The missile's on its way."

Amid cheering, Rusty typed instructions that would cause the computer to print on one of its video screens an overlay of the area. He pointed to a meandering, snakelike dot matrix pattern. "That's the Mississippi. And the flyer is coming right down the middle. The missile will show up as soon as it attains enough altitude to—"

"There it is! And look at that sucker go." The blip that was the missile raced across the screen with ever-increasing speed as its flight path leveled out and more of its fuel expenditure went to pushing it horizontally instead of gaining altitude. The two electronic signals were converging rapidly.

There was nothing to do now but sit back and watch, but Rusty leaned forward and gripped the console tightly. "This is just like the simulators back home. We've done this a hundred times, haven't we, Scott? As soon as the two blips touch they'll disappear. That's the destruct signal."

"There's no evasive action," Scott said.

"They don't even know it's coming." Rusty's fingers hovered over the keyboard in case the automatic tracing sensors gave out.

"It appears that the altitude signals have matched," Doc noticed.

The blips were only a hairsbreadth apart. Quickly they merged into one, the smaller missile signal swallowed by the snowy flyer. Tension gripped Doc's stomach, then knotted into despair as the flyer blip continued unabated along the Mississippi.

"The warhead didn't go off," Scott groaned.

"It was a dud." Rusty sat back heavily. "And we've lost the advantage of surprise."

Feeling their disappointment, Doc placed a heavy hand on Rusty's shoulder, and tousled Scott's golden crewcut, now growing long. "You did your best, I'm sure."

Sandra pounded the console top. "Well, don't just sit there. Arm another one. Quick."

"Wait!" Rusty leaped up out of his seat. All eyes went back to the screen, as if the collective willpower could bring down the craft. And as they watched, the blip slowly faded. With each sweep of the antenna its image became less intense until it disappeared altogether.

"What happened?" Scott said.

"I'll check for a malfunction." Rusty played with the keyboard, his fingers a blur. "Oh, no. I don't believe it." He sat back and stared up at the ceiling, his eyes dancing from the fluorescent lights.

"What is it?" Sandra thwacked him on the back of the head. "Speak up."

Rusty laughed, and shook his head. "There's no malfunction. It's just that I'm used to working on simulated displays, with instantaneous feedback. But in real life the enemy craft doesn't blow up and vanish—it crashes. And the image stays in contact until the ship drops below detection range. We made a direct hit, and the flyer sank in the river. *Whoopee!*"

The room burst into a bedlam of cheers, whoops, and backslaps. Even the stoic savage joined the fun. If the flyer held its usual compliment of troops, a hundred dragon soldiers had just been sent to their happy hunting ground.

"I congratulate you all, my young friends."

Scott grinned, and rubbed his hands together. "And this is only the beginning."

CHAPTER 18

"Here comes another one," Scott said smoothly.

Rusty jerked upright in his seat, not even aware that he had fallen asleep. He rubbed his eyes and took control of the attack computer while Scott prepared another missile.

"I've got a go on pad two."

Very soon afterward, Rusty lifted his hands from the keyboard. "Fire when ready."

Scott lifted the protector cap. "Do we have time to call the others?"

"I have a hunch they'll be here as soon as the walls of Jericho start tumbling down."

"Okay. Then, here goes." He pressed the button. The warning light flashed, giving them ten seconds to abort the flight. When the delay time terminated, the familiar rumbling sound started, and more plaster rained down from the crumbling ceiling. Almost immediately, Death Wind and Sandra ran breathlessly through the open door, followed a few moments later by Doc, hobbling on his cane.

The scene that followed was virtually a replay of the previous occasion. It was almost anticlimactic. The dragon flyer followed the same course up the river.

Doc said, "They are undoubtedly looking for the wreckage of their other machine."

The missile whipped across the screen with extreme speed and unerring accuracy, and intersected the flyer in almost the same place. As before, the blip stayed on the screen a few anxious seconds before fading away. The computer graphics indicated another success.

"Just like a turkey shoot," Sandra said.

"Two down, four to go," Scott said dryly.

Rusty swelled with pride. "If this keeps up, the skies will be clear inside of a week. Then we can plan our assault on the city."

"You boys have sure put new spirit into these old bones. In all the years of dragon domination I've never seen such triumph. I never in my wildest dreams imagined—imagined . . ." Doc's voice broke off with a tremor, and his eyes grew glassy.

Rusty's lanky arm encircled the sagging shoulders. "Don't worry, Doc. This time we've got them on the run."

"I'm beginning to believe you."

* * *

It took longer for the next contact. It happened three days later when Sandra ran into the missile complex screaming, crying, and bleeding from a nasty gash on her hip.

"They've got Death Wind. They've got him cornered. You've got to go help him." Fainting from the pain of the wound, she keeled over and slid down the cement wall.

Doc caught her in his arms. "Oh, my."

Scott jumped up so fast that he knocked his chair over backward. "Let's go." Rusty ran out after him. He stopped in Doc's ground-level room long enough to pick up the forty-five, while Scott donned the power pack. Already beamer blasts could be heard outside.

Just as they got outside, a tree on the perimeter of the clearing burst into flames. Fire raced up the trunk as palm leaves crackled into ash. Death Wind leaped from behind it and charged for the protection of a nearby depression. A bolt of lightning flashed over his head and discharged its energy uselessly in the grass a hundred feet beyond. He leaped up and loosed another arrow, straight into the breast of a soldier dragon. But the lizard was undaunted, and plucked at the shaft with its forepaws while hissing in anger and pain. The distance had been too long for the deep penetration of a killing shot.

Coming upon them unawares, Scott and Rusty had the advantage. The dragon never knew what blew its head off. But a dozen yards away another dragon returned Scott's beamer blast with one of its own. It scorched the earth next to Rusty, but he had not forgotten Death Wind's training and kept in motion.

Rusty emptied a cartridge into the flank of the dragon. While it groped wildly in the air, hissing in pain, Scott severed its neck with a well-aimed shot. Death Wind had already accounted for four dragons with his deadly arrows. One still moved, and the savage sank another flint-tipped shaft into its throat. Then it lay still.

The forest was a charnel house of dead bodies and smoldering vegetation. Smoke rose up from the ground where the tall grass had been singed, but the flames were dying out. This jungle was far too damp to support a fire for very long. Even the burning tree had been quenched: now its bark smoldered, and black wreaths slowly curled skyward. Death Wind stepped close to the last dragon he had shot and recovered his arrows from the still warm corpse.

Scott looked down at the elongated neck, bent around backward so the top of the scaly skull touched the bony protuberance of the back. "What happened?"

"Dragon lie in wait. Sandra and I walk, pick flower. Then they shoot. We dodge, and shoot back. I cover for Sandra while she go for help. You arrive in time."

"I think you would have taken care of them anyway."

"How is Sandra?"

Rusty blew on the hot barrel. "She's got a pretty nasty burn on the—"

Before Rusty could finish a titanic explosion rent the forest, knocking all three of them backward. Metal shrapnel, slivers of wood, and chunks of bloody gore flew up in all directions, and dropped back down.

"What the heck—" Rusty uncovered his face, but another explosion cut him off. This time they all fell to the ground in a heap. When the debris settled Rusty saw his companions covered with blood. "Scott! Death Wind! What happened? How badly are you hurt?"

"I'm not hurt at all, but you are."

Rusty looked down at his own body, and gasped. He was covered with blood, but a finger wipe revealed that it was not his own. It was dragon blood!

Scott got to his feet. "Hey, somebody's dropping bombs on us. Let's get out of—"

Another explosion took place, this time farther away. Death Wind took the others by the collar and dragged them back to the bunker. "Dragon blow up."

"They haven't hit anything but their own soldiers."

Rusty stopped by the door. "No, don't you see." Two more explosions went off almost simultaneously. A tall palmetto dropped to the ground as if it had been felled by the blow of a giant's axe. "It's the power packs. They're blowing up."

As they watched, the last dragon warrior that had died with Death Wind's arrow in its throat burst apart in a fury of blood and guts.

"But how?"

"I don't know, but there's not enough of them

left to find out. Maybe Doc can tell us."

Scott paused at the doorway. "Death Wind, did any get away?"

"They are all dead."

Rusty scowled. "What troubles me is, I don't think they found us by accident."

Inside, Sandra lay on the cot Doc was using as a replacement for the confiscated radar antenna. He put the finishing touches on her wound when they walked in.

"Don't make such a fuss, girl. It's a superficial burn that took off a few dermal layers."

"That's easy for you to say, old man. You're only looking at it."

"Is she going to be all right?" Scott said.

"Where's Death Wind?" As soon as she saw him step through the doorway she cried, "Death Wind," and pushed Doc aside as she jumped to her feet. She threw her arms around the savage, and sobbed softly.

"She must be all right, Scott."

"Of course I'm all right. But, what happened to you?" In disgust she drew her hands away from Death Wind. They were wet and gory. "You look awful."

"How about if you lie down and let me put a bandage on that wound?" Doc pulled Sandra back to the cot and eased her down. He took up his ministrations where he had left off.

"Well, what are you guys gaping at? Haven't you ever seen a girl's skin before?" Doc had cut away the dinosaur hide all the way up the side.

Scott stifled a snicker. "Not that part of it."

"Oh, you men!"

"My dear, would you please control your temper. The increased blood pressure is likely to prevent the necessary clotting."

"I can't help it. I'm mad. I should have known better than to go out without my gun. Next thing I know, a beamer blast hits me below the belt and sets my clothes on fire. While I'm rolling on the ground to put out the flames, Death Wind has to tackle a whole squad single-handed. I was about as much help as a barnacle. I had to get up and run for help. Me, running away."

"The practical thing to do, under the circumstances. Even if it did leave Death Wind in a somewhat vulnerable position."

She shoved Doc away. "Yeah, well, what did you expect me to do, lay there and fry."

"Ah, the beamer must have affected your hearing, too, since you heard something other than what I said. I repeat for your benefit: it was the practical thing to do under the circumstances."

"Yeah, well, I don't like your tone of voice."

"Please do not read into my statement meanings that stray from what I've said. Now, may I please get this bandage on?"

Her eyes burned like fire, but she let Doc place the gauze across the burn. She redirected her anger at Scott. "I'm glad to see you two could drag yourselves away from your precious computer."

"It was safer out there than it is in here," Scott said.

"You shut up, you, or I'll launch one of those missiles down your throat."

"Why don't you let the doctor handle the tonsillectomies?"

"Please, please, please." Doc smoothed adhesive tape over Sandra's thigh. "Can we put an end to this banter and try to evaluate the situation? My dear, you can get up now, but don't do any obtuse bending. The glue on these bandages is long since out-of-date. Now, tell me what has occurred, other than that you successfully vanquished the enemy."

As Sandra vacated the cot to stand by Death Wind's side, Doc sat down and swung his bad leg into a comfortable position. Without interruption he listened as Scott and Rusty cleaned themselves off with rags and outlined the incidents of the fight. When they were done he sat quietly for many minutes, stroking his white beard. His eyes became narrow, coal-black discs, his lips a tautly drawn line. When he spoke, it was with a deep, reproachful voice.

"I must apologize for a grievous error in judgment. I've underestimated these devils, and now they've stolen a march on us. I did not anticipate such shrewdness, perspicacity, or adaptability in the plodding dragon brain. Slow thinking they may be, but stupid they are not."

Sandra leaned back against Death Wind and stared up at the ceiling. "Can you speak plain English for once?"

Doc pursed his lips. "Yes, well, it seems that while we've been sitting here waiting for them to put up another target for us, they've taken the initiative to investigate the demise of their machines. The fact that they discovered us so quickly and so easily demonstrates both their understanding of the situation and the capability of their science. Once their suspicions were aroused they triangulated our position and dis-

patched a patrol to probe the area in question. The booby-trapped beamers proves the precautionary measures they've developed. I would not be surprised now if a signal were also sent back to their high command."

"To make a long story short, it's time to hit the road."

"I'm afraid that sums it up. After all, we're fighting a guerrilla war, and the task of a guerrilla is to hit and run: mobility is the key to success. I haven't thought along those terms for so long that I've let it slip my mind."

"But we can't leave now," Scott said. "The greatest weapon we have is at our fingertips. If we lose it we may never have another opportunity."

"An unfortunate circumstance, my friend, but perhaps the only viable one."

"Good. Let's stop playing computer games and go in for the kill."

"My dear, please try to constrain your vivacity. Let's think this thing through before we jump from the frying pan into the fire."

"I think she's right," Rusty said. "I think we should attack."

"What did you do, pick up an extra backbone out there?"

Rusty ignored her. "For the last few days I've been—well—playing computer games. I've been trying to work out a self-operating program. The problem is that with only one radar antenna I only have single line feedback. But now I know something else: all the flyers, sooner or later, must enter or leave the city. By having the radar stationary, and aimed at the city, I can have the computer launch a missile automatically as soon as one of them tries to take off, or comes within range to land.

"But that's not all! I can also design an auxiliary program that will fire the missiles at will, and I can rig a homing beacon that the guidance control will respond to. We can launch our two extra missiles directly at the city—and blow up the time transporter!"

There was a moment of dazed silence while this idea was digested. The result of such a plan, however, was obvious: for then no more supplies, weapons, or dragons could be sent from the past. The outpost would be isolated.

Doc raised bushy eyebrows. "Please excuse my ignorance but, how does this homing beacon work?"

Rusty was nonchalant. "Well, it's really very

simple. It's just a radio transmitter set on a pre-selected wavelength. When it's actuated, the computer will treat it as a target and home in on it. I've got enough spare electronics from storage to—"

"I don't think I understand. How does it inform the computer where the target is? How do you point it?"

"You don't point it, you place it. You have to put it on the target."

"Now we're talking turkey. Let's bust into that city and show 'em we mean business."

Doc was still cautious. "It's not as easy as it sounds."

"I don't care. Rusty's plan gives us the chance to get in there and find my mother."

Doc sighed. "Tell me, what is the explosive force of these warheads? How much earth and rock can it blast through?"

This was Scott's department. "These missiles are designed to knock down opposing aircraft or missiles. It doesn't have to obliterate its target, just make it aerodynamically unstable enough to cause it to crash. I'd say it won't penetrate more than a few feet of rock. Why?"

"Because the time warp equipment, and the transporter room, are conveniently located inside a mountain, with only a narrow tunnel entrance."

Rusty thought for a moment, and tried not to show his dejection. "Well, we can still drop two missiles on the city and cause some damage."

"Not until we find out where my mother is."

Doc used his best bedside manner. "Child, would you please listen to me. It grieves me to have to say this to you, but for your own good I must. You can't keep thinking of your mother as being alive."

"She is alive. I know what I saw."

"She may have been alive when you saw her last, but remember who are her captors. I'm afraid the best you can hope for—is that she died quickly."

Sandra stared at him with daggers in her eyes. Torture was something no one wanted to think about, but why else would the dragons want to capture an enemy they had tried so hard to annihilate? Perhaps they were using human subjects for some inhuman experiments.

Scott interrupted. "Wait a minute. I've got an idea."

Doc looked at him, sighing again. "Whenever one of you boys comes up with an idea, I get the strangest feeling in the pit of my stomach. I know this is going to scare me, but please proceed."

"Well, we've got two missiles that are non-functional—at least as far as missiles. But there's nothing wrong with the warheads. We can take out the explosive canisters, drop the other two missiles somewhere else in the city to create a diversion, then sneak into the cave with the time transporter, and set off the charges electrically."

"And while we're in the city we can look for my mother—before we set off any bombs."

"You know, you boys are forcing me to think like a warrior again. And to think that I used to plan raids against the dragons."

"You—a fighter?" Sandra laughed. "I don't believe it."

"It's true, my dear. That's the only reason I agreed to go along with your schemes in the first place. It takes me back to my own deeds of daring, in my younger years. Killed a dragon or two in my time. But I thought I had retired from all of that. Now it looks as if I'll have to do more than take you to the city—I'll have to guide you through it."

"All we need is the map," Rusty said. "You can draw it for us.

"No, I must do more than that. As I stated before, I would like to be there at the finish. I feel—I feel the old scout in me resurfacing. After listening to you two my heart is full of the old enthusiasm, my mind is full of ideas. I—I want to do something. I've fought against the dragons all my life, but never before have I had such an opportunity as this."

Doc paused for a moment, put his leg down on the floor, then stood up and tested his weight on it. "Even the pain is gone, now that I no longer need it as an excuse. Yes, and I'm beginning to think along the old lines." He lowered his voice to a confidential whisper. "Listen to me, this is what we're going to do . . . "

CHAPTER 19

Scott held a small battery in his hands, to which he attached two wires, while Rusty unraveled the extension cord that led to the switch. They both nodded to Doc at the same time. Doc nodded back. Rusty closed the knife switch.

Several hundred yards away a thunderous explosion blew dirt, plaster, and several tons of re-inforced concrete into the air. When the roar subsided and the dust settled, the only thing left of the above-ground bunker, the entrance to the missile complex, was a mound of unrecognizable rubble.

"That should cover our tracks fairly well," Doc said. "When they send their army out here the next time they'll find nothing but ruins."

Scott coiled the wire over his arm. "Let's hope they don't decide to dig through the debris, or they may find more than they bargained for."

"I certainly hope not, or that would ruin my well-laid plans."

Sandra huffed. "You've already got a lame leg. Try not to break your arm patting yourself on the back."

"I promise to be more reserved in the future. Death Wind, Scott, check all the silo coverings for damage. Sandra, check the antenna."

"I've checked it three times already."

"Thank you, but please check it once more. I know it's well hidden, but I want to make sure the explosion didn't loosen any connections. And make sure the cables are out of sight."

Sandra grumbled, but went anyway.

"Rusty, how is reception?"

Rusty picked up the control box. It was twelve inches square and six inches high. The top panel held a double row of toggle switches and indicator lights, and a ten-keyed numerically assigned input board. He punched in a sequencing code and watched as the tiny globes lit up. "All my readings are affirmative. And the green light means I'm receiving the signal from the antenna."

"With the radar dish in the thicket, will you still be able to pick it up from the city? Doesn't the drop in elevation affect its range and sensitivity?"

"It depends on the frequency, but we should get atmospheric bouncing like a short-wave radio. And I still have manual control."

"And you're sure it will stay dry in there?"

Rusty placed the control box in a clear plastic container and snapped it shut. "Absolutely. The rubber gasket makes it airtight. It's standard equipment for spare electronic components." When it was securely stuffed in his pack and the straps were cinched tightly, he put the battery and cords in a similar container and put it in Scott's fanny pack.

"What about the explosive canisters?"

"Water won't affect them one way or the other. They're completely stable and can only be detonated with a blasting cap."

"Hey, Doc," Scott called out, returning from his errand. "We walked right on top of them and they didn't even creak. Death Wind did a terrific job covering the openings with sticks and brush. Those dragons will need second sight to find the silo openings."

Sandra returned at the same time. "That's what lizards use the other brain for."

"Yes, they say two heads are better than one." Doc climbed to his feet and hoisted up his pack. Now that everything was checked out he was eager to get underway. "And I guess that goes for brains as well. They may be retarded in hand-to-hand combat, but they are particularly shrewd when given the time to think things through." To Sandra he added, "I take it the antenna survived the concussion?"

Sandra merely scowled. Doc accepted this as an affirmative. The rest donned their packs. Death Wind carried the heavy explosive canisters from the dismantled missiles. Around his waist he knotted a rope which would shift some of the weight off his shoulders and onto his hips.

Doc took the lead, not only because he knew the way but because he had to set the pace within his limits.

Rusty settled the delicate electronic equipment more comfortably on his back. "How long will it take us to reach the city?"

"As a young scout, traveling light, I could make it in two days—swimming part of the way. But now—we've got to take a circuitous route in order to avoid possible dragon war parties; we have heavy loads; we have lakes to cross; and then, we've got an old man not in the best of health. I'd say four days at least."

Hobbling forward on his cane in a rambling, uneasy gait, Doc took a bearing with his compass and set the course. The brush was thick, and clinging vines barred the way. "Death Wind, I think you had better break trail for a while. I'm only carrying the medical kit and already I'm exhausted."

Once pointed in the right direction the savage needed no further bearings, for he steered by the sun. Even in the dense jungle he simply followed the shadows, altering course periodically to make up for the fifteen degree change per hour as the day star traversed the sky.

Scott hung back to talk with Doc. "What's

this about the double brains?"

With the cane he knocked limbs and vines out of his path. "It's probably a misnomer to call the spinal enlargements brains. All large dinosaurs have a thickened bundle of nerves at the base of the spinal column, but it was not a thinking brain: it merely controlled movement of the hind legs and tail. Some, like the Jurassic stegosaurus, had three brains, the third being in the shoulder."

Sandra, carrying most of the food, the rifle, and the remaining two hundred rounds of ammunition, stayed close to Death Wind. "Doc, look at these trees with flowers on them."

"They're dogwoods, my dear." They were only a few minutes on their way and already the jungle was becoming denser, more luxuriant, and more tropical. "The dragons come from a magnificent era in Earth's history, for it was a time of change. Conifers still ruled the plant world, but deciduous trees and flowering plants were coming into their own. The age of ferns was giving way to laurel and sassafras, magnolias, and dogwood. It was what you might call the best of both worlds."

Death Wind had his knife out now, and used it like a machete to cut through the thickening vegetation. Underfoot, the ground became soft and squishy. Logs and tree trunks were dotted with large crawling insects. Flying bugs buzzed everywhere, and high in the treetops lizard birds cawed raucously from their sanctuary.

"Doc, what about the brains?"

"What? Oh, yes. Well, I've dissected more than one dragon in my time: their carcasses were always left to rot when we managed a kill and returned several days later. They have a thinking brain that is quite a bit smaller than ours, although just as complex. But since they have two other brains to handle motor coordination, it can all be used for cogitation and interpreting the senses. It's very concise in that respect, and accounts for their rise above the beasts of the time. But it lacks efficiency because of the time lag while messages are being passed between the fore brain and the secondary brains.

"It's like a military chain of command, where the general tells the colonel who tells the major who tells the captain who tells the lieutenant who tells the sergeant who tells the corporal who tells the private. By the time the message reaches the worker, the information is outdated. Dragons have the same trouble catching you in their

sights as you have in trying to catch a butterfly. Your eyes can follow the insect, but by the time you instruct your hand where to grab, it's no longer there."

The land dipped considerably, and the dense mass slurped at every step. Their moccasins soaked through, but it did not matter. They waded knee deep through a bog with an oozing, muddy bottom. The water was stagnant, and stank with marsh grass. Rotting logs and stumps blocked their way. And the insects grew larger.

"Halt." Death Wind's command was soft, but urgent. Sandra unslung her rifle and crouched beside him. She chambered a round and thumbed the safety. Death Wind forced the barrel down into the ground. "Do not shoot."

"What is it?" Doc drew up behind the savage. He looked out over the pond, but saw nothing. Scott and Rusty likewise peered over his shoulder, scanning the water. There was not so much as a ripple.

On the other side of the pond, a scant hundred feet away, the trees parted. Out stepped a bipedal dinosaur, fifteen feet in height and counterbalanced by a long, thick tail. With jerky motions of its stocky forepaws it pulled leaves off a willow tree and stuffed them into its drooling mouth. The sun shone down and reflected off smooth, brown skin. The curious skull was a rounded, bony knob two feet long, half of which was forehead. Around the eyes protruded a collection of nasty-looking spines and bumps.

"A bonehead," Doc whispered. "Not particularly dangerous unless you happen to frighten it."

"Will it run if we make some noise?" Scott asked.

"Probably not. Generally speaking, dinosaurs with armor attack anything that threatens them. It's a survival instinct that protects them from the carnivorous predators of their own time."

Sandra fingered the trigger. "So what do we do? Sit here like boobs and wait for it to go away?"

Doc was unruffled. "Either that, or walk around it. Experience has taught me never to attack them unnecessarily. It is that warlike aggression you harbor that has caused mankind so much discontent in his internecine past."

"Cut with the philosophy and let's do something."

"Well, if you won't accept *my* advice, why don't you ask Death Wind for his opinion."

She did. Death Wind's curt comment was, "Wait." So, they waited. It seemed as if the boneheaded dinosaur would never fill its monstrous stomach. It browsed noisily, ripping and tearing limbs off trees with its paws, then chewing off the leaves with long, flattened teeth. After a half hour it had eaten its way through enough jungle so that it was out of sight, although not out of hearing. Cautiously, the war party made its way around the pond and veered diagonally away from the feeding animal. Sandra grumbled the whole time.

Rusty slapped at his face. "Ouch!" Grimacing comically, he pulled away a two-inch-long, partly squashed beetle that had dropped on him from above. A sticky ichor oozed out of the crushed abdomen. He tossed it away as if it were poisonous. "I don't think I'm going to like this."

"I think you're going to hate it." Scott laughed, then slapped his arm. "Beetles I can live with, but I don't like all these mosquitoes."

"Here, let me show you a trick." Doc looked around until he found a bright green, treelike plant with a broad, flat leaf that was a tiny parasol some eighteen inches in diameter. Breaking it off at the stem, he crumpled it up in his hands until they were coated with a sickly green liquid. Then he rubbed his hands over his face, neck, and exposed portions of his lower legs, and around his waist where his shirt left a gap. "It's not exactly the scent of perfume, but take my word for it that most of the insects will like it even less."

Following his example, they all applied a generous portion to their bodies. "Need any help?" Scott said to Sandra, while she was rubbing it on her midriff.

"If you lay a hand on me you'll regret it. Yeech!" She pulled a multi-legged creature resembling a toy tank from under her blouse, and hurled it to the ground. "I don't mind dragons or dinosaurs, but these things give me the creeps."

As the sun dropped lower in the sky and the jungle grew darker, the fauna grew louder and bolder. The air was filled with a cacophony of barks, howls, and shrieks. Four-legged dinosaurs abounded. Some were the size of squirrels, and lived in the trees. Others were the size of alligators. Some danced rapidly out of the way, others squatted, or clung vertically to the smooth bark of trees with needlelike claws, and watched with apparent unconcern as the people walked by.

Doc arched his neck and peered up at the purple, cloudless sky. "I think we'd better look for a place to camp."

Sandra said, "I haven't seen a place flat enough or dry enough to stand on, much less lie down."

"You haven't been looking in the right places. It isn't safe to spend the night on the ground. What we need is a nice, comfortable perch."

CHAPTER 20

"This is for the birds." Sandra straddled two thick boughs a hundred feet above the jungle floor. While Death Wind busily cut off branches with his knife, the others tied them with vines athwart a framework of heftier, parallel branches.

"I thought you liked living out on a limb." Scott leaned against the trunk of the giant oak and twisted several creepers together to make a stout rope.

"Can't you do anything without making wisecracks?"

"Someone has to make up for your gloom. Say, did anyone ever show you how to smile?"

Sandra flashed a mouthful of even, white teeth with something more like a grimace than a grin. She brushed her silky hair out of her face and shoved a hacked-off branch at Scott, thwacking him in the abdomen.

"If you two are done trading witticisms, and have completed your work on the upper berths, you can come down for some food." Doc looked up from a lower limb, where he felt his climbing expertise had been sufficiently strained.

"Be right down." Scott drew a tight knot around the last set of branches, and put the finishing touches on the sleeping platform. Now it was ready for a makeshift mattress of soft leaves. That was soon accomplished, and the three of them climbed down to where Doc and Rusty sat on a lower platform. He had the food out and ready for distribution.

"Ah, just like the good old days." Using a small penknife he sliced off several pieces of meat, passed them around, and chomped into a large chunk he left for himself.

The climbing had not bothered him as much as he had thought it would: there was still plenty of strength left in those old arms, and he delighted in the exertion of pulling himself upward. His leg was propped up perfunctorily, but exercise and incentive had done much to ease the pain.

Dark clouds were rolling in, eclipsing the low sun even more than the tall trees and dense foliage. A welcome coolness accompanied the early dusk.

"We'll have to be careful from here on in. We're near the stockades where the domesticated dinosaurs are kept. And that means there will be guards around the perimeter; only a few, but they'll be armed." Doc looked directly at Sandra. "We don't want to announce our presence, so we'll do everything we can to avoid trouble."

Sandra ignored him, but Scott said, "Hey, did you hear that?" There was a plopping sound overhead, then another, then many. "What's going on?" The pattering increased in intensity for a minute. Scott looked up. "Hey, something's dripping on me."

Rusty held out his hand. "It's—water. The leaves up there must be leaking."

Sandra let out a loud guffaw. "Don't tell me you guys have never seen rain before?"

"Well, uh, as a matter of fact—" Scott caught some of the large drops in his mouth.

"I would heartily suggest that we seek the protection of our beds, or we're likely to get very wet—and cold." Doc crawled into his aerie with the rest of his meal, where the broad leaves of the mattress quickly became umbrellas. There he spent the rest of the night shivering slightly from the sudden drop in temperature—and scratching from the number of insects that desired to share his shelter.

He awoke stiff and cold, and was happy to get underway. The ground was soggier than ever, and the air clammy. It took an hour for him to warm up. Then they stopped at a small rivulet of fresh water for breakfast.

Doc smelled the green, algae-filled liquid. "We have to be careful what we drink now. Much of the water is polluted by the outflow of the pens." He pointed a quivering finger at a structure that was barely visible through the moss-covered trees.

At first it looked like a wall of gold, but that was just a trick of the sun. Without the glare it was dull orange. Ten feet high, and broader at the base than at the top, it wound sinuously through the jungle without true definition. It was made of a material that was basically amorphous, but covered with ropy contours.

"Plastic. It's extruded from nozzles and poured without a mold until it conforms approximately to the shape they want. The dragons do not care about art or architecture—only form and function."

As they walked along the wall, the squeaks and bellows of dinosaurs on the other side could be heard. Doc led them away from the alien structure.

"There used to be houses and highways here a hundred years ago—even a few good-sized towns. Now, there's no trace of human habitation. What time hasn't destroyed, the dragons have demolished. They level an area with their disruptor beams, let the wind cover it with sand and dirt, then seed it according to their own specifications." His voice took on a tone of sadness. "They've not only exterminated mankind, they've obliterated every vestige of his civilization."

"And we're gonna take it back. They'll be sorry they ever set foot in this time."

"My dear, why do you have such pent-up—hatred?"

"What should I have—love for what they've done to me, and my life. Do you think I like skulking around in this jungle, in this heat, in this filthy water? Do you think I like having to fight to survive? Well, damn it, I don't. I hate the dragons, and I hate everything about them. And I'd like to blow every damn reptile off the face of the Earth."

"Surely you don't mean that? Remember that our enemies are the dragons, not a herd of dull-witted dinosaurs."

"Yeah? Maybe you should remember it yourself. A little hatred wouldn't hurt you. It might even make you more dedicated."

Doc's voice showed no anger. "My loyalty is not in question. Nevertheless, I don't hate the dragons any more than I hate a growth of cancerous cells. I recognize that they must be removed in order to ensure my own survival. They are merely a force to be reckoned with."

"Then let's stop arguing and start reckoning."

Scott said, "Sandra, I think you and I agree again."

"Good. Then let's go."

"Yes. Let's." Doc knew that the dispute was futile. They both had the same aims, but their motivations were different. Still, he would rather have her on his side than against him.

As they trudged along, the jungle thinned out until it was more of a swamp: watery lowlands with aquatic plant life interspersed with slightly elevated drylands on which abounded groves of oak and willow, with a few palms at the water's edge.

The procession continued on a course parallel with the orange, plastic wall. Several times they stopped and climbed up massive oak trunks in order to peer over the top. Subdivisions kept different kinds of dinosaurs apart. Doc named a few of them, but many were species unknown to human paleontology. It was as strange an array of animal life as one could possibly imagine.

When the sun was straight overhead, Death Wind raised his hand and called a halt. There were noises from in front, and he moved up alone to investigate. When he came back, he said, "Big water ahead. Many lizards swim. We need to build raft."

Scott and Rusty started hauling in logs, while Doc hacked vines off nearby trees and dragged them to the bank. Sandra helped Death Wind with the lashings. The lake was half a mile across, and dotted with small, tree-covered islands.

Suddenly Sandra screamed. When Doc looked around, his hackles raised, he saw a huge monster rising out of the water only a few feet from where Sandra had fallen back. Water dripped off an enormous arched head with a duck-billed mouth. Dull eyes opened and transfixed the girl as she scrambled backward, tripping over a pile of rotting sticks.

She rolled to where she had leaned her rifle against a tree, swung it around, and was tightening her grip on the trigger when Doc plopped down beside her. He pushed the barrel up into the air.

"Don't waste your ammunition. It's only a harmless tracodon."

With a flurry of leaves and underbrush Scott arrived with the beamer trained on the fearful head. Death Wind had drawn his bow, but at Doc's command lowered it slowly.

"They're not usually belligerent. When caught on land they tend to run away. And in the water they're safe from their natural predators. It's only curious."

"Yeah, well, its curiosity scared the daylights outa me."

The massive head moved toward them as if on a conveyor belt. It rose higher out of the green water until the neck appeared, then the thickened body. Small hands came into view, but the beast then started submerging until only the top of its head, its eyes, and the glossy upper surface of the flattened bill showed. It stared at them.

"I used to swim across these lakes, and never had one bother me. They're really very docile, and sometimes quite playful. They have powerful hind legs with webbed feet, which they use for swimming. They used to glide gracefully alongside me, like ducklings after their mother."

"Thanks for the nature talk, but I'm not swimming in this lake with that thing in there."

The tracodon backed away and when it reached deeper water it submerged so slowly that only the barest trace of a ripple showed where it had gone.

"Of course you're not, my dear. We can't afford to let that wound get wet or it will become infected, so you'll have to ride on the raft with the rest of the baggage."

And that is what she did. Sitting astride the packs and weapons, she acted as lookout while Death Wind, Scott, and Rusty paddled alongside and pushed the raft. Doc trailed off the rear on a long vine: he was not up to pushing, but neither did he want to be a drag. He was able to swim for himself.

During the crossing they were not bothered at all by tracodons, although several smaller swimming reptiles left wakes under the surface. Once away from the banks, where the green algae tended to grow thick, like a sludge on the water, the lake became bright blue and crystal clear. Logs and stumps could be seen on the bottom, as well as some of the larger denizens.

"Remember, the dragons brought no carnivorous dinosaurs with them," Doc said, to instill confidence. "Unless some sneaked through, of course."

They camped that night on a dry, raised knoll, where Doc assured them they would be safe. The more hostile dinosaurs, like the triceratops and styracosaurs, liked the dry, open plains. The scurrying reptiles of the lush jungle were behind them, while those that inhabited the swamps lurked in solitude, avoiding contact.

The stars came out and lit up the sky with their silvery, twinkling brilliance. And later, the waxing moon arose, casting long shadows on the ground. They could not afford themselves a fire because it might be spotted by dragon guards. Yet, they experienced a tranquility and warmth that could come only from close companionship. There was a serenity of thought that belied their differences of opinion, and the seriousness of their mission.

Doc was almost asleep when he heard Sandra yelp. "Hey, what did you mean by 'the rest of the baggage'?"

CHAPTER 21

For two days the party prowled through the marsh: swatting insects, rubbing on leaf sap, sweating it off, and swatting more insects. The water became more and more polluted as they neared the city, so whenever they could they ascended to high ground, and dry ground. But so did many of the smaller reptiles, and they became an increasing problem by their sheer numbers.

On the final approach there lay a series of wooded hills that were rough and cragged, and separated by long shallow lakes which, because of their elevation, had escaped the contamination of the lowlands. While the clean water was welcome, each crossing ment the time-consuming construction of another raft.

One of these lakes was bordered by a low cliff line some ten feet high, with no beach on which to land. Finding a place where the rocks created a broken ledge a body's length above the algae-filmed surface, Sandra held the raft close while one by one the others climbed out of the water, onto the raft, and up the rock face. Death Wind let Sandra climb up before him so he could pass up the packs.

Once the raft was emptied, the Nomad severed the vines that held the logs together and let the timbers float away. It would not do to have something so obviously manmade discovered by dragon patrols.

Doc surveyed the area. "I believe we are very near, perhaps just over the next rise."

They rested for several minutes in the tall grass, picking leeches off their skin and squeezing their clothes dry. Sandra peered ahead, always on guard. Then they donned their packs and prepared to move on.

A stick cracked in the forest. Doc heard a faint hiss. In the fading light from a setting orange sun, shadows moved softly behind a line of trees. Thick bodies and long necks were vague silhouettes moving through green foliage.

"Dragons," Sandra whispered. They dropped flat into the cover of the waving green blades.

Doc heard the click of the safety. "Careful. Let them pass."

"No way. This is what I came here to do."

Doc reached over and deftly disengaged the cartridge clip from the rifle. But Sandra always had one round chambered, and that shot would be enough to give them away.

Sandra rolled out of his reach. "Damn you." By this time the dragons had withdrawn into the protection of the trees. She pulled another clip from the bandolier.

Death Wind loomed over the top of her, bent slightly under the weight of his pack. With fingers like steel springs he wrenched the rifle out of her hands. Sandra was too startled to do anything more than grunt. When she recovered from her surprise, she reached out for the gun and kicked with her powerful legs.

The moccasinned feet struck the savage in the solar plexus. Caught off guard, air puffed from his lungs as if from a bellows. He stumbled backward and caught his heel, the weight of the explosive canisters in his pack bringing him down. As he twisted sideways and placed a hand on the ground for support, the pack was still levering him over. He slipped on the moss and in an instant he tumbled over the brink and cartwheeled into the water with a resounding splash.

Doc scrambled through the grass to peer over the edge. There was no sign of Death Wind, only the sloshing, stirred-up algae. The pack dragged the savage right down to the bottom. The splashing stopped and settled down. Ripples cascaded gently against the base of the rock wall. The water became still. Nothing moved.

"Do something!" Sandra screamed, heedless of the retreating dragons.

Without thinking, Scott wriggled out of his pack straps, stood up on the top of the cliff, and dived. He carved a small hole in the smooth surface of the lake, then was gone. Long moments passed with no further movement other than dying ripples. Doc strained his eyes, but could see nothing below. It was as if the lake had swallowed them both.

Anxious moments later, as the water cleared, a dark shape could be seen through the patchy algae. As it grew larger Doc could make out flailing arms. Then a blond head broke the surface and sputtered for air.

Scott splashed from side to side. "Where's Death Wind?" Without waiting for an answer he took a quick, deep breath, and dived again. This time the water had not had time to settle before he reappeared, clutching the savage's inert body. Cradling his head so it was out of the water, Scott did a one-sided dog paddle until he came to the rock wall. But from this level it was impossible to climb up—and the raft had already been broken up.

"I can't hold him," Scott said between gasps. He coughed and sank, then clawed his way to the surface again. Rusty jumped into the water and grabbed hold of Scott. "Get him, not me."

Rusty paddled around and took Death Wind by the shoulder. Together they kept him up. Then a vine dropped into the water and fell across the savage's unmoving chest.

"Tie it under his arms," Doc ordered.

Rusty found a finger grip on the smooth rock and held on tightly enough to take the burden from Scott. He immediately began looping the vine around Death Wind's chest, under the armpits, and in a knot in front. He fumbled more than he should have, kicking and staying afloat at the same time.

"Pull him up," Scott shouted.

Death Wind's face lost its ruddy hue, and was slowly purpling. It was obvious to Doc that he had stopped breathing. He and Sandra pulled, Scott and Rusty pushed. The body came up out of the water by inches: far too slowly, and with far too much effort. Doc knew that he and the girl did not have the strength necessary to haul up the weight of a fully-grown man.

"This isn't working. Let him down," Doc said. He wasted no more time. As soon as he was sure that Sandra had a good grip on the vine, he held his nose and leaped into the water. He came up right away, and one stroke put him in touch with the struggling trio. Now Scott and Rusty held onto the vine for additional support. They kept Death Wind's face out of the water.

Doc floated between Scott and the savage. Pinching Death Wind's nose with his fingers and tilting his head back, he placed his mouth over the other's. He blew deeply, watched the bronze chest expand, released his mouth, and felt warm air expel slowly from the lungs. He blew into Death Wind's mouth again, watched the chest expand, let him exhale. He did it again—and again—and again, while the rest waited in anguish for some result, for some sign of life.

"The water's full of blood," Sandra shrieked. Then, she snugged the rope around a rock outcrop.

Doc wondered only briefly about the noise they had made, and the proximity of the dragons. Then Death Wind went into convulsions, his body jerked spasmodically, and almost pulled him under the surface. But Doc held him up, and turned his head to one side as water and vomit spurted from his mouth. The surface of the lake was a witch's brew of bile and green algae stained red with blood.

Death Wind stopped convulsing, and merely gagged. But at least he kept breathing. His body suddenly went limp. His eyes opened to a narrow slit, but rolled up inside their sockets. The obstruction cleared itself from his throat, and he passed out, breathing lightly.

"Climb up the vine," Doc said. Scott scaled the wall easily. Rusty had a little more trouble, but as soon as he got within reach Scott extended a hand and pulled him up the rest of the way. Doc pulled the rope up under Death Wind's arms so it would not tighten on the chest. "All right, now pull."

Pulling together, they hauled him up the ten-foot rock wall until he was almost at the top. Leaving Sandra holding the vine, Scott and Rusty grabbed the limp form by the armpits and dragged the body onto the soft grass.

Doc waited awhile before calling out. "Excuse me, but could someone please throw me a line?" He calmly treaded water and awaited rescue. Scott slipped the vine from around the savage's body and dropped it to the doctor. He climbed into the loop and allowed himself to be hauled up the rock face while he scrabbled for footholds. Then he squirmed over the brink. "Are there—any dragons—about?"

"I forgot all about them," Scott said.

"They'd have been here by now if they had heard anything," Rusty said.

"Doc." Sandra cradled Death Wind's head in her lap, and combed the matted hair from his forehead. There were tears in her eyes. "He's got blood all over him."

Doc crawled on hands and knees, and lifted the savage's eyelid. "It's all right, my dear. It's not internal." With practiced fingers he examined the gash on Death Wind's abdomen. "It's not deep, but it will take some tending to."

"It was the waist rope," Scott said. "He couldn't get out of the pack, so he cut the knot with his knife. I got there in time to help him out of the shoulder harness and push him to the surface, but he must have passed out on the way up."

Lying restfully in the warmth of Sandra's lap, Death Wind's eyes flickered open for a moment. He coughed, spitting up water. Then he rolled over and tried to climb to his feet.

Sandra clung to him, and Doc gently pushed him back. So weak was the Nomad that he could not resist Doc's gentle pressure. "Rest now. Just rest."

"I'm sorry. I—I'm sorry." A tear fell from Sandra's eye, rolled down her cheek, and dripped onto Death Wind's broad, naked chest. "I didn't mean to—please forgive me."

Death Wind nodded faintly, closed his eyes, and fell asleep.

Sandra continued to cry. "I didn't mean to. I didn't mean to—now I've ruined everything."

"My dear, life is like a soap bubble: a thin and tenuous film buoyed up by a moving, unstable force. It is the most fragile thing in the universe and, once burst, can never be repaired. But his life force is strong. His bubble is safe." Doc patted him on the arm, as if to share a secret between them. "Let us all be thankful for that."

They made camp where they were, while Doc dressed the laceration with first-aid supplies from his pack.

Sandra was inconsolable: she would not allow Death Wind to be moved from her lap. She spent the entire night in a crouched, uncomfortable position, dozing fitfully, and awakening whenever her patient moved. She stroked his hair absently.

"I'm so sorry."

CHAPTER 22

The morning sun had barely cleared the sky of its reddish glow when Scott dived off the rock ledge with a coil of freshly cut vine peeling out behind him. He cleaved the water with a splash, and started kicking.

He held his breath during the descent, working quickly on the bottom to locate his objective and perform his job. The water was still for almost a minute before he casually came to the surface and shook his head clear. Triumphantly, for all to see, he held up in one hand a bow and

a quiver of arrows. "And the knife." He held up the other hand and let the sun glint off the steel blade. Then he slung the bow and quiver over one shoulder, put the long blade between his teeth, and scampered up the vine like an agile monkey after a banana.

Scott dropped his treasures to the ground. "I've got the vine through both straps." It took but a moment to haul the pack full of explosives to the surface, over the rock face, and onto the grass.

The pack was still dripping as Death Wind lifted it to his shoulders. "I will carry." He grimaced in pain, and slowly twisted to the side and sank to his knees. Scott took the weight of the pack and set it down. The Nomad rubbed his side where Doc had applied some salve and taped a string of compresses. "Too much pain. I cannot carry."

Sandra bit her lip. The packs were shuffled around so that Scott wound up with the heaviest, carrying the explosive canisters; Rusty took the beamer; and Death Wind took the instrument package.

Doc put a finger to his lips. "We'd better go quietly from here on. I've never seen patrols so far out, so I suspect something must have them stirred up. Losing two flyers must have hit them in a sensitive spot."

Like snakes in the grass they slunk through the forest: toward the city, toward the dragons, toward their destiny.

*   *   *

Doc stood on the very edge of the rocky bluff, and let the binoculars drop slowly down his face. "It hasn't changed as much as I would have thought." He handed the glasses to Rusty. "It's grown some, but mostly in the other direction, on the other side of the central mountain. That's where the transporter is housed."

The dragon city had no tall spires, no majestic landscapes, no architectural wonders. Instead, it was more like a rough cast Roman village: cluttered streets lined with two- and three-story buildings, uneven walls that bordered not-quite-rectilinear atria, parapets that were blobs of frozen magma. The whole fortification looked like something a child might build out of clay.

Rusty put down the glasses. "It's plastic! Orange plastic, just like the stockade walls in the jungle."

"Dragons are not known for their artistic design," Doc said.

Scott tussled with Rusty for the binoculars. After a moment of viewing, he said, "It's like an anthill down there. There must be thousands of them, scurrying all over the place as if someone had disturbed their nest."

"They have a caste system much like the hive insects, with three different ranks which I've named leaders, technicians, and workers. The workers are the most numerous. Less than slaves, they are more like beasts of burden. They are raised like livestock, live in corrals, receive no education, wear no clothes, and are expendable. Their soldiers come from that group.

"The technicians are superior in dragon hierarchy in that they live in barracks and are highly educated. They are transported here already schooled in their specialties. And they are distinguishable by the litheness of their bodies as well as by the tool vests they wear. The leaders are the elite: they do no manual labor, but direct the course of others. They'll be the fat ones in the highly ornamental capes."

"Hey, I can see three flyers over there." Scott pointed to the high-walled revetments, with black-stained decks.

"I've seen them land. The disruptor beam melts the landing pad if the craft is brought in by unfamiliar hands. The plastic becomes malleable, but resolidifies quickly after the beam is turned off. The ramparts prevent the molten plastic from running off. But an experienced pilot can land it quickly without damage."

Doc took a step closer to the cliff edge and peered down over the jagged precipice. He saw something, then nodded slowly to himself.

"Where's the hatchery?" Scott said.

"Toward the eastern end of the city."

Scott panned the binoculars. "Yes, I see it. And the nursery, too."

"Hey, do you mind sharing the peepers?" Sandra jerked the glasses out of Scott's hands.

Behind her, Death Wind scrutinized the city with eagle-sharp eyes.

"Anybody hungry?" Scott reached for the food pack. "As long as we have the afternoon to kill—"

"My palate can be twisted, but that does not mean that we have time to waste."

Rusty took a slice of meat. "We can't enter the city in broad daylight."

"And besides, you said the dragons don't come out at night."

"What I said was that lizards become extremely sluggish in the cold because they have no thermoregulatory system: they rely on the sun for heat. The only way they can raise their own body temperature is by the friction of their muscles. Ambient temperature is—"

"Hey, there are people down there," Sandra screamed.

Scott said, "I don't think dragons are civilized enough to be called people."

"No, you fool. I mean *real* people." She shoved the glasses back at Doc. "Human beings. There!"

Doc put the binoculars to his eyes, aimed them where Sandra was pointing, and stared for a long time. He gasped once or twice before he found the ability to speak.

"Oh, my. I do believe you're right." His eyes were still riveted to the lenses. "I—I just don't—understand it." When he passed the glasses on, his face was as white as a sheet. "Damn. I keep underestimating those devils. Their tactics are—changing drastically."

There was triumph in Sandra's voice. "Now you'll believe me when I say my mother's down there."

Doc stroked his snowy beard, clearly disturbed. "My dear, I understand your plight, but remember too that the mission is all important. We can't afford to endanger our chances of success. This may be our last opportunity to beat those devils at their own game. This may be—"

"Screw the mission. I'm going after my mother."

"Child, I truly empathize with the depth of your concern. In your moccasins I'm sure I would feel quite as strongly, but—"

"Shut up, old man."

"—there is more at stake here than the life of one individual, or even a host of people. We're fighting for the survival of the human race as a species. It would do us no good—"

"I'm not listening."

"—to save your mother at the expense of the greater sacrifice. It would only ensure her death at a later and not too distant time. But I promise you this: as soon as our main objective is attained, I will turn all my energies to the rescue of your mother, and all the helpless prisoners with her."

"Promise anything you want, old man." Sandra's face was twisted into an agonized caricature. "I'm going after my mother—with or without your help. But either way, that's what I'm doing. And you can't stop me."

"Oh, dear, I was hoping you would be a little more reasonable."

"It's my neurosis. Take it or leave it."

Doc sighed heavily, and surveyed the other three faces. They were looking to him for advice. Slowly, he nodded consent. "All right, we'll go after your mother. But, we'll have to do it my way. I see no reason why we can't think of some manner in which to accomplish both objectives at the same time."

"Don't lie to me—"

Doc held up his hand, and looked hurt. "I promise. Just leave everything to me. So finish your food and let's get started."

Scott started wrapping the meat. "I still don't see how we're going to walk across this city in broad moonlight."

A sardonic grin spread across Doc's leathery face. "I must have forgotten to mention. We're not going to walk *across* the city, we're going to walk *under* it—through the sewers."

CHAPTER 23

Viscid green liquid dribbled out of the eight-foot-high rectangular tunnel and fought to get into an evil-smelling, scum-covered pool. A bluish-green smoke ebbed in and out of the entrance, like an ocean surge, carrying with it effluvium and carrion. Willows surrounding the outflow drooped more than usual, and the lower bark was eaten off at the waterline. Nearby fallen trunks were etched, as if with acid. And where the pool drained into the forest there was a distinct perimeter of death.

Stifling the urge to puke, Scott pointed to something lying in the shallows. It was a thick bone, bleached by the organic soup in which it lay half submerged.

Doc nodded grimly. "That is how they dispose of their old, their sick, their infirm. They're cut up into small chunks and shoved down the culverts."

"You gotta be kidding." Sandra waved her hand in front of her face, warding off fetid fumes. "You're not gonna get me in there."

Doc maintained a straight face. "You do want to see your mother again, don't you?"

Sandra rolled her eyes, but said nothing.

Doc pointed to the plastic grate that barred their entrance. "Burn a small opening down by the water."

Rusty held the weapon awkwardly, stood back, squinted his eyes, and pressed the firing stud. A bolt of lightning arced into the grate, melting a sizable hole but one not large enough to climb through. He fired again, wincing at the thunderclap the beamer made.

"I think that'll do." Scott plunged into the foul water. He sank almost knee deep into sticky ooze underneath the grate, stooped, and crawled under with his face a fraction of an inch from the floating stench. He stood up inside the sewer and resumed breathing. "It doesn't smell as bad in here. And there's some high ground out of the water."

Doc waded in next. He had a little more difficulty crouching through the low opening: his back was not as limber as it used to be. "Death Wind, bring those torches in." His voice reverberated strangely inside the tunnel.

The savage ducked in, careful of his wound. He found the sand ledge on which Doc and Scott were waiting, unlimbered his pack, and struck a flint at one of the homemade torches. In the yellow light they could see Sandra, holding her long hair in a knot in order to keep it out of the putrid water. Rusty was right behind her.

Sandra let her hair fall back over her shoulders. "I think I'm gonna be sick."

Doc took the flaming brand and held it high. "Death Wind, get the rest of those torches going. Scott, Rusty, take some of this silt and build up a mound by the hole. I don't want to give away our entrance. Sandra, is that bandage still dry?"

Sandra mumbled in assent. The savage took the loose bundles of sticks, tied with vine, and dipped them into a bladder containing dinosaur oil. He lighted each one from the first, and stuck them into the island of sand and silt.

With the opening covered, Scott washed his hands in the foul water. "Doc, that beamer didn't seem to have the punch it used to. I think it may be running out of power."

"Yes, well, I'm rather surprised it lasted this long. We should try to go easy with it."

Now they congregated on the island. The vagaries of flood and run-off left half the tunnel sanded in, and half carrying the current. In the flickering light of the five torches, weird shadows seemed to jump about the orange, plastic walls.

"This is the main tunnel, running right up the

middle of the city. In order to get to any of our assigned destinations we'll have to take side pipes."

Rusty was a stickler for details. "Are you sure you'll remember which pipes to take? After all, it's been a long time since you've been here."

"I put markings on the walls when I made my original survey. And I used a code I'd not be likely to forget." With great effort he extracted his cane from the muck, peered dubiously as globs of mud stretched like cotton candy from the end and fell off. Then he started slurping down the embankment. Soon he was padding in shallow water where the walking was easier. The rest followed.

Very soon they came to a mud bank that rose more than waist high, and choked with strange organic remains: stripped bones, bent limbs, and laughing skulls. There was also a flurry of motion as rat-sized reptiles with long tails, dazzled by the incursive light, ducked into their burrows.

"Carrion eaters." Doc's voice sounded priestlike in the hollow echo chamber of the sewer. With the mud taking up so much of the tunnel, the water became deeper. "They're afraid of the light." Using the openings of their holes as footholds, he climbed onto the sticky mound and continued up the tunnel. Inquisitive, beaked snouts and beady eyes peered out in the flickering, yellow light. "Come on. They won't hurt you."

"This place gives me the creeps." Sandra's whisper was hardly audible.

Undaunted, Doc was far in front.

For fifteen minutes they sloshed through ooze. With only four feet of clearance they had to walk hunched over like gnomes. There was an eroded pathway through the middle of the tunnel, winding like an ancient river, but that was where the carrion-eating reptiles were the thickest. They made no outcries, but could be heard scurrying about in the shadows. Finally, the mud bank receded, and they were able to take a more upright posture. Doc groaned as he stretched his aching back.

The stink, if anything, was worse. Half-seen gooey objects floated by in the underground soup. Long strips of plastic hung down from the ceiling like stalactites, where the once soft compound had dripped between molds during construction. The walls were overgrown with slick, glistening mold.

"I need a rest." Scott panted under the weight of the pack. A small circular tube intersecting the main tunnel at waist height trickled with black, viscous liquid: a drooling tongue. He backed up to it and let it take the weight off him. He wriggled out of the straps and stretched upright. Faint scratching sounds emitted from the pipe. "How much farther?"

"It's another quarter mile before the first main cutoff. At this speed it should be dark by the time we're ready to go to work, so we won't have to sit it out until sunset."

"You're crazy if you think I'm going to sit in this stuff." Sandra stayed in the middle of the channel, far away from both mildewed walls.

"Merely a matter of speech. What I meant was that our timing is going perfectly. We'll be able to complete all our topside work before the moon rises."

"Less chance of being shot at."

"Oh, my, no. Never fear being fired upon, my boy. This city has been without incident of enemy attack in its hundred-year history. There are no guards. And during the night, except for a few technicians wandering the streets on wayward missions, the dragons are securely hidden in their quarters like chickens in a coop. They don't like the dark, or the cold."

Death Wind passed around his water pouch. Sandra rinsed out her mouth. "You mean in all your trips into this city you never had the urge to stick a spear into one of those sleeping demons?"

"I can't go as far as to say that, but the purpose of my excursions was strictly exploratory. If I had yielded to such temptation the dragons would have been put on their guard, and we would not be able to enter this city today with the ease with which it has been accomplished. Of course, I always had in the back of my mind a general assault of this nature, but I never had the arms or the manpower."

"So you did nothing instead."

"Killing individuals does not win wars, only battles. Shall we proceed?"

Without waiting for a reply, he slurped onward through the muddy tunnel. Death Wind repacked his canteen, and the four youths started out after the aging scout. There was a spring in his step, a purpose, which the rest found hard to match. The mud that slogged them down seemed to leap out of his way.

Still, Doc leaned on his cane with every step. His renascence was more mental than physical.

Fifteen minutes later Doc stopped beside a four-foot-high side passage that veered to the right. "Well, here it is." A torch cast into it did not shed light very far, but it was enough to send the local denizens scurrying away. The walls were wet with condensation, and an unsightly trickle of effluence flowed down the middle. It did not look very inviting.

"Are you sure this is the right one?" Scott said.

"My mark is still on the wall." Doc held his torch high so they could all see it above the entrance. Rough-hewn letters were cut into the orange plastic.

"No mistaking that code," Rusty allowed.

Death Wind leaned close, and read with newly acquired knowledge, "To airport."

"Nice going, Death Wind," Scott said.

"The dragons do not read English. Nor would I expect them to come down here to look for engravings." Doc grinned at his own wit. "Now, if you'll excuse me for being a perfectionist, let me go over this with you two again. You'll pass under half a dozen street accesses with ladder rungs. Look for a slightly smaller tube on your right, with the words "To flyers" printed above it. That will take you to an access near the flight bay. It's pretty open up top, with very few walls for protection, but it's usually not guarded, either. But don't loll around too close in case they turn on the disruptor beam. There may be some technicians about getting ready for a night flight. It's rare, but it happens."

Scott shrugged off the pack and laid the explosive canisters by the entrance. "Got it."

Rusty transferred the beamer to Scott. "Where will we meet you?"

"About half a mile up the main tunnel, on the left, is the tube leading to the hatchery. After we set our homing beacons we'll stay there and wait for you."

"When do we rescue my mother?"

"That's farther up the tunnel. But I want to make sure we're all together, and safe, before we make another move. It's important that all the homing beacons be set so we can do the most damage and have the optimum amount of diversion when we make our attack on the transporter."

"Yeah, well, what happens if one of those flyers takes off in the meantime and triggers the computer automatically—aside from the fact that our little experts get fried?"

Rusty swung Death Wind around and removed the plastic utility box. He took out three homing beacons, then returned the box and cinched down the straps. "You'll have the control box with you. All you have to do is push the button, and when the red light comes on you're home free. Doc knows how."

"So if we get cooked, you still get your mother," Scott added. "But don't worry about those flyers getting away. If they try to take off, the missiles will launch as soon as the flyers gain enough altitude to reach scanning height. So we'll get them one way or another."

"You guys have really thought of everything."

Scott flashed a smile. "You forget, we're experts in our field. Sarcasm isn't the only profession."

Sandra glared.

Doc passed his pistol to Rusty. "And boys, do be careful." He squeezed their hands warmly. "I don't want to lose you—even for the world. I've grown to love you too much:"

"Uh, thanks."

"Yes, we'll watch our step."

They ducked into the tube with torches in front of them, and started off half stooping, while Doc, Death Wind, and Sandra turned toward the hatchery.

CHAPTER 24

"Doc forgot to tell us this tunnel got smaller," Scott groaned. He did a duck waddle and at the same time tried to straddle the flow of fetid water that ran down the middle of the plastic conduit.

"Ouch!" Rusty surged ahead, then stopped several feet away and looked back by tucking his head between his legs. "Don't get so close with the torch, will you?" He swatted at the bottom of his lizard-skin shorts, where they had been singed.

"Sorry." Scott held the torch back a respectable distance. He tried not to slip on the slimy floor. More than once they passed patches of unidentifiable goo. Smaller side pipes brought in fresh streams of putrid liquid stained red with chemicals so they looked like gushes of blood. And always, beyond the feeble glow of light, there was the scrabbling sound of tiny reptilian feet.

At last they reached the first street access. If

Rusty had not been standing up in it, Scott would have missed it. It was already nighttime so no light shone through the small holes in the grate. Scott stood up in the narrow vertical shaft and leaned against the ladder rungs to take the weight of the power pack off his back. Rusty's face was only inches away. Looking up, he could see stars through the grating, twinkling in the hot summer sky.

The next moment the stars were blotted out, and the lid crunched overhead. They both crouched as a large leg stepped off the grating; a tail dragged by behind it. They thrust their torches into the horizontal tunnel.

After a moment of breathless silence, Rusty said, "Let's get going."

Scott did not argue. Back in the lame-duck position, they plowed on. Scott had crawled through many maintenance tunnels in his day, but never any as revolting as this. It was quite a few minutes before they passed under another grating. This one was sticky with goo.

Rusty went by without pausing. "If this keeps up we'll be hours getting to the airport."

Carrying the heavy power pack in this unnatural position was becoming a strain for Scott. "I think Doc's memory for distances is a little off."

Fortunately for his aching back, they passed the next three accesses in quick succession. There was only one more to go when, impossibly, the tunnel shrank again. Now, instead of doing a duck waddle, they were forced to crawl on hands and knees. Scott had to stoop even lower because of the pack, and his face was practically in the viscous liquid.

At last they reached the sixth access. The torches were already growing dimmer, but with the conduit so small it was hardly noticeable. Out in front, and closing in behind them, the scampering carrion reptiles stayed out of the cone of light. Sharp claws clicked dully against the plastic. They lived in the multitudes of small inlet pipes, only inches in diameter, that lined the sides.

Rusty stopped and turned around. He faced a side passage that was barely two feet across.

"I hope you're kidding," Scott said.

Rusty pointed with the torch. Inscribed in the plastic at the junction were the words: To flyers. "At least Doc got the number of accesses right."

Scott worked his arms out of the beamer straps. "Yes, but I wish he was more explicit on size. I'll never get the beamer through there."

Rusty shoved the torch into the pipe. A gentle breeze bent the flames back. "Leave it. The soldiers should all be cuddled up in some nice warm place. The technicians won't be armed. And besides, I've got the forty-five."

Scott set the beamer upright on the floor. "You don't have to twist my arm."

Rusty slithered forward on elbows and knees, holding the torch out in front. "Don't get too close." Scott could not answer: he was holding his torch in his teeth.

The air in the small pipe was thick. The fumes were not noxious, but there did not seem to be quite enough oxygen to go around. Soon they were both gasping. The smell alone was enough to make Scott pass out. And it appeared hotter than before, but that was probably due to his own exertions.

Scott opened his mouth and let the torch fall out. "Hey, hold up."

"What is it?"

Scott jerked his thumb in the semidarkness. "You missed it." With his face down Scott almost had not seen it himself. Because there was no room to turn around, Rusty had to crawl backward.

Scott wedged his torch behind the lowest rung and climbed up ten feet to the grating. He listened intently for several seconds, heard nothing, then pushed gently on the grimy cover. It did not budge.

"It's stuck." But being close to fresh air quickly renewed his strength. He braced his back against the wall and shoved hard. The lid popped off so easily that it clattered and rolled away before Scott could reach up to grab it.

Rusty's voice echoed from below. "What are you trying to do, make a formal announcement?"

"It was an accident. Leave the torch and come on up." Scott climbed out of the manhole—as he called it in his mind—and recovered the lid.

Rusty poked his head up, but kept it at street level. He glanced around in the starlight. "I don't see anything."

Scott plastered himself against the base of a seven-foot-high wall that ran along the edge of the street. On the opposite side was a two-story structure that extended a hundred feet in either direction. It must have been a tenement house, for it was lined with doorways, although there were no actual doors. "I thought we were supposed to be at the docking pens."

Rusty climbed out and joined Scott by the wall, where the shadow seemed to offer protection. "We are."

Through gritted teeth, Scott said, "What makes you so sure?"

"Doc hasn't been wrong yet."

"His distances haven't been too close."

"All right, so we look around" Rusty slipped out of the slender pack and looked up and down the empty street. "It must be around here somewhere." He studied the wall at Scott's back. Then he sprang up and grabbed the lip with his hands, and pulled himself up until he could see over the top. He stayed there for several seconds, then dropped back down. "I guess he *has* forgotten a few details. But we're only twenty feet from the edge of a flyer."

Scott rolled his eyes at his own stupidity. When he stepped away from the wall he could see all three flyers. "Did you see anybody?"

Rusty shook his head. "Not a soul."

"Forget religion. Did you see any dragons?" Scott flashed a set of teeth that shone whitely in the dark.

"No, but you'd better take this anyway." He took the gun out of his pack and handed it to Scott. Then he grabbed the three homing beacons and tucked them under his belt. He dropped the pack down the shaft, and fitted the lid over the hole. "All right. Let's do it."

With athletic ease Scott vaulted to the top of the wall and balanced on the foot-wide, rounded ledge while he lent Rusty a hand. Rusty jumped up, allowed himself to be pulled onto his stomach, then pivoted around and dropped to the other side. Scott alighted beside him.

Like a giant toadstool, the flyer was an immense disc resting on a tall central column which was open on one side where a ramp descended. The hundred-foot-diameter underbelly was covered with gleaming nozzles that protruded down like stalactites: exhausts of the disruptor beam. They were dark cones eight feet in length.

"Cover me."

Scott nodded, and held out the gun so its smooth surface glinted in the starlight.

In the light of the stars, Rusty inched toward the supporting column that was a retractile part of the flyer. His lizard-skin moccasins made no sound on the plastic landing pad.

When he reached the ramp his body was outlined in a weak cone of light that spread out from inside. He glanced briefly upward. Then he slipped a homing beacon from under his belt and slid it out of sight under the edge of the metal ramp.

A moment later he was back at Scott's side, smiling confidently. "One down, two to go."

Scott returned the grin. "This is almost too easy."

They sidled along the wall toward the next flyer pen. A rampart separated the two, and probably had a door in it somewhere. But Scott did not want to waste time looking for it. After a quick glance over the top, he clambered onto the wall and dragged Rusty after him.

"There's not even a sign of a dragon," Scott said. The docking bay was dark and quiet, yet he looked around warily. He followed Rusty while he planted the beacon, then together they proceeded to the other side. They repeated the wall-climbing procedure.

Scott was trying not to make the mistake of overconfidence. Yet it all seemed so simple. They approached the ramp. Rusty took the last beacon and shoved it under the bottom step. Metal groaned overhead. Scott lifted his eyes and saw a dragon's clawed foot on the top step, and another one descending.

He grabbed Rusty's tunic and pulled him out of the light. Then they dashed to the far wall and crouched in the shadow. By that time the dragon was halfway down the ramp. Its head was bent down on its snakelike neck, and red eyes squinted through nictitating eyelids at the inside of the revetment. Scott wished he were a turtle so he could cringe into his shell. He willed the creature to look the other way.

The dragon reached the plastic deck and rotated ponderously, its tail swinging in a slow arc. The gray vest it wore identified it as a technician. It was unarmed.

Scott held the forty-five in a hand that shook slightly. The dragon peered myopically around the compound once, then a second time. It seemed to sense that something was wrong. It stopped with its lanky body pointed at Scott and Rusty.

Then, with curiosity, it started walking toward them.

* * *

"Here it is." Doc pointed with his torch to the side passage. He held the light close to the wall where years ago, as a lone scout, he had first entered the city, mapped its complex tunnel system, and scratched street signs at the intersections. The opening was only slightly smaller than the main tube. A noxious, yellow muck flowed slowly, like molasses. Ugly reptiles ran for the darkness.

"To hatchery," Death Wind pronounced.

Sandra screwed up her face. "What do they do, drop their bad eggs down the drain?"

"The sulfur smell is more likely from chemical waste than rotten eggs. The plastic manufacturing plant is on the other side of the hatchery."

Death Wind stepped into the circular side passage and set the instrument pack in a dry spot high on the curve. He let slip a grimace of pain, which brought Sandra in after him. She placed a hand on his side, but said nothing.

Doc took the two remaining beacons from the protective housing and put them in a pocket. "My dear, I think it would be most propitious if you would wait here for Scott and Rusty, in case we're not back before they arrive."

"Not me. I wanna go where I can shoot some dragons."

"And that is precisely why I want you to wait here. We're not going to shoot anything: stealth is our prerequisite. We want to do more than kill a few stray slaves—we want to clean out the nest."

"I always was a good housekeeper, so I'd be glad to help with the spring cleaning."

Doc took off his pack and laid it beside the other. "My dear, I understand the vengeance you feel, but if you want to do the best for your mother you'll see to it that everything goes according to plan."

"Don't start pulling that stuff on me. I'll—"

She was cut off as Death Wind squeezed her arm. "Sandra, it is best this way."

Sandra scowled as she peered into Death Wind's eyes. After a moment she spoke in a lowered voice. "Well, okay. But I don't like the idea of being left alone with these creepy lizard rats."

Doc knocked caked-on mud off his cane. "Just keep the torch brightly lit and they won't bother you. They abhor light. Well, then, are we ready?"

Death Wind gave his usual single nod. He readjusted his bow and quiver, squeezed Sandra's arm again, then followed Doc's sucking footsteps.

The stench grew worse as the old doctor and the young Nomad, men of two different worlds

yet bound together by heredity, penetrated deeper into the black sewer. The torches did little to dispel the gloom, for the walls were stained with ooze that absorbed the feeble flames. They waded through muck that was several inches deep, and cold and unctuous to the touch as it seeped through shoes and moccasins.

After several minutes they came to a fork where the tunnel split into two smaller passages. Without reading the signpost Doc automatically veered to the right. Here the atmosphere was too noxious even for the carrion eaters. The remains of tiny dragon dolls lay scatted in the mud in various states of decomposition. Some of the dolls were perfectly formed, others wildly distorted.

"The dragons dispose of their malformed and unwanted without proper burial. They are merely discarded, sometimes still living. Sandra's opinion of their barbarous nature is vile enough without her having to see additional evidence."

Death Wind nodded. "Dragons do not care about the ones, only the many."

"Yes, that's true. But there were also nations of men who cared nothing about the individual—to them it was the state that was sacred. Individuality and personal happiness were sacrificed for the goals of the government. Let us hope we can learn something from this. We cannot change our past, but given the opportunity we can use our knowledge to shape the future."

With torches held high they skirted around the decaying bodies. But there were more ahead. And from the sides smaller conduits were choked with pieces of rotting flesh, skinny white bones, and strips of skin like parchment. A sticky fluid as thick as paste tried to fall to the mud-covered floor. The odor was nauseating.

Doc swooned, and would have collapsed had not Death Wind caught him. He held the older man in his arms for a moment while he recovered.

"I'm not as young as I used to be," Doc rasped. "I'm afraid that my scouting days are numbered."

"I will help you. Lean on my shoulder."

"Yes, thank you, son. I do need your help. I—I'm having difficulty breathing, but we must go on. It's only a little farther."

It was with difficulty that Doc pulled his feet from the thick, clinging mire. He allowed Death Wind to pull him along, and ease his exhaustion.

"This is it. I'm sure of it." The tunnel constricted ahead, and a side passage led to the left. Doc stopped on his own. "It's only a few more feet."

The starlight did not penetrate through the grating, but the rungs were visible in the torchlight. Doc ducked down, leaning forward on his cane, and waddled the few feet to the shaft. Death Wind kept one hand on his belt to steady him.

Doc stared at the engraved arrow that pointed up. "From here on we travel the alleys and corridors. Up you go."

Death Wind left his torch on the floor and climbed up the filthy rungs. The lid slipped aside easily, and in a jiffy he was out and motioning Doc to climb up after him. Doc put his torch next to the Nomad's. A moment later he emerged into a courtyard bounded on four sides by twenty-foot-high walls which were inset with doorways and window openings.

While Death Wind replaced the cover, Doc sucked in the cool night air and regained his composure. He wiped sweat off his forehead. Slowly the color came back to his face and he breathed more easily. After a five-minute rest, he was ready to continue. Again he took the lead, stepping through an arched doorway that emerged into utter darkness.

"Use your ears," Doc whispered. As his eyes adjusted, he could see that the room was furnished with low stools, each with a circular groove on one side of the seat. "An indoctrination center. Baby dragons sit in these chairs, and their tails fit comfortably in the grooves."

They passed through the room in a few seconds, into a large yard that was a playground. It was empty now, and they used the hundred-yard-long plastic field as a way of reaching the building at the far end. This had several rooms in it, each of which was crammed with stools and tables. They passed through this into another playground, but stopped halfway across.

"Look over this wall and tell me what you see."

Death Wind's fingers wrapped over the seven-foot-high parapet. He hoisted himself up. He stayed only for a second, then dropped back down. His expression was quizzical. "Many dragon babies. They look—innocent."

Doc nodded wearily. "You'd better let me see." Death Wind interlaced his fingers and made a step. Doc put his foot into the cupped hands and allowed the savage to lift him up.

He saw hundreds, possibly thousands, of baby dragons, from hatchlings to puppy size, crowded together for warmth. Each one was a tiny ball, with long neck bent and head tucked under its tail. Like babies of any kind, they jerked and moved spasmodically, rolled in their sleep, and kicked their siblings when their legs twitched. Every now and then a sloe-eyed, reptilian head arched on its long neck as a half-aroused infant hissed in discontent.

Doc stepped down. "Ah, yes, I understand your sentiment, my friend. They are the unsuspecting children of the future: without sin, without evil intent, but waiting to be imprinted. Nevertheless, by the nature of their heredity they are our enemies."

Doc fumbled inside his shirt and brought out a hand-sized homing beacon. "Place it on top of the wall. I couldn't bear to see their faces again."

As soon as the simple task was performed they moved to the other end of the courtyard, and into the next building. Here there was no furniture, but an odd variety of, for lack of a better word, playthings. They were models of simple hand tools, designed to fit the miniature alien paws. Doc did not give Death Wind time to look around, but immediately mounted a flight of plastic stairs.

In the second level a long corridor stretched interminably toward a pinpoint of light at the farthest end. It seemed to Doc that he was looking through the wrong end of a telescope. They passed room after room, with only the faint glow of the stars peering in through tiny portholes. It took a full minute to pass all these classrooms, and when they did they found themselves on a walled parapet.

"The hatchery." Doc swept the scene before them with his wrinkled but still strong arm.

Below was a network of cubicles, a virtual maze of tiny, roofless rooms, extending hundreds of feet in all directions. The walls that separated the cubicles were wide, like platforms, and in between was filled with a dry, strawlike vegetation. Here and there white ovals showed through where they were insufficiently covered.

"At night the eggs are covered to prevent heat loss. During the day, workers pluck them out with rakes so they can have the full benefit of the sun."

Death Wind nodded dumbly. After a long surveillance he turned to Doc. "They are still the enemy, for when they grow, they will kill."

"Yes, I'm afraid it's true. They are our potential foes of the future." He stared out over the thousands of living but unborn usurpers. "We do what we must—but let us do it with remorse."

Doc leaned over the low wall, found a suitable niche in the uneven plastic wall, and secreted the other beacon.

From behind came a loud hiss, like the sound of escaping steam. Doc snapped around. Death Wind stood between him and a leering dragon's head that strode forward quickly on a stout, strangely clad reptilian body.

The mouth gaped wide, revealing double rows of gleaming white teeth and a menacing, darting tongue. It was so close that drooling saliva stained Death Wind's hair as taloned paws reached out for his throat. . . .

CHAPTER 25

Scott slowly and silently pushed the safety lever to the off position. He was reasonably certain that a well-placed slug would kill the inquisitive beast on the spot. But the resultant pandemonium might not only compromise their escape, it might ruin all they had planned for.

Before he was forced to pull the trigger, the curious dragon's attention wandered, and it veered off to inspect some other imaginary disturbance. For several minutes it poked around the revetment in a seemingly random pattern. Then, with broad tail swaying, it ascended the ramp and entered the flyer.

Scott breathed a sigh of relief and tucked the gun away. Without a word, Rusty sidled along the wall back the way they had come. Scott trailed along behind. But the night was not as quiet as it had been.

There seemed to be some commotion in the other landing pad, so Rusty pulled himself up cautiously and peered over the partition. After a quick look he dropped down beside Scott. "Five dragons—technicians—prowling around."

"Do you think they found the beacon?"

Rusty shrugged.

Scott said, "Well, we can't stay here. Our friend may get restless again. Let's assume they're just making a routine check—" He clamped his mouth shut when he heard another tread upon the flyer's ramp. A clawed foot appeared in the light. "We can't stay here and wait

to get caught."

"The street. It's our only chance."

Without waiting for Scott's confirmation, Rusty leaped to the top of the wall and squirmed to get over. Scott gave him a shove from below that tossed him clear over and into a pile on the plastic road surface. Then he leaped over after him almost without touching the top. He crashed into the street and rolled over.

"Are you all right?"

Rusty sat up and dusted himself off. "A few broken bones is all."

"Better than a laser beam." Scott looked hastily up and down the avenue. "You know, I thought Doc said they never come out at night."

"He said they *seldom* come out at night. But still, it does seem funny that—"

Scott suddenly slammed him against the partition, then pointed with his chin up the wall-lined street. "Here come some more seldoms."

A whole squad of dragon soldiers was marching toward them, claws clicking on the plastic. They were carrying beamers, and they were holding the triggering mechanisms in their reptilian paws.

"I think they mean business."

"Time to go." Rusty took off, running crouched and keeping close to the wall. Scott ran along expecting any moment that a beamer blast would cut them down. But it seemed as if the soldiers had not observed them—yet.

"Hold up. I think we passed it."

Rusty stopped and looked beyond Scott. They had outdistanced the plodding dragons. "No, it's right up ahead. I can see it." He crawled out into the middle of the street and removed the lid. An instant later he was at the bottom of the shaft, and Scott climbed down the ladder far enough to ease the cover back in place.

"The torches are almost out." Rusty held them both upside down, nursing the flames.

Scott descended the rest of the way and took one. "They're not going to last much longer."

Scott blew meager life into the dying reeds. "Neither are we if we don't get out of here. I'm not sure they didn't see us."

Rusty ducked down and entered the narrow conduit. He backed out a second later. "Hey, the pack's gone."

"What do you mean, it's gone?"

Rusty remained in a crouch. "I dropped it straight down the shaft, but it's not here."

"It's got to be here. It didn't get up and walk

away." Rusty parted Scott's legs and thrust his torch in the other direction. "It's not here either."

"Well, come on. We haven't got time to look for it."

"But it's got our spare torches in it."

Scott said, "If we hurry we won't need them. Now let's get moving. I don't want to be here if someone decides to look down."

Rusty swung back and started slithering along the pipe. "Maybe it floated away."

Scott ducked in right behind him. "Or maybe the scavengers dragged it away."

Rusty added a sigh to his grunts. "I can do without the moral support." There was a hiss, followed by, "Darn, I dropped my torch in the water."

"Where did the water come from," Scott said sarcastically as he kept his elbows and knees out of the sludge that seeped down the middle of the pipe. "Do you want mine?"

"Never mind. I don't want it passed up between my legs." A moment later, he screamed. "Aaaagh."

"What is it?"

"I bumped into something."

"Maybe it's the pack." There was not much flame left in his torch, but Scott held it low so the light would pass under Rusty's body.

"Yeech." Rusty crawled back a step. "It's not the pack." He hunched his back and cringed past the object.

"I see what you mean." Scott clambered over the torn limbs and ripped body of a carrion-eating reptile that was still oozing warm blood. He tried not to touch it, or to breathe as he passed over it.

"Hey, here's the beamer." Rusty entered the larger pipe and stood up. Scott crawled out behind him and felt the cool plastic of the power pack. "And there's what's left of the pack."

Tatters of material, pieces of strapping, and a chunk of flint were all that remained. "I guess the reptiles got it after all. And that one back there lost the fight."

"The torches are gone."

Scott grunted resignedly. "Well, at least we can't get lost. It's a straight shot from here to the main tunnel." He handed the torch to Rusty and in the fading light slipped the power pack harness over his shoulders. When he felt the bulge of the forty-five in his belt, he took it out and handed it to Rusty. "Here, you hang onto this."

Rusty nodded, and tucked it in his own belt.

Then, holding the dying torch in front at arm's length, he scuttled down the sewer like a racing spider. By the time the pipe broadened, and they reached the first street access, the torch was reduced to little more than a glowing ember. Scott was happy to be able to stand up for a moment, despite the prospect of coming darkness.

But Rusty allowed him no rest. "All we can do is keep moving." He ducked into the tunnel. Scott arched his back, but was forced to follow. A few minutes later the torch went out. Blackness hammered in with a tangible clap.

"I can hear noises up ahead." There was a slight tremor in Rusty's voice. One thing Scott had not banked on was that the light was all that was keeping back the hordes of carrion-eating reptiles.

"Yes, and they're behind us, too." Scott knew that they were also on every side, peering out of the small drain pipes. "If they get too close I'm going to turn around and kick them." He tried not to let his imagination run wild. It was all too easy to imagine the darting tongues and leering faces that were probably only inches away in the Stygian darkness. He held onto the stub of the burned-out torch, ready to stab at anything that touched him.

With agonizing slowness they passed under the accesses, and reveled in the brief amount of light that each one offered. The clicking noises were getting louder, the reptiles more bold. They were beginning to close in on them.

When they stopped under the next access, Scott took the lead. "I've got an idea. Let me go first."

"Be my guest." Rusty followed so close to his friend that whenever Scott made a misstep, he bumped into him. In front the noises grew louder, as if the carrion eaters were licking their lizard lips. Finally, Scott decided it was time to put his plan into action.

Bending low, he leveled the laser gun and let loose with a bolt of lightning that arced down the sewer pipe with blinding brilliance. In the strobelike flash Scott saw scores of little lizards walking on the slimy floor or clinging to the curved wall. In the ensuing darkness he could hear the frenzied motion of clawed feet scurrying for cover.

"I guess that will show them."

He picked up his pace. With his legs spread wide he straddled the ichorous fluid that collected in the middle of the tube. The curvature helped guide him through the inky dark. Whenever the reptiles became too audacious, Scott let loose with the beamer and sent them scampering for cover.

As they passed under the sixth access, counting backward, Rusty tapped Scott on the shoulder. "I don't think the warheads will go off, but wouldn't be a good idea to burn through the canisters."

"Right." Now that he could stand straight, Scott did not mind kicking the scurrilous beasts out of the way—until he encountered something more solid. "Hey, I think this is it."

In the pitch-black he felt the contour of the explosives pack. By feel, Scott handed the beamer back to Rusty while he threw the other pack over his shoulders.

"Now what?"

Scott stepped into the main tunnel. "Now we just head upstream until we see a light. It's not likely there will be anyone else down here."

"Suppose there's no light? We might get to the junction before they get back."

Scott nodded, forgetting that Rusty could not see the gesture in the dark. "All right. You walk up this side and I'll walk up the other side. Just keep dragging your hand along the wall."

"Through this crud?"

Scott thought about the slimy covering on the sides of the passageway. "Do you have a better idea?"

"I wish I did."

Instead of dragging his hand, Scott just touched the wall with one finger at each step. Often he heard the scurrying reptiles, but they were not as profuse as they had been in the smaller pipe. Separated by the width of the tunnel, Scott listened for Rusty's footsteps in the slurpy mud to keep abreast of him. He did not want to talk because of the eerie echo effect. He searched for a glimmer other than the coruscating points that haunted his eyes in the total absence of light.

Time passed.

Suddenly the darkness in front burst into dots of fire, punctuated almost instantly by the hammering of explosions that reverberated deafeningly in the long chamber. The air was full of flying debris that ripped past Scott's face, thudded hollowly into the walls, and plowed furrows unseen in the mud.

They were blind, alone, and under attack!

* * *

If the dragons had a slow reaction time during the heat of the day, their responses were that much more sluggish at night, when their blood thickened and their muscles were stiff. Death Wind, acting with trained Nomadic impulse, ducked and stepped aside. Reptilian paws clapped on empty air.

At the same time, Doc's cane swept up from ground level and smashed into the beast's lower jaw, breaking bone and snapping off teeth. Hissing with pain, the dragon backed away with its paws to its face. Doc swung again, and the dragon was unable to ward off the blow.

Death Wind took but a moment to unsheathe his long knife. He lunged under the flailing paws and stabbed hard through the clothing and into the massive chest where the two-chambered heart pumped torpidly. With an overhand swing Doc's cane crashed across the skull. The knife was whipped out of the savage's hand when the wailing beast twisted away. This gained it no respite.

With the knife buried in its chest, and Doc still beating it about the head, the dragon technician died in stages. While the long serpentine neck slowly drooped, the oversized hind legs kept walking backward in retreat. When the paws dropped and the head literally hung on its belly, it was already dead. Still it moved backward, until it bumped into the wall of the corridor and could go no farther. Then it finally stopped moving.

"Quick! Help me drag it into one of these rooms." In the adrenaline flow, Doc forgot all about his pain and fatigue.

The creature had died on its feet, in a squat. Together they upended it and dragged it on its back into a dark corner of the room. Death Wind recovered his knife while Doc picked up his cane.

Doc was breathing hard. "Whew. That happened so fast that I quite forgot to limp." He wiped sweat off his brow. In the aftermath of the fight he did not forget to scan the area for other insomniac dragons. "I think it's time we withdrew, before another mentor is awakened by the clamor."

As quickly as they dared, they retraced their steps along the darkened corridor, downstairs, through the courtyards, to the tunnel access. There was no further incident.

They found their torches going dim, so before they started out they took spares out of the pack and lighted them from the still-burning brands. The used ones were doused in the water and buried in the fetid muck.

They moved fast through the mélange of tiny, rotting bodies and the thick, noxious atmosphere. With a lungful of clean, topside air Doc was able to get through the worst of it easily.

Then there was nothing to bar their return but mud and distance.

The faint light from Sandra's torch was already in view when the tunnel ahead erupted into a cacophony of loud gunshots that came so quickly because of the echo effect that it sounded like one continuous roar.

"Sandra!" Death Wind did not wait for the older man, but charged ahead stringing his bow as he ran. By the time Doc reached the pair, Sandra was crying hysterically, and from down the tunnel came the frantic shouts of Scott and Rusty. Death Wind held the girl to his breast and brushed her hair with his hand.

"Sandra, what's wrong? What happened?" She was sobbing so hard that she could not answer Doc's question—or even return to a rational state of mind. Doc stepped into the main tunnel with his torch held out. "Scott. Rusty. Are you all right?"

"We will be if you can keep that madwoman from shooting at us." There was no mistaking Scott's furious voice.

"It's all right." Doc waved the torch. "But, what are you doing there in the dark?"

Rusty moved cautiously into view. "Our torches went out and we lost our spares."

"What's gotten into that crazy girl? We've got enough problems without having a trigger-happy kid on the loose."

Sandra tore free from Death Wind and stepped out of the side pipe. "What the hell's the idea of sneaking up on me in the dark? This place is creepy enough without you two playing hide-and-seek."

Scott tried to match Sandra decibel for decibel. "We weren't playing games. Rusty already said we lost our torches."

"And how did you do a stupid thing like that?"

"It's not as stupid as screaming and losing your head."

"I didn't scream. I never scream."

"Yeah, and how do you think we heard you that day in the ruins? Because you were whispering for help?"

"You shut up, you, or I'll jam this rifle right—"

Doc chose drastic measures and clamped a hand over her mouth. "Please, please, please. Can we calm down before we wake up the whole city?"

"What does she think, that we were out for a moonless stroll in the sewers?"

Sandra pulled Doc's hand from her face. "Get off my back, will you?" She tried to strike Scott, but Doc prevented her.

"Children, please." Gently he pushed Sandra back to Death Wind. The savage held her tightly. "Scott, please control yourself. Now, Rusty, can you tell me how this eventuality occurred?"

Rusty gave a concise account of their activities. Doc harrumphed. "Yes, we had a slight altercation ourselves." He tendered a brief account of their own foray. "And the beast was wearing clothes. Unheard of. Something is afoot, or our presence is compromised. Now, if you two can reconcile your differences, at least temporarily, we are a wee bit behind schedule. . . . "

Neither combatant said a word, or even deigned to exchange glances.

"Fine, well, now that that's settled we can continue. But I must warn you—I'm somewhat concerned about the midnight peregrinations of our reptilian counterparts. We must exercise utmost caution." Then he added, for Scott's and Sandra's benefit, "And quiet."

The patrol started out again, deeper into the hostile city.

CHAPTER 26

"This is where we split up." Doc held his torch against the sharp angle that formed the base of a Y, where the sewer split. "This way lies the stockade, that way the time transporter."

Rusty handed his torch to Scott and helped take the instrument package off Death Wind's back. "Time to shift gears."

Scott dropped the explosives in the inch-deep water and reached for the beamer that Rusty was still wearing. "I hope this thing doesn't die on us."

With deft fingers Rusty unlatched the clear plastic storage box and flipped open the lid. He pressed the switch that connected the battery circuit. Stored-up power surged through the wiring to the roughly soldered electronic components. He placed the toggles in the ready position, punched in the sequencing code for a quick check, and sat back on his haunches.

"Seems to be all right. All I have to do is push this button and the missiles will be on their way."

"How can you be sure?" Sandra asked, more with reproach than with concern.

"This 'signal received' light will come on. Then, as the missiles leave their silos, the annunciator lights will change from green to red."

"How far are we from our target areas?" Scott asked Doc.

Doc tugged on his beard; it had stayed amazingly white during his perambulations. "I should say not more than fifteen minutes to either one. We should be in position before the missiles arrive."

"Then let's cut the gab and get a move on. Push that damn button."

"Okay." Rusty pressed down his index finger. In the flickering torchlight it was difficult to see the glass lenses because of the glare. Rusty tilted the box into the shadow and pressed the button again.

"Is something wrong?" Doc inquired softly.

Rusty lifted the block of components out of the plastic housing and inspected the wiring. He pressed the button a third time, shaking his head. "I'm not getting a positive return."

"That's just great," Sandra said. "All dressed up and nowhere to go."

"Could there be something wrong with the filament?" Doc said.

Rusty shrugged. "Well, there could be—if the bulb got broken in transit. But most likely the signal's not getting through. I think these plastic walls are damping the broadcast. We've got to get topside."

"I'll start looking for an access," Scott said.

Death Wind pointed with his torch. "We pass access one, two minutes ago."

"One can always trust a Nomad for constant vigilance. I suggest we retrace our steps." Doc let Death Wind lead the way. Rusty picked up the instrument package and hand-carried it as they backtracked down the sewer. The savage entered a large side passage where, only a few feet in, a faint glimmer of light shone down.

"The moon might be up by now," Doc said. "I'm afraid we may have lost our cover of total darkness."

Rusty looked up at the pattern of dots filtering through the grate. "Let me try it from the top of the shaft. That might be all it needs." He cradled the instrument package in the crook of his arm as he climbed up the plastic rungs with one hand. At the top he wedged himself tight so he could fiddle with the box. A moment later he was back down.

"It's no use. The signal's too weak to get through all this plastic. It must be an almost perfect insulator. I've got to get above where there's no interference." He jerked his head upward. "And I couldn't get the cover off. It's stuck."

Doc issued orders. "Death Wind, go up first and see if the coast is clear. Scott, cover him. Rusty, get ready to follow."

"Hey, what about me?"

"You hold the torches."

Death Wind beat against the grating with his massive shoulders until it broke free and rolled away. "Clear." Then he leaped into the street and notched his bow.

Scott clambered out right behind him, and took up a station facing the opposite direction. Rusty climbed out awkwardly with the instrument package.

Right behind him came Sandra. Scott said, "Hey, what are you doing here?"

"Hell, I'm not gonna stay down there an' miss the action."

Doc poked his head and shoulders out of the hold. "Head-strong lass."

The quarter moon had risen, and shed a stark light over the dull orange architecture. This street, like all the others, was bounded on both sides either by buildings, or by walls that enclosed courtyards. The entire city seemed to be one vast molded plastic model: without relief of color or style, without art, without trees or flowers, without any form that was not strictly functional.

"It's still not working," Rusty murmured, more to himself than to Doc. "I'm going to have to get higher—above these walls."

"How about that watchtower?" Scott gestured with his chin toward a structure that rose three stories high. External steps connected the walkaround porch on each level.

"That should do."

Doc looked nervously up and down the street. "Do you realize that this is a public thoroughfare?"

Sandra stood with legs spread apart and the rifle butt resting on her hip, the barrel pointed skyward. "If any dragons come this way, they're gonna hafta pay a toll."

"Keep us covered." Scott escorted Rusty up the stairs to the first level.

Rusty pushed the button. "Higher." On the second level the moon sent silvery beams that lighted his features and cast shadows. Again he shook his head. On the third, where the porch was wider, a solid railing a body-length high cast a dark umbra. Rusty pursed his lips and looked up at the roof some ten feet above. "I have to get higher."

Scott nodded, thinking about the antenna hidden in the bushes. It was low; very low. "Climb up on my shoulders." He stepped onto the orange railing and leaned inward so his hands were against the wall.

Rusty cradled the signaler under one arm, steadied himself with Scott's aid, and jumped first to the railing. Then he shinnied up Scott's back, using the power pack as a footstool.

When he stepped onto Scott's shoulders he pushed the box onto the roof, then clambered after it.

Slowly, he stood up on the platform. His angular figure was silhouetted against white clouds drifting low across a purple sky. Standing on his toes, he held the box overhead in outstretched arms, as if he were supplicating to the gods. He could go no higher. He pushed the button.

Two things happened almost simultaneously: a tiny red annunciator light flashed on, and the plastic box with its delicate electronic components exploded in his hands with a burst of light and a loud report.

Rusty was thrown backward. He rolled off the edge of the platform, collided with Scott, and both of them fell into a snarled heap behind the solid railing.

For a span of about two seconds there was a stunned silence. Scott untangled himself and tried to see what was going on. The still of the night was again broken, this time by Sandra's burping rifle. She stitched a line of bullets so neatly across a dragon's neck that its head was practically severed from its trunk. The beamer it had fired at Rusty blasted twice more from the falling gun before the restless fingers got the message that the dragon was dead.

As the creature slumped to the side, another dragon's head appeared behind it, leering over the wall of an adjacent courtyard. But by the time its beamer rose high enough for a shot,

Death Wind buried an arrow in its throat. Gurgling, it fell back and dropped from sight.

Scott pushed Rusty unceremoniously out of the way, and rushed toward the stairs. "Come on." He was not abandoning his friend, but joining the fight. On the second level he leaned out over the railing with the beamer in hand, and sent a blast at a dragon that was ambling up the street behind Sandra and Death Wind. Lightning burned a hole through the lizard hide into vital organs. The creature hissed as it fell, smoldering.

He fired again at its replacement, but the beamer refused to discharge its deadly bolt. Faintly, he could hear the drawn-out whine as the capacitor strove to reach full charge. By this time both Sandra and Death Wind, warned by Scott's beam, pivoted and fired. Another dragon hit the ground, dying from lead and flint.

Rusty, weaponless, fumbled past Scott and down the stairs.

From his vantage point, Scott covered him until he reached the manhole from which Doc had just ducked out of sight.

Another dragon peered over the courtyard wall beneath Scott. The beamer still would not discharge. "Death Wind!" The savage turned around and let loose an arrow into the gaping maw before the beast's gun elevated. The reptilian head was so close that when the point of the arrow penetrated the neck, the feathers were touching the outstretched hand that held the bow. With unbelievable audacity the savage reached out and plucked the arrow from the wound, then turned and fired it at another dragon that was stepping out of the opposite doorway. Both dragons died in seconds.

Rusty dropped down the hole at the same time that Scott charged into the street from the lower level of the tower. Beamer blasts converged from all angles as dragon patrols converged on the disturbance. Remembering Death Wind's training, he danced across the street faster than the soldiers could draw a bead on him. "Let's get out of here!"

Death Wind was closest, so he jumped into the manhole. Scott fired over his head and zapped a dragon that was slinking out of a doorway. Then he waited for the beamer to recharge. He skidded to the opening. "Sandra, come on."

But Sandra had ideas of her own. Her face was contorted into a leer, as if in the heat of battle she was being overtaken by primal blood lust. She picked off dragons left and right with well-aimed, single shots. Scott realized that she was having the time of her life, and had no intention of leaving.

Until her gun jammed.

Crouched right in front of the sewer access, she was a sitting target for the dragon soldiers. "Sandra!" She looked up, saw the danger, and dodged her head slightly to avoid a lightning bolt. Her hair was singed as the heat ignited the dark strands and burnt them away. Then she calmly pulled back the bolt of the rifle and cleared the round in the chamber.

Scott rammed into her and knocked her aside just as another laser beam would have transfixed her. Bracing on one knee, he raised his gun and aimed at the dragon that was approaching and getting ready for another shot. For an awkward few seconds Scott held his fire, until he saw the dragon drawing a bead. At the last possible second he fired. The dragon's hide sizzled, but the beast did not fall. Scott's beamer was running out of energy.

Dark, steellike fingers wrapped around Sandra's ankles and pulled her to the hole, then down the shaft. As soon as her head dropped out of sight, Scott sprang after her. As he landed in the muck at the bottom of the sewer, Sandra was still struggling in Death Wind's arms.

"Whudja do that for?" she screamed. "There were more of 'em coming."

Scott appreciated Death Wind's knowing when to talk and when to act. The savage threw her over his shoulder, picked up two torches that were standing in the mud and ran along the pipe.

Sandra beat him on the back with clenched fists. "Put me down. Put me down."

Scott grabbed the last torch and chased after them. Doc and Rusty were waiting in the main tunnel. Then they all splashed through the water to the fork.

When Death Wind put her down, Sandra was still swinging and kicking like a tigress. "What the hell's the idea?"

Death Wind's eyes were ignited black pools. "We have mission."

"Our mission's to kill dragons."

"You not understand mission. You get us killed because you have no sense."

"Listen, buster, I have enough sense to know the more dragons we kill now, the less we hafta worry about later. And I didn't run out on you."

"Sandra, please calm down. Death Wind is

right. Your foolhardiness is likely to compromise our lives as well as the mission—which, as you may recall, is to blow up the time transporter." As an afterthought, Doc added, "And to rescue your mother."

"The mission's already compromised because wonderboy's box didn't work. Now we gotta shoot our way through this burg."

"Oh, it worked," Rusty said matter-of-factly. "The light went on just before the box got hit."

"So what? The box blew up."

"That doesn't matter. If the light went on it means the signal was transmitted and received."

Scott added sarcastically, "The missiles are on their way."

Sandra clamped her mouth shut, and stared from eye to eye. After a long silence, she plucked a torch out of Death Wind's hand and stared into the flame. "Oh. Well, how was I supposed to know?"

Slowly, the tension eased.

Scott smiled. "In a few minutes the dragons are going to have real egg on their faces."

Sandra looked up at him. Her face mellowed. "You know, you're really slinging my lingo."

"It's from hanging around in bad company."

Doc's chest finally stopped heaving. "If I can interject some commentary into this pleasant diatribe, I would like to mention the obvious—that it would seem we have lost the advantage of surprise. If, indeed, we ever had it."

"You think they knew we were coming?" Rusty said.

"I'm sure of it. I'm afraid I've underestimated their cunning again. That patrol on the outskirts of town was no accident, as I thought. They must have been expecting some kind of action, even if they did not know from which quarter it would come. I wonder what other precautionary measures they've taken."

Scott waved his torch to make it glow brighter. "Listen, Doc, I've got an idea."

Doc rolled his eyes. "Every time one of you boys gets an idea I have a premonition of fear."

Scott flashed a quirky smile. "Well, the beamer's almost dead—"

"So that's why you took so long," Sandra interrupted.

"—we're almost out of bullets, and pretty soon Death Wind's going to have to use his bow as a banjo. Why don't we get resupplied?"

Doc chewed his lip. "I'm afraid I don't follow you."

"Right now we don't have the firepower to assault an anthill. And the dragons are armed tooth and nail. If we split up we'll be practically defenseless. So, why don't we take over the armory—beamers for everybody?" For Sandra's benefit, he added, "Including the prisoners when we let them loose."

"Now we're talking turkey!"

"Oh, dear. If I live through this I think I'll retire from scouting for good."

Rusty said, "I think it's got a chance."

"Plan is good," said Death Wind.

"But the armory is locked—and probably guarded," Doc said.

Sandra playfully punched Scott on the shoulder. "I'll bet it won't be guarded when those missiles start making scrambled eggs."

Doc shivered. "Levity at a time like this."

"You gotta keep your sense of humor."

Doc merely shook his head. "Far be it for me to stand in the way of—" He coughed once, then again. He seemed unable to catch his breath.

Scott slapped him between the shoulder blades when he started coughing. "Take is easy, Doc."

Among the putrid smells of the sewer he picked out one that sparked his memory and sent chills down his spine. In the flickering, yellow flames a green mist appeared, and a stinging sensation gripped him by the back of the neck.

The dragons had gassed the sewers!

CHAPTER 27

Scott braced himself with one hand on the rung of the ladder, and stared up the shaft that led to the surface of the dragon city. He could go no farther along the tunnel because he detected a whiff of gas coming from up ahead. The dragons were trying to seal them off.

Death Wind jogged up next, wearing the heavy explosives pack. The bandage on his side was tinted red, but if he felt any pain his face did not show it. Sandra, too, ignored her injuries, both the beamer blast that had burned her hip and the one that had singed her hair and blackened the side of her face.

"I'm going up." Scott started climbing as soon as Doc and Rusty were close enough to hear.

"Wait!" Sandra reached out and stopped him on the third rung. Scott had tucked the beamer

gun in its holster; it was almost useless except for charring meat. She swung the rifle off her shoulder and thrust it at him. "Here, take this."

Scott summed up the significance of the act with a brief glance. "Thanks." He no sooner reached the top of the ladder that a shadow moved across the grating. Visible through the slots was a dragon's face so close to the cover that the forked tongue behind the mouthful of shiny teeth could be seen licking outward. Instinctively he brought up the rifle and sent three short bursts through the slots into the leering face.

The dragon was jerked up by the force of the bullets, away from the grating. With his head hunched forward, Scott rammed the manhole cover with the top of the power pack. The lid shot two feet into the air, crashed on its side, and spiraled away. He leaped out of the hole and rolled to the side just as a bolt of lightning seared the leading edge of the opening. The rifle burped again, followed by the thud of a body.

Death Wind, Sandra, and Rusty poured out of the hole like flies escaping a trap. All three turned to help Doc, whose strength had been severely sapped by the poisonous fumes.

A laser beam chased Scott across the street. The dragon that had fired the bolt was trying to adjust its sights to the rapidly moving youth. Scott wasted no time in firing two quick shots from the prone position into the tawny breast. The beast was dead, but the paw with the beamer was still moving in a slow arc—and firing. Scott jumped out of the way, trying to conserve ammunition, and watched as the dragon slowly heeled over and crashed into the street. There were no other soldiers visible, but the fight was sure to bring a patrol to investigate.

Scott was afraid the battery pack was booby-trapped. "Let's get out of here. Quick!"

Sandra flung back her hair. Bits and pieces broke off where the strands had been seared. "Which way?"

Doc sat with his head between his legs, hyperventilating. He glanced up at the moon, still low on the horizon. "We have to go south and east. Let's follow this street and look for an intersecting alley." He pushed himself to his feet with his cane and hobbled off past the dead dragons.

They found an alley before being discovered by any more dragon soldiers, but several were visible in the distance. The seven-foot-high walls were tall enough to hide the skulking humans, but low enough for dragons to see over—and be seen.

"Do you mind if I rest for a moment?" Doc leaned heavily against the plastic. "I'm afraid I'm not as young as I used to be."

Rusty was fidgety. "We've only got a few minutes before the fireworks begin."

"And we've got to have those weapons so I can get my mother."

Scott said, "Give him some time, will you. He got us this far, he'll get us the rest of the way. A few more minutes won't matter one way or the other."

"That's easy for you to say. You don't have a mother—" She gritted her teeth. "I—I'm sorry. I didn't think—"

Scott ignored the tactless blunder. "Forget it."

"No need to argue. I'm ready." Doc straightened up. "And she's right. We have no time to waste."

At the end of the block, Death Wind scrutinized the street in both directions, dashed across to where the alley continued between two rows of three-story buildings, and motioned the others to follow.

"This is a barrack district."

They passed many openings that led to the black recesses where sleeping dragons undoubtedly lay. But so far only the soldiers had been aroused. The general populace was blissfully unaware that an invasion was happening. And the dragon leaders had no idea of the calamity of what was about to happen.

At the next street they had to wait in the shadows as a dragon patrol marched by slowly, dragging their tails. They were about to run across the street into the next alley when Doc gasped and fell back. Clutching his chest, he sagged to the ground writhing in pain.

"Doc, what's wrong?" Rusty's voice rang out too loud. Scott caught the man and watched helplessly as his face contorted horribly.

"I—can't—go—on," he said, through gritted teeth. Then, his face relaxed. Breathing hard, Doc bit his lip after each word. "The strain has been—too much. I'm too old for this kind of thing."

"What can we do?" Scott said.

"Complete the mission. Go on without me. Remember that it is not individual life that matters in the long run, but the survival of the race. We are ephemeral, but we live on in spirit in the hearts and minds of others."

"Keep your words of wisdom for later," Sandra said. "Scott's right, we need you."

"I'll only slow you down. And it's only a few hundred more feet—"

Sandra was adamant. "We don't have time to argue. You're coming with us even if we have to carry you. Right?" Sandra looked sharply at Scott and Death Wind, her large brown eyes flashing brightly in the moonlight.

Scott helped Doc to his feet while Death Wind approached from the other side. Together they lifted the white-haired man, each holding an arm and a leg as if he were a chair. Sandra led the way across the next street while Rusty brought up the rear. They jogged along the alley with their parcel as if he were nothing more than a sack of potatoes. They did not put him down until they reached the end of the alley.

"How ignominious," Doc huffed, dusting himself off. Then he pointed with his chin across the open expanse of a wide street. "There's the armory, and I don't see any guards."

The building was constructed of the same orange plastic of which the entire city was made. It had no windows, and only one entrance—a ten-foot-high double door that glinted metallically. A massive shackle held the two swinging portals together.

"How do we get in?" Sandra said to no one in particular.

Doc pointed to the beamer. "You'll have to melt off the hasp."

"I don't know if there's enough power left in this thing. It takes forever to recycle, and when it does the energy output is weak."

"The missiles should be here any minute," Rusty said.

Sandra pushed him aside. "The hell with the missiles. There's nobody here. I say let's get started now." She dragged Scott by the harness into the deserted street. Death Wind and Rusty followed, leaving Doc in the shadow of the alley.

The street was slanted, rising upward to the east and descending slowly in the west to the mountain that housed the time transporter. The quarter moon cast a white glow of serenity over the dragon stronghold. The gently undulating plastic streets and buildings had a look of surrealism as the low orange shapes merged with the darker shadows. It was the calm before the storm.

Rusty bent close to examine the lock. "I think it's steel—and the hasp, too."

"All right, stand back." Wincing slightly, Scott aimed the gun at the shackle of the alien mechanism. There was no way of telling how the lock was supposed to work, but the idea of a shackle was universal. As he pressed the firing stud an arc stabbed out of the nozzle and struck the metal only a foot away. There was a ball of lightning the size of an orange. When it receded, the metal glowed a bright red.

"It melted a little." Rusty inspected the shackle, then jerked on the recessed door handle. "Hold it closer this time."

On Scott's back the power pack was struggling to recharge its capacitor. The firing circuit was temporarily deadened while the storage battery was being sucked dry. A precious minute passed.

"Hurry that thing," Sandra said.

Scott fired again. Barely more than a visible spark jumped the gap between the nozzle and the still radiant shackle. Rusty looked again. "One more might do it."

"Dragons come," said Death Wind calmly.

As all eyes looked up. Doc scurried across the street to join them. "I don't mean to rush you, but I think the enemy is precipitating an advance."

"Can't you ever say anything short?"

With a wry look, Doc said, "I promise to try to please your predilection for brevity in the future—if we have one."

Sandra rolled her eyes, but readied the rifle, too. She nudged Scott with the butt. "What're you waiting for—an invitation?"

"I can't help it. This thing's just about dead."

"And so are we if we don't get this door open right away." She looked up and down the high-walled street. The dragons were drawing nearer—from both directions. "I'll get them while they're still outa beamer range."

Dropping to a kneeling position, Sandra rested the rifle against her leg. She fired one round at the leading dragon on the downslope. The bullet went through its head and out the back, blasting away face and skull. Without waiting to see it fall, she spun around and fired at the first dragon on the upslope. She misjudged the rate of fall: the trajectory carried the bullet into the lower jaw where it tore out bone and muscle but did not kill.

Instantly the dragons started to return her fire.

From several hundred feet away, on either side, laser beams with full potential lashed out. The air in front of the armory crackled with electric discharge.

Sandra burped off two more shots. "I can't hold them off forever."

"Flyer in air." Death Wind pointed northward with his bow. Everyone looked, including the dragons, as the flyer rose on a shimmering purple heat wave and began to move laterally out of its pen.

"It's going to get away," Sandra shrieked.

Rusty shook his head confidently. "No, it's not."

"Damn." Sandra threw down her rifle, seemingly in disgust.

"What are you doing?" Scott yelled.

"I'm outa lead. It's up to you now."

The dragon soldiers lumbered onward like slow freight trains. The momentary distraction caused by the flyer taking to the air no longer held their attention. They were close enough now that the full power of their laser beams could be felt. Blobs of molten plastic were blown off the street and gouged out of the walls. They were uncontested as they moved in for the kill.

Death Wind notched his last arrow and prepared to let it loose as a final challenge. The airborne flyer climbed for elevation along a well-worn track that had already been burned through the jungle hundreds of times over. A second flyer was rising slowly on its disruptor beam.

Scott put the point of the gun right on the shackle and pressed the firing stud. One last weak, almost ineffectual charge trickled through the mechanism and warmed the sagging steel.

A laser beam skittered overhead, then two more from the other side. The dragon soldiers were getting the range. Doc shoved Rusty aside and raised his cane in the air. A lightning bolt sheared it in half. Undaunted, he took the shortened stick and with all the force he could muster struck the shackle while the metal still glowed. The weakened steel snapped apart. Then, using the cane as a pry bar, he bent the connecting bolt out.

His shout was nearly drowned out by the crackling of beamer blasts. "Open it."

Scott grabbed the right-hand door while Rusty fought with the other. They were heavy, and moved ponderously on squeaky hinges.

Laser beams ricocheted off the steel barriers as Doc ducked into the opening—

—right into the leveled beamer of a dragon guard!

In the next instant Doc knew he was going to die, for he had neither the willpower nor the strength to move his fatigued and aged body. But before the clawed hand could squeeze the trigger there was a twang close by his ear. Death Wind's last arrow buried itself triumphantly into the open mouth. Sandra tackled Doc, and as the two crashed to the ground the already dying dragon fired its last shot. The electric bolt burned the savage's bow in two.

Then the five of them fell, stumbled, and crawled into the armory with beamer blasts gouging large holes in the steel door. The wounded dragon, hissing madly, fell forward in its death throes and was immediately baked by the crossfire of hostile lightning bolts.

At the same time a streak of fire descended from the sky. An enormous explosion rent the air, and the flyer that was making for the river shuddered wildly. The disruptor beam winked out, and for long seconds the flyer continued on its course as an act of momentum. Then, it angled down sharply and crashed with a fiery blast that leveled a large area of jungle and started small blazes.

Sandra jumped up and down. "You did it! You did it! You shot down the flyer."

Rusty peered out the door at the spectacle, with a look of smugness on his face. "You mean you doubted my word?"

Before Sandra could reply, the second flyer cleared the landing field and exploded violently. It fell back and crashed into the adjacent buildings. Almost instantly the third flyer blew up in its revetment, sending flaming slivers of molten metal into the sky in a bright pyrotechnic display.

Rusty could hardly conceal the pride in his voice. "I had the computer set on automatic override. Even if the homing beacons got melted during takeoff, the missiles were programmed to revert back to antiaircraft mode."

Scott threw off the dead power pack. "That's great. When you think you can get your hat back on, how about helping me get these beamers off the shelf."

Death Wind shrugged out of the pack with the explosive canisters and slid it close to the door. He spun a power pack around and backed into it.

While the others were arming themselves, he stepped into the street and fired an accurate and deadly volley at the stunned dragon soldiers. They were frozen in their tracks by the awesome spectacle of destruction. The savage cut them down like so much wheat. Sandra joined him and in moments the street was a smoldering wilderness of dead and dying dragons. The seriously wounded hissed horribly.

The armory was stacked from floor to ceiling, and along shelving in the middle of the room, with power packs. Doc walked all around the room, surveying its contents. He noticed that not all the power packs had pistols attached to them.

"You know, I think the dragons must use these modules to power all their portable equipment, whether it be weapons or tools. Depending on how the energy is released—in one full burst or with a trickle discharger and diffusing system—they can be used for many functions."

"Terrific, Doc. Can we discuss it later?" Scott rigged the straps of a power pack to fit his body, then drew the gun out of its holster.

Rusty checked through the pack carrying the explosive canisters. He pulled out coils of wire, blasting caps, and a handful of dried-up flowers. Death Wind must have been carrying them for some reason. He tucked everything back in, next to the battery. It was all he could do to get the pack on his back.

"How's it look?" Scott stepped outside behind Death Wind and Sandra. The battle was still raging, but the dragons were definitely on the rout. He shot down two dragons before he got an answer.

Sandra sent a beam of energized light into the street opposite. "Watch out for the alley."

Even as they talked two silver streaks dropped out of the velvet sky, like shooting stars, and impacted in the middle of the city. A huge cloud of fire and burning plastic globules erupted upward and outward. Streamers of flaming orange cascaded in the air, casting temporary daylight over the battlefield.

Cheers arose from the armory. Even the usually stoic Nomad grinned and issued war whoops. Sandra holstered her gun long enough to throw her arms around Rusty and plant a kiss on his freckled cheek. Rusty turned a shade of red that matched his hair. Then she hugged Scott unabashedly.

"The day I ran into you three turned out to be the most important day in my life—until today."

Scott showed mock surprise. "That's funny. The way I remember it we ran into you."

Sandra flashed a smile. "Have it your own way."

Doc stuck his head out long enough to take in the situation, then ducked back in and explored the rest of the armory. He puttered around the many strange devices, wishing for the time to study them. He rubbed his gnarled hand over the clear plastic casing of a large cylindrical object that lay horizontally on a dolly. Seven feet long and half that in circumference, each end spouted brass end caps. Through the transparent plastic he saw a whirling, hypnotic maelstrom, a constantly rushing cyclone of gas, rainbow hued like a volatile oil slick.

Rusty appeared suddenly by his side. "What's that?"

Doc was somewhat dazed. "Why, I think it's a bomb—a dragon death bomb waiting to be dropped on some far corner of the Earth."

"Well, it looks like we got here just in time."

Now the rest of the war party gathered around. Sandra wrapped her soft, warm arms around Doc and kissed him resoundingly. "They're gone. They're running away. Like ants after their eggs."

"Yes, I should imagine they are." Doc still had a faraway look in his eyes; his thoughts were somewhere else. "Well, I—I guess we had better get on with the mission. I've done just about all I can do. It's in your hands now."

"Aren't you coming with us?" Scott said.

"I could do nothing but slow you down. This has taken so much out of me. And I'm quite confident in your abilities. I think it would be best if I were to stay here and—stand guard over the weapons."

"Good idea," Sandra said.

The smell of burning plastic filled the air, and with it was the horrible mephitic stench of scorched flesh. The loud hissing sound that was carried with it was not all due to the consuming flames: many dragons, young and old alike, were being destroyed in the rampant conflagration.

Sandra stared hard into Doc's eyes. Her own brown eyes flashed with the scintillation of polished jewels. "Doc, I—I'd like to say thanks. For everything. And I'd like to apologize for, well, for the way I—"

Doc pulled her close for a hug. His eyes were squeezed tightly shut. "Think nothing of it, my dear. You've certainly done your part. And done it well, I might add. You all have."

Doc held back tears. He was overawed by the gripping sense of fellowship that this venture had brought to him. As she stepped back, he swept away her partially singed hair. His eyes shifted to the tiny pendant that hung from her delicate lobe. He was caught by its luster. Then he felt in him a queasiness that sapped the strength from his already weakened legs. "My dear, where did you get that?"

Sandra pulled away slightly, and laughed. "Doc, this is no time to admire my jewelry."

But she was trapped in his suddenly iron grip. "Where did you get it?"

Sandra beheld his astonished gaze. "If it means that much to you, my mother gave it to me."

Doc seemed to wilt where he stood. "Ah, I suspected as much." His teeth gnashed together like a squirrel grinding nuts. "My child, all of you, warriors and killers of dragons, you've done a fine job. No matter what happens now, no one can ever take that away from you. But the most important part of our task yet remains. For humanity's sake the time transporter must be destroyed, and the prisoners must be rescued. Now flee. Flee all of you. And may honor and righteousness guide your way."

He ushered them to the giant doorway.

In the orange glow of flames the four warriors, who had fought together through so much, hugged and shook hands. The street had been deserted ever since the dual explosions. Only the dead and dying remained.

Then Sandra turned to Scott and Rusty. "Take care of yourselves. I love both of you." She nodded to Death Wind, and together they left the armory and ran up the slanted street. Scott and Rusty took off in the opposite direction, downhill.

Doc wistfully watched them go, for he loved them all. But years of training and hardship had taught him that duty comes before joy. There was still important work to be done.

Back inside, he studied the death machine that lay in its cradle. Softly, almost lovingly, he ran his hand over the alien mechanism, sensing through his fingers the awesome power that it contained. A wry grin touched his weathered lips.

"Oh, boys, if you only knew," he said, thinking aloud. "This time I've got an idea of my own—and it scares me to the very depths of my soul."

CHAPTER 28

Scott and Rusty sneaked up on the intersection. The street was thick with dragons, streaming by only a few feet away from where the two crouched in the shadow of the wall. Yet, none so much as glanced in their direction. They all had only one thought in mind: the hatchery.

Rusty drooped under the weight of the explosives pack. "How are we going to get through that stream of traffic?"

Scott shoved the beamer back into the holster. These were unarmed slaves, and not dangerous. "Over this wall?" He jumped up and took a look. Below him was a courtyard, but visible in the distance were flames leaping a hundred feet into the air as the fire, which had started to die down after the first furious blast from the twin missiles, found more fuel. The dry plant growth in which the eggs were covered during the night kept feeding the blaze, while the air rushing in to fill the void fanned it out of control.

He dropped back down. "It's all clear." Automatically clasping his fingers together, he held his hands down low so Rusty could put his foot into them. Then he boosted his friend up and Rusty clambered up onto the ledge. Scott easily swung himself over, jumped down, then helped Rusty to the patio floor.

For a moment they had been in almost full view of the dragon throng, yet none had taken the slightest notice of them. The slaves were too dull, too stupid, too mechanical to know better. They were programmed for simple functions, and beyond the scope of their training they were helpless.

They worked their way through the darkened enclosure, around scattered furniture. At the other end the twenty-foot-high wall of a house provided the only means of egress. The tall, oblong doorways were like monstrous mouths waiting for victims. Scott stepped inside, beamer in hand. The room was deserted. With Rusty right behind him, he bounded up a set of poured plastic stairs.

The second floor was full of doorways, one of which led to a common porch that was a parapet connecting the entire block, like a private sidewalk ten feet above the crowded street. From this height Scott could easily see the cave opening that was the entrance to the time transporter. It glowed with an eerie blue light that coruscated slightly and spilled out into a plaza that was surrounded by the same seven-foot-high walls that lined all the streets. From only several hundred yards away the mountain looked like a giant gumdrop, granite colored, set in orange plastic as if it were a caramel candy.

"They don't even know we're here." Scott led the way along the parapet completely unopposed, while below scores of dragons rushed in exodus toward the hatchery, attracted like moths to a flame. Interspersed among the numerous naked slaves were vested technicians and several richly caparisoned leaders with flowing capes. None bothered to look up.

When they got to within a hundred yards of the cave entrance, the block of plastic buildings curved around and veered off. This close to the plaza there was very little traffic. The dragons Scott saw now were mostly soldiers milling around haphazardly like any military outfit. They did not appear to be an attacking force; rather, they were a rear guard with little to do.

Scott lowered himself to an alley, then turned to help Rusty. "I can't make it down with this pack."

"All right, then hand it down." Scott reached up and took the explosives at arm's length. When Rusty alighted beside him he placed it on his back.

Scott took careful stock of the situation. They were in an alleyway that opened directly into the main thoroughfare, pitching down into the plaza and straight into the glowing entrance. The half dozen dragons that were lounging around, weapons holstered, did not appear to present any tactical problem. But an uncounted number might be waiting just inside the cave opening.

"Let's take them on the run."

Rusty took a firm grip on the straps. "Okay, but I can't run too fast with this weight on my back."

Scott pulled out the beamer. "Just do your best. I'll cover you."

Rusty took a deep breath, and nodded. Scott stepped out into the moonlight. For several seconds no one took notice of them.

Then, a wary soldier swung its long neck in their direction, registered surprise with a hiss, and started to draw its gun. Before the beamer was halfway out of its holster, Scott's laser stabbed into the tawny breast with a surge of power that stunned the wielder: the capacitor must have been supercharged, for the dragon was literally cooked on the spot as the beam went straight through its body and exploded in the bushes that covered the mountain.

"The jig is up!" As quickly as he could, Scott beamed down three more guards before their reptilian tripartite brains had time to handle the concept of foul play. Daggers of light transfixed them with the same violent intensity that had slain the first: they were burned to a crisp.

Blasting right and left, Scott ran into the midst of the no longer unsuspecting dragons. Enemy laser beams poured out of niches and doorways. "It's a trap!" But it was too late to back out now. They were committed.

"I'm right behind you." Rusty lost his footing for a moment over a sudden dip in the street, but regained his balance by skipping along awkwardly without slowing down.

The soldiers chose him for a target, shooting from all corners of the plaza. Half a dozen laser beams lashed out over the shuffling redhead. One dragon was cut down by a bolt of lightning that was shot by another. Blobs of molten plastic flew in all directions as the walls were picked apart.

Rusty raced into the cave unscathed, while Scott was still outside shooting cover fire. Then the blond ran in after him. They had run the gauntlet successfully.

But in the weird light that pulsated with an electrical charge that made his hair stand on end, Scott suddenly felt his heart sink. Barring their way to the time transporter was a stout, floor to ceiling, case-hardened steel gate.

* * *

Doc inspected the bomb carriage and discovered that it had roller-bearing-type wheels. Six axles distributed the load evenly. A long handle either extended straight forward for pulling, or folded over the top for storage. It had two mechanical calipers that were brakes as well as a steering mechanism: squeezing the left caliper caused the chassis to swerve in that direction, and vice versa. There was no motor, for with unlimited slave power there was no need.

Even though the bomb must have weighed hundreds of pounds, it moved easily on its lubricated and closely machined wheels. Leaning back with all his might, he was able to move the carriage by himself. And once started, it took equally as great an effort to stop it.

Straining, pushing, pulling, and twisting the handle, Doc managed to extricate the cumbersome device from where it was wedged between shelving and miscellaneous equipment. He crashed it back and forth until it was free.

By that time he was exhausted; his bad leg ached where it was forced to bend against unused muscles. Still, he worked the carriage out from the back of the armory. He had to get that bomb out of there.

The future—and presence—of humanity depended on it.

* * *

Sandra and Death Wind stalked up the street like two thieves. There was nothing in their way for the first block except dead dragon bodies stretched out helter-skelter. The odor of burnt flesh permeated the air, not only from the still blazing nursery but from the roasted soldiers as well. To Sandra's nostrils it was the scent of victory.

When they reached the first intersection they slunk into an alcove filled with street-cleaning tools. From among the long plastic handles they watched the panic-stricken horde of dragons sweeping along the wide avenue. Not all were slaves, for many caped individuals were tagged by their covering as belonging to the high echelon. But all shared the mindless terror that drove them relentlessly onward, unaware of their surroundings.

After several minutes it became apparent to Sandra that there was no end to the stampede. "Come on, let's cut a path through this mob."

"We cannot shoot. There are no soldiers."

Sandra was not bound by any sense of fair play. She was prepared to immolate every dragon that came between her and her mother. Without any qualms she stepped out into full view of the passing parade and cleared a swath through the street, beaming down slaves with unmerciful abandon. Dragons hissed hideously, perishing sequentially as the separate brains fought to coordinate their inputs. Some of them were literally half dead.

"Come on, shoot the bastards." Sandra could not understand Death Wind's immobilization, or Nomadic ethics. All she knew was that this was the enemy, that they were on the rout, and that this was her opportunity for revenge. "Kill them!"

Sandra pulled the trigger mindlessly, blasting left and right. Then, as if a traffic signal had decreed it, all dragon movement came to a standstill. The two long-haired youths casually scuttled across the street by weaving between parboiled bodies. Glazed reptilian eyes did not even follow their hasty track, but merely waited a suitable period of time before resuming their instinctive pilgrimage. The dead and dying were completely ignored.

Death Wind had not yet fired a shot. "Prison this way." He cut through a maze of alleys and cross streets that avoided further confrontation. Sandra shot off a bolt at every stray dragon, but the savage would not slow down simply to fight. He seemed determined to get to the captives with the minimum amount of squabble and at the maximum speed.

Before long, Sandra was grateful that he had. Bright flashes warned her of discharging beamers ahead, while screams of pain and cries of anguish cast evil foreboding.

The prisoners were being massacred!

* * *

Rusty stared at the insurmountable obstacle in front of them. "Now what?"

"Start beaming the hinges." Scott aimed at the massive metal joints on which the doors swung. Rusty averted his eyes. With the supercharged battery pack, the beamer cut through steel like a steak knife through hot butter. After a dozen blasts both doors sagged. Scott ran forward and kicked the locking mechanism with a high thrust of his foot. The gates swung open and tore off its hinges, then crashed in an upright position against the rock walls. Scott put the heel of his hand against his forehead. "Oh, no. It wasn't even locked."

Then they hurried through the rest of the short tunnel and into the immense inner chamber that housed the time transporter. Two hundred feet across and a hundred feet high, every available space on the arched walls was covered with power packs identical to the ones that charged the beamers. Protruding out of each one was a single, ten-foot-long needle that resembled closely the disruptor beam nozzles that buoyed up the flyers. Crammed side by side, the inside of the hollowed-out cavern bristled like an inverted porcupine skin.

In the middle of the room was an intensely blue spherical shield at which the needles were aimed. The shield was coruscating with the leakage of static charge that continuously pulsed from the focusing nodes. Along the circumference of the floor stood huge whining generators that were even now winding up the capacitors to full charge.

So potent was the energy in the cave that each individual needle tip glowed with a purple luminescence that filled the air with an eerie, and tangible, shimmering light. Every hair on Scott's body stood up from the electrical inductance, and his skin crawled as if covered with slimy worms.

Rusty stood with mouth agape, studying the raw potential, the advanced technology, the stupendous scientific apparatus that they were about to destroy. Then he was jerked aside as Scott yanked the pack off his back and flung it to the floor.

"We don't have time to admire it." He started removing the cylinders from the dismantled warhead. With an armful of explosives he dashed away and started depositing them at strategic locations: between pairs of generators. His will to live was stronger than his sense of marvel.

Hurriedly, Rusty unrolled the spool of detonation cord and started walking it out, leaving a long loop at each canister. The idea was to wire all the charges together so they would detonate simultaneously with one gigantic bang.

There was a commotion at the entranceway. "Uh oh, here they come." Scott raced back and fired half a dozen bolts of lightning up the tunnel, then took another armful of canisters. His job was done easily, so while Rusty made the connections he kept the dragons at bay. They were trying to sneak in along the rough-hewn wall, hiding in jagged, rocky corrugations. Scott ran back and forth inside the opening so he could direct his beamer at both sides. He picked them off one by one as they became either too bold or too careless.

"We've got them good. They're afraid to shoot." Any laser beams that went past him were sure to hit some of the delicate and complicated time transporting equipment.

Halfway around the curved cavern, Rusty attached blasting caps to the explosive canisters. He pushed them against the wall when they were connected, so the resultant blast would use the walls and floor as a springboard to hurl the destructiveness upward and outward, and destroy the capacitor banks as well as the generators.

"Hey, watch out."

Rusty was concentrating on his work when a dragon technician stepped out of a work cubicle in front of him and swung a heavy tool at his head. Scott was too far away to shoot accurately. He started running, aghast, as he saw his friend swing around. He did not have time to duck before the metal object made contact with his red hair.

* * *

The wagon with the plague bomb was taxing Doc's strength.

He had ruined half the armory working the carriage around and past the plastic shelving. He would struggle to get it moving only to have it crash into a wall or stanchion before he could get it to turn, for its forward momentum kept it going where it was aimed. Then he would have to back it off and push it forward again.

By now he was panting heavily, and rubbing his injured leg where the bone had not healed properly. In addition, his chest pain had returned, although not as severely. He had completely forgotten that he was supposed to guard the armory against infiltration. It suddenly seemed as if the most important thing in the world was to get this bomb out of there.

Finally he could see the light. Just around the corner of the doorway, the dying embers of the conflagration wrought strange, flickering shadows. Doc wiped sweat off his forehead, and rubbed his damp palm across his mouth. Positioning himself in front of the wagon, he gave a mighty tug and started it rolling. Now there was room to maneuver, so he used the alternate brakes to steer.

He cast a glance over his shoulder. One of the shadows coalesced into an eight-foot-tall form, squat near the base and sinuous near the top. Silhouetted against smoke and flame, the dragon lifted its paw and pointed it at the man. The golden gun gleamed brightly.

Behind it two more tall forms lurked. And behind them were more—many more. There seemed to be no way out.

* * *

Four dragon guards walked along a parapet that surrounded the stockade. A caped leader was there, too, hissing orders to his troops. The soldiers fired their beamers downward, into a crowded throng of humanity—one of whom was Sandra's mother.

There was no compassion in the girl's heart as she lashed out with the stolen weapon. She zapped the two closest dragons before they were aware of her presence down in the dark street. By the time the other two turned around, one of them had its head blown off. The first two had not yet crumpled from their posts.

Death Wind ran ahead while Sandra dispatched the last dragon soldier. He tried to get into position to shoot the leader, but two more dragons stepped out of a guard shack and opened fire. Dodging quickly, he got out of one beamer's path, while another crackled by his ear. He fired twice, his aim as straight as his arrows. Both soldiers fell, but the leader slunk away.

"Darn." Sandra sent a beam of light after the beast. She melted plastic, but nothing more.

"Let us hurry. It will bring more."

Sandra nodded. Through the barred gate she could see people picking themselves up from the ground. She concentrated her fire on the thick jambs and blew away the mounts for the steel hinges. The entire structure crashed to the ground.

Inside the stockade a mass of people, perhaps fifty in all, were reacting to the attack. Most of those that wore complete lizard-skin outfits huddled against the far wall. Those dressed in loincloths and breast skins stood poised to leap erratically in order to evade beamer fire. They had been in a constant state of movement during the whole operation in a bold attempt to outwit the slow-moving dragons and their slower response systems. There was mumbled surprise when they saw the two desperate youths limned in the garish glow of the moon.

"Sandra! Is that you?"

A trim but ragged woman with long, dark hair and fair features ran out from the crowd. She was taller than Sandra, and more mature, but the resemblance was immediately apparent.

"Mother!" Sandra let the gun dangle by its power cord and ran toward the woman's open arms. They came together in the middle of the stockade, mother and child, hugging and kissing and weeping openly.

Now the prisoners began to realize that the crashing of the gate was an act of liberation, not an incursion of dragon soldiers. More people climbed out of cubicles into the courtyard, milling with those who were already there, until the crowd swelled to several hundred. Excitement ran high, the din of voices crescendoed. To those who had been incarcerated for so long, it was impossible to believe that they were on the verge of rescue.

One man cheered as he wrapped his arms around Sandra and her mother. It was Ned, ragged and much the worse for wear, but alive. The three made a happy spectacle.

"Sandra, how did you find—I mean—how did you—Sandra, what are you doing here?"

"I came to get my mother."

Only a few feet away another man strode forward. He was tall, gaunt, and dark-skinned—his bearing was unbroken by the harshness of captivity. Long, black hair covered his shoulders; a breechcloth hid his hips and muscular thighs. Deep-set eyes peered from behind a face that was firm and stolid, but in which swelled unfathomable depths of emotion.

"Son."

"Father." Death Wind stood at arm's length, and spoke in a monotone that belied his feelings. But to a Nomad, that one word exchange expressed volumes.

Death Wind's father placed two strong hands on his son's broad shoulders. Death Wind returned the gesture. It was the Nomad family greeting.

A woman only slightly shorter, and dressed in a lizard-skin breechcloth and halter top, came to stand next to Death Wind's father. With a quick glance Death Wind acknowledged her presence. Releasing his father's embrace, he stepped to one side and kissed the woman on the cheek, where tear tracks were already glistening. She returned his kiss.

"Son."

"Mother."

Many Nomads crowded close behind the chief and his wife, watching the event in controlled admiration. Beyond were other Nomads, from other tribes, as well as oddly dressed strangers who must have been itinerants much as Sandra's mother.

Death Wind faced his father once more. In a voice loud enough for all to hear, he said, "Talk later. Fight now. Follow me."

Without further word or expression he turned on his heels and trotted out of the open stockade gate. Behind him every able-bodied Nomad, whether man or woman or child, took up the trot. And behind them, slower to respond, came the rest. They all understood that the fight was not yet over.

Indeed, it had just begun.

CHAPTER 29

It was pure instinct that made Rusty duck, but it was training and experience that permitted him to roll to the side and draw the forty-five from his belt. The blow on the head stunned him, but was reduced in severity by his movement away from it. When he rolled up onto one knee the weapon was already in his hand. In the next instant, before the metal tool descended, he burped the last three slugs into the monster's grisly face.

The two antagonists froze in this position: Rusty with arm outstretched holding the now useless gun, the dragon dead with the signal not yet received in its alien brain. Then they both collapsed, Rusty into unconsciousness and the dragon into death.

When he came to, Scott was hovering over him. "Are you all right?"

His scalp was bleeding where a chunk of skin was torn off. He groaned and shook his head. "I—I guess so." Without thinking he brushed his hand through his hair, winced with pain. He made an enigmatic laugh that came out like a huff. "That was a close shave."

"More like a haircut." Scott glanced at the entrance. "Can you make the rest of the connections by yourself? I've got a whole roomful of dragons just dying to get in here."

"If I can't, I'll call for help. I'm just a little dizzy, that's all." Rusty followed Scott's gaze. He had to look right through the center of the materialization ring; the swirling, coruscating image accentuated his dizziness.

"Okay. I haven't got time to chat." Without waiting for further acknowledgment, Scott ran around the perimeter of the room, staying as far away as he could from the cyclonic central sphere. The eerie purple glow was gaining in strength. It flickered like a strobe, highlighting his motions like sequences cut from poorly adapted stop-action photography. At the node, half-formed images, like wraiths, soughed into and out of focus.

Rusty quickly worked his way back to the entranceway. A dragon entered the time warp room but before it had time to swing its head around on its snakelike neck, Scott fried it. An ugly gash was seared through the potbelly, spilling organs and intestines. Before the beast hit the floor, Scott took up a new station and sent blasts along the corridor as fast as his power pack would recycle. Some of the soldiers had taken refuge in the corrugations and stayed there for protection. Scott's shots seared rock but did not hit any more dragons. At least he was holding them at bay.

Overhead, power packs hummed and the long needle points whined and danced with fire. The capacitor bank was nearing full charge. It suddenly occurred to Rusty that if they did not hurry, they might find a party of dragons materializing right in their midst.

"Would you hurry up and blow that thing? This stalemate isn't going to last forever." Scott fired two more blasts up the tunnel. Molten chips of granite exploded into the air, but no dragons were hit. The weapon that was their greatest offense now proved their downfall, for they had no shield against it.

There was an impasse between reptile and human.

Rusty crabbed across the floor, trailing the detonation cord behind him. He dragged the battery out of the pack and started wiring the last connection.

"I can't hold them off much longer." Scott fired one shot at each side of the tunnel just to let the dragons know that he had not fallen asleep. They were advancing erratically from one corrugation to another. "They're bound to think of something."

Rusty worked wordlessly, sorting out the wires with attached alligator clips. His head throbbed, dulling his concentration.

There came a crashing sound from the outside entrance of the cave. Dragons erupted from the walls where they had been hiding. Something that looked like a huge battering ram sped past the downed gates with unstoppable momentum.

"I need a few more seconds."

With grim determination Scott stepped out into the open, beamer in hand. He had lost so much already, so long ago in that other world in which he had once lived, that it was easy for him to make one last sacrifice.

*   *   *

Even had he wanted to, Doc could not have stopped the bomb-laden carriage. Once he had the mass moving, the tremendous kinetic energy was not so easily lost.

He ducked under the outstretched arm of the nearest dragon and trundled past. There was a pain-filled hiss as the front wheels rolled over extended reptilian digits, crushing claws and bones. The next two dragons were raising their weapons to fire as Doc slipped between them, shoving for all he was worth on one good leg and one slightly misshapen one. By the time they fired he was no longer there, and the crossed laser beams gouged plastic and hit one soldier in the leg.

Once on the slanted street, the carriage began to get away from him. He hobbled alongside trying in vain to keep hold of the handle that controlled the brakes. But they were not holding. Metal was grinding against metal as the roller bearings heated up and shrieked mechanically.

Laser beams flicked overhead. Human shouts chorused in the background. But Doc was in no position to make explanations. As he barreled through the dragon army, he heard Death Wind's whoop and Sandra's cry as they led the newly drafted troops into the Armory.

He had both brake handles squeezed tight and was still not able to keep up with the wagon. He grabbed the metal collar on the bomb as he ran alongside. This did not help slow it down; instead, it swept him along faster than he could run. He clung desperately to the rampaging vehicle. It was no longer under his control.

Before he knew it he was approaching an intersection where thinning dragon hordes were still rushing toward the blast areas. With resignation he swung his left leg, the bad one, over the top of the bomb as if he were mounting a saddle. He clung precariously to the carriage for several seconds before he was able to climb onto a more stable position. Then he was riding the racing bomb like a wild cowboy on a bucking bronco: lying down hugging it with both legs as he kept a firm grip on the reins: in this case the steering handle.

He held this pose for only a second. Then, as he entered the crossroad he released the squealing right brake; the continued pressure on the other caliper caused the carriage to slew to the left. Skidding sideways, the wagon upended as the wheels on one side left the ground. As they did so they also lost their braking power, and the wagon straightened out until it fell back down with a crash and the brakes took control again. The wagon banged up and down in this manner while Doc negotiated the turn and miraculously threaded a path through nonplussed dragons, crashing into more than one and bowling them over like tenpins.

He was knocked from his perch when the wagon first slammed down, so that he rode the side of the bomb like an Indian warrior riding his pony into battle. His long white hair and beard streamed back in the wind. He grinned maniacally at the adventure. He felt like the young, reckless scout he had once been.

The wagon barely made the turn without flipping over. It made such a wide arc that his back scraped the opposite wall and his shirt was torn to shreds. The screaming brakes were a warning that he was on the warpath, but startled, slow-reacting, and dull-witted reptiles could not get out of his way in time. Then he clambered back on top.

He gripped the steering handle and swerved drunkenly through the mob, trying to avoid the worst collisions. Glancing blows knocked dragons to the ground and sent some reeling into others. The street was soon turned into a madcap replay of the Keystone Cops.

He grazed the left retaining wall for only an instant, but that was enough time for one of the two retaining straps that held the bomb in place to wear through. The flayed strap dangled uselessly, flapping in the breeze. The cylindrical bomb was still nestled firmly in the grooved floor.

By this time Doc could hardly see where he was going, for there were tears in his eyes as the air bit savagely into them. His hair billowed out like a lion's mane. With the brakes still screeching like a banshee, the bomb carriage was like some mythical monster swooping through the city.

The wagon hit a dip in the roadway with such speed that it traveled ten feet forward in the air before its roller bearings touched the plastic roadway. The resultant jolt not only broke Doc's grip on the collar, but it knocked the bomb sideways in the carriage. The rear strap took up the strain, but threatened to snap. The bomb was half out of the groove now, sticking off at an angle. Doc's leg slipped to the ground with a painful jar. A few seconds contact with the smooth plastic surface at this speed was enough to rip several layers off his skin.

He lost his grip on the steering handle and the front of the bomb veered too close to the wall. It hit with a jarring crash.

* * *

At first Scott could not tell what was happening. The flickering purple light behind him cast an eerie glow of light up the tunnel. By the awful sound of things, the dragons were engaging some new kind of weapon, for he could hear it winding up like a charging capacitor.

All he knew for certain was that some large object was about to run him down. He leveled the beamer. Licking his lips, he cast a glance at Rusty.

The redhead looked up just then. "I'm almost ready."

But there was no more time. The battering ram was there. The only thing left for Scott to do was to try to blast it apart, or stop it with his body.

* * *

The bomb carriage veered sickeningly to the right and rose high up on one side to the point of overbalance. With strength he did not know he had, Doc pulled himself back up onto the bomb, which was now pointed at an oblique angle to the forward motion of the wagon. The carriage came down onto all its wheels with a crash. The bomb would have slid off had not Doc retained his grip on the metal collar.

Instead, it reseated itself into the curved groove, the one retaining strap preventing it from rocking out of the cradle on the other side. It happened so quickly that Doc rolled over the other side of the bomb, as if he were an acrobatic stuntman performing tricks. He almost had to laugh at himself.

Ahead he could see the brightly lit maw that was the entrance to the cave. The plaza in front of it was filled with soldiers and technicians, milling and hissing hysterically. They did not even notice his approach, despite the still shrieking brakes.

Doc carefully aimed the wagon to avoid congregations of dragons. So fast was he moving that the soldiers did not have time to draw their weapons as he zoomed past. Then he was in the clear, for there was a long corridor that was empty of dragons, as if they were afraid to stand where the purple light spread like a beacon.

Then he was in the tunnel, rushing forward with jetlike speed. The time warp node was dead ahead, in the middle of the cave. With his peripheral vision he noticed dragons hiding in the corrugations along the side of the tunnel. But in front of him there was only one barrier.

"Get out of the way," he shouted when he recognized Scott standing in his path.

Scott was too stupefied to move at first, until

his eyes focused on the white head, the long-flowing beard. "Doc?" At the last second he jumped aside as the wagon thundered past.

"Blow it up," Doc shouted as he rode by. "Blow it up now."

Then Doc, the plague bomb, and the lumbering carriage sped into the high arched cave. The purple radiance was noontime bright, and the focusing nodes glowed and sparkled with potential merging on full capacity. The time warp was wound up to full excitement. Electricity arced and crackled; the smell of ozone was thick in the air.

The last hundred feet was covered in a matter of seconds. Then Doc rolled off the bomb and was swallowed up by the miasma of pulsating purple haze that was emitted from the warp screen.

There was no time to jump for cover. Rusty made the last connection, touched the battery terminal with a bare wire. The entire cave seemed to detonate at once. Hundreds of power packs were discharged at the same moment the explosive canisters were detonated.

Scott crashed into Rusty and hurled him into an alcove by the entrance. At the same time the dragons in the corridor, hearing the violent discharge, evacuated their hiding places and ran as fast as their lizard legs would carry them. It proved to be their undoing.

The discharging warp field was accentuated by the destruction of the generators, power packs, and focusing nodes. Every piece of equipment in the transporter room was ripped from its foundations, flung outward, then spliced through the wreckage of equipment flying inward from the opposite wall. Part of this debris was blasted violently into the time warp. But the dragon bomb, if it exploded, was already sixty million years in the past.

The cave was at once a moving, chaotic pit of hurtling metal and plastic shards. Showers of sparks, electrically as well as frictionally generated, scintillated among tons of passing parts. Sophisticated electronic components were converted to shrapnel and spun around the circular walls like water in a maelstrom.

The burst of heat melted plastic and made metal glow. The hot expanding gases could not be confined in the cave, and were forced out the entrance tunnel like a blast from a cannon. The dragons that were caught in the barrel were wiped out in an instant, their dismembered bod-

ies vaporized and spread across the city like so much stew. The funneled discharge leveled buildings and disintegrated plastic ramparts, leaving orange globules in its wake smoking.

The mountain shrugged under the tremendous impact, and expanded for a moment like a balloon. Then it deflated as uprooted trees were shed like falling hair. Thousands of tons of dirt slid down the gumdrop-shaped exterior to leave a naked granite mountain behind, and burying all that lay at its base.

In the tunnel, in an alcove, two huddled, blackened bodies sought to extricate themselves from the dust and debris. They had stopped breathing while the heat wave passed. Their clothes were virtually burned off their backs. They had scores of cuts and bruises. But they were alive.

Somehow, when Scott had grabbed him, Rusty had held onto the pack. Now he rummaged through it for a couple of torches, and a flint and stone with which to light them. In the darkness, Scott poured oil over the bundled sticks. Rusty struck a spark, and gloom was dispelled. Then they climbed over the heaps of rubble into the center of the cave.

All was quiet.

There was a tinkle of glass. Shadows moved in the torchlight. A confusion of wire and electrical parts and blobs of fused plastic, like some weird mechanical monster, rose up out of the ash, shedding shards and components like leaves off a tree in autumn.

"You could lend an old man a hand," said a soft, familiar voice.

"Doc!" Two voices rang out simultaneously.

Scott and Rusty dashed forward and in a flash pulled him clear of the trash. They cheered, hugged, slapped, and jumped up and down—and never noticed that his snowy hair had turned black.

"What happened to the bomb?" Rusty said.

Doc raised bushy eyebrows that were covered with soot. "It was sucked into the vortex of time and sent back to its makers. Peace be with them."

With their arms around Doc's weary shoulders, they half carried the tired old man out of the cave, through the entrance tunnel, over the mound of dirt filling the plaza, and into the cool nighttime air where the stars shone overhead and the moon glowed like a beacon of hope.

A cheer arose as the three stood in the open,

torches held high. Several hundred yards away, with beamers flashing in exultation, hundreds of people, the freemen of the world, honored those who had released them from bondage.

Then came another sound, high-pitched and ominous. The vibration in the air filled everyone with dread, for there were none who did not recognize it—or fear it.

"Oh, no." Doc looked with despair up the hill toward the armory.

Way up in the coal-black sky, but descending purposefully on shimmering disruptor beams, the last of the dragon warships was returning like a maddened hornet to its molested nest. Already it touched the tops of the tallest buildings, melting them down like icicles under a blowtorch. The hundred-foot-wide swath meant destruction for the city, and for all who stood in its path.

In victory, there is death.

CHAPTER 30

People ran for their lives: along the streets, over walls, into buildings. They scattered as widely as they could. Beamers fired at the flyer like wolves nipping at the heels of their prey, inflicting damage. But it came on relentlessly, suicidally.

The stockade was incinerated in a flash, and the flyer moved quickly along the street after pockets of humanity. Walls and ramparts melted into garish puddles. Multi-story structures sagged into squat masses, or twisted over on their sides in molten blobs. Orange plastic ran in rivulets.

Screaming people ran toward the sanctity of the cave. Sandra spared a second to glance over her shoulder at the awful spectacle. The flier was dangerously close, but it seemed as if they might make it—until someone fell headlong and could not get up.

It was her mother! Sandra stopped and dashed back to help her up. She was dazed, and only half conscious. When Sandra tried to pull her to her feet she was like a dead weight. The purple radiance loomed practically overhead, blotting out the sky.

Suddenly Death Wind was at her side. With one easy motion he threw off the power pack, lifted the slender woman onto his shoulders, and trotted off with his burden as if she were noth-

ing more than the haunch of a deer. Sandra lagged along with him while everyone else made for safety.

The flyer hammered on mercilessly, its deep-throated humming filling the air with a presentiment of death. The glowing disruptor beams stabbed at their heels; Sandra's legs felt the warmth, then the heat, then the burning.

Then there was a helping hand beside her. Death Wind's father grabbed hold of the woman's legs and took some of the weight off his son's shoulders. With the shared load they surged ahead, moving faster—but not fast enough. The pounding in Sandra's ears told her that the flyer was drawing inexorably closer, that no power could make them move any quicker, that they would never reach the cave where Doc, Scott, and Rusty were beckoning.

They reached the loose dirt and debris from the hillside. Sandra slipped, fell, tried to get up, and could not. She crawled on her knees, watching Death Wind and his father carry her mother onward. She did not cry out for help. She rolled over and brought her own beamer to bear. She would not die without a fight.

A meteor descended from the star-studded heavens with incredible speed, pushed by a needle of bright yellow flame. Sandra could hardly comprehend what was happening when it contacted the flyer with a dull thud, followed immediately by a loud boom and a billow of bright gas.

At first the flyer absorbed the shock, dipping slightly with the thrust of the impact. Then half the disruptor beams winked out, and the flyer canted to an acute angle, propelled by only part of its power nozzles. The still-working light beams unstabilized the flyer, driving it around in a circle. It seesawed crazily, retracing its route, then lost altitude until its leading edge crashed into a watchtower. The fiery beams acted as a lever, flipping the flyer upside down and flattening walls. Then it blew up violently as the pent-up power in its capacitor banks was released all at once. The pyrotechnic display sent flaming metal parts thousands of feet into the air, and lighted what was left of the dragon city with solar brilliance.

The last missile, fired automatically when the flyer came into sensing range, vanquished the last dragon defense.

Doc sank heavily to the ground as Scott and Rusty ran forward past Death Wind to Sandra.

Scott cradled her head in his arms. "Sandra, are you all right?"

She was slow to respond. She shook her head from side to side, blinking her eyes. "Three strikes and you're out. The next time a flyer comes after me it's sure to get me. I hate having to thank you guys again for saving my life."

Scott laughed. "There won't be a next time. They're all gone. It's just a mop-up operation now. We'll just kill off the one's that are left."

Sandra slid her arms out of the straps of the power pack. When she sat up it stayed on the ground. "Most of the soldiers are dead. And we left the slaves alone."

"Then you leave it to me. I'll kill every last one of them."

"Scott, you don't have to. They're only slaves, and they're unarmed."

"They're dragons," Scott snarled. "They're the enemy, remember? And we came here to kill them. All of them. If you're too squeamish, then get out of the way. Here, Rusty, take this beamer."

Scott pushed Sandra aside and lifted the power pack to put on his friend's back. Rusty hesitated. "You know, maybe she's right."

"She's not right; she's just selfish. Now that she's got her mother she doesn't care about our fight." He gave Sandra an angry look. "Always thinking of yourself, aren't you? You don't care about anyone but you. All right, if you don't want to fight, I can't make you. But don't try to stop me." Looking up at Rusty, Scott gestured with the power pack. "Are you with me?"

Rusty glanced at Sandra, then back at Scott. He demurred for a moment, then nodded wordlessly. He donned the pack and palmed its golden gun.

Then Death Wind approached, with his father by his side. "Let us go. We have work to finish."

"Not you, too. You wouldn't—" Sandra bit off whatever she had to say because Death Wind was no longer there. He was gone along with the rest of the Nomads, women and children included, and all the people who had been captured by the dragons in their sweep across the continent. "It doesn't matter, now. We've won." But there was no one there to hear her.

Then her mother was by her side. Sandra buried her face in her breast and cried. She did not know why.

"Hello, Helen." Doc was lighted by the glow of the still burning flyer. He smiled, and tenderly reached out with one blackened hand.

"Hi, Dad." Helen's lips twitched and formed a tender smile. She placed a palm lovingly against Doc's face, then kissed him on the lips. "Just like old times, isn't it?"

Now it was Doc's turn to smile. "It seems as if I'm always getting into trouble."

"You'll never change." Helen shook her head with chagrin. Sandra watched the exchange of words completely baffled. Then her mother looked down at her. "Sandra, I'd like you to meet your grandfather."

"I'm happy to make your acquaintance, my child."

Sandra's jaw hung slack. She looked from mother to grandfather to mother, and repeated the process until the slow realization crept into her brain. "But how can you—that is, I didn't know—I mean, why didn't you say—"

"Until recently I only suspected myself. The resemblance was striking, to be sure. And you had your mother's courage, individuality, vanity, and lack of respect."

"Dad!"

Doc ignored Helen's pout. "But I was not really certain until I saw—" Here he swept back her long, dark hair, now mussed and singed, and pinched the shining pendants hanging from her lobes. "—your earrings."

"Dad gave them to me when I was a child. I passed them on to you because it was part of the family heritage. And he was no longer around—he had a world to conquer and there was no way of stopping him."

"It was not easy for me to leave, you know?"

Helen pursed her lips. "Yes, I know that now. But I couldn't understand it then. I needed you."

"But, Doc—er—Grandfather—er, Dad—Heck, what do I call you now?"

Doc laughed out loud. "That's for you to decide."

"But, what's going to happen now? What are they doing?" Sandra made a sweeping gesture over the city. Beneath Sandra's blood-splattered shirt lay a troubled heart. She had had enough of killing, of death, of destruction, of fear and anger.

Doc's smile faded. "They are putting an end to dragon rule."

Twin pearls of water rolled down Sandra's quivering cheeks, washing away the dirt. Her own ruthlessness faded. She was only a girl who did not understand the cruelties of life.

"But why must the slaves, and the babies, be killed. Death Wind says the enemy are the leaders, and the soldiers. It seems so—brutal."

"Remember, my dear, that the dragons killed four billion human beings without so much as a warning—or an afterthought."

"And you don't know what it was like being a prisoner. We were beaten, starved, kept thirsty, waiting for the day when we would be dragged off and used for their inhuman experiments. None ever returned from the torture chamber. At least, not in one piece."

Sandra's heart was in turmoil. "But these are just slaves, mindless animals. They aren't responsible, and they can't fight back. It just doesn't seem right."

Doc held her chin in her hand. "Not because it is right, but because it is necessary. There is a time for strength, and a time for righteousness. Now is the time for strength. Let us hope we do not lose our sense of righteousness."

The orange flames from the downed flyer were dying out. But beyond, a brighter ball of fire was rising. The eastern sky was tinged with color as the deep blue of the night slowly faded. The stars were gone, and the moon was a pale ghost dipping westward.

Doc took the weight off his bad leg and leaned against Helen. She put one arm around her father, the other around her daughter. "You haven't changed at all, have you, Dad?"

Doc suppressed a smile. "I've tried not to. I did get lost along the way, but these young people found me and nudged me back onto the right path. And in my own way I nudged them along as well."

Sandra wiped the tears from her eyes. "Grandpa!"

"Yes, my dear?"

"Nothing. I just like the sound of it. I think I'll call you Grandpa."

Helen and Doc looked at each other, and laughed. "Well, you've always called me exactly what you wanted in the past. And I suppose I still have no control over you. Yes, Grandpa has a nice ring to it. I accept it."

Still entwined, the reunited family strode across the dirt-filled plaza to enjoy the first free dawn of humanity's new beginning.

* * *

It was a weary group of warriors who straggled into the slag heap that had once been a broad courtyard. Death Wind led Scott and Rusty to where Doc set up a temporary command post, and reported on operations. "Guards all set. Dragons no escape."

"Guards! What guards?" Sandra wanted to know.

Scott shrugged off his beamer, then helped Rusty with his. He scowled with contempt. "They wouldn't let us kill them all—only the ones who wouldn't give up. The rest were rounded up and herded into makeshift prisons. I think it's a big mistake."

"My boy, mercy is the one quality that differentiates raw intelligence from civilized learning. It is that social grace—our humaneness—that separates humanity from the dragons. To their dishonor, it is what their culture lacked."

"You knew it would turn out this way, didn't you?" Sandra asked.

White teeth showed on Doc's newly scrubbed face. "I know the Nomad way, and had faith in them."

Rusty shrugged. "I guess I'm not sorry we let them live. In a way, it shows we're better than they are."

Death Wind doffed his own beamer and stood next to Sandra. He drew her closer to him. She bent her head against his brawny, naked chest. Helen looked at the couple perplexedly.

"Or more stupid." Scott shook his empty canteen. "Come on, Rusty. Let's go get some water. I need a drink."

They left through one melted opening in the courtyard just as two Nomads entered through another on the other side. "Death Wind!"

Death Wind saw his father approaching. He was puzzled, because he had not yet told him what name he had conferred upon himself after completion of his trial. He was even more puzzled when his father shook Doc's hand in the Nomad greeting and exchanged the ritualistic "Men stick together. It is code."

"From what your boy told me I never thought I'd see you again, Bold One. Nor you, Slender Petal."

"Dragon destroy village, kill many people, capture others. We live, but no escape." Turning proudly to his son, he smiled and placed a strong bronzed hand on his shoulder. "Son rescue."

Death Wind was now the proudest person alive, for he had earned more than the Nomad title of warrior; he had earned his father's respect as well. But there were still things he did not understand.

Addressing his father, he pointed to Doc. "You know?"

Bold One nodded. "Know for many moons. Killer of dragon, helper of old, healer of sick. We fight together, side by side. He is great man, brave scout. We call him—Death Wind!"

Death Wind, the Nomad, recoiled in horror. Suddenly things became all too apparent: Doc's knowledge of the world, his knowledge of Nomad ways, even his hauntingly familiar face. Vaguely, Death Wind saw images in his mind of when he was a child playing with toy arrows. He remembered the strong, oddly white-skinned man who had lived and fought with his tribe during their migrations.

Doc laughed heartily. "Yes, it's only one of the many names I picked up during a rather long and hazardous career. I borrowed it myself from a Western writer named Zane Grey. Now I fear I'm getting too old to maintain the image. I think the name would do better on a younger man, someone bold and brave, some killer of many dragons—someone like yourself." Pausing dramatically, Doc added with glee, "Therefore, I hereby bestow upon you the name of Death Wind. May you carry it faithfully for a long and useful life."

Death Wind grasped arms with Doc. "Men stick together. It is code."

No sooner had they completed the chant when there was another shout of "Death Wind." Rusty raced back into the compound swinging his canteen. His carrot top looked lop-sided now that he had combed the hair away from his scalp wound. Scott walked sullenly behind him.

Death Wind cringed, for he saw the quizzical expression on his father's face. Bold One had no way of knowing that Death Wind had already chosen that name for himself.

Rusty stopped in front of the Nomad. "Death Wind, uh, I was wondering if that offer was still open. You know, when you said we could come and live with you. I don't know what's going to happen from here on out, but I'd still like to be, well, part of the family."

Bold One looked seriously at his son. The simple nod he received carried with it reams of Nomad understanding. He stepped up to Rusty and put his hands on his shoulders. "Son." Then he held out his hands for Scott. The blond came forward reluctantly. "Son." Then Bold One stepped back and waved his hands in a way that included all who were present. "Family."

Rusty beamed, but Scott was not so easily put off. "What about the dragons? What do we do with them now?"

"Those that have survived will be allowed to live out the rest of their days," Doc said. "Perhaps we can even get some work out of them."

"Do you think that's smart?"

"Dragons have intelligence, but man has wisdom. We will do what is just, as well as what is wise."

"And those in the past?"

"Time is like an endless river: it has no past or future, only flow. The dragons made their own destiny, now we must make ours."

Doc shielded his eyes from the hot, bright sun. He grinned apishly. "And right now, my destiny lies with breakfast. What say we scrounge around and try to scare up some food. I'm famished." He leaned on Helen and took the weight off his bad leg. "And by the way, someone's going to have to carve a new cane for me. I can't depend on my daughter's support forever."

"On the contrary, I don't think you can live without me. And anyway, I don't intend to give you the chance. You need me." She fluffed up his long white hair. "And when was the last time you washed behind your ears?"

Amid the laughter of all, Doc stared at the sky as if to plead with a higher authority. "It seems as if I've freed everyone except myself."

There was a great deal of work to do. The pieces of the world were waiting to be picked up. In order to pick them up properly it was important for men to stick together.

It is code.

Dragons Past

CHAPTER 1

Scott dragged the heavy power cable across the floor, dropped it behind the computer console, and pulled off the access panel. He reached into the maze of wires, felt along the gray insulation. It took him a minute to find the wire he wanted. He worked his fingers to the terminal, stabbed it with an arc welder, and pulled it free. He scraped the insulation off the power cable, applied the arc welder, and attached the new leads to the still-hot terminal.

"There, that should do it."

Rusty flexed long fingers. "Are you sure? I can't keep having power failures in the middle of a program. I have enough trouble as it is."

"I'm never sure when I work with dragon hardware." Scott moved around the console, behind his friend, and thumbed the power switch. "But if my deductions are correct, we should be on a different circuit, and I don't think we'll have any more overloads. Give it a try."

The annunciator board glittered with yellow, incandescent lights. Some shone for a moment, then winked off. Others flashed sequentially, each with its own tone. The viewscreen brightened.

Rusty took a deep breath and sighed. He pulled on a pair of thin hide gloves that had sharpened wooden pegs protruding from the fingertips. "Okay, here goes."

With deft manipulations, Rusty flicked toggles along the side of the alien keyboard, inserted pegged fingers into pointed depressions, and palmed plastic levers. Strange, indecipherable symbols ranged across the screen, and a speaker emitted discordant intonations. Rusty played the input valves with practiced ease.

"That is quite a display of talent for so young a lad."

Scott spun around. "Oh, hello, Doc. I didn't hear you come in."

"Stealth is a faculty that I still retain, although my bones do creak a mite if I bend too much." Doc hobbled closer, leaned against his wooden cane. "What kind of chicanery are you performing now? I thought this machine broke down yesterday."

Rusty's eyes kept their focus on the foreign calligraphy that appeared on the screen.

"No, it just uses so much power that it was causing a voltage drop." Scott fanned the room with a large bronzed hand. "What with all the peripheral devices going at the same time, the main distribution circuit couldn't handle the load. The computer kept glitching on us."

Doc watched the proceedings, absently playing with his long white beard. "I'm still amazed at what you boys have been able to learn about dragon technology, as abstruse as it is."

"No technology is incomprehensible once you understand the basics. Look at it this way. Last week you set Helen's broken leg which, to me, is an absolutely incredible accomplishment."

Doc rubbed his own bent extremity. "I hope I did a better job on hers than I did on my own."

"But you had medical training and experience that made the job a simple one—for you. And I'll bet you could just have easily set a dragon's leg."

"Yes, well, the physiology is essentially the same despite evolutionary variations. A bone is a bone, and a leg is a leg. They all grow alike, and they all heal according to established biological precepts."

Scott grinned. "Exactly! And the same holds true for technology. Granted the dragons built things differently, partly because of the materials at hand, partly because of their physical differences, and partly because of their lizard way of looking at things. They didn't have large oil and coal deposits, so they had to reach atomic energy directly before they could form a centralized power network."

Rusty stabbed a kill switch that cleared the screen. "And they designed their tools and machines to suit their own anatomical dimensions." He held up his gloved hands. "Sandra sewed extensions into the fingers that approximate their clawed digits. Now, I can run the computer as fast as a dragon technician."

"Faster," Scott said.

"I can poke all these indented buttons with fake talons, and snap switches with the curled ends. It took a little getting use to."

Scott picked up a coil of wire. "And look at this. Dragons are color blind, so it would be senseless to color code their electrical leads. Instead, they have a notching system similar to Roman numerals. That way they can feel the ciphers without having to look at them. And under the insulation is plain old copper wire, just like we use. Doc, electrons don't care who manufactured the filaments, they flow just the same."

"Yes, well, I guess you've got something there."

Rusty started the computer again. "I can even get their computer to work. I can load programs, I can enter the data banks, and I can print a hard copy on that laser printer over there. But I can't make it do anything."

Scott laughed, long blond hair shaking. "He can even get it to sing, if you can call that noise a song."

Rusty squirmed on the uncomfortable alien stool. "More like a funeral dirge if you ask me."

Doc watched the computer light up. The beeping tones followed a simple monotonous routine. "How do you know what you're doing?"

Rusty's fingers danced across the complicated keyboard. "I've learned certain functions that lead to the same results. Watch." For several seconds he flipped switches and punched buttons.

"I do declare," Doc said slowly. "Have you memorized an entire twenty-two character sequence?"

"Twenty-three. But all I'm doing is defining parameters. I don't understand what any of it says."

Lights flashed on and off, the speaker twanged in cadence up and down the music scale. Unfamiliar symbols appeared fleetingly on the screen. The laser printer clattered, then started humming as a lamina of white plastic spit out the left side.

Scott took a few steps, waited for the machine to stop, and ripped off the finished copy. "The printer doesn't use ink, it burns holes through the material. To see the figures you have to lay it down on a black surface. This board is a reader." He placed the sheet on the movable panel. "It doesn't need lights because the black shows through the holes."

"Ingenious." Doc took the reader and ran a crooked finger across the odd figures. "Do you read it from left to right, or right to left."

Rusty switched the computer to a different mode. It emitted lights and tones. "Who knows? Maybe they read from the bottom up."

Scott humphed. "It's all pterodactyl scratch to me."

Rusty pressed a lever. A clear cube, each facet an inch across, popped out of a hidden recess. He opened a compartment that held identical cubes stored like eggs in a carton, each slot padded with soft cloth. He exchanged the cube in his hand for another, held it up.

"This is how they store information. It's a crystal matrix that can be inserted into this receptacle with any one of the sides facing the scanner on the bottom. Each facet is notched with a specific symbol, and each side loads a different program. So far, I've been able to figure out how to count to six."

Rusty dropped the cube into the aperture, ran through another sequence on the keyboard. More dragon hieroglyphics filled the screen. "I'm still looking for a computerized Rosetta Stone. Now, I can convert this into a series of dots and dashes, but, of course, I can't read that either."

"Incredible."

The computer went into its song and dance routine, the printer clattered, then began humming. As the plasticized laminations appeared, the pitch changed from a uniform hum to a Dopplering whine.

Rusty's eyes pinched. "Hmmnn. I've never heard it make *that* sound before."

Scott froze with his hand on the printout. He bent over, put his ear close to the fluctuating dials. "It's not coming from here."

Doc turned ever so slightly, faced the doorway. "If I didn't know better, I'd say that sounded like a—"

* * *

"Mother, please." Sandra jerked her head

away, but her long tresses stayed with the comb. "Ouch."

"Well, if you would stay still for a moment and let me get the witches out, it wouldn't hurt at all. You have such fine silky hair, why do you let it get knotted like this."

"I already brushed it once today."

Helen cleaned black strands from between wooden teeth. "Stop it. If you make me break this comb, Death Wind will be awfully mad. It took him half a day to whittle it for you."

"He's the one who likes my hair smooth, not me. I don't care if it gets a little rustled."

"Sandra, at least show some appreciation for his effort." Helen held her daughter close. She twisted the long hair into a simple braid that would keep the loose strands from flying in the breeze. "You can't start letting yourself go just because—"

"Mother, stop treating me like a child."

"I'm treating you like you deserve. You'll understand when you have children of your own."

"Ha! Not in this world. I've got better things to do than pamper some little brat—"

"You said it." Helen stuck the comb in the back pocket of Sandra's shorts and patted her on the rump. "And I'm still your mother, no matter what he is to you. There, you're all done. Now go outside and play."

Sandra scowled, but headed for the door. Outside, she leaned against a blobbed plastic railing. From the uppermost roost, once occupied by dragon officials, she had a view of the entire city: low-roofed structures, open courtyards, flyer landing pads, the hatchery, slave quarters, all stitched together by rolling, narrow streets. Much of the city was amorphous orange plastic, melted by fire and flame, now caught running and solidified in a permanent blackened mass.

"I'm glad they're dead. Every last one of them. I never want to see another dragon."

Bending her splinted leg and moving awkwardly on crutches, Helen stepped out into the sunshine. The radiant rays softened the lines of hardship on her face. "They were only slaves, dear."

"I don't care. If they're dragons, I don't like them."

"They weren't responsible for anything." Helen leaned up against her daughter. She was a head taller than Sandra. "They couldn't help what they were."

Sandra pressed against the warm touch. "So

what did they die from?"

Helen shrugged. A light breeze played with her tawny hair. "Loneliness? Homesickness? I don't know. The Nomads fed them, and took care of them, just as they would any wounded animal. But they just withered away. Slaves are never healthy, because they don't have a purpose, or any real reason for living. When you live by doing the bidding of others, your own life doesn't have much meaning. You have no reason to care."

"Mother, did—did they torture you much?"

"The technicians?" Helen stood on her good leg, placed the crutches in front of her. "Yes, but it wasn't done cruelly, as you might think. It was—well, it was kind of how they communicated what they wanted done. The dragons don't have vocal cords, so they can't speak. What they did was shoot us with stinging rays that made us move. And if they wanted us to do something, they just kept stinging us until we figured out what it was they wanted us to do. Then, they stopped stinging. Unless someone got out of line. After a while, you learn to get up and start moving as soon as they arrive. You anticipate what they want, and you get hurt less."

"They treated you like animals, like beasts of burden. The dirty—"

"Sandra, I told you to stop using those words."

Sandra grimaced. "I didn't say anything bad."

"But you were going to."

"So what? I couldn't say anything bad about the dragons that isn't true. They're lousy bastards, every one of 'em. And I'd never knuckle under 'em, no matter what they did to me."

"Sometimes, dear, even if you don't want to, it's easier to just go along with things. To stay alive is the primary motivation. You can always plot. And we did. We were working on schemes when you rescued us. But they would have cost lives. There would have been sacrifices."

"You know, sometimes you sound just like Pop."

"Well, he *is* my father."

"Yeah, he's a neat guy. I wish—DW!"

Death Wind, tall and dark, walked along the parapet. His bulky musculature was overtly visible since he wore only moccasins and a loincloth. Long shaggy hair hung down to his broad shoulders.

Sandra ran to him, threw her arms around his back, lay her head for a moment upon his chest.

"Where've you been all day? I thought you were going to help me make the bed."

"We make it—we will make it—tomorrow. I will get more padding from the nursery, and cut the legs from a workbench. Today I helped Scott move machinery. He shows me how to make electrical connections."

"Oh, him." Sandra drew away, jumped backward onto the flat-topped railing. The courtyard was at least fifty feet below. "He's always working on something."

"Honey, get down from there before you fall." Helen placed her crutches under her arms, limped to her daughter, pulled her by the arm. "Death Wind, you're going to have to watch her. She tends to be so impetuous."

The savage's expression did not change. "That is Sandra."

Helen laughed. "I know, but she can afford to change."

"Mother! I'm a grownup now. I proved it a month ago."

"I didn't say you weren't, and I said nothing about growing up. All I said was there was room for growth. We all grow, throughout our lives. The day we stop growing, we die."

"Nomads learn always: about their people, about their land. It is the only way." Death Wind raised a thickly veined arm, gestured toward the jungle beyond the city limits. "My people must work together, and learn together. It is the only way to survive. We collect wisdom always, even without need. If it has no use, we pass it on to our children. Maybe they need."

Helen leaned on her crutches, formed a triangle with the two youngsters. She placed a hand softly on his shoulder. "Death Wind, do you miss your people, your mother and father? They've been gone over a week."

His forehead furrowed, his eyebrows pinched. "They go home, where they belong. They cannot stay in one spot, for it is in their blood to move. And now that the land is free from dragons, they roam in peace. Later, I will visit." He raised his fist and thumped his breast. "I carry them with me always, whether they live or die."

"A good attitude." Helen pursed her lips, nodding slowly. Her dark eyes dropped. "I wish I could adopt it. I will always miss . . . "

"Hey, whaddaya say we go get some chow? I'm so hungry I could eat a dinosaur." Sandra dragged Death Wind by the arm, indicated with her chin for her mother to follow. "They killed a fresh one from the pens this morning."

Death Wind placed one hand on his sheathed knife; with the other he patted his belly. "I have tasted it already." Slowly, his stern features relaxed. "But, I can eat more."

"You can always eat more." Sandra laughed. "Come on. Let's go."

Helen's eyes widened. She peered over her daughter's shoulder. "Why—why is the sun—moving?"

Both Sandra and Death Wind followed her gaze. The golden globe shimmered, grew larger, veered slantwise.

Then Helen twisted on her crutches and looked at the real sun. "Oh, my god."

CHAPTER 2

Heart pounding, Scott charged for the doorway. The sky was clear and blue, with only a few scattered puffy clouds coasting along the horizon. He spun toward the thrumming sound, southward. A golden object hung in the sky, riding on a column of heat waves.

His stomach twisted into a knot. "It's a dragon flyer!"

Rusty was suddenly standing next to him, technician's vest flapping. "Where the heck—"

"Not from Shangri-la, that's for sure."

Doc poked his cane between the two, pried them apart, and stepped through the opening and onto the portico. "I do say, this is rather unexpected. I thought we had seen the last of them. I'm afraid this is going to pose quite a problem."

"Problem, hell. It's going to start a war. Let's go!"

Scott took off, with Rusty on his heels.

"But where—"

Doc's question was cut off as a large object crashed onto the ground. Death Wind landed on his feet, legs bending to take up the shock of the fifteen-foot drop to the lower level.

"Armory," the Nomad said. "Quick."

"I'll race you," Scott shouted.

As the three of them ran off, Sandra screamed down from the penthouse, "Wait for me."

But no one waited. They bolted into the street and along the narrow corridor of orange plastic. They cut through an alley that emerged on the walled lane leading to the weapons storage building. Others, captives that the dragons had collected during their rampaging sojourns into the wilderness, were there ahead of them.

The huge doors were already open, and anxious people were inside the armory passing out power packs and laser pistols. Three warriors joined the melee, donning weapons that were constantly charged. Men and women dashed madly about, shouting orders and observations. There was no confusion: they were all warriors, trained by a lifetime of fighting.

Scott adjusted the straps across his chest, as he had done so many times before. "Let's get back to Computer Central."

"What are we going to do?" Rusty said.

"I don't know. I guess we defend ourselves."

Rusty straggled out of the armory with a backpack slung over one rounded shoulder. "But what's our plan?"

Scott was already in the street. "Stay alive."

Death Wind wore one power pack, carried another by the straps. "This not good. Could be other death machines coming."

"Let's hope not." Scott weaved through the crowd. People crisscrossed along the street, heading back the way they had come, back to their dwellings, to their families. "We'll have our hands full with just one."

The dragon saucer stopped at the perimeter of the city. The shimmering force field was a pylon that kept it high in the air. It hovered over the revetments, but made no attempt to lose altitude. It seemed to be watching—and waiting.

Rusty gasped under the weight of the pack. "Is it my eyes, or is that flyer bigger than the others?"

Scott glanced aloft as he ran, trying to keep up with Death Wind. "I'd swear it's twice the size. Look how much wider it is than a landing pen."

"It is moving," Death Wind observed. He skidded around an intersection and down a side street. Apartments lined both sides, vacant now that the dragon contingent had died off. "It comes to the tower."

"They're staying high, though." Scott pulled the pistol out of the pack-mounted holster, felt the weight in his hand. "They don't want to vaporize the central computer with their force field."

"If they're afraid of doing damage, maybe they won't land in the city," Rusty said.

"Look, someone's shooting."

Laser beams flashed up from the ground.

With sharp intensity the penciled lights cleaved the air, reaching out for the cone-shaped energy funnelers on the saucer's undercarriage: "It's too high. They're not doing any damage."

The dragon flyer thrummed, moving over the city but staying out of range. Its shadow crept over the streets and low structures. A port split the curved edge, a circular bank of nozzles poked out and pointed downward.

"It's about time you guys got here." Sandra's voice trembled as she dashed out of the portico. "Whaddidya do, stop for tea on the way?"

Scott was breathing hard, but controlled. He stayed out from under the canopy and kept an eye on the approaching flyer. "They had a fresh batch brewing. Rusty, hurry up. It's starting to descend."

Rusty trudged in from the street, leaned his scrawny body against a plastic column. "This thing—is so—heavy."

Sandra turned around, arms behind her, back to Death Wind. He slung the power pack over her shoulders. She humped it up high, cinched down the straps, reached behind and pulled the firing mechanism out of its holster. "Yeah, but it'll blow 'em to kingdom come if they get close enough."

"Pardon me for interrupting your bandying conversation, but I think you should realize that you're up against an adversary without true remorse. If that is a troop flyer, the soldiers may not be aware of the intrinsic value that this humble structure has to their more informed superiors. I suggest that when dealing with an unknown quantity, one seek concealment."

"Go stick your head in a hole, Pop." Sandra held the laser pistol out under his nose. "This is the only quantity I need to know."

"My dear—"

The top of the portico exploded in a shower of molten plastic. Hot, searing blobs flew outward like drops of water splashed from a stomped puddle. Scott felt tiny pinpoints of it stinging his face, his hands, his bare legs. The explosions kept coming in a continuous line, arcing around them, blasting the top of the portico, scything through the supporting colonnades. The roof sagged.

"Inside, everyone!" Scott grabbed Rusty by the arm, shoved him ahead through the doorway. Death Wind and Sandra piled in behind them. "They've got a laser machine gun."

Sandra crouched inside the opening. "I hate

it when he's right."

The portico was eaten up in a series of blasts. Then the wall began to melt as fire was redirected. Several beams pierced the doorway, hitting a charging generator and igniting an electrical cabinet. Sparks spit out of the plastic casing as high-voltage leads were short-circuited. The air smelled of ozone and burnt insulation.

The enemy machine dropped lower, the flaring tip of its multitudinous dischargers touching the roof of an adjacent building. The entire structure metamorphosed: doorways and window openings became drooling stalactites of plastic. Orange turned to black. Like a cube of chocolate in the hot sun, the building softened, sagged, poured into rivulets of molten polymers.

"Help! Help!"

"Mother!" Sandra leaped into the doorway.

"Don't—" Scott's warning was ignored. He charged out after her. Death Wind held a piece of her blouse in his hand; the material had ripped free when she broke from his grasp.

From half a dozen different directions laser beams shot upward at the descending flyer. People were converging and concentrating their fire on the needlelike power cones. The laser Gatling gun swiveled, returning blast for blast. Small explosions followed in the wake of its rotating barrels.

Scott jumped back for cover, his moccasins singed from the molten puddles. He crouched half outside. Helen crutched down the outer ramp. Scott aimed his pistol at the flyer.

Death Wind firmly pushed his hand down. "Do not attract fire."

Scott realized that the flyer's attention was occupied by the flanking attacks. "Good idea."

Sandra reached her mother, jammed a shoulder under her armpit, and hopped with her along the still-smoking floor. "Come on." She yanked the crutch that kept getting, in the way. Together they hobbled down the ramp. Death Wind and Scott, guns holstered, rushed to meet them.

Street defenders continued to pour laser beams into the hull of the flyer. Three more gun turrets opened, and with the firepower of four concentric Gatling lasers, the surrounding structures were swept with awesome and death-dealing energy. Explosions blew holes in thermoplastic barricades, routing the attacking garrisons.

Lasers raked the demolished portico, stitching a seam through the hobbling foursome. Scott

screamed and fell, clutching his right leg. Death Wind bundled the women through the doorway, turned to help his fallen companion. With laser beams discharging all around them, he picked up Scott and half dragged him to safety.

The air smelled of acid. Doc threw another glass bomb at the electrical panel. The ruptured casing spat gaseous fumes that extinguished the fire. Fanning the air, he receded on his cane. "I had to use carbon tetrachloride to put out the fire. Lucky the dragons thought of such safety devices."

Scott grimaced with pain. "Yes, well, right now they're not being so thoughtful."

"Helen, are you all right?"

"Yes, but I can't run with this cast."

Doc nodded, bent to examine Scott's wound. "Let me see that leg."

An ugly hole, still smoking, cut through his calf. Scott gritted his teeth. "Forget it. Let's just get out of here."

"We'd better hurry, too." Rusty held a cloth up to his face as he chucked another firebomb at the front wall. "They're going to melt their way in at any moment."

The staccato report of hits on the outer rampart was followed by bulging panels. A hole appeared next to the doorway. Energy continued to pour in with unerring accuracy. Outside, the oversized flyer settled down on the remains of the building opposite the courtyard, cut off its engines, and stood on its central column like a giant toadstool. As the plastic around its base resolidified, a ramp was let down from the column. The wall of the building dissolved under constant fire, and beams of light shot across the unprotected room.

"Out the back way!" Rusty pawed at his face, wiping away tears, as he headed for the doorway.

Injured and wounded, they limped and staggered out the other entrance, into a courtyard bounded on all sides by high plastic walls. Dragon furniture lay strewn about, and abandoned eating stations stood idle.

Scott leaned heavily against Death Wind as the savage pulled him across the orange pavement. "Into the mechanical room." They veered toward the wide opening as the sky brightened with a flood of laser beams. Rusty's power pack was hit, the casing bored. Shorted contacts arced and smoked. He shrugged off the pack and tossed it down a garbage scuttle just as its pent-up energy let loose. Expanding gases and molten plastic burst out of the hole like an erupting volcano.

One of Helen's crutches was burned in two; she fell in a heap. Sandra stopped and grabbed her arm. Another heat beam seared the back of her head, lopping off the twisted braid and singeing the rest of her hair. "I'm on fire!"

Death Wind fell on top of her, rolled her head against his belly, put out the blaze. The air stank of burning skin and hair. All six crawled through the opening as the Gatling gun fired sizzling laser beams all around them.

"It looks as if they temporarily have the best of us," Doc said.

Sandra's eyes flared red. "Brilliant deduction, Sherlock."

"I thought so, myself." Turning, "Scott, does this room have another exit?"

"Directly into the street. That's why I picked it. They used it to get heavy equipment in here without going through the command center."

"Who the hell cares?" Sandra screeched. "Let's get our own equipment out of here."

"A less than prophetic statement, but a useful suggestion. Helen, can you manage on your own?"

"I don't think so, Daddy. Not on one leg."

"I will carry." Death Wind scooped her up.

Scott got to his knees; his body was covered with blisters, and blood dripped down his injured leg. "I can't handle the gun." He shrugged off the backpack. The wall behind him was slammed with energy bolts. "Back between those transformers. Quick!"

The wall facing the courtyard suddenly blew in. Storage cabinets, mounted junction boxes, motors, and cable trays vaulted across the room in wild disarray. Through the gap Scott saw dragon soldiers marching robotlike out of the ruined computer center, spraying deadly energy beams ahead of them.

Scott led the way, tumbled through the wide opening into the street. "It's all clear."

Doc thrust his cane out first, followed it with sharp glances both ways. "The proximity of dragon soldiers demands a propitious retreat."

"I ain't hightailin' it." Sandra poked her head, hair still smoking, into the street. "I haven't even gotten off a shot."

"You always were a hothead," Scott said, managing a weak grin.

"Shut up, you!"

"Can we continue this exchange of ideas in a different location?" Doc stepped aside to let Rusty, Death Wind, and Helen out of the shambles of the mechanical room. Another explosion roiled behind them, showering sparks and metallic debris through the tepid air. "I have a suspicion that that Gatling gun can be set to fire all its barrels simultaneously with a largely inevitable result, the object of which I would not like to be."

Rusty ran across the street, ducked into another opening. "In here."

The battered squad followed him. Scott limped badly, dragging the foot of his injured leg. He was the last to reach the doorway. As he spun around, he saw the flyer lift off the crushed building, rotate its turrets, move toward him on its power beams. Ramps, walls, and barriers melted under the concentrated energy. The thrumming crescendoed as the focusing needles heterodyned. Death Wind set Helen down on a pile of matting.

"Can we get into the sewers from here?" Scott shouted above the shooting and thrumming. He searched eagerly for an exit:

"Not unless you've got a pick and shovel." Rusty surveyed their surroundings. "Hey, there's no doorway into the next courtyard. This is a dead end."

Doc peered out the opening. "We've got patrols coming from both directions—and through the mechanical room. And the flyer is circling Computer Central high enough so as not to destroy it."

"Nice going, redhead." Sandra dashed around the darkened room, kicking aside brooms and pushcarts. "You've got us into a fine pickle."

"How was I to know it was a street maintenance storage facility?"

"You look before you leap."

"I didn't have time for a detailed inspection."

"This is most strange," Doc said softly. "The soldiers have halted their advance, and the flyer is hovering directly overtop of us. I should think if they meant to kill us—"

"If anyone's interested, here's a trash chute." Helen scrabbled along on her knees, dragging the calf-length cast. "Maybe we can—"

"It's clogged," shouted Scott. He dug frantically in the chute, trying to clear an opening. The flyer's engine whine rose in pitch. The sonic vibration pierced his eardrums, knifed through his skull, and bulged his eyes.

Loose gear rattled. Shelving peeled off the walls. Storage containers crashed down and splattered their contents. Helen was crushed under an electric street melter. Blood ran from her head.

Scott put his hands to his ears, felt icy fingers caressing his brain. A heaviness built up inside his skull that could only be released by screaming. He did his best to relieve the pressure. He let out a long, painful yell that was absorbed by the freezing thrumming. His head was going to explode.

He continued to cry in his dreams long after he passed out.

CHAPTER 3

When Scott regained consciousness, his whole body ached: not just the muscles, or the joints, or the skin, but everything. He felt as if he had been run over by a tank and then caught in a rocket blast. His eyes were painful blobs of fire, radiating outward. When he went to rub them, he found that his elbows were clamped to a bar behind his back, which was part of a waist band shackled to a bulkhead.

He squeezed and squinted, fighting off red-hot needles. He saw his legs stretched out in front of him, and knew that he was sitting. The room was dark, lit only by annunciator lights on the far wall. In the faint yellow glow he could make out his companions: Doc to his right, Rusty, Death Wind, and Sandra his left. None of them moved; they huddled in contorted positions on the smooth floor, heads lolling, cuffed by wires.

"Anybody awake?" His throat scratched in agony, the words came out barely a grated whisper. His lips were dry and cracked.

"I am, but I'm afraid to open my eyes." The voice sounded like no one he ever knew, but from the direction it was Rusty's. "Did we get crushed in a sandblaster?"

"My powers of perception are somewhat limited, but I do believe that I have returned to some form of consciousness." Doc and drew his knees up to his chin. "This unnatural sleeping position has not done my back any good."

Sandra kicked spastically. "Are my teeth still in my mouth? I feel as if my gums have been rubbed over an electrified washboard."

"You look okay to me," Scott said.

"Then why do I feel so awful?"

Sensitivity to light, as dim as it is. We all appear to be physically intact, with no more injuries than we had before that rattling vibration." Doc ran a practiced eye over his body. "Other than a bent fingernail, I'm relatively unscathed."

"Goody for you. I've lost five years worth of hair. DW, move or say something, so I'll know you're alive."

The Nomad shuffled. "I am here."

"I can see that, you big lunk." Sandra stretched out a leg, wrapped it around the savage's bronzed calf. "Are you hurt?"

Death Wind stared at her expressionlessly. "Yes."

"Where?"

"Body."

Sandra scowled. "DW, where on the body?"

"Body."

Rusty grimaced as he changed position. "I'm a little better off. I only hurt from the ankles up. My feet are numb."

"You've probably cut off the circulation," Doc said. "Try flexing your muscles."

"Doc, how can my hair hurt?" Scott wanted to know.

"That tingling sensation is in the scalp, but the pain sensors transmit the information to the brain where its interpretation is suspect due to overload. If my suppositions are correct, we were engulfed in a sonic field that was phased to trick the synapses into believing they felt pain— a kind of direct neural stimulation. A very sophisticated cattle prod that is effective in its goal, but otherwise not harmful."

Sandra squirmed in her trammels. "I feel a lot better now, Pop."

"I rather preferred when you called me Grandpa."

"Get used to it." Sandra inched closer to Death Wind. "DW, how's your tummy?"

Death Wind did not bother to look at the singed hair and skin on his abdomen. Strands of Sandra's hair, where he had put out her flaming brand, mixed with his own belly pelt. He shrugged.

Scott struggled, stretching and testing the strength of his bonds. He felt the slick surface of wristlets, bound together by several inches of wire. Behind him, a joint connected the combination waistband and arm bar to the wall by two feet of thick cable. He could move his body slightly, as well as his hands, but not his arms.

As the general pain eased off, he became more aware of a sharp stinging sensation in his right thigh.

"Doc, is there something wrong with my leg?"

Doc leaned as close as he could. "It's rather dark to be sure, but I think you've got a nasty welt from that laser blast. Probably another one where it came out: right through the muscle of the calf, but it looks as if it missed the bone."

"I swear I can still feel the burning."

"They drilled you, huhn?" Sandra said. "And I never got a chance to squeeze my trigger. That's what makes me so mad."

"Have you given any thought to the demise of your mother?" Doc said calmly.

Sandra perked up, her face dropped. "Hey, where is she? I can't see anything in this damn dungeon. Mother!" A silent moment later, she screamed, "Mother!"

The door swung open, bright ceiling lights flared on. A dragon soldier stood in the opening, gun in hand. The prison was devoid of furnishings, and Helen was nowhere in sight.

"What have you done with—?"

The squat dragon body lurched into the room on taloned feet, fat tail swinging. The leering head peered down from the stalklike neck. The soldier took a post to the side while a technician came in behind it. It fumbled through the pockets of its equipment vest, brought out a metallic instrument, scanned the prisoners with it. It stepped to the other side of the doorway, the instrument still panning.

A gaudily caparisoned dragon swept slowly into the room, golden cape flowing. It moved with a grace not normally attributed to the awkward-moving reptiles. Its claws wrinkled and clutched at the air. Long talons clicked across the hard plastic floor. It stopped in front of Sandra.

Sandra was goggle-eyed, her jaw slack.

When the dragon leader worked its fingers in front of her face, she jerked back. Burnt strands of hair dropped off the back of her head where it banged against the wall. She drew her legs away from the scaly reptilian feet.

The dragon reached out, clutching. It passed its paws by her as if to grab, but kept out of her reach. It sidestepped, stopped in front of Death Wind. The savage returned its leering gaze, neck arched upward at the eight-foot-tall creature. The dragon feinted with its hands, but the

Nomad did not flinch.

Rusty shrank back when the reptile stepped in front of him, but made no other movement. The dragon moved sideways. Scott could smell the fetid breath, feel the foul air blowing against his face, hear the rasping of hot air grating through pointed teeth. A long, daggerlike tongue darted in and out of grim lips. The eyes were red beads with tiny round pupils.

Scott steeled himself for the clutching feint, refused to respond or be intimidated when the dragon reached out for him. Clawed fingers worked in front of his eyes with quick, hypnotic movement. Several scales dropped onto Scott's outstretched legs.

The creature moved on, paused in front of Doc. Its fingers jerked epileptically. Doc swallowed, but made no other outward motion. The dragon finally turned toward the door, still maintaining its senile activity.

The waiting technician stowed the shiny device in a vest pocket, took out a small stringed instrument, like a miniature harp. It played its claws across the tightened gut. The sound was deep, bass, discordant. If it was a tune, it was a completely alien one. Scott could find no rhyme or repetition in the chords.

The caped dragon again faced the captives, glared at each one. The long tongue stuck out, and it hissed like a snake.

"The same to you, pal."

The creature blinked, its head curling back at the sound of Sandra's voice, like a cobra preparing to strike. It approached her, reached out with long fingers wriggling.

Sandra let out a startled yell.

The guard fired its weapon. A jagged, lightninglike bolt sparkled across the room, crackling and engulfing her in a momentary display of shooting stars. Sandra writhed, her mouth open, but no sound emerged. She flopped on her side, straining at her bonds, and vomited violently onto the floor.

The dragon leader eyed her silently, tongue darting.

Sandra curled into a fetal position and opened her eyes. She gasped as she looked up at the dragon. "You'll get yours, buddy. You'll get yours."

Again the guard fired upon her. The dazzling fireworks flared around her like a glowing spiderweb. Her body was outlined in brilliant white pinpoints, like a child's connect-the-dots drawing. Her body spasmed, and her arms and legs flopped about as if driven by hidden springs. She coughed and gagged, vomited again.

"Shut up! They don't want you to talk."

Scott barely got out the words when he saw the pyrotechnics billowing out of the needlelike gun barrel, like a ball of scintillating water. When it hit him, he felt his skin burning as if it were on fire. Deep ice picks of pain stabbed into his muscles, he jerked and twitched involuntarily. His insides revolted. A bomb exploded in his stomach, singeing the lining with acid. Hot, stinging fluid exploded up his throat, out his mouth, through his nostrils. Long seconds passed before he could breathe; then, each breath was fire.

The dragon gathered in its cape, turned, and trundled through the doorway. The technician played a few more notes on the harp, then departed. The lights flickered out as the guard closed the door.

In a hushed voice, Doc said soothingly, "Are you two all right?"

Scott was still coughing, but he managed a nod and a groan.

Sandra gasped, "About as all right as you can be after swallowing a volcano."

"The dragons have a curious array of weapons, and I think it is less than wise to offer overt resistance when they can retaliate with such impunity."

"The power pack was the same as ones that energize the laser guns, just the output nozzle was different."

"Shut up, redhead. This isn't the time for technical observations. " Sandra cleared her throat, spat on the floor. "I've just had my guts ripped out."

"Even a fish would stay out of trouble," Scott croaked. "If it kept its mouth shut."

"Shut up, you. I don't need any of your witticism." She coughed again, slithered away from the malodorous puddle. "I've got enough troubles with one dragon wiggling his fingers under my nose while another one plays the harp. The next thing you know they'll start singing to us."

"If they do," Doc observed calmly, "I hope you will be more attentive to their musical inclinations. I don't think they'd enjoy being booed off the stage by a pugnacious lower life form."

"Pop, I can live without the platitudes."

"My dear, I'm just trying to point out that a

prisoner must act in accordance with convention."

"And I'm not going to be humiliated by a bunch of lizards. If they——"

The room took a sudden lurch. Scott felt his stomach rise up into his throat. The floor buffeted sickeningly, then straightened out.

"What the heck . . . "

Rusty said, "We're in the air. We must be inside a flyer."

The old man stroked the bottom of his long white beard, the part that he could reach with his arms bound. "Yes, lad, I agree. The dragons are obviously taking us somewhere."

"But where?"

"I will be very interested to find out," Doc said. "However, I do not suppose we will know until we get there."

"And what did they do with my mother?" Sandra wailed.

"The last thing I remember," Scott said, "was the shelving collapsing on top of her. Maybe she got buried and the dragons didn't see her . . . "

Sandra's shoulders slumped. "I just hope . . . she's . . . all right." She straightened, and threw back her shoulders. "Cause if she's not, I'm gonna kill somebody——"

The lights flared into brilliance, the door swung open. An armed soldier entered the room, gun at the ready.

Death Wind kicked Sandra hard. He whispered, "Do not speak."

Right behind the guard came a slave, carrying two plastic pails. The dragon worker shuffled across the room, set the pails in front of Sandra, retreated backward until it reached the doorway, then turned and left. The guard backed out, gun nozzle pointing. The lights doused with the closing of the door.

Rusty broke the long silence. "What was that all about?"

Sandra reached out with her feet, hooked a bucket between two petite but dirty ankles, and pulled it close between her legs. She bent her head and sniffed. "It's pig slop." She kicked it aside.

Death Wind stretched out a moccasinned foot and deftly maneuvered the pail in front of him. With his elbow bound he could not reach his hands into the bucket, so he dropped his face right inside the circular rim. He slurped for a moment, then straightened. "Food." His head dropped again, and he sucked the ingredients into his mouth like a snorting swine.

Sandra dragged the other pail across the floor. "Hog wash."

Death Wind pushed the first bucket to Rusty, dragged over the second one. He bent and slurped. "Water. Funny water."

"Funny! The stuff's got enough iron in it to attract a magnet."

"Give me some of that," Scott said.

Rusty's head came up out of the bucket, lips covered with gray ash. "It doesn't taste too bad, but it won't win any contests." He pushed the slop jar toward Scott.

The blond tasted the broth, coughed, and sucked in great mouthfuls. "This isn't exactly dining at the Ritz." He shoved the pail to Doc.

Doc ducked his chin so as to keep his beard out of the mess. "Hmmnn, it tastes rather like some form of grain, although oddly tainted. It's probably highly nutritious."

"Hey, let me have some of that porridge," Sandra said. "Before you guys finish it all."

"I thought you didn't want any," Scott taunted. He took another couple mouthfuls when Doc passed it back to him, then nudged it toward Rusty. The other bucket came his way, and he swallowed great quantities of foul-tasting water, soothing his cracked lips and parched throat. He offered it to Doc. "The stuff is dilute iron oxide. With a slightly higher mineral content it'd be solid."

Doc sampled the brew. "Well, at least we know they're not going to starve us to death."

Sandra brought her head out of the food bucket. "No, they're gonna poison us." Despite her protests, she continued to suck in the slop. The buckets passed back and forth among the prisoners until the nearly empty food pail wound up in front of Sandra. She managed to tilt the rim with her fingers, work it onto her lap, and pour the remaining contents into her mouth. She licked her lips of the remaining fodder. "Is there any more of that liquid ore?"

Scott leaned back against the wall, staring off into the darkness. He salivated so as to clean his mouth and lips, then spat into the pile of dried vomit. His stomach churned. "I wonder what's for dessert."

The door opened again, and light filled the room. Two guards entered, took opposite stations. Two technicians lumbered through the opening, each carrying an eight-foot-long pole with a lighted box near one end and a yawning,

two-pronged claw on the other. One dragon posted itself by the annunciator panel. From a distance the other poked Sandra in the stomach with the mechanical grab, withdrew the pole, and released a spring which snapped the clamp on the wire that bound the wristlets.

The other technician stabbed a flared button with its paw. The cable attached to the waistband retracted into the wall. The dragon pulled Sandra forward by the wrist shackles.

"Hey, whaddaya think you're—"

A scaled finger pushed a lever on the lighted box. A coruscating ring traveled down the eight-foot length, burst like a bubble on Sandra's fingertips. She screamed. The dragon dragged her to her feet, backed toward the door.

"You bastards. Wait till I—"

Another circle of light raced toward her balled fists, enveloped her fingers, shot up her arms. She shrieked again, louder. She ran forward on the pole, kicking, but could not reach the dragon with her feet. She fell, got up, and kicked again.

This time the ball of light reached her shoulders. Sandra gasped, but no sound emerged. Her eyes widened. After a moment, she gulped in air like a beached flounder. She was drawn slowly out the door. The first technician stepped around behind her, attached the other pole to the back of the waistband and elbow clamp. Together they prodded her out of the room.

Sandra was not struggling when the door closed behind them.

CHAPTER 4

"Uh-oh. I have to do something unpleasant. I don't think I can hold it in any longer."

Doc hunched his shoulders, stifling a groan. "Don't worry about it, Rusty. I've been doing it all along. There's no way to stop nature from taking its course."

Scott retreated from his own puddle, but could not shut off the nauseating smell of his own vomit. His skin was hot and clammy, his arms ached from their unnatural position. He struggled in his bonds. The plastic rod binding his elbows would bend, but not break, and the attaching cables were beyond his strength. He lay hunched over on one side, exhausted, sickened.

"How's the leg, my lad?"

Scott did not raise his head from the floor. "Sore."

"You're lucky. It appears to have missed the bone. What we would call a 'flesh wound' in the field."

"Terrific."

"Did you know that your skin is blistered?"

"Yes, I can feel it."

"Death Wind, how is everything with you?"

"Okay."

"Do you know what happened to Helen? Back there in the city?"

"I put her down. The roof caved in. I did not see."

"Ah." The sibilant sound was Doc's only epithet.

The lights flickered on, the door opened, two guards shuffled inside. A technician pulled on a long pole attached to Sandra's wrists, while another pushed at the small of her back from the end of another. Both held tightly onto the insulated grips. A subdued Sandra, whimpering, clothes torn to shreds, allowed herself to be uncoupled from behind and reshackled to the bulkhead. She continued to cry softly.

Bloody gashes streaked her legs, her back, her chest, as if she had been mauled with a garden trowel—or a dragon's sharpened claws. She made no attempt to cover her exposed breasts.

As soon as the forward clamp released its hold, Scott heard a loud snap. Death Wind's hands suddenly shot out, grabbed the end of the electric prod, wrenched it out of the unsuspecting dragon's paws. The savage brought his feet under his haunches and bounded sharply. The rear cable ripped out of the already broken waistband, and he launched himself straight at the offending technician.

The glowing end of the rod rapped the dragon in the jaw and caught the extended tongue in mid dart. Before it could hiss, Death Wind swung the pole around like a pugil stick, and slammed the clamp end alongside the dragon's narrow skull. The head lolled over on the long neck.

The two guards fired almost simultaneously, but Death Wind was protected from their blasts by the bulk of the technician that was slowly falling over. It took the brunt of the static discharge.

"Go get 'em, DW."

Wielding the prod like a sword, the Nomad charged the other technician, parried, and flicked the pole out of its grasp. He jammed the clamp around its neck and shoved the lever forward as far as it would go. The light ring burst into the dragon's face, coruscated over its head and down its slender, snakelike neck.

As the dragon began to collapse, Death Wind swung his weapon, but was caught first in one blast, then in another. He was flung backward by spasmodic muscles; he skittered across the floor.

Scott reached out with his good leg and hooked his heel over the glowing prod. A lightning zigzag caught him on the calf. His leg reacted galvanically, and twitched painfully. He fell back with a cry of pain. A guard lurched on powerful hind legs and scooped up the fallen pole.

Death Wind lay inert.

A guard backed against the opposite bulkhead, stabbed a mushroom button. A yellow light came on, flashing, and harplike tones played out of a hidden speaker. In moments a squad of soldiers charged sluggishly into the cell, spread out with gun nozzles aimed. A contingent of technicians followed them, paws flying as they gathered their fallen comrades and dragged out their inert bodies.

Rusty's whisper was barely audible. "Don't say a word."

To the tune of music, a technician brought in a new waistband and attached it to the unconscious savage. He was hauled by the legs across the floor to his former location. Rusty and Sandra cringed away from the lumbering dragons while Death Wind was reshackled to the wall mount. Slowly, the dragons retreated, first the technicians, then the soldiers. The music stopped. The lights went out.

Sandra could barely reach Death Wind's outstretched leg. She touched him tenderly. "DW. DW. Are you all right?"

Rusty bent over as far as he could and picked up the limp hand extended his way. "He's still got a pulse."

"Those lousy bastards." Tears ran down Sandra's face. "Those lousy, no-good lizards. I'll burn 'em all, down to the last scale."

"My dear, squeeze his calf for muscle response. Rusty, chafe his wrists if you can. I don't know what crisscrossing beams might do to the circulatory system."

"He's still breathing," Rusty said.

"How about his eyes? Can you see that far?

Are his pupils dilated?"

Rusty struggled against his bonds. "No, I can't get any closer. It's too dark anyway."

"Why don't you—"

The lights came on, and every eye turned toward the door. It opened slowly, and a lone dragon duckwalked ponderously into the room. The naked soldier cradled a nozzle that was ten times the diameter of the lasers and stunners. An enormously fat connecting cable trailed into the corridor.

Scott gulped, flattened against the wall. He was looking right into the mouth of the tube. With the other paw the dragon pulled a foot-long lever. Scott saw a sparkling bubble emerge, soar across the cell, growing larger, expanding, attacking, engulfing. He closed his eyes just as the force hit him, dousing him with cold, stifling his breath. His body was jerked around to the limit of the shackle, washing him back and forth with awful power. His body tingled with icy stabs of pain. He sputtered for air.

Then the awful feeling was gone, and Doc was deluged with the spray. He was buffeted around like a feather in a gale, his body flopping unmercifully. After several seconds the spray washed over Scott's head, then concentrated its power on Rusty. He was totally inundated until the nozzle drenched Death Wind's motionless form, making his body dance like a dime store manikin. Only Sandra screamed when she was hit.

The power died down, the nozzle ceased its effluence, the soldier backed out of the cell, the door closed.

Scott sloshed around on the floor, pushed wet hair out of his face. He felt amazingly refreshed. "The next time they decide to give us a bath, I hope they use fresh water."

Death Wind shuddered. Slowly, he contracted his limbs and crawled to a sitting position. He shook his head like a wet hound, then stared at his companions. "Doc is right. Resistance is no good."

"Oh, DW, are you all right? I thought they hurt you badly."

"Hurt, yes." The Nomad ran his hands over his body. "No damage. You?"

Sandra shrugged. "I got a little rough handling when they tried to pin me down, but once I stopped resisting they let up on me. The scratches aren't deep, but rubbing salt in the wounds doesn't make me feel any better." She

extended a hand, managed to touch his fingertips. "Thanks for what you did."

Death Wind gave a slight nod.

Scott rung out his shorts. "Well, now that we're all cleaned up, I guess we're ready for round two."

"They've already won by a technical KO." Rusty pushed puddles away with the flat of his hand, clearing a dry spot around him. The bulk of the water drained through a grill in the middle of the floor. "Boy, when I heard that music, I thought for sure the angels were coming to take me away."

"Yes, the dragons appear to have eccentric behavioral patterns of which I was not previously aware," Doc said. "I'm sure there is some significance to the playing of the harp, something outside my experience."

"Kinda like the cavalry blowing the trumpet during the charge," Sandra offered.

"Possibly, although I did not know the dragon intellect was musically or artistically inclined. I thought their only method of expression was the stick symbolism of their writing."

Sandra scowled. "Pop, can we stop studying them long enough to hate their guts?"

"My dear, knowledge of one's enemy is the most important weapon in the arsenal. Previously, we have fought only against military forces and soldier mentality. Now, we have a unique opportunity to study the dragons from the inside, and to learn more about how their leaders operate."

"Pop, I hate to burst your bubble, but—we're prisoners of war. Get the aitch two oh out of your noggin."

Doc laughed whimsically. "No, my dear, the human mind is never made prisoner by a cage alone. It is the failure of the will that makes one a captive of enemy forces. We have more freedom now to study dragon hierarchy than we ever had before, and we must take advantage of our position. The fate of the world may rest upon it."

"Pop, I don't think I'm getting through to you—"

"No, he's right," Rusty interrupted. "Don't you see. We thought we had conquered the dragons, but we didn't. We haven't won the war, only the first battle. If there are more dragons alive—anywhere—or anywhen—we've got to annihilate them. We've got to make sure there's no chance of future retaliation."

"Yes, we must resolve ourselves to see it through." Doc wagged an extended digit. "We must learn everything we can about their world, their society, their culture. Before, I was able to study them only from the outside, or from the rare and clandestine excursions into their stronghold. And you saw how valuable that intelligence turned out to be. But if there are more of them, if there are other outposts, we must continue the fight. The only difference is that now we wage war from the inside."

Sandra was quiet for a long moment. "You know, sometimes I don't think I understand you. Other times, I know I don't."

Doc laughed again. "Then you must learn to think as a warrior, not as a woman."

"And you'd better stay on his heels," Scott said, "or he'll always be one step ahead of you."

"Well, has it ever occurred to you that we may be in danger? Dragons don't show much compunction about wasting human lives."

"In the wild, that's true. They treat us like vermin. But think of all the prisoners who were kept alive at the city. It seems that a human, once captured, takes on a different role and instead of being exterminated is somewhat pampered—in a POW sense, of course. And I don't believe they would have harmed you if you had not talked out of turn, or fought their guards. No, I think they have plans for us."

Rusty shuddered. "Maybe they want to torture us because we took over their turf."

Doc shook his head. "Again, no. To my knowledge dragons do not waste time on revenge. They are, as far as I have been able to ascertain, totally without emotion. They respond to logic, killing when necessary to attain their goals. What we must do, in order to thwart them, is to discover those goals. And if we do not show any overt resistance, I think we can do some useful underground work."

"Yeah, well, all I want to do is discover my way outa here." Sandra folded the shreds of her blouse as best she could, tying knots in some of the loose strands. "Without a scaled escort."

* * *

Seven feeds and two hosings later, and to the tinkling of bells, a horde of guards and technicians filed into the jail cell. Prods were clamped to all the prisoners, front and rear, and they were marched out wordlessly and unprotestingly.

Scott was truly amazed at the sheer size and inner convolutions of the flyer. The corridors seemed to curve on forever, with ramps connecting various levels. He saw scores of hatches; those that were open led to cubicles similar to the prison cell.

Machinery and exposed wiring crowded the corridor. Hundreds of battery packs lined the walls, some connected to cables that led directly to massive charging generators. He recognized a coolant system that could feed only a nuclear reactor. Except for copper conductors and terminal points, almost everything else was constructed of synthetic resins bonded by epoxy compounds.

They approached a spacious balcony, overlooking the central exit chamber. The retractable core was extended and open, and cooler air found its way inside. Dragon slaves were hauling gear and pulling handcarts down the massive ramp and out into the sun. Their shadows were long.

Scott made as many observations as he could, wishing he could reach into his pocket for the stylus and notepad that for some reason had not been taken from him. He exchanged glances with Doc and Rusty whenever he saw something interesting, and pointed with his eyes.

Three gurneys trundled out of a recess, scraping on plastic wheels. The slaves paid no attention to their cargoes. But Scott took special notice of the stiff technician, still wearing its vest, lying under the clear plastic wrap. The second gurney carried another vested dragon.

"Mother!"

Sandra struggled, but was held firmly in place by her jailers.

Each pushed the stunning lever, and she was caught in twin coruscating balls of light. Her back arched forward, and she fell to her knees, sobbing.

"Stay still, my dear. There's nothing you can do."

"They've got her covered in plastic. She can't breathe."

"She doesn't have to. Don't you see the rigidity of her limbs."

Scott clenched his jaw, staring at the passing parade. Helen lay partly on her side, one leg drawn up, and one arm bent and held upward against the force of gravity, frozen. "Rigor mortis," he breathed.

Sandra was hit with another pair of bolts. She collapsed to the floor, gasping from electric shock overload. Death Wind jumped toward her, but took only a step before his rear guard zapped him in the small of the back. The waistband glowed for an instant, but he stayed on his feet. He stopped wrestling.

"My dear, you are only making it worse."

"Those bastards!"

Every guard, every technician, stopped in their tracks. The only sound was that of Sandra's wailing. The gold-caped leader, neck bobbing and forelegs working, clicked across the balcony toward the prisoners. It waved its paws ominously, clutchingly, as if it wanted to strangle them.

Death Wind remained perfectly still. "Sandra, you must not resist."

Chest heaving, Sandra slowly climbed to her feet. She stared at her mother's body, then at the chief dragon. It hissed, tongue darting.

"All right for now. We play it Pop's way. As long as I get to kill that one."

The caped dragon waved its paws, the funeral procession began again. Behind it, the five prisoners marched solemnly, resignedly, into a sun-scorched dragon land.

CHAPTER 5

"Out of the flyer and into the flying pan."

"Shut up, you."

Scott tilted his head. "I was just trying to keep up morale."

With the back of her arm Sandra wiped sweat off her brow. "Yeah, well, you're not doing a very good job."

"After all, we're not all wearing ventilated clothing."

"I said, shut up!"

Rusty paced the floor of their cell, four steps up and four steps back. "Doc, if you're cooking up a plan, you'd better get on with the recipe. With the sun shining through that transparent dome, we'll be well done in a matter of minutes."

Doc folded his body into a corner. "I do not believe the dragons found any humor in Sandra's rejoinders about their incestuous parental activities."

"What was I supposed to say when that guard goosed me with the prod?"

"My dear—"

Sandra held out her hands. "Okay, I'm cool. From here on out I promise not to lose my

head—unless somebody tries to take it. I just wish one of them dragons would bend over in front of me, 'cause I'd love to do some kicking."

Doc slumped into his own lap, breathing hard. "Right now, my dear, I could do with a little less hot air."

Scott doffed his tunic, crouched in front of Doc, and fanned the older man. "They didn't bring us all this way to knock us off. I think they just want to soften us up."

"If I get any softer I'm going to melt away. I need water."

"Hang in there while I call room service."

Doc's laugh was barely audible, but his smile was there for all to see. "I like it, Scott. Despite what my granddaughter says, I enjoy your wit."

"I'm glad someone appreciates me."

Rusty used his own tunic and took over the fanning. "I need the exercise. My arms are still stiff from being locked into that brace. Doc, where do you think we are?"

He shook his head weakly. "I forgot to bring my compass."

Scott dabbed the doctor's forehead, dried his damp hair. "Have you ever heard rumors of other—dragon outposts?"

"Not in the North American continent."

"South. We are south." All eyes turned toward Death Wind. The savage sat calmly against an orange plastic wall. "I watch the sun. It is higher."

"That's because it's noontime, silly," Sandra said.

Doc looked up at the sky. "No, he is quite right, although I had not taken particular notice. The inclination above the horizon is much higher here. Nomads have a constant awareness of stellar activities, as it guides them on their migrations. Now that I think about it—" He paused and rubbed his chin. "The sun is nearly perfectly overhead, almost as if we were . . . "

"On the equator," Rusty finished.

Scott wiped his freely flowing forehead. "Then, unless we crossed the Atlantic Ocean, we must be in South America."

"So this is Montezuma's revenge," Sandra said slowly.

Scott pounded on the thick door. "Hey, out there, let us out of this oven." He heard harps, and backed away immediately. "Uh-oh. Here comes another serenade."

The door swung open. Two squads of guards, armed with stunners, created a gauntlet. The gold-caped leader blocked the end of the double column, while behind him stood a technician strumming a bass harp.

With Rusty's help, Doc struggled to his feet. "I guess this means they want us to come out. And remember, my dear, no more aspersions about their unwed ancestral heritage."

"Don't worry. I've been zapped enough." She stabbed a stiff finger at the leader. "But I still want him."

"All in due time. Scott, I'm afraid I'm going to need someone under my other arm. That's good. Thank you." The doctor led with his chin. "Shall we?"

Sandra held onto Death Wind's hand, followed the trio out of the heated cubicle. "Easy on the trigger digits, fellas."

Scott looked up at those leering faces mounted on stalklike necks. Some of the soldiers hissed, flecking outward with vibrating tongues; others revealed rows of sharpened teeth; all exuded foul breath. There were never less than two stunner nozzles aimed at his midriff. Scott gulped.

The gold-caped leader waved them on with wriggling fingers. Doc hung heavily between Scott and Rusty, his game leg made worse by dehydration. The twin files of soldiers kept up the slow pace along the broad corridor. A hot breeze flowed through glassless windows.

Scott whispered into Doc's ear. "Can you see those plowed fields out there? I didn't know dragons went in for gardening."

"I'm at a loss for an explanation. Even the slaves at the city ate ground dinosaur meat."

Rusty squinted his eyes in the glare. "Looks like mostly soybean, but there's also corn, peas, and carrots."

"And lettuce and spinach, too," Scott added.

Doc's head struck back, his cheeks pinched. "You can differentiate the vegetation this far away?"

Rusty humphed. "Of course. We grew all that stuff in our hydroponic gardens. The foliage patterns are distinct, although I can't see the leaves from here. Might be romaine lettuce."

"Aren't those peanuts—"

The gold-caped dragon turned around slowly, cocking his head.

Sandra poked Scott in the rib cage. "Pipe down, you. You wanna get us all electrocuted?"

The dragon waved its paws, resumed its course.

Scott whispered over his shoulder, "You're stunning enough to get even with them."

The cortege wound up a great circular ramp. The orange plastic motif was unchanging and unadorned. Dusty sunbeams filtered down through a louvered dome of clear material, similar to the roof of their prison cubicle. Vertical slots in the wall admitted light as well as air.

The ramp leveled off at the end of a great hall with a high flat ceiling. A throng of dragons, wearing capes of various color schemes, milled throughout the unfurnished chamber. They were in constant movement, chugging along pigeon-like, heads bobbing, and working their arms and paws nervously. Some hissed as the humans passed.

Technicians mingled among the dragon leaders. The vested lizards carried small harps and strummed tuneless chords on them. Scott thought he discerned a repetitive measure being played, although the deep sound had no tonal qualities to it.

"Just what we need, a symphony orchestra."

Sandra punched him in the ribs again. "I'm warning you."

Dragons shuffled out of their way. A canopied area appeared, occupied by a lone dragon wearing a silvery, reflective cape. It hunched forward on a plain plastic stool with a notch in the backrest for the thick tail. The point of the tapering appendage flicked slowly from side to side. The scaled breast heaved sonorously.

"The head honcho."

Scott turned his head, gave Sandra an expression of horror. Guiltily, she covered her face with her hands.

The gold-caped dragon stepped aside for a vested technician, which played its harp with irregular strains. The silver-caped leader waved it aside with gnarled claws, then reached out clutching for the band of people. By watching its dextrous motions, Scott had the impression that it wanted to strangle them.

He watched the flailing arms, the curving digits, the drooling, bloodless lips, the beady red eyes, the sagging scaled skin. This lizard was *old*. It stuck out its tongue, red and darting, and hissed. The head sagged on the long, slender neck, and it was forced to look up from the downward curve.

Another technician neared its side. It played a stringed instrument directly into the head dragon's external ear opening. After a few notes it was fanned away by the drooling leader. With short jabbing motions, the silver-caped dragon punched the air. The half-closed lids gave it an odd sleepy appearance.

More harps came into play. The gold-caped leader walked sluggishly to the five people. Scott cringed as the dragon reached out and grasped Doc's free hands. The eight-foot-tall beast lifted Doc's stark white fingers, squeezed them, let them go. Doc did not move, but kept his arms at half mast.

The dragon swung around at its leader. The silver-caped oldster punched the air again; the harp played by its side. Scott saw the paw reach out for him, felt the dry, leathery touch, the gentle pressure on his knuckles. When the dragon let him go, he was shaking. The technician plucked strings, the gold-caped dragon stabbed the air in front of Scott's face with threatening, daggerlike claws. Scott pulled his hands to his sides.

As the aged leader made more punching motions, the harp by its side sang discordantly. The gold-caped dragon hissed, then walked past Scott and grabbed Sandra by the shoulder.

She cringed, but allowed herself to be dragged aside. She remained perfectly silent.

The dragon feinted at her face, missing her by a hair. She stood her ground. The dragon hissed, turned toward its leader. Claws reached out. Then, the gold-caped dragon released Sandra, marched past her and between the columns of soldiers. It turned once, cape swaying, stabbed with a crooked paw, then continued on its way.

"My interpretation of the action is that the interview is terminated," Doc whispered. "It has shown off its captives. I suggest that we follow Goldie out of the presence of his eminence."

They all swung around, Sandra and Death Wind leading. The guards did not fire, but moved along with them at the gold-caped leader's pace. They left the hall to the accompaniment of hissing dragons, paraded down the circular ramp, then along a narrow corridor away from their previous prison.

The procession angled down ramp after ramp until it passed out of the sun and into the cooler air of a subbasement. Angled mirrors funneled meager reflections into dark corners and shone weakly through the grill of the door that closed behind them. Overhead, inlaid crystals let in light through the ceiling.

"Let me sit. Please." Doc faded from Scott's

grip, fell into a heap on the plastic flooring. "I'm just about done in."

"Damn it, they didn't give us any water," Sandra shouted. She went back to the door and banged on it with her fists. "Hey, you lizards. How about some refreshments."

Death Wind checked out the walls of their cell, reached into a trough at the far end. Scott heard crinkling sounds, saw the savage pull something up to his nose and sniff.

Sandra joined him. "Hey, DW. Whatcha got?"

"Food." The Nomad took a bite, crunched it slowly. "Fresh."

"What? Let me at it." Sandra dug into the trough, pulled out some leaves. "Ugh, what is this stuff?"

Rusty tasted a leaf of green foliage. "Hmmnn. It's lettuce. And good, too." He took a handful to Scott and Doc. "In fact, this may be the best lettuce I've ever had."

Doc crunched it greedily. "It's even wet."

"Water in bottom of trough," Death Wind said.

"Come on, Doc, let's get you a drink." Scott shoved a handful of lettuce into his mouth, and chewed as he helped the old man to his feet. "You're right, Rusty. This stuff is great. Better than any we ever grew at home."

"Salad," Sandra spat. "There's nothing in here but rabbit food."

Doc dug his hands into the vegetation and brought cupped water to his lips. "As long as it's edible, my dear, that's all that counts."

Rusty rummaged through the torn lettuce leaves. "There are beans floating in the water." He chomped down on a mouthful. "They're hard, and uncooked, but very nourishing." He passed them around.

Scott heard a scraping sound from the wall in front of him, then a dull thud. In the dim light he saw several intersecting creases in the plastic. He felt a ridge along the wall. "Hey, there's something here. A trapdoor, or something. But I can't get it open."

"Let me try." Death Wind ran his fingers across the top of the trough, traced out a one-foot-square panel. He took his knife out of its sheath and dug it into a crevice.

"Hey," Sandra shouted. "Where'd you get that knife?"

The Nomad was taken aback. "From Father."

"But, how come you have it with you?"

"Always carry."

"I mean, didn't the dragons take it away from you? They took our guns."

"I still have."

"Then why didn't you pull it out sooner?"

"No need. I kept it hidden under loincloth. Now I need."

Sandra sighed, her exhaled air blowing singed hair off her forehead. "DW, sometimes I don't know what to do with you."

"You should know by now," Scott said.

"Shut up, you."

The Nomad pried the panel open, got his fingers inside, and pulled. The small door popped out, swung on a top hinge, and a flood of vegetable matter flowed down a chute into the trough.

"Wow, look at all the food!" Rusty exclaimed. He ran his hands through the fresh vegetables. "Look at this! Tomatoes. And bananas."

"And oranges."

"And pears."

"And—what the hell's this spiked thing?"

Scott took the strange fruit from Sandra. "Rusty! Look! It's a pineapple. I've only seen these on tape." He lifted the unstuck lid and shouted up the chute. "Hey, you have any pomegranates up there?"

"Scott, this is a cornucopia." Rusty stuffed his mouth with the various foodstuffs. "I haven't eaten like this since . . . " His voice trailed off distantly.

"Don't start thinking of home, now," Scott said, enjoying the feast. "This isn't the time for nostalgia."

"Excuse me, but could I get over there where the water is a little deeper. I sorely need another drink."

"Sorry, Doc." Scott sank his teeth into an orange as he moved out of the way. "I can't believe the dragons are treating us to a banquet. This stuff is delicious."

Sandra nibbled on a pear. "Don't get too excited. They're probably fattening us for the slaughter."

Scott stopped in midbite. "Hey, you don't think—"

The dungeon door creaked open, a broad shaft of light spread across the floor. A dragon guard, stunner in paw, stepped back. Two people were shoved into the room. The door clanged shut, the bolt shot into place.

The girl's only article of clothing was a G-string. Long, tangled dirty blond hair cascaded across bobbing pink breasts. Under the dirt-smeared face were the bright blue eyes of a teenager. Thin brows pinched as she studied each of the five prisoners.

The man was of medium height, well built, and wore a loincloth that was made of only slightly more material than that of the girl's. He, too, was barefoot. Straight, jet-black hair reached down below his ears, blended with the curly beard. He took a couple steps forward, tilting his head and pinching his dark eyes. He looked at each of them in turn, then spoke in a guttural, throaty voice.

"Well I'll be a son of a bitch. What the hell do we have here?"

Sandra fell back between Scott and Death Wind, clung to them both. Scott put a hand on her back, felt her heart racing. She was breathing hard. Suddenly she pulled away, stepped hesitantly toward the bearded newcomer. She stared at him hard, peering up in the dim light. Then she screamed and jumped at him.

"*Daddy!*"

CHAPTER 6

"Toad?" The bearded man bent down, peered deeply into her eyes. "Is that you, Sandy?"

"Oh, Daddy." Sandra threw her arms around him, buried her face in his chest, and sobbed softly. The top of her head barely reached his chin. "Daddy, I don't believe it."

The man blinked. "Well, I'm not too sure myself this is really happening. It's—it's unbelievable."

Doc limped closer to the entwined pair. He stretched out a gnarled hand and placed it on Sandra's back, in the tatters of her blouse. "Hello, Sam. Fancy meeting you here."

The man's jaw dropped, was snapped back in place by Sandra's bobbing head. He seemed not to notice. "Henry? What the hell is going on? Am I dreaming?"

"If so, we all are."

Sam reached out over Sandra's still heaving body, wrapped his fingers around Doc's neck, pulled him closer. "Henry, I just can't believe this. Of all the godforsaken places to meet, this is the damnedest. And after all these years—"

"Fifteen or twenty, I reckon. Before she was born."

Sam pulled Doc into his other arm, and the

three of them hugged and cried for several minutes.

"I thought you were dead," Sandra said, when they broke free. "When you didn't come back—"

"I know. I know how it must have been. I thought about how you must think I failed you. I'm sorry. There was nothing I could do about it. They killed—the others. Somehow I survived—knocked unconscious, I guess. When I woke up, I was here, in this city. A prisoner. I've thought of escaping, even made plans. But I can't do it alone. I need help. I—Henry, who are your friends?"

"Ah, many pardons. I suppose I should introduce you. Scott, here, is our mechanical genius. Rusty is a computer wizard. And Death Wind—"

"A Nomad, isn't he?"

"Yes, and somewhat related—"

Sandra went to the savage, melded into his side, under his brawny arm. "DW's my—that is, we—uh, I mean—"

"They got hitched, Nomad style," Scott supplied.

"Shut up, you!"

Scott smiled, held up his palms. "Just trying to help."

"My god, you mean you're married?" Sam breathed. "You found someone strong enough to tame you?"

"Daddy!"

Sam ran a hand through thick hair. "Sorry, Toad. But I guess—I just never thought it would happen. Not in my lifetime, anyway. Well, congratulations, uh, Death Wind. You sure have your hands full."

The savage nodded, showing white, even teeth.

Sandra pounded him on the chest. "Hey, you don't have to agree with him."

"Oh, I almost forgot." Sam turned around, held out his hand. The young girl came forward hesitantly, into the light. "This is Jane. Or, at least, that's what I call her. She didn't have a name until I gave her one. She lives here. A native. Say hello, Jane."

Her mouth worked silently for a moment, as if her lips were trying to wrap around the words. "Hel . . . lo."

"Tell them who you are."

"I . . . am . . . " She looked up at Sam, her face twitching. He nodded. " . . . Jane."

Sandra sneered. "What's wrong with her? Is she retarded?"

"No, she just doesn't speak. None of them do."

"Whom do you mean by 'them'?" Doc asked.

"The people who live here, in this city."

"You mean, with the dragons?" Rusty practically shouted.

Sam nodded slowly. "Yes, they've been here for generations. Ever since the takeover. Henry, I've learned so much about the invasion—"

"Yes, we've had some rather intimate contact with the details, too. We'll have to compare notes. But, why can't they speak? Is it congenital, or do the dragons perform laryngectomies?"

"Nothing so drastic. No, they're just not allowed to talk. Any vocal noise other than a hiccup has historically been treated with electric shock: a great deterrent. So, today's generation has lost the knowledge of speech." He pulled Jane close, hugged her tightly. "I've taken her under my wing, like my own daughter. We met in this very dungeon, right after I got here. This is where they put people who are caught making noise, like humming. The dragons think this is torture—the dampness, the cold. They don't realize that we like it here, that we come here to escape the work details, so we can study, and learn. I'm teaching Jane some English, poor tutor that I am."

"She hasn't made much progress," Sandra huffed.

"On the contrary, I think she's done pretty well. A lot better than I have learning dragon."

"Do you mean to say that the dragons have the faculty of speech?" Doc said.

"No, but they do have a language, and an amazingly complex one, at that. They talk with hand signals. The placement of each digit—"

"So that's why they kept waving their dirty paws in front of my face," Sandra exclaimed.

"Yes. And have you heard their strings?"

Scott laughed. "Sure. They just treated us to some of their chamber music."

"It's not music. The notes correspond to codes that the dragons learn from egghood. Jane can interpret that code, just as easily as you can read a book. And she knows dragon sign like the back of her hand. She's a natural linguist, and picking up more from me every day."

Rusty was enthusiastic. "Can she make sense out of their calligraphy, too?"

"Yes, she's a keen observer, apparently with total recall. I just wonder what she could have accomplished by now if she had had an education."

"Doc, this is great. If she can read their computer lingo I can figure out how to work their programs."

"That's assuming that we can gain access to a terminal. We don't exactly have the run of the house." Doc made exaggerated motions of feeling his clothing. "And I forgot my keys."

"Getting out of here is no problem." Scott walked over to the food trough. "The way they restock the salad bar is our highway to heaven. Someone thin, like Rusty or Sandra, can shinny up the chute, then come around and slip the bolt on the door."

"You're not getting me in that rat hole," Sandra said.

"Scott, I think you've got something—"

Sam cut Rusty off. "Wait a minute. We don't want to leave now. We just got here."

"An unusual way for a prisoner to speak about his cage. Excuse me, but do you mind if I sit down. This leg has had about all it can stand." Doc squatted on the floor, and the others crouched or sat in front of him. "Now, Sam, I believe you mentioned several escape routes you've been working on. Would you care to elucidate on them?"

"Well, sure, but like I said, I'm going to need help. I'm pretty sure we can get out of here, especially since the dragons are so short-pawed. For some reason they've been leaving in herds, so there's only a small contingent left behind."

"Have you any idea where they're going?"

"Sure. Right here." Sam snickered at the upraised eyebrows. "The question is *when* are they going. No, that doesn't sound right either. I never was too good in grammar. Anyhow, the warp field's been working overtime. Or maybe undertime. I don't know. Whatever the case, they're going somewhere in time—and not coming back. Jane says it started about the time I got here. They're migrating somewhen else."

"Now what do you suppose they have on their minds?" Doc said.

"Scales," Scott chuckled.

Sam jerked a thumb at his daughter. "You've been hanging around this one too long. She used to drive me and her mother crazy with her wisecracking." His eyes widened, his face fell. "You know, I've been so overwhelmed by recent events I plumb forgot to ask about your mother."

Sandra drew in her breath, put her fingers to her mouth.

"What—what is it?"

Doc cast his eyes down, fidgeting. He took a deep breath, raised his bushy white eyebrows, and stared straight at his son-in-law. "Sam, I don't quite know how to tell you this, but—"

"She's dead, isn't she?"

"Sam, she was with us. She—"

"Is she dead, or not? Don't beat around the bush, just tell me."

"She was wrapped in plastic when they took her off the flyer. She had hit her head, and—"

"That's enough!" Sam held up his hands. "Spare me the gory details. I—She's—The bastards. I'll kill 'em all. She's the only reason— It's just that she's so—she's—the only—woman I've ever loved . . . " Great, quivering tears streamed down his cheeks, dropped off his angular jaw onto his hairy, heaving chest. The confident, muscular stature drooped, deflated like a punctured balloon.

Sandra sucked in her breath, coughed back her own tears. She kept her hands tucked into her lap. Death Wind jabbed her with his elbow, made motions with his hand. Sandra sobbed louder, but reached out and placed her trembling fingers on her father's bare leg, squeezing. He grappled with her hand, brought it to his breast, hugged it, then raised it to his lips and kissed her palm.

"I love—you too—Sandy. It's just—"

"I know, Daddy. I know. But I'll take care of you now. You can count on me."

Father and daughter fell into each other's arms, crying openly. Scott gulped, found tears rolling down his own cheeks. He could hardly swallow. And he was afraid the others would hear him sniffing.

Doc's soft hand reached out again, to comfort. "I know it's difficult for you, Sam."

"My thoughts for her were the only thing that kept me going. Now—"

"I understand. Helen was my own flesh and blood. I raised her from an infant. I will miss her, too. But life goes on, and so must we. She will be alive within our hearts as long as we live, and we will carry her with us always. Helen was one who touched everyone she met, helped everyone she knew, giving of herself unselfishly. But at least her suffering in this world has ended. We must carry on her tradition, as she would expect us to. We can't give up now. She wouldn't allow it."

Sam ran his fingers through his daughter's

singed, shortened hair. He clutched her tightly against his chest. "I know you're right, Henry. You always are. And I don't intend to give up now. Not by a long shot. We're gonna blow this dragon land to kingdom come."

"You said it, Daddy."

"We still need a plan. We must have your ideas, and Jane's intimate knowledge of her community. And the people. We must free the people."

"That's not going to be easy. The people don't want to be free. Not the natives, anyway."

"Slaves enjoying their condition? That is contrary to the human psyche. Surely they are not so well off that they would accept domination."

"No, it's—well, it's hard to explain. You see, Jane's people have been here since this place was put together. In fact, they helped build it. Most of them were miners, caught underground. Because of their breeding, because they've never been allowed to talk, they have—retrogressed. They have the intellect, but not the—will. No desire. They're—pardon me for saying this, Jane—but they're mostly just dumb animals. Draft animals. Some of them till the fields, plant food, raise crops, reap fruits, grains, and vegetables. But most work for the dragons as either laborers or personal servants. You see, our dexterity is something the dragon slaves don't have. So, humans are treated like trainable monkeys."

"They ain't gonna treat me that way!" Sandra said vehemently.

"You see, Henry, the problem isn't that they don't want freedom. It's that they have no idea what freedom is. They've been kept in total ignorance. They don't know any other way of life. They're like living automatons, sleeping, eating, and doing what they're told. Trying to get them to revolt is like trying to convince cattle to stop giving milk.

"Now, the captives are different. There are others, like me, who've been—collected—most of them quite recently. We're a small but growing faction, whispering to each other when the dragons aren't paying attention, making plans at night, purposely hindering any employment we happen to be included in. If we get sent out in a work party, we try to sabotage the native workers' construction. Not enough to be obvious— we don't want to get anyone sent to the pens. But we conduct subversive operations, chinking away at their armor." Sam shrugged. "It's not

much, but we do what we can."

"Do you, or your people, know the layout of the city?" Rusty said.

"Every inch of it. Our duties carry us everywhere. And since the dragons look upon us as inferior animals, because they're so used to dealing with the native population, they don't think we have the capacity for learning—or revolt. What we really need in order to overthrow the bastards is a guiding influence." Sam stared hard at Doc. "Henry, you can provide that. You haven't lost any of your charm over the years, so I doubt if your political talents have faded. You got us together once before, you taught us how to fight." Sam stabbed a finger into the plastic deck. "You can do it. You can spark us where no one else can. And the natives have potential. Jane is proof of that. They don't lack intelligence, just initiative. If we can only get through to them . . . "

Doc rubbed his bearded chin. "Your praise fills me with trepidation. However, as far as reaching into their souls, cultivating their repressed inhibitions, liberating their true potential as thinking, self-aware beings, that's going to require some tangible powers of which I am not possessed. How can I reach them when they cannot speak, or understand speech?"

Sam hugged the native girl. "Through Jane. She's a natural messenger. She's been trying to communicate her whole life, but until recently she's been stifled by her environment. She can talk to the people in sign—"

"You mean, all the natives understand dragon finger speak?" Scott asked.

"Sure. How do you think they receive orders? The main problem is in teaching Jane to vocalize."

Doc placed a professional hand on the girl's throat, ran it up and down the tiny Adam's apple. "Say ah." He turned Jane's open mouth toward the light coming through the grille in the door. "Her larynx appears to be normal, and in good shape, although possibly underused. However, it's not a muscle, so it can't atrophy. It does not require constant exercise. Increased use may cause soreness, nothing else."

"Well, I guess I'll continue my lessons," Sam said.

"Scott is better." All heads turned to Death Wind. Sitting cross-legged, he pounded the blond on the back. "He is a good teacher. I learn from him better English. He teach Jane very well."

"Scott, what do you say? I admit I'm not too good at it." Sam smiled at Jane, while pointing a finger at Scott. "Would you like to have a new instructor? I'm sure he can teach you more than I ever could."

Jane looked at Scott. He blinked back at her. Slowly, she let her full lips part, revealed the glimmer of a smile. She held out her hand. "We are . . . friends?"

A huge grin spread across Scott's face. "You bet."

Jane arched an eyebrow.

Scott realized he spoke in the vernacular. "Yes, we are friends." He gestured widely with his hands. "We are all friends."

"Take good care of her," Sam said. "She means a lot to me."

"I'll do my best."

CHAPTER 7

Sam winced as he plucked a flea out of his beard. He rubbed it between thumb and forefinger, then placed it on his thumbnail and quickly rolled his other thumbnail over it. The small snap was a satisfying sound. "That's an amazing story, Henry."

Doc scratched leathery skin under his tunic. "Only the highlights, of course. I wouldn't want to bore you with details."

"You haven't lost your grand flair for adventure, that's for sure. And this private army you've recruited seems like it can tackle anything you throw at them. I'm sure if we put our heads together, we can break out of this place. Although, getting home across two continents presents quite a problem."

"We don't have any home," Rusty lamented.

"That's not true," Doc countered. "Wherever you are is home."

"Pop, come back to reality. A prison is not a home. Hanging curtains on the walls and carpeting the floor will never make it home. It'll always be a prison."

"Whatever happened to Grandpa?"

"It was one syllable too long. And stop trying to change the subject. I'm for breaking out of this berg and heading for the hills. Once we're on the outside, we can figure a way to blow the place up. You wanna play spy, you stay here with the rest of the retards."

"My dear, please be fair. Jane is the product of a disadvantaged community. She lacks education and opportunity, not intellect. If we can get through to her, we can get through to her people. You can help by showing some respect for her situation. We are all human beings, and we are all in this together."

"And I say forget the local yokels. Let's stir up the captured outsiders and make a run for it. They'll fight, at least."

Sam plucked another flea from his beard. "Toad, I thought your mother and I raised you better than that."

Sandra turned on him with a sneer. "You raised me to be a survivor. All right, I'll do whatever I have to do to save me and mine, but I won't risk my neck for a bunch of domestic sheep following the herd to slaughter. If they won't do anything to save themselves, I don't wanna have any part in doing it for them."

Death Wind placed a hand on Sandra's shoulder. "These people need help. Their minds are crippled, but can be healed. We can heal them."

"They can heal themselves. Why do we have to do it for them?"

"Men stick together. It is code."

Sandra jerked back as if struck. Death Wind's statement was not only the Nomad code, it was part of the Nomad marriage vow. Clenching her teeth tightly, she stared at him with dark, penetrating eyes. Death Wind did not stare down. Sandra climbed to her feet, and stalked two paces into a corner where she stood facing the plastic wall.

The silence in the cell brought a strident whistle to Scott's ear, a ghostly monotone that seemed to emanate from his head. He squinted with pain as he drew his wounded leg close to his chest, with knee to chin. After a long moment, he said, "Okay, folks, let's try to plan for the future and figure where we go from here."

"Not where, but when," Doc said distantly.

"Whatever, as long as—" Scott drew in his breath as a new wave of pain hit him. "Doc, all of a sudden it's hurting a lot. Could it be infected?"

"Not this soon." Doc bent forward, took Scott's foot, and stretched out the leg so it rested in his lap. He inspected the wound. "It takes longer than a few days for infection to set in. No, I suspect that in the healing process the blood is gorging the injured vessels. Let's try elevating the leg so that gravity draws the blood away from the extremity."

"Doc, I don't want to lose it. Is there anything we can put on it to prevent infection? Some kind of salve. We used to have medicines in Maccam City that—"

"Antibacterial ointments merely cover up the wound; once applied, they then become a bed of infection. All we have to do is keep the scab sterile. Under these conditions, clean will have to suffice. The bleeding is actually to your advantage. Perhaps . . . "

Jane dipped her hand into the trough and brought out a wad of crispy lettuce. "I . . . help." She knelt by Scott's side, swung his leg around so that it lay in her own lap, and rubbed the lettuce leaves delicately over the burn holes. Scott flinched at first, until he felt the coolness. Jane used the crinkled leaves as a washcloth; she patiently cleaned away the dirt, and debrided the wound.

Doc pursed his lips and nodded slowly. "Exactly what I would have done. This girl knows much more than we give her credit for. Simply because she cannot communicate her knowledge, and her feelings, does not mean that she is devoid of such intangibles."

"The natives know how to shift for themselves," Sam said. "They have no other choice."

When Jane finished cleansing the holes in Scott's calf, she ran the fingers of both hands along the back of his thigh. He felt a strange tingling sensation that was not confined to the area she was touching. Her long hair swung outward, and he could not help but stare at her bare breasts: they reminded him of firm, ripe pears. Jane did not look up at him; one hand stopped at a spot halfway up his thigh, and squeezed, while with the other she raked her long nails over his skin. Gradually, the pain in his leg faded until, it was little more than a dull throb.

Scott covered his lap with his hands. "Hey, that's really great. You've got the magic touch. The pain's almost gone."

Doc murmured, "She is obviously expert in the art of pressure points. A valuable asset, under the circumstances. I think we have much to learn from this backward and unsophisticated young lady. Sam?"

Sam crushed another flea between his thumbnails. "Yes."

"In your contact with these people, have they ever exhibited any special talents? Any—habits, or seemingly primitive proficiencies—that we may put to our advantage?"

"Well, I haven't been with them that long, but they do seem to have a natural acumen for anticipating dragon movements or demands. I mean, they seem to know exactly what's expected of them, and act without direct instruction. Almost like an innate ability to read dragon minds."

"Telepathy?"

"No, nothing like that. No, they just—well, I guess they've lived with dragons for so long that they know how the lizards think. They understand dragon psychology. Some of it is reading dragon methods of communication, of course, but it seems like they can interpret dragon body language—not just individual dragons, but overall patterns. They know intuitively what is expected of them, and they do it. It prevents them from getting zapped, or ending up in the pens."

Doc nodded thoughtfully. "A valuable survival skill."

"Excuse me, Sam." Rusty leaned forward over folded, lanky legs. "What are these 'pens' you keep referring to? Are they some kind of outside prison cells?"

"No, they're—they're not." Sam stared down at the floor. "They're where bad people are sent. People who do not conform, or who become sick and can't work. It's where old people go, and babies who die in childbirth, or infancy. It's where the dead are taken."

Rusty squinted in the dim light. "Is this a real place, or an allegorical heaven."

"Oh, it's real all right. And it's anything but heaven. No one who goes there ever comes back."

A long silence ensued, broken eventually by Jane's gasp and retreat. She dropped Scott's leg as she backed against the wall and covered her mouth with her hands. Her eyes blazed with abject fear.

Sam slithered to Jane's side and put his arms around her slender shoulders. "It's okay, honey. It's okay. Try to put it out of your mind."

The girl broke into uncontrollable sobs. She buried her face in Sam's chest.

"She doesn't understand everything we say, but she knows about the—" Sam broke off with gritted teeth. He covered her ears with his hands and continued in a whisper. "Her mother was taken to the pens. Her father died a long time ago. She's an orphan."

"Her sensitivity to the subject is understandable." Doc patted the girl on the leg. To Sam,

"Do you think we can reach these people through her? Can we open a line of communication? Do we have a chance of breaking them free of their Pavlovian training? Can we foment revolt?"

Sam slowly released Jane from his grasp. She eased back to a sitting position, wiping tears from her cheeks with callused palms.

Sam sighed. "Henry, I don't know. I haven't seen much initiative here, at least among the native population. Other captives, like myself, will jump to the cause—given the slimmest chance of success. Most of them would rather die fighting than live cowering. But there aren't that many of us—certainly not enough to carry off a revolution. We have no weapons, no tools, no outside allies . . . "

Doc nodded. "Other than Death Wind's knife, the only weapon that we possess is our collective knowledge. Psychological warfare notwithstanding, mental prowess is the best armament in any conflict. And solidarity, of course."

"We can get the captives to stick together, no problem, but we're only a couple dozen strong. They're real scrappers, like you: brought up fighting the dragons, and suffering losses. But our only hope of reaching the natives is through Jane. We need an interpreter so we can talk to these people."

Scott moved his injured leg into a more comfortable position. "I don't know how well I can pick up tone talk or finger speak, but I'm sure I can teach English to Jane so she can translate for us."

"And I want to learn dragon scratch," Rusty added. "Once I figure out what those squiggles mean, I can crack their input codes. You let me loose inside their computer and I can do some real damage."

Sam shook his head. "You people are incredible. Listening to you, I'd believe we were winning this war, and only stamping out pockets of resistance, instead of being jailbirds with a life sentence."

"One must always maintain a positive outlook," Doc said.

"But you're halfway between inspiration and the absurd. Why, if I didn't know you better, I'd think you were insane."

"A modicum of madness is what keeps the dragons guessing." A quixotic smile touched Doc's lips. "I've always relied upon the irrational approach in order to keep them off balance. If we're going to win this time, we must strike when they least expect it. This girl, and her people, may be the key to victory."

"All right, I'm sorry." All eyes turned to Sandra. She stepped out of her corner and through the middle of the powwow, then knelt by Jane's side. She held out her hand. "Maybe I flew off the handle."

Jane stared at the outstretched palm.

"She doesn't understand what you mean," Sam said. "Her people don't greet that way."

Sandra looked nonplussed. "How do they demonstrate friendship?"

"They groom each other."

"Huhn?"

"They go through their hair, picking out fleas, ticks, and lice."

"How barbaric. What do they think they are, a bunch of chimpanzees?"

Sam took his time before answering, then spoke slowly with exaggerated enunciation. "Sandra, these people do not live in a style of choice. The dragons keep them rigidly controlled. They work in the fields, they live in a corral, and they have no bathing facilities. Once a week the dragons irrigate the stalls with high-pressure hoses. They are surrounded by vermin of every kind. Prisoners of war are forced to act according to their jailers' bidding—or suffer the consequences. The natives have simply developed a mode of living that fits the conditions that have been forced upon them."

Sandra said in a huff, "Look, I just felt sorry for her. Okay? I didn't ask for a sermon." She plopped down next to Jane, extracted the comb from her back pocket, and ran it through the native girl's long tresses. The hair was tangled in knots that pulled sharply, but Jane gave no sign of minding painfulness. Sandra pulled the curly locks over the other girl's tanned shoulders. "As long as we're cooped up together in this cell, we may as well make the best of it."

Sam grimaced at Doc, who winked back with a quirky smile.

Scott dragged his eyes away from Jane's bared breasts. "Sam, tell us about this place. What's the layout? What do we need to know to stay alive?"

"The most important thing is to do as you're told. Dragons tolerate no disobedience. All the guards have pain guns, and even if they have two brains they don't think twice about using them. They—"

"Excuse me, Sam, but the enlarged sacral plexus, where the spinal cord passes through the pelvis, is used for motor control of the hindquarters rather than for expanded cognitive processes. It is not even an afterthought."

"Henry, I'm not a vertebrate anatomist, or an animal physiologist. I was just speaking colloquially."

Doc spread his hands. "Please continue."

"Thank you. Well, like I was saying, dragons may be slow on the draw, but the guards have real itchy trigger fingers. Sometimes, if you sense it coming, you can avoid the pain shot by jumping out of the way. You act as if you'd been hit, and they don't know any better. But the best thing to do is to follow instructions. When they call, you come. When they tell you to get to work, you do it."

"That'll be hard for us," Rusty commented. "We don't know their lingo."

Sam nodded. "Yes, I had some trouble at first, and got zapped a few times because of it. But I learned to do what everyone else was doing. If they were picking fruit, I picked fruit. If they were digging holes, I dug holes. If they were hauling trash, I hauled trash. If they were called upon to pick parasites off the dragons' backs, that's what I did. I've picked up some of the tone commands, so I can understand the simpler orders, like get up, walk, run, and come here."

"Picking parasites?" Scott said with disgust.

"That's our greatest occupation. Human fingers are nimble enough to pluck out the insects that infest their scales, something they find impossible to do themselves. It's easy work."

"Yuck." Sandra stopped combing in midstroke. "It sounds nauseating. You ain't gonna get me to touch one of those slant-eyed lizards, unless it's to slip a knife in its throat."

"My dear, I completely understand your revulsion," Doc said sympathetically. "I would sooner swim in raw sewage than pet a dragon, but the alternative for resistance is less desirable. You would be well advised to curb your antagonistic attitude in favor of survival."

"And maybe you should butt out—" Sandra thrust the comb onto her lap. After a few seconds of thoughtful silence, she picked it up and resumed dressing Jane's hair. "Well, you may have something there."

"As usual, your grandfather is infallibly correct," said Sam. "Oh, we're all used to being zapped with the pain guns. They keep them on low power so no one gets incapacitated: crippled slaves don't work well, and too many high-power hits does permanent damage to the central nervous system. The guards strike at random just often enough to invoke their might, and as a reminder of their authority."

"So we go with the flow," Scott said. "What about the city? How big is it, and what keeps people from getting out of it?"

"It's about five miles across and designed like the cross section of a tree, with a central core surrounded by concentric rings. Right in the middle is the time transport structure: a clear plastic dome embedded with power nodules aimed inward. It looks like a transparent porcupine turned inside out. It's the tallest structure in the city, so you can see it from everywhere: especially at night, because of the coruscating . . . focusing nodes. Is that what you call them?"

Doc nodded, and Sam went on. "Anyway, encompassing that are a couple of nuclear generating plants, mechanical spaces, transformer stations, and guard shacks. The next ring is administrative. All the bigwigs live and work in a girdle of two-story houses interconnected with courtyards. The Silo, as I call it, where you met the head cheese, is in the northern quadrant. There are alleyways that pass through the living quarters to let technicians reach their workstations.

"Outside that you've got a separation zone filled with storage sheds, soup vats, vegetable hoppers, granaries, freezers, meat larders, and miscellaneous warehouses. Beyond that are the slave quarters, both dragon and human, then come the cultivated fields and the dinosaur kennels. I call them dinosties; they smell worse than pigs. Oh, and the landing platforms are at the extreme perimeter. That's where the rampart takes over. Looks like the Great Wall of China, only the parapets are thicker. And the battlements are heavily defended with casemated laser guns. It beats me who they think they're going to fight off. The range is full of dinosaur herds, but they're not going to attack. It's just dragon offensive psychology, I guess."

"Or offensive dragon psychology," Scott quipped.

"Do they have communication links?" Rusty wanted to know.

Sam nodded vigorously. "Hard wire. And slave-drawn carts for transportation. This whole place is a weird mix of primitive encampment and futuristic technology."

"If the walls are slick plastic, we'll never storm them," Scott said. "Are there external stairs, or ramps, or do we have to break in through armored doors?"

"Doors that hinge open from the bottom, but without the moats. I've only seen them from a dis—"

"None of that matters," Doc interrupted with a wave of a gnarled hand. He stretched out his bad leg and kneaded it absently. "The outer barricade is the least of our problems. What is important is getting back in time."

"In time for what?"

"Oh, we'll get back," Sandra interjected. "If we have to crawl, walk, or skip to ma Lou. No walls ever held me in before, and they ain't gonna stop me now. I'll get outa here if I have to huff, and puff, and—"

"This is not the time for fairy tales," Doc said abruptly. "That time is past. And that's our way out of here—through the middle."

Scott placed a hand on the old man's forehead. "Doc, are you feeling all right? Can I get you some more water?"

"Dehydration must be affecting—" Rusty started.

"No, no, no. I'm all right." Doc gently pushed Scott's hand away. He stroked his long white beard. "Listen to me for a moment. Hear me out. Now, tell me, where do you fight a fire?"

"Huhn?" said Sandra.

"I said—"

"At base," Death Wind intoned.

"Right. And how do you beat an enemy?"

"Cut off head."

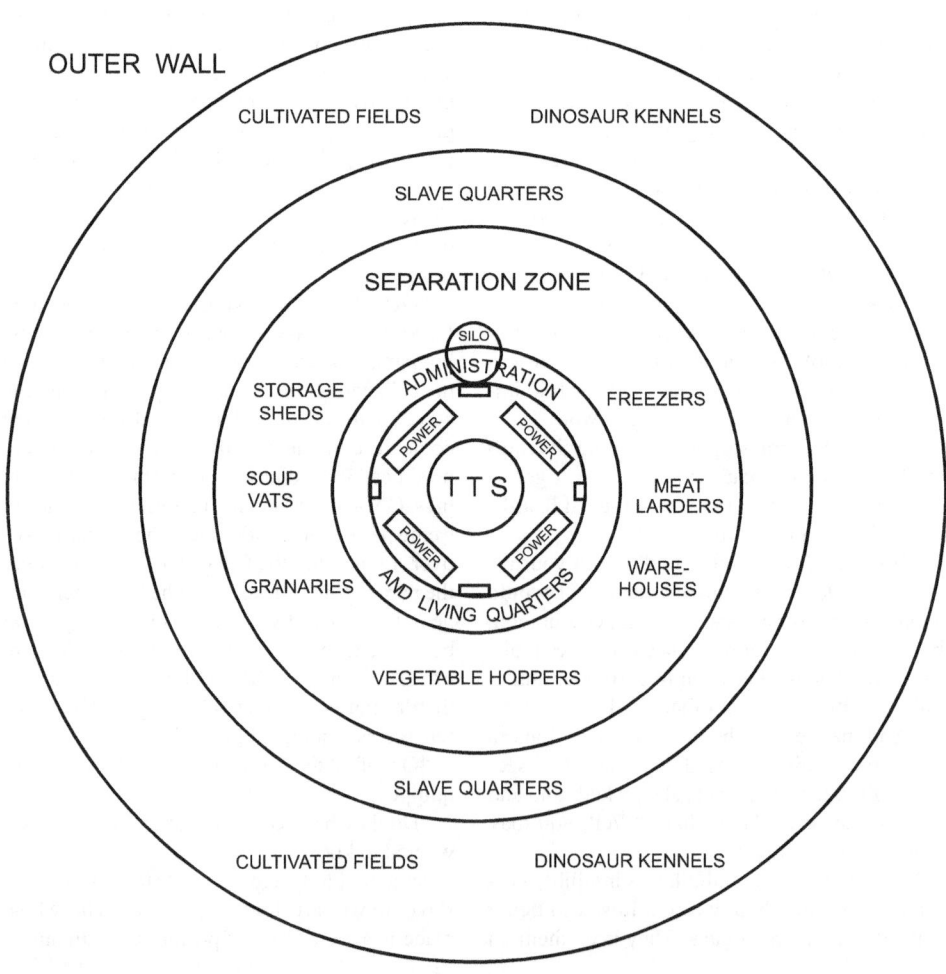

"Exactly. You don't squirt water on licking flames, and you don't conquer a foe by slashing away at his arms. Every Nomad knows that."

Sandra said in frustration, "Quit talking in parables and spit it out. What the hell are you trying to say?"

"I'm saying that we do not want to escape. Not yet. We have come a long way to get here, but we have farther to go before our war is won. We have worsted our opponent in only one battle. In doing so, we have learned that our adversary has more extensive holdings. That means that we must strike again—not just at this stronghold, but at the origin of evil."

Doc paused, and stared each one in the eye. "We must fight the dragons when and where they come from. Their present is our past, and unless we destroy them *then*, we will have no future. Our plan of attack is clear: we must go back in time."

CHAPTER 8

Doc surveyed the crowded barn with professional interest. Nearly naked natives lay strewn about the plastic floor like a crateful of rag dolls dropped through a chute; they were dazed by torpor. The heat in the auditorium-sized room was unbearable, the stench even worse. The slaves were crammed together under the shade of the roof, preferring the torridity of bodily contact to the near combustion temperature of the adjacent, sun-baked corral.

"So, what do you think?"

Doc mopped his expansive forehead with a dirty piece of hide. "Are they always like this?"

"What? Listless? Thoughtless? Moving like automatons?" Sam shrugged his shoulders. "Can you expect anything more?"

"I don't know. I've never encountered a condition such as this. They lie about like sated sloths. It's frightening. I had no idea what we were up against."

"You can understand how exceptional Jane is among this bunch."

"Even the children do not move about. They do not play."

"They're not allowed to play. They're not allowed to learn. They're not allowed anything but a food allotment and a place to sleep."

Doc gulped. "It is a truly pathetic human condition."

"Now you understand how getting them to fight for their freedom is as useless as convincing a rock to walk uphill. The captives show a little more spirit—the more recent ones, anyway. Eventually, after they're here long enough, they lose their will, their incentive; they become like the rest. Maybe we can cure some of them—those that still retain the power of speech and the capacity of independent thought."

Doc sighed. He knelt by a woman whose skin was shriveled with age, whose body was wasted through overuse. Tiny breasts like sagging prunes quivered as she panted like a dog in an overwarm cage. Her stare was vacant, her eyes sunken into her skull. Doc held her wrist and counted her pulse.

"She's not far from the pens," Sam said sadly. "She hasn't moved in three days. The workload has been light, and they haven't needed every available hand. But if she's still comatose the next time they clear out the barn, she'll take a one-way stretcher ride."

Doc stood slowly, his eyes riveted on the pitiful package of humanity. "The dragons do not care for the sick, or the aged, or the infirm, or the insane. That is what separates them from humanity."

"You're right. They dispose of the useless. I guess they figure there are more where they came from."

"And the pens? Where they bury the bodies. Is that where the mercy killings take place."

Sam jumped, as if his whole body had been struck with spasm. "Who said anything about mercy killings?"

"Why, I thought you said . . . "

"I said . . . I said . . . " Sam's face sagged like melted plastic. "Oh, Henry, can we step over to the side?" Without waiting for an answer, he picked his way through the insensate forms. Doc hobbled along behind him. They stopped at the edge of the barn. Sam stared out into the blazing sunshine and the dirt-filled corral. In the distance, the fortress wall dominated the landscape. "Henry, I . . . "

"What is it, son?"

"Henry, I—" Sam gulped in several deep breaths of fetid air. "I killed an old woman the other day just like that one," He jerked a thumb over his shoulder. "Two of them, in fact."

Doc's voice was craggy. "What do you mean? Were you treating them?"

"I had been, yes. But they were too far gone.

Even a cursory examination must have shown you that there's not much we can do to cure disease, or relieve their suffering. I have no instruments, no drugs. The dragons would have taken them to the pens . . . "

"I don't understand." Doc's bushy white eyebrows pinched sharply. "If they died under your care, that is not the same as killing them. Every doctor, when he takes the Hippocratic Oath, swears to attend people to the best of his ability. But sometimes, a patient's condition is beyond human attention. You mustn't blame yourself—"

"No, Henry. I strangled them. With my bare hands. I—I couldn't stand to see them dragged off to the pens for—extermination. I . . . " Great, glowing tears rolled down Sam's sweat-covered face and were soaked up by the black beard. His smooth features convulsed into a caricature of Sardonicus. His chest heaved. "I had to do it."

Doc leaned against his son-in-law and placed a fatherly arm around the taller man's shoulders. "Sam, what is it about the pens that is so awful. What do the dragons do to people there? Do they use them for—food?"

"Worse. Much worse." Sam wiped the tears off his cheeks. He broke Doc's embrace and turned to face him. "They have these vats—like giant mixers—with sharpened cross grates that are pulled back and forth manually. Dragon slaves operate the machine. All leftover organic material is dumped into the hopper. The grates slice it all up, very slowly."

Sam took a deep breath. "Garbage, bones, domesticated dinosaur meat, dead dragons and humans. Nothing is wasted. And if the people are still alive when they are dropped in—you can hear them scream as their flesh is macerated, and piece by piece they are ground into—fertilizer."

* * *

"How's the leg, Scott?" Rusty whispered.

"Could be worse." Scott crawled into the shade and massaged his sore calf. "It itches like crazy, though."

Rusty folded his lanky form into an imitation chain link. "Remember what Doc said. Don't scratch it."

"Don't worry. I'm scared to death it'll have to be amputated."

Jane sidled up against the orange plastic wall, out of the direct rays of the sun, and stretched Scott's wounded leg into her lap. Gently she kneaded the flesh. "Better?"

"Yes, much better." He pointed a finger at her and smiled. "Hey, that's another new word for you." "I—speak—learn—English?"

Scott pronounced his words with care. "Yes, you are learning to speak English very well."

"Well?" Jane spelled out a dragon equivalent with her fingers. "Water—ground."

"No, not that kind of well. This well is like good. The word that better is the superlative of—I mean, it's like—"

"You're confusing her with syntax," Rusty said.

"Then help me."

"Well, you're the teacher."

"Well?" Jane said again, frowning.

"Now you've confused her more." Scott shook his head. "Jane, forget it. Just—we'll start over. When I say—"

Jane abruptly let go of his leg and stood up. She motioned with her hands for the boys to follow suit.

"There are no dragons around—"

Rusty grabbed Scott by the armpits and hoisted him to his feet. "I don't see any either, but she hasn't been wrong yet."

"Great, the only break of the day, and the first time we get to talk, and they have to cut it short. I wish we could get back into solitary confinement. It was cool there, and nobody bothered us."

Jane silently shuffled off along the roadway.

"Shut up, Scott." Rusty dragged Scott after the girl. "I got zapped twice this morning, and I don't relish another dose of nerve juice."

"What's the matter with us, Rusty? We never talk any more."

Rusty jabbed him in the rib cage. "Quiet." Now he heard the faint strumming of a harp, plucking a tune that was indecipherable to him. Slaves marched in from all quadrants. Rusty was hot enough without the press of bodies closing in on him. Worse than the confined heat was the mindless stare of the native slaves: bleak, inanimate eyes glimmered slightly less than chunks of burnt-out coal. Human slaves went about their assigned chores as sluggishly as their dragon counterparts.

Scott whispered out of the corner of his mouth. "I've seen vegetable soup with more life than these folks."

A dragon guard pivoted ponderously on stalk-like legs. Its tongue darted out with a hiss. If half drew its stun gun, but replaced it when the twang of a harp commanded movement. Jane, Scott, and Rusty tagged along with the mob. If Jane knew what their next job was to be, she did not vociferate such privity. She never spoke when dragons were within audible range.

The roadway was bounded on both sides by parapets over which the dragons, whose grotesque heads crowned elongated necks, could see. Rusty, tall as he was, stayed constantly frustrated by the high-walled corridors. The overall city plan was simplistic, but the map he was building in his mind was intended as an aid for eventual overthrow.

"Looks like field work," Scott muttered. "Unless they're taking us home."

Rusty glanced behind him and observed their position in relation to the shimmering time transport structure that dominated the foreground. After sweeping foul-smelling private quarters all morning, he would be glad to work in the open air. Although the fruits and vegetables were grown naturally in the ground, instead of in troughs of chemical liquids, the farm work reminded him nostalgically of his youth in Maccam City—now a painfully dim memory.

They were brought up short by a tonal command. For a long time natives milled like cattle in the hot sun, under the baleful stare of dragon guards. Several technicians pushed through the throngs of people. As one passed him by, Rusty studied its equipment vest and made mental notes of the strange instruments it carried. One technician stopped in front of a formless plastic building, with a typical blob facade, and inserted a slender metal rod into a narrow slot. Two guards then pulled back on large handles, sliding open a ten-foot-tall wall panel on greased tracks.

A blast of icy air erupted from the opening. The white mist that touched Rusty's bare arms was a wet condensation that made him shiver. At first, contrasted to the noontime heat, the cold felt good; but soon the frigid temperature became a discomfort. He tried to hang back when the crowd moved forward, but the pressure from behind was too great. He marched with the others into the sanctum of the cold storage locker.

"Get a whiff of that ammonia," Scott muttered. "They could use a little maintenance on those loose solder joints."

"Are you volunteering?"

"Sure. I could fix the refrigeration so it would never work again."

Rusty hugged his chest and rubbed his arms vigorously. Already his teeth were chattering. Beside him, although he saw goose bumps rippling her skin, Jane seemed not to mind. She emplaced an extended index finger perpendicular to her lips, the way Scott had showed her to indicate silence. Rusty nodded affirmatively.

Ahead of them, natives were piling sides of dinosaur meat onto four-wheeled dollies, and pushing them back in fire brigade fashion. Rusty adopted a station where all he had to do was give each cart a shove toward the door; the next person in line did the same.

The building was actually a catacomb of separate freezers, each with a different type of stores. Thickly cloaked technicians directed the work force using a combination of tone talk and finger speak. They were clearly in a rush. The guards wore long ponchos, but carried power packs and stun guns on the outside where the armament was immediately accessible. There was no cause for a show of force, for the natives, not afforded the luxury of extra clothing, labored with feverish abandon.

With the clattering of wheels, the drone of machinery, and the hubbub of activity, Scott and Rusty had little difficulty in making observations and exchanging a few words. Scott forged ahead and entered one of the side chambers with part of the native crew. He stepped out a few moments later, after the room was emptied of its supply of flesh, and joined Rusty in loading the frozen slabs on a three-tiered cart.

"Quit an assembly line they have here."

Rusty's teeth were chattering so hard that it was all he could do to nod.

Scott finished packing the lower tray and pushed the cart on its way. "Come on, let's check out this place."

Jane shook her head vigorously when she saw Scott and Rusty mix with the throng of natives, and work their way deeper into the freezer complex. Rusty desperately wanted to run outside where the sun was hot enough to fry eggs. He was afraid that he would shake apart like a motor with an unbalanced flywheel. His curiosity was tempered by the biting pain of cold. Only Scott's decisive conduct forced Rusty onward.

"Let's see if there's a way of sabotaging this place," Scott said. He squeezed through the crowd of uncomplaining natives, pulling Rusty along by the hand. "Maybe we can break a few pipes and spoil some meat."

A guard took notice of their surreptitious movements. Its hiss was lost in the clamor of activity, but Rusty saw the pink tongue dart out a warning. He and Scott joined a group that was unstacking collapsible stretchers. They grabbed one of the flattened litters and, following the direction of the others, unfolded the wheels from the undercarriage. When they were done, they had a waist-high gurney.

"I wonder what they use these for?" Scott asked.

Rusty clamped his mouth shut; his teeth hurt from chattering so hard. He saw another gurney being pushed toward an oblong doorway, so he followed suit. He waited next to a distracted guard, suffering from the cold worse than Scott, until an opening appeared in the line entering the room. He pushed his cart inside right behind another. The nearly naked native stumbled suddenly, fell to his knees, then crashed to the floor with a dull thud. Rusty jumped to his aid.

As he rolled the old man over, a searing bolt of pain engulfed him from behind. He had only one glimpse of the old man's face, the rough craggy beard, the cracked and withered skin, the gaping mouth that tried to suck in air, the purpling cheeks that was a sure sign of cyanosis; then he was flung back by reflex action as his muscles went into painful spasms. He rolled aside, an instinctive reaction to avoid a follow-up shot. He came to rest against a frozen shank.

Every nerve ending in Rusty's body screamed for mercy. The cold was temporarily forgotten. He looked up quickly at the leering guard; it was making no attempt to fire again. It simply stared down at him, working the fingers of its free paw. Rusty nodded and got halfway up. His legs were frost-nipped; his muscles responded grudgingly. He fell back down, on top of the rock-hard slab of meat.

For a moment his eyes closed. He swallowed as a wave of nausea threw his stomach contents into a maelstrom. The pain ebbed. Slowly, he became aware of his surroundings. The cold hammered at him again. He pushed himself off the frozen steak. He stopped partway to his feet, immobilized.

After a long moment, the urge to vomit was rekindled. Fear galvanized his legs like those of Volta's experimental frogs. He kicked away until he came up hard against the thick tail of a dragon guard. He leaned back on the lizard for

support, unable to take his eyes off the grisly scene before him.

Cold eyes stared sightlessly back at him. This was not just another dinosaur steak sliced for the stew pot. It was a frozen human corpse.

*   *   *

Sandra glared at the technician that had just finished waving its paws at her. All morning she and Death Wind had picked cotton with a group of natives: work they learned easily. The afternoon had been spent in weaving thread in a mill; neither had ever seen a loom before, requiring them to team up with natives who knew the job by rote. Now, the couple had been singled from the crowd.

When he saw Sandra's mouth open, Death Wind took her by the arm and pushed her forward. Together they approached the finger-speaking technician. Out of the corner of his eye, the Nomad saw a dragon guard reach for its stun gun; the reptile paused with its paw on the handle, the weapon undrawn, when the human pair stopped and looked up at the lizard in charge.

The technician turned on its clawed feet and clicked on the plastic flooring out of the building. Death Wind pushed Sandra along. The guard followed.

"What do they want?" Sandra said in a barely audible voice.

"Follow."

Sandra shrugged out of Death Wind's grasp. "I don't need two bosses."

Death Wind hung back far enough to miss tripping over the dragon's swinging tail. They were marched at a slow pace out of the factory. The sun was low on the western horizon; the temperature was not uncomfortably hot. They were led along a narrow roadway to a main thoroughfare where other people joined the exodus that was heading toward the center of town.

The blue coruscations of the time transport structure were hypnotic. An azure ring of energy started at the base of each cone-shaped focusing node, ran along its narrowing length, and burst with a snap at the pinpoint tip. The cycle repeated itself with increasing speed and intensity. The ball of potential energy grew brighter with each coruscation. Multiplied a thousand times, the clear plastic dome was a mind-boggling aura of pure power.

Death Wind was looking at the mountain-sized transporter when it discharged its pent-up static charge in one huge explosion: like a sharp peal of thunder of magnificent proportions. A thousand shooting bolts of electricity directed at the central core left searing lines embedded on his retinas; for several long seconds he was blind. As his sight returned, the eerie coruscations started recycling, and the transport nodule was prepared for the next passage through time.

Sandra and Death Wind were herded into a compound where a throng of natives milled. The Nomad took the opportunity to tank up from a water trough. After a while the people were prodded through a gate, led along a narrow alley, and lined up along the perimeter of the dome. Not a single person spoke. Death Wind observed his fellow men, and saw none with any curiosity in their eyes about what they were about to experience.

"DW, look at that!"

Death Wind poked Sandra in the rib cage. She shut up immediately.

A long line of gurneys was being wheeled along the streets, two natives to each. The procession stopped at the edge of the dome. Upon each stretcher was laid a naked human body, stiff with rigor mortis. A technician inspected the grisly cargoes, then waved each team through the arched opening.

"What are they doing?"

Death Wind poked her again. It was easy to see through the thick clear plastic what was going on inside. One by one the gurneys disappeared into the house-sized transfer zone. An opaque, blue effervescent light obscured further observation. The dragon slaves waddled back out. The stretchers kept on coming until a score was swallowed by the electric curtain. As the discharging nodes whined in their final excitation, Death Wind closed his eyes tightly. The transfer was as loud as an overhead thunderstorm, the brilliant incandescence like a solar prominence. It was over in an instant.

"Something crazy is going on. What the hell do they want with a bunch of dead people?"

Dragon slaves reentered the transfer zone. They exited with crates and boxes and bags, all manufactured from plastic pulp or woven of resinous thread. They dropped their loads at the dome entrance. The natives who had wheeled in the gurneys were ordered to pick up the heavy loads and carry them away. When that work force was depleted, the group of which Sandra and Death Wind were a part was put to the task.

Like automatons the natives lumbered along the roadway. Sandra hoisted a sealed carton to her shoulder and followed wordlessly. Death Wind did the same. A heavily armed escort accompanied the train of laborers through the power generation sphere. The air reverberated with the clatter of machinery and humming transformers. Heat exhausted from the cooling towers made the passage nearly unbearable. Overhead, a sealed, clear plastic tube that was suspended from a track afforded a comfortable atmosphere for technicians making the trek through the mechanical works. Straight ahead was the Silo, the dragon administrative complex.

Led by an armed guard, the natives filed through a narrow archway. Tone talking, a technician directed them where to pile the goods. A caped administrator appeared when it was Sandra's turn to unship her carton. Its harp twanged shrilly. Sandra froze with the carton waist high. Behind her, Death Wind halted in midstride. He did not understand the signal, but knew that its command overrode that of the technician. Lizard fingers wriggled silently, then the caped dragon turned and waddled off.

"Follow," Death Wind whispered. Already, a guard was pulling out its gun. Death Wind placed a hand on Sandra's back and shoved her forward. "Follow."

The guard tagged along at a discreet distance. Its gun was drawn and aimed. The caped dragon slowly preceded them up a ramp to a second-story balcony. It entered private quarters where two guards stood in waiting. The room was sparsely furnished with utilitarian seats and tables. The eight-foot-tall dragon perched on a stool behind what could have been a workbench. Piercing lizard eyes glared at the human slaves.

Death Wind moved forward and placed his package on the workbench in front of the dragon. Even sitting, the lolling head was a foot higher than the Nomad's. When no stun bolts stabbed out at him, he knew that he had made the right interpretation. As he stepped back, he stared silently but meaningfully at Sandra. She deposited her carton next to his.

The dragon leader ripped open the plastic package with curved talons. With a dexterity that Death Wind did not know the dragons possessed, it pulled out a clawful of slender metal tubes. Each was the size of a rifle barrel, one end of which was enlarged to fit the dragon palm.

After laying the tubes on the bench top, it deftly picked up one in each claw.

It aimed the narrow end of the instrument at Sandra. The. scintillating burst of light caught her in the midriff. She gasped, bent forward at the waist, and fell to the floor in a heap.

Death Wind was caught in midleap by the burst of light from the other instrument. He did not see the floor hit him in the face.

CHAPTER 9

"Rusty, my boy. Rusty!" Doc shook the lad as hard as he dared. In the dim light of a waning moon he could see little more than a long, writhing form. "Wake up, my boy."

"Wha—what." Eyelids flickered weakly for a moment, then opened sharply. Eyeballs darted in their sockets like bouncing marbles. Rusty shivered with ague. "Doc, is that you?"

"Yes, my boy." Doc placed one hand on Rusty's sweaty forehead, the other on his wrist. He counted Rusty's pulse in relation to his own, a procedure that he had perfected after years of practice.

"I'm so cold—and yet I'm hot. My head—"

"You're getting over a fever, my boy. Try to relax—"

"Doc! There's a guard coming in from the corral." Scott scrambled on all fours along the straw-filled floor. Breathing hard, he slid to a stop next to his young companion. "It must have been the noise—"

"Where is Jane?"

"I thought she was here."

"She left right after you. Didn't you—"

A cone of light stabbed through the barn door opening. The dragon guard was illuminated by the backlash of the brilliant searchlight attached to the power pack slung over sloping, scaled shoulders. Another dragon marched behind it, this one armed with a stun gun. The beam of stark white light passed over sleeping forms with the intensity of the noonday sun. Awakened by the disturbance, natives squirmed in their straw matting.

Doc threw several handfuls of straw over top of Rusty. "Quiet, lad. Just rest easy until they pass." He buried himself under a layer of bedding so he could watch the proceedings without showing his eyes to the guards. He lay barechested and without his sandals. When the light swung in his direction he closed his eyes tight. The light lingered overlong. He half expected the kick of a clawed foot or a stab of pain from the stun gun. At long last, darkness returned and the dragons continued their inspection of the other prisoners. Many minutes passed before the guards left the barn. Doc realized that he had been holding his breath. "I do say, that was a close one."

"What's going on?" Rusty squeaked

"Are you okay," Scott wanted to know. "We've been worried about you."

"Well, I feel a little weak—"

"The fever is broken." Doc examined Rusty's hands and feet as best he could; his eyes had not yet readjusted to the darkness. "You had a touch of hypothermia from your sojourn into the freezers, and a bit of frostbite as well. How do your fingers and toes feel?"

Rusty made exaggerated motions of testing his extremities. "Well, they feel a little funny—kind of numb."

"That will pass. They got you out of there before any permanent damage was done."

"Who did? The last thing I remember—" Rusty winced as he rubbed his temples with his knuckles.

"We stood you up and walked you out. Jane and I—where the heck is she?" Scott twisted around. The rustling of straw attested to minor movement within the barn, but that was nothing more than native folk getting back to sleep. "Doc, are you sure she followed me?"

"Quite sure." Doc reached over Rusty and touched Scott on the arm. "You needn't worry about her. She is quite capable of taking care of herself."

"That's not the point. I just don't like—"

Jane alighted from the air with a stealth that neither made a sound nor moved a stalk of straw. She crouched on the balls of her feet, poised like an animal about to pounce on its prey. "I—am—here."

Scott reached out for her. "Jane."

She took his hand and held it to her breast. "You—okay?"

"Sure, I'm fine."

"You gone?"

"Just for a little while. When Rusty started calling out in his sleep, I ran out to the corral as lookout. Good thing, too. But where did you disappear to?"

Jane pointed toward the ceiling.

"I don't understand."

She made scratching motions with her hands. "I climb."

Scott shook his head. "Doc, do you know what she's talking about?"

"I can think of a possible interpretation, but I prefer not to accept it without a practical demonstration. Jane, would you mind showing us?" He pointed to her with a crooked finger. "You—climb."

In a flash she leaped upward—and did not come down. She clung momentarily to the crude plastic wall, then scampered along the vertical barrier like a nimble mountain goat traversing a rocky ledge. She ascended twenty feet to the ceiling, hung there for a moment, then returned to the floor level by a different route.

Scott looked at her, his jaw sagging.

"Ah. Just what I thought. I saw some of the other children playing a similar game the other day—without her awesome agility, of course. She is indeed a person of rare talent."

"You like?"

"Yes, my dear. I do indeed like."

Jane pointed at each of them in turn, including herself, each time extending a finger. She held up her hand with her thumb withdrawn. "Where Sam?"

Doc said, "He went on a scouting mission. He may have gone through the corral into the next barn."

"Dra—gon?"

"I'm sure he will take great care. He is quite an enterprising individual. I am more concerned about Sandra and Death Wind. While we were on KP, they got picked up for some other detail. They have not come back. Hopefully, Sam will bring some news of their whereabouts. Rusty, exercise your arms and legs for me, please."

The redhead stretched and curled and did some sit-ups. "Whew, I'm still a little stiff. Mostly my back. And my memory's a little fuzzy—" He sat still for a moment, head tilted. "I remember the cold—the awful cold. And other people—"

Scott ran his hands along the walls. "The surface is lined with horizontal swellings, as if the plastic extruded through slits in the forms when it was still molten, but I still don't see how she can climb like that. The lips don't stick out more than a quarter inch."

"Scott! Was I seeing things, or were there really people—bodies—in that last freezer com-partment?"

"Sorry, Rusty." Scott sat down next to his friend and folded his legs Indian fashion. "It was pretty scary. There were rows and rows of them, all stacked up like books on a shelf. I thought for sure the guards were going to gun us down when we carried you out, but you weren't the only one to drop from the cold. Doc, it wasn't cold like snow, it was—it stung. It burned—like a hot coal, or a soldering iron."

"Yes, it sounds more like dry ice—solid carbon dioxide." Doc squeezed his chin and ran his hand down his long white beard. "It freezes at over a hundred degrees below zero. It is used as a refrigerant in systems—"

"Doc! Forget about dry ice." Rusty leaned forward, shoulders back. "The important thing is, why did they freeze those people? What are they going to do with them? And where were they taking them?"

"Well, uh, Sam had some interesting observations in that vein." Doc glanced at Jane. From the expression on her face, she was painfully aware of what he was saying. "However, there is no need to go into it now. As long as you survived the experience—"

"A lot of others didn't," Scott interjected. "I saw half a dozen natives pass out either from the cold, or from the sudden return to the outside heat. The dragons just dragged them away by the legs, the same as you'd drag dead game."

"I believe we have firmly established that the dragons have no sense of moral obligation where human beings are concerned; perhaps even where they themselves are concerned. They consider us a lower life form to be utilized as they see fit: as draft animals, as food, and as—whatever. Let us accept that. Instead of flinging incriminations of their heinous activities, let us concentrate our energies on circumventing their master plan of extinction of the human race and the dominance of dragons. That is what we should think about."

Rusty sat back on his elbows. "Sure, Doc, I guess you're right."

"And the sooner the better," Scott added. "Let's start by ganging up on the guards the next time they make the rounds. After what I saw in the freezers, I want to spill some blood—lizard blood."

"You are beginning to sound as impetuous as my granddaughter, which alone should warn you that your methods are unsound. Killing a couple of dragons prematurely would jeopardize our chances for success of the overall campaign. I don't want to tip our hand. I think it is paramount that we continue to gather intelligence, especially as our position here is fairly stable. No one has ever infiltrated the dragons' ranks as we have."

"We get shot to pieces, bound hand and foot, beat half to death, and you have the audacity to call it a tactical maneuver. Doc, you never cease to amaze me."

"Why, thank you. I accept that as a compliment. On the other hand—"

"Sam!" Jane jumped up and ran toward a loping figure that was momentarily silhouetted in the broad entranceway. She threw her arms around him and hugged him tight. "Where— go?"

Sam returned the hug. He ran his hands up and down her bare back and kissed her on top of the head. "I was doing a little scouting." The pair walked side by side to the corner that Doc, Scott, and Rusty inhabited. "Rusty, good to see you up and about. How do you feel?"

"Not bad, considering I almost got turned into a block of ice."

"How did the mission go?" Doc asked.

"Pretty good." Sam disentangled himself from Jane, and the two of them squatted on the straw-covered floor. He took a crumpled piece of material from where it was tucked into the back of his G-string and handed it to Doc. "Thanks for the shirt. There was a slight chill in the air. I needed it."

Doc nodded grimly, understanding fully the coded message. At least one old woman would not be carried off to the pens in a stupor. "Think nothing of it. Did you make contact with any more outsiders?"

"Yes, and I've enlisted a few more recruits, too, who are eager to cross swords whenever we're ready to mobilize. I even picked up a few homemade weapons. But the big news is, I got word of Sandra and Death Wind. They were spotted last night in a barn on the other side of town."

"Are they okay?" shouted Scott.

"Are you sure it's them?" said Rusty.

Sam's teeth glistened in the faint orange glow of first light. "The description fits: tall, dark, quiet, broad-shouldered, high forehead, and swept-back ebony hair, mated to a feisty, big-breasted woman with a singed scalp. Those

aren't my words," he apologized to Doc. "That's the way I heard it. There's not another couple like them."

"I daresay," said Doc.

"It's as I suspected. They ended the workday in a different quarter, and the dragons took them to the nearest barn. It happens all the time. It's tough when mothers are separated from young children. Days, even weeks, may pass before they're reunited." Sam shook his head slowly. "An egg laying lifestyle doesn't suit a familial culture. The dragons could care less."

"That seems to be tonight's topic of discussion," Doc said.

"Hey, take a look at these." Sam extracted two slender needles from the material of his loincloth and handed them to Doc. Each was nearly a foot long. "A guy named Wendell gave them to me. He likes to be called Windy."

"A simple but formidable weapon." Doc inspected them and passed them on to Scott and Rusty.

"They're plastic stalactites. He broke them off from a poured roof, where the excess plastic had dripped over the edge. You know how tough this stuff is. He spent hours honing the point till it's as sharp as a tack."

Scott touched the point with the tip of his finger and drew blood. "Kind of dangerous to carry around. It'll make a pin cushion out of your leg if you keep it on your belt."

Sam nodded. "I'll bet Jane can weave a sheath for it, out of straw. You'd be surprised what she can do with her fingers."

"Not after seeing her make a monkey out of herself." Scott jerked a thumb over his shoulder. "She climbed that wall like it was a ladder."

"Yes, she's quite agile. She can do things average folks never even thought of." Sam mussed her hair and smiled at her. "Can't you, honey?"

Jane grinned. "If you say so."

Sam laughed raucously. He rocked forward so far that his face brushed straw. "Scott, did you teach her that?"

Grinning, Scott said, "You've got to watch her. She's like a parrot: she mimics whatever we say. And the more she learns, the more that makes sense to her, so she's picking up the language in a geometric progression. The problem I'm having is that she's very easily influenced by what she hears, and she's hearing words and phrases that I don't want her to know: slang expressions, improper usage, and colloquial grammar. It would make my job a whole lot easier if you people would mind your p's and q's; then I wouldn't have so much to unteach her."

"English was never my strong point, but I'll try to contain my penchant for the vernacular." Still smiling, Sam continued, "You know, I haven't laughed, or even smiled, in months—ever since I was captured. Being a prisoner hasn't been nearly as bad as being separated from my family. Becoming united with my daughter, and my long-lost father-in-law, and meeting you boys has meant a lot to me. I—I wanted you to know that in case—well, in case everything doesn't go the way we plan. I mean, if we get separated for some reason."

"We will have to ensure that that eventuality does not occur." Doc kneaded the cramps out of his bad leg. "Let us remember, however, that the group objective has greater importance than individual caprice. There can be no peace while dragons live, and no security for the future—indeed, for the future of mankind—until we eradicate from the earth every vestige of dragon influence. Personal sacrifice is our watchword, survival of the species our goal. And lest you think I am being heroic, or histrionic, understand that my will is governed by my genes. We are what we are because that is the pattern of our evolution. If we were any different, we would have died out long ago—or perhaps we never would have originated. The question that remains to be answered is—can we live up to our potential?"

CHAPTER 10

"I haven't done this much doctoring in a turtle's age."

Sam humphed. "I've been making rounds ever since I got here. Why, in two months I'll bet I've treated half the community for one thing or another. Usually, all I can prescribe is a poultice, or barn rest. The natives are good that way: when one of their number is sick, the others hide him like they do the elderly. At reveille, when the guards come in to make up work crews, the strong, healthy adults stand out in front."

"Traditional herd instinct." Doc finished touching up the bruise above Death Wind's eye. "There you are, my boy. The next time you faint, try throwing your arms out in front of you."

"He didn't faint," Sandra said belligerently.

"And neither did I. We were shot by some new kind of self-contained gun."

"Please excuse my metaphorical reference; humor is part of my bedside manner. I did not mean to be imprecise."

Sandra sneered, but did not comment further.

"What worries me is the implication of rearmament." Scott tucked his thumbs in the front of his shorts and perambulated around the corner of the barn that the squad had appropriated. "Why do they think they need more weapons? Could they possibly know about our plans for insurrection?"

"Maybe they're just playing it safe," Rusty offered. "Because so many dragons are going back in time, the natives now outnumber the local dragon population ten to one. This small firearm is the perfect defense for a technician that can't carry a power pack to operate the larger unit. It'll tuck right into a spare vest pocket."

Doc sat down and hunched over his knees. "Perhaps it is part of an ongoing plan. Sam, you said they've been sending personnel back at an ever-increasing rate?"

"Yes, but it had nothing to do with your arrival. The activity began soon after I got here, although I'm not paranoid enough to believe that my presence posed such a threat to them. If anything, it seems to coincide more with your destruction of the North American outpost. Toad, how many cartons of these self-contained stun guns came through the transporter?"

"Must have been a dozen, at least, Daddy. And it looked like each box held ten to fifteen."

Sam shook his head. "One gross of guns compared to three to four thousand natives and outsiders is negligible. Besides, there's no history of rebellion to cause such a change in tactics."

"It might have been only the first shipment."

"That's not right. It may have been the first shipment," Scott said.

"That's what I said."

"No, you said, 'might have been.' Might is the past tense of may. I'm trying to teach Jane correct conjugation. Your jargon keeps confusing her."

"Who gives a damn?" Sandra shouted, hands on hips.

"Listen, Toad, I'm just trying to help her—"

Sandra lunged at Scott and slammed him up against the wall. She scrunched up the folds of his shirt and pinned it against his throat. "Nobody calls me that except my daddy. Got that?"

Scott glared down at her, hands at his sides. "I got it without the body language. I can still hear, you know."

"Then don't forget it." She released him and stalked off toward the barn entrance.

Scott tugged his shirt back down to his waist. He cleared his throat and called out to her retreating form. "I'm sorry. Okay?"

Sandra did not reply.

Scott glanced at Death Wind.

The Nomad winked at him.

"Anyway, the guns are the least of our worries. They've already got enough armament to kill everyone in this compound three times over. All we've got is one steel-bladed knife and two plastic knitting needles."

"Garrote?"

Scott looked down at Jane, sitting on the floor weaving straw into rope. "Yes, although I think dragon necks are too strong to strangle. But that lasso may come in handy. Doc, now that we're all together, I think we should start formulating our plans. A week and a half in this place and already I'm going stir crazy."

Doc snorted. "That is quite a statement, coming from a lad who has spent most of his existence hermetically sealed in an underground chamber whose largest open space was a closet."

"That was different, Doc. I didn't feel cooped up then because I didn't know any other way of life. What I don't like is being penned in against my will."

"The real prison, then, is not these walls of plastic, but the barriers of your mind."

"That may be true, but it doesn't make the feeling any less genuine."

"Mere orthodoxy. You have free will; you can always change the way you think."

"Doc, you are amazing. You could find a silk lining in a pile of manure. If I had your—"

"Hey! Cut the philosophy session and let's talk about getting the hell outa here." Sandra stood with legs spread wide and hands on hips; except for her stature and her thoracic bulges, she could have passed for the Colossus of Rhodes. "I've been zapped one too many times by these living fossils. Let's revolt before the revolting lizards get on to us."

"A sensible suggestion," Doc said. "Rusty, would you mind removing your lanky limbs from our sketch?"

Rusty stood up and kicked away the straw

that covered the plastic flooring and the map of the city that was carved into it. "I've added a little more detail since last night. Windy's been collecting data from everyone who talks, and Jane has interviewed as many natives who will finger speak with her."

"Excellent."

"My people not dumb. They not understand spoken language." Jane enunciated each word precisely. "Some will help."

"I thought as much. You see, Sam. There are subversive elements in every tyrannized colony. They merely need a directing, cohesive force to channel their energies."

"It took a man like you to get the ball rolling," Sam said.

Doc waved him off. "You were stymied only by lack of communication. Long before our arrival you laid the groundwork by taking this girl under your wing and by spreading discontent among those prisoners who were captured from the outside."

"Can we pat each other on the shoulder later and get on with it?" Sandra knelt by the circular layout. The others gathered around the perimeter of the map. "We've got no time to lose."

"On the contrary," Doc said with his quixotic smirk. "We have a great deal of time to lose: about sixty million years. These aged bones can use the time reversal to good effect. Perhaps by visiting the past I can enjoy a second childhood."

"Pop, sometimes I think you're already in your second childhood. This plan of yours scares me. I'm only going along with it because it's crazy enough to work. Now, I've been all over this burg working for these slave drivers. The way I see it, we've got to slip out under cover of darkness, hightail it through the separation zone, sneak through the dragon quarters, run like hell through the machinery spaces, charge into the transporter arena, and—whammo—look out dragon land, here we come. I'm no mathematician, but I think we've got about one chance in a thousand of making it all the way."

"Your vote of confidence is appreciated, my dear. But I've got another idea that I think is more viable."

"Forget it, Pop. I'm not crawling through two miles of sewer pipe. Besides, if they blow our cover it'll be too easy to gas us. We'll die like— aaagh! What the hell is she doing with that rat?"

Jane sat with her back to the wall. She was facing the circle, but with one hand she fed crumbs to a furry rodent. She looked up in surprise. "Me?"

"Yes, you. Are you looking for a case of rabies?"

Jane raised her eyebrows at Scott. "Rabies?"

Scott shrugged. "Doc, that's your department."

"It is a viral disease transmitted by the bite of infected mammals, via the saliva. I've never seen a case of it. It was effectively wiped out when the mammalian population was exterminated. Besides, rats were not a common carrier. Historically, the fleas that prey on rats were responsible for epidemics of bubonic plague that decimated—"

"I don't need a clinical description. I know all about rats. We had droves of them in the tunnels where I grew up. They're disgusting!"

Sam said, "Sandra was scared by one when she was a toddler. It crawled into her pajamas when she was taking a nap. She's had a morbid fear of them ever since."

"I do not! I'm not afraid of rats any more than I'm afraid of the dark. But I don't feed the damn things, either."

Jane sat, wide-eyed, "Rats are also prisoners."

Sandra placed a hand on her forehead and covered her eyes. "I don't believe this girl. Okay, that settles it. I'm for getting out of here tonight, moon or no moon."

Jane continued to feed her pet.

"After hearing your and Death Wind's report, I am entertaining a daylight flanking maneuver. Of course, it will mean that we must disguise ourselves—"

"Daylight! Pop, are you completely out of your skull?"

"Audacity often carries off the battle."

"Cut the military aphorisms. I—"

Scott said, "I didn't know you knew such big words."

"Shut up, you! Pop, what are we gonna disguise ourselves as—a bunch of cabbages?"

"I had in mind—natives."

"What do I look like—an eight-foot-tall lizard?"

"No. You look like an outsider."

"Pop, we all look the same—to a dragon. One lizard face looks like any other to me, I'm sure all people look the same to them."

"Can you tell the difference between an ad-

ministrator and a technician?"

"Of course. The administrators wear capes and the technicians wear vests. What's that got to do with it?"

"I believe our clothes have been giving us away and attracting undue attention. I do not think it was mere coincidence that you and Death Wind were selected as subjects for experimentation. I have noticed a subtle disparity in the treatment of outsiders, almost as if the dragons do not trust us as they do the natives. Our clothing gives us away. Ergo, we go native."

"Now, wait just a minute." In a huff Sandra jumped up to her knees. She held out her arm and pointed a rigid index finger at Jane. "If you think I'm going to wear nothing by a few grains of straw like that—like that hussy, then you've got another think coming."

Jane looked inquisitively at Scott; he held out his hand and quelled her question.

"And you keep out of this," Sandra shouted at Scott.

Nonplussed, Scott said defensively, "I didn't say a word. All I—"

"I know what you were thinking."

"My dear, there is more at stake here than vanity. We must use all the wiles at our disposal. I am less proud of the condition of my body than you are of yours—"

"Who's not proud?"

"—but we must do what is necessary in order to achieve our goals. I am certain that if we divest ourselves of our rather ostentatious attire, we can travel through the city with less notice than we have been attracting. It is paramount to my plan that we join the daily food delivery unit." Doc ruffled his fingers through his beard, scratched his chin, and deftly extracted a tiny black flea. "You see, I thought we were going to have to escape into the past. Instead, the dragons are going to take us there of their own volition. We are going to escort some of those bodies through time."

CHAPTER 11

The native work force gathered in front of the icehouse, awaiting further orders. People milled aimlessly while bored dragon guards leered down from the sidelines. No guns were drawn. The seven warriors huddled together in the middle of the crowd.

Scott said, "Well, getting in the right labor party was easy enough. It's a good thing Windy tipped us off."

"Pop, what'll we do if they don't want anything but meat?"

"Patience, my dear. Patience. Our strategy is sound, but the time for its execution must be appropriate."

"Does that mean we wait?"

Doc nodded slowly. "If necessary."

"Well, I can think of some executions I'd like to perform in the meantime."

"I'm sure you can, but please try to curb your appetite."

Sandra suddenly turned on Scott. "What're you looking at, mister?"

"Who? Me?" Wearing nothing but a G-string, Scott's entire body turned visibly red. "I was just—"

"I saw you staring." Sandra positioned the long dark tresses in front of her bare breasts. For the hundredth time that day she checked the makeshift clips that kept the slender strands fastened to her own foreshortened locks. "You look at me once more, buster, and you'll be wearing that smile on the other side of your face."

Ever watchful, Death Wind stoically ignored them.

Jane fluffed out her hair. So selectively had Death Wind cut the individual strands from her head that she seemed to still have a full-bodied coiffure. She pulled the braids back from her chest. "You like?"

Scott rolled his eyes. He felt terribly exposed in his brief apparel. "Don't these people have any inhibitions?"

Sam laughed. "Hang-ups are a cultural trait, something of which these people are totally naive. When I first got here—"

"Pipe down!" Rusty whispered harshly. "We're on the move."

Harps played on both sides. The horde of natives lurched forward like the sections of a caterpillar. The tall icehouse doors opened outward, and a mist of cold air rolled over the front ranks. The natives entered the building without hesitation.

"Remember, linger in the back until they finish loading the meat and vegetables. Jane, keep translating for us."

"Yes, Doc. Dragons give the signal enter. Pick up. Carry out. Follow."

The frigid air caressed Doc's skin like a mid-winter snowstorm. Goose bumps rose instantly. As the pack surged ahead, he was thankful for the warm touch of their bodies. He tried to stifle his limp, but without a cane his game leg ached constantly. In the handling room the people spread out as they marched into the various cubicles to gather their loads. "Let's mill a bit."

They kept moving, but in such an ineffective way that they each described small circles that kept them in the same area. Enough unused prisoners were left that the dragon guards noticed nothing unusual.

"It's at the other end of the hall," Rusty breathed. "On the right."

The natives were quick to work: the sooner they grabbed a haunch of steak or a basket of vegetables, the sooner they could leave the freezing confines of the icehouse. They did not need to be tone talked into working fast.

"Harp say go that way." Jane pointed with her eyes.

"Okay, here we go," Scott said enthusiastically. "Look out yesterday, here we come."

Natives gathered around the stack of gurneys. Working quickly, they teamed up in taking one down from the pile, unfolding the legs, and pushing it into the freezer compartment, where they picked up a frozen corpse and gratefully trundled it out of the building and into the heat of the sun. Due to the arctic conditions, only three heavily-bundled dragon guards oversaw the work; they merely stood and looked threatening. The natives needed no further encouragement.

Sam shoved through the throng. "This is the first time I've ever seen these people work with a will."

Death Wind was the first of the group to reach the gurneys. With muscular arms he easily pulled down one in each hand, passed them out, and grabbed two more. Several natives tried to take them away, but they were pushed aside. In a few seconds, the four gurneys rolled on plastic wheels toward the corpse-filled freezing unit. Natives were already rushing out with their human cargo.

Just as they got to the door, Doc heard the thrumming of notes from a harp. He looked sharply at Jane. "What are they saying?"

"They say stop."

Rusty wrapped his arms around his shivering body. "Stop? Why?"

"No reason. Stop."

"But, we need to get those bodies," Scott protested. He gave the gurney a shove toward the doorway. "We can't stop now."

Sam held him back. "Don't disobey. It'll only get us in trouble."

"But, it'll ruin the plan. We may never get this opportunity again."

Doc said, "Sam is right. If we act out of order the guards will surely take notice. We cannot—" Doc suddenly looked down at the stretcher before him. His brows knitted in intense concentration. He looked around at the dragon guards, saw that their attention was otherwise occupied. With scores of bustling natives in the handling room, no one was paying particular mind to their activities. Doc tugged the knot that held his G-string in place. As it fell away he rolled over onto the stretcher, and tucked the puny piece of material under the small of his back. "Death Wind!"

Scott said, "Doc, what're you doing?"

The Nomad needed no explanation. He slipped out of his loincloth and jumped onto the plastic padding.

Sandra stared down at his naked body. "DW, what the hell—"

"Start pushing, folks," Doc urged in his calm, quiet voice. "Before they notice that we did not get these bodies from the freezers."

Rusty and Sam nudged the gurney forward. Doc, lying flat on his back, winked up at them. "That leg was beginning to bother me, anyway."

"Come on, Jane. Let's go." Scott abandoned the gurney he was pushing, and took his side by the one on which Death Wind lay. "And, Death Wind, I know this'll be hard for you—but try not to smile."

"Hey, wait for me." Sandra ran a few paces and caught up with them. "This is the craziest—"

"We're committed now. Let's just hope they didn't take a body count. Hey, let's get past those guys."

As they merged into the stream of natives emerging from the meat lockers, the confusion masked their scurrying to bring the gurneys out of the building ahead of the others. Scott banged people out of his way, passed Doc's gurney, and reached the outer door right under the sloe-eyed gaze of two dragon guards. The lizards took no notice of the shuffling for position.

"Henry, if you don't stop shaking you'll give us away."

"Sorry, Sam, but I got a bit chilled in here. My boy, how are you holding up to the cold?"

Rusty's teeth were chattering so hard that they sounded like clattering drum sticks. "Another minute and I'd be as cold as those stiffs."

The procession slowed down as it reached the sun-filled courtyard. All around were natives carrying food goods. Harps vibrated with instructions. People were directed along different roadways for destinations yet unknown. The dragons did not give advance information, only orders.

Jane held up two fingers and pointed at each of the counterfeit gurneys. "Scott. Three bad."

Scott's brows beetled for a moment, then he nodded. The dragons may get suspicious of three people pushing a stretcher when only two were prescribed. He bounded through the crowd to the preceding gurney and roughly shoved aside the native holding one side. "Sorry, pal, but this is for your own good." Scott looked back and flashed the okay sign: a fist turned inward with the thumb up.

The two counterfeit gurneys mingled with those that were headed for the time transport structure. With the strumming of its harp, a technician led the way along the alleys that separated the living quarters. Doc got an ant's-eye view as they passed through the machinery spaces. Overhead cable trays carried power from the nuclear generating station to storage accumulators from which the mobile batteries were recharged. Massive motors droned, and transformers hummed monotonous tunes.

"I have to hand it to you, Henry. When a situation doesn't present itself, you make one up." Sam kept a wary eye on their surroundings as he spoke. "You're always three thoughts ahead of everyone else."

Doc carefully peered from side to side. "When expediency is called for it does not pay to hesitate. Audacity often succeeds where temperance fails. Indecision is anathema: any action is better than none."

Rusty murmured, "Doc, do you have a book of these proverbs, or do you make them up as you go along?"

"Hush!" Sam put a forefinger to his lips. "Something fishy is going on."

The funeral procession halted. A squadron of guards and a host of technicians blocked the opening of the plastic dome. Like a herd of draft animals, the natives stood by their gurneys awaiting instructions. Other natives, carrying loads on their shoulders, milled in the courtyard.

"Are any caped—" Doc got his head only an inch off the stretcher pad.

Sam placed a sturdy hand on his father's-in-law forehead. "Don't move a muscle, or you're dead."

Doc relaxed. "Appearances can be deceiving." He let his head loll slowly from side to side, so he could observe events. Scott glanced over his shoulder, and shrugged.

Death Wind lay like a cadaver; he breathed so shallowly that not even his chest moved. But his hawklike eyes watched every movement. Jane and Sandra stood poised for action.

Out of the milling crowd came an outsider, wearing a shirt, shorts, and sandals. He was taller than Sam, but stooped. His wiry beard only partially hid a craggy, rough-hewn face. "Don't know what's happenin', but I seen 'em act this way before."

"Windy," Sam breathed. "What's it mean?"

"Could be some bigwigs comin' through. Got a couple of capers watchin' the proceedin's. An' they been sendin' back all kinds o' slaves. Mus' need a awful lot o' dragon power back then. Frozen carcasses, too. I never seen nothin' like it."

"Are any natives going through?"

"A couple. Mostly, it's lizards an' corpses. Right now, the dome's empty."

"Damn. Doc, what'll we do?"

"This two-way transfer procedure complicates things. One never knows whether one is coming or going. Windy, how long has it been since the last transfer?"

"Few hours. The 'pacitors're jus' 'bout ready fer another discharge. You kin tell by the cracklin'."

"That must mean that instead of balancing the load by transporting equal amounts from past to future and from present to past, they are sending a big shipment from their time zone to ours." Bushy eyebrows bounced. "Theoretically speaking, of course. That is a calculated guessometry."

"So, what do we do?" Rusty said. "Call it quits and try another day? Or wait for the next transfer and hope that we can sneak through?"

Doc pondered the situation for a moment. "We cannot back out. Dragons did not invent time travel by being stupid. When they see the empty stretchers they will know that something

is wrong. Bodies do not just get up and walk away. On the other hand, if we hang around, they may decide to take the laborers on another work detail. Death Wind and I may get through, supposing they do not think to check our body temperature."

"Or put you back in the freezers until tomorrow," Rusty added.

"Whatever yer gonna do, do it fast," said Windy. "Now I got the bug, an' got a burr under some o' them deadheads' saddles, I wanna git this kit an' caboodle movin'. Been a POW too long to suit *my* fancy."

Sam took a firm grasp on Windy's forearm. "Can you make a diversion?"

"Whatcha mean?"

"Draw their attention."

Windy looked over the reptilian overseers. "Sure. It'll cost me a shot with the pain stabbers, an' maybe a coupla days inna clink. Whatcha got in mind?"

"No time to explain. Just do it," Sam fairly shouted. The air smelled of ozone, and the focusing nodes were heterodyning. "And if all goes well, we'll see you back here in about sixty million years."

Windy hesitated for a moment. When resolution caught up with him, he was off in a flash. He ran screaming through the crowd, knocking down natives and spilling their packages. Half a dozen dragon guards drew their guns. They fired into the masses, not bothering to aim. People yelled in pain, fell to the plastic flooring, and writhed in agony.

"Make up a motto, Henry. We're on the move."

Doc felt the gurney lurch. Caught off balance, he had to grab onto the sides to stop from sliding off. "Sam, what are you—"

The gurney mowed down two natives who were thrust aside like billiard balls. Doc hung on for dear life. Rusty shouted and tried to keep up. Doc saw Scott's stunned face among the bystanders. The gurney ricocheted off a pair of dragon knees. The stunned technician rocked back; its thick tail formed a tripod, so it did not fall down, but it hissed in surprise and pain.

Sam shouted over his shoulder, "Come on."

Death Wind was up and running, dragging the girls behind him. A dragon guard swung its stun gun toward the charging brawlers. Before it could squeeze the trigger, the Nomad sliced through the power cable with his knife. The circuit was shorted in a momentary shower of sparks. A split second later the battery pack exploded with a tremendous roar. The dragon disintegrated as the blast tore through its back and ripped muscle from flesh. A volcano of blood and guts erupted into the air, splattering natives, guards, technicians, and visiting dignitaries with a mountain of gore. Death Wind and the girls were knocked down by the blast, but were protected from injury by the mass of the dragon's body: the dismembered parts flew over their heads. A moment later they struggled to their feet and continued running.

All around people screamed, guns fired, and pandemonium reigned.

The gurney raced through the main entrance of the time transport structure. Flanking guards were waddling out into the action as Doc and Sam rolled between them. One guard fired. The shot was way too late; the laser beam bored into the opposite guard's broad belly. The dragon hissed painfully as it teetered sideways. Rusty ducked under the falling neck. Scott jumped over it as it hit the ground. The standing guard fired again, missing altogether. It swung around as Death Wind attacked with his deadly knife. He did not try to cut the connecting cable; they might not survive the blast of another exploding power pack. Instead, he slashed the lizard's forearm and severed its tendons.

Doc stared up at the kaleidoscope of flashing needlepoints: the tips of the focusing nodes coruscated like effervescent haloes. The pitch of the whining capacitor circuits was almost beyond audible range. The air was alive with static electricity; Doc's scalp tingled, and his snowy white hair stood straight out. Only the shimmering blue curtain that surrounded the transfer field stood between them and the Cretaceous.

They passed through the curtain and entered a sphere of eerie soundlessness. Sam dragged his heels on the plastic flooring. The gurney skewered sideways. Doc felt himself slipping off. He held on harder, but the gurney overturned, depositing him on the floor. He went into a controlled tumble and rolled hard against something rough and unyeilding. The silence was palpable, as if all molecular motion had ceased. He blinked his eyes to clear them. Then something wet and slimy splattered on his arm. He rolled back and looked up. A dragon technician leered down at him, tongue lolling.

"Doc!" Rusty screamed.

A huge, clawed hind leg hovered in the air above Doc's chest, and descended slowly. Sam scrambled to his knees. Scott entered the sphere at a dead run and never slowed down. He charged right into the fracas. He smacked the drooling dragon mouth with the side of his fist. The technician was knocked off balance by the force of the blow. With its upraised hind leg still in the air, it flailed its forelegs for a pawhold. It executed a short dance step and regained its upright position. Scott jumped up and swung on the neck just behind the head. The added weight was too much for the beast. Its neck twisted around nearly a hundred eighty degrees as its body fell with a thud.

Scott was underneath the elongated neck as it hit the floor. He had a death hold on it, but was losing his grip. "Help!"

Sam was there in an instant. He pulled the plastic needle from the straw sheath that was tied to his waist, paused for a second until he located the right spot, then plunged the sharpened point into the dragon's ear hole. The needle easily punctured the tympanum and went straight into the brain. The dragon died instantly, although its hindquarters continued to squirm.

Scott crawled out from under the limp neck. "Thanks, Sam. I—"

Another vested dragon stepped into the blue haze. It pulled something long and slender out of a pocket, aimed it at Sam, and—

Death Wind burst through the blue curtain right behind it, vaulted off the thick tail, and leaped onto the dragon's back. Corded thigh muscles bulged as he wrapped his legs around the technician's lower throat. As the leering head lunged upward with a hiss, the Nomad sank his knife into the side of its neck. Quickly he pulled it out and stabbed again—and again. The dragon dropped its instrument in its struggle to dislodge the savage from its back. Claws raked Death Wind's calves, leaving streaks of blood. The Nomad kept stabbing. The lizard leaned forward and kept right on going. As its face crashed into the floor, Death Wind released his grip and did a somersault over its plated skull; he came up on his feet, knife poised for another attack. The dragon lay in a growing pool of reptilian blood, gasping its last.

"Nice going, Death Wind." Scott crouched with another plastic needle in his hand. His voice was eerily damped, as if the sound waves were absorbed by a partially evacuated medium.

"You and Sam must be the first people to ever kill a dragon in hand-to-hand combat."

If the Nomad heard him, he gave no notice.

Sam gawked at the bloodied needle in his hand. "It all happened so fast. I didn't know what I was doing."

Rusty scooped up the technician's fallen instrument, looked it over hastily, and tucked it in the loop of his G-string. "The question is, what do we so now? How do we get this time machine in motion?"

"Actually, I do not believe the support structure moves at all. It merely ruptures the fabric of space-time in such a—"

"Save the physics course for later, Pops. We're surrounded."

"Sorry, my dear. Rusty, do you see any mechanisms that would discharge the capacitor circuits and catapult us into the past?"

Rusty quickly glanced around the pulsating blue sphere. The seven of them stood in varying defensive positions, but nothing else was visible. He shrugged his shoulders and held up his palms. "No."

A long moment of stunned silence ensued.

Sandra put her hand on her hips. "Well, this is just great. Here we are all dressed up and nowhen to go."

"Here, Rusty. Here." Jane waved frantically with one hand and pointed down with the other.

The group circle closed on the spot that she indicated. Rusty dropped to his knees and examined the clear plastic panel in the floor. Underneath it was an annunciator panel full of flickering lights, an array of gauges both digital and needle, and several rows of throw switches.

Rusty ran his fingers around the perimeter of the panel. "There must be a lock somewhere—"

Doc said, "Locks are superfluous in the dragon hierarchical system. Natural biological stratification keeps unauthorized personnel from—"

"Ah-ha!" Rusty found a circular depression in a corner of the panel, but was unable to get a grip on it with his finger. "It must be a lifting hole, but it's designed to fit a dragon claw. Scott, give me your needle."

Scott handed over the plastic stalactite. "You'd better hurry."

Rusty inserted the point and pried. The clear panel popped open. He pulled it up and over its hinges and laid it down flat. "Now what?"

Jane pointed to a line of scratches above a large circular disk. "This mean—" She hesitat-

ed, with one hand wrapped over her eyebrows.

"Come on, girl, what the hell does it mean?" Sandra shouted. "We haven't got all day."

"It mean—it mean—" Jane bit her lower lip. "I think it mean—begin."

Rusty jammed his palm down on the disk. A flash of sparks flew out of the electrical contacts beneath it, and all the indicator lights went out. "Uh-oh. I think I just blew a fuse."

CHAPTER 12

"That's great," Sandra screamed. "That's just great. What the hell do we do now?"

"We're in a time machine," Scott said. "I say we call for time out."

"This is no time for jokes, mister. Any second now a whole dragon army's gonna come pouring through that haze."

"Dragon dragoons, huh?"

Sandra's looks alone could have killed half a battalion.

"Rusty, my boy, is there any chance that you can reset that breaker?"

"Maybe. I could also jumper the disconnect switch if I could trace the wiring." Rusty grasped the annunciator board, but it did not move. "I'll need some time—"

"How ironic that we are trapped in a time transport device, yet have no time to spare." Doc pursed his thin lips. "You keep working on it, lad. The rest of us must take the defensive." He glanced up at the others. "I suggest that since neither electromagnetic radiation nor molecular vibration propagates through the force field, we take up stations in adjacent quadrants and prevent physical passage."

"Why don't we take the offensive and attack?" Sandra said.

"We are underarmed for such a military tactic."

"Listen, Pop, if we're going down for the count, I'm gonna take a few of the bastards with me. I don't care if I don't have any weapons. I can lift up a dragon's tail and kick it in the gonads. I may not kill it, but at least it won't spawn any more little lizards."

"My dear, I think it wiser to gang up on them one at a time as they come through the barrier. If we can dispatch an unwary soldier we will be at least one weapon stronger."

Rusty held up the foot-long metal tube that he

had picked up from the downed technician. "You can always zap one with this." He tossed the instrument to Sandra. "If you can find the firing mechanism."

Doc turned at a clattering sound and saw Death Wind dragging the equipment vest off the technician whose throat he had minced. "Good idea. It may contain something valuable. Sam—"

Sam was already cutting off the straps that held the vest onto the other dragon's chest. "Not only that, but this one's got another one of those miniature zappers." He pulled it out and held it up triumphantly. "Jane, you'd better hang onto this one. I've still got my darning needle."

Jane took the instrument, ran her hand over the smooth plastic surface of the enlarged handle.

"I can't find any trigger," Sandra said.

Jane cautioned her with a splayed palm. "Do this." Several times she made a fist with her free hand. "Dragon tool work."

"What?"

"She says to squeeze it," Scott explained. "The dragons have other tools that work that way."

"But how do I know how hard—" A technician waddling into the time zone forced her hand. Sandra aimed and squeezed. A ring of light burst off the tip of the barrel like an iridescent smoke ring, flashed instantaneously across the intervening space, and engulfed the dragon's ugly head. The beast toppled like an oak tree struck by lightning; it hit the deck with a thud that was absorbed by the eerie acoustics of the temporal sphere. Sandra blew smoke off the end of the tube. "I guess it works."

Sam scampered to where the felled dragon lay. He knelt down and placed his ear against the bulbous abdomen. "It's breathing. It's still alive."

"Gimme that knife, DW. I wanna finish it off."

"No! Wait." Doc hobbled across the sphere and stood between Sandra and the unconscious lizard. "I want it alive."

"What're you, crazy?" Sandra stood with legs spread wide and arms akimbo. "Any millisecond now this place'll be swarming with dragons, more'n we can shake a stick at." She waved the weapon tube in the air. "What if this guy wakes up in the meantime?"

"I understand your concern, and your point is well made. But the validity of your statement is suspect. I think we've got all the time in the world."

"Pop, either the time warp has warped your brain, or you caught some backlash from this tube." Sandra brandished the barrel in his vicinity.

Doc gently pushed the weapon aside. "My dear, if the dragons proposed to launch an assault, they would not have telegraphed their charge by sending ahead a solitary technician. Dragon psychology does not possess diplomacy. I doubt that it came to plea for our surrender."

"You're right, Doc." Scott closed in from the position he was guarding. "Something strange is going on. But what?"

"I suspect that we have some advantage of which we are as yet unaware. Perhaps they have no way of knowing that temporarily we cannot trip the transfer switch."

Death Wind and Sam maintained their guard at the far side of the sphere. Doc stared at them. When no one was talking, or moving about, the silence described such total absence of perception that he felt like a fly at the bottom of a glowing vacuum bottle. The Nomad nodded at him from his faraway universe, turned, and stepped through the blue haze. He disappeared from view.

"Death Wind!" Sandra wasted not a moment. She charged across the sphere after her husband. Before she reached the point at which he had vanished, he reappeared. Sandra stopped short. The expression on Death Wind's face was one of puzzlement. "What is it? What did you see?"

"Outside—it is—different."

"Different? Whaddaya mean, different?"

"Dark. No dragons. All still."

Sandra spun on her heel. "Pop, they've cut the power."

"Yes, it could be. Or else . . . " Doc rubbed his beard to a point.

Rusty got his legs under him and assembled his lanky body to its full upright posture. "Or else when I shorted out the switch, the surge passed through the branch circuit breaker so fast that it tripped the main disconnect. If that's true—"

"You do not understand," Death Wind enunciated slowly. "The sky is dark."

Scott ambled across the sphere. "Hey, Rusty, when you trip a fuse you really do a job on it. Somebody's going to be awfully mad at you when he finds out what you did to the heavens."

Rusty's jaw hung down to his chest. He was speechless.

"I think we had better investigate this, uh, rather incredible phenomenon." Doc favored his bad leg as he walked across the sphere toward Death Wind. He held his hand out like an usher. "Would you care to lead the way?"

Death Wind turned and walked through the hazy blue curtain.

"Hey, wait for—"

Doc did not hear the rest of Sandra's plea because he stepped outside the time transfer zone. An instant later she bounced through the soundproof, sightproof barrier. One by one the others followed.

The focusing nodes imbedded in the inner wall of the time transport structure showed not the faintest scintillation. Through the clear plastic, the visible sky was a purple, star-studded canopy. Nowhere was there a hint of movement, or a trace of sound. Then, from the distance, came a hooting the likes of which Doc had never heard before.

"Could it be nighttime already?" Rusty asked.

"Maybe time passes quicker inside the shield," Scott offered. "As if we were accelerating. Or maybe our sense of the passage of time slows down."

Doc pursed his lips and stroked his beard. "Even though I do not profess to understand the principle behind the dragons' time transporter, I rather doubt that. It is too illogical."

"So's time travel," Sam said.

"True, but even though time travel is illogical to the finite human mind, it can be proven mathematically. Why, even in the twentieth century, physicists postulated that the neutrino, that evanescent subatomic particle almost impossible to detect, existed in a plane that allowed it to travel through time. That may indeed be the—"

"Pop, get your mind out of the past."

As the small band of humans filed out under the dome's arched entranceway, Doc craned his neck and peered up at the unfamiliar stellar backdrop. Faraway stars twinkled as the light they emitted millions of years previously passed through the heat inversions of Earth's lower atmosphere. "For the moment, I do not believe that that is possible. Would you agree, Death Wind?"

All eyes rose to the firmament. The Nomad said, "I agree."

"Where did everyone go?" Sandra said in bewilderment.

"Nowhere, my dear. They are exactly where we left them. It is we who have traveled."

Scott shouted. "Hey, where's the Big Dipper?"

"It does not yet exist, my boy. The stars that form the constellations as we know them will not move into positions we can recognize for another sixty million years. Welcome to the Cretaceous."

CHAPTER 13

"This is not exactly what I had in mind," Doc said. "I wanted to remain in the ranks of the slaves and study from the inside the society of dragons past. Now it looks as if we shall have to become renegades."

"That suits me fine, as long as I get to take it out of their hides."

"My dear, we did not come all this distance in time just to snipe at reptilian flanks. We already know how to destroy. We came here to learn *what* to destroy. And now that we've consummated an unplanned escape, we will have to fight our way back into the dragon stronghold."

"Hold your eohippus, Pop. This gal ain't going back to prison."

Doc smiled whimsically. "I did not mean to infer that we will allow ourselves to be recaptured, only that if we are to disclose our adversary's weaknesses, we must penetrate their defenses."

"I want to get past their security codes," Rusty said. "With Jane as my cryptographer, I may be able to crash their central computer."

Jane smiled wordlessly.

Scott emerged from the semidarkness, announcing his arrival by tapping a crooked tree limb on the plastic flooring. "You let me loose in their generating station, and I may be able to gum up their power production." He handed the smooth-barked limb to Doc. "Here you go, Doc. I found a cane for you."

"Why, thank you." Doc took the piece of wood and stretched his arms along its length. "Feels like the right size. Where did you get it?"

"There's a forest out that way, a few hundred yards from the perimeter."

Doc sniffed the aromatic wood. "Hmmnn, smells like sassafras."

"That's what I thought. Some things never

change. There seems to be a clearing—"

"Ahoy, there." Sam waved his arms over his head as he returned. "Is Death Wind back yet?"

"No," said Sandra. "And I'm getting worried."

"Don't. He went looking for water. That boy can take care of himself. Doc, we appear to be in a secluded area, surrounded by fields, trees, and shrubbery. There's a road at the bottom of the hill, but I couldn't see anything beyond that. And the whole place is abandoned. No guards—nothing. Only that one technician."

"It was probably left as a caretaker. There is no reason to post guards when there is no enemy to guard against. Sam, I agree with your assessment of the situation. Whatever special dragon contingency was waiting for transportation must have gone forward at the same time we came back. Our streams crossed somewhen in the intervening space-time continuum."

One section of the sky was brightening. Tall trees stood silhouetted on the horizon as stars glimmered overhead. The humidity was high, the temperature slightly lower than the comfort range. The world was alive with sounds: the buzzing of flying insects, the faraway calls of animals. The time transport structure glowed faintly as the focusing nodes began to store new energy after the recent discharge.

Sam said, "Rusty, what did you learn about operations?"

"It was too dark for me to see much of anything. Other than the dome and a warehouse, the only aboveground building is a control room. I went inside, and by the light of the annunciator panel I could see a keyboard, but I didn't want to touch anything until I know what I'm doing. I heard capacitors recharging under the floor, so my guess is that the machinery and storage batteries are buried. There's probably an access hatch nearby, but we'll have to wait for sunrise before we can spot it."

"It all makes sense to me, Sam." Doc leaned back on his newfound cane. "In our time the dragons built a city from scratch. They necessarily began with the time transport structure, then expanded concentrically around it—a city planned properly from the beginning. But in dragon land, this technological experiment was an outgrowth of previous construction—a laboratory addition which they built away from the mainstream of their civilization. I think we'll find that the electrical energy needed to run this establishment is transmitted from a remote station. By the way, did you take care of the bodies?"

Scott said, "Yes, we dragged them off the plastic and behind a bush, then covered up our tracks afterward."

"That was good thinking."

"Death Wind's idea. The live one is trussed up with some wire we took from its vest. We didn't find much in the pockets—"

"I still think we should waste the bastard." Sandra folded her arms under her breasts. "It'll never talk."

"Not orally, perhaps, since it lacks the vocal chords that are necessary for true speech. But we cannot overlook the opportunity to interrogate a living dragon; it has never been done before. With Jane as our translator, we may unravel mysteries of dragon aristocracy that we can put to great advantage." Doc shifted his position and stretched out his bad leg. "As far as the dead ones go, the only dragons I have ever examined were soldiers. An autopsy on a technician may provide inestimable information about the structure of the hierarchical dragon brain. How does it differ from that of a soldier? What makes its bearer more intelligent: heredity or education? Does the brain possess Broca's area, that convolution that grants only man among all Earth's creations the ability to speak?"

"Spare me the biology lesson. This may be a field trip to you, or a science experiment, but I came here for revenge."

"Not a very admirable quality."

"Maybe not, but it makes me feel good. You can call me shallow if you want, and I won't deny it." Sandra jerked a thumb at her heart. "Your motivations may be pure, old man, but mine are simple—"

"Toad!" Sam angrily confronted his daughter. "I've stood by long enough without saying anything about your behavior, but now you've gone too far. You may be a married woman, but you're still my little girl, and I won't allow you to talk that way—"

Death Wind charged across the plaza with imperative speed. He stopped a few feet in front of the group, breathing normally and showing no strain over his exertions. "Dragons come."

All eyes turned to the Nomad.

"From the road. In a wheelbarrow."

"A what?" Scott asked.

Death Wind pinched his brows. "A cart on many wheels that moves by itself."

Scott's hand flew to his temples. "They're coming by bus. We've got to get out of here."

"Bus?" Jane said, perplexed.

"I'll explain later. Come on, people, let's move it." Scott pulled Doc up by the hand. "Do you have any suggestions?"

"Run like hell, as my granddaughter would undoubtedly put it."

Death Wind trotted in the direction that was opposite that of the road. The others straggled along at various gaits. The sky was bright enough to light their way across the plaza, around the dome, and to the perimeter of the time transport complex. The Nomad halted as his naked feet hit the dirt under the knee-high grass of the surrounding plain.

Scott stopped next to him. "Yes, what do we do with it?" Behind a large mulberry bush lay the captured dragon, its legs lashed together like a pig dressed for the spit. The eyelids fluttered, partially exposing the dark orbs beneath. The long tongue lolled out of the half-open mouth like a length of flattened garden hose. A thin stream of saliva collected into a pool below tight-set lips.

"Kill it," Sandra growled.

Doc caught up with the rabble and leaned hard against his cane. "Can we take it with us?"

"It's pretty heavy, Doc," Scott said. "It took two of us to drag it out here."

"Kill it, and let's go," Sandra insisted.

Death Wind knelt by the beast's head. He held his knife limply.

"It knows where we came from," Scott said with more serenity than Sandra. "When we came from."

The knife hovered between the leering lizard head and the foreleg lashings.

"It is already a vanquished enemy," Doc intoned. Death Wind looked up at Doc with clouded eyes.

Sandra screamed, "Butcher the beast, will you, and get it over with—before we end up on a laser shish kebab." Doc took in a deep breath and swallowed slowly. "It must be done, Death Wind. Our lives are at stake. Consider it not murder, but a coup de grace."

The Nomad dropped his gaze. The knife slowly rose in the air—and hesitated. After a long, lingering moment his forearm muscles tightened, and the knife plunged. When the

blade entered the throat the dragon lurched and kicked helplessly. Death Wind held down the twitching head as he worked the knife back and forth until the steel blade severed a main artery. Blood spurted out in a thin, sickening stream. Still the dragon struggled. Death Wind withdrew the knife; his hand was covered with the lizard's sticky blood. The dragon's life force gradually departed; finally, it lay still.

Doc placed a warm hand on Death Wind's sagging shoulder. "Come on, son. We have to go."

Death Wind squeezed his eyes tight, waited a long moment, then stood up tall. His hand still dripped blood. "Yes."

The seven renegades raced through the tall grass for the protection of the trees. A gentle breeze rustled through Doc's silvery mane. Despite his barefootedness, he found the going easy; the downward slope made him seem to fly.

"I knew it was too good to be true." Sandra skidded to a halt, almost sliding off the brink into the wretched bog that separated them from the tree line. Stumps and clots of weed poked through a bubbling, sulfurous-smelling morass. Bright flowers in hues of crimson and yellow softened the evil-looking appearance. "Anybody bring a raft?"

Gasping for air, Doc caught up with the group. He was thankful to have a cane to lean against. "I guess going around is out of the question?"

Sam shook his head. "It curves back in both directions. The way the banks are cut vertically on both sides, I'd say it's a natural feature artificially extended—to keep out unwanted intruders."

"And I thought man invented the moat to keep out dragons," said Scott.

"I doubt," said Doc, taking his time between breaths, "that man has invented anything that dragons have not already perfected—except for the elements of emotion."

"So, what do we do?" Sandra wanted to know.

"Fortunately, my dear, I brought my wading boots." Doc slid down the embankment and hit the film-covered water with a splash. "Not so bad. It is only ankle deep." He steadied himself with his cane and delicately placed one bare foot in front of the other. "Although there is quite a bit of sharp debris on the bottom."

The others followed his lead.

"Yuck! You didn't say anything about the ooze." Sandra scrunched up her face as she slipped into the swamp. "It feels so slimy."

Scott and Jane held hands as they sloshed through the quagmire. Death Wind took the opportunity to wash his hands and clean the blood from his knife. Sam and Rusty did their best to hop from stump to soggy island to grassy clump. Doc found himself practically groveling as he fought the suction at every step. His cane was useless most of the time; its narrow tip buried itself in the soft mud.

The stars were gone, and the sky was bright enough to dispel the gloom of early morn. Sticks cracked underfoot. Strange chirps and whistles emanated from all sides like a weird stereophonic orchestra. The air hummed with oddly patterned bees seeking the day's first nectar. Extraordinary insects buzzed like bombers.

Sandra's scream pierced the air. She punched frantically at a dragonfly the size of a large bat. The two-foot wingspan enabled it to move with incredible celerity. The prop wash tossed her hair around like autumn leaves in a windstorm. "Help." Sandra stepped into a deep hole and sank in over her head. She came up sputtering words and phrases that, at that day and age, had not yet been coined.

Scott scooped up a floating branch and hurled it at the double-winged monstrosity. The wet clump of wood and attendant moss ricocheted off the dragonfly's extended abdomen, and swept it aside, but appeared to do no other damage. It soared off with an angry droning sound. "Doc, I didn't know they had biplanes in the Cretaceous.

"I have no doubt we will encounter many curious forms of life. This is a time that was—or rather, is—replete with—" The high-pitched scream that cut him off issued from Jane's larynx. She pointed at a ripple coming her way in the water. The creature's skin tone perfectly mimicked the green scum. Only a pair of wide-set eyes gave it away.

"It's a gator," Scott shouted as he whipped out his plastic needle and pushed Jane behind him.

Sandra yanked free the miniature stun gun, aimed, and squeezed. "It's not working!"

A moment later the swimming beast was enveloped in a momentary electrical display. It writhed only once before it stiffened. Rusty held up his tube weapon like a western gunslinger. "Right between the eyes."

Forward momentum took the creature close to Scott before its gaviallike nose dipped beneath the surface. Death Wind sloshed past Scott, reached underwater, and caught the thing before it sank to the bottom. He held the four-foot-long specimen by the eyeballs.

"A crocodilian of some sort," Doc observed. "A small one."

"You mean, there could be bigger ones?" Rusty said.

"Undoubtedly—perhaps ten times as big." Doc ran his hand over the coarse, knobby exterior. The skin was rough, like sandpaper, and the protrusions were sharp. "Amazingly good camouflage."

"A nice set of dentures, too." Scott took Jane's hand and pulled her along. "And I don't want to be wearing them."

Death Wind trampled after them, dragging the crocodilian through the water. As he climbed up the fern-covered embankment at the edge of the swamp, Sandra said, "What're you gonna do with that?"

"Make breakfast."

Sandra gulped and curled her upper lip. "Yeah. I guess I've eaten worse."

"Food comes in strange packages," Doc said. "And they will probably get stranger."

They headed for the trees. Behind them, high on a hill, the time transport structure glowed brightly as its capacitors recharged. The shrubbery that dotted the field was like none that Doc had ever seen before. The landscape was one of dampness and dense foliage, jungle and swamp, patches of high, open ground: an amalgamation of geological features. The sweet scent of flowers mingled with the fetid odor of dank rotting vegetation.

The red sun rose, bringing with it heat, spreading before it prismatic colors borne of a dust-laden atmosphere, and illuminating a primitive, antediluvian world that had never known the step of man. For the squad of human desperadoes, this was the dawn not just of a new day, but of a new era.

CHAPTER 14

Using both plastic needles as darning tools, and Death Wind's knife to cut slits in the material, Sandra pleated one of the pilfered vests so it would fit more comfortably around her narrow shoulders. She had lost a hairpiece in the swamp, so her ample left breast was unabashedly exposed. She worked quickly to cover herself. "If it gets any hotter, I'll melt."

"So put on a jacket," Scott said with feigned sarcasm.

"Shut up, you."

Scott shrugged and returned his attention to Jane. She drew squiggles in the dirt: symbols that represented dragon scratch. Scott and Jane continually reversed their roles as teacher and student, each learning from the other.

Rusty looked over Jane's shoulder and memorized the drawings that looked like a cross between Egyptian hieroglyphics and Chinese picture writing. At the same time, he went through the pockets of the three vests and tried to make sense out of the oddly shaped tools and instruments. "How about that? I've just figured out that this is a pad and pen set."

"Hey, that's something we can really use." Scott took one of the rectangular plates that Rusty handed him. "Why are the words smeared?"

"Because I—hello, Doc, Sam. What did you find?"

"An earthworm about six feet long," Sam said, smiling. "I thought it was a python at first. Scared the hell out of me. Some flying beetles the size of boxcars: you need antiaircraft guns to shoot 'em down."

Doc smiled as he crossed his legs under him and slid down his cane like a fireman down a fire pole. "Death Wind is watching the road. At the moment there is no activity in either direction. However, having a highway through the jungle will certainly mitigate our transportation problems, as well as provide a direct route to dragon headquarters. Rusty, what were you saying about stationery supplies?"

"Huhn? Oh, the writing materials." He held up. a fat cylindrical metal dowel with a point at one end. "This is an etching tool, and—Scott." Rusty, took the plastic slate back from Scott and demonstrated how the surface could be carved by the etcher. "Then, when you want to start over, you can erase the board with this." The box fit awkwardly in his hand. It hummed after he squeezed it, and when he ran it over the writing surface, the scratches disappeared. "It's a low-power, battery-operated heating unit. It wipes the slate clean by melting a coating of thermoplastic—that's a chain-type polymer with

no chemical bonding between chains."

"Ingenious."

"And, it's got a hole in the top that matches exactly the hole in the handle of the stun gun. I think it's a charging port."

Scott said, "And neither gun is working. Apparently, the self-contained battery is good for only a single discharge—a one-shot deal. I don't think Sandra's was damaged at all by the water—it had already shot its bolt. Rusty's doesn't work now, either."

Doc nodded and arched his bushy white brows. "I am happy to see that you boys have not been sitting idle."

"I also performed that compass experiment you suggested, and you were right." Scott placed before him a tiny plastic cup filled with water. "These are all things we got from the vests, uses unknown. I shaved off this sliver of iron, pounded it with a blunt instrument—what I call a screwdriver, although the tip is triangular instead of slotted and—" He dropped the filing into the water. Surface tension prevented it from penetrating and sinking. Slowly, he rotated the cup. The orientation of the iron filing did not change. "Voilà! It points north and south." Scott aligned his hand with the longitudinal axis of the sliver. His fingers pointed toward the setting sun. "But not the north that we know."

"Further proof—if, indeed, we truly needed it," Doc said, "that we have entered an era not our own. Pole reversal is an old story in geological chronology. The Earth's magnetic field wanders constantly, and sometimes shifts drastically. Add to that the concentration of Late Cretaceous land masses, before continental drift and plate tectonics began to spread the continents into their future positions and orientations, and compass needle deviation is not unexpected."

"There, that's better." Sandra donned her new blouse and, after the front was closed with the original thongs, she plucked the remaining hairpiece from her head. "Jane, thank you for the loan of your hair."

Jane smiled. "You are welcome. Cover breast?"

"Yes, and they're going to stay that way."

"You didn't always used to be this shy," said Scott.

Sandra scowled at him, then turned to Doc. "Pop, you'll have to pardon me for that outburst this morning. I guess I was a little impetuous.

I'm sorry."

"My dear, we are all under a bit of a strain. Think nothing of it."

"Toad, I can't get over how—grown-up—you've become. I've never heard you apologize before. You've become quite mature. And you've—grown out, as well," Sam added with a smile.

"That's just because you haven't seen me for a year or so."

"Time flies, but it hasn't been nearly that long."

"More like sixty million," Scott said. "Or can you say time is passing when you're going through it backward? This is all so confusing that—" Scott jerked around suddenly. "There it is again. That honking sound. Only this time it's closer. I wonder what it is?"

The deep bass tone reverberated again.

"Whatever it is, it's coming this way," Rusty said.

Scott jumped to his feet. "You know, I really wasn't that curious."

"I believe there is more than one." Doc climbed up his cane and peered into the woods.

"More than one what?" Sandra said.

In quick succession two more toots rang out.

"More than one—source."

Scott said, "Jane, could that be some kind of dragon tone talk?"

As if she had done it all her life, Jane shook her head. "I not hear sound."

"What're you, deaf?" Sandra shouted.

"She means she's never heard it before. Jane, could it be some kind of dragon machine?"

She shook her head again.

The toots proliferated, louder than before, and were accompanied by grunts and the crashing of trees.

"Never mind," Sandra admonished. "We'll see it any moment."

Branches snapped off a nearby tree, and a blanket of vines fell to the ground. A green shape the size of a small tank pushed through the underbrush. The thing grunted.

Rusty crouched behind a moss-covered log. He held a palm frond in front of his face and peered through holes in the broad leaf. "It's an armored vehicle."

The tank that sauntered out of the shrubbery had four fat, stumpy legs, a thick caudal appendage that terminated in a swelling that made the tail look like a flexible club, and a body that

was covered with pointed knobs and sharp spines. The. snub-nosed beak rooted noisily through the grass. The cheeks puffed out as mouthfuls of foliage were crammed into the giant maw.

"What the hell *is* that?" breathed Sandra.

Rusty cast a glance at his mentor. "Doc?"

Doc seemed preoccupied, his eyes glued to the scene before him. "Oh, sorry. What was it you said?"

"What *is* that?"

Without interrupting his observations, he said, "Obviously an ankylosaur of some species or other, although not quite what I expected from studying their fossil remains. It appears to have a longer neck and a more upward stance than is usually pictured, and the tail is not as—"

"Pop! Just tell me whether it'll eat us."

"Do we run or hide or fight it off?" said Scott.

Doc shook his head. "I suppose we could shoo it away, or—"

The triangle-shaped head perked up. Beady little eyes peered out from under a ridge of bony plates. The beast looked straight at Rusty. The arm holding up the palm frond slowly lost its strength. The ankylosaur snorted. Then came a loud honking from behind it. The trees were thrust aside as a much larger but hunched-over dinosaur scuttled out of the herbage. Short forelegs exaggerated the size of its rear quarters.

"Now we run," Sandra said.

The ankylosaur spun around with agility that seemed out of place for one of its bulk and design. It wagged its tail like a happy puppy, but the swinging club was anything but a gesture of friendship. As it backed away from the intruder, its hindquarters came dangerously close to Rusty's place of concealment.

"Easy," Doc cautioned. "Easy. Do not alarm it."

"Who's alarmed?" Sandra fairly shouted.

The hunched dinosaur stood up on thick hind legs, to a height of some twenty feet. It balanced for a moment on its tail and looked down at the ankylosaur. The head was ornamented with a comb that protruded from the back like a trombone slide. The comparatively tiny mouth chewed a wad of conifer leaves. It swallowed. A moment later the air was rent with a loud, deep-pitched honk.

The ankylosaur turned tail and ran. Jane and Sandra screamed. Rusty fell to the side. Doc and Sam rolled out of the way as the armored dinosaur charged through their midst. Scott was bowled over like a tenpin. The ankylosaur kept right on going.

Scott clambered to his knees, feeling his body. "I'm okay."

The tall dinosaur honked again. In the distance, another of its kind honked in return. Short arms stripped leaves off a nearby tree and stuffed them into its mouth. Wide-set eyes stared down at Rusty. Out of the corner of his eye he saw a bronze statue poised for action.

Death Wind stood in a clearing with a crudely fashioned spear aimed at the tall beast's throat.

"Do not attack," Doc called out in a scratchy voice. "It is only a hadrosaur."

"So what is that, an endangered species?" Sandra said angrily.

"They're all endangered here," Rusty said.

"So are we. But I'd feel better if they're more endangered than I am. Pop?"

"No need to worry, my dear. They are harmless herbivores."

Death Wind lowered his weapon. The hadrosaur paid him no mind, but went about its business of consuming leaves. It swung its mottled brown body broadside and ignored the band of people. It continued sounding its horn as it browsed.

"Nothing twenty feet tall or with a body full of pikes is harmless. What I want to know is where these things came from."

Scott dusted himself off. "Eggs."

"I know that. But I thought everything was supposed to have been wiped out. How come these guys survived?"

Doc sat up and composed himself. "Probably because they do come from eggs. Shell material is not gas permeable, so any eggs laid prior to the arrival of the death bomb could still hatch healthy chicks if properly incubated."

"That monstrosity was no chick," Sandra complained.

"Pardon my lack of precision, but I do not think the English language has invented a word description for hatchling dinosaurs. I rather think the presence of livestock explains that wall." Doc indicated direction with a wave of his hand; nothing was visible but a grove of oaks and willows. "This is a game preserve for herds of domestic dinosaurs. That hadrosaur over there—more specifically, a parasaurolophus—is a farm animal."

The hadrosaur rose up on its hind legs, honked, and meandered out of sight.

"By the way, the hollow crest atop its skull is merely an elongated sinus passage from nostril to windpipe—a resonating chamber that functions as a recognition signal between individuals, or for warning of predators, or perhaps even as a mating call."

Scott readjusted his G-string. "Doc, how come you know so much about dragons and dinosaurs?"

"I have studied them. It pays to know one's enemy." Doc's smile faded as he glanced at the surrounding forest. "Invaders are at a distinct disadvantage because they are unfamiliar with the territory and its inhabitants. That is why we survived against the dragons who invaded our time, and that is why we must move cautiously in the dragons' time."

"Right now I move that we get the hell out of this dude ranch," Sandra said. "I'll feel a whole lot better on the other side of that barricade."

"My sentiments exactly. Death Wind, what did you find?"

The Nomad stood tall with the butt end of the spear pressing into the soft soil. The honed tip rose two feet above his head. "One guard on each side of gate. Drawbridge opens in middle, controlled from either side. If we kill inner guard, outer guard is warned."

"Ah" was Doc's only comment.

"Hey, Jane's got the solution to that," Scott said. "She's been using her weaving skills again. Go ahead, show them."

Jane untied a coiled vine from where it hung down off her hip. "I make rope."

"You made a rope."

"I made a rope." She held it out to Doc. "It is a vine. I—plaited?"

"That's right." Scott kissed her on the forehead. "Not only does she absorb information like a sponge, she's highly creative—an inborn trait that's been stifled by a life of bondage."

Doc inspected Jane's handiwork. "She has both skill and natural aptitude." Doc patted her hand. "My dear, you are going to get us out of this mess. Shall we go?"

"We climb?"

"We climb."

The wall was thirty feet high and solid enough to keep in the largest of the multiton beasts of burden. The orange plastic had been poured into crude forms without regard for architectural elegance. Rough protrusions and extruded plastic produced a surface that Jane's long fingers and toes gripped with prehensile ease. She scaled the wall as if it were a ladder. After she reached the top, she tied the bitter end of the rope around a notched protuberance, and dropped the other end to the grass-covered ground.

The rope uncoiled into Scott's waiting hands. "Who's first?"

"I'll give it a try." Sam was strong. He leaned back and had no difficulty in walking up the wall like an experienced mountaineer.

Death Wind tossed his spear up like a rocket; Sam grabbed it. Then the Nomad scampered up with the agility of a red squirrel.

"Next?" When no one stepped forward, Scott offered the rope to Sandra.

Sandra looked down at the loose fold of material hanging from her G-string. "Thanks, but I'll go last."

Scott smiled. "Your pleasure."

"I guess I'll go." Rusty wrapped the rope around his wrists. He threw his feet against the wall and struggled for several seconds without getting anywhere. His lean arms could not lift his entire body weight. He clung to the wall like a limpet and sought the bulging knobs as purchase for his feet. He was thankful for the wraps of hide made from the skin of the morning's breakfast package; they protected his soles from serious scraping. The others cheered him on, but it was a long hard climb full of frequent rest stops. Most of the time he had his eyes closed. His strength was nearly gone when Death Wind grabbed his hand and vaulted him over the top. Rusty collapsed on the broad platform, sweating profusely inside his appropriated technician's vest. "Thanks."

"I do not think my performance will be much better. These old bones are not what they used to be."

"Come on Methuselah, I'll make it easy for you." Scott tied a loop around Doc's chest, and snugged it under his arms. The bunched material of the dragon vest offered padding. "Okay, take him away."

Death Wind and Sam hauled him up like a sack of potatoes. "How ignominious," Doc said.

When the rope was let down, Scott offered it again to Sandra. "How about for *my* pleasure?"

"Not on your life."

Scott winked at her, grasped the rope, and raced up the wall only slightly slower than Death Wind. "That leg is still a little sore." As he climbed over the top, he pulled up the rope just enough to keep it out of Sandra's reach.

"Hey, you, let down the rope."

"Did you want to come up?"

A hadrosaur honked in the distance. Sandra glanced frantically over her shoulder. "Scott, you drop that rope this instant," she screamed.

Scott smiled at the Nomad. "Death Wind, I sure hope you don't mind me teasing your wife."

Death Wind shrugged. "Someone must."

CHAPTER 15

After Scott dropped the end of the rope, Sandra climbed the plastic barricade unassisted.

From the top of the wall the view was almost unlimited. The landscape ranged from gently rolling hills blanketed with luxuriant green foliage and dotted with sequestered stands of conifers, magnolias, and dogwoods, to lowland swamps steeped with palmettos, ferns, and placid ponds.

"It looks like we've got a long way to go," Sam said.

"So this is the land of the 'terrible lizard.'" Sandra coiled the rope and handed it to Jane. "I never thought it would be so beautiful."

"Looks can be deceiving. What is smooth from a distance is often rough upon close inspection. The terrain may be more difficult to traverse than it appears." Doc leaned against his cane. He untied the thongs and let his vest flap in the breeze. "Notice the predominance of angiosperms, and the lack of ferns—"

"What kind of sperms?"

Doc smiled. "Flowering plants that produce seeds that must be fertilized. They dominate the swampy forests of the Cretaceous, but soon will yield to plants like the fern, which reproduce by dispersing pollen to the wind. For some reason, the fertile ground of the Tertiary was kinder to the germination of airborne spores. It has been theorized that a worldwide forest fire may have decimated the angiosperms, and ferns, being smaller and growing more quickly, took over afterward. It is, of course, only one part of a biological cycle. Angiosperms eventually grew again—but the dinosaurs that fed upon them never did."

"That's okay by me. I don't ever want to see another one of them oversized crop crunchers."

Doc rubbed his beard thoughtfully. "Even though the dragons undoubtedly nurtured the hatching of the domestic fauna we have just encountered, we may come across some survivors in the wild: stragglers, so to speak, who lived beyond the dominion of the world's overlords."

"Yeah, well, we'll burn that bridge when we come to it. I say let's blow this burg and get some miles under our feet. I'm antsy."

Doc rolled his eyes. "Sam, why did you let this child watch so much video?"

Sam shrugged. "Growing up in a subway tunnel wasn't easy. At the time, video seemed like a good way to show the kids what the world used to be like."

"I do not think it was ever like the way it was portrayed on video." A shiver of revulsion coursed through Doc's thin frame. "Shall we be on our way?"

"I go first." Jane threw out the rope, stepped over the edge, and walked down the wall backward.

Doc went next, and one by one the others followed.

Sandra was last in line. It was not until she was halfway down that she saw Scott grinning up at her. "Scott!" she screamed. She lit beside him and threw a punch at his naked chest. "You beast. You're more prehistoric than that 'ankle sore' back there."

Scott partially deflected the blow. "I was just steadying the rope for you."

"Do me a favor, and don't do me any favors."

She stalked off across the field and did not speak for nearly an hour. The ground was soft and loamy. The short grass buzzed with attendant insects that all too easily transferred their attentions to her bare legs. She continually reached down to dislodge the little biters, none of which she recognized.

Doc plucked plants and bunches of fern, and inspected them minutely.

"Pop, we didn't come here to study the wildlife, you know."

Doc chewed thoughtfully on the leaf of a small shrub. "My curiosity is more than academic. The first priority of any invasion force is to find food. We are at a distinct disadvantage because most of the indigenous flora is foreign to us, and we certainly do not want to consume vegetation that is inimical to our systems."

"What difference does it make, Pop? Meat is meat. Leave the herbage for the grazers. I'll stick to steak."

Sam rustled through a patch of thin, waist-high stalks resembling wheat. "Toad, ever since you were a baby your mother and I had trouble getting you to eat your vegetables. Now—"

"Now I'm a big girl, and I can eat what I want."

"How many times have I told you that the human body can't sustain itself on a diet of meat."

"I know all about uremic poisoning, Daddy, but I'd rather take my chances with that than eat leaves." She pointed to Doc. "How do you know that stuff isn't full of deadly toxins?"

"Well, I—Henry, how *do* we know? Aren't you taking an awful big risk sampling unknown substances?"

Doc held out the macerated stem. "In the case of this particular leaf, I am not. I observed the ankylosaur eating it. I also recognized several varieties that the dragons transplanted to our time. I cultivated some of them myself."

Rusty said, "In Maccam City we lived almost entirely on vegetable protein extract."

"Listen, you guys wanna eat fodder, be my guest. Me, I'm going after the first game we see. Right, DW?"

The Nomad shrugged. "Food is food."

"I knew you'd agree."

Death Wind handed the spear to her.

"What's this for?"

He pointed to the edge of the clearing, where the long trailing limbs of a willow tree shimmered in the breeze. "Look close."

Sandra pinched her eyes. She saw movement, like leaves blowing across the ground. "What is it?"

"It's not an it. It's a them." Scott pulled out his needle and held it like a dagger.

Sandra saw a greenish, rabbit-sized creature scuttle through the underbrush. Then she saw another—and another—and— "They're all over the place." She crouched low and stalked silently through the grassy field. She placed a finger across her lips. "Shush."

The ground was alive with scurrying, lizard-like animals. As Sandra approached, they spread out in the woods, some climbing trees and others scampering over moss-covered rocks. A few stopped and peered back with dark, curious, bulging eyes. Swinging the spear around her head, Sandra dashed into the middle of the flock. The little creatures suddenly stood up on two legs, tucked their forelegs along their sides, and bolted in all directions. Sandra lowered the spear so it grazed the ground at grass-top level. She caught one animal in the head and swept the legs out from under another. She stamped on the injured one and pinned it to the ground. The other had a crushed skull.

Scott chased futilely after the fleet runners; he never even got close. "These things are fast."

Sandra picked up her trophy by the scrawny neck and held it out triumphantly. "Now this is what I call dinner."

"But what are they? And what are they covered with?"

Doc took the still-living creature and examined it closely. "Feathers." He wrung its neck, then plucked a handful of dark plumage from its back. "Not true bird feathers. They look more like flaky, elongated scales that continually bifurcate until the tips resemble fanlike filaments. It must represent some dead-end evolutionary offshoot of avian ancestry."

"It's a blizard," Scott said triumphantly. "A cross between a bird and a lizard."

"Let's get a couple more." Sandra picked up a fist-sized rock and hefted it for weight. "Watch me pick off that turkey on the boulder. I'll cook his goose."

The round, grayish boulder was the size of a small bungalow. One bird-lizard perched on its hind legs and flapped its arms, while two others struggled up the craggy surface on all fours.

"That's strange," Doc ruminated. "Everything else is covered with moss or fern—"

The rock struck with a dull thud just below the clawed feet of the uppermost bird-lizard. The creature blinked and jerked his head, but made no other movement until the boulder on which it stood rippled. Then all three of them scampered into the underbrush and dashed away.

"What the heck—" started Rusty.

The boulder trembled like a giant blob of gelatin. The woods came alive with madly racing bird-lizards. Jane screamed as part of the flock swept past her in their curious upright, tucked-in posture. Sandra was too shocked to strike out at them. The boulder seemed to grow in height, as if it were being pushed up out of the dirt. Two massive, treelike columns lifted the gray mass like hydraulic pistons. A fat, ridged appendage

unfurled, reminiscent of an elephant's trunk; it swayed from side to side.

"Uh-oh," said Sandra.

One hook-toed foot left the ground, tearing up logs and leaves and clinging vines. The beast pivoted. As the tail swung out of sight, the drooling, leering head came into view. Long, dagger-like teeth filled a mouth that measured over five feet in length. A protruding brow ridge topped dark eyes that burned with anger. The thick tongue darted out with a screech that sent chills down Sandra's spine. Her legs went limp when the animal rose to its full vertical height; it was as tall as a skyscraper.

"It's an allosaurus," shouted Rusty.

"No, allosaurs lived in the Jurassic. I rather believe it's a Tyrannosaurus rex. Notice the ridiculously tiny two-clawed forelimbs—"

"Forget the taxonomic classification," Scott shouted. "Let's get the hell out of here." He grabbed Doc by the vest, spun him around, and shoved him off. He gathered Jane in his other arm and pulled her along. "Come on."

The tyrannosaur roared again, precipitating a complete rout.

Death Wind snatched the spear that was hanging limply from Sandra's hand. "Run!"

She needed no other urging.

They raced across the open field that skirted the antediluvian swamp forest. Shrubs with pointed stems stabbed Sandra's legs, but she hardly noticed. The weakness of fear left her body as the adrenaline took hold. Her heart fluttered wildly. She glanced over her shoulder and saw the portly behemoth stride out of the trees. Its stance was not upright but angled forward, the enormous head counterweighted by the bulky tail. White teeth glimmered in the sun. The beast swung its snout in ever-widening arcs, as if it were trying to locate its prey.

Its screech fulminated across the field, sending chills down Sandra's spine. The hideous head pointed directly at her. Its nostrils flared as if it could sniff her human odor. The head lowered and the tail raised, forming a body-line that was perpendicular to the ground. With another piercing screech the tyrannosaur charged. Taloned feet ripped up the earth at ten-foot intervals. This was no slow lizard: the carnivore advanced with the speed of a cheetah.

Sam veered for cover. "Head for the trees!"

The party in flight followed his example. A wall of shrubbery rose waist high in front of the palmettos, while five-foot-long segmented leaves cascaded down like a pall. Sam hit the leafy barrier first; he was stopped as surely as if he had hit a brick wall. He clawed and fought his way through the dense, closely packed bushes.

Death Wind leaped into the air, grabbed a low-lying limb, and swung over the barrier. Scott dived headlong, hit the ground on a roll, and came right up onto his feet. Rusty's long legs easily vaulted over the shrubbery. Doc hit the ground and crawled under the foliage. Jane executed a scissors movement with her legs, and ducked her head under the palmetto leaves. Sandra fought her way through the leaves behind her father.

Scott grabbed Doc's hands, dragged him out from under the bushes, and yanked him to his feet. "Come on!"

Jane hung back and parted branches for Sandra. "Hurry!"

Sandra raced past Death Wind, who stood grimly facing the field with his spear raised over his shoulder, ready to launch. From far ahead she heard Sam shouting "This way!" and spotted Rusty crouched and waving her on. She stopped to wait for her grandfather.

"Come on, Pop. Get the lead out."

Doc hustled by, half dragged by Scott and Jane. Sandra ran just fast enough to keep in front of them without losing sight of them in the brush.

"Over here," Sam called out. His naked chest was covered with scratches. As the group closed on him, he turned and made off through the trees. From behind came the feral screeching of the enraged tyrannosaur.

Sandra hopped across a tiny brook. Tangled tree roots eroding out of the shallow embankment snagged her foot. She fell down in a heap, but was up and running in an instant. "Watch it," she yelled back. She heard what sounded like a giant threshing machine mowing down the woods. By the clamor she judged the beast was less than a hundred feet away.

Splashing noises from ahead kept her attention on where she was going. She broke out of the trees onto a grassy bank that dipped gently to a slow-moving creek that stretched perhaps fifty feet wide. Sam was already halfway across, in water up to his crotch. Rusty plied through knee-deep water along the edge. Sandra leaped into a pile of what appeared to be lily pads except that

the floating leaves were the size of pillows. The rubbery leaf bent under her weight, but she did not tear through. Instead, her momentum carried her forward. She felt like a frog as she slipped off the green pad into the warm water and submerged completely. She floundered about for a few desperate seconds until she realized the depth was only a yard. She got her feet underneath her, waded into the shallows, and continued her flight.

"Come on." Scott pushed Jane and pulled Doc into the creek. They followed Rusty onto a sandbank in midstream, then across a reed-filled swamp. Jane tripped over a partially submerged log and went completely under water. She came up sputtering. As Scott straddled the log it moved sinuously beneath him, tossing him five feet to the side. He landed sitting, in water up to his neck. "Watch it, Doc!"

The thirty-foot-long crocodilian writhed between them. Its body was covered with brownish leathery plates; its head looked like a frying pan with the long snout stretched out like the handle. Doc fell back, his jaw ajar and his eyes bulging. Scott whipped the plastic needle from its sheath. With a mighty swing he plunged the point into the depression between the two periscopic eyeballs. The needle promptly broke in two.

The crocodilian lurched forward with a powerful sidesweep of its broad tail. The wash knocked Scott down. Doc gulped. Scott slapped his hands against the surface of the water, regained his balance, and reached forward for Doc. "Come on."

The monster bent its body double, lunging back at the trio. Death Wind entered the arena with his spear, which he snapped down on top of the knobby head. The shaft broke in two, but the mouth full of cruel teeth was driven beneath the shimmering surface. Death Wind leaped past the crocodilian before it came up for air. He grabbed Doc under the armpits and plucked him out of the water like a child would pick a flower.

"No waste time." Death Wing hauled Doc to the opposite bank.

The trees were sparse and offered no places of refuge. The terrain was mostly semi-open forest angling upward onto dryer land. The ankle-high grass blanketed the earth as it would a pasture. Fields of yellow flowers contrasted brightly against the vivid emerald background.

"Hey, there's the road." Scott pointed to a

horizontal elevation that carved an artificial orange path through the verdure.

"Let's start hitchhiking," said Sandra. She looked back at the creek just as the tyrannosaur crashed through the swamp forest on the other side. "And now!"

They took off running. The tyrannosaur teetered at the water's edge, tail swishing angrily.

"I hope that thing can't swim," Rusty said.

The tyrannosaur crouched like a hen about to squat on her eggs. It screeched and bounded upward as if a colossal spring had released under its tail. The tremendous leap carried it halfway across the stream. Its huge feet swung forward with the claws outstretched. It landed with one foot on the crocodilian's head, pinning it to the sandy bottom. The tyrannosaur bent forward with its cavernous mouth agape, its lips pressed back exposing a horrible array of teeth. In one incredibly swift rending motion it clamped its jaws on the crocodilian's plated back and ripped out a chunk of flesh that weighed as much as a large man. It tossed its head back, devouring the bloody meat in a single gulp. The crocodilian writhed in the tyrannosaur's unyielding grip; part of its backbone was gone, and what was left of its organs slopped into the water. Then the tyrannosaur bit the crocodilian between the shoulders, tore out another huge chunk of flesh, and swallowed without bothering to chew. The crocodilian lay still, surrounded by an immense pool of blood that stained the creek a frothy red.

Sandra wanted to throw up, but did not have time. She clambered up the rough, extruded embankment, and onto the flat orangetop. The poured plastic roadway extended as far as she could see in either direction, straight as an arrow but undulating with the terrain.

Doc bent forward at the waist, huffing and puffing. "Need a—moment to—"

"We're not out of the woods yet, Pops." Sandra watched the tyrannosaur finish its meal. It stood up on its haunches, licking its gruesome, drooling lips. "Come on, gang. Let's keep moving."

"I don't—think—"

"You can do it, Henry." Sam took Doc by the arm and urged him along. "You have to."

"That thing looks like it's still hungry," Scott warned. "And it's caught sight or scent of us."

Doc nodded weakly. His cane tapped on the road surface as he picked up the pace. "We can't

outrun it."

"It's on the move and coming this way," Rusty said. Scott took off at a trot. "I'll scout ahead for a place to hide."

"It's our only chance," Doc said, breathing easier, loping hard.

The tyrannosaur galloped across the open field with a speed that seemed impossible for a beast of five tons. Great clods of earth flew up from behind its taloned feet.

"There're no buildings, no—" Sandra looked around frantically for anything that might offer protection. "DW, come on."

Death Wind hung back with his truncated spear poised.

The tyrannosaur gobbled up distance like an express train. It stopped momentarily at the steep embankment and cocked its head from side to side, as if deciding how to negotiate the climb. It crouched and jumped, and in an instant stood atop the orange roadway. It screeched like a banshee.

"Hey! Down here!"

Sandra saw Scott sliding down the embankment to the grassy field. He plunged through some low scrub into a narrow brook. "It's a culvert."

Rusty and Jane plowed through the brush after him. Doc slipped on the scree and tumbled down the slope into the soft earth.

Sam skidded down after his father-in-law. "Quick! In here."

Sandra's feet hardly touched the ground as she skipped down the angled roadbed. Death Wind leaped completely over her head and landed with a plop in the muddy water. With the tyrannosaur screeching wildly right above her, Sandra ducked under Death Wind's upraised spear, stumbled, and fell headlong into the circular opening. Death Wind ducked in behind her, spun, and jabbed the point of the spear into the tyrannosaur's gaping, cellarlike maw. The beast chomped down on the spear and snapped it as if it were a toothpick.

Foul, fetid, carnivorous breath gushed into the cylindrical drainpipe. The beast gnashed its teeth and howled in crazed frustration. The head forced its way into the culvert, but the twisted neck and bulbous body prevented farther advance. Sandra wrapped her arms around Death Wind's chest, and looked past him into the glaring dinosaurian eyes only a few feet away.

The beast retreated. For several seconds the

air was rent with its awful, screeches. Great gray legs swept past the opening. The monstrous head reappeared and pecked at Death Wind. Sandra's scream reverberated throughout the short tunnel, and the vibration knocked dirt off the ceiling, but the Nomad did not flinch.

The tyrannosaur pulled out its head. It continued to stalk the culvert entrance, occasionally stooping to screech in rage at the prey that cowered just barely out of reach. It was a long time before the beast finally wandered off, a longer time before its howls were no longer audible.

Inside the culvert, no one moved or spoke. They huddled together like a brood of baby rabbits. Sandra's heart pounded so hard that she was certain that Death Wind could feel it.

Eventually, the sun set and ended their first day in the Cretaceous.

CHAPTER 16

Sandra sniffed the meat suspiciously. "DW, where'd you get that?"

"You kill."

"Death Wind, I thought I taught you better than that." Scott gladly accepted the chunk of meat that the Nomad handed to him. It was raw, but he was not about to quibble. He gave his portion to Jane.

"Yes. Sandra, you killed it. Before big lips." Death Wind cut another strip of flesh and held it out to Scott, who passed it farther down the line. "I picked it up, tucked it under belt."

"Wow, I was so startled by—big lips, as you call it —I forgot all about the little bird-lizards."

Death Wind shrugged. "No sense to leave behind."

Scott cringed, but did not correct Death Wind's English this time. He knew how often he could point out the Nomad's curt speaking mode before he would clam up completely. "All I had on my mind was hightailing it out of there. You know, we only made it into this culvert by the skin of our teeth."

Rusty chewed on a tough meat strip. "More by the skin of *its* teeth. Did you see the size of its tonsils?"

"Are you kidding? I almost died of dinosaur halitosis." Scott scooted his backside higher up the mud bank. There was not enough room to get his feet out of the trickle of water that flowed through the sewer pipe. "Doc, how big do you

think that thing was?"

"My powers of observation were unfortunately diminished by what I would like to call the exigency of the situation, but which I cannot in all honesty refer to as other than pure fright. My altered sense of perception tells me it was the size of a small mountain. However, upon careful reflection, I would estimate that stretched out in running mode it spanned a full fifty feet from tip to tail, somewhat less than half that in erect posture. A postmortem would undoubtedly provide paleontology with long-sought enlightenment on details not available in the fossil record."

Sam's deep voice echoed in the darkness. "My clinical interest ended when I saw that thing grin with a mouthful of croc."

Scott extracted another thorn from his macerated thigh. "Mine ended when it first stood up. Sandra, I think you should let sleeping tyrannosaurs lie."

"Shut up, you." Sandra's eyes were undoubtedly spitting fire, but in the total darkness of the culvert, Scott could not see them.

He mocked her in a high-pitched voice. "'So this is the land of the terrible lizard. I never thought it would be so beautiful.' "

"You're cruisin' for a bruisin', buster."

Scott patted her knee. "Nothing personal, my dear. I'm just experiencing a normal human reaction to traumatic events. It's called post fear syndrome. I've been scared silly, and I'm trying to laugh it off. Right, Doc?"

"I thought psychiatry was a defunct profession."

"Naw, we all studied it in Maccam City, didn't we, Rusty?"

"Yes. Part of our programming was the recognition and treatment of mental disorders arising from our highly confined and artificial living conditions."

"Rusty, get the computer lingo out of your head. Logic circuits are programmed, people are taught."

Rusty said, "Same thing."

"Yeah? Well, I'll tell you what my reaction is." Sandra stretched her legs across the narrow confines of the culvert, placing one foot between Scott's legs and one between Death Wind's. "I'm tired of being chased by nightmares that should have been dead for sixty million years."

"I'm just plain tired," Scott mumbled.

"I want guns. I wanna kill someone. I wanna

blow something up."

"My dear, I have no doubt you will have your opportunity. Excuse me, son, but is there any more of that delicious meat?"

Death Wind served a second course.

Scott leaned forward and melded his chest to his knees, then arched his back as best he could in the cylindrical pipe. He was sore, tired, and dreadfully uncomfortable—but glad to be stuffed into a place where the rapacious tyrannosaur could crawl. "It sure has been a long day. Somebody wake me up when—"

"Quiet!"

Scott instantly froze. He could not remember Death Wind ever raising his voice. No one moved, or breathed. Scott listened intently, but heard nothing other than the hollow echoing of air—like the sound of a seashell held up to the ear. He knew that the Nomad's senses were finely tuned, his perceptions acutely sensitive: the result of a lifetime of training that Scott, in his underground upbringing, had not developed.

Soon he detected a faraway wail, like the pleading call of a night creature. At first the sound was steady, without modulation, but soon it rose in pitch and loudness. A faint glow suffused from both ends of the culvert, detectable only because of the otherwise stygian blackness.

The sound became a whine. Peering cautiously out of the tunnel, Scott discerned shrubs and trees in the growing light. The shadows rotated with ever quickening speed. The whine dopplered to a roar. With a loud whoosh something passed overhead. The light reached full brightness and began to fade as the sound receded and dropped in pitch.

Death Wind tumbled out of the culvert.

"DW!"

Scott climbed over Sandra's legs and splashed into the open. He scrambled up the slope, his eyes glued to the ball of light that shot down the road like a flaming meteor. "It's a car! It's some kind of dragon vehicle."

Sam crawled out the other side of the tube and climbed up onto the orangetop. "Battery driven, I'll bet. Everything else they operate is run on storage batteries."

The rest of the group came out of hiding. They looked like strange caricatures in the ghostly white fog that enshrouded the nighttime landscape. A few stars poked through the mist-filled sky. The slight drop in temperature with the setting of the sun was more than offset by the high humidity.

"I daresay you are correct." Doc rolled his shoulders and flexed his arms. "I detect no carbon monoxide or other exhaust fumes that are usually associated with the internal combustion engine." Scott stared at him dumfounded.

"There were still a few around when I was a lad. Well, as long as we're up and about, I suggest that we follow that cab."

"Aw, come on, Doc. I'm beat. We've been up for two days straight, and constantly on the go—to say nothing of what we've been through, including the time barrier. How can you even think of staying up another night?"

"It is not a matter of choice, my boy, but of necessity. Our position is precarious. Apparently, even though the death bomb decimated the indigenous population, enough predators survived, or were hatched afterward, to harass the unarmed and unwary traveler. The gauntness of that tyrannosaur is an indication of how scarce a commodity the local prey must be."

"Doc, the thing was as fat as a tub."

"I think not. The dispatch with which it assailed us so soon after gorging itself on that crocodilian demonstrates its near starvation. I think we would be safer prowling at night and resting during the day."

Scott sighed deeply. He could not refute Doc's logic. Where did the man get his energy? "Okay, Doc. You win. Let's start walking. If I stand here another minute I'll fall fast asleep."

Jane placed her arm around Scott's middle. "I help."

Scott managed a weak smile. "Thanks."

The motley squad ambled along the orange road in the direction the speeding car had taken. Scott's feet dragged listlessly along the plastic. Even the warmth and tenderness of Jane's touch did not arouse him from his lethargy. He barely paid attention to the conversation the others resorted to as a way of staying awake. He heard only snatches of overlapping dialogue.

"Dinosaurs had quite a cosmopolitan distribution, so it makes sense that a few sur—"

"Did you see those withered hands, with only two useless fingers—"

"—the contrary, the dinosaurs were amazingly successful. They dominated the earth for over a hundred and thirty million years. Man has existed in his present form for a mere hundred thousand—"

"—no problem. Lots of drinking water and

plenty of culverts to—"

"—must have a high speed of growth, to go from egg to adult in a few mon—"

"—like deer dropping their kids, they have to get up and walk—"

"—much more cursorial than specula—"

"Hey, you got any skin scrapings on that pelt? I could eat a dinosaur."

"—without pharyngeal speech the dragons have done quite well for themselves in the art of communication—"

"—than being eaten—"

"—what is sluggish to us. The dragons survived despite the speed of contemporary predators the same as man survived against the fleet-footed lion: by stealth and—"

"—all we need is a nocturnal—"

"—a genius at dactylology: deaf-mute fingers-and-hands speech. I saw her signing with a tech—"

"—intelligence, not wisdom—"

"—can find tubers—"

"—dragons are descended from lizards that were cold-blooded, or ectothermic. The body temperature is environmentally dependent: they bask in the sun to gain heat, hide in the shade to shed heat. At night they become inactive, although the friction of muscle movement can generate—"

"—gimme a bazooka and I'll show 'em who's—"

"I wonder if they hibernate in the winter?"

"Mammalia and dinosauria coexisted for millions of years, but mammalian evolution was stunted by the dominance of dinosaurs. After the Great Dying there was nothing to prevent mammalian growth—"

"—diversification of species—"

"Are you kidding? She's as smart as a whip. You're just envious—"

"—high basal metabolism of warm-blooded animals, whether dinosaurian or mammalian—"

"Mesozoic and Cenozoic are eras; Cretaceous and Tertiary are periods."

"—never had to kill anyone. But she has other—"

"What do you call a dinosaur that knows a lot of synonyms? A rogethesaurus."

"—thermoregulatory—"

"No, I think the oceans absorbed the contaminant and killed off everything from ichthyosaurs to plankton."

"—called minimum population density. Sure,

a lot of individual animals survived the holocaust, but you need a large gene pool for the species to propagate. Extinction is a function—"

"—think there's a lot more going on between you two than a simple father-daughter relationship. I've seen the way she hugs—"

"—purpose of sexual dimorphism. By having both male and female gametes there is a greater chance of—"

"A scute is like a scale, isn't it? Like the plate on a turtle shell?"

"—glue them together to make a 'scale' model—"

"Because I've seen you two kissing, that's why. You never kissed me—"

"—not quite true. The hind brain of the stegosaurus, for example, was twenty times the size of the brain in the head."

"—two heads are better than one—as long as you only put your heads together—"

"Cockroaches have been around for three hundred million years—from the time of the Coal Age. I am sure they will outlive all of us."

"Just the same, I don't like her pawing you."

"—speaking, they are not dinosaurs. The plesiosaurs—"

"Yipes! Look at that!"

Sandra's scream shattered Scott's reverie. His eyes popped open. He saw a huge, bright orange ball rising up from the road ahead. The fog had cleared, and the stars shone down brilliantly except in a large arc above the fantastic orange globe.

"Wha—quick, get off the road!" He dragged Jane to the shoulder. "Come on!"

The rest of the squad just stood there. Scott implored them with one arm outstretched. "Hurry!"

Rusty grinned and slapped his knee. "Scott, you look so funny."

Scott glanced at the mysterious ball. It was larger than any object he had ever seen in the sky except the sun and—"It's a flyer!"

Sandra put her hands on her hips. "Don't be silly. It's just the moon."

Scott look again. "But it's so big."

"Due to refraction through the Earth's atmosphere, the apparent diameter is always larger when the moon is low on the horizon," Doc explained. "But it is closer now than it will be in our time. The tides must be higher as well. Beach front property must be rather wild and ephemeral."

The adrenaline was still flowing through Scott's veins. He held Jane tight as he watched the near-perfect sphere break contact with the ground. He breathed a sigh of relief. He did not even mind when everyone laughed at him.

CHAPTER 17

"Scott. Wake up."

The voice that reached Scott's ears was dim and faraway. It was part of a dream.

"Come on. It's time to go."

Every muscle in his body ached. He moved sluggishly, and squinted through narrowly parted eyelids. A shaft of light stabbed into one corner of the room, glinting off dust motes that jiggled and danced in the sunbeam with the random pattern of Brownian motion. For a moment Scott had no idea of where he was—or when he was. He dug his fists into his eyes and rubbed out the matter that had collected there like clots of earth. Rusty's image slowly took shape in the mists of his mind.

"What's the rush? I won't be born for another sixty million years."

"If you don't jump to it, you may become the first person to leave this Earth before he entered it."

"Maybe my future body is a reincarnation of this previous life."

"We can discuss semantics later. Right now we've got a coach to catch. It leaves in ten minutes."

"Save me a front row seat." Scott gathered his legs under him and pushed himself upright. He stretched languorously. His body was covered with sweat; there was no circulation of air in the cubicle, and the heat of the day was stifling. "Where is everybody?"

"Working."

"Yeah? On what?"

Rusty slipped past the barrier that was intended to keep large marauding dinosaurs and their smaller cousins out of the now-empty storage shed. Immediately beyond the doorway stood a wall that crossed the opening like a tee. The narrow corridor extended twenty feet in either direction, under a thick plastic ceiling, and was barricaded by a swinging mesh of woven acetate fibers that was fitted with a simple latch.

"Jane's been translating instruction plaques, so we've been able to gain access to the main yard and operate some of their mechanisms."

"No kidding?" Scott followed Rusty into the sun-filled lot. The highway ran through a shaded concourse that was straddled by a complex of fenced-in buildings and enclosures. "Why didn't you wake me earlier?"

"I tried. So did everyone else."

"What can I say? I need my beauty rest."

"It didn't help." Rusty ran a hand through his curly red locks. "You look like you combed your hair with an eggbeater. Anyway, it's apparent that besides being a substation—you heard the transformers humming—this place is also a maintenance facility and stopover point. It was crawling with dragons an hour ago, and—"

"With dragons?"

Rusty blinked at him. "Yes, you know—the guys with the long necks? The eight-foot-tall lizards that walk on two legs?"

Scott rubbed his scalp vigorously and brushed the tassels of blond hair back over his head. The cooler air of evening was a welcome relief. "They were here?"

"Scott, the road goes right through this place." Rusty spread his arms, indicating the small outbuildings, the canopied areas, the electrical compound, and the sprawling structure on the other side of the road. "It's like a pony express stop—traveling dragons can eat, sleep, and change vehicles. The corral's this way."

"Whoa. Wait a minute. What are you talking about?" Scott looked both ways before crossing the highway. He saw no traffic in either direction. The sun was about to drop below the horizon. "You mean, there were dragons and vehicles running around and I didn't hear them? Where are they now?"

"Gone. I'd guess in its heyday a labor contingent stayed here full-time, to patronize truckers servicing the time transporter. Now, with the population deficit, there aren't enough left to dragon the place. The convoy carried trained workers with them."

"Hey, the gates are wide open."

"I told you we got in." Rusty's long legs ate up the plastictop. "The dragons don't lock things for privacy, only against danger. Because of their biological predilection and their highly structured class system, they probably don't have theft or other crimes of possession. That's what Doc says, anyway, after listening to Jane's descriptions."

Scott shrugged. "Makes sense to me. I always

thought doors were sound barriers. I never saw a lock until we had to leave—" He flashed back to those final hectic moments when he and Rusty were forced out of Maccam City as acidic gas crept up the ventilator shafts corroding everything it touched. While Scott was usually able to ignore his feelings about the catastrophe, he knew how sensitive Rusty was about the loss of home, family, and friends. He rushed on, "Did the dragons leave the gates—"

"Wake up, Scott. I told you, Jane's been reading all the operation signs. The motor contactor is actuated by an external switch. We just had to flip up a protective cap, press the button, recite 'open sesame,' and entry was ours. Actually, we watched the dragons do the same thing. Still, Jane was a big help once we got inside."

They walked into a huge parking lot filled with vehicles of all descriptions, from single passenger models to tractor-trailer rigs. Each sat on a thick plastic chassis whose wheels were protected by armored fenders. All storage compartments were enclosed in bubbles of clear acrylic. The smaller cars were equipped with single rotating turrets, while the trucks and multipassenger coaches sported any number up to four; a laser nozzle poked out of the top of each turret.

Scott ran his hand lovingly over the squared-off, purely functional body of the nearest vehicle. "Look at these machines!"

"I knew you'd be excited. Anything with moving parts fascinates you."

"Hey! Over here." Scott turned at Sandra's shout. She leaned against the forward turret of a jitney and stroked the barrel of the laser gun. She thrust out her fist with the thumb up. "Now let one of those bastards get in my sights."

Scott whispered out of the corner of his mouth. "Sandra's got her security blanket." He smiled at her as he approached. "You know, you look your best when you're wearing a gun."

"Hey, man, I'm dressed to kill."

Sam climbed out of the front door. "Toad, remember that we're to use the gun for defense only."

"I hear you."

To Scott, Sam said, "Some people are trigger-happy, but she's trigger ecstatic."

Scott put his hands on his hips and surveyed the situation. "Rusty, when you said the bus was pulling out, you weren't kidding. How's it work?"

"Like everything else, it runs on universal, chargeable, interchangeable battery packs. Retractable cables pull out of that wall and plug into the charging port. The dragons either stop long enough to recharge their batteries, or a maintenance crew changes battery packs, or they turn in their vehicle for one that is fully charged. And look at this." Rusty held up the single-shot stun gun. "There's an adapter for fitting this into the receptacle. It's rearmed and ready to fire."

"And where are the transformers fed from?"

"Underground. The main power cables run under the highway. I can only see where they come out of the packing glands in the service tunnel, but I suspect the plastic road surface is poured over the top of the wires as added insulation and protection from damage."

Scott nodded. "Telephone poles wouldn't last long in this country. The tyrannosaurs would use them as scratching posts. I would have thought—"

"Well, well, my boy. I see you're up at last." Doc carried a large plastic carton under one arm. Jane was one step behind him. "Did you get your nap out?"

Scott smiled sheepishly. "Sure, Doc. I was really exhausted. Jane, what's in the boxes?"

Jane held out the plastic container so he could see inside. "Rations."

Doc tossed his own package into the bus. "It is not exactly what I would call living off the land, but the food is quite good once one gets used to the added preservatives. The cafeteria has not been restocked for quite some time, but we managed to scrounge up some victuals. Are you hungry?"

"When isn't he?" Sandra called down from her perch in the turret. "Hey, here comes DW. Let's get this caravan on the trail."

Death Wind carried a double armful of slender branches. "Bow and arrows."

"Rearmed, recharged, and rarin' to go," Sandra sang out. They all climbed aboard.

"This is all going a bit fast for me." Scott sat down in the oddly shaped window seat behind the driver's compartment. He noticed the cutout in the backrest where a dragon's tail was intended to slide. "Now I know how an infant feels in an adult chair." Furniture made to fit squatting dragons was not molded for the human form.

Sam took his place in the driver's seat. "All aboard?"

"Are you sure you can drive this thing?" Scott said.

"No. But what better time to learn."

Jane thrust an open plastic box into Scott's lap. "Eat?"

Scott sniffed the concoction in the container. It smelled awful and looked worse: bloody red chunks of meat the size of his fist. The grumbling in his stomach forced him to taste the unappetizing rations. He screwed up his face as he gulped it down. "If this is dragon cuisine, I'd rather have grubs."

Sandra laughed raucously. "Scott, that's the first time I ever saw you make a face at food."

Sam fiddled with the controls. The dashboard annunciators came alive. "Jane, which button was the searchlight?" Jane pointed to a tag covered with scratches.

"Thanks." He applied power to the electric motor by pushing a rheostat lever. The coach rolled smoothly ahead. "The joystick makes the bus go forward and backward, applies braking action by reversing current flow, and alters the direction by forcing one set of wheels ahead of the other in a scissors movement: every pair of wheels is mounted on a split axle." He demonstrated how the coach drove at an angle to its facing axis. "It's extremely responsive, and if you pull the tiller all the way to one side it'll go around in circles. So far, I've only pulled it out of its parking spot." Sam demonstrated the turning radius in the lot., "If you want to stop you can either slow it down gradually by cutting the power, or throw it into emergency braking by applying reverse power. Hang on."

He yanked back on the lever. The polymerized wheels screeched on the orangetop. Scott was thrown forward by his own momentum as the coach skidded, halted, and started off in reverse.

Sam brought the vehicle under control. "It's fast and has tremendous torque. And with every wheel independently powered, it can probably travel off-road just as well as on. It's quite a machine." Sam veered in a large curve and steered the coach out the gates. "Death Wind."

The Nomad leaped past Scott and out of the coach. He touched an inset switch on the garage wall. The massive gates swung closed. When Death Wind was back in his seat, Sam closed and sealed the armored hatch. Ventilators opened and airflow fans switched on automatically.

"Next stop, dragon land city," Sam announced to his passengers. "Sandra, keep a sharp eye open." The coach rolled smoothly onto the highway, but went into wild gyrations when Sam pulled the lever to the side to execute a turn. The vehicle zigzagged like a drunken sailor until he got it facing in the right direction and resumed a straight course. "The steering's going to take a little getting used to."

The sun had dipped below the trees, and the first stars of twilight were upon them. The highway maintained its arrowlike course through the swamp forest. The coach accelerated with a quiet whine up the gentle slopes, and coasted noiselessly downhill. A ground mist hung low above the bogs, creeping eerily across the road. Trees on high ground had been cut back to offer an unobstructed view in case of stalking predators. The night orchestration of prehistoric insects was damped by the acoustical properties of the acrylic housing.

Scott tossed down another chunk of preserved meat. "This is too good to be true: the dragons providing us transportation not only into the past, but to their city. And I thought we were going to spend weeks trudging through the swamp and fighting off dinosaurs. Unbelievable."

Jane winked at him.

Sam adjusted the temperature controls for maximum comfort. "We can only travel at night, though, when the dragons can't see who's driving this bus."

"Wait a minute." Scott squirmed in his seat. "You mean, we're not going to run off the road at the first sign of another vehicle?"

Doc chuckled. "There is no reason to, my boy. They will not expect to find us driving so boldly along a main thoroughfare."

"But what about when the future dragons relay information about our escape into the past? Won't they be on the lookout for us?"

"I have no doubt they will, but not in a stolen vehicle. No, I think we should maintain a course of intrepidity. The way to win a war is through active aggression. We should never allow—"

Rusty placed a hand on Doc's forearm. "Please, Doc, no more dictums."

Doc stopped with his mouth open. He slowly turned his gape into a smile. "Quite right, my boy. Quite right."

"Besides, we can always blast our way out of trouble." Sandra climbed down from the turret.

"DW, gimme another one of them tubers."

Death Wind handed her what looked like a maroon banana. "Already cleaned."

"Hey, what's that?" Scott said.

Rusty took another one out of a plastic sack. "It's actually a bulb." He gave it to Scott. "And quite tasty."

Sandra took a bite off the end. "Not bad for a vegetable."

"Honey, would you mind closing the hatch?" Sam said.

"Sure, Daddy." Sandra climbed back up into the turret and sealed the upper hatch. She sat on the gunner's chair and hunched forward over the firing mechanism, but her feet reached nowhere near the rotation control pedals.

"Sam, watch out!" Scott practically choked on his food.

The coach swerved sharply as Sam yanked the joystick back and to the left, forcing the vehicle to slew sideways with the wheels racing in reverse. The coach bumped off a grayish shape, lurched to a halt, then backed up until Sam let go of the lever and stopped the engine altogether.

Scott twisted around and saw the dinosaur standing in the middle of the road. It was quadrupedal and sported a splayed neck shield with scalloped edges. Tiny horns, little more than enlarged thorns, topped each beady eye, while one long fat horn jutted off the snout. It twisted its neck and looked at him with obvious lack of concern, chewing a mouthful of vegetation. Scott swallowed the unchewed bulb at a gulp.

"It's a triceratops, and you broke off its horns."

Sandra slid off her seat and jammed the foot controls. The turret spun until the gun pointed in the dinosaur's direction. Then she jumped back into the seat and lowered the elevation of the barrel.

"Don't shoot! Don't shoot!" Sam shouted.

"I ain't gonna, unless I hafta."

Jane squeezed into the seat next to Scott. She snaked one arm around his middle. "Okay?"

"You, me, or it?" Scott kept his eyes on the creature as Sam switched on the searchlight and stabbed the beam in its face. It had a beak like a parrot, a body like a cow, and a thick tail that rested on the ground. "I don't see any blood."

The dinosaur let out a loud bleat that rose Scott's hackles. It lifted its multiton mass halfway up on thick hind legs, pivoted, and charged off like a scared rhinoceros at a speed inconceivable for a beast of its bulk. It trampled down brush and small trees as if they were grass. Sam kept the bright beam on the creature until it disappeared among the trees.

Scott felt Doc's hand on his shoulder. "I doubt if it was hurt."

"But the horns—"

"It is a member of the short-frilled ceratopsians: a monoclonius. It is supposed to have only one large horn. Sam, if we have not sustained any damage, I suggest we proceed with caution."

Sandra scowled. "You'd think they'd have a dinosaur crossing sign."

"We're out of here." Sam applied power, and the coach eased ahead at a snail's pace. "I can see that one of the first rules of driving is to keep your eyes on the road. I'd better concentrate on what I'm doing."

Uneventful hours later they came to a crossroad.

"So now what do we do?" Sam brought the coach to a halt. "Wait for a dragon vehicle to lead the way?"

"Jane, my dear, are there any hidden symbols to guide us?" Doc asked.

"I still think we oughta go back to the time transporter now that we're armed, go back to our time and blow the structure to kingdom come." Sandra drummed her fingers on the laser gun's power amplifier. "We got the might, we got the right."

"My dear, we have already settled that issue," Doc said.

Scott was in a quandary. "We have?"

"While you were asleep," Doc explained. "Our principal aim is not to destroy, but to learn. We do not know what secrets we may uncover unless we seek with an open mind. Wonders of the universe may unfold—"

"Doc!" Rusty screamed.

"Sorry, my boy. But it is in our best long-term interest to storm the walls of dragon land before we retreat, to ensure that when we close the portal to the Cretaceous it remains closed forever."

"Seems like I missed a lot by oversleeping," Scott said.

Rusty whispered, "An argument with Sandra is something you can afford to miss."

"I heard that, you worm!"

Rusty cringed and rolled his eyes.

Jane peered out the windshield as Sam played

the searchlight beam across the road surface. They were surrounded by open fields of tall grass. No buildings marked a way station, and no poles indicated direction of travel.

"There." Jane pointed down at the middle of the intersection. "Dragon scratch." Her thin brows beetled as her eyes raced across instructions etched in the plastic surface of the road. She held out her right arm. "There."

Sam executed a right turn. He left the searchlight pointed straight ahead, illuminating the road in front of the coach. Thirty minutes later they passed a lone building sequestered in a desolate tract of forest. It was dark and seemingly abandoned. A few minutes after that they came upon a cluster of sheds constructed of universal poured plastic. Just beyond was a rural complex consisting of single unit structures of different sizes and shapes.

"Nobody's home," Scott said.

"We must be on the outskirts of a city," Doc said. "We may soon encounter occupied dwellings."

"Hey, what was that?" Sandra dropped out of the turret and hit the floor with a thud. "Over there, to the left."

Sam brought the coach to a halt and swung the searchlight to where his daughter was pointing. A huge mound of freshly dug earth towered next to a deep hole. A truck-sized vehicle with a blunt grille was parked next to a pile of dead dragons that were stacked like cordwood. Sam took the coach closer to the grisly scene. The pit was crammed with the bodies of naked dragons. Long necks intertwined with protruding legs and paws and snakelike tails. Leering faces glared up at the stars. White teeth gleamed sardonically.

"There must be thousands of them," Rusty breathed. "Millions."

A flock of pteranodons fluttered over the decaying remains with rapid motions of their twenty-five-foot wingspans. The ungainly monstrosities pecked with long beaks at sightless eyeballs and lolling tongues. With the rear cranial ornament protruding as far to the rear as the toothless beak stuck out in front, the pteranodons presented an otherworldly profile as they hastened to consume the proffered morsels.

"The dragon metropolis must be a charnel house that is yet being cleansed." Doc leaned back in his seat and closed his eyes. "I fear; my friends, that we are about to enter the city of the dead. Let us do so with as much trepidation as daring. The future of the world is in our hands."

CHAPTER 18

A long dragon convoy trundled by in the opposite direction. The leading vehicle was a flag-car filled with caped dignitaries, the rest were heavily armed freight cars. Sam maintained speed to allay suspicion. He slunk down in his seat, and hid his face behind a curtain of dino-hide. The others lay flat on the floor.

"All clear," Sam sang out.

Scott stared out the rear window at the retreating searchlights. "You're right, Doc. They must assume we have a right to be on the road."

"Dragon psychology—the best weapon in our arsenal."

"I'd still rather beam off their family jewels," Sandra glowered.

"My dear, besides the trivial biologic fact that lizards do not display external genitalia, we have a better chance of preventing dragon reproduction by continuing our clandestine crusade. Silence is our watchword, stealth is our method, and bold—" Doc peered at Rusty. "Anyway, you get my point."

"There are more lights up ahead." Sam did not slacken speed. "But they appear to be stationary."

The moon had long since risen. Scott was getting used to its increased apparent diameter. A steady stream of pure white light shone down on the landscape, highlighting a jagged escarpment that rose thousands of feet above the surrounding prairie. Castellated ramparts were plainly visible.

"It's a fortress," Rusty shouted.

"The size of a city," Scott added. The battlements extended as far as he could see to either side. "A big city."

"That long talus slope must be the entrance ramp. Sam, slow down so we can see what we are getting ourselves into." Doc said to Jane, "My dear, let us know of any scratched warning we should heed."

"Yes, Doc." Jane positioned herself by the windshield. "I read."

"Sandra, I am not expecting trouble, but you be ready to man the gun—er, woman the gun—should the need arise."

"When it comes to blasting dragons, I'm always ready."

"Scott, please stand by the rear turret."

"Gotcha. "

"Death Wind, how are your weapons systems coming along?"

The Nomad carved the finishing touches on a wooden shaft and held it out for inspection. "Wood is strong, it make good arrow. Feathers okay." Fitted into the sliced grooves were the coarse scale-feathers from the carcass of the turkey-sized creature Sandra had clubbed to death. He twanged the taut bowstring. "Plastic line not so good—too much stiff."

"In your hands, I am sure it will be exceptional armament."

Death Wind hefted his new spear. "This is very good." The shaft was shorter than that of the other spear, before it had been reduced to a ruler splintered at both ends, but it was tipped with a formidable, finely honed white point.

"Where'd you get that?" Scott said.

"From tyrannosaur mouth. It broke off when I stabbed in culvert."

"Death Wind the dentist. Extractions free of charge." Scott admired the six-inch tooth that was lashed to the end of the spear. "I have to hand it to you, you are some scavenger. You don't miss a trick."

The highway headed straight for the cliff face. Other pikes merged from both sides. Abandoned vehicles lay scattered across the shoulders where they had apparently been towed. Many were smashed beyond repair. The lights ahead did not seem to be getting any closer: in the open, desertlike expanse leading to the dragon aerie, perspective was distorted by distance.

Many minutes passed before the coach came within clear view of the huge concourse that siphoned all the highways into a seemingly single broad orangetop entrance that measured hundreds of feet wide. Two searchlights were mounted atop tall gun emplacements on either side.

"That must be how they keep marauding tyrannosaurs out of the city," Doc commented dryly.

"But how do the dragons keep the traffic in order?" Rusty wondered. "In all the video movies I've ever seen, cars had lanes—"

"That must be what these ridges are for," Sam said loudly.

"I've been driving right over them. Jane, what do these scratches in the road mean?"

"In. Enter. Come."

"Close enough. Well, Henry, we didn't get shot to pieces by the first defense, so I guess this is going to go as well as you thought. What do we do next."

Sandra said, "I still say let's just find a cache of explosives and leave a delayed charge in the time transporter, and blow the thing after we go through."

"My dear, we will do that eventually, but we have priorities of more importance. We must explore this magnificent city, not just out of idle curiosity, but to gather knowledge about the dragons as yet unknown to us, and which may be of monumental importance to future events. They have at their digittips a power of awesome strength and a technology of incredible complexity. We cannot simply destroy their time transporter, we must ensure that they do not build another and escape once again from their proper place in the geological history of the world."

Sandra grimaced and pounded the back of the seat with both fists. "I hate it when you're right. Okay, Pop, we do it your way." A broad smile split her face. "You just let me know when I can do some damage."

Doc nodded gratefully. "My dear, your cooperation is deeply appreciated, and serves as a fine illustration of deferring tactics to strategy. You are to be commended—"

"Sam. There." Jane pointed to the left. "Follow symbol with two line."

"Lines, Jane." Scott stood behind her and rubbed her shoulders. "Two implies the plural."

Jane smiled. "Okay."

"Looks like we're coming to a tunnel." Sam hunched low and peered upward. "No wonder. There's a sheer cliff above us."

The coach entered a conduit wide enough for a dozen vehicles. Ripples in the dull orange plastic lining gave the appearance of a lava tube. It was dimly lighted by solitary fluorescent fixtures spaced at hundred-foot intervals.

"Looks like they're conserving electricity," Rusty observed.

The grade was no more than fifteen degrees; it may have slowed down a heavily laden freight car, but the coach hummed along at its normal gait.

"Stay in line," Jane read.

"I'm sorry." Scott laughed. He jerked his hands off her shoulders. "I wasn't trying anything funny."

Jane's thin eyebrows pinched together. "I not under—stand."

"Jane, your linguistics is improving at a fantastic rate, but you're not yet ready to embrace the pun." Scott winked at her. "But I'll teach you."

"Don't do her any favors." Sandra leaned against the turret ladder. "Maybe she didn't learn much from Daddy, but you can ruin her."

Sam huffed. "I think she did very well in the two months we had together. She at least caught the rudiments of the language so Scott—"

"Why do you keep saying two months? What were you doing the rest of the time?"

"The rest of what time? I was only there for two months."

"Where?"

"In the dragon city. Where Jane lived."

"So where were you before?"

Sam winced. "I was home, of course. With you."

"What the hell are you talking about?" Sandra came erect, and her voice became a squeal. "That was a year and a half ago."

"No, dear, get your times straight. The hunting party was out only a week when we got—" Sam's eyes clouded over.

In front of them the lights grew brighter. The tunnel flared out as the ripples in the road surface curved away from the middle. The ceiling yielded to the open canopy of the sky; faraway stars twinkled through atmospheric heat inversions. Shapes hovered in the ground shadows below the searchlight stations.

"What's happening up ahead?" said Rusty.

Sandra ignored him. "And that was a year and a half ago."

Scott's mind filled with comments about all the incidences taking place in the future, not the past, but his attention was split between Sam's evident consternation and disorientation, and the spectral display they were fast bearing down upon.

"I—I—can't remember—it seems as if—"

"Hey, those are armed soldiers!" Rusty screamed.

Sam shook his head. He stared out the windshield, but his mind obviously was not taking in the scene before them. He was frozen.

As the coach leveled out where the ramp split into half a dozen thoroughfares, a bank of searchlights burst into full brilliance. The inside

of the coach was illuminated as if by the noonday sun. An entire panzer division lined the walls of the tunnel outflow. Ground troops filled the spaces between the armored tanks.

Sam shrank back in his seat, oblivious to his surroundings. When his hand left the lever, it automatically resumed the middle position. The coach slowed down. Doc leaped forward and jammed the joystick as far forward as it would go. At the same time, a barrage of laser blasts crisscrossed in front of them. Two energy beams penetrated the windshield and left smoldering holes in the acrylic.

"It's an ambush!" Doc shouted.

The sudden acceleration threw everyone to the floor. A second volley arced through the side windows, blasting holes through the seats or going out the other side of the coach.

Doc kept his hand on the joystick. "Sandra, I believe that your wish for action has been granted."

Sandra sat up, her face showing signs of shock. "What?"

Scott braced himself against a backrest, wrapped his hands around Sandra's waist, yanked her off the floor, and thrust her against the turret ladder. "Shoot 'em." He climbed over Death Wind and scrambled up into the rear turret. His legs were not long enough to reach the foot pedals from the seat; he stood awkwardly with his spine bent backward in order to rotate the turret while he adjusted elevation manually.

His first shot went wild, gouging a hole in the orange road surface. His second shot barely missed a dragon soldier taking aim with his pack-mounted laser gun. Doc turned the coach away from a vehicle blockade, throwing Scott to the side; his hand clutched the trigger as he grabbed the discharge mechanism for balance, and he succeeded in blasting a hole in a second-story balcony.

The coach turned in a wide circle just inside the lethal perimeter. Scott spun his gun to starboard, shooting bolts of electronic lightning as quickly as the capacitors recycled. He and Sandra pasted a deadly broadside into the dragon ranks, felling soldiers and drilling chassis. One lucky shot hit a vehicle's recharging unit; the battery exploded in a shower of sparks and flying debris.

"Way to go, Toad!" Scott shouted enthusiastically. His fighting blood was flowing. He braced himself against the clear plastic walls of the turret, aimed down the barrel, and cut down the dragon hordes with reckless abandon. The slow-moving soldiers, made more sluggish by the nighttime chill, responded lethargically to the passing high-speed coach.

"It's a turkey shoot," Sandra yelled over the sounds of battle and exploding fusillades. "Give 'em hell, Scott."

The heavy-duty laser cannon reeked with raw power. Scott worked the trigger like a lab animal jolting itself with bursts of gratification through brain-stimulating electrodes. Every deadly discharge released pent-up emotions. He was more alive than he had ever felt before. For a fleeting moment during the heat of battle he understood that Sandra's aggressive nature was not prompted by feelings of hostility or inadequacy, but by a sense of almighty dominance over a situation of previous impotence. He was the weak devouring the strong, the innocent conquering the culpable. He was getting even.

An enemy laser beam bored through the turret; Scott winced as hot fire touched his abdomen. His moment of reverie was gone. He was scared again.

Sam suddenly came alive in the driver's seat. The windshield was riddled with holes, and smoke poured out of the dashboard. Jane huddled in a heap where she had been thrown against the hatch. Doc lay in a prone position; he kept his hand on the throttle and directional control. "Henry, I've got it." He thrust the lever from side to side, causing the coach to dodge erratically. Bolts of pure energy stabbed at the vehicle; the fenders may have been proof against tyrannosaurs, but the laser beams penetrated the plastic guards like hot foils through butter.

"There're too many of 'em," Sandra shouted. "Get us outa here."

Sam steered for an opening in the barricade of vehicles. Soldiers from the after ranks moved forward to take the place of their fallen comrades. They wore cloaks to protect their bodies from the cool air. Hand-held weapons leveled at the coach.

Sandra blasted away from the front turret. "I'll make Swiss cheese outa them."

Scott, frustrated at not being able to direct his fire forward, picked off troops along the sidelines. His turret was punctured by three laser beams almost simultaneously. The breech of his gun was blown asunder. Scott fell back, ricocheted off the seat, and dropped like a stone into the cab.

Death Wind softened his crash to the floor. "You okay?"

With a shake of his head, Scott said, "I think so."

A rending crash sent them both forward. All the windows on the port side blew in as the coach scraped alongside a building. The coach leaped into the air as the wheels rolled over a dragon soldier. The coach reeled at so sharp an angle that Scott thought it was going over. It righted itself with a crash. The follow-up gyrations were not caused by Sam's lack of control; the coach had suffered serious structural and mechanical damage. A fire raged in the rear compartment.

Sandra plopped down on the floor. "I think it's time to abandon ship. My gun's on strike."

An awful screech emanated from under the floorboards; the misaligned axles were grinding to pieces. The coach looked like a sieve. Seats and bulkhead insulation were smoldering. What was left of the windshield was splattered with the blood of the run-down soldier. The ambushing vehicles had broken formation, and a full battalion of dragons was creeping along the street.

Doc squirmed out of the miscellaneous wreckage on the floor. "I think a propitious retreat is appropriate."

"I've lost the hydraulics." Sam punched buttons on the darkened instrument panel. "The door won't open."

Death Wind slung his bow and dinohide quiver over his broad shoulders. He climbed through the cluster of bodies, grabbed hold of an overhead rail, and swung his feet through the remaining glass. He kicked out the windshield, then hopped through. "Spear."

Scott picked up the weapon as the others climbed through the opening. He waited until the rest were off the coach before passing the dangerously tipped spear to the Nomad. Splinters of glass pricked his feet, but the dinohide moccasins were tough enough to prevent the shards from breaking through. "Now what?"

"We should take a lesson from the lowly flatworm and move away from the disturbing stimulus," said Doc.

"Go where the dragons aren't," added Rusty.

Jane screamed at the same moment that Rusty discharged his one-shot stun gun at a leering lizard face. The soldier dropped as if pole-axed.

Jane shook her head. "No good door."

Death Wind buried the tyrannosaur tooth into the heart of the soldier that took its place in the doorway. "Run." He led the way along the sidewalk.

The human squad scuttled after the Nomad. Searchlights roved along the roadway and illuminated building walls. The abandoned coach blew up with a tremendous roar of fire and flame; a chunk of quarter panel knocked over a passing single-turret vehicle, and burning fragments scythed through nearby soldiers with the devastation of a grenade. The flaming roof turned end over end until it smashed into a third-story balcony. The chassis separated into its component parts; wheels ricocheted from walls like billiard balls off cushions.

As they ducked into a narrow alley, Doc looked back at the scene of destruction. "So much for stealth."

CHAPTER 19

Doc reconnoitered from the top of the watchtower. The dragon metropolis sprawled in front of him as far as he could see. It had not been built from scratch like the concentrically designed outpost in Holocene South America; it was a hodgepodge of slave pounds and domiciles, barns and sties, industrial plants, warehouses, and lofty spires that punctuated the urban scenery with add-on irregularity. The city was bigger by many times than any that modern man had ever constructed.

"Here you go, Doc." Scott pounced into the room with a handful of supplies. "We raided another storage locker and found all kinds of good things to eat."

"Yeah, and he's already sampled most of 'em. You'd better chow down before he consumes the whole lot." Sandra unloaded her booty by the door. "With the elevators out of order, this is quite a hike."

Doc said, "That is the idea—to deter dragon scouts from locating our base camp."

"No chance of that. They're spread as thin as dielectric on a resistor." Scott handed a faded brown, fist-sized cube to Doc. "Processed meal, probably made for the slaves."

"Thank you." Doc gratefully accepted the dried, compacted food bar. "Did you check the basements?"

"Yeah, there's not a soul anywhere," Sandra said. "Not any that haven't already gone to heaven. Man, there are bodies everywhere. Millions of 'em. It'd take a month of Sundays to clean 'em all out."

Scott chewed on a mouthful of meal. "And the cellars go on forever. There's an underground maze all interconnected with the topside structures. I'll bet you can go anywhere in the city without getting a suntan. And, Doc, we've got the key to the city. There are abandoned cars all over the place, charged up and rarin' to go. I even tried my hand at the stick."

"Yeah, and he almost creamed Jane when he lost control."

"It's not as easy as it looks."

Doc sighed. "Perhaps I'd better come down from my aerie and perform some useful work. All I've done all day is stare out the window. Oh, yes, I scared some pterodactyls out of the attic—or was it the other way around?"

"But, Doc, that's what you were supposed to do."

"What? Scare pterodactyls?"

"No. Watch the city for movement, for military maneuvers, for dragon activity."

Sandra harrumphed. "While those lizards are busy hatching eggs, you better be hatching one hell of a plan."

"Yes, well, that is what bothers me. For once in my life I have no plan. My grandiose scheme to delve into the world of dragons past has so far gained us no advantage. Nor can I excogitate a discernible future plan. I keep waiting for an inspiration—for some direction. But three days cooped up in this lavish apartment"—he swept his hand to indicate the plush furnishings, the alien architecture, the convenience appliances silenced by the loss of electric power—" and I haven't got a clue as to how to proceed. I underestimated the dragons once and it nearly ended our campaign. I do not intend to do it again. I need more input from you young scouts."

"I wanna stop skulking around like a pack rat," Sandra said, "and eliminate some lizards— if I can find where they're hiding."

"Not an easy task in a city that is designed to house tens of millions, and occupied by a mere pawful. They must have a stronghold that I fear must now be heavily defended. The dragons do not seem to have made the mistake of underestimating human ingenuity."

"Yeah, they sure knew when we were coming, and how."

"That is precisely why we must tread with caution. I realize now that they have been studying our psychology as much as we have been studying theirs."

"There isn't much they could learn about this outfit by watching those dunderheads back in the present—or the future—or whatever you call it." Sandra strode to the window and glanced outside. The sky was a clear deep blue with practically unlimited visibility. Clouds like cotton puffs floated serenely overhead. "So how could they do that?"

Doc was caught off guard, lost in thought. "Do what?"

"Study human psychology. Did they read Freud's *Beyond the Pleasure Principle*, or did they experiment with two-legged guinea pigs?"

Doc jerked back so hard that he almost tripped over a tail rest. His jaw hung slack, and he was momentarily speechless. When he regained his composure, he said haltingly, "My dear, whatever possessed you to peruse such an erudite volume?"

"Hey, I didn't spend all my time as a kid watching movie vids—just most of it."

"I don't know," Scott said with a smile. "It sounds like a title that would attract her attention."

Sandra pinched her brows and poked out her finger as if she were going to yell. Instead, she threw back her shoulders and said calmly, "Scott, I may have some personality flaws, but at least I'm working on them."

Scott rolled his eyes. "I guess I asked for that. I apologize."

"Accepted. So what—"

Rusty and Death Wind joined the powwow. "We've had an interesting morning," Rusty said.

"DW!" Sandra threw her arms around her husband and gave him a resounding smack on the lips. They had not seen each other in several hours. "Where's Daddy—and Jane?"

"They stay behind."

"Together?"

"Alone is not safe."

Sandra pouted, "I don't like it when those two—"

"Hey, don't you want to hear what we found?" Rusty interrupted. "A library."

"You mean, with books?" Scott said enthusiastically.

"Made of the sheerest synthetic vellum. I'm telling you, there's nothing the dragons can't do with organic polymers. They read it, wear it, build with it, drive on it —I wouldn't be surprised if they eat it, too."

"Yes, well, judging by the taste of this stamped-out cubic nutriment, they do." Doc placed the partially-eaten food bar on a countertop, and wiped his mouth with the back of his hand. "As food for thought, I hope what you have to say about this prehistoric atheneum is more digestible."

"Unless you're a termite or a silverfish, you'll love this." Rusty paced the room with the practiced gait of a thespian. "There are more books on these shelves than the legendary Library of Congress—or was that real?" He shook his head. "It doesn't matter. The important thing is that Jane can read practically everything but the technical journals. Did you know that when she was a little girl she stole grammar books from the schoolhouse? She was studying dragon scratch when she was supposed to be sweeping the floors." Rusty flung his hand past his ear. "Anyway, the information retrieval system is serviced by computer and, knowing the dragon's penchant for uniformity, I'll bet it operates in identical fashion with the one I played with in the North American dragon outpost."

Scott jumped for joy. "You mean, you can enter through a keyboard terminal and access their data files?"

"No."

The expression of glee on Scott's face took a long time to fade into a frown of misunderstanding.

"They've turned off the electricity to the entire complex." Rusty faced Scott and placed his hands on his friend's shoulders. "But our mechanical and electrical wizard can trace the wiring circuits back through the distribution panels and plug us back into the main power supply. Then we'll show these lizards some mammals in action."

CHAPTER 20

"Uh, Henry, can I talk to you for a minute?"

"Of course, Sam. What seems to be troubling you?"

Sam looked both ways, saw that they were alone in the dark, underground corridor, and said in a hushed voice, "It's about—my amnesia."

Doc pinched his eyebrows. "Is some of your memory returning?"

"No, not exactly." Sam pursed his lips and again checked the empty hallway. The only illumination emanated from the battery-operated lantern at his feet. "That is—I've been thinking about it a lot and, well, I've been waking up at night with the shivers. My chest feels like a block of ice."

Doc wiped perspiration off his brow. "Not the reaction one would expect in this heat."

"It's the dreams, Henry. It's coming back to me: a sensation of—utter cold. I can remember when I woke up—after being shot. I was freezing. My teeth were chattering, I was shaking like a leaf, my skin was frosted—"

"Not an uncommon response to the temperature suppressive affects of anesthesia on the hypothalamus. Vasodilation coupled with long-term immobility—"

"No, Henry, this was different. It was intense cold, like—I don't know—like I'd been buried in an iceberg."

"When I was practicing medicine in my younger days, back east, I often saw similar responses in patients after long surgical procedures. People sometimes suffer memory loss after a traumatic accident."

"Did they lose a year out of their lives?" Sam said desperately.

Doc tilted his head. "No, of course not. But then—"

"This was different. I wasn't shot with a stun gun. I remember looking down the nozzle, I saw the burst of light, I felt the laser beam drill through my chest like a red-hot branding iron. And, Henry, I don't even have a scar."

"The mind often plays tricks on the brain; it can go awry like the printed circuits of a computer. Oxygen starvation to the cells will cause synaptic breakdown—"

"I know my physiology, Henry. I studied under the best doctor in the profession—you. I'm also a wise enough physician to know that a doctor is his own worst patient. That's why I'm telling you . . . my impressions. Please don't explain them away so hastily. Just—think about what I've told you. And remember what I'm going through. I'm trying to account for a big gap in my memory. I'm trying to reconstruct—"

Death Wind padded along the corridor like a breath of wind. Only the intentional thumping of his spear warned of his approach. "Scott says

throw the switch."

Sam nodded and glanced away. He ducked into the electrical closet, held the lantern up high, and wrapped his hand around the engaging device of the liquid circuit breaker.

"Sam, do not look at the contact blade in case it arcs."

"Right." He closed his eyes as he rotated the mercury-filled vial that made the electrical contact. "Hey, no sparks." The vial stayed in the horizontal position, instead of spinning to the vertical and breaking the flow of electrons. "Let's go upstairs and see if we're in business."

By the time they threaded their way along the convoluted corridors and up the stair towers into the library, Scott had his instruments clamped to the exposed wiring in the central distribution panel. He touched the probes to various terminals. The window on the plastic meter box flashed runic symbols.

"How's it look?" Sam said.

"So far, so good."

Sam looked over Scott's shoulder at the readout. "How do you know what all that stuff means?"

"I don't," Scott said matter-of-factly. "I never have. At least, not most of it. And Jane's dragon vocabulary doesn't extend into technical jargon. But I used the same kind of instrument to check wiring circuits on the dragon computer in our time. I know I'm checking voltage because the lead goes from a hot wire to ground; amperage is gauged by putting the meter in series with the circuit. These scratches are integers to base eight—dragons apparently developed their numerical system by counting their toes. I figured this out through interpolation. How many volts or amps, or what amount of resistance we've got, I just don't know. But it doesn't matter, as long as I remember that the numbers are consistent with the readings I made before. So, let's give it a shot."

Scott rotated the mercury tube until it rested against the detents. As slow as the dawn, the light in the room waxed from nothing but lantern glow to the equivalent of bright moonlight to the luminous intensity of the rising sun.

"Dragons have an interrupter rheostat that prevents power surge from popping the fuses again. It's quite clever. Well, let's go see if there's enough light to read dragon tales by."

"I do not believe I fancy getting close enough to a dragon to read its tail."

"Doc," Scott said with surprise. "Aren't you getting our roles reversed? You're the serious one; I make the jokes."

"Solemnity is a condition of inflexibility to which I refuse to adhere. Do not let this cane confuse you: my bones may be aged, but my wit is sprightly."

They passed under an arch that could have been the center span of the Brooklyn Bridge. The grand exhibition chamber that housed the principle book collection was a ten-story-tall geodesic dome whose walls were crisscrossed with ramps that began at four points on the floor and which took off in alternating directions: a quadruple helix that wound upward to the transparent ceiling with inward protruding study platforms at the intersections.

Rusty sat at the computer console in the middle of the vast room. He was surrounded by a vast complex of keyboard terminals and tiered monitors. Sandra lounged against a printer station. Jane ran her finger along a row of labeled switches and read out their meanings.

"Is it hot?" said Scott.

"The place ain't exactly air-conditioned," Sandra retorted.

Scott ignored her. "Rusty, do you have power?"

The redhead did not look up. He wore a newly made pair of gloves with claw extensions sewn into the fingertips. He tapped away at the keyboard. The control panel lit up like a Christmas tree. Rusty grinned like a Cheshire cat. He flexed his hands. "All the power I need."

Using pointed thumb and forefinger like ice tongs, he plucked a program capsule from a storage bin and inserted it into a square depression in the control panel. The weight activated a servomotor that siphoned the matrix cube out of the capsule and introduced it into the scanning recess. A bank of monitors sprang into life; their display screens filled with line language.

"This model is highly sophisticated. It can boot all six superficies at once."

"Huhn?" Sandra said, frowning.

Rusty waved a hand over the hundreds of other capsules. "Each one of these crystals contains an operating format and memory unit that is coded at the molecular level, and containing as much information as every volume in this library."

"Get outa town," Sandra said.

"No, I'm serious. Microminiaturization is the key to dragon dominance of the world. It enabled them to produce a computer that worked better than their own brains."

"So what? We had computers that could out-think people."

"No, we didn't. We had computers that could calculate faster and store more information and retrieve data quicker than their programmers, but they could not think. They were simply programmed logic circuits that operated at the rate of electron flow—essentially the speed of light. By comparison, although the human brain carries thoughts at a snaillike pace, it has the ability to create ideas."

"That didn't help me any on my math homework."

Rusty went on without interruption. "Early computers using vacuum tube technology took up a five-story building just to add simple figures. Second generation computers used diodes and transistors, analogues for neurons in the human brain, and became much more efficient. But this"—he stabbed a clawed finger at the control panel—"using a multilevel scanning system, reads data stored in a finely grown crystal lattice in terms of the positions the atoms occupy within the lattice. Perpendicular laminations provide internal access—"

"Whoa, whoa, whoa." Sandra waved her hands in front of her face as if she were warding off a horde of hornets. "Just give me the short version. My brain can't even keep up with an abacus."

Rusty sighed.

"He hates being cut short when he's on a roll," said Scott.

"If I may interpolate," Doc said, "it may help to understand that the human brain is biologically superior to—that is, its construction is more complicated than—the lizard brain. At least, in the accumulation and processing of data. Which is not to say that we are necessarily smarter, only that we reach conclusions more quickly—and sometimes jump to them."

Rusty said, "The dragons have designed a computer that is better than their own brain, possibly even better than ours. The internal search and seizure interval is almost instantaneous, giving it the semblance of true thought. Of course, it can't make decisions that it hasn't been programmed to give. That's the difference between memory capacity and intelligence."

"From my experience with dragon soldiers,"

Doc added, "they function either by instinctive reaction or conditioned response. That is why they will fight to the death. Technicians have the ability to learn. Administrators can actually think for themselves, although almost always within predictable parameters. On the other hand, the mammalian orders are somewhat adaptable to situations of stress. In man, this flexible response to circumstances has reached the highest degree of versatility. The irrational approach to uncomfortable predicament is called emotion, my dear, and it is one of your greatest attributes."

Sandra stared slack jawed at her grandfather. Before she could cry a rejoinder, Doc, smiling quixotically, rushed on, "And I intend that as a compliment. You see, one of the most effective ways for a numerically inferior force to overcome a stronger adversary is to catch him off guard, to attack from an uncertain direction, to do the unexpected. Your compulsive conduct under pressure often leads to unpremeditated victory. That is why, although I chastise you for your hasty actions, I always forgive you. You exercise a genetic quality that has a positive long-term effect."

Slowly Sandra regained muscular control of her mandibles. "I'll remind you of that the next time we get in a tough spot."

"I am sure you will."

Sandra picked up a cube and held it so that it glinted in the light. She pushed open the slider; the crystal dropped out of the clear plastic housing and into her hand. "Oh! I'm sorry. Do I have to be careful of breaking it, or scratching it?"

"You can't hurt it. I've already dropped a few without ill effect. The data is locked permanently into the crystal lattice; the bonded carbon atoms can't be dislodged by shock, magnetism, or electricity. And since it's diamond, you can't scratch it either."

"Diamond!" Sandra held the gem by the corners and admired it with newfound awe. Like a prism, the crystalline structure split white light into its component parts. The rainbow spectrum that played across her palm disguised in colorful ostentation the true value of the jewel. "How many carats?"

Rusty shrugged. "I don't know. But its storage capacity is in the hundreds of gigabytes. Each one of these cubes holds uncountable reams of dragon knowledge."

"All of which we can use to our advantage," said Doc.

"Capturing the enemy battle plan is the ultimate victory in a spy operation." Scott pounded a fist into his palm. "With all that information at our control we can wage a guerrilla war that'll blow the dragons to kingdom come. We'll be a worse plague against what's left of the lizards than the Great Death was against mankind. I think it's time to get to work. What do you think?"

Rusty flexed his fingers, tapping his clawed gloves against the keyboard in front of him. "I think we're about to make history."

CHAPTER 21

"I have a plan."

"I knew you would come up with something eventually, Pop."

Doc pulled the shish kebab off the fire, inspected the chunks of canned meat, then put it back over the flame. "I am sure it is one that will meet with your approval, my dear, since it involves dragon bloodshed."

"Now we're talking turkey."

With his teeth, Scott pulled a bite of meat off another steel spit. "Tastes more like stegoceras to me. I wish they had pictures on the boxes, so I could be sure."

"May we dispense with the repartee and get down to business?" Doc waited for a moment of silence. Scott and Sandra exchanged raised eyebrows, the others nodded silently. "Thank you. Now, we all understand how important it is for Rusty to familiarize himself with dragon science and technology via the library computer terminal. Whatever we learn about our enemy may play a significant part in our triumph over the survivors who would bring dragon rule back into the world. But the library computer is not a control computer; it can only read and access data. It is not tied in to the defense network, or other actionary devices. I think it is equally important, therefore, to explore more than the dragon state of knowledge. We need practical intelligence as well. And we need to disrupt and demoralize their ranks. I propose that we do this by coordinated sniping."

Sandra grinned. "Tell me more."

"We split into three teams. Rusty will stay at the computer console, with Jane to help with translation. Death Wind and Sandra will work as a combat unit, Sam and Scott as an exploration party. We go out only at night, and we forage as far and wide as vehicular operation will allow during the hours of darkness. I want everyone to report back at daybreak."

"Pop, I love it."

"Sounds great to me, Doc." said Scott.

Sam tossed more trash onto the fire. The courtyard in which the rebels dined was surrounded on all sides by five-story living accommodations. "Do you have specific objectives?"

"Only those we've already discussed. The main emphasis should be placed on crippling their utilities. Since virtually everything in the city operates on electricity, shutting down or disabling the generating plants is the number one priority. Scott, you must study the distribution system in order to ensure that we do not cut power to the computer."

"Hey, what about the time transporter?" Sandra wanted to know. "This is a nice place to visit, but I don't wanna live here."

Doc raised bushy white eyebrows at Scott.

"Sure, Doc. No problem. That substation where we stole the bus is an electric facility as well. I'm sure there's enough battery power there to make several time transfers."

"Good. I always feel comfortable having a backup. Sam, keep an eye open for dragon operations. If we can determine a specific survival plan we may be able to circumvent it."

"Right, Henry."

Doc held up his walking stick. "Death Wind, Sandra, your main objective is to act as a diversionary force by raising Cain. Kill, loot, plunder, burn, do anything you want—but always on the opposite side of the city from where Sam and Scott are conducting their activities. We will operate in random fashion so the dragons never know where we will strike next. Do not conduct major assaults, just hit-and-run warfare. That is the strength of the guerrilla tactic." Doc paused and glanced around at his meager but multitalented squad. "Are there any questions? I am always open for input."

Doc took the skewer out of the fire, tasted the meat, and found it favorable. He slid the other pieces off the spit and onto a plate, then passed the feast to Jane. She smiled. The first chunk of charred flesh she offered to a shrewlike creature that she cuddled in her lap.

"Does she always have to keep vermin?" Sandra said through clenched teeth.

"My dear, it is only a pet, and keeping pets is part of human nature: one of the distinguishing characteristics that separates man from the lower animals." Doc held out a tiny morsel, smiling as the cute critter wrinkled the nose on its long snout, and nibbled at the proffered food. "Who knows? Perhaps someday the descendants of this little fur ball will evolve into the larger mammals of the Tertiary—perhaps even into the Primates. We certainly wouldn't want to take the chance of killing it, would we?"

Eyeballs roved, but no one spoke. The plate circulated around the group of warriors, returned to Doc with several bites left. Sam poked the fire with an iron rod. Death Wind rotated another skewer in the yellow flame.

"I suggest that we finish eating and get a good day's sleep. We have a world to change, and, despite the availability of temporal displacement service, very little time in which to do it."

* * *

Death Wind stole along the open street toward the lighted building, whooshing before the hot wind like a leaf in an autumn gale. His tooth-tipped spear led the way.

He stopped jut outside the cone of light and melted into the shadows. He stood as still as a bronze statue. He detected no movement inside the doorway, he heard no sound; but he smelled the ripe odor of lizard flesh. Dragons were nearby.

All his Nomad instincts welled within him. With his back pressed tightly against the plastic wall, Death Wind peeked around the jamb. A sleepy guard perched on a stool; the tip of its tail flicked to the slow rhythm of a lizard heartbeat. The long neck looped like a horseshoe, letting the guard's lower jaw rest on its scaled breast. It wore a cloak of thick dinohide. On the floor, leaning against its hindquarters, stood a battery pack and laser pistol.

Death Wind rushed into the room, a wraith with a will. He buried the tyrannosaur tooth into the dragon's chest and punctured the three-chambered heart between beats. The guard did not have time to breath its last.

The tripod formation of tail and legs kept the motionless lizard on its stool. The only sign that it was dead instead of asleep was the viscous flow of blood that dripped over its fat belly and pooled on the floor. Death Wind slung the backpack over his shoulder and readjusted the long straps to their shortest extension. The battery pack rode uncomfortably on his lower back beneath the bow and quiver, but could not be raised higher. He doffed the backpack and left it with his spear by the door. Bow in hand and arrow notched, he strode farther into the building.

A palatial spiral ramp coiled clockwise from the floor of the antechamber. Only nightlights were lit. Death Wind crept up to the second floor. A long corridor stretched out before him. A guardroom stood to one side, occupied by two lounging lizards. The Nomad slipped past them quietly. He stopped at the next room, lifted the latch, and eased open the heavy door. He ducked into the darkness.

When his eyes adjusted to the gloom, he saw that the apartment was tenanted by a lone dragon lying naked in the sunken pit that served as a berth. A gold cape hung on a wall rack. Death Wind slowly released the tension on the bowstring. He put the arrow back in the quiver. He drew his knife.

Crouching low, he flowed across the room at a glacial pace. Every sense was alive, every muscle attuned. Unfamiliar insects buzzed in the air like dive-bombers. A winged monstrosity landed on Death Wind's bare shoulder; he ignored it. The knife rose in the air. Death Wind balanced on the balls of his feet as he lowered himself to within striking range. His nostrils flared and his chest expanded as he forced air into his lungs.

Scaled lids fluttered, the squat body stirred.

Moonlight glinted briefly off the steel blade as it plunged downward with all the force that Death Wind's corded muscles could bring to bear. The dragon lurched in slowly dawning awareness. The knife sheared off the breastbone at the same time that the long tail whipped around and caught the Nomad in the head. He was flung backward by the force of the blow. He crashed noisily over a stool and into the hard wall, absorbing most of the concussion with his brawny back.

The wounded dragon hissed as its head rose up like a rattlesnake's, tongue darting. Blood spurted from its chest. Death Wind regained his feet and charged. He leaped into the air, came down at the base of the dragon's neck and vaulted over the clutching claws. Death Wind executed a perfect roll. When he came up, the dragon's head lay flat against the mattress. It gurgled once, then went limp.

Death Wind yanked out the bloody knife. He wasted no time in flinging open the door and whisking down the corridor. One guard was already half out of the watch room. It was in the act of bringing its stun gun to bear when the Nomad bolted by with his knife upraised. The razor-sharp blade rasped across the tough underside of the leathery throat. The guard recoiled, but by that time the Nomad was halfway down the ramp.

He stopped at the junction of the hallway and let out a series of war whoops. The uninjured guard waddled to the railing. In one smooth motion Death Wind pulled an arrow out of the quiver, notched it, and let it fly with deadly accuracy. The honed plastic tip buried itself in the soft, fat underbelly. The guard hissed as it clutched the half-buried shaft with one paw and grabbed the balustrade with the other. It steadied itself. Still hissing, it turned and waddled off.

Death Wind stood there for several minutes, waiting for something to happen. Escape at this point was too easy. When a squad of soldiers finally appeared on the landing, he whooped once, turned, and ran before their stun guns could be brought to bear.

He snatched up the spear and backpack on the way out, then hung around the doorway and waited for the dragons to catch up. When he was sure they had spotted him, he jogged in full view down the middle of the street. He stayed just beyond stun-gun range. Dragons did not move fast, but their long legs carried them far with each step. Several of them fired their guns.

Death Wind let out a whoop as he approached a darkened alley. He stepped over a thick rope that was stretched across the street. When the dragons reached the same spot, Sandra pulled the rope taut and snugged it around a hydrant. The first two soldiers were caught in midstride and went down headlong. The next three reacted too slowly to stop their forward momentum; one of them tripped, the others leaned beyond their balance points, but flung their tails out backward and remained upright. The two in the rear crashed into the melee, knocking them all down.

"Gimme that laser gun!" Sandra shouted. She burst from the alley like a jet from an aircraft carrier's boosting track. She jerked it out of Death Wind's hand, flipped off the safety, and fired. The power pack recycled again, and again, and again. The street filled with smoke, and with the stench of burned flesh.

When Death Wind finally convinced her to stop shooting, there was nothing left of the dragon soldiers but fried meat.

Sandra wiped tears from her cheeks. "Take that, you bastards."

*   *   *

Sam swung the dragon lantern nonchalantly. "If anything is in here we'll see its light a long way off."

The corridor was as black as a coal bin, and every bit as dusty. Scott held up his lantern and cranked up the rheostat. The light gradually grew brighter until he could see the pipe racks along the ceiling. "Still the same coding." Scott referred to the plastic tablet. "According to Jane, a loose translation would be something like 'main power circuit district eight'."

"Did you bring the dictionary?"

"Yes, but I'm not that proficient at using it. I'm not as quick a learner as Jane."

Sam nodded. "A bright gal."

"A veritable Rosetta Stone as far as I'm concerned." Scott held the lantern next to the pipes on his side of the corridor. The markings had not changed. "Jane is . . . Sam, I—can I ask you a personal question?"

"Of course."

Scott dimmed his lantern until it threw out barely enough light to show the way: more as a mask to prevent their discovery. "Sam, is—is there anything—between you and Jane?"

Sam answered calmly and forthrightly. "Yes."

Scott gulped. He stared straight ahead. "Oh."

"But not the way you think."

Scott stole a glance at his companion. "How do you mean?"

"You've been taking too much stock in Sandra's innuendoes. Sandra sometimes sees what she wants to see, the result of insecurity mixed with childhood fantasy. She means well, but she's confused about her feelings, and *by* her feelings."

"I thought she was the most secure person in the world—next to Death Wind."

"Considering there are only seven of us in the world—this world—that's not saying much. Actually, her outspoken audacity is merely a cover-up for the fragile person inside. It's not her fault, really. We did a lot of traveling when she was a baby—either chasing after dragons or running from them. Until we stumbled on the subway people, we lived in caves, in tents, in demol-

ished buildings: always hiding, always on the lookout for the enemy. Then, after we moved into the subway, we were apart a lot. I was foraging, or hunting, and she was stuck in the tubes watching videos with her mother. She's never forgiven me for what she perceives as abandoning her."

"But, Sam, it wasn't your fault that you had to go out for food."

"Oh, I know that. And she knows it, too. But the child inside her doesn't know it. She needs love and acceptance, but doesn't like to have to need it. That's the conflict she faces. And until she comes to terms with it, until she finds a situation in life that she can live with, she will be an unfulfilled woman. As her father, all I can do is understand her—and love her. I love Jane the same way—as a daughter. The great, fulfilling love of my life has been lost, and once lost can never be regained. You'll understand that someday."

"Well, I . . . "

"Scott, it's blatantly obvious that you're smitten with Jane. The eye embraces, the touching, the long walks together: they all give it away. Don't try to resist the temptation of longing; go along with it. I would—if I were in your moccasins."

"But you—"

"Forget about me. I'm not a competitor. Whatever relationship Jane and I have is not affected by your relationship with her, nor vice versa. If anything, they complement each other. Now, what do you suppose that glow means up ahead?"

Startled, Scott looked up. He had been staring at the floor for so long, and in such emotional turmoil, that he had forgotten their mission. "This must be it. We must be close to the generating station." The corridor broadened, and the pipe racks spread outward in various directions. "This is how it looked in the nuclear power plant in the outpost in our time. This is a much larger scale, of course. We should see a—" Scott drifted toward a plastic retaining wall on which were mounted lighting distribution panels, insulated pipe lines, and equipment shelves and cabinets. "Here it is: a radiation counter."

He pulled the device out of its compartment, flipped a switch, and watched with satisfaction as the clear plastic faceplate lit up. "This is unbelievable!"

"What? High levels of radiation?"

Scott shook his head. "No. There's nothing but normal background emission. But now that I know something of the dragon language, I can understand the readings. It never made sense to me before. Come on." Holding the radiation counter in front of him, Scott led the way through the maze of duct work. "The reactor should be nearby."

"I can't believe there aren't any guards," Sam said.

"According to Doc, it all has to do with dragon hierarchy. They have a class system of such enforcement that no dragon would ever think of entering an area for which it wasn't authorized." Scott shrugged. "It doesn't seem strange to me. Where I come from the ideal of community welfare was taken for granted. And even though we've been raising hell in the city for the past two weeks, they don't have enough soldiers to guard against intrusion."

"Let's not get overconfident." Sam warily scanned the sidelines. "It's getting brighter up ahead."

Scott found himself whispering. "Better switch off the lanterns."

They entered a mechanical space full of humming motors and clacking contactors. Emergency lights suspended below the overhead pipe racks shed an eerie yellow glow. The room was as big as a house. A pump started, and the discharge of water was clearly audible in the distance, reverberating in the tomblike structure.

"Shouldn't a nuclear power plant be humming with technicians?"

"Naw, they're fully automated," Scott explained. "Back home, in Maccam City, the only time we had more than two people watching the monitors was during a core change. But there may be a maintenance crew wandering around—if they have the personnel to spare on anything but emergencies. As long as we stay clear of the control shack we should be okay."

The floor inclined upward; dragon architecture did not include stairs. Since the pipes ran horizontal they gradually dipped beneath the plastic surface. Soon the auxiliary generator room was behind, and Scott and Sam found themselves in an enclosure the size of a large stadium. The monstrous structure that occupied the center stage was a sleek-skinned, five-hundred-foot-long lozenge whose lower portions were cribbed with external crossmembers that doubled as an interlocking series of catwalks.

Stars shone through the transparent dome.

Scott stopped in his tracks, ogling the ultramodern structure. "This is the strangest nuclear containment system I've ever seen. I don't see any access panels for the exchange of fissionable materials."

Huge magnetic coils protruded from either end of the five-story lozenge. Peripheral machinery whined steadily. The smell of ozone was thick in the air. The floor thrummed with power, sending a tingling sensation through Scott's feet.

"Oh, no."

"What is it?" Sam jerked his head from side to side. He drew the laser pistol from its holster and thumbed the safety. "What's wrong?"

"I can't believe it."

"Talk to me, dammit!"

Scott walked forward slowly. His arms hung limply at his sides. He paused at an engineering station long enough to stare at the cluster of gages and the dazzling array of annunciator lights. He passed under the catwalk ramp. He did not stop until he was within arm's reach of the dull orange surface of the generating lozenge. When he held out his hand, every hair on it stood on end as a result of the static charge.

"Scott, what is it?"

Scott's mouth was full of cotton. He licked his lips and swallowed hard. "It's a plasma shield. After a reflective pause, "This is a fusion reactor."

CHAPTER 22

"Rusty, my boy, wake up. Wake up, lad."

Rusty sat on the tripod stool with one arm dangling down and the rest of his body sprawled across the keyboard and function switches. His curly red hair was matted where his head had lain against his hand. He groaned, but did not move.

Doc clutched a sheath of foolscap against his chest. Half a dozen printers clattered behind him while reams of newsprint collected on the floor and threatened to inundate the library. "You may as well lie down if you are going to sleep."

Rusty's head lolled. The circles under his eyes were dark. "No time to sleep," he mumbled. His voice was craggy and barely audible. "Work to do."

"Yes, I understand." Doc deposited his fanfold on a workbench. When he lifted Rusty off the stool; the youth's legs buckled under him. Doc let him down as easily as he could.

Rusty curled into a ball. "Incubator." He breathed deeply and evenly.

"He is okay?" Jane said in an unfaltering tone. She stopped scribbling English transliterations long enough to stoop and place her hand on his forehead. "He is hot head?"

Doc smiled. "It is the other way around, but never mind. He has a mild fever. Nothing to worry about. Just overwork. He has been glued to that console for more than thirty-six hours straight. His longest stretch yet."

Jane pinched her eyebrows and looked up at Doc. "What is incubator?"

Doc rubbed his beard thoughtfully. "It could be the beginning of future adversaries."

* * *

A dragon soldier waddled out of the building with its gun drawn. Behind it marched a vested technician. The armored car squatted only yards away, engine idling; gunners sat in their turrets.

Death Wind loosed an arrow from a second-story window across the street. It was a long shot that glanced off the soldier's scaled flank. The twin turrets slowly rotated, the gun barrels elevated. By the time the laser beams stabbed through the opening, blasting away the framework, the Nomad was long gone.

Sandra fired her pack-mounted laser from half a block away. She did no more damage than to crease the pavement between the technician and the car. She was forced to duck the blast from a second soldier who was leaving the building. As soon as her gun was recharged, she poked the nozzle around the corner of the alley and let go a wild shot. The concentrated fire from ground troops and gun turrets bit into the walls and street surface around her, blowing out droplets of molten plastic.

She ducked back and threw her arms across her face as protection against the incandescent blobs. She scrabbled to safety on all fours. With her aim to draw fire accomplished, she stood up and ran. Ten minutes later, and half a mile and three subbasements away, she met her husband in an abandoned storeroom.

"It ain't as easy as it used to be," she said, breathing hard.

Death Wind nodded. "They are on guard. We must keep them that way."

* * *

Scott huddled in a corner of the library, using crumpled papers for a makeshift mattress. He heard a rustling behind him. When he rolled over, he saw Jane holding out a steaming mug of tinted water. Scott smiled at her. "No matter how far people go, in space or time, they take their customs with them."

Jane grinned. "You like tea?"

"Very much." Scott pushed himself to an upright position, leaned against a shelf of books. He took a sip of the brew. "Hmmnn, it's good. What's it made from?"

Jane shrugged. "That means I do not know."

"I know what it means." Scott gave her a peck on the cheek. "Do I say good morning, or good evening?

"You wake up, so it should be morning. But it is dark outside."

Scott humphed. "I don't know. Leading a nocturnal existence for a couple months throws one out of perspective. I think it's a matter of choice."

"Do always have choice?"

"Yes. Always. Or at least, you should. I know that's hard for you to understand, being brought up as a human slave." Scott took another sip and raised his eyebrows in consternation. "That's why we're fighting this war. So we can have a choice in what we do with our lives."

"I understand. It is difficult to make up mind after years of—dragon telling. I think—I like it. I not like dragon control. I not know this before." Jane placed her hand on her breastbone. "I have turnings in here."

"Feelings, Jane. Those are feelings."

Jane sidled closer on her knees until their skin was touching. "I have other—" She chewed her lower lip. She clenched her hand into a fist and lightly tapped her chest. "Pain in here—but not hurt."

"Huhn?"

"Not the words." She took Scott's hand and pressed it against her bare breast. "What is—love?"

Scott was caught between a gulp and a tingling in his groin. "Where—where did you hear that?"

"Sandra say it with Death Wind. Say 'I love you.' What is love?"

"Well, it's, uh, it's a word that—has to do with feelings, and with the heart. Not the physical heart. That's just a poetic description, I guess, because when your feelings are hurt you feel pangs in your chest. Actually, the seat of emotion is in the brain. It's part of your personality, part of your being, part of—your soul."

Jane looked at him blankly.

"All right, I guess I'm not explaining this too well. Love is—the way you feel about people. Not that you love everyone. At least, not in the same way. It's a feeling of—warmth, I guess, of wanting to be near—of wanting to touch."

Jane brightened with glee. She rummaged through the accumulation of scrap paper until she found a plastic box whose sidewalls were full of tiny cutouts. She unsnapped the lid, reached inside, and pulled out a furry rodent with a long snout and twitching whiskers. "I touch. I feel warmth."

Scott rolled his eyes. "That's not exactly what I meant." He went on quickly when Jane started to pout. "I mean, you can love your fur balls, but that's only one kind of love. There are other kinds of love. Like—do you remember your mother?"

Jane nodded expressionlessly.

"Well, you had feelings of love for her. And it hurt very much when—she was taken away. That's the bad side of love. Some people aren't even aware of love until they lose it. But love is a very great thing. It describes the depth of your closeness to someone; it's a bond between two people; it's a one-word summation of a million mixed-up emotions that are too complicated to explain. And you can love people in different ways, and on different levels. You have one kind of feeling for your fur balls, another for your mother, and yet another for Sam, and Doc, and the others."

Jane stroked her pet as she pondered Scott's description. "What kind of feeling I have for Scott?"

Scott inhaled deeply. "That's something that only you can know."

* * *

Doc rolled the six-foot-diameter hemisphere across the floor of the library. He shuffled through papers that were strewn everywhere—tens of thousands of pages filled with laser-burned dragon scratch. The sheets of vellum were also piled high in every available nook and cranny of the main level. When he reached the space that had been allocated for the half globe, he let it fall; it rolled around in circles for nearly a minute, winding down like a child's top, before it came to rest.

"There it is: the great continental mass of Cre-

taceous dragon land." Doc dusted off his hands. "Although it is not exactly the way geologists reckoned it would look."

"A hundred-foot change in water level could make a big difference in coastal contours," Sam offered. "Polar ice pack could account for it."

Everyone gathered around, sitting on stools or lounging on deck pads that had been brought in for bedding.

"It was believed that the supercontinent of Pangaea split up long before the Cretaceous." Doc ran a gnarled finger along a separation zone on the raised surface. "I can see here what may represent fault lines, the rifts of modern day plate tectonics, but I believe that we will have to rethink our theories about the time scale of prehistoric geological processes that created Gondwanaland and Laurasia, and eventually the continents and subcontinents as we know them. Empirical evidence takes precedence over—"

"Pop, this is all very interesting, but what does it have to do with your plan of attack?" Sandra sat cross-legged, one arm crooked around Death Wind's elbow. "Wouldn't we be better using the city map?"

"Quite right, my dear. I was simply trying to set the stage for Rusty's discourse: to give an overview of this microcosm in which we find ourselves. We do not want to rush into anything that we do not fully understand. Rusty?"

Rusty bounced to his feet with a sprightliness that he had not shown in weeks. He passed a wand over various dark splotches of the curved map. "These are dragon municipalities, fortifications actually, in various portions of the world. According to the videos—"

"Videos!" Sandra shouted. "You mean while we've been out there tailing dragons you've been watching videos?"

Rusty's face was a blank. "Part of the time, yes. Uh, may I continue?"

Sandra maintained her frown.

"Thank you. Now, according to the videos the dragons maintain a feudal state in which remote rulers occupy tracts of land surrounded by fenced-in forts, or plastic castles, whose sole purpose was to provide a place of refuge from marauding carnosaurs. There were no battles between warring vassals: they all paid homage to the central government. Toward the end of the dragon regime they managed to wipe out most of the wild predators while corralling many of the herbivorous dinosaurs. The newsreels end with the coming of the death bomb that Doc sent through the time transporter, devastating the continent, but it's fair to assume that all the border legions died in the great genocide. However, some of the slave population here in the city managed to survive because they lived cooped up in underground units. The bigwigs lived in the multistory apartments and were all killed. I believe that most of the administrators and technicians returned here from our time."

Sam raised his hand like a schoolchild. "Doesn't this social and technological disparity seem strange? On one hand we have a highly advanced science that has harnessed the energy of nuclear fusion, while on the other hand we have a civilization that relies on slave-drawn carts. And in between is a pervasive and unemotional desire to kill off an intelligent race that is predisposed as inferior. There's no evenness in their culture."

Doc grimaced as he tugged his beard. "I daresay we can find appropriate parallels in mankind's recent history: one country living in riches and comfort while another lives in squalor, the hunting of animal species to extinction, even pogroms against adjacent nations. Dragons may not be fundamentally different from mankind, only more ruthless. And where man chose space flight as a way to leave his planet and expand the race, the dragons opted for time flight. Just because we do not understand the physics of time transport does not mean that it is an esoteric science."

Rusty plucked a diamond off the computer console. "I may not understand it, but this crystal lattice does. Each cube is a data storage packet programmed on a specific topic—with a great amount of cross-indexing. I hold in my hand the secret of time travel."

"Let me see that," Scott said.

Rusty tossed the carbon crystal to him. "One facet is also a history module. Initially, the dragons built a sending unit large enough to handle their death bombs. When the coast was clear they sent through the personnel and materials to build a reciprocal unit—the push-pull system is far more efficient. The time transporter then becomes a harmonic device that can both send and receive in the same space at the same time, with interlocked safety features that prevent passage into a space that is already occupied. Once synchronized, the double transfer utilizes hardly more power than a one-way dispatch—operating on the same principle as an elevator with a counterweight."

The wand touched a spot on the semiglobe. "Not knowing what they were getting into, the dragons built their time transport structures in the boondocks. Here is the one we came through. And here, given sixty million years of geological displacement, is the North Atlantic TTS that we blew up: an outpost intended as the first phase of their expansion program. Eventually, they would have built more transporters in the Cretaceous to correspond with the positions of the continents in the Tertiary. Because of the chaos created by the death bomb that massacred the home force, it took months for them to send the relief mission that captured us. I suspect they thought that we were previously captured outlanders and not responsible for the 'accident.'

"All that is in this little cube?" Scott held the diamond so the beam of light shining down through the transparent dome focused on the floor in prismatic design. "I can't see it. But seriously, Rusty, how about skipping the history lecture and getting on with the plan."

"Uh, sure." The wand danced across the land mass that was concentrated in such a way that a full globe was not necessary to depict it all. "The city is built on this escarpment that according to my geographic knowledge doesn't exist in modern times. Perhaps future tectonic movement—"

"Rusty!"

"Sorry." Rusty moved the pointer. "The distance between the TTS and the city is several hundred miles—"

"Several hundred miles!" Sandra called out. "We were only on the road a few hours."

"You probably didn't notice how fast we were going because of the dark. Sam kept the throttle pushed to full acceleration. Anyway, the lizards never got around to building the other transporters because their existence was terminated by a new order of intelligence—the mammals. Uh, Doc, how about bringing out the city map, please? I'll point out the objectives, then you can take over."

"Of course, my boy." Doc slid the hemisphere across the floor. He was still crouched over it when a beam of light flashed under his nose. A hole appeared in the middle of the supercontinent. The odor of burning hair wafted across his nostrils. "Wha—" As he stood upright he felt heat against his chin. His beard was smoking.

"Dragons!" Death Wind tackled Doc just as

another laser blast arced across the room. The Nomad rolled in the air so that he hit the floor under Doc and padded the older man's fall.

There was a mad scramble for weapons. Lightning bolts ionized the atmosphere as soldiers poured into the room through the archway. Two dragons wearing strange harnesses stooped down on all fours; on their backs they carried heavy-duty Gatling guns with barrels the size of saplings. Gunners straddled the bearers' tails and fired with abandon. In seconds the library was a psychedelic light show. Books were blasted off the shelves, shelves were blown off the walls. Fires started among the litter.

Rusty ducked under the console as pulses of pure energy lashed at the computer station. Monitors exploded from direct hits, showering glass and electronic components all over him. He scooped up a sheaf of papers and tucked them inside his vest.

"What the hell're you doing!" Scott crashed down beside his chum. He held the nozzle of his laser pistol over the countertop and fired blindly. "Start crawling toward the ramp before they think to cut us off."

"I need these notes."

Scott grabbed Rusty by the collar and dragged him backward, keeping the computer terminal between them and the dragons. "You need your life, too."

The laser Gatling guns chewed so many holes through the control panel that it looked like a colander. The room was a mass of flames fanned by the nonstop machine-gunning. A solid wall of soldiers advanced through the flickering orange fire, kicking the burning paper out of the way with clawed hind legs.

Rusty worked his legs ineffectually. Sandra plopped down next to him and took a fistful of material. She and Scott dragged Rusty so fast that he was strung out like a mannikin. He was choking on the hide collar that bunched around his neck.

"Where's Jane?" Scott shouted above the tumult.

As the three of them rolled down the ramp, Jane yelled, "Here." She cowered by Sam's legs as the man provided cover with a laser gun.

Doc and Death Wind were behind Sam, halfway down the ramp. Scott disentangled himself from the twisted limbs of humanity. Sandra pulled Rusty to his feet. The squad beat a hasty retreat to the lower level. The precautionary barricades they had built across the underground passageways were being blasted apart by flanking soldiers.

"Down the escape shaft!" shouted Sam.

They all piled into an electrical closet. Scott closed and barred the door behind them. One by one they climbed down the raceway opening where cables and conduits came up from the subbasement. The trays that fastened the components to the wall doubled as ladder rungs. When they finally came to a halt, at the lowest level, they were all sweating from their exertion.

Sandra gasped, "Pop, I'm all for rushing this plan of yours—whatever it is."

Doc fingered his singed beard. "My dear, I hadn't intended to implement it with such expedition, but circumstances force me to agree with you."

"Wait a minute," Scott rejoined. "We can dodge these slowpokes from now till doomsday. There are millions of places to hide. I could spend years studying dragon machin—"

"And I love a computer with overbyte," Rusty added. "There's so much data to assimilate."

"Love?" Jane asked questioningly.

"I'll explain later," Scott told her. "Doc, the dragons have built a truly magnificent metropolis. We've got all the time in the world, why rush it? There are other computer centers where we can set up a base camp. Let's not run like scared rabbits the first time they swipe at us."

"Speed of flight does not necessarily connote abdication, nor withdrawal surrender. Any goal must be set with limitations, and I feel that we have reached a point where further ambitions can only be approached asymptotically. As Sandra would undoubtedly state it colloquially, it is time to cut bait and be satisfied with what we have already caught."

Sandra nodded fervently. "Right on. Besides, it's becoming almost impossible to find dragons anymore. They're really on their claws. And when we do stumble over a work party, they're so heavily guarded we can't get close enough to count coup. We can't get a shot in edgewise. They've been withdrawing to a tightly knit perimeter around their precious reactor."

"You see, Scott, I am afraid that if we do not act soon, we may not be able to act at all." Doc hunched into a corner. He picked up his bad leg and massaged it with his fingers. "We can study dragon culture ad infinitum and never understand it completely. Man never reached an understanding of his *own* culture, and he evolved with it. With soldiers nipping at our heels, I believe the time has come to execute our grand design. We must stop living in the past and look toward the future. That is where our destiny lies."

CHAPTER 23

"As far as I have been able to ascertain, there is no genetic distinction or specialization. They all come from the same eggs."

Sam scratched his black beard. "So they're not like ants, creating drones and soldiers and workers and queens by chemical injections or forced feeding?"

"Not at all, no." Doc watched Rusty splice the remote computer terminal to a multistranded cable. Scott and Death Wind were stringing wires inside the access trunk. Sandra stood guard at the end of the corridor. Jane ran her finger along the wiring diagram as Rusty referred to his notes. "Dragon class structure is social convention. Impulsive promiscuity between administrators, or kings, and female slaves, or drones, confers universal gene pooling. Hierarchical division results from aptitude: the smarter ones become administrators, the stronger ones become soldiers, the active ones become workers, the listless ones become drones. Some dietary management during the rearing process increases physical bulk, but that is not analogous to the gross anatomical distortion that is achieved by ants. After all, dragons are lizards, not insects."

"A dragon in any other vest would look the same," Sam misquoted.

"Precisely."

Death Wind peered down through the open ceiling panel. "Steady ladder."

"Got it." Sam braced the giant A-frame against his shoulder as the Nomad clambered down the makeshift rungs.

Scott climbed down next, carrying a satchel full of dragon tools and instruments. "The place is a maze of ventilator Shafts, conduits, junction boxes, and terminal boards. We were only inches away from a maintenance worker. He never knew we were inside the incubator computer console. It was unbelievable."

"What about the heat exchanger," Rusty wanted to know.

"This is one mammal that's going to destroy a whole nest full of lizard eggs. I jumped the temperature control circuit so they'll never know when things start to heat up. By the time they figure it out and shut down the power, it'll be too late. Every egg in there will be soft-boiled—a generation gap the dragons'll never overcome." To Rusty, "Now that the heat's off us, are we ready to sabotage the reactor?"

"Almost. Thanks to Jane I'm fairly fluent in dragon scratch, which is what shows up on the computer screen, but they use a line language for programming that's something like Morse code. We've got to make three-way translations without making any mistakes. You just get me to the reactor control room, and I'll patch in the interrupt circuit. The time delay will give us twenty-four hours to get to the TTS before shutdown occurs."

"I know you can do it."

Rusty shrugged. "I'll finish the programming in the car."

Doc clapped his hands. "I am already forgetting the past and planning for the future. Sam, how is traffic this time of night?"

* * *

"No wonder we haven't found any stray dragons in the past couple weeks," Sandra said. "They've all been at the same party."

The dragons had established temporary accommodations in the buildings that surrounded the fusion reactor containment structure. Dragon administrators and workers slept while drones milled in the courtyards. In the gloom of night it was impossible to see all the fortifications, but by the static glow emitted through the reactor dome, Doc could discern that the entire area was cordoned off by a girdle of armored vehicles like a wagon train in circle defense against a tribe of attacking Indians.

"Even the guards have guards."

"It all makes sense," said Doc. "Your ambushes were so successful that it forced their paws. They retreated to the most vulnerable part of the city while they sent out shock troops to track us down."

Rusty leaned over the parapet. "I'll bet they got onto us by tracing power consumption. They must have switch gear to detect load peaks. Even though we kept the lights off, their technicians could trace where the electricity was going. And a computer that size draws quite a few amps."

Jane still wore nothing but a G-string and the coiled rope clipped to her waist, but she now carried her large dinohide bag by a strap over her shoulder—like a twentieth-century designer outfit. She took out a sheaf of computer print-outs and Doc's carefully drawn map of the city with a detail of the power plant. She pointed to a thirty-foot-high featureless rampart. "We get in there."

Sandra scowled. "What're we gonna do, melt our way through with these." She pulled the laser pistol out of its holster and ran her finger along the notches she had carved into the handle. "I wanna get them dragons as much as you do, but this time I wanna get 'em all. No more pickin' 'em off one at a time. Right, Pop?"

"My dear, you are becoming a master strategist. I compliment you." Doc stroked his beard; another group of whiskers that had been blackened by the laser blast broke off in his hand. "It is indeed frustrating to have such well-laid plans come apart at the seams."

"Don't break your arm patting yourself on the back."

"I take no credit for the original ideas. I merely took the observations of others and put them together into a cohesive whole."

Scott, Sam, and Death Wind joined the others in the tower. Sam said, "It's no good, Henry. They've corked all the basement corridors with blobs of plastic. You'd need a division of tank-mounted laser guns to melt through that kind of barrier. And they've probably got guards on the other side."

"Dragons move," Jane said calmly.

Everyone rushed to the balcony. Two blocks away and several stories below, milling lizards did not appear to exhibit any untoward movement.

"Finger speak say leave."

"That means our electric frying pan's in action," Scott said gleefully. "If we're going to strike, one way or another we'd better do it now."

Sandra said, "Yeah, let's act emotionally and throw 'em off balance. We'll go in with guns blazing. You know, Pop, that mammal trick that their lizard brains can't grasp."

"Odd that you should remember that so well. Jane, what is this plan of yours for gaining access?"

"I climb wall." She patted the coiled rope attached to her G-string. "I drop rope for Sam. We

open door."

"Henry, it sounds simple enough to work."

Doc rubbed his beard. "Yes. It is so direct and against such odds that it is not an option I would normally consider. Therefore, we will do it. But—" He pointed an errant finger at Sandra. "No blazing guns."

Sandra crossed her heart by drawing diagonal lines between her breasts. "I promise."

Doc gazed at the lightening sky. "The sun is almost upon us. Let us make this our last day in dragon land. And let us make it the last day for dragons."

CHAPTER 24

"Excuse me, Sam, but could I, uh, talk with Jane before you go? Alone?"

Sam pinched his eyebrows, then nodded slowly. "Of course." He scuttled back into the shadows of the alley, toward the tall rampart that surrounded the fusion reactor building.

Scott fidgeted for a moment; if his G-string had had pockets, he would have shoved his hands into them. Instead, he kept his eyes plastered to the ground while he nervously untied a leather cord from the connecting thread of his brief apparel. When he brought up his hands he held a crystal that sparkled in the bright light of the setting moon. He held the jewel between his face and Jane's.

"I hung onto it when Rusty tossed it to me because I—well—because I wanted to present it to you, uh, as a token of my, uh, my feelings. For you. I couldn't find a setting for it. Besides, it's too big for a ring. But I bent this platinum wire around it and made a loop for a thong. It'll have to be a pendant. It's the best—I could do."

Jane stared at him expressionlessly.

Scott stumbled on. "Uh, you're supposed to wear it. Around your neck. It's a custom that signifies—very close friendship. When you look at it, you're supposed to remember the one who gave it to you." He spread the leather necklace with his fingers and worked it over her head. After it fell around her neck he spent several awkward seconds pulling her waist-length hair through the loop. The diamond lay snugly against her throat.

Jane took Scott's open palm and cupped her left breast with it. "I remember you always— here." She looked deeply into his eyes. "I love you, Scott."

"I—I love you, too, Jane." He gulped loudly. "I have—for a long time."

"Sixty million years?" she said innocently.

Scott broke into a broad grin. "At least. And I will love you forever. Now, uh, you'd better get going before the sun comes up—and something else as well." He gave her a peck on the cheek.

Jane clutched him when he pulled back; she drew him close. She pressed her lips against his. Scott ran his hands down the smooth skin of her back and pulled her hips tight against his. She kissed him long and hard. "We make love later?"

Scott felt the blood rush to his face. "Yes. But we've got work to do now." He spun her around, patted her on the seat, and gave her a little shove. "Now move it," he said, smiling, with more cheer than he felt. The wrenching inside him was not all longing, for it was tempered with thoughts of what they yet had to face. "I'll be waiting."

He promptly turned and rushed back to join the others. They took up their vigil by the roadway that led to the reactor stadium's loading platform. And there they waited—and waited—and waited.

First light glimmered, casting long shadows across the courtyards. Dragon slaves stirred in preparation for dawn: The temperature skyrocketed as the sun made its debut. Neither Sam nor Jane put in an appearance.

Doc sat down next to Scott. "Are you worried about her, my boy?"

Scott jerked to attention. He had not realized he had been so deeply lost in thought. "Uh, not really. She can take care of herself. Besides, if anything went wrong, I'm sure it wouldn't have gone wrong quietly."

"Quite right, my boy. Quite right." Doc leaned back against the wall. He unbuttoned his vest. "I always experience the jitters before I go into battle. I almost wish for the kind of fight that comes unexpectedly. Fear itself is short-lived, but the continued anticipation of fear can rack one's nerves. So much of my life has been subjected to the anxiety of imminent death that I sometimes take survival for granted."

Scott humphed. "You do come off pretty blasé."

"Do not interpret a calm exterior as a defiance of my own mortality. I am too well aware of such inevitability. Life is a commodity to be savored, for who knows when that vital spark shall be forever quenched. And even though I believe to a certain extent that what will be, will be, yet I strive to alter the world in which we live along precepts that I find personally acceptable. We have but one life, therefore we must life it to the fullest."

"I've certainly learned a lot about life since getting my head out of the ground," Scott said. "Although I can't say that I accept it with your equanimity. To be honest with you, Doc, I've been bored to tears the past couple months. Don't get me wrong: taking apart dragon machines and vehicles to see what makes them tick has given me a great deal of satisfaction. That's a side of me that I've always had. But ever since I entered the real world, ever since I joined the war against the dragons, I've been developing a need for—excitement. For danger. I actually revel in it. And it bothers me because it's something I never felt before; or, at least, was never aware of before."

"The maturation process induces changes in the hormonal balance of the prepubescent body. Growth induces modifi—"

"No, Doc, this is more than chemical stimulation. It's a psychological dependency: an adrenaline rush that I can't get enough of. It's become an addiction."

"Adrenaline is a chemical—"

"That is emotionally induced. Its physiological effects can't be denied, but control of its release is a matter of inner security. And I'm finding out that I don't have the security I thought I had. That's what hurts. I want to be like Death Wind: strong, austere, confident, a man of the forest. Instead, I end up acting like Sandra: wild and irrational."

"Perhaps you should concentrate instead on being more like Scott. We are all born with our own strengths and weaknesses. One should cultivate one's strengths and protect one's weaknesses. Who you are, and who you can be, is greater than your desires otherwise."

Scott tilted his head resignedly. "Sure, Doc, I understand all that. My problem is a condition of too much self-awareness. I know from within that I'm looking forward to what we're about to do. I'm enjoying the destruction of this world, and that feeling is destructive to my inner being. I should want to build up, not tear down."

"When a house falls into disrepair it is necessary to remove dilapidated walls before constructing new ones."

"There you go, talking in parables again." Scott shifted the backpack and pulled the laser pistol out of its holster. He slapped it in his palm. His hands tingled with the knowledge of the power he held. "Maybe you're right. I guess a planet can't be restructured without a little damage first. And dragon land isn't long for this world." Shaking his head, he stared at the plastic surface between his feet. "You know, I have the feeling I've done this before: cracking their eggs while we sneak in the back way. We did that a few months ago along our time stream, but sixty million years in the geological future. It's so confusing—like a case of pre-déjà vu. Let's call it préjà vu. And they still don't know what's coming. It almost seems unfair to play the same trick twice. It's so unoriginal, even though in universal time sequence it's never been done before."

"Semantics aside, would you rather give them a warning?"

"Doc, I'm not that confused. Besides, we've come such a long way to get where we are. Every time Sam and I sabotaged one of their fission reactors, I knew it was leading to this moment."

"You did an excellent job of concealment, I might add. It was a master stroke disassembling the control panels and performing electronic lobotomies where the dragons could never see them, then putting the external circuitry back together so it appeared that the reactors were simply shut down, and not permanently impaired."

Scott shrugged. "They can be repaired, but it'd take years and a whole lot more personnel than they have available to do the job. I didn't want them to have alternate resources in case this job doesn't go as smoothly as planned. Once they're out of power, their civilization comes to an end. And the sooner we can get on with our own lives."

"What does that mean for you—now?"

Scott thought for a moment. "I know I could never go back to my old lifestyle. I love the outdoors, and the freedom of movement. Maccam City doesn't seem real anymore. It's a dream I just woke up from." He looked into Doc's eyes. "I want a world of my own choosing. I guess— I guess I want Jane to share it with. There's probably a lot more I want. I just haven't had time to think of it yet."

Doc raised bushy white eyebrows. "It is 'want' that provides motivation in life. It is that quantity that keeps us moving forward, that prevents stagnation. Of course, we do not always get what we want. We sometimes have to roll with the punches."

Scott made a fist. "I'm going to throw a few punches first. Then I'll—"

Sam and Jane ran briskly into the alley. Death Wind maintained his vigil at the terminus as the duo stopped to catch their wind. Scott jumped up, leaving Doc to climb slowly up his cane.

"It's all set," Sam gasped. "The door's open." He took a few more deep breaths before going on. "We got up the wall with no problem, but we had to stay out of sight till the techs abandoned their stations. Once the eggbeater started going full speed they left like rats deserting a sinking ship."

Jane pouted and hugged her gadget bag closer to her chest. She pulled out her pudgy rodent pet and stroked its sleek fur.

"Sorry. No aspersions intended against present company. Anyway, they left a few guards behind, but we can take care of them, no problem."

Scott threw his arms around Jane's slender shoulders and kissed her on the forehead. "That's my girl."

Jane fingered the diamond brooch. "I not forget you."

Laughing, Scott said, "I should hope not. It's only been an hour."

"Hey, if you two can stop smooching, we've got a job to do." Sandra drew her gun and stroked the barrel with the same tender motions that Jane had used on her protomammal. "Let's get in there and pull the plug on them lizards. I got a date for tomorrow that I don't want to be late for."

Rusty said, "Your date's not for sixty million years. But if we hurry we can make it before we die of old age."

"Lead on, wise man."

The guerrilla squad double-timed into the outer compound. After months of roaming deserted streets, the lack of dragon personnel did not seem out of the norm. None of the inner doors possessed locks. In a trice they found themselves skulking along silent corridors. "There's likely to be a couple of meter readers on watch," Scott cautioned. "Be careful not to zap any gauges or electrical cabinets."

"You afraid of damaging what you're going

to put out of commission?" Sandra said haughtily.

"I want to shut this reactor down right. Jane, do you have the computer printouts?"

Jane pulled a sheaf of fanfold out of her handbag.'

"Good." To Sandra, he explained, "Remember that I've never worked on a fusion reactor before, so I'm a little out of my depth. From what I can make out of that dragon scratch, the control circuits are pretty much the same at the monitoring end. The main difference is what effects they cause. I'll follow the same procedures I would follow for a fission reactor shutdown—except that we'll use Rusty's delayed action device to give us getaway time. Once I've got—"

Death Wind held his hand up high, signaling for silence. Everyone froze. The Nomad crouched and advanced cautiously on the balls of his feet. He was a mountain lion stalking its prey. He bent back his wrist and grasped the spear halfway along its length. He hefted it once or twice for balance. Very slowly, he bent until his knees touched the floor. He laid down the spear.

He peered around a doorjamb. When he stepped back it was to notch his bow. Quickly he stepped into the rectangle of light. His shadow spread behind him like a huge black giant. Three arrows thwacked into the room, a low murmur of a hiss escaped. When he bent to retrieve his spear, he nodded once.

The three dragon technicians lay sprawled on the floor, each with its throat transfixed by one of Death Wind's plastic-tipped arrows. The Nomad quietly went about recovering his ammunition.

Scott slapped the Nomad on the back. "Death Wind, you make it all seem so easy."

"Death is always easy."

"Yes. I guess it is. The shame is that it's necessary. Oh well." Scott unlimbered his tools while Jane spread the blueprints across the desk. "Rusty, have you got that timer programmed."

"For about an epoch and a half."

"The Mesozoic doesn't have epochs, only periods."

"Lucky Mesozoic," Sandra chafed. "Scott, can you get on with it? I'd like to leave the Cretaceous before I become a grandmother."

"I didn't know you were trying."

"Shut up, you."

Scott held up his hands in defense. "Sorry.

Just remember that you can't hurt me until I make these connections. Sam, take down that panel with the flow gauges. Death Wind, make the solder connections. Rusty, get into the CPU and follow what I'm doing on the simulator."

Jane took the soldering iron out of her gadget bag and gave it to the Nomad.

"Is there anything I can do?" Doc asked.

"Help Sandra watch for dragons. This is going to take some time."

Sandra marched out of the control room with her gun drawn. "The Cenozoic's right around the corner."

Three hours later, except for the dead technicians, no one would have known that the reactor station had been compromised. The timing device was concealed behind a panel, the reactor was generating its full load of electricity, and none of the gauges indicated pending trouble. Sam and Death Wind dragged out the bodies and hid them in a pump room.

"Just like clockwork, Doc. I feel like an old hand at this."

"The booby trap is set?"

"Yes. If some smart cookie does figure out what's wrong, it'll blow up as soon as he tries to disconnect the timer. Otherwise, we've got twenty-four hours to reach the transporter before the bomb goes off and demolishes the main control circuits. Then the reactor quietly shuts itself down and the power begins to fade. Even if the focusing nodes are discharged when we get to the TTS, as long as the transmission lines are intact, the reactor will recharge the capacitors to full power in a couple hours."

"And they can't restart the fusion reaction?"

Scott shook his head. "It takes an immense external power to supply heat and compression. Once fusion is started, the reactor is self-generating, but with all the fission reactors down, they won't be able to initiate the system. Batteries just can't generate the amps."

Rusty said, "I'd still feel better if we could have cracked the main containment hull, or fractured the magnetic generator housing."

"Both are made out of pure iridium, one of the heaviest metals in nature. We'd need explosives a lot stronger than a shorted battery pack to split foot-thick walls."

"Then the countdown has begun and there is no turning back." Doc nodded slowly as he rubbed his beard. "So this is the way the world ends; not with a bang, but a whimper."

CHAPTER 25

"Doc! Doc! We got dragons breathing fire down our necks!" Sandra skidded into the control room with her laser gun drawn. "It's a whole horde of techs and a coupla battalions of soldiers. They're onto our ruse. The jig is up."

Scott hastily threw the battery pack over his shoulders "Come on, Doc. It's propitious retreat time."

Jane grabbed her handbag and took out the single-shot stun gun. "This time I fight."

Scott spun her around and shoved her out the door. "Let's hope we don't get that close to them. Rusty, get the lead out."

They raced along the corridor and into the reactor room. Sam and Death Wind met them with weapons in hand.

"There's a squad of soldiers coming in the back way," Sam shouted. "But they didn't see us."

"They will now." Sandra jerked a thumb over her shoulder. "There's half an army right behind us, and they ain't just whistling Dixie."

Doc pointed his cane in the direction from which Sam and Death Wind had just come. "I believe the path of least resistance is that way."

The words were barely out of his mouth when the vanguard emerged from the control room corridor. The wall of lizard flesh waddled into the open. The lead soldier hissed loudly as Death Wind's arrow buried itself into the flesh above its forelimb. It dropped its gun, but kept coming. There were two more behind it, ready to fire.

"I believe you," shouted Sam as he turned to run.

It was strangely quiet in the reactor room despite the sudden call to arms. The only sound dragons were capable of making was a sibilant hiss. The roar of atomic fusion was damped by the thick iridium walls of the plasma bottle. The clacking noise of auxiliary motors and pumps was absorbed by the acoustic properties of the plastic structure. The action progressed like a reel from a silent movie.

As the rebel squad approached the emergency exit, the rear guard shuffled into view. Scott saw the trained gun nozzles. He stopped so fast that his moccasins slipped out from under him. In an uncontrolled skid he crashed into a dynamo casing. The ring of fire from the upheld weapon burst into the air like a great green amorphous bubble. The coruscation dissipated harmlessly over Scott's head.

"Hey, they're using pain guns instead of lasers," Sandra shouted. She crouched by Scott and sighted along the barrel. "That means we can outrange 'em."

"They don't want to damage the equipment," Scott observed. "And neither do we."

The others took up defensive postures in the cluster of machinery adjacent to the plasma containment lozenge.

"It doesn't make any difference at this point. They know we're here."

Doc spoke with a deep, calm timbre, "We would like to keep the electricity flowing until we effect our passage through time. Unless you would like to become a permanent teratology major."

Sandra pulled back her wrist and aimed the nozzle at the faraway ceiling. "Oh, yeah."

Death Wind let loose another arrow that caught the dragon blocking their path of retreat squarely in the breastplate. The long tongue shot out its mouth, but no hiss emerged. It kept walking forward even as blood spurted between jagged teeth and curled lips. It finally fell forward like a wooden cigar store Indian.

As dragons converged from both sides, Sam peeped over a cooling coil. "We've got to shoot our way out, Henry. There's no other choice."

Another arrow twanged through the air.

"I must concede to logic," Doc said. "Here, let me hold that spear for you, Death Wind." Doc glanced quickly at the attacking minions. "Commence firing at will."

"But be careful!" Scott called out. He took careful aim and drilled a back door dragon in the gut. It clutched at the hole in its abdomen as it reeled to the side like a drunken sailor.

Sandra blasted one in the face as it emerged from the control room corridor; its head exploded as the laser beam tore out the back of its skull. Sam caught another at the base of the sinusoidal neck. Because of the distance between gun and target, the energy field was spread out at the point of contact: it gouged a large gaping wound rather than burning a needlelike hole. The end result was the same either way: death by invasive maneuver.

"Hey, there're techs slipping along the walls!"

Scott looked where Rusty was pointing his stun gun. "If they're trying to outflank us, why aren't they doing it with armed soldiers?"

"Beats the pants off of me," said Sandra. She zapped one before it waddled out of sight behind a computer console. "But as long as they're afraid to shoot back with real beams, I love it."

Rusty shook his head. "They've got to have something up their sleeves: gas bombs, or knock-out beams, or something."

"You might be right, my boy," said Doc. "They can't take chance on wrecking their only source of electricity. If I were—"

"Up!" shouted Jane. "Up!"

All heads turned toward the catwalk overlooking the plasma injector at the far end of the fusion reactor. A lone dragon stood on an observation sponson; a long, golden cape flowed around taloned hoofs. Half-lidded eyes watched the fight that was taking places several stories below, while claws plucked at the strings of a harp.

"That's the one! That's the bastard that got me." Sandra drew a bead on the bulbous body. "Buddy, you just crossed your last time zone."

"Don't!" shouted Scott.

Sandra checked her fire, frowning. "What's wrong?"

"It's standing in front of essential control circuits. If you miss, you may fry the output electrodes."

"Damn." Sandra pounded her knee with her fist. She glared at the caped dragon with staunch resolution. "Oh, well, it's so far away, I probably can't do anything more than give it a good hotfoot. All right, I say it's time to bust outa here."

"A sensible suggestion, my dear." Doc stood up, held spear in front of him like a lance, and hobbled toward soldiers blocking the emergency exit. "Char-rr-rr-rge!"

Caught unawares, the rest of the team were still clambering to their feet as the white bearded scout halved the distance the back way. Sam and Scott spread out behind him and fired crossing beams past his head. Two dragons fell smoking. Sandra stabbed out with her laser over Doc's snowy mane and grazed another soldier in the chin. A red tongue darted out with a hiss as the beast veered into a wall.

Another soldier lurched into its place. Doc buried the tip of the spear—the tyrannosaur tooth—into the creature's heart. The jaw dropped and the dark eyes widened in pain. Still, the sagging soldier brought its gun to bear on its attacker. Doc grabbed the scaled forelimb and

shoved it aside just as the soldier squeezed the trigger of the stun gun. The blob of light that burst from the nozzle narrowly missed the old man. Coruscations of energy wrapped around a capacitor bank that protruded out of the floor. Sparks flew into the air. A miniature lightning storm raged over the device, crackling explosively and erupting blobs of molten plastic like a toy volcano.

"Uh-oh."

Scott, Sam, and Sandra poured a deadly volley of laser beams into the escape corridor. Soldiers armed only with stun guns were unable to retaliate effectively. So many energy fields were discharged in such a short amount of time that the air simmered. The static charge built up enough to make Scott's hair stand on end.

Death Wind leaped past Doc and buried his knife into the throat of the soldier that Sandra had wounded. It died squirming. He then braced his foot against the other beast's breast and yanked out his spear.

"What have I done?" Doc shuffled backward across the floor away from the pyrotechnics. The floor bulged in front of him, accompanied by a deep-throated whump. "What's happening?"

Scott grabbed Doc by the armpits and pulled him to his feet. "I think the capacitors overloaded and burned out the magnetic flux accelerator coils."

"Nice going, Pop."

"I do not feel the need to apologize for my audacity, although the result was unanticipated. The final action was only in self-defense."

"It's too late to worry about it now, Doc." Scott fired into a distant mass of reptilian flesh. The distance was too great kill, but the beam of energy checked the speed of the advancing soldiers. "It just shortened our getaway time a bit. There's still enough reserve power to last for days."

"Then I may as well cook my goose." Sandra took careful aim and fired a bolt of electricity at the gold-caped dragon some five hundred feet away. The energy field reached it in such a weakened condition that it merely singed its scales, but the harp strings melted in its paws. Having talked its last tone, it turned and ducked into a control cubicle. The blackened cape fell away in ashes; its back smoldered like a dying ember. "Bastard."

"Scott! Take at look at this." Rusty stood in

front of a panel of gauges, the labels of which Jane hastily translated. "We're in trouble."

Scott recognized most of the symbols from his study periods with Jane, when he was learning how to sabotage the reactor control boards. "Uh-oh."

"I believe I already said that," Doc said. "How serious is it?"

Internal detonations continued to emit bass sounds dampened by the plastic flooring. Needle gauges and numerical readouts were on the rise, although the fusion reactor demonstrated no distress.

Sam fired his laser gun down the escape passage, keeping the way clear. "Come on. Let's get going before they send reinforcements."

Sandra kept the advancing hordes at bay. "I could use a little help. This ain't supposed to be a one-woman stand."

"Real serious." Scott ignored the importunities. "The power surge shorted the high voltage transformer coils and fused the flux reinforcing bus bars."

"I fail to comprehend the significance of that." Doc rubbed the remnants of his beard more quickly than usual. "Does that mean the loss of electrical power sooner than expected?"

"Worse than that. It means we can't shut down the reactor at all. The feeding circuits have been isolated into a self-generating loop. Without a load it'll pour all that power back into the magnetic deflectors that are buried in the floor."

Sandra joined the caucus. "Ain't there some kind of interrupt circuit? We can always blast our way back into the control room—or come back another day."

"No good, Sandra." Scott's spine crept with chills as he watched the mounting figures on the dials. "Our booby trap is irrevocable."

"What about triple redundancy—"

"I wrecked all the backups. And there isn't going to be another day." Scott did a quick mental calculation. "Doc, you'd better start whimpering, because this thing's going off with a bang. In about ten hours, this city will be a hole the size of the Mediterranean Sea."

CHAPTER 26

Not only was their escape vehicle in ruins, but the cleverly disguised ambush nearly caught them unawares. Only Jane's timely warning kept the fleeing squad from the clutches of dragons.

"Danger! Do not touch!"

Sandra jerked her hand back from the trip wire that was stretched across the open seal. "Now what? Ain't it bad enough they smashed in the windows—"

Jane pulled Sandra a safe distance from the nondescript black box. She indicated the squiggles on the plastic sidewall. "It say danger."

Sam placed his hands on his daughter's shoulders. "It's a good thing Jane can read that dragon scratch. They've got the whole coach rigged with explosives. One touch—"

Death Wind loosed an arrow that caught a skulking technician in the midriff. The tip penetrated the hide at an angle and lodged against the hip joint. The dragon hissed as it limped behind a road barrier. The Nomad stared up at the tall buildings that surrounded the parking lot. "More with no guns."

"Get away! Quick!" Doc dashed for the protection of a sidewalk partition. "It's a command detonator."

The others followed his example without further explanation. No sooner had they leaped for cover than the coach exploded with a deafening roar and a tremendous sheet of flame. Burning debris and molten plastic rained down for nearly half a minute. Scott was caught in the open and slammed into a storefront by the expanding gases. His face was numb from the blast. When he convinced his battered muscles to move, he found that his body was relatively unscathed; but his vision was blurry. Something hung down over his left eye. When he brushed away the obstruction, he saw clearly for only a moment before a shadow again fell across his eye.

"Hold still, my boy." Doc knelt by Scott's side and cradled the blond head in his callused hands. Sandra screamed, and Jane thrust her fist into her mouth. "I'll have this fixed up in a jiffy."

"What is it, Doc? What's wrong?"

"Jane, give me some of that vellum, please."

Jane fumbled with her handbag and handed Doc a sheaf of computer printout. She stifled back a tear.

"Doc, what happened? What's wrong with my eye? It's blurry."

Doc quickly but professionally wound the continuous roll around the top of Scott's head, across the side of his face, and under his chin.

After several wraps he tucked the loose end under the bottom fold. "There. That ought to hold." He peered into Scott's eyes one at a time. "Your eye appears to be all right. But a flap of skin was burned off your scalp and fell across your brow. It may sting some when the shock wears off."

"It stings already." Scott fingered the makeshift bandage. "I think it's bound too tight."

"No, that's the epidermis drying and stiffening. You'll have to suffer with it, my boy."

Scott felt a laser blast near his head and heard Sam's capacitor recycling. With his good eye he saw soldiers emerging from an alley. Sandra fired with telling effect.

Scott stumbled to his feet. "Why do I feel like a planarian?" He staggered a few steps in the direction away from that of the oncoming soldiers, until Rusty wrapped his lanky arms around him and yanked him to a halt.

"That's it. That's exactly what they want us to do. React in a prescribed manner to a specified stimulus."

Scott's jaw did not move well because of the shriveled skin the vellum wrappings. It was an effort to talk. "Let's go! This isn't the time for philosophical dissertations."

Rusty gripped Scott with uncommon strength belied by the emaciated look of his arms. "That's exactly what they want us do: move away, and probably into another ambush. What we should do is the exact opposite."

"Sounds like a good emotional response to me," Sandra said. "Let's rush 'em."

Doc raised bushy eyebrows. "I do not think it is truly emotional once one takes the time to reason it out. But the result should be the same."

The rebel squad launched a frontal attack against the remaining soldiers in the alley. Scott lumbered along uselessly, his gun undrawn. He was barely conscious enough to observe the proceedings. The next thing he knew, Jane was dragging him past dragon bodies and into a waiting troop transport.

"Rusty, you're all right in my book," Sandra shouted with glee. "Daddy, can you run this thing?"

"Can a pterodactyl fly?" Sam switched on the power train and engaged the drive controls. The annunciator lights flashed on silently. "All systems are go." When he advanced the throttle, the motor hummed softly and the vehicle moved forward with a barely perceptible lurch. "Hang on, people. We're homeward bound."

Scott fell into a seat like a lump. The side of his face felt as if it were pressed against a hot iron; his left eye was full of gravel. Jane sat next to him and cradled his head against her breast. Her nipples were erect and hard against his cheek, but he was in too much pain to take pleasure in the fact. She worked her fingers around his temples in a circular motion. The warmth and the love of her touch was a greater comfort than Scott had imagined possible.

"I don't want to beat a dead dinosaur, but are you sure there's no way we can stop the fusion process." Sandra climbed into the forward turret and fondled the laser Gatling gun lovingly. "Can't we blow something up that'll do the trick?"

"Not unless you've got an atomic bomb in your back pocket," Rusty replied.

"Wouldn't that set it off?" Sam asked.

Rusty shook his head vigorously. "No. There is no 'setting off' a fusion reactor. But a big enough bomb would crack the casing. The magnetic field would instantly collapse, and the plasma would leak out. You'd still get a hell of a blast, but that would mostly be from the nuclear explosion. With the reactor isolated from the control circuits, there's no other way."

"Meaning, of course, that the dragons are as powerless as we are." Doc rolled his baby blue eyes. "Once they figure that out . . . "

"Yeah, well, it looks like they already have." Sandra rotated the turret as the truck sped through an intersection. Cutting in from the right was a two-dragon convertible. Long lizard necks peered through the tall windshield while blue capes were buffeted in the slipstream. "Hey, Pop, can I send these guys to their maker?"

"Please do."

With a rapid-fire staccato, Sandra riddled the smaller vehicle with laser beams. Holes appeared in the bonnet and fenders. Sandra found the range on the occupants as the car veered away. She injected the bulbous bodies with bolts of energy until the vehicle went out of control and crashed into a building. The car scraped acrylic across plastic until the front wheel carriage hit an entrance ramp; then it careened on its side and skidded into a projecting rampart.

"Damn. I missed the batteries, and it didn't even burn."

"Good shooting, my dear, especially considering a five-foot-two tyke is firing a gun that was designed for a seven-foot-eight lizard."

"I'm still frustrated. I want to blow something up, and while I'm picking off dragons with a peashooter, you set the whole damn world on fire."

"An honor of which I am not particularly proud, although in retrospect I can see now that it was inevitable. It is curious how we are bound by the dictates of the past, as if we were predestined to be here at this time in order to perform the changes necessary to ensure our own future. The mind boggles."

"Yeah, well, while you're boggling, how about consulting your crystal ball and tell me what it says about us getting the hell out of here before dragon land becomes an inland sea."

"I would not care to speculate, my dear. No course of action is a surety. I suppose the future holds secrets aplenty to keep us guessing for a long time—perhaps forever, if we can imagine such an infinite quantity. The past holds the key to the future only in a statistical sense which we as minor inhabitants of the microcosm—"

"Sam, do you know where you're going?" Rusty said.

"To Hell in a hand basket. Of course I know where I'm going. While you had your head buried in a computer console, Scott and I were taking a grand tour of the city. Maybe I don't know every corner and back alley in the red-light district, but the streets move in a pattern of right angles that're pretty easy to follow even without a road map."

Sam did not spare the amps. The army truck rolled through the deserted city like a sports car on a freeway, dodging vehicles parked in random fashion where they happened to have been when the death bomb appeared out of time and destroyed all life on the planet's sole supercontinent. Many vehicles still held the remains of their drivers: their bodies desiccated after many months of microbial action.

It seemed to Scott like quite a while before he recognized the approaches to the tunnel complex that led down the escarpment to the plains below. This time no blockade awaited their passage. The sun was suddenly blotted out as the troop carrier entered the underground tube.

Doc hopped to the back of the truck and dabbed at a trickle of blood that was seeping through the vellum on Scott's face. "My boy, how certain are you about that time limit?"

Scott snorted. "It could be plus or minus fifty percent. I just made an assessment on the short-term accretion ratio and measured it against the danger markings on the dials. But if the rate of increase is exponential—"

"Hmmnn. This is not as bad as it looks, although I daresay you will have a bit of a scar once it heals. There's some inflammation in the eye, but it is more like a flash burn than an injury. Assuming we survive the next ten hours you should return to good health in a few weeks."

"That's a pretty big 'if'."

"A positive attitude is the key to success in any campaign. Will can win where might may fall. One cannot achieve greatness without striving to be great. Triumph comes to he who tries. Good fortune smiles—"

"Doc!" Rusty screamed. "Can we skip a couple of chapters?"

Lines creased Doc's forehead. He cleared his throat. "Forgive me, lad. I disguise my fear with rhetoric."

Jane continued to rub Scott's temples. "What will be, will be."

"That is a truism." Doc resumed his seat, then turned and raised his eyebrows at the girl. "My dear, I do not remember you being present at the conversation where that utterance was extemporized. Unless you were around the corner the whole—"

The troop carrier burst into sunlight at the end of the tunnel at the same time that a tremendous explosion ripped through the aft end of the vehicle. One third of the gear train was gone, along with a significant portion of the passenger compartment and the rear turret.

"We've hit a land mine," Sam shouted.

Death Wind whipped into the open rear.

Sandra dropped out of the turret and hit the deck between the seats. "DW, are you okay?"

The Nomad stood up plucking shards of plastic from his back and sides. The seat fell away from under him, crashed onto the orangetop, and bounced end over end until friction brought it to a halt. Sandra dabbed at Death Wind's blood-smeared body with a cloth that she pulled from one of the vest's many pockets.

Rusty shouted above the roar of air, "That means they were waiting for us. Watch out for—"

Two laser blasts from the main gun emplacements tore up the road in front of the vehicle.

"Evasive action." Sam jockeyed the throttle to and fro and from left to right. "Sandy, keep 'em busy while we run the gauntlet."

Sandra careened back and forth as she dashed up the aisle to the turret hatch. The troop carrier gyrated in a random escape pattern. Scott did not have the energy to man the gun in the middle turret; he gripped Jane to keep from being hurled out of his seat.

"I can't keep up the speed with two of our axles missing," Sam complained. "Good thing each wheel runs on independent motors."

A gigantic bolt of energy from one of the enemy laser cannons chewed up a chunk of road surface next to the truck, spattering the sidewall with blobs of molten plastic. The acrylic windows melted in splotches. The wind whistled in chorus through holes of various sizes.

Sandra's shots ran wild. "Daddy, I can't hit a thing jolting around like this."

Sam maneuvered recklessly. "I ain't gonna stop just so you can get your jollies. They'll get our range."

Because of their size, the laser cannons recharged slowly. A beam from the right hit aft of the racing vehicle and dangerously close; another from the left creased the roof with its heat, causing the supports to sag and the center to belly inward.

"That was a close one." The carrier swerved crazily as Sam rotated the throttle in a way it was never intended to go. The undercarriage was a bed of indecision as the wheels swiveled in a circular motion that stressed the chassis in all its dimensions. Sam sang out, "Catch me if you can."

Jane dragged Scott off the seat and onto the floor next to Doc and Rusty. She clasped Scott to her breast like a mother would hold her child, rocking gently. With one eye closed Scott peered out the window. Death Wind crouched in the aisle on one knee, holding onto the seats for stability. Then they were past the centerline between the two embattlements.

"Not as easy getting out as it was getting in."

Sam swung the control lever sharply in order to avoid a blast hole in front of the truck. The left wheels trundled over plastic moguls and caught the liquefied edges of the furrow. The vehicle launched itself into the air, throwing the occupants against the inner panel. It banged down hard and continued on its way with solidified masses of synthetic plastic bonded to the

wheel treads. The multiple motors hummed along to the tune of the bumps hitting the orangetop with jackhammer regularity.

"Hit something, Toad. Will you?"

"I'm trying." Sandra's body was stretched out between pedals and gun sight. She could aim only by eyeing the bottom of the barrel with her target while rotating the turret in the approximate direction. "I'm just not built for this."

Sam thrust the joystick all the way forward for maximum speed, while alternating its sideway motion haphazardly. The truck yawed with sickening caprice. Another laser blast gouged a huge crater right in its path. The wheels left the ground as the truck soared across the open space where the road used to be. The front axle hit the opposite side of the trough with such a bang that the whole vehicle shuddered with the shock. It squished through the plastic lava without slowing down. The front axle was smashed out of alignment, adding further torment to the truck's aberrant course. The wheels were recapped with a new coating of plastic.

Gradually they outdistanced the effectiveness and accurate range of the laser cannons. A few parting shots seared the road surface in their vicinity, but the energy field was so diffuse as to cause little damage.

Sandra dropped down into the cab. She pulled Death Wind's face against her side and kissed the mop of long hair that was blown in wild disarray. "Scott, are you okay?"

"No, but I'll live."

"Hey, I never thought I'd say this, but during the fight I missed your repertoire of wisecracks."

"I'll mention that the next time you disparage my drollery."

"Hey!" Sam called out. "We're not out of the woods yet. There's a roadblock up ahead."

Sandra leaped to her gun station. "Clear for action. I wanna blow the gizzards outa them lizards."

The two tanks that were parked broadside across the highway were not big enough to prevent passage of what was left of the troop carrier. But the guns they mounted were portable models of the stationary laser cannon.

Sam tacked furiously from side to side in order to forestall attack. "Sandy, I'm gonna keep dodging until they both fire. Then, while they're recycling, I'll straighten out to give you a chance to aim. But be quick about it."

"Gotcha."

Watching through the windshield, Scott saw the burst of light from the mouth of one of the laser cannons. The beam of energy seemed to be coming straight at him. The laser cut through a corner of the clear acrylic window and went right out the open back of the truck. The air inside rippled with intense heat. Scott broke into a sweat that was not all temperature dependent. The second beam contacted a guardrail to the left of the truck; shrapnel soared into the sky, but fell harmlessly behind.

"Now!" Sam steadied the vehicle on a diagonal track.

Sandra pulled the trigger and kept it depressed. Her gun was not as powerful as the laser cannons, but it recycled faster. She got off three shots before the enemy returned fire. Neither damaged the other.

"All right, I've got their charging time figured." Sam threw the truck into a long curve that evaded the follow-up shot from the other cannon. "Eight seconds, Toad."

As the truck straightened out, Sandra picked her target and opened fire. Her first shot clipped an armored fender, the second slammed into the main body, the third missed high, and the fourth grazed the base of the turret. Sam swung the truck as the other tank let loose its bolt. A dazzling beam of amplified light dug a long trough in the highway shoulder and splattered hot plastic along the truck's left side.

"The turret's jammed on the one," Sam yelled. "I'm gonna head straight for the other."

Sandra locked the turret in the zero position and concentrated on the elevation. The first shot was short, but three in a pronounced devastating damage on the hull. Sandra kept shooting. Beam after beam arced into the tank. No fire was returned.

Sam did not veer off course until the last moment. He narrowly avoided a collision. Both tanks were silent. "All in a day's work."

"Damn." Sandra shook her fist as the tanks were left behind. "Neither one exploded."

CHAPTER 27

"Daddy, can we make a pit stop."

Sam jerked his head around so fast that his neck cracked. "What're you, crazy? The continent's on the verge of being blasted off the face of the Earth, and you wanna take a break? Go off the back of the bus like everyone else."

Sandra's face was pale. She clutched her stomach tightly as she made her way to where the truck terminated in jagged pieces. She knelt on the floor, gripped the last seat for support, and vomited into the void.

"Motion sickness," Doc said, low enough so she would not hear. The troop carrier skewered along the road on a wobbly front axle and plastic-blobbed wheels. "How is your injury, my

"It hurts, but it's not too bad." Scott snugged the vellum against his nose. "My eye's still blurry. I can see better with the good eye when the bad one's covered."

Death Wind pulled up a floor panel and handed it to Rusty. "Smoke comes from battery. I can disconnect."

"That means we lose more power," Rusty said.

With four wheels blown off the rear, and the resistance from drag on the front axle slowing them down, half the drive train was already out of action. The six working wheels were overloaded.

The Nomad severed the cables one at a time, and covered the wires with slashed seat-covering material. "Cannot help. This will catch fire soon." Slowly the flow-through ventilation cleared the smoke out of the cabin.

They sure don't build 'em like they used to." Sandra claimed her seat at the base of the forward turret. "Whatta we got—half speed?"

"Less," said Sam. The screech of grinding axle parts came through the dashboard. "We gotta ditch this buggy at the first pony express stop. It's got more rattles than a hill full of snakes."

The truck thumped and wheezed along the highway. They were out of the city environs and passing through lush swamp forest that buzzed with insectivorous life, most of which found its way into the troop compartment through the massive hull breaches. The sun was high, the heat and humidity unbearable. The force of time passed poignantly.

"Oh, no. What the hell is that?" Sam pulled back on the joystick and let the vehicle coast. "Looks like we got a brontosaurus sleeping on the road."

Doc crouched next to the driver's seat. "The brontosaurs lived during the Jurassic and have been long extinct. This is more likely a smaller descendant, the titanosaurus. It looks full grown. Dinosaurs must have a phenomenal growth rate in order to reach maturity in such a short—"

"Henry, we don't have all day to listen to your scientific speculations. And I don't care what you call it. It's got the road blocked. We're all likely to be extinct if we don't get around it." The truck screeched as Sam pulled back the throttle and threw the strained motors into reverse. The titanosaur's body lay stretched out from shoulder to shoulder, while the thick neck and tail draped across the culverts. As soon as the forward motion stopped, he punched the door release. Nothing happened.

"The hydraulic system must be out." Sam climbed out of seat and kicked the door until it sprang open enough to squeeze through. The rest followed him out.

Scott felt more energetic than he had in hours. "What a mountain of flesh." The body was so thick that he could not see over it.

Sandra placed her ear next to the abdomen. "I can hear all kinds of gurgling inside. The damn thing is taking a nap."

"I think not," Doc commented dryly. "I am not surprised that in a creature of this size, organic processes continue after death. After all, twitching nerves cause muscle movement in animals long after they die. A body of such mammoth proportions must die in stages."

Sandra stepped back shaking her head. "I don't get it. Why did the dinosaur cross the road?"

Scott groaned, but felt more like his old self. "Since this is the Cretaceous, that must be the oldest joke in the world."

"A joke on us if we don't get around—"

"Here!" Death Wind pointed his spear toward the grass divider between the road surface and the tree line. A man-sized monster lay on the ground, with smoke pouring out of a gaping hole in its chest. "Laser did that."

"So our dragon counterparts have been here recently," Doc mused. "Judging by that wickedly enlarged hind claw, I'd say we're looking at a deinonychus: a vicious carnosaur that—"

"Look! Over there. Tracks." Rusty indicated an area where two parallel paths flattened the grass. "If they went around, so can we. Let's go!" He dragged Doc by the arm. They all piled into the truck.

Sam jumped into the driver's seat and flicked the controls. "I don't know if this baby can hold together off road." He backed up until he reached the spot where the dragon vehicle had left the orangetop. "But it doesn't seem as if we have much of a choice."

"Notice the bloody longitudinal gashes on the titanosaur's throat. It is astounding that a six-foot-tall predator can dispatch a brute weighing tens of tons. Of course, it was common for a pack of hyenas to bring down wildebeest in the African savannah—"

"Doc!" Rusty placed his hands on Doc's cheeks and turned the older man's head toward him. "Cut it out. We've only got a couple hours—"

"Hang on back there." Sam yanked the throttle to the side and eased it forward. The split differentials spun in their joints, turning the wheels to the left while applying power. The troop carrier veered off the prepared surface and down the sloping embankment on a steep angle. The front wheels groaned as they impacted with the mushy grassland. "That wasn't so bad."

He throttled down as the truck bounced across the uneven ground. Clods of dirt spun out of the drive wheels like an arched rooster tail. The truck skidded and swayed as the tread dug up the grassy covering and churned the damp earth underneath into a muddy mess. He stayed in the grooves made by the earlier passage. As the path curved back toward the road, he gunned the motors to full power. The truck ran up the slope on an angle, sideslipping as the gritty shoulder offered little traction. The wheels spun futilely, without the torque necessary to mount the final hump. Instead, with wheels spinning madly and motors whining, the truck moved horizontally just below the crest of the shoulder.

"We ain't gonna make it."

Scott gripped his seat and willed the truck upward. His stomach muscles tightened. He let out a gasp when he felt the truck slip backward. "Come on, baby. Come on. You can do it."

Smoke poured out of the armatures. The pungent odor was distinctive to Scott; he was used to working with motors and burnt-out windings. The treads issued a musty stink from the pulverized plastic. Still describing a diagonal heading, the weary and battered truck seemed about to rattle apart when the left wheel trains caught a slick of extruded plastic that bestowed solid traction.

The truck scratched upward, pounced over

the shoulder and onto the orangetop facing sideways. Sam pulled back the joystick as the truck raced across the road and nearly went over the other side. The tortured wheels spun backward and brought the truck to a halt just before it careened down the opposite embankment. Scott felt like a billiard ball caroming off case-hardened cushions. Sam pulled the lever to the side, rotated the vehicle like a top, then thrust the lever all the way forward as soon as the broken bow was aligned with the lane marker.

Sam wiped sweat off his brow. "Whew."

"Way to go, Daddy."

"Expert handling, Sam." Doc breathed a sigh of relief.

"Anyone got any water?" Rusty said. "I could use a drink."

"We have no supplies, and I do not think we have time to stop by a convenient puddle. Other obstacles may await us."

"Hey, who are those guys up ahead?" Sandra's hand quaked as she pointed to a bunch of stick figures standing in the road"

"I don't know, but they're coming this way," Sam said.

Scott at first thought it was a human road crew, until one turned aside and he saw the long tail stretched out behind it. "They look like that carnosaur back there in the grass, except these are alive."

"Deinonychus," Doc pronounced slowly.

"You didn't say they traveled in herds," Sandra fairly screamed.

"The fossil record is devoid of behavioral characteristics. Bones tell us about an individual, not—"

"Forget it, Doc," Rusty said. "Sam, don't pick up any hitchhikers."

"We're going full speed, and if they don't get out of the way they'll be wearing plastic."

The carnosaurs stood upright on hind legs, balanced by whiplike tails. Clawed fingers graced humanlike hands that were held at half-mast. Their heads were shaped like fat beaks. Fernlike roughage covered their bodies in the way that feathers covered birds. They were two-hundred-pound packages of meanness looking for a scrap.

Sam steered the truck for the middle of the flock. Tails rose and heads lowered as the carnosaurs ducked into a running mode, seemingly undaunted by the approaching vehicle. As the distance closed, the beasts split to the side—

except for one deinonychus that leaped straight at the windshield with both hind feet stretched forward like an osprey clutching for fish in the water. It hit the clear acrylic talons first. The windshield splintered as the clawed feet came through, narrowly missing Sam's head. The edge of the roof caught the beast at the base of the short throat. The plastic snapped off in chunks, but retained enough structural integrity to fling the brazen carnosaur in front of the charging vehicle. The truck vaulted over the squirming body and hit the road with a crash.

"I guess that'll show 'em."

If the carnosaurs had the faculty of cerebration, they expressed other ideas. With catlike agility they reversed their direction of flight and fairly flew after the onrushing truck. They had no trouble keeping up the pace.

"Look at 'em go," said Sandra with consternation.

"They're catching up!" Rusty shouted.

Sandra dashed for the middle turret, which now stood at the end of the truncated troop carrier. "I'll slow 'em down with a light show." She climbed up the trunk and took a position at the breech of the laser gun. One deinonychus ran so fast along the shoulder that it caught up with the straining vehicle.

"It's coming in the doorway," Rusty shouted.

Death Wind's spear was too long to maneuver in the confines the troop carrier. He knelt on the landing next to Sam, bow hand. Wind rushing in through the shattered windshield blew long hair about his head. He notched an arrow and pulled back until the bow nearly curved back on itself. The deinonychus's throat was only a yard away. With a loud twang the arrow leaped instantaneously into the gaping, tooth-filled mouth and emerged from the back of the neck. The carnosaur's head swiveled around as if it had been jerked by a lariat; it fell dead in the road.

"Watch out the back!" Sandra screamed.

Scott was so intent on the Nomad's action that he forgot about the other carnosaurs. When he twisted in his seat he saw with his right eye that another deinonychus was climbing in the rear opening. Sandra screamed as the monstrous head darted up the turret tube. Scott rudely thrust Jane aside, grabbed Death Wind's spear, and, unable to turn it around in the narrow compartment, butted the carnosaur in the chest as hard as he could. The creature fell backward, but clawed fingers grabbed the backrests of the last two seats. Scott butted again, in the throat. The deinonychus screeched as it clutched for the object of pain, lost its balance, and fell out the back of the truck. It flailed in the air for a moment, but landed on its feet with uncanny litheness. The forward momentum carried it onto its face. A pack member leaped over its back. A moment later, the downed creature regained its feet and continued the chase.

"They're too close." Sandra dropped out of the tube and landed on her buttocks with a slap. If she was hurt, she paid it no mind. "I can't depress the muzzle enough."

Scott searched frantically among the seats. "Where're the guns?"

"Gone with the rear of the truck," Rusty said.

Sandra climbed into the forward turret. "Hold 'em off a minute."

"With what? My good looks." Scott held his stance with the spear as two carnosaurs fought to climb in the jagged opening while the truck rolled along at highway speed.

Rusty pulled out the stun gun he had been carrying all these months. He climbed over the starboard seats and jabbed it in the face of the closest deinonychus. The single shot paralyzed the beast; it fell limp onto the road. Scott thumped the other one in abdomen, but it had too good a grip on the backrests. The hind leg came up so high that the extended talon brushed the ceiling. Scott fell away as the carnosaur gashed downward. The hoof hit the floor, and the other one came up to repeat the procedure. Death Wind stepped over Scott and picked up the fallen spear at the same time that a laser blast burst through the roof and drilled the creature neatly through the head; the beam continued lengthwise through its body, frying its insides. It fell dead on the floor.

Sandra did not stop there. She raised the barrel and fired at the bloodthirsty entourage. She blew out most of the roof doing it, as the rear turret was in her line of sight. She knocked down one deinonychus, but since she could not see well through the roofing material, most of her shots went wild.

"There's a rest stop up ahead," Sam called out.

"And a stagecoach pulling out with a fresh charge," Doc added. A double-turreted vehicle turned out of the driveway and headed toward the time transporter. "Now I understand. The deinonychus herd killed the titanosaurus, then

was interrupted by the dragons. The carnosaurs did not like having their repast disturbed, and chased after the dragons. Since the dragon vehicle was undamaged, our lizard refugees soon outdistanced—"

"Who gives a hoot?" Rusty screamed. "We've got monsters behind and monsters ahead. What'll we do?"

"We gotta changes horses." Sam eked as much power as possible out of the dying troop carrier. "This one's on its last amps."

Scott let Death Wind pull him to his knees. "Don't those things ever give up?"

Half a dozen carnosaurs galloped behind the truck, heedless the bolts of death punching the orangetop around them. Sam not slow down as he turned onto the staging platform, but beasts cut across the hypotenuse and raked their claws along what was left of the windows and sidewalls.

"Hang on, guys." Sam steered the truck toward the stockade, yanked the joystick over hard, and threw the vehicle into sharp turn. The side with the clinging carnosaurs bounced along the wall, scraping off two of the monsters and crushing a third under the wheels.

The stockade doors swung open. The motors screamed in protest as Sam spun the joystick in a circle. The truck veered away from the heavy gates, but spun out and stalled. The cab was full of smoke.

Coughing, Scott swatted the air in front of his face. "What the hell's a tech—"

An enraged deinonychus reached the vested dragon in a flash, raised its hind leg high in the air, and with one swift downward slash ripped open the slow-moving lizard from neck to groin. Razor-sharp teeth clamped onto the snakelike neck as the dragon's organs spilled over the roadway.

A passenger coach full of technicians trundled out of the stockade and was immediately set upon by the remaining pair of carnosaurs. No soldiers were ready at the guns. The two rampaging beasts clambered through the open front door and wreaked bloody carnage on the dragons that were hissing within.

Sandra fired a well-aimed blast at the deinonychus that was hurriedly swallowing the entrails of the dragon that it had disemboweled. She waited until all sounds of lizard hissing ceased before emptying her magazine on the coach. When the power finally died, the coach was a mass of flames. "Damn! It didn't blow up."

Sam kicked open the door and helped the others out of the wreckage of the troop carrier. "End of the line for this bus, folks."

"I have never seen such a feral, ferocious, single-minded animal—"

Rusty grabbed Doc's elbow and hauled him into the stockade. "Later, Doc."

Scott let Jane lead him into the newly selected vehicle: a low-slung, double-turreted sedan with barely enough room for them to fit. Rusty pulled the charging plug before squeezing inside. Sandra climbed into the forward turret, Sam took the joystick, the rest crammed into the two passenger seats and cargo space.

Sam wasted no time in switching on the motors. "Hey, the power grid says we're only half charged."

"The electricity was off in the complex, too. None of the indicator lights was lit." Rusty turned to his companion, his face locked in a grimace of horror. "Scott, do you know what that means?"

"Yes." Despite the blurry eye, Scott could see all too clearly. "It means that no more power is being transmitted along these lines: either in or out. If the time transporter is operating off its own reserve power, it'll send through only one more shipment. We've got to get to the TTS before the dragons in the bus ahead, because the only ones who get away—are the ones who gets there first."

CHAPTER 28

"No sign of 'em. They must really be hauling." Sam held the joystick all the way forward; he moved it slightly from side to side in order to correct his course. "I wonder if they know about the reactor."

"With the power out, the commlinks are down," Rusty said. "Since we didn't pass them on the road, they must have left the city before we did. Ergo, they are probably on a routine assignment."

"Yeah, they shuffle techs back and forth like they were telegrams." Sitting in the turret seat, Sandra spoke down the entrance tube. "You just get close enough, Daddy, and I'll send 'em on their last mission."

Sam shook his head. "Scott, I sure hope you

know what you're doing. I still think we should have taken a couple of single-turret speedsters instead of this lumbering coach. The batteries are so weak that I'm losing speed."

"I took enough rigs apart to repair them blindfolded. Open the door. I want to get rid of another seat."

Sam hit the hydraulic switch that operated the portal piston. Gale force winds whipped into the cubicle as Scott and Death Wind held the bench seat in the air and manhandled it over the other seats and thrust it out the door. It tumbled off the shoulder in one piece and plowed a furrow in the grass.

"Good. Now, get that other access panel off."

While Death Wind removed the floorboards, Scott worked with unwieldy dragon instruments on the cable connections. Jane held the tool box in her lap and with uncanny prescience handed him the strange devices as he needed them.

"Are you sure the overload will not damaged the motors?" Doc asked.

"Sure. It'll destroy them. But by the time it does, we'll either be sixty million years away, or it won't matter."

"Don't you dare disconnect my turret," Sandra called down. "We may need this Gatling gun before the day's over."

"Oh, you just want to blow something up."

Sandra fumed. "True. So what's your point?"

Scott wrapped a wrench around a copper bolt and loosened it enough to slip out the terminal prong. "Besides, I'm shunting the laser power in such a way that either gun will work, but not both together. You're a fast gal, but you can't be in two places at the same time." To Doc, "By putting the other power module and storage battery in series with the power train I can increase the voltage to the drive motors. They'll run faster than they're supposed to, and the extra heat will eventually burn out the windings. But dragons built things to last, and I'm betting the motors will hold up beyond their design specs at least long enough to get us to where we're going."

"It is a calculated risk that we are forced to take, considering, the alternative. Today is judgment day for us as well as for the dragons."

Sandra said, "Yeah, well, as long as the better man wins, the lizards don't have a chance."

"Is that proverb or prophecy?"

"It's propaganda. To keep up *my* spirits more than any else's."

Scott tightened the final connection. "Sam, you want to take off the load while I make the crossover?"

Sam idled the motors by pulling the joystick into the middle position; he could still steer the coach by shifting the lever from side to side, but the power linkage remained in neutral. "All clear."

The coach decelerated slowly on nearly perfect bearings.

"Okay, Death Wind, you can close the knife switch."

There was a momentary spark as the Nomad closed the contacts.

Scott kept his good eye on the built-in meters. "Looks good. Ease it into gear, Sam."

As he slowly thrust the joystick forward, the motors hummed until they sang at a higher pitch than they ever had before. The coach exceeded its previous top speed by twenty-five percent. After the initial load there was no more arcing.

"Dragons are good engineers." Scott smiled. "They have their faults, but none of them are electrical."

"Soon their only faults'll be geological," Sandra commented wryly. "An observation we should leave to them. Come on, Daddy, move this thing like there's no tomorrow."

"An unfortunate choice of words," Doc muttered, "phrased such that they are likely to prognosticate before they become clichéd."

"Whatever that means." Sandra stood on the seat and arched her toes so that her head touched the turret canopy. "Hey, I can see the bastards up ahead. Battle stations, folks. Get ready for a shootout."

Scott readjusted his bandages. "There's nothing we can do, Sandra. You've got the gun, so it's all up to you."

"Has it occurred to anyone that without power the drawbridge may be inoperable?"

"Pop! Why the sudden pessimism? What're you trying to do, destroy morale?"

"I was merely pointing out the obvious so that we can prepare for every eventuality."

"Well, if worse comes to worst, we climb the wall again. Jane must still have her rope. She has everything else in that bag."

Jane smiled innocently as she pulled out the coiled vine. "I have."

Doc smirked. "My dear, it certainly did not take you long to join the ranks of civilized women."

"The next thing you know she'll be wearing a blouse," Sandra scoffed.

"Okay, I can see 'em now," Sam said. "Whoops, they just went over that next rise. Sandy, I'm gonna come straight up on 'em so you can lock the swivel on zero degrees."

"Gotcha."

As the coach topped the hill, Scott saw an orange barrier several miles ahead. The time transport structure was not in line of sight with the road, and, even though it sat high on a hill, it was hidden by nearby trees. "It's going to be close."

"You know, if there isn't any power, it may not make any difference," Rusty said. "No one is going anywhen if the transporter isn't fully charged."

"Hey, cut the gloomsday predictions," Sandra yelled. "Let's cross each bridge as we come to it."

"I was just pondering the possibilities."

"Yeah, well, what're you guys gonna dream up next?"

"Flyer in sky," said Death Wind without intonation.

"Just what we need," Sandra said sarcastically. "DW, don't you start going funny on me, too. I've got enough worries—"

"Hey, what's that mountain moving across the road? Daddy, do you see that?"

"Yeah, but I can't make it out. It's as big as a house. It must be some kind of moving van."

"That is certainly going to complicate—"

Doc was cut off by Rusty's poignant shout. "It's not a vehicle. It's a dinosaur."

"And it's not just *any* dinosaur," Scott gasped. "It's a Tyrannosaurus rex. Maybe the same one we woke up before."

"This time I'm ready for 'im," Sandra said through gritted teeth. "I'm gonna put 'im back to sleep—permanently."

Sam pulled back on the throttle. "We sure as hell don't wanna run into it."

The road in front of the coach erupted in a violent orange display of molten plastic. Exploding globules splattered against the windshield and bubbled the acrylic.

"What the hell—"

The coach drove straight through the tempest of flying debris; it emerged intact, but with the front window opaque. "I can't see—"

The coach still streaked along the road faster than full speed.

"Watch heads!" Death Wind bellowed.

Everyone ducked as he swung the access panel like a discus. It sliced a neat horizontal slit in the acrylic windshield. Sam squinted as hot air hit him in the face. Straddling the highway like the Colossus of Rhodes, the tyrannosaur screeched angrily at the oncoming vehicle. Two-fingered paws clutched futilely as a cavern full of teeth gnashed the air in strident expectation.

"Holy—" Sam jerked the joystick.

The independent axles swiveled so sharply that the coach skidded fifty feet before beginning to describe a vector. The heavy storage cells in the chassis gave the vehicle such a low center of gravity that there was no chance of the vehicle overturning. As the coach's forward motion curved to the left, Sam slammed the throttle forward and to the right. He narrowly missed driving off the edge of the embankment. When the coach swerved right, it grazed the columnar hind leg of the tyrannosaur and ran over the beast's tail. The crash with the caudal appendage tossed the vehicle sideways. It skimmed along the opposite embankment and came to a halt teetering over the edge.

"I got no power," Sam shrieked. "Musta blown a fuse."

"DW was right. It *is* a flyer. And my gun is jammed. Sandra tumbled out of the forward turret and scrambled along the narrow aisle and up into the after turret. "Damn. This one's dead, too."

Scott saw the tyrannosaur spin around and stare directly at him through the rear window. Close-set eyes gave the beast binocular vision and depth perception that Scott was temporarily lacking.

Sandra punched the trigger uselessly. "Scott, I thought you said—"

"They just went through the gate, and they're closing the drawbridge behind them," Rusty shouted.

"Ten o'clock high, and it's taking aim."

The tyrannosaur hunkered down low and charged.

Doc inhaled sharply in the sudden shocked silence. "Sometimes I wish I hadn't been born. And in a time such as this, I realize thankfully that I haven't."

CHAPTER 29

The explosion next to the coach jolted Scott to action. He leaped off his seat and in one smooth motion ripped off the dashboard access panel and reset the electrical breaker.

Sandra must have had her finger clamped to the trigger mechanism because as soon as power was restored, Scott heard the staccato drumming of the laser gun. Through the clear thermoplastic turret he saw the flyer veer off as bolts of energy bit off its power nodes in bursts of bright sparks. Sandra rotated the turret and let loose a blast at the oncoming tyrannosaur.

Sam fanned the master control switch; all drive motors came on-line at once. The accumulated torque jarred the coach's delicate balance; it tilted forward over the edge of the steep shoulder. Sam engaged the wheels at the same time: most of them turned vainly because they no longer contacted the road surface. But the two axles that provided the pivot point offered enough reverse motive force to catch the coach before it plummeted off the road. It slammed down hard. As the rear wheels bit into plastic, the coach shot backward, knocking all but Sam and Sandra to the floor.

The joystick banged against the turning detent as Sam tried frantically to prevent the coach from darting across the road and over the other shoulder. The odor of burning plastic wafted upward through the disassembled floor as the wheels spun against the road surface. The coach gyrated sharply, aligned itself with the direction of the highway, then smashed its back end into the tyrannosaur's low-slung abdomen. The rear window splintered inward, showering the cab with slivers of plastic.

Sandra was knocked from her perch by the impact, pitched down the turret tube, and deposited with a thud in the aisle. The tyrannosaur leaned forward like a steam shovel and with one monstrous crunch bit off the after turret. The gun was ripped from its mount. As the power cables separated, a pyrotechnic display of thunderstorm proportions burst in the tyrant lizard's face.

Rubbing her posterior, Sandra scuttled away from the missing turret; chunks of metal and shards of acrylic fell away from the opening. "It didn't even faze—" She grabbed a backrest to keep from being hurled into the cascading debris as Sam jammed the joystick all the way forward and propelled the coach out of the tyrannosaur's kissing embrace. The spinning wheels created so much foul-smelling smoke that the beast was hidden from view.

Doc said, "Warm-blooded metabolism requires tremendous amounts of food, but I did not think that—"

Another blast from the laser cannon gouged the orangetop between the coach and the tyrannosaur. The twenty-foot-tall monster spat out a mouthful of plastic parts. As soon as the volcanic eruption subsided, the tyrannosaur leaped fearlessly across the puddle of molten road surface and dashed madly after the careening coach.

"Sandy! Get up in that turret." Sam fought to keep the vehicle under control. He headed straight for the rising spans of the drawbridge. "You gotta blow up the guard shack and demolish the hydraulic system."

Sandra clambered up the tube in a flash. "What about the flyer?"

Preceded by its long shadow, the tyrannosaur galloped along the highway right behind the still-accelerating coach. Rows of rapacious teeth chomped the air. Sam did not dare slow down. "It can take care of itself."

"Undoubtedly full of administrators escaping the city. The dearth of pilots—"

Doc was again cut off by a laser blast, this one uncomfortably close to the starboard side. The windows blew in, and the bulkhead dented, but held.

"In the future, Rusty, I shall keep my thoughts to myself. Dragon methods of negative reinforcement are much stronger than yours."

Sandra blasted away at the bottom of the saucer. Power cones blew into pieces from her accurate fire, dissuading the flyer from following too close. Then she redirected her rotating barrels at the armed and armored guardhouse that was coming into range. Bright flashes of light attested to enemy alertness. The green bolts of energy seared the roof of the coach and melted one side of the turret. The blockhouse laser cannon was akin to a shotgun: it was intended to fight off encroaching carnosaurs, so its beam was spread for maximum close-range coverage. At a distance, its effect was lost in the scatter.

Sandra kept her finger pressed tightly on the trigger. The Gatling gun emitted burst after burst of high-powered, pinpoint energy. Sam steered the coach without deviation. Every bit of speed and forward motion was necessary to stay ahead of the rampaging tyrannosaur. Sandra poured a deadly hail of fire into the guard shack. Excess energy poured into the blockade wall behind it, causing the plastic to sag like a collapsing mud bank.

The drawbridge's upward motion halted when the opposing spans were raised a third of the way, leaving a gap in between them. They jerked up and down as if they were slipping a cog.

"Hit it, Sandy! Hit it!"

Between shots the black hole of the laser cannon's barrel was clearly visible. Sandra put an energy bolt right down the tube. In an instant the blockhouse, guard shack, and dragon soldiers were converted to molecular particles as a titanic explosion ripped outward from the supercharged battery packs. An orange ball of expanding gases created such intense heat that nearby trees were stripped of their leaves and left as smoldering, blackened sticks of charcoal. The grass was turned to cinder.

Flames billowed into the sky and across the road, completely obscuring the drawbridge from view. Sam's hand never wavered from its position on the throttle. The coach hurtled headlong into the seething cauldron, passing so quickly through the conflagration that, except for a brief finger of flame that darted through the windshield slit, the heat did not have time to penetrate the cab or ignite the undercarriage.

The coach lurched sharply when the front axle hit the angled span. Scott felt his stomach drop as he was launched out of his seat. Only a death grip on the backrest of the seat in front of him kept him from crashing into the roof. All he saw out of the bubbled windshield was the purpling sky. The silence was palpable. The coach seemed to hover in the air on gossamer wings as the coach flew across the open space between opposite spans.

Time was frozen.

Scott was several feet above his seat when the crash came. An instant later he was slammed against the floor and wrapped into a ball under the next seat forward. He floated through another bounce, then hit hard again when the coach contacted the roadway for the second time. The vehicle went into an uncontrolled skid, left the road, and dug up the lawn for a hundred feet before sliding sideways to a stop. The cab was full of dust.

Scott blinked in the eerie silence that followed. His ears were ringing. He inhaled deeply, gratified that he was still alive. But every muscle in his body was battered and bruised. He moved slowly. A long while passed before he could focus his good eye. Then he saw Jane crumpled on the floor next to him. She was limp and unresponsive.

In a daze, Scott pulled her head onto his lap. Long golden hair flowed around his legs like strands of silk. He tried to talk, but the lump in his throat prevented his vocal chords from working. A tear rolled down one cheek as he brushed her hair back from her face. She looked so lost, so forlorn. They had been through so much together that he could not bear to lose now. He would rather die himself. He bent down and brushed his lips across hers.

Jane's eyelashes fluttered. She blinked, but did not otherwise move. Then she twisted her head suddenly and gazed into his eyes. She snaked her hand out of the wreckage and placed it against his cheek; she wiped away the lone tear. "We are alive?" Her voice was soft and mellifluous.

"Oh, Jane." Scott hugged her tight. Her bare chest felt so good against his.

Jane returned his embrace, lingered in his arms for a moment, then pushed him away. "The others?"

Scott coughed. The cab was filling with smoke. "Doc! Rusty!" Both companions lay prone under a blanket of dirt, plastic, windowpanes, and ceiling insulation. He pulled Doc out from under the debris. His face was white with powder. "Doc."

Death Wind rose up out of the wreckage like the mythological phoenix, and brushed himself off. "Sandra."

The turret seat had torn free from its mounts and lodged in the access tube. Sandra hung onto the gun by the breech. She kicked out wildly, gained purchase with her feet, and climbed back onto the turret shelf. "I'm okay."

The Nomad turned his attention to Rusty, who was pinned under a broken bench seat. Death Wind tore the seat off its one remaining stanchion and shoved it aside. The redhead blinked his eyes and spit out a clot of mucus. As the Nomad hauled him an upright position, Rusty went into a coughing spasm that did not end until he emptied his nose of inhaled grit.

In Scott's arms Doc finally started breathing. Acrid fumes wafted up through the floorboards.

Scott clamped his hand over Doc's mouth and dragged him toward the opening where the windshield used to be. Sam lay on the grass twenty feet away. "Help me, Death Wind." Scott lay Doc on the floor, climbed out the opening, and reached in. The Nomad picked up the doctor and handed him to Scott, who carried the limp form to where Sam lay motionless.

Carrying her always present handbag, Jane helped Rusty out of the coach, then went immediately to Sam's aid. She placed her hands on his forehead. "Sam. Sam."

Sandra screamed at Death Wind. "Lemme go. I said I'm okay."

Death Wind struggled with the jammed seat. "Coach on fire."

Scott could hardly see the Nomad through the smoke and rising flames. "Get out of there before it blows." He turned his attention to Jane. "Come on, let's get them farther away." He dragged Doc across the grass while Jane and Rusty did the same for Sam.

"Leave me alone." Sandra undogged the seals, leaned back, and kicked open the upper hatch. "I'm clear."

Still wearing his quiver and bow and carrying his long-shafted spear, Death Wind ducked and jumped through the windshield opening. He dashed across the lawn to where the others scrabbled away with their charges. "We have trouble."

Scott looked to where Death Wind pointed. The flames of the blockhouse explosion were nearly extinguished. Out of the smoke stalked the angry tyrannosaur, its head darting pigeon-like as it lumbered along the partially raised drawbridge. It balanced skillfully on the upper edge, tilted his head, and without hesitation leaped across the gap to the inboard span.

A laser gun fired explosively. Scott nearly jumped out of his moccasins until he realized that Sandra was the shooter. The dazzling laser bolts seared rectilinear paths through the air—not at the storming tyrannosaur, but upward at the descending flyer.

The enemy flying machine veered away from the landing pad adjacent to the brightly glowing time transport structure. The thrumming of the saucer's power cones filled the air in concatenation with the electrical crackling of the time portal focusing nodes. Scott's hair stood on end from the static charge in the air.

The flyer's laser cannon fired at the smoldering coach and succeeded in demolishing the driver's compartment. Sandra nipped away at the saucer with smaller blasts that did no major structural damage, but which chewed up the undercarriage with telling effect. The flyer gradually lost altitude.

"What an unfortunate time to be deprived of one's faculties." Doc shook the gravel out of his snowy white hair and rubbed the back of his head.

"Doc!" Scott yelled. "I thought you were—are you hurt?"

"Abrasions and contusions, but nothing serious. I seem to have misplaced my cane. Could you help an old man—"

"Dragons! Up there." Jane indicated the technicians that were piling out of their vehicle, next to the transport dome.

"They're headed for the control bunker," Rusty shouted.

Sandra redirected the Gatling gun long enough to stitch a line of laser beams through the waddling horde. Then she spun around as fast as the turret would rotate and zapped the tyrannosaur in the fattest part of its abdomen. The befuddled creature stopped in its tracks. Shriveled, two-clawed paws clutched at the site of sudden pain.

"Hell, I've lost turret power." Sandra climbed out of the hatchway and onto the roof of the coach. The compartment below her was a mass of flames. She reached into the turret, removed the trunion clamps, and lifted the heavy Gatling gun off its mount. Resting the muzzle on the lip of the turret, she fired again at the settling flyer just as it released another blast that tore a long blazing furrow in the grass.

Jane implored to Doc with one outstretched hand. "Sam is hurt."

The tyrannosaur's scales smoked. Instinctively, the huge head tried to bite the hole that was causing such internal distress. Its attention was diverted for only a moment. Then the great coal-black eyes locked on the struggling humans on the lawn. Primitive mental associations racked its prehistoric brain. It screeched like a speeding freight train with its wheels locked on steel rails.

Scott's hackles rose as he jumped up and ran waving his hands. "Here! Over here." Nimbly, he darted across the grass and ran a zigzag pattern up the hill toward the hovering flyer. His ruse worked, and the dim-witted carnosaur

charged after him.

Doc knelt by Sam's stationary form. He placed his ear against his son's-in-law chest. "His heart beats weakly."

Sandra danced from foot to foot as the plastic heated up. She picked up the Gatling gun, held it in both arms, and carried it as far away from the smoke-filled turret hatch as the power cable would let her. She poured a deadly stream of fire into the flyer's extended pedestal. With the saucer now practically on the ground, her laser beams enfiladed the undercarriage and blasted through the forest of power cones. The flyer wobbled as it struggled to maintain a level attitude for landing. The pedestal was still ten feet above the nonmelt orangetop when the flyer, deprived of most of its force field channelers, dropped suddenly.

Because of the uneven destruction of its power cones, the flyer was listing considerably when it contacted the ground. The impact of the crash sheered off the cylindrical pedestal where it periscoped out of the base of the saucer. The flyer pivoted; one edge banged hard against the landing pad. The power ceased, and the whole weight of the flyer collapsed on the side of the displaced landing pedestal, crushing it.

Sandra immediately pirouetted and aimed at the dragon technicians who had been convinced to steer clear of the control bunker. Now they were making good their escape by converging on the dome. "Oh, no, you don't." She fired a controlled burst into their ranks, then kept a solid line of deadly beams between them and the portal entrance. The focusing nodes glowed with spectacular brilliance, ready at a moment's notice to discharge their pent-up energy and disrupt the space-time continuum.

Scott nearly collided with the caped dragons that were emerging from the wreckage of the flyer. They descended from the central opening, where the saucer was supported by the flattened pedestal, and crawled along the landing pad on all fours. Scott brazenly kicked the lead dragon in the chin, heard the resounding clack of breaking teeth, and slipped past it under the edge of the flyer. A soldier clambered out behind the stunned administrator, gun in hand.

With a terrific bound the tyrannosaur leaped into the fracas, chomped off the caped dragon's head, and swallowed it like a mint. The soldier fired point-blank into the carnosaur's mouth. The laser burned a hole through the thick jaw, but it served only to enrage the beast. The tyrannosaur stretched its neck under the flyer and took such a huge chunk out of the soldier's body that all that was left was four limbs and a curved backbone.

Leaving the tyrannosaur to complete its carnage, Scott dashed back to where Death Wind guarded his companions who were huddled on the lawn.

Jane pulled the strap over her shoulder and laid the gadget bag on the ground. A whiskered, furry head poked out of the end folds. The antediluvian rodent wrinkled its nose and sniffed the grass with innocent curiosity. Jane dumped the bag. Eight baby rodents the size of thimbles tumbled out behind their mother; the newborns lay in a mass, kicking silently.

"Where'd they come from?" Scott asked incredulously. Jane stroked the mother as it nibbled at the young and corralled them into a hollow next to a small rock. "Here." She indicated the birth canal. "They are strong. They will survive." Sam twitched.

Doc quickly ran his hands along Sam's arms and legs, feeling for broken bones. "Yes, and they will bring after them a new order of life to the face of the Earth—an order that will dominate the next era just as the dinosaurs dominated this. Their descendants may very well—Sam. Sam. Can you hear me?"

Sam rocked his head and struggled to open his eyes. "Where am I? When am I?" He groaned as he sat up, and grabbed his neck. "Oh, do I hurt."

"Likely a case of whiplash. That was quite a pitch you took," Doc examined Sam's pupil response by swaying in and out of the light of the setting sun. "There are no breaks or apparent concussion. Do you think you can move? It is imperative."

Sandra let out a yell. "Damn. Just when I was having fun." She pulled the trigger several more times, but the laser gun refused to fire. She thrust it aside and leapt off the roof as it sagged from the heat and jumped ten feet to the ground. She landed on her feet, went into a roll, and came up running. "Clear the decks!"

The electrical wiring short-circuited, detonating the batteries. The resultant explosion blew apart the coach and sent flames and debris a hundred feet into the air. The rebels covered their faces as shrapnel and burning chunks of plastic fell like hot hail. When Scott uncovered

his eye, the ground was littered with flaming debris: a graphic restoration of Hell.

Death Wind was the first to stand. "We hurry. Dragons make for dome."

As the tyrannosaur gobbled down the lizards that were struggling to escape from one side of the flyer, a pair of armed soldiers led their superior officer out the other side. What remained of the technical crew that had survived Sandra's withering fire gave up on their previous objective of attaining the control bunker; now they waddled as fast as their lizard legs would carry them to the top of the hill and toward the shimmering blue curtain at the center of the time transport structure. The sky was a blaze of red: the pageant of early twilight.

"Hey, they're gonna go through," Sandra bellowed.

Rusty clambered up on hands and knees. "There's no more juice coming in. Once the capacitors are discharged, there's no way to recharge them."

"Come on, DW." Sandra charged the technicians that were approaching the dome's entrance portal. She was completely weaponless. "Let's get 'em."

Death Wind was right behind her, and Scott behind him. The Nomad tossed the spear to Scott in a running lateral pass, then in one smooth motion drew an arrow from its quiver and notched it on the string. He shot the arrow past Sandra's head and into the back of a vested dragon. The lizard let out a hiss as it clutched at the shaft stuck deeply in its flesh.

"Way to go, DW." Sandra swooped up behind another technician, grabbed its tail, and kept running. Caught unawares, the dragon was twisted around and yanked off its legs. It no sooner hit the plastic then Death Wind leaped on its chest and buried his knife in the snakelike throat.

Scott passed the skirmish and buried the spear tip in the hindquarters of another dragon. The powerful beast turned so quickly that Scott, still holding onto the spear, was swept aside like a fly. He maintained his grip on the shaft. The dragon kept turning, but Scott dug in his heels, found his footing, pulled out the spear, and quickly plunged it into a more vulnerable spot. Blood spouted like a geyser as the spear sliced into the chambers of the heart. The dragon collapsed like a marionette whose strings had been cut.

"Good going, Scott." Sandra patted him on the derriere as she brushed by him. "Now, how do we take down those soldiers when all we have are sticks?" The question in the air did not slow her charge.

The only technicians left were sorely wounded and no longer a problem. But the oncoming soldiers had their guns drawn. A laser bolt whipped past Scott and exploded in the control bunker bulkhead.

"Don't let them damage the transmitting station," Rusty called out as he and Jane dragged Sam, too injured to move on his own, up the hill and onto the orangetop. Doc limped along painfully on his bad leg.

Scott, having to dodge another laser blast, angled to a spot where the bunker was no longer behind him. Sandra and Death Wind spread out in the other direction, thus dividing the fire of the enemy soldiers.

"It's him!" Sandra screamed. "The one with the gold cape."

The cape was a mere shred, singed black; the dragon's scales were charred.

The moment of inattention nearly cost her life as one of the soldiers zapped her. The searing bolt went through her vest and left an ugly black furrow across her rib cage. She fell to the ground clawing at the smoldering material. Death Wind loosed a bolt that ricocheted harmlessly off the offending soldier's backpack.

The Tyrannosaurus rex licked bulging, blood-stained lips. Having devoured all the lizards within reach, it looked for other prey to feed its voracious appetite. It did not take long to discover the battle between dragons and humans.

The tyrannosaur bounded away from the flyer. Tusk-sized talons gouged the plastic surface, affording perfect traction. In the time it took Scott to gasp, the creature reached the caped dragon and with swift retribution chomped down on its sloping back. The tyrannosaur stood up like a derrick two stories tall. The dragon squirmed and hissed in its mouth. Massive jaws crushed the morsel while sharp, lancelike teeth rended effortlessly through flesh and bone. As the monster munched what was little more than a tidbit, it eyed the next course. The long tail lashed from side to side, knocking down first one then the other soldier.

"Time to leave." Scott stood his ground, holding the spear menacingly as Death Wind helped Sandra to her feet and whisked her toward the time transport structure. In the gathering darkness the dome glowed with awesome brilliance; the focusing nodes crackled with stored energy. With one last look at the towering tyrannosaur, Scott turned and ran. "Hey, wait for me."

Doc and Rusty dragged Sam through the dome's arched portal. Despite Sandra's burden, Death Wind paused to help. "I'm all out," Doc said, resting.

Jane stood resolutely and waved. "Hurry, Scott."

Scott took only one step when the world jumped up and hit him in the face. For a time interminable he saw nothing but blackness. When he again opened his good eye and sucked in the breath of life, he felt the ground shaking violently. His body bounced like that of an acrobat on a trampoline. He struggled to get on his hands and knees, to crawl across the heaving orangetop toward the time transport structure.

The clear plastic dome vibrated shrilly; the focusing nodes spat static overcharges. Rusty dragged Sam out of sight through the ethereal blue curtain. Sandra fell to the floor, groaning and clutching her wounded side. Death Wind scooped her up and plunged out of sight.

With a tremendous zap the focusing nodes channeled their energy into the stasis field, rupturing the fabric of space-time. In a split second the time transport structure was as dark and silent as a tomb. The control switch had been tripped prematurely by the quake.

The earth continued to rumble, gaining in vehemence. It shook the very foundations of the dome. Fracture lines appeared in the sleek, curved plastic. The ground rippled.

Jane appeared out of Scott's blind side. Crying, she dropped to her knees and threw her arms around him. "Oh, Scott."

As Scott buried his face in her neck, he saw a sight that was beyond his comprehension: where the sun had but recently set, there now rose a furious fiery sphere.

Somehow, Doc managed to make his way along the quaking ground. Above the roar of noise, he said, "The others got through safely."

Scott stared openmouthed. Then he heard a savage screech that made him weak with fear. He broke Jane's embrace and twisted sharply. The tyrannosaur towered overhead, switching its tail and glaring down with bloodthirsty eyes. The lips curled in anticipation of a meal that might prove to be the last supper.

CHAPTER 30

It was when the tyrannosaur reached out with its hind leg that the shock wave reached them. The blast of air from the thermonuclear explosion knocked the carnosaur off balance. Its tiny arms flailed as it crashed through the plastic structure and rolled across the floor where once had stood the blue containment curtain. Tornadolike winds whipped across the top of the hill and lashed the tall dome.

Scott was lifted off the ground, and Jane with him. Doc was bowled over like a tenpin. All three lay flat and clutched the ground.

The defunct transport structure shuddered under the tempestuous impact. Plastic that was already fractured snapped loudly as tiny splinters grew off the major cracks. The focusing nodes ripped out of their mounting brackets and, like giant spears, crashed to the floor and splintered to pieces. Then the entire dome collapsed of its own weight and fell in on itself. The tyrannosaur was crushed under tons of plastic and steel.

"Hang on," Doc yelled above the rush of air. "It will pass."

The ball of light on the horizon was already double the apparent diameter of the sun. Scott allowed himself only a brief glimpse of the nuclear fire. The trees in the swamp forest were bowed like saplings; many had broken off. Scott realized that they were experiencing only the forefront of the shock wave: as the gases expanded from the point of detonation, they pushed before them the Earth's entire atmosphere. The intense heat and radiation could not be far behind.

He held onto the ground, and to Jane, for what seemed like an eternity before the pressure wave subsided to gale force. Then he dared to pick up his head. The pain under his chest was the thick shaft of the spear. He rolled off it and sat up. He hunched over with his back to the wind. The sky was brighter than noontime. "It's over. It's all over."

Doc, too, picked himself up. "Our friends at least have been saved. We can be thankful for that."

Jane rubbed her hand over Scott's back. Her hair whipped about her face. "We are alive."

Scott scowled. "And about to become extinct."

"There is always hope for the living," said Doc.

"Tell it to the dinosaurs."

The wind continued to howl. The orangetop was a sliding conveyor belt of dirt, sand, sticks, leaves, and plastic parts, all rasping in discordant strains. The ground moved again: a long sliding motion, as if the entire land mass was rolling on greased runners. The rubble of the time transport structure settled raucously—except for a section of cables, batteries, charging generators, and broken focusing nodes that rose up against the force of gravity.

The tyrannosaur shrugged off tons of debris like a dog shaking water off its back. It seemed not to notice the raging storm. It took but a moment for the beast to spot the three people sitting on the ground.

Jane screamed. Scott leaped up and pulled Doc and Jane with him. "Quick! Into the control bunk—"

Nothing but a pile of disjointed plastic remained where the building had once stood.

Doc limped away with Jane in tow. "Perhaps we can hide in the rubble."

The tyrannosaur did not pause dramatically to weigh the situation. Its primitive brain did not house thoughts of tactics—it acted merely on instinct. It crouched low, bunched its leg muscles, and with a froglike jump cleared the wreckage and landed on the orangetop. It hunched over and charged.

Scott fumbled for the only weapon he had—Death Wind's spear. Knowing that the five-ton battering ram would simply knock it out of his hands before the tip managed to penetrate the thick-scaled hide, he jammed the butt into the ground. With one eye bandaged, it was difficult for him to judge distance—it seemed as if the twenty-foot-tall monster was on top of him instantly. Scott raised the shaft at the exact moment that the tyrannosaur hunched for the bite; he tried to aim it perpendicular to the bulging abdomen.

The speed and momentum of the descending body forced the spear through the hide like a straw piercing a potato in the famous parlor trick. If the tyrannosaur realized that its heart had been punctured, such knowledge did not slow it down. The Volkswagen-sized head split across the middle to reveal rows of jagged teeth that put railroad spikes to shame.

Scott ducked under the drooling mouth and without even thinking ran out between the tyrannosaur's columnar legs. He hid for a moment beside the massive hindquarters, watching the swing of the tail, before dashing away. The tyrannosaur pivoted and lashed out. Scott leaped. The sticky tongue caught him in midair, wrapped around his leg, and halted his flight with a jerk. He was sucked into the tyrannosaur's mouth upside down, swinging like a pendulum. He felt an awful pain in his foot. Then, at the opposite end of the swing, he was flung clear of the carnosaur's muzzle. Scott's body crashed into the orangetop with a wallop. He lay insensate.

His next sense of awareness was Jane's high-pitched scream. As he rolled onto his back, he saw only a few feet away a dragon soldier lying battered and broken where it had been swiped by the tyrannosaur's tail. The dragon made a dying effort to aim its laser gun at Scott's chest. Jane slid between the two adversaries and fired her stun gun at point-blank range into the dragon's face. The dazzling coruscation wrapped around the reptilian head and along its neck. It went limp without a hiss.

The tyrannosaur, still impaled on the spear, staggered in circles as it tried futilely to break off the shaft with its feeble forelegs. It reeled toward Scott, tottered drunkenly, then stumbled the other way.

Doc dropped by Scott's side. Quickly he shed his vest and wrapped it around Scott's injured leg. "You will be all right, but I need to stem the flow of blood."

Scott was becoming drowsy, his senses were leaving him. Doc and Jane were fuzzy shapes acting in pantomime. They made a cradle by interlocking their arms and picked him up. "What good—" He felt a curious numbness all over his body.

"Let us wait in the wreckage of the dome. It will be a while yet, but we must be ready."

Scott had no concept of the passage of time. When he lapsed into the pleasant void of mental blankness, he knew that his life in this world had ended.

* * *

Voices.

In his head.

Distant and far away.

He wanted to open his eyes, and slowly came to the realization that they were already open. He seemed to be looking through a thin diaphanous veil. Everything was so fuzzy.

"—be coming out of it, my dear. Perhaps you should be here when he awakens."

"I'll go tell the others, Doc." Rusty?

An amorphous shape swam into view—a giant blur that gradually coalesced into the face of an angel wearing a halo of blond, silken hair. His mouth worked, but no sound came out. He felt a soft touch upon his forehead.

"He is—conscious?" Jane. The voice was Jane's.

"I believe so."

She leaned close to him. "Scott? You are awake?"

Scott contracted neck muscles into what he hoped would be interpreted as an affirmative nod.

The diamond pendant sparkled. "I love you." Jane kissed him tenderly on the lips—his first kiss in ages.

He must be in heaven. He regained control of his muscles and formed his lips into words. "I—love—you—Jane." The voice was craggy and hardly recognizable as his own.

"Ease him up a bit, my dear, while I put this pillow under his head."

Jane applied even pressure to his shoulders.

Doc tucked in the pillow. "Now, we don't want you sitting up yet. The rush of blood will likely make you pass out, so just lie quietly."

Scott got used to the elevated position. He saw that he was in a room that was formed of orange walls. Diffused light entered through a window opening. He breathed deeply. "So—what—happened?"

"I guess I lost that bet. I said you would ask 'Where am I?'"

"It's that—emotional—response—that keeps them—off balance."

Doc's face split into a broad grin. He looked so clean and neat. "And you have proved the worth of that."

He forced himself to wink. "Was that Rusty's voice?"

"It was, and he should be back anon."

"How did—he get—here?"

"The question you should be asking is, how did *we* get here. Or put more properly, how did we get back to now?"

Jane sat by his side and held his hand. "We are home time."

Scott was beginning to feel better. His words came more quickly. "Thanks for the clarification."

"It is Rusty's story, and—let him tell you himself. Here he is now."

The redhead appeared in front of Scott. He was smiling and full of energy. He squeezed his friend's arm. "Hey, old buddy. How's it feel to be back among the living?"

"I'm not sure. I feel kind of—numb."

"A medication that Jane supplied," Doc interjected. "Distilled from local vegetation. You've been out for three days."

"A lot's happened while you've been sleeping off a hangover," said Rusty. "The dragons are gone, the city is ours—"

"Whoa, whoa, whoa. One thing at a time. First of all, how did we get back if the time transporter was demolished?"

Doc and Rusty exchanged conspiratorial smiles. "The system wasn't demolished—only the transfer structure in the Cretaceous. Everything on this end was fully operational. Remember, once the dragons established themselves in this city, they engineered the push-pull system so they could send and receive at the same time with an economical expenditure of energy. After we came through, I set up the force field for reception only—a one-way transmission. Of course, most of what we got was the junk from the collapsed dome, but Doc and Jane had carried you into the perimeter of the force field— then sat down and waited."

"I knew he would not let us down," Doc explained. "It was just a matter of time. Naturally, I could not be sure that we would not come back into dragon paws, but I figured that a prisoner at this time had benefits not available to one in the Cretaceous." He shrugged.

Scott said to Rusty, "What did the dragons do—just hand you the controls?"

Rusty slowly shook his head. "There weren't any dragons left."

"You mean—Windy rallied the troops to revolt?"

"No. I mean, yes. He did rally the troops—at least, those who'd been captured from the outside. But they didn't take over the city until most of the dragons had already gone—of their own volition."

"But—where did they go?"

"We figure they went into the past, to try to reconstruct their civilization from the technology that already existed. You remember they were sending back technicians by the busload. They—hey, Windy, you tell him."

Windy looked as ragged as ever, but he strutted into the room with newfound pride. "Hello there, feller. Heard tell you was up 'n about. How's it feel ta be back inna present?"

"I'm not sure yet. My thoughts are still in the past. I guess I'm still lacking presence of mind."

Rusty groaned and rolled his eyes. "Now I know he's getting better."

"Windy, Rusty was just about to tell me how you got the dragons to chase their tails."

"Di'n't do it. Oh, we was ready fer the big fight, a few of us was. But little by little the dragons skipped out on us. Left a skeleton crew behind, never thinkin' we had the guts to mutiny. Soon's we had the upper hand, we slipped inna their beds at night an' knifed 'em with plastic needles. Once we had weapons, we done in the techs an' capers. Then we sat by the dome and did 'em in as they came through. Damn near killed your lot before we recognized 'em. Hell, we give up on you weeks ago."

"What about the natives? How are they making out?"

Windy scrunched up his face. "We lost a lot of 'em. The dragons took 'em away—an' a bunch o' corpses, too. Guess they're gone for good, now. But the rest're doin' okay. We're teachin' 'em to be independent. With Jane here as 'terpretor we're makin' a lot more headway."

Death Wind and Sandra slipped into the room. Sandra threw her arms around Scott and gave him a restrained hug. "I'm still sore from that laser shot."

"From it, or about it."

Sandra tilted her head. "Both."

Death Wind placed a firm hand on Scott's arm; Scott returned the Nomad arm shake. "You killed Tyrannosaurus rex. You are greatest brave of all."

Scott's spine tingled, and an intense heat flowed through his body. He knew that he was blushing. Death Wind's pronouncement was the most noteworthy praise that Scott could imagine. It was his proudest moment.

Rusty added, "You're the only man in history to ever kill a tyrannosaur."

"I'm only one of seven who've ever seen one. Besides, what killed the tyrannosaur was Death Wind's spear, tipped with a tooth out of its own mouth. When you think about it, it actually bit itself to death." His gaze shifted. "But Doc, here, is the real hero: a past master who moved more than mountains—he moved continents." He winked. "If you get my drift."

Doc grinned sheepishly. "I have tried to do my part in shaping history. But it is not something that I could have done alone."

"I've got something I couldn't have done alone, too," Sandra said proudly. She hooked her arm around her husband's. "I'm going to have a brave little brave."

Scott's eyes widened. "You mean—you're pregnant?"

Sandra wagged a finger at Jane. "You'd better watch this man. He catches on quick."

"Quickly," Jane said.

"Whatever."

Scott thought for a moment. "Do you realize that you must be carrying the oldest human being in the world? A sixty-million-year pregnancy. The mind boggles."

Sandra shook her fist in mock anger. "I'll boggle your mind, buddy, if you keep up the jokes. I think I liked you better unconscious."

"You wouldn't strike an invalid, would you?"

"Don't press your luck."

"Hey, what's this? A fight in the infirmary?" The voice was unmistakably Sam's. His face came into view over Jane's shoulder. He kissed her hair, and pressed his cheeks against hers.

"Sam! It sure is good to see you're all right."

"We all got a bit battered, but you took the cake."

Rusty groaned again.

"How do you like my bride? Isn't she prettier and younger than ever?"

Scott looked at Jane, who was smiling, and his heart sank. He gulped, unable to command his voice.

"Move over, honey." Sam sidestepped and pulled another woman into view. At first, she was too far back for Scott's distorted vision to make out. Then she came closer.

"Helen!"

"Hello, Scott. It's been a long time."

Scott's jaw fell open. He was too stunned to make a wisecrack.

"I kept her on ice so she wouldn't get any older while we were away," Sam said. "It was the freezers, Scott. None of those people in there were dead; they were in hibernation, or suspended animation. Another dragon technological achievement. Usually, they reserved the treatment for their own dignitaries—those that've

been injured. You see, the body continues to metabolize, but at a very slow speed. One of the side effects is that the natural healing process is not hampered. So, you take a wounded caper, stick him in the icebox, and melt him down a couple months later, completely healed."

"The only good dragon is a heeled dragon," said Sandra.

"Quiet, Toad. Anyway, they got the bright idea of freezing people so they'd have slaves on hand when they needed 'em. Now I understand why all of us POWs 'arrived' about the same time. We'd been captured months before and refrigerated till needed. After the dragon slaves died off, people suddenly became a valuable commodity. Helen was in the spring thaw."

Scott managed to find his voice. "But, why the pens?"

"The freezing process heals, it does not cure," Doc explained. He placed his hand on Scott's forearm and squeezed gently, fatherly. "Neither can it replace."

"What—what do you mean?"

Doc sighed deeply. "Your right foot, my boy, was bitten off. I amputated the stump just above the ankle. It was a sacrifice that undoubtedly saved your life, but not an easy one to live with. I'm sorry."

Scott held his breath as he rose slowly off the pillow. He bent his knee to bring his leg into view. The thick bandages wrapped in a ball did not hide the fact that nothing extended beyond the lower calf. He choked back his tears. Triumph was so quickly followed by tragedy.

Jane bent down and laid her bare chest against his. Her silent tears fell on his parched skin like the soft petals of a rose.

Life would never be the same. Life never *was* the same. Change was the definition of life. And one could not move forward without leaving the past behind.

Scott's strength gave out. He sank back, but Jane held him firmly and eased him down onto the pillow. He would never have to worry about falling, for his friends, and his love, would always be there to catch him. He swallowed hard.

There was a brand new world out there. He made up his mind to greet it—and to go on with no regrets.

No Future
for Dragons

CHAPTER 1

Scott signed off his work crew by manipulating his fingers in dragon finger speak. Natives gathered the tools and trash, and carried everything away. "That's it, Doc. The core change is done."

Tapping the checklist with an errant finger, Doc looked up and cocked one bushy eyebrow. "I thought it was going to be a much more complicated procedure."

Scott tucked a screwdriver in his belt pouch. "I have to give the dragons credit where credit is due: they were technological geniuses, especially in design and construction. They built products to last, and assembled them so they were easy to service."

Doc nodded. "Their machines were wonderful; it was their machinations that led to the destruction of their civilization. I have often thought that if they had not embarked upon a course of world domination, the Cretaceous never would have ended, and they might have continued uninterrupted as the dominant species on this planet. In a way, they were responsible for their own demise."

"The dragons didn't shape the world the way it is today, Doc. You did."

"I played my part." Doc shrugged and rubbed his white beard. "We all had our roles. We still do." His forehead wrinkled in consternation. "But my mind is full of wonder and trepidation. Are we indeed actors on the stage of life, exercising free will; or are we merely puppets locked in an unalterable script written by cosmic prerogative?"

Scott took Doc by the shoulder and urged him out of the reactor room. "Let's base our plans on physics, not metaphysics. Besides, if you truly believed in predestination you'd simply lie back and let the world run its course, instead of working so hard to alter its direction. And nobody has

made more earthshaking changes in the world than you."

Doc allowed himself to be led along the corridor. "You instill me with confidence, my boy."

"We all need our strokes. But this is the first time I've ever seen you lacking self-assurance."

Doc shuddered, as if a blast of icy wind had struck him across the back. "Perhaps that is because in the past my method of attack was somewhat spontaneous. I did not have time to envision the potential consequences of my actions. Now that we have all the time in the world, this premeditated campaign has me justifiably concerned. I have no idea where—or when—this path will lead us."

"One never does. But that won't stop us any more than it stopped the caveman from playing with fire. He burnt his fingers a few times, I'm sure. But if he had been the kind of man to run and hide from what he didn't know or understand, we'd still be living in caves. Instead, he took his chances and learned to harness his fire. We aren't just walking blindly into the future; we're being pushed by our heritage."

Doc thought that over as they turned at an intersection and followed the curved corridor along the outside bulkhead. "That is very clever of you to paraphrase my own words."

Scott laughed out loud. "It's impossible to psychoanalyze a psychologist. You're always one foot ahead of me."

"For one in your condition that is a curious use of words."

Scott exaggerated the clumping of his prosthesis on the plastic flooring. Long pants hid the bulky brace that was strapped to his right leg. The only part of the artificial limb that was visible was the plastic extremity that extended below the cuff, and the padded heel plate. "Some things you have to learn to live with."

Doc ignored the twinge of pain in his bad leg. "And you have done quite well, my boy." When they reached the ramp and ascended to the next level, Doc leaned forward and pushed harder on his cane. "With my tapping and your padding, we make quite a duet."

Scott laughed as he threw an arm around the smaller man's shoulders and hugged him tight. "Yes, but we're playing an overture, not a swan song."

"I will remember that as we charge headlong into perpetuity—or oblivion."

"Doc, let's not start this operation on the wrong foot."

Now it was Doc's turn to laugh. "It seems to me you made that very same statement once before. Your sense of humor in situations of imminent peril or dire straits is indeed an inspiration."

"Part of my charm." They passed another landing, then got off the ramp when it next leveled out. "Hey, Death Wind. How goes it?"

The Nomad pulled his head out of an electrical cabinet. His long black hair was pinned back in a ponytail. He wore a tool pouch over his loincloth, and held a screwdriver and pliers in his hands. "I am tightening all connections to the power grid."

Scott nodded. "Did you draw a schematic for the auxiliary focusing nodes?"

"On vellum. Jane is inputting data into computer."

"Great. But I want a hard copy kept in a safe place just in case."

Death Wind stared back expressionlessly. "Level Two lockbox."

"That's fine." Scott slapped Death Wind on the back. "Keep up the good work."

Scott and Doc continued along the corridor. They had to wind through the bustling horde of natives who were storing supplies in the rooms and compartments. Although they chattered constantly in their newly discovered language, whenever their hands were empty they continued to use sign as an adjunct to speech. It was not only a matter of habit; it allowed them to be understood above the racket.

"Doc, I can't believe how much progress these people have made." Scott yelled in the doctor's ear in order to make himself heard. "It seems like only yesterday they were a rabble of cow-eyed slaves. Now they're men and women with a will, infused with the desire to work and learn and run their own lives. The change is amazing."

Doc waited until they reached the central ramp and left the hubbub behind before commenting. "Freedom has a strange effect on people. Even the most slothful will flourish with zeal when liberated from the bonds of captivity."

"I understand the process. But I never thought they would react so—explosively. These people have burst out of oppression like lava from a volcano."

Doc shrugged. "Look at yourself. Did you ever imagine that once released from the confinement of Maccam City you would have become who you are?"

Scott led the way up the circular ramp. "Well, I used to dream about escaping into the world above—"

"Howdy, pardners. You all ready fer the launchin'?" Windy was clad in beige attire of his own manufacture. The shirt's long sleeves were rolled up past the elbow, the pants were bloused at the ankles, the moccasins were made of heavy-duty dinohide with reinforced soles.

"I do say, Windy, you look positively resplendent in uniform." Doc eyed the ammunition belt around Windy's waist. Clipped to the synthetic material were water pouches, one-shot stun guns, and ditty bags for provisions. "That is an ensemble that any soldier would be proud to wear."

"Thanks, Doc. We got ever'thin' but the medals. Decided we ain't gonna have none. We'd haf to do a whole passel o' damage to catch up with you fokes, so we'll jus' stay 'nonymous."

"The true mercenary spirit."

"How's the name calling?" Scott asked, smiling.

"Me an' the boys thought up a coupla monikers. Split ourselves inta company units with separate captains, 'stead o' jus' one big army. Figgered that kinda structure'd give us more leeway. Mine's the Texas Rangers. The other chaps're callin' themselves the First Fusiliers, under Broderick."

"I'm sure they look dashing."

"Their outfit's darker 'n ours so's we kin tell us apart. Got lots o' natives to join up, too. More 'n makes up fer the outsiders that 'lected to stay behind with their wimmenfoke. Even got a squad full o' ladies callin' themselves the Femme Fatales. That was Sandra's idee. Hope I don't hafta tangle with 'em; they're real mean scrappers."

Doc and Scott exchanged guffaws. Doc said,

"Who is in overall command?"

"The vote was fer Death Wind, but he di'n't want no parts of it. Kinda independent like, that feller; fancies bein' a scout. So Sam gots the job. We call 'im the Gennelman Gen'ral. Kinda fittin', doncha think?"

"I'm not sure he would agree," Doc said. "Although he has got a good sense of humor. In any case, I suggest you keep that honorific for private consumption."

"It don't make no never mind. He's a good egg."

"But he can't take a yolk." Scott went on quickly as Doc rolled his eyes, "Windy, this bird's almost ready to fly. Who's taking care of the crew list? We don't want to leave anyone behind."

"Me an' Broderick's responsible fer our own outfits, but Sam's got the main printout on the bridge." Windy jerked a thumb upward. "He's double-checkin' it now. Some job, too, 'cause most o' the natives never had names before, so they don't know who they are when they're called. Anyhow, I gotta do a last-minute weapons check. Catch ya later."

As Windy descended the ramp, Doc and Scott continued on up to the command bubble: the superstructure dome that perched atop the saucer-shaped flyer. The bridge was a large hemispherical room whose lower bulkheads were crammed with control panels full of switches and annunciator lights, and whose upper works consisted of alternating window-panes and computer screens that went completely around the perimeter. In the middle sat an octagonal console with eight terminals facing outward.

Rusty glanced up from the command seat. "I'll be right with you. The diagnostics test is still running." He looked haggard; fine lines grew under his eyes, and his curly red hair was long and bushy and hung down across his forehead and around his ears.

Scott nodded, and walked across the bridge to where Jane sat at an auxiliary terminal. He leaned down and kissed the top of her head. "How's it going, sweetie?"

Jane smiled, tilted her head, and offered her lips. Scott kissed her again. Her fingers flew across the keyboard without missing a key. "It is much easier since you declawed the equipment."

It had been a comparatively easy task to re-design the input pads with pin extensions that conformed to the tips of human fingers; now programming and data entry could be handled without taloned gloves. Scott huddled up to Jane, rubbing her shoulders. "Anything to make life easier for you."

Doc cleared his throat. "I think I'll leave you two lovebirds alone." He winked as he sidled around the central console. On the opposite side, Helen tapped control keys at an identical station.

Sam leaned over her with his eyes glued to the monitor screen. "Okay, honey, that's enough. Give me a printout."

"You know, you could learn to do this yourself."

Sam shook his head. "I can do it myself, but it takes twice as long. My motto is 'always hire an expert'." Sam looked up at Doc's approach. "What do you think, Henry?"

"I think Rusty prefers that I keep my bromides to myself." Doc nodded in the direction of the youth, who was deeply enmeshed in his work and made no sign to indicate that he heard Doc's words. "He says they put him to sleep."

"Does that mean you're going to quit prescribing them, or make them more complicated?" The printer clacked as sheets of white vellum spun out of the burning tube. "Never mind." Sam grabbed the top sheet and slid a black-faced reader under it. The holes seared through the vellum stood out as legible typeface. "I'll bet the dragons never thought their computers would be spitting out orders in English."

Helen said, "I'll bet they never knew someone as brilliant as Rusty could crack their matrix code and reprogram it."

Rusty made no movement at the mention of his name. He was completely preoccupied.

Sheets of vellum continued to drop into the collection bin. Sam skimmed each one. "Well, folks, I'd say the People's Expeditionary Force is ready to get under way."

"Sam, how is our star genius?" Doc tilted his head toward Rusty. "I am quite concerned over his health and psychological well-being. Since we began this project he has concentrated enough energy on it to kindle a small nuclear furnace."

"And he still has power to spare."

Helen leaned against the chair's makeshift backrest. "He seems to have retreated into himself. He doesn't talk about anything but the mission. We have to force food into him. When he becomes so exhausted that he can't work, he sleeps at his console. He hasn't left the bridge for days. He keeps digging for data in that crystal, as if it contains all the secrets of the universe. I have the feeling that he's harboring some deep dark secret—as if he's discovered something that he's not yet ready to reveal. Whatever he knows—or thinks he knows—he's keeping to himself. And it's eating him up inside. Frankly, Dad, I'm worried about him."

Sam raised his eyebrows. "I've been keeping an eye on him, but I guess a mother's observations are instinctively more astute than a country doctor's."

Helen swept her hand past the surrounding viewscreens. "This computer has become his whole life. He sits there for hours on end, running programs, accessing data, making computations. I understand that the work needs to be done, but without dragons breathing fire down our necks, we've got all the time in the world to do it."

"Henry, it's almost incestuous the way he fondles that keyboard. But I can't say that it's necessarily bad for him. He's naturally introverted anyway. Scott's the only one who can get through to him; they grew up together. And Rusty took it pretty bad when the dragons gassed his family and friends. It turned his whole life around. Emerging from the womb of Maccam City into the reality of a dragon-infested planet was quite a shock for him, and a blow to his security. Maybe he's just working out those pent-up emotions by delving into the sanctum of his mind. These mental exercises are probably as important to him as physical therapy is to Scott. Both need to stay in shape: one mentally, the other physically. Rusty might be headed for a nervous breakdown; or he might be on the road to catharsis."

Doc pursed his lips and squeezed his beard. "That's a well thought out medical opinion for one who professes to be only a country doctor."

A broad grin split Sam's bewhiskered face. "I have been keeping an eye on him. The diagnosis is subject to change, if there's a change in the subject."

"I'll change the subject," said Helen. "How about some chow? The granary is overflowing, the galley is stocked with fresh fruits and vegetables, the last of the livestock has been butchered and salted, and the freezer is full of prepared meals. And when I passed by there ear-

lier, the galley slaves were baking bread."

"I'm easy," said Sam.

"You always were," Helen chided. "Father?"

"There is rarely a time when this stomach is not grumbling. But with all these good victuals so handy, I'm going to have to watch my waistline. Starting tomorrow." Leaving Sam and Helen laughing behind him, Doc tapped his cane across the deck. "Scott. Jane. Would you care to join us for a mild repast?"

Scott looked up from the monitor. "I'm as hungry as a dinosaur."

"You always are." Jane pushed back her chair and stood up, surrounding Scott's midriff with her arms. "He is an eating machine."

"Good." Doc pattered across the orange plastic deck to where Rusty sat in front of a bank of terminals and viewscreens. The redhead was completely absorbed in the dragon line language that flashed intermittently on the display monitors. Doc was barely able to focus on the coded symbols before they disappeared and were replaced by others, but he knew that Rusty was scanning every line with complete comprehension. Doc slipped his hand between Rusty's face and the computer screen; he waved to gain attention. "My boy, do you think you can break away long enough for a bite, and perhaps a short rest? You look awfully run-down."

The blank stare that was returned seemed to be a million miles away—or a million years off. Rusty's face was gaunt and haunted, and his tan had long since faded. He squeezed his eyes tightly, opened them, then blinked several times. "Wha—what?"

"As friend, physician, and father-figure, I heartily recommend some time off."

"Time?" The lone word lingered in the air like the dying croak of a frog. Rusty blinked some more. His eyes were red from the lack of sleep. "Time?"

"We cannot take off on this venture with our bodies debilitated by fatigue, any more than we can fly this saucer in a state of disrepair. We must be fit to meet every demand. I think, perhaps, you are overtired."

There was silence on the bridge.

Rusty squinted as he surveyed those around him. "Tired? Of course I'm tired. And you know what I'm tired of? I'm tired of legendary lizards and prehistoric monsters ruling my life. I'm tired of dragons popping up in every millennium. I'm tired of living in fear of what tomorrow may bring. I'm been on the run too long, and I'm not running anymore. The dragons have reigned supreme one time too many. We chased them out of the present, we destroyed their past, and now we're going to make damned sure there's no future for dragons. One time they came after me; now they're hiding. This time I'm going after them—anywhere, anywhen. And this time there will be no survivors."

CHAPTER 2

"I christen thee *Ark*."

Helen officiated the ceremony. After delivering the incantations and pronouncing the name chosen for the modified dragon flyer, she smashed a plastic container of local manufacture against the telescoping entrance pedestal. The jar broke, splattering water over Helen, the landing pad, and the loading ramp.

A great cheer arose from the throng that was crowded in the shade of the saucer. The overhanging undercarriage bristled with lifting cones and double-acting focusing nodes, now quiescent for the official commissioning. The casemates were hinged open, and the guns protruded from their blisters like giant insect stingers. The warship was fully charged, the weapons systems functional, and the power train operational. It was ready for launching.

"I can't wait to try this baby out." Scott grasped Rusty's forearm in the Nomad greeting style. "Now we can really make some time."

For the first time in weeks, Rusty had the strength to stand up straight. He thrust back his shoulders and worked out the cramps. The forced feeding and round-the-clock snooze had done him a world of good. He was able to face the future with renewed energy and outlook. "I'd be willing to forgo the pomp and circumstance, and get on with the performance trials."

"Don't worry about that. The *Ark* will pass the tests with flying colors. She'll do her job anywhere, anytime."

Rusty nodded absently. "I believe in execution, not theoretical prediction."

"She's a machine, Rusty. More sophisticated than most, but still a machine. And like any other machine, she'll do exactly what she was built to do. You don't call it a prediction when you press the trigger of a laser gun and it burns a hole through a bulkhead, or when you drop a

ball and it bounces on the ground. It's called design and natural law. The *Ark* is simply the greatest machine and the grandest design ever conceived, operating on sound principles of natural law."

Scott's enthusiasm was gradually breaking through Rusty's self-doubts. "I'm sure you're right, Scott. I'm just afraid of being disappointed."

The slap that Scott landed on Rusty's back nearly bowled him over. "Come on, you old skeptic. Is this the same Rusty who programmed missiles to knock down dragon flyers and never thought twice about success?"

Rusty forced a grin. "The same one, but older and wiser."

"Then fight off senility and get with the program. We've got to stay one foot ahead of the dragons." Scott tapped his peg leg on the landing pad. "Tyrannosaurs, too."

"How can you joke about something like that?"

"I can't let it get me down. Life is what you make of it, not what it makes of you."

"Have you been taking proverbial lessons from Doc?"

Scott bowed in laughter. "I guess a lot of him has rubbed off on me."

"Me, too." Rusty reconnoitered the crowd. People were celebrating the event like Roman soldiers marching off to war. "Uh, listen, Scott, I'd like to avoid the festivities and take care of a few last-minute details. Will you make excuses for me?"

"No way. You're staying right here. With the amount of time we've got ahead of us, the detailed minutes don't count." Scott glanced around at the merrymaking. "Sandra." The jollity was so loud that his voice was lost in the hubbub. "Hey, Sandra!"

She was only a few feet away, clinging to Death Wind like bark to a tree. She saw Scott, waved with her free hand, broke her husband away from the mob, and piloted him to the corner of the entrance ramp where Scott and Rusty huddled out of the stream of well-wishers. "I've never been to a party before, but this is an awful lot like they looked on video. Hey, sourpuss, did you have a nice nap?"

The corner of Rusty's mouth turned up in the semblance of a smile. "Thanks to a potion that someone slipped into my salad."

Sandra held up her hands, palms outward.

"I'm innocent. I've been exerting all my feminine wiles on my husband. He thinks that just because I'm—" She rubbed her hands over her distended abdomen. "Well, never mind. It's just an old Nomad custom that I'm not accustomed to."

Death Wind looked on expressionlessly.

"That watermelon seed you swallowed looks like it's about ripe." Scott pointed a finger at her belly. "Have you thought of a name yet?"

"No, but we're working on it." Sandra's hair was growing back in. When she swept the loose strands over her ear, the frizzled ends brushed her shoulders. She leaned close conspiratorially. "Death Wind Junior is not among the choices."

"No offense meant, but I'm glad. That's too much of a mouthful for a godfather to say." Scott held his hands out like a supplicating priest. "So how do you like our pincushion. Think it'll get off the ground?"

In addition to the lifting beams of original installation, the *Ark* was equipped with all the focusing nodes from the dismantled time transport structure, as well as the battery packs to operate them. The extra cones were mounted atop as well as beneath the saucer, and along the curved perimeter. Only the gun turrets, command bubble, and landing platform were uncluttered by forcefield units.

Sandra jabbed Scott with her elbow. "I think the *Ark's* gonna show us a great time. Whoops, sorry, I'm slipping into dialect. Going to show us a great time. The hardest part about teaching language to the natives has been cleaning up my own lingo. If I don't speak properly or enunciate correctly, they pick up my bad habits."

"Have you chosen your replacements?"

"A local gal we named Susan is taking over for Jane in basic; it's important to have someone who understands finger speak and tone talk in order to converse with the natives. An outsider named Bethany is taking my place in advanced." Sandra shook her head. "I never thought I'd be an English major."

Scott winked. "You're only a captain, but there's still hope."

She faked a scowl. "You may think you're funny, but you don't have a kernel of wit."

Scott groaned as he buried his head in his hands.

Rusty roared out loud. "She got you that time." He could not stop laughing.

Even Death Wind smiled.

The noise attracted Doc, Jane, Sam, and Helen. Jane slipped her arms around Scott's chest. Sam and Helen lounged in each other's embrace. Doc pinched his eyebrows at the continuing laughter.

"Is this a private conversation, or can anyone join in?"

Rusty completely lost control. He laughed so hard that his cheeks hurt. Scott fell back against Jane as if in a fit of weakness. Sandra joined in with a chuckle.

Doc was still nonplussed. "I fail to comprehend the nature of such merriment, but the condition is certainly infectious."

Natives and outsiders clustered about and joined in the revelry. The commissioning ceremony was more than the simple naming of a renovated aerial warship, or the official transfer of control to human hands. It was a preflight gala, a celebration for those who were about to embark on a mission of mercy—and a campaign of all-time war.

"Can you give me a general idea what it's all about?"

Rusty bent over double; his sides ached as he bellowed and cried at the same time. Grinning broadly, Sandra shook her head. Death Wind was no longer the stoic Nomad: he was taken over by a deep-throated snickering. Sam and Helen joined in the rejoicing, but did not know why. Jane had her hands full with Scott.

When Rusty got control of himself, he managed to squeak out, "It's a matter of corporal punishment."

By this time everyone was roaring uncontrollably. The townspeople who now owned the erstwhile dragon city caught the fever and cheered their compatriots who were about to leave for battle. Those who elected to remain behind had responsibilities, too. They had the backbreaking job of adapting the city for human habitation; of starting a new civilization from available resources; of teaching a new generation about freedom, fraternity, and individuality; of learning the rudiments of dignity.

They named the city Charon—after the mythical boatman who ferried the dead across the River Styx to eternal life in the underworld. The modern-day Charon was the departure point for mankind, the portal through the Stygian flux of time into the great unknown of dragon purgatory. Little wonder that the eve of decampment should be attended by such jollity—otherwise, dread and depression might prevail.

The revelry continued until long after sunset, under the artificial light provided by minimum power to the lifting cones. The stroboscopic effect kept the cabal in high spirits: singing, dancing, and enjoying the last night before battle.

Later, after it was all over, Rusty returned to the command bubble and shut down the outside power circuits. The flyer's plastic insulation stifled the clamor of Rangers and Fusiliers who were bedding down in the barracks, of couples slipping into their staterooms. The bridge was a refuge of silence and solitude.

"No one but us bachelors to mind the midnight watch."

Rusty spun around at the deep-throated voice. "Doc, I didn't hear you come in."

"My bones may creak, but I still retain a modicum of stealth." Doc tucked his cane under his arm and eased himself into the copilot's seat. His lion's mane of white hair and his bushy bleached beard were damp from a recent shower. The luxury of indoor plumbing was one of which everyone partook. "It is my resolve that reverberates."

"Don't tell me you're having second thoughts."

Doc humphed. "The wise man never stops having thoughts, for then he is undone. In this case, however, it is my imagination that runs riot. When one contemplates the paradox of time travel, one realizes that in an infinite universe in which one may roam at will, there is time for as many thoughts as one wants. All this confabulation about alternative continua and parallel universes does not conform to my primitive, nonmathematical concept of space-time. The complexities are paramount. I remain agnostic to the notion that the cause-effect of our actions is interdependent upon our origin as well as our destiny. Going backward and forward in time has altered my perception of reality."

"Time isn't a treadmill with a beginning and an end. It's a simultaneity. Mathematically, space and time are two coordinates that are perpendicular to each other. There are many spaces, and many times. Events can occur at one space at many different times, or at one time at many different spaces. By definition, an event is something that occurs at a specific space at a specific time. It's a mutual exclusivity."

Doc raised thick eyebrows. "And your explanation, my boy, lacks pellucidity."

Rusty smiled. "Sorry, Doc. I wasn't trying to be pedantic. It's just that you're used to traveling in space, but not in time. I'm sure our existence is equally incomprehensible to a being who travels in time, but not in space."

"Do you postulate such an entity?"

"I admit only the possibility because time travel has the same mathematical validity as space travel. The dragons' time transport structure is a prime example. It has the capability of moving objects anywhen in the time stream, but it's static in space. That's why we filled in the area with twenty feet of poured plastic: it invalidates the use of the TTS for as long as that space is occupied. The time dragons can't suddenly appear in our midst. The force of a material object recoiling off already occupied space would destroy the sending unit with incredible devastation.

"Let me give you an example of apparent nonsimultaneity. Once we were prisoners in this flyer, now we command it." Rusty held out his hands. "Is that a paradox?"

Doc shook his head.

"That's because the events occurred at different times. Easy enough to understand. But suppose I said we are sitting here and we are lying on the deck in the brig."

"You're merely confusing the issue with semantics—"

"No, I'm not, because the statement is true. I just left out the time axis referent. But that's not cause for invalidation. I could just as easily have left out the space axis referent by saying that you are six years old and you are sixty years old."

Doc cleared his throat ominously. "Neither of which is true."

"Both of which are true—sometime, somewhere, but not anywhere at the same time, or anywhen at the same place. We can't be two places at once any more than we can be twice in the same time. That's a universal given."

"In other words, you can't bump into yourself."

Rusty grinned. "Doc, you have a knack for reducing the most complicated concepts to simplistic analogical terms."

"A minor talent,"

"But let me go one step further."

"Do we have to?"

"I'll keep it simple. Besides, it was you who said that time is an endless river with no past or future, only flow."

Doc brightened measurably. "How nice of you to remember."

"I always pay attention to wisdom."

"Thank you, although that may have been one of my less lucid apothegms. I believe I was just being philosophical."

"Nevertheless, it was an astute physicalistic statement. Between you and me, Doc, you know a lot more than you let on, and understand more than you allow."

Doc pursed his lips, but made no comment.

"Anyway, in spatiotemporal terminology, the flow of time is more accurately defined as upstream and downstream. We think of it as backward and forward for the same reason we think of north as up and south as down—that's the way we draw our maps. We relate to time according to our psychological orientation to it. Since our movement through time from birth to death gives our bodies existence on the time axis, we imagine time to be moving. And it *is* moving relative to the cosmos, the same as the Earth moves through space: rotating on its axis, revolving around the sun, spinning with the solar system through the Galaxy, swept along with the Galaxy through the universe. But we're not aware of all that motion. All we can perceive is that the ground beneath our feet is steady.

"If you were to view events in time from an external frame of reference equivalent to that of a station master able to see what was going on inside every car of a train, they would all appear to be occurring simultaneously. You'd see me sitting here in front of you, you'd see me running from a tyrannosaur in the Cretaceous, you'd see me attacking the Outpost, you'd see me living in Maccam City, you'd see my birth—and you'd see my death. Every event in the time stream is visible from the proper perspective, which means that every event is universally simultaneous. It's the same as standing on a mountaintop and observing four different people, one in each quadrant. Those people can't see one another; in fact, they have no awareness of the others' existence, because they are out of sight from each grounded observer's point o view.

"So here we are flowing downstream in time, sighting each event as we pass it by. Now the dragons have invented a machine that can journey through time the same as an airplane flies through space. It's not quick enough to reach simultaneity, and paradox, but it permits us to go

faster than our life flow allows, and permits us to go further in either direction. You can't walk to China: your lifeline isn't long enough, and the physical barriers are insurmountable. But a jet can fly you there in a few hours. The dragon time transporter works the same way, but along the time axis instead of the space axis."

Doc said, "Then you are assuring me that, even with the refinements that you have incorporated, the fabric of space-time is not so fragile that mere mortals can disrupt its continuity."

"Exactly."

Doc inhaled deeply. "I guess that is what I needed to hear."

"Good. Now we both feel better."

CHAPTER 3

The throttle control was an electronic rheostat that was operated from the pilot's console by a series of buttons, or tap switches, each of which applied eight times the thrust of the next lowest button in line. Rusty made sure that the perimetric gyroscope had reached full stabilization before switching on the electric drive. He tapped the lowest button once. A light appeared on the flight annunciator panel, denoting a single increment of vertical thrust.

He tapped it again; another light came on. A dazzling array of gauges and digital readouts fluctuated slightly with the added energy potential. A third tap caused the bridge to shudder, like a sail struck by a gust of wind. Rusty glanced at the anxious faces around him. He realized that he was holding his breath.

"It must be all the extra weight—"

The fourth tap brought a bump. Rusty studied the screens whose linked cameras brought external images into the command bubble. The power nodes glowed dimly. Thermocouples registered outside temperature readings, while telemetry equipment sufficed where hardwire was impractical.

"I think this is it." Rusty tapped again and felt the floor push up against his feet. The inclinometer did not waver. The momentary pressure eased off; there was no more sense of motion. Rusty broke into a broad grin. He could not keep the elation out of his voice. "The *Ark* is airborne."

A loud cheer rose around him, but he had to ignore it in order to keep his mind on the unfamiliar controls. As he continued to tap the vernier buttons, the thrust grid illuminated brighter by degrees.

"Way to go, Rusty!" In the copilot's seat, Scott kept his eyes on the readouts. "Look at the down monitor. You can see the ground getting farther away."

"Steady as she goes." Rusty kept all the power on the vertical axis. Until the *Ark* attained more altitude, he did not want to drift away the landing pad and fry the surrounding buildings. Onlookers had been warned to maintain a safe distance during takeoff. Reprogrammed transponders displayed the elevation in Arabic numerals. "Relative altitude is just passing a hundred feet."

"The sky's the limit," Scott shouted.

"Is it?" said Sam. "How high will this thing go?"

"She's not a rocket, so she can't fly in a vacuum. The power nodes need to push against a substance. The thinner the air, the slower her rate of ascent." Scott pointed to a sectional viewing screen. "The altimeter is calibrated to about twenty-five thousand feet, but there's no reason to think that's her true ceiling. After that, she probably becomes increasingly unresponsive to vertical lift."

"Passing two hundred." Rusty gulped as he tapped the next highest button. The power input jumped by a factor of eight. His stomach dropped into his pelvis, giving him a queasy sensation that he had never felt before.

"Hey, what're you trying to do, cause a premature birth?" Sandra gripped her belly with both hands, fingers intertwined, as if she were making a cradle for her unborn offspring. "You'd better slow down unless you want a baby born on your bridge."

"Sorry."

Jane stood behind Scott, rubbing his shoulders. "I have climbed walls, but never air. It is strange."

Rusty flipped on the external microphone. The vibrant thrumming of the lifting beams filled the command bubble, lilting in cadence with the purple pillars of light that coruscated along the needlelike energy focusers.

"That's a sound I never thought I'd be happy to hear," Helen said.

Doc exaggerated a shiver. "It still fills me with apprehension. The depths of emotion are not readily overridden by reason, nor can a life-long association of that sound with death be shrugged off so simply."

"I've got a few chills myself." Rusty tapped the level two thrust button again. Another burst of power surged through the *Ark*, launching the flyer upward at ever-increasing acceleration. Less than half the lights on the flight annunciator panel were aglow—there was power to spare. "Altitude one thousand feet, elevation nine hundred." The hundred-foot difference was the height of Charon above sea level. "Scott, you want to start displacing thrust from the vertical axis to the horizontal?"

"With pleasure." Scott manipulated the axial displacement controls that tilted the energy needles off their baseplates in any selected direction, thus providing lateral thrust. The copilot's console contained a flight panel similar to that of the pilot's console, except that the lights glowed in accordance with power applied to the horizontal axis. The vernier buttons controlled angular thrust. "Honey, this may get a little rough. You'd better tell everyone to hang on."

Jane was the communications officer. "Okay." She squeezed Scott again before taking her place at the intercom station. Dragons did not possess the laryngeal apparatus needed to issue vocal commands; all audio transmission was given in the form of musical tones played on a stringed instrument, or, in the case of shipboard intercommunications, on a digital synthesizer. Jane typed the appropriate coding signals. Loudspeakers in the rooms and corridors below decks chimed the message.

Scott flexed his fingers. "Going for level one displacement." He selected his direction from the gyrocompass and locked it in. "Headed east."

As Scott tapped the lowest vernier button, Rusty added another increment of power from the fusion drive. The result should have been a smooth transformation from pure vertical rise to vertical rise with lateral movement. The actual consequence was a sudden drop in altitude because the energy cones were deflecting their power at a slight angle, propelling the *Ark* laterally; not enough power had been added to correct for the loss of upward motion.

"Add power! Add power!"

Rusty responded to Scott's shouted entreaties by tapping rather casually on his control panel until the altimeter leveled out. "Looks like we've got a three or four to one ratio for vector translation. At least, at this altitude. Air density probably makes a difference."

Scott wiped sweat off his brow. "Didn't mean to panic. I just don't like feathers in my stomach."

"I think this is going to take some getting used to." Rusty decreased power by flipping the reverse switch and tapping the power buttons. Lights faded off the flight panel. "Reading the manual isn't the same as flying."

"You said it." Scott studied the gauges spread before him. "We're headed east at about one mile per hour."

The *Ark* maintained an even keel, without pitch or yaw; the gyromechanisms were functioning perfectly. The ex-dragon flyer glided smoothly across the landscape. Starting at city limits and heading away from the plastic structures, it soon cruised over thick green jungle along the bank of a broad river.

"Let's practice our maneuvers at two thousand feet." Rusty flipped back to positive feed, tapped, and brought the *Ark* to the determined height. "That'll give us a safety margin in case I'm slow on the draw."

"I don't want to hear talk like that," Sandra said.

Scott smiled at her. "Don't worry. There's an emergency switch that immediately transfers all power to vertical lift." He touched the lever lightly.

The sarcasm in her voice was feigned. "I feel much better." Beside her, with arms folded across his broad chest, Death Wind watched the proceedings wordlessly.

Rusty explained. "Of course, we'll still coast on the same bearing until friction brings us to a halt. Forward motion is canceled by retroversion: tilting the cones in the opposite direction and exerting a compensating thrust. This crosshair base recorder"—he indicated a graphic monitor—"bounces a laser beam off the ground so you can judge your drift."

"What happens if you're over the water?" asked Helen.

"It doesn't matter. The beam reflects off bedrock whether it's at the top of a mountain or at the bottom of the ocean. But the most complicated maneuver is turning. When thrust is applied in a different orientation, the machine describes a curve that's the result of both directional components, much like a vector. Well, as long as there aren't any peaks to bump into, let's put the *Ark* through the paces."

*   *   *

Death Wind glanced over his shoulder. The leading edge of the *Ark* was barely visible through the jungle canopy: a gold rim in a sea of green foliage. He readjusted the bow and the quiver of arrows that were slung across his broad, naked back, and continued the slow jogging pace that he could maintain for hours.

He felt free in the woods, the kind of freedom that he had known as a youth, before he had become a brave and his life had changed so abruptly, so drastically, and so irrevocably.

After such a long spell living the life of a city dweller, shrugging off the reins of civilization was like tossing aside iron shackles. As a captive in Charon, a guerrilla in dragon land, or a liberated citizen, he was confined to the indoors: a situation he bore with patience and Nomadic stoicism. Science and technology did not hold for him the fascination of the woods, the lore and the lure of the open spaces.

The air caressed his bare skin with silken pleasure; the woodland odors assailed his nostrils like perfume. He loved running free. He prized his physical prowess. The heaving of his chest, the dripping of sweat, the ache of muscles too long restricted: all brought back memories of simpler, happier times. The touch of lush ground cover under his moccasinned feet was pure ecstasy. The faculties of reason were important to him, but his body was life itself. In the jungle Death Wind was at home.

His peripheral vision captured the minutest details around him: birds flitting in the treetops, insects buzzing among the branches, tiny lizards slithering underfoot. He ran on and on. He leaped over logs, slogged through the wet marsh, sprinted madly across the glades where he could put his mettle to the test. He was so sorry when, after an hour of independence, he heard sounds in front that were not natural to the forest.

Death Wind crouched by a thick bole, his bow unslung. Whoever, or whatever, was approaching did so with slow deliberation. Others were farther back. They were spread out at intervals that were as even as the trees and terrain allowed. They were quiet; hardly a twig cracked. But the Nomad's sensitive nose detected them with unerring precision. Confidently, Death Wind waited until the point man came into view.

The Nomad made his presence known.

"Greetings!"

Like a felled oak the man dropped to the ground. He crawled behind a clump of tall grass. Only the battery pack protruded above the green stems. From all around came the clatter of weapons and falling bodies.

Death Wind made no foolish movements. Scared men were too quick on the draw, too likely to shoot at the merest provocation or hint of danger. He remained snug against the tree trunk until an unnatural silence reigned supreme. He sensed half a dozen laser barrels pointed his way; they were close enough to cleave the tree from its roots.

The Nomad waited for a bird to stop trilling. "Men stick together. It is code."

Death Wind heard rustling in the underbrush. Then he saw a head pop up above a bush.

"It's a Nomad." The startled expression matched the surprise in the man's voice. "It's a goddamned Nomad."

Death Wind stood tall and stepped into the open. He held up his right hand, palm outward. "Greetings, Ned. Many moons have crossed the sky since we last spoke. And much has happened."

CHAPTER 4

"You sure gave us a hell of a fright. I mean, buzzing over the city like that reminded me of before, when you folks were taken away." Ned threw his arms around Sam and hugged him tight. Tears flowed unabashedly. "And you—We thought the dragons got you years ago."

"They tried to interrogate me, but all they got was an icy stare." Sam winked at his wife. "Helen gave them the cold shoulder, too."

Ned pushed away from Sam so he could hug Helen again. "You don't look a day older than when I saw you last."

"Aging is arrested during hibernation, while the healing process is promoted," Helen sniffled. Tears of joy rolled down her cheeks. "Daddy says the preparatory chemical injections shift the body's hormone balance."

"A diagnosis partially substantiated by a computer scan of dragon medical records," Doc explained. "I followed their prescribed therapeutic procedure to thaw out the few corpsicles that were left behind after the dragon exodus, and they all revived in better condition than when

they were frozen."

Ned used his short sleeves to wipe his face dry. "I'm still stunned. This reunion—and what I know from the quick briefing that Death Wind gave me on the way here—well, it's just incredible." He swept his hands around the bridge. "This flyer." He shook his head. "And a time machine." He rolled his eyes in awe. "And you went back to the Cretaceous. It's just—incredible." He faced Doc. "Only your outfit could have pulled it off."

Doc shrugged. "My own part was relatively small."

"Although he did have a few earthshaking moments," Scott added.

"The most frightening part of the whole venture," Sandra tendered, "was Scott's humor—or attempt at it."

Scott tapped his stump on the deck. "I lost a few bones in the past, but not my funny bone." He gripped his upper arm. "Despite my loss, I've kept my humorous disposition."

Sandra rolled her eyes. "Uncle Ned, are you sure you missed all this?"

Ned laughed uproariously. "Every bit of it. I love you people. And the town will go wild when they hear about your return—and your revenge. Abolishing the fear from the past will offer hope for the future."

"Do you think your squad's had enough time to reach the Outpost and warn them?" Rusty fidgeted in the pilot's seat. "So we can get going?"

"Oh, sure. Death Wind met us about halfway, and we walked back pretty slowly. I kept prying him with questions."

"Jane. All aboard." Rusty spun around and faced the console. He checked the power grids while Jane toned the departure warning. When the all-clear signal was returned from the entrance ramp, Rusty tapped the vernier buttons. With a week's flying under his belt, the *Ark* lifted off the ground so smoothly that not a single stomach fluttered. This time, too, he did not forget to actuate the hydraulic ram that withdrew the telescoping landing tube into the body of the saucer. "Next stop, the Outpost."

Ned seemed unaware that for the first time in his life he had left the ground. Mentally, perhaps, his head was already in the clouds. "Sandra, what's happened to my little girl?"

"I grew up."

"And out," added Scott. "If she gets any bigger she won't fit through the doorways."

"You're just jealous because I'm having our baby before Jane's having yours."

"No, I just like teasing you. It's one of life's little pleasures."

Sandra ruffled Scott's hair. "I think I liked it better when we fought all the time. Sometimes I miss seeing you cringe."

"And no two people fought longer than we did—all the way from the Cretaceous onward. Ned, did anyone else ever get away with calling her Toad?"

"Watch your tongue, you!"

Scott smiled. "Never mind. I got the reaction I wanted."

Sandra hit him playfully on the arm. "Careful, blondie, or I'll crack your humorous humerus."

"If you do, I'll slap your gluteus maximus."

"Don't you wish." Turning to Ned, she said, "You can tell we love each other. We quarreled constantly before we got married—to our prospective mates. Honestly, Jane, I don't know what you see in this hunk of flesh."

Jane opened her mouth, but did not join the repartee. "Sandra, please. You two can spar later. Let Ned tell us what's been going on since we left."

"Not much. Fortunately, Scott and Rusty trained enough people in reactor maintenance that we've been able to keep the electricity going. I mean, we're holding our own, all right, but we haven't made much progress in converting the Outpost, as you call it, to a human habitation. Oh, we've got some of the houses renovated, but since the Nomads left, and then you were taken away, that left us shorthanded and not very motivated. We didn't know when the dragons might come back again and recapture the whole town, so we've been living on the edge ever since. Got quarters near the city limits, and moved the whole armory into the jungle for safekeeping.

"We've been concentrating our efforts on cultivating the crops and repopulating the swamp with dinosaurs. I know that's what the dragons wanted to do, to change this world into a latter-day Cretaceous, but we don't have much choice. We need meat, and without any other stock, dinosaurs will have to be the fare for the future."

"I could eat one right now," said Scott, from the copilot's seat.

"You always could consume a triceratops right down to the shield and horns. I see you haven't changed any." Ned ran his hands through his hair and wiped them off on his shorts. "So what's this Death Wind was telling me about computer crystals and seeding farms? That fellow still don't talk much."

Doc snickered. "Once a Nomad, always a Nomad. Despite his recent education, he still harbors his native ways. But then, I guess we all do."

"Thanks for answering my question, Doc."

The aging doctor shook his head and came out of his reverie. "Sorry, I have a tendency to wax philosophical these days."

"No comment," said Rusty. The *Ark* skimmed along the top of the jungle just high enough so the energy needles did not singe the upper branches. Once the course, speed, and altitude were established, and locked into the automatic pilot, there was little to do but sit back and watch the gauges and monitors. Coordinated ground-scanning radar maintained the *Ark's* height above the ground at all times, while lateral proximity sensors warned of oncoming cliff faces that might obstruct passage.

"As you were saying," prompted Ned.

Doc stroked his cottony beard. "I never understood how love could conquer the world, but in this case it has certainly given us the weapon to do so."

Ned stared openmouthed. "Huhn?"

"We have Scott and Jane to thank for that. Scott for demonstrating his love so thoughtfully, Jane for requiting it in such fiercely feminine fashion. It was the diamond that prompted so traditional an engagement: a diamond that was a crystal memory lattice and the key to the future."

"Oh, sure. That makes perfect sense."

"Forgive me if I ramble, but so much mental disorientation has occurred in recent months that those events seem like ancient history. We are now engaged in a totally different but every bit as serious battle with dragons. They lie in wait for us in the future—our future. And world domination is again the stake for which we are playing."

"It's getting clearer already."

Doc continued on his own track, gazing most of the time into space. No one offered to prompt him. "Death Wind's thumbnail sketch undoubtedly covered the destruction of the time transfer structure in the Cretaceous, and the disabling and dismantling of the TTS in Charon. But the latter action merely ensures that dragons cannot suddenly reappear at that specific space-time coordinate. The information contained in the crystal brought back from the past along with Jane's slender neck confirmed Rusty's deduction that, while the geographic location occupied by the TTS in Charon was the same throughout the ages, other way stations existed along the time stream. The Charon TTS was not a terminus, but a stopover point that was operated for the specific purpose of making the land fertile for later dragon occupation. A seeding farm is what we call it; the Outpost was built later for the same purpose. More plantations were planned, but never reached the construction phase."

"Whoa. Hold on a sec." Ned held his hands out in front of him. "I'm more bewildered than ever. Can we go a little slower."

"For us, time is no longer of the essence. I do understand that, not having spent countless hours discussing the probability of events, the issue must seem somewhat perplexing to you. Let me add detail. You see, Ned, soon after the dragon's serendipitous discovery of time travel, came the startling revelation that their race as well as their rule was doomed to extinction. They did not know how, nor how soon, only that despite their best efforts it must occur. They firmly believed in the absolute inevitability of events; that is, they perceived the flow of time as an immutable conveyor belt that began when the universe was created, and that will end when entropy causes the universe to run down.

"Rusty, here, possesses no such preconceived notions. He has been instrumental in convincing the rest of us that nothing in the universe is absolute except the zero mark in the scale of atomic motion: that point at which all nuclear activity ceases, and when for all practical purposes the structure of the atom collapses into a form of degenerate energy."

"Uh, Doc, you're getting a bit beyond me."

"An unnecessary digression. To clarify, atomic motion is what we perceive as temperature. Its relevance to the present is metaphysical and somewhat out of context with our initial and for now primary purpose. I was musing in terms of the Grand Design of the universe. To resume, on their very first downstream time jump, the dragons descried that warm-blooded dinosaurs and cold-blooded lizards had relinquished their predominant place in the scheme of life to an order of animal that had previously been considered

little more than a nuisance: the mammal. Dinosaurs died out altogether, while lizards survived in a subservient role. The erstwhile tiny protomammals would shortly grow to great proportions and evolve competitive intelligence. Am I boring you?"

"Not at all. I'm sure it all means something."

Doc frowned. "I will try to be more specific. The dragons, despite their dogmatic acceptance of the unalterable flow of time, were quite understandably loathe to yield either their lives or their power. They conceived a master plan that was commensurate with their credence: to populate the Earth at some future time when the climate was suitable to their way of life. Only one thing stood in their way."

"Let me guess. Us."

"A minor impediment, which they abolished without quibble or qualm. Dragon shortcomings lay not in the technologies of mass murder or obviating the time barrier, but in the humanitarian sciences. No, the chief hindrance was an unstoppable geological process leading to global glaciation: what we refer to as the Ice Age."

Ned sighed and glanced at the others on the bridge. "The Pleistocene Epoch?"

"The same. And what may eventually come to be referred to as the Pleistocene Epic. You see, when the dragons laid siege to our time period, the Quaternary, they did so with the knowledge that the last of the Pleistocene glacial advances was over. That was why they selected this particular interregnum in which to make their invasion. It made little sense to start some millions of years into the Tertiary Period, knowing full well that most of the Earth would someday lay buried under billions of tons of ice.

"Biological survival was not the problem. Many species have lived through the four glacial advances that occurred during the Pleistocene; many also died. Most managed to cope by adapting to conditions, a process known as evolution. But the dragons did not want to evolve, or be forced to undergo the hardships of living through global freeze-ups lasting hundreds of thousands of years. They wanted to maintain the status quo of their civilization, and eventually transport it in its entirety to a ready-made Garden of Eden. They did encounter a few problems, however, in carrying out their stratagem.

"They had all of time to dabble in, but their time transport apparatus was limited by two constraints: power and imprecision. This station, what we have termed the Holocene Station, represents the furthest time downstream that their equipment in the Cretaceous could reach."

"You mean, they couldn't focus enough energy to punch through more than sixty million years?"

Doc was taken aback. "Why, yes."

Ned smiled at the sea of faces. "Go on. It's beginning to come to me."

"It is?" Doc cleared his throat. "Of course it is. In any case, their problem was not the lack of raw power, but, as you surmised, the technology required to concentrate enough energy through the focusing nodes to further penetrate the barrier of space-time: in correlative terms, to get further into the future than our own present. At the time of their demise, it appears that the dragons were on the verge of making the technological breakthrough that would have allowed them to extend their temporal range with ease.

"But the reptilian intellect operates differently from the intellect of mammals. Just as the ectothermic body is more primitive than the heat-producing body of the mammal, so is the structure of the lizard brain more primitive. Dragon gray matter has vast potential, but it works more slowly. What this means in evolutionary terms is that dragon progress, both biological and cultural, takes place over a period of time that we would consider abnormally long."

"I'm way ahead of you," Ned said proudly. "Dragon verge is not the same as human verge, am I right? Industry that took the dragons hundreds of thousands of years to develop could be invented overnight by man."

"Perhaps an oversimplification, but approximately true."

"Which means that given dragon science and technology as a starting point, mankind can push ahead dynamically and accomplish what dragons could never even dream of. The good old hyperactive human bean is better than the dragon noodle."

"Vegetative aspersions aside, yes."

"Which means that we're going places while the dragons are still making up their minds to blink."

"I wish you would not make it all sound so elementary."

"Doc, you didn't have to go through all that rigamarole to arrive at a simple conclusion. All you had to say was we got what it takes, and they don't."

Doc raised bushy eyebrows at his companions. "I'm afraid I have gotten completely off the subject of our goals, both short-term and long-range. Ned, you must understand that we do not have complete knowledge of the dragons' latest activity or state of advance, because the crystal salvaged from the Cretaceous was a backup crystal stored in a data retrieval facility. However, the fact that was the most clearly delineated and not subject to change was their plan of campaign. And while we have destroyed both dragons past and present, there are others that exist in a time frame that can still do us harm.

"What we need to do immediately—if you will allow a word which within the parameters of time travel has no relativistic meaning—is to spike the Outpost's TTS in order to prevent dragons from entering this particular spatial reference, and to recruit an army to track down all the surviving dragons—wherever and whenever they may be—and stamp every last one of them out of existence." Doc wiped sweat off his brow. "That may sound pathetically brutal, but given the history of dragon intrigue and tenacity it is the only choice we have. Dragon and human cannot coexist. There is space-time for only one of us."

CHAPTER 5

"Father."

"Son."

"Men stick together."

"It is code."

Death Wind and Bold One clasped each other's shoulders in the traditional Nomad familial embrace.

"You come in flyer," Bold One stated flatly, not just as an observation, but as a summation of all it implied.

Death Wind did not need to concur. "Much has happened."

Bold One waited patiently for an explanation. The hot sun beat down on the open prairie, baking the sandy soil. The grass was withered and dry except along the banks of the nearby creek. There was no breath of wind to rustle the brittle stems, or to sift through dark, shoulder-length hair. Except for the creases of age, father and son were as alike as two kernels on a cob.

The land felt good under Death Wind's moccasins. A deep-seated longing crawled out of the soil and held him there like the roots of a quaking aspen. Here, with his father, with the rest of the tribe looking on, he was home. That other world, in the dragon flying machine, surrounded by space-age technology, no longer seemed real. That was where he lived; this was where he belonged. Death Wind was suddenly homesick for the freedom and lifestyle of his youth.

"We fight. Many dragons die. Take flyer. Fight more. Need help."

Bold One stared long and hard. He held the finely crafted spear in front of him, butt on the ground, and stood as tall and immobile as a cigar-store Indian. His naked chest was broad and bronzed, his belly flat with abdominal muscles finely delineated. His stance was that of a warrior about to pounce: legs spread wide, knees slightly bent, upper body tilted forward at the waist.

Dark, fathomless eyes peered out from under a wrinkled brow. "Come. We talk."

Bold One spun on his heel and took off at a jog. Death Wind followed his father at the same pace. The tribe was spread out among the bushes, out of sight to all but one experienced in the ways of the Nomad. Death Wind strained his eyes to pick out the protruding arrow here, the tip of a spear there. The men and women themselves blended with the terrain; the children lay huddled under the leaves of shrubbery, or behind the trunks of stunted trees. They were the wraiths of the plains.

The older Nomad stopped in the middle of a shallow depression. He jammed his spear into the loamy soil, cupped his hands, and emitted a loud call that was the perfect imitation of a hoot owl. Slowly people came out of hiding. They emerged from the ground, they crawled out from under blankets of leaves, they descended from the low piñon pines. First the braves: men and unattached women; then the young and elderly; then mothers with children and babes-in-arms.

Death Wind kissed his mother and exchanged greetings of love. "Son, you have come home."

"Not to stay, Mother. Take away. In flyer. Fight dragons."

Slender Petal nodded once, almost imperceptibly. "More?"

"We find. We must destroy."

Slender Petal nodded again.

The tribe gathered in the hollow. Bold One, as their chief, raised his arms skyward for attention. There was no noise or clatter, no fussing or fidgeting—only the occasional whimper of diaper-clad infants and the choral cooing of their mothers. The air was still.

Bold One's voice was deep and sonorous. "Death Wind speaks." He dropped his arms and stepped aside.

Death Wind took his father's place. He gazed at the faces of the people—his people—making eye contact with each and every one before opening his mouth. He had never spoken to the tribe as a member of the council of war. Yet, he felt no anxiety or lack of resolution. Many times during his youth he had squatted while others offered counsel. They were always treated with respect, and their ideas were accepted with great regard.

"I have come far in dragon flying machine. Since we last met we have killed many dragons, we have captured other city, we have destroyed their homeland. But others exist to menace us. Not now, but in future. We build great army to fight them, to rid them forever from our world, to make this land free for our children for all time. To do this we need help. I have pledged my tribe to conquer dragons because men stick together. It is code."

Every person of speaking age repeated the litany. The intonation sounded like one voice with a hundred different pitches.

Bold One raised his arms once again. "Members speak."

There was but a moment's hesitation before the first brave, a woman, stood up and jabbed her spear at the white, puffy clouds. "Fight!"

A wizened, old man bent with age climbed unsteadily to his feet. "Fight!"

One by one, then en masse, the tribal members jumped up. Men and women, young and old, warriors all, shouted their subscription to wage war against dragons. It took but five minutes to gather weapons and personal belongings, to load the travois, to start the march toward the shimmering golden saucer that perched serenely on the horizon like the rising sun. Once before, against their will, these people had been herded into such a flyer; now, by their own prerogative, they rushed forward eagerly to meet their fate, and to play their part in deciding the fate of the world.

* * *

The surface of the Earth was a dizzying

patchwork quilt of muted colors some six miles below. The images received on the downward viewscreen were interspersed with puffy cumulus clouds. The lateral viewscreens showed a faded blue stratosphere and fleecy strands of cirrus; the sky above was a deep purple canopy punctuated by the bright, untwinkling pinpoints of stars.

"It's a complex formula that took me months to develop, despite the fact that I knew both the problem and the solution: that is, where/when in space-time the dragons departed, and where/when they arrived. What I had to determine was how to get from one synchronistic point to the other. In actuality, I worked from both ends toward the middle, or, in scientific terminology, from one synchronism to another."

"Rusty, I don't think of myself as an ignorant man, but talk like that humbles me." Ned scratched his balding head. He wore an expression of perplexity that was fast becoming his normal mien. "If it hadn't been for Scott boning me up on your gobbledygook I'd be a regular flibbertigibbet."

Rusty squinted hard. "Huhn?"

Now it was Ned's turn to laugh. "I've been picking up some of Windy's argot. It has a right nice twang to it."

Scott raised his eyebrows innocently. "He didn't ask for a course in spatiotemporal navigation, just for the short version of why we're practically going into orbit to make the jump."

Rusty rolled his eyes. "It's not easy to condense a textbook that hasn't even been written into one easy lesson."

Still smiling, Ned urged him on. "If I get stuck on the big words, I'll let you know."

Rusty looked from one to the other, took a quick glance at the flight grid, gauges, and control screens, and inhaled deeply. "I'll try to make it as simple as possible, but I've had to make up words to describe some of the transtemporal phenomena."

Scott winked. "You don't need sixty million years to take him from the Cretaceous to the Holocene, but you don't have to do it in two high intensity minutes, either."

"Actually, the transfer through time is instantaneous in both the objective as well as the subjective sense because universal isochronism dictates the parameters—" Rusty stopped with his mouth open, realizing what he must sound like.

"Just take it slowly," Scott warned.

"Right." Rusty took a deep breath. He paused for half a minute before proceeding. "Okay, look at it this way, Ned. The mathematics of physics recognizes four dimensions, which are descriptions of convenience that we call length, breadth, height, and the passage of time. Understand, however, that these measurements are artificial representations that are designed to fit human perceptions: finite quantities that portray a picture of infinity. Are you with me so far?"

Ned screwed up his face. "Just barely. Are you saying that dimensions aren't real?"

"Almost." Rusty wagged an index finger. "What I mean is that dimensions lend corporeity—no, forget that." Rusty held up his fist and circled it with a bent finger. "Here's an electron spinning around an atom. All of this in here is empty space. But when we put millions, or billions, of atoms together, with their outer shells touching, we get this chair. It's tangible, something that we can see and feel, but we know it's made up mostly of tiny bits of matter that are held in place by electromagnetic force."

Ned nodded slowly. "I got you so far."

"What we perceive as solid is composed of a bunch of hollow spheres whose shells are jammed together like a bag full of soap bubbles. And we don't even know if protons and electrons are solid—they too may be forces whose subatomic interaction is manifested as humanly perceived solidity."

"I'm not sure—"

"Forget it." Rusty dissolved his hydrogen atom and waved his hands in the air. "Just think of the universe as a force field, not as a physical substance. But let's use our dimensions to create an analogy." Rusty placed a dragon notepad on his lap. With an etcher he drew a square on the plastic facing. "Here's a two-dimensional world that exists on a single plane. It has length and breadth."

"Not bad breadth, I hope," Scott intruded.

Rusty sighed, but otherwise ignored his friend. He slid his finger along the pad. "To a two-dimensional stick figure, the interior of the square is hidden." His finger bumped into the etched lines on all four sides. Then he raised his finger in the air above the pad, and slowly brought it down inside the square. "But a figure that exists in three planes can see and touch any point in the square."

Ned's face brightened measurably. "Hey,

that's pretty neat."

"Now just take that one dimension further, and you begin to understand how points of view exist that we can never be aware of. But it doesn't mean that with the proper instruments we can't detect those points of view, or that with sophisticated enough technology we can't utilize forces that we can't comprehend. We can't see electrons move through a conductor, but that doesn't stop us from using electricity. Our eyes perceive only a narrow band of light, but we have detected and used the entire scale of electromagnetic radiation. Short waves existed before the invention of the radio. Our ears translate pulsations—"

"Okay. Okay. I get the point. Molecules vibrate when a tree falls in the woods, even if no one is there to hear it."

"Very good. Now let's assume that time is another dimension. We don't pay any more attention to it than we do of the Earth speeding through the Galaxy. We just take it for granted. We're a kind of universal flotsam, or an interstellar plankton, swept along with the tide of space-time. And we're stuck there just like this square is stuck to the pad. As three-dimensional observers, it's easy for us to understand that the square could invent a machine that could lift it off the pad.

"And so the dragons discovered a way of stepping through time. They stumbled over the physical principle that allowed them to peel off the three-dimensional world in one spot, and drop back down in another spot."

Scott interrupted his friend. "You see, Rusty. You don't have to use all that technical jargon. We'll make a teacher out of you yet."

"Don't do me any favors." He redirected his attention to Ned. "But as long as I'm on a roll . . . The dragons didn't want to drift aimlessly with the currents of time. They never operated in random fashion. They had a specific goal in mind—a direction, a purpose, and a destination. They knew about the two-hundred-fifty-million-year-ice-age cycle. If they were going to begin a new civilization, why not begin after the next glacial advance? That's when they ran up against technological problems. The state of development of their time transfer equipment was extremely crude."

"Stay away from feedback gap circuits and use the cog analogy," said Scott. "Ned isn't an electronics expert."

"I was going to." Rusty rankled at the intrusion. "Picture a wheel whose rim is a series of teeth. Two wheels: one is the wheel of time, the other a machine wheel." Rusty held both hands in front of his chest, fingers spread wide, and interlocked them. "When you put the two together you've got a time machine, because you can move freely from one to the other and back again. But the number of teeth on the time wheel is infinite, while the manufactured wheel has only as many teeth as the dragons were able to machine. The teeth are all the same size, but they can mesh only at certain intervals. Are you with me so far?"

Ned frowned, but nodded silently.

"Okay, the dragon cogs are about a million years apart, give or take a few hundred thou, depending on space-time variables that we needn't go into. That means they couldn't go anywhen they wanted, but were forced to jump to times that coincided with the circuitry of their time transfer equipment. They were on the threshold of refining the infinite-time transfer vernier, that would have given them ultimate precision, but they met their maker first. How's that, Scott? Did I use simple enough words?"

"I like it."

"Now I get the picture," Ned said, his voice lilting. He stabbed a finger at the redhead. "And that's what you discovered."

"Extrapolated is more accurate. The dragons already had the raw data; all I did was carry it one step farther. Even then, I probably wouldn't have thought along those lines—"

"Or space-time continua," interposed Scott.

"—if it hadn't been for Scott coming up with the idea of removing Charon's TTS focusing nodes, mounting them outside the hull, and reversing the polarity. Converting this saucer into a flying time transport structure was a brilliant concept—"

"I thought so."

"—that revolutionized transportation. Now we can move through space *and* time—"

"Now, or then, or simultaneously."

"—with equal impunity. At least, as far as our power resources allow. The *Ark* is the perfect all-continuum vehicle—"

"I was partial to naming her the Magic Carpet."

"—because it can move in—"

"She can *move*."

"—all four dimensions. We can circumnavigate the globe here and now, or then and there. We can go wherever we want whenever, or whenever we want wherever. All the reaches of space and time belong to us."

"The world is our oyster, time is our pearl."

"And that's what brings us to this altitude, and my calculations."

"Our rate of ascent is slowing down dramatically." Scott leaned forward and fiddled with some dials. "We appear to be leveling off at about thirty-four thousand feet."

Rusty glanced at the flight grid and saw that all available power was being translated along the vertical axis. "The data in the crystal gave the coordinates of the dragon retreat. The spatial reference is the same because their time transport structures are fixed in space. When they left Charon in droves, they didn't go all the way back to the Cretaceous. That would have required incredible energy for the number of transfers they made. Instead, they went back only one click in their time wheel—to a TTS they had installed in the Pleistocene—a short jump, relatively speaking.

"The equation for calculating a course to those coordinates is complicated—it has to be integrated in four dimensions—so the comptime is incredibly long. The other factor is power output, which is a function of the distance traveled in time, the mass of the object, and friction. Just as dynamic drag reduces the speed of an object moving through air, so a time transfer is affected by the density of air at its point of arrival. When a vehicle moving through space contacts a solid object, it crashes; when an object transferred through time tries to displace too much matter at the point of its arrival, it backfires explosively and destroys the transfer capsule—in the dragons' case, the TTS.

"That's the reason for the force field: the staging area is partially evacuated so that fewer molecules need to be pushed out of the way when the transferred object arrives. By climbing into the stratosphere we are doing two things: making sure we don't transport ourselves into the middle of a mountain, and reducing the friction at the other end of the transfer.

"But you don't have to worry." Rusty cocked an eye at Ned. "Remember what I said about instantaneity. If there is something in our way at the other end of the time tunnel, we'll never know it."

CHAPTER 6

The *Ark's* bridge control octagon was crowded for the big moment. Rusty and Sam sat in the command seats, Jane took over the communications console, Doc monitored the reactor station, and Helen and Sandra held places at data input terminals.

Scott stood by the all-important time transfer post that he had rewired from an auxiliary steering station. "I wish we had time to check this baby out." Dragons designed all their systems with triple redundancy, but when Scott cannibalized Charon's TTS, he found the equipment so massive that there was room in the *Ark* for only one working model.

"We're taking the time, right now," Sandra scowled. "And we have all the time in the world."

"You know what I mean."

Sandra jerked a thumb at Scott while she glowered at Jane. "You see how serious he gets when it's *his* shirt on the line."

Jane smiled demurely.

Like a skulking lion, Death Wind padded off the last curve of the circular ramp. "Preparations complete. The crew is ready."

Since the saucer was constructed as an armed troop transport, and since dragon psychology permitted only a strictly utilitarian use of space, the *Ark* contained no amenities that would have been built into a human warship. There were no wardrooms, game rooms, or scuttlebutts. Whoever did not have an assigned battle station was forced to remain in quarters, or to roam the corridors.

"Okay, Sam, put us into a glide so we don't drop like a rock when we shift power."

"Don't take more than ten percent of the load," cautioned Rusty.

Sam tapped the vernier buttons and gradually transferred energy from the vertical drive cones to the lateral thrusters.

"Let me know as soon as we're stable, Rusty." Scott kept his eyes glued to his station monitors. "I want to lose as little altitude as possible. The thinner the air, the better."

"Gyros are on full, deviation is zero."

"Halfway there," said Sam as the thrusters diverted five percent of the available power.

"Let's not rush it." Scott wiped sweaty palms across the front of his vest. "I want to make a last-minute check of the chronometry circuits."

"Stop biding your time," Sandra quipped. "I'm not getting any younger."

Jane switched on the external mikes. The thrumming of the lifting cones whined down while the thrusters emitted a low, deep-throated roar. The *Ark* flew too high to detect any visible motion across the green jungle below.

"We're at maximum glide," said Sam.

Doc looked up from his monitors. "The reactor is still making little atoms out of big ones."

"Remember not to look directly at the screens," said Rusty.

Scott took his last Holocene breath. "Infinity, here we come." He jammed his finger down hard on a button that needed only to be tapped.

Deep within the bowels of the *Ark*, huge contactors shunted the main transmission lines so that all generated nuclear energy flowed into the time transport circuits. The interval of diversion lasted either an instant or an eternity. The bridge lights dimmed. The lifting cones and thrusters went dark. The revamped flyer dropped suddenly. The inverted focusing nodes burst into full brilliance with the speed and intensity of a high-power strobe light, and discharged as quickly with a loud clap that sounded like a truncated peal of thunder. Power reverted to its normal mode. The bridge lights brightened. Lift and lateral thrust were restored. The *Ark* cruised on.

Scott inhaled deeply. Despite sealed ventilation ducts and electrostatic filters, the air was tainted with the pungent odor of ozone. "Well, something happened." He scanned the gauges and digital readouts. "We lost a hell of a lot of stored power. The capacitors are reading zero potential, and every battery in the ship is stone dead. All that electricity must have gone somewhere—or somewhen."

"Or maybe it stayed there and we went," said Sandra.

"The fabric of space-time does not tear easily." Doc tapped a few buttons on his console. "The reactor is straining under the load demand."

Rusty issued orders in a raised voice. "Sam, cut the thruster power completely. Doc, switch off the charging circuits till we reach the ground. I'll cut back on the cones so we can drift down. Jane, tell the crew that everything's under control. Helen, run a logic check. Sandra, get Sirius."

"I'm always serious."

Rusty grimaced. His fingers flew across his keyboard. He repeated a phrase that was still on his mind. "You know what I mean."

Sandra lolled back in her seat. "Hey, redhead, I don't need to fix our position relative to the Dog Star to know that we've moved." She stabbed a finger at the viewscreens in front of her. "A sun sighting will tell me that."

Each console had its own set of external camera monitors. Rusty looked up, frowning.

"Either we've been in slumberland for eight hours, or somebody moved the sun on us. It was morning when we left—where we left."

The words poured out of Scott's mouth like molasses in winter. "Hey, she's right."

"The logic circuits check out," Helen said perfunctorily. "But there's a memory gap that looks as if the computer couldn't find itself for a microsecond or two."

"Look at the downscreen," Sam screamed. "It's all white."

Rusty was standing now, crouched over his keyboard while he craned his neck at the monitors. "Clouds?" He tapped the power grid in reverse; the *Ark* lost altitude in a controlled rate of descent.

"No way, man. The sky's clear as glass." Sandra waved her hands at the cluster of viewscreens. "The only nimbus out there is around the *Ark*."

The purple halo was the result of raw energy from the lifting cones being swept away in the downward rush of the flyer. Ionized vapor curled up around the saucer's rim, glowing in conjunction with St. Elmo's fire.

"I believe the monotonous expanse of bleached achromatism is a broad blanket of snow." Doc smiled proudly. "As we drop lower we should see some relief—"

"Hey, I got something on radar."

Scott leaped to Sandra's station and engaged the image enhancers. "Nothing on visual."

"It's too far away for proximity warnings, but it's coming our way." Sandra was unruffled by Scott's intrusion. The blip hung in the lower left corner of her screen. "What the hell is it?"

"Climbing fast." Scott skipped around the bridge like a nervous chipmunk. "Sam, what's our lateral speed?"

"We're still in a slow glide, momentum only. Say, fifty mph."

"Rusty—"

"I know. It's altering trajectory to match our course. Whatever it is, it isn't natural."

"Jane, tone a warning."

"It's closing vectors." Rusty's downscreen showed a growing blotch of red.

Sandra shouted. "Hey, the damn thing's gonna hit—"

"Brace for impact!"

The object suddenly filled the downscreen, then wiped it out. The *Ark* reeled with the concussion, bucking like a bronco with a burr under its saddle. The perimeter scanners showed chunks of metal and bits of plastic flying into space like broken toys from a shattered piñata. The *Ark* absorbed the shock and the damage, then settled down with a slight wobble.

Scott was bounced momentarily off the deck. He hovered in the air for a second, then touched down on the toes of his one foot like a performing ballerina. "What the hell—"

"That was a missile!" Rusty yelled.

Sandra was laconic. "Strange way of saying your prayers."

"Not a missal! A missile!" Rusty realized how stupid he sounded. "A guided missile."

"Jane, get a damage report from below." Scott shoved Rusty back into his seat and stood behind him with his hands gripped on the backrest. "How's our flight pattern?"

Rusty pounded out instructions on his keyboard. "Everything's operational. We lost a few cones and some focusing nodes, and the gyro's a little out of kilter. Lucky the damn thing was a dud."

"We might not be so lucky with the next one." Sandra drew attention to the radarscope. "There's another blip rising to the occasion."

"If you'll pardon my intrusion at this time of emergency, I suggest that we consider evasive maneuvers. The dragons obviously have a launching pad stocked for immediate delivery."

If Rusty heard him, he paid no mind. "We're coming down too fast. I've got more cones short-circuiting." His fingers were a blur across the keypad. "I can balance the load by increasing power to the other cones, but we're destabilizing. The gyro—"

The *Ark* wobbled sickeningly, like a child's top running down.

"It's getting close," Sandra warned.

Jane played her keyboard like a piano. Melodic tones sang over the ship's loudspeakers. "I'll tell the gun crews to shoot."

"Great idea," Scott said feverishly. With Rusty at the conn, and the other navigational consoles already staffed, there was nothing for Scott to do now that the time transfer had been accomplished. He made a continuous circuit around the octagonal control center. "If the warhead goes off even close—"

"Do you suppose it's atomic?" Sandra said.

"If it is, we haven't got a chance."

Sam screamed, "Rusty, give me some power. I'll take a random course."

"Take as much as you want. I just need enough to smooth out the oscillations. Let's go into a controlled dive, the faster the better."

As Sam applied full tilt to the thrusters, Rusty counteracted the circular gyration and nosed the *Ark* downward. The saucer picked up speed. The g-forces were noticeable as the *Ark* plunged into the thickening atmosphere.

With the downscreen out of action, the alien missile could not be traced visually from the bridge. It appeared only as an electronic blip on Sandra's radarscope. She locked on the ranging circuits, normally used to determine distance to the ground or surrounding obstructions, and forced the digital evaluations onto the tracking monitor. "It's gonna be a close one."

Laser cannons pivoted down in their sponsons. Gun crews opened fire while the speeding missile was still out of range. Unlike ballistic cannons, which required close calculation due to the lag between the time the projectile left the barrel and the time it reached the position of a moving target, laser fire traveled at the speed of light. For all practical purposes, a laser bolt was instantaneous: it was not necessary to lead the mark.

Sharp thrusts to port and starboard skewed the *Ark* haphazardly. Energy bolts fired at will seared lightninglike tracks in the air and left jagged condensation trails. But it was neither the skillful handling of the craft nor the accuracy of the fire that saved the *Ark* from calamity. The saucer's power dive was so fast that the missile could not alter its trajectory fast enough to veer and catch up. The rocket-powered projectile flew harmlessly past the *Ark* in a tight curve that forced it to spiral back down to the surface miles away.

"Whew. That was a close one." Rusty wiped sweat off his brow.

"Pure luck," Sandra said calmly. "But the next one seems to be coming in low enough to intercept our dive pattern."

"There's another one on our tail?" Scott

dashed frantically around the bridge and stared at the radarscope. Death Wind stepped back out of his way. "Damn."

"Rudder response is slow," said Sam. "I don't have much chance of avoiding it."

"Jane, tell the gunners it's up to them." Scott did another lap around the bridge. "If they don't blow that missile out of the sky, you'll be playing your harp in heaven."

Electronic tones sang again over the intercom. In the lateral viewscreens, Rusty watched the guns swivel on their trunnions as the latest threat became visible to the naked eye.

Jane monitored the return messages. "Cannons are not firing."

"What?" Scott screamed. "What's wrong?"

Doc supplied the answer. "I'm afraid the first artillery barrage drained our firepower. And since warping time depleted our energy reserve, I can recharge the cannon capacitors only at the expense of the propulsion units. Our choices are fight or flight, but not both."

"I'm for fighting," said Sandra, without hesitation. "Give 'em all the power they need."

Rusty shook his head. "The *Ark* isn't a hot-air balloon. It won't float. Without power to the lifting cones, she'll fly like a brick.

"If we didn't outrun it before except by a stroke of luck, we won't do it now against a better aimed missile," said Helen.

"Make up your minds." Sam fiddled with the controls. "We got about two minutes before we'll be wearing uranium."

Scott spun Rusty around in his seat. "Just take the power you need to keep us from going into a tailspin and let the guns have the rest."

Rusty immediately saw the logic in it. "Agreed. Doc?"

"Shunting." Doc threw switches and twisted dials. "Jane, you may let the gun crews know that they have been resupplied."

Tones sang over the loudspeakers.

Sandra said, "This better work, 'cause I didn't bring my parachute."

"The hull is heating up," Helen said.

Rusty turned back to the controls. "Altitude is fifteen thousand. The friction's not slowing us down any, but it's adding calories to the heat shield." A thermal-resistant lamination protected the undercarriage from ablation and from heat generated by the lifting cones. "Sam, cut the thrusters. Doc, give me a tad more power so we don't hit the ground like a blazing mete-orite."

Doc executed the transfer. "Use it sparingly."

As Rusty leveled the *Ark's* glide pattern, the craft began skipping on the dense atmosphere like a flat stone across the surface of a pond. "The saucer shape is amazingly aerodynamic. I'll bet from a high enough altitude we could glide halfway around the world. Even with all the extra weight—"

"Save it for the after-action report," Sandra chided.

The first laser cannon blast reverberated throughout the bridge, the sound carried by the external mikes. To Rusty, with the downscreens out of action, the dogfight was a mental exercise. He felt a strange tingling sensation creep up his spine. The *Ark* was flying faster than it had in any of the trials; any moment he expected the shear strain to split the hull apart at the seams, or the deck to bulge up beneath him from the explosion of a warhead. One part of his mind reveled on the genius of dragon construction—until he realized that the attacking missile must also be of dragon manufacture.

"Hey, catch the rearscreen."

The missile was just visible, captured by the video camera's wide-angle lens. Then it popped into the portscreen as well. The missile was nosing over to intercept the *Ark's* predicted position. Rusty threw the saucer into a steeper dive, hoping to duck under the missile's path as he had done the last time. But this missile was staying right on the *Ark's* tail, changing its heading to compensate for the *Ark's* drastic loss of altitude.

"That thing's going ten times faster than we are," Scott breathed.

"Beam propelled," added Sandra. A long streak of blazing blue flame followed the shiny warhead like a pencil under an eraser.

The forward battery was frustratingly silent. Only the rear and the two lateral cannons could keep the missile in their sights; they pummeled away as quickly as their capacitors recharged. The gunners must have jammed the firing mechanisms in the on position while tracking the target.

The missile leveled out. As the *Ark* dived toward the ground far in excess of what Rusty thought must be its design speed, the missile closed the gap from the rear. "I'm out of tricks." With the ice-covered ground dangerously close, he raised the bow. The screaming sound that droned through the intercom was the wind whipping past the microphones. "It's up to the gunners, now."

Bolts of energy lashed out, but not far enough to reach the missile. The gunners checked their fire to conserve power.

"Broderick is handling the men like an expert," said Sam.

"Once that missile gets in range, they're not gonna have much time to hit it." Sandra watched the digital readouts on the radarscope. She rubbed her bulging abdomen. The baby inside might not survive to see the new world. Death Wind stole up behind her and gripped her shoulders. She tilted her head to the side to kiss the back of his hand. "I feel so helpless."

Half the screen was filled with angry blue flames. The missile looked close enough to leap through the lens. Then all three bearing cannons opened fire at once. Laser beams crisscrossed in front of the silver cone and maintained a deadly barrier of energy. The missile flew blindly ahead, right into the web of beams. It was hit by two charges at once, and another a split second later. The double-barreled cannons let loose a second salvo that raked the missile's sides. The explosive charges penetrated the hull. The missile exploded in a titanic ball of expanding gas. The picture went blurry as the yellow incandescence overtook the after rim of the *Ark* and melted the lens.

The next explosion came from inside the bridge, when everyone leaped up and cheered. Even Death Wind let out a war whoop. Doc stood up without his cane, waving his arms over his head. Scott scooped Jane off her feet and swung her around in an improvised do-si-do. One advantage of dragon building dimensions was that, because of their tall, bulbous bodies and long tails, there was always plenty of room on the human scale.

Jane disentangled herself from her husband, gave him a peck on the cheek, and sat down at her console to tone the all-clear signal.

Sandra clutched her belly and screwed her face into a grimace. "Uh-oh."

Smiles melted into frowns. The *Ark* plowed along on its own.

Sandra leaned toward the radarscope. Her hair fell forward and framed her face.

Scott said tremulously, "Another blip?"

"No, it's—" Her eyebrows formed twin steeples. Slowly she raised her head. "In front. Half the screen—"

Rusty looked up sharply at the forward viewscreen. He saw a huge expanse of white that was hardly distinguishable from the cloud-filled sky. Only a single jagged, windswept peak gave it away. "It's a mountain."

CHAPTER 7

Rusty plopped into the pilot's seat and slammed his fist down on the uppermost vernier button. Instantly, full available power was applied to the lifting cones. "Doc, give me whatever you can spare."

The cones that were still working burst into purple brilliance. The deep thrumming sound echoed in the bridge. Forward momentum was unaffected, but the *Ark* rose upward on dancing electric beams. With the gyrostabilizer out of kilter, and the energy levels to the cones no longer controlled separately, the saucer pitched and yawed.

Without sitting down, Doc worked the controls at his station and transferred all reactor output to the guidance systems. "It's yours."

The snow-covered mountain loomed closer. The summit was a black granite point that rose unbelievably high. The *Ark* could never gain enough elevation to clear the frozen ridges on either side.

"I can't hold her steady and keep her climbing at the same time," Rusty shouted.

Scott picked up Rusty bodily and deposited him on the deck. "I'll take over." He cut the power to the perimetric gyroscope. The *Ark* no longer fought its mechanical directive to fly parallel to the ground. The wild circular plunging stopped immediately. The port side of the saucer dipped due to the inoperative lifting cones that were destroyed by the first missile. "Cut the lights, Doc. I want everything."

"Good idea. I should have thought of it myself."

The bridge blacked out. The darkness was accentuated the glow of control panel lights, annunciator globes, and computer display screens. Below decks, isolated batteries switched on automatically to energize the emergency lighting system.

Scott took advantage of the drop. He added power to the forward and starboard lifting cones. The deck tilted sharply as the *Ark* careened port side down. Because the forward cones pointed at an oblique angle, the *Ark's* bow was jetted to port. The saucer turned in an arc like a fighter plane peeling out of formation. Momentum kept people and objects within the *Ark* oriented to the deck.

The picture through the viewscreens was out of whack. The port screen showed the dirty striations of an enormous glacier's medial moraine; the starboard screen showed nothing but overcast white and occasional patches of blue. Looking forward, the mountain was a crazily canted monstrosity of rock and ice. The angulation was making Scott dizzy.

"Helen, peel back the awning."

Rapid-fire typing on her keyboard actuated the dome port. The opaque filter opened like an iris, flooding the bridge with ambient light. The mountain loomed large and menacing above the saucer. Scott used the black and white checkered face as a visual reference until the *Ark* inclined so far that the horizontal axis lay perpendicular to the Earth.

Rusty picked himself up off the deck and stood behind the pilot's seat. "I think it'll work."

"It better," Scott said grimly. "Or we'll be eating rock."

The *Ark* described a high-speed parabola that brought its radiant undercarriage dangerously close to the cliff face. Purple beams melted a broad swath through snowdrifts and started an avalanche. The ridge curled toward the speeding saucer, matching curves. Scott transferred more power to the front cones, forcing the *Ark* into a tighter turn. An overhanging rock face momentarily blotted the starboard screen. It looked for an instant like the saucer's bow would crash into an icefield. The cliff dropped into a bergschrund—the crevasse that separated the solid ice pack from the living, flowing glacier—and the *Ark's* port rim sliced through it, taking off a few layers of white fluff.

Ahead was open sky.

Scott sank into the seat like a snowman in a furnace. "I don't have the energy to cheer."

Apparently, neither did anyone else.

Scott squinted several times and dug his fists into his eyes. "Doc, you can return power to the auxiliaries. Sam, hit the forward thrusters." Scott manipulated the energy levels to the cones, reactivated the gyrostabilizer, and brought the *Ark* onto an approximately even keel. "Let's see if we can find a place to land this baby."

Rusty pounded his friend on the back. "I'll

bet that's one maneuver that's not in the crystal."

Sandra sat limply in her seat, hugging her belly. "Great work, Scott. I thought we were gonna get stoned for sure."

Scott looked at her askance. His face was a mask for at least five seconds before he grasped her meaning. Then he managed a weak smile. "Never take anything for granite."

While she groaned, Jane circled the bridge and threw her arms around Scott. She gave him a resounding kiss on the cheek. "Please, Jane. Not in front of a crowd."

"Go ahead, Jane," laughed Helen. "He deserves it."

Scott pushed himself out of the pilot's seat. "Rusty, can you take the conn?"

"If you'll let me have it." There was no sarcasm in his voice.

"I'm sorry I had to relieve you of command, but—"

"No apologies necessary." Rusty took his seat, nodded to Sam as he transferred power from the flight grid to the thrusters. "You saved me from engraving our tombstones with hull plate."

Death Wind said, "Scott has saved our bacon."

Scott slowly turned his head, an expression of amazement on his face. "Where did you ever hear an expression like that?"

Death Wind smiled proudly. "From Windy. He is full of localisms."

Scott jabbed a finger at the Nomad's chest. "Don't go falling for any of that dialect that he has the effrontery to call language. His kind of talk will throw English back to the Stone Age."

"I hate to burst your bubble," Sandra said. "But if we went when we were supposed to go, we're *in* the Stone Age."

Scott held up his hands. "I know. I know. The world out there is full of Neanderthals and Cro-Magnons. But just because we're in their space-time doesn't mean that we have to start acting like them. Windy's a nice guy, and I like him a lot, but he just won't knuckle down and learn to speak properly."

"Only Neanderthals have arms long enough to knuckle down."

"If you will pardon me from interrupting your customary repartee, I would like to point out that the terrain below has changed from an icy, windswept polar panorama to a luscious, luxuriant green verdure." Doc gestured to the viewscreens. Then, pointing upward, he added, "And the sky has taken on a delicious shade of blue."

Sandra said, "How did we get from the Arctic to the tropics during the course of a conversation? We're not going that fast."

"My dear, I do not wish to comment on your loquacity. But while you were engrossed in digressive palaver, we flew out of the mountain regions and are now descending into a broad valley where Ice Age glaciers have not yet reached. If we can find a suitable clearing in which to land, I daresay we will find the countryside not only charming, but free of dragons. Perhaps we can settle down to effect repairs, and to plan our next course of action."

"Whew. And you accuse me of being long-winded." Sandra rolled her eyes. "But I like the part about being free of dragons." She patted her belly lovingly. "I don't want my children growing up under reptilian rule. So what're we waiting for?"

"For one thing we don't have a downscreen, so I can't see what's below us, and for another the landing pylon hydraulics aren't working." Rusty watched the speed indicator. "With all this extra weight, I don't know if the balance stanchions will support the *Ark*. Crushing the lifting nodes would have an adverse effect on future liftoffs."

"I get the picture, already. So what do we do about it?"

"Come on, Death Wind. Grab your tool pouch and we'll hop down to the cargo bay." Scott took an instrument kit out of a storage bin and slung it over his shoulder. In the aftermath of battle, in the release of stress, he was euphoric with the feeling of vivid animation: almost a resurgence of life. "Jane, tone some techs to meet us there and tell them to be snappy about it." Scott scraped his stump across the deck. "This is no time to drag our feet."

"Scott!" Sandra singsonged.

He winked at her as he left the bridge. Death Wind was right behind him. They followed the central circular ramp down to the upper platform deck, then took a corridor to one of the perimeter ramps. The center of the flyer was the reactor room and machinery spaces, with limited access points. They met Windy on the lower level.

"You boys sure had us shakin' down here. I

was in the for'ard turret with Broderick an' some o' the boys when you was playin' chicken with that mountain. Why, I thought them rocks was gonna shear off the barrel. The port turret's plumb full o' snow."

"It was a close shave," Scott acknowledged. "We've got enough gray hair on the bridge to weave a carpet. And I want to compliment you and the gun crew. For your first time in battle you did a hell of a job. And a moving target, no less."

"Weren't nuthin' to me. Was the boys in the back that did it." Windy shuffled along with a stiff-legged, stooped gait. His wiry beard only partially hid a craggy, rough-hewn face whose blanched features expressed more anxiety than his words allowed. A slight stutter, perhaps in dire memory, confirmed his agitation. "I smell a ra-rat. Where the hell d'you figger that blasted missile came from?"

"The dragon stronghold, no doubt. We've got the whole thing recorded on tape. We can triangulate the launch site when we review the log. But why they should be prepared for an aerial attack is beyond me. The local landowners can't be that much of a threat to them."

"Never underestimate dragons," Death Wind said. "They are smart."

"That's fer damn sure. Them guys in the capes always got somethin' up their sleeve."

"Windy, I've been meaning to ask you if you'd like to sit in on Sandra's advanced language course."

"Me an' her had a confab about that already. I don't think I got much to teach them native buggers from Charon. Leastways, not in the manner o' talkin'."

Scott wearily rubbed his temples. "That's not exactly what I had in mind. I was thinking more in terms of her, uh, let's say, helping you with your vocabulary, and diction, and whatnot."

"You tryin' to tell me I don't speak good?"

"In a manner of speaking, yes. There's no reason you can't improve your communication skills. Death Wind used to talk in clipped Nomad dialect, but under my tutelage he learned modern English. Now, Sandra's taken over the English department, and she'd like you to join her for a few lessons." They arrived at the mechanical room above the telescoping landing pylon. "Never mind. We'll discuss it later."

Several men and one woman were waiting inside. They had already removed some of the cover plates, exposing the electrical wiring and hydraulic lines. Scott had trained them well.

Scott climbed down into the maintenance pit. He crawled completely around the plastic cylinder, then poked his head up. Some of his golden, curly locks were smeared with grease. "No structural damage."

Death Wind touched a test probe to terminal screws and buss bars. "Disconnect okay. Leads hot."

"Probably a hydraulic break, then." Scott was in his element. He checked pressure tubes and vacuum gauges until he found the leak. "It's just a crimped pipe that split and lost some fluid. Windy, tone Rusty I've located the trouble and will have it fixed in a jiffy."

"You got it, boss." Windy stayed by the intercom and toned back and forth with the bridge.

Scott left the actual work to his technical staff, most of whom were Charon natives. They needed the practice. In short order the pylon was ready for deployment. Jane telegraphed the order to stand by for landing. Scott, Death Wind, and Windy stood by the pylon pump.

"Someday, when I have time, I'm going to replace the tone lines with telephones."

Death Wind took off his tool pouch and stuck it into a storage nook. "You always want to repair, or renovate."

"I love machines," Scott allowed. He understood machines. They were predictable and perfectly logical. When they broke, they could be fixed. A mechanical fault could be reduced to a formula that was as straightforward as a mathematical problem, except that there were no unknown quantities, no irrational numbers, and no unsolvable equations. He felt secure dealing with manmade, or dragonmade, devices. He pounded the bulkhead with his palm. "Especially this one. She's my baby."

"She is hurt."

Scott's face clouded. "Yes, the dragons didn't treat her very well. But I can heal her. That's what I do best. And, you know, Death Wind, as a mechanic you're becoming pretty good at maintenance and repair."

Death Wind shrugged. "It is necessary." He watched calmly as the pylon descended smoothly. Despite the radiant heat of the lifting cones, a blast of cool air found its way up the ramp and blew dark hair off his shoulders. "I always do what is necessary. That is the way of life—of long life."

The fat cylinder extended twenty feet downward. The cargo bay was filled with the thrumming of the lifting cones; the purple glow flooded the opening, shedding a garish light on the three faces that stared down at the verdant green forest.

"But you don't like it, do you?" Scott said. "You don't really care about machines and mechanical marvels."

The Nomad shrugged again. "Life does not always concern itself with likes."

"I go along witchu on that," Windy piped up. "Ya live one day fer the next, an' don't plan any farther."

Scott shook his head. "As an animal, for sure. As a prisoner, perhaps. But as an active, free-thinking, imaginative human being, the future is something we dream about. It's not a full belly or a grassy pasture that keeps us going. We've become creatures of intellect. And that is what humanity is all about."

"If it's all the same witchu, I'll take the simple life."

Clutching a handgrip, Death Wind leaned out over the void. The *Ark* slowly settled into a clearing. Emerald fields of grass were burnt; long, knee-high blades shriveled and died, never to live again. But beyond the perimeter of deadly flame stretched a verdant, virgin forest that had never known the step of man. The simian, quasi-human creatures that lived in the Pleistocene were too wrapped up in their own individual survival to appreciate the woodland beauty.

Death Wind did not shrug, but his manner shrugged for him. "Different people have different dreams."

CHAPTER 8

Scott snipped the wires at the base of the shattered lifting cone, peeled them back, and applied a dollop of molten plastic to the ends; this prevented a short circuit in case the electricity should be turned on by accident. He shoved the still-warm capping tool into the holder on his waist, then coiled the copper conductors into the junction box. The terminal block was damaged, but reusable.

"How bad is it, my boy?"

Scott climbed down the ladder and propped his prosthesis against a lower rung. Too much standing or walking often sent twinges from his nonexistent foot. Phantom pain hurt just as much as the real kind. "Not as bad as it looks. One advantage my profession has over yours is the availability of spare parts. When thine cone offends thee, I pluck it out and replace it."

Doc fluffed his snowy white mane and aligned his face with the breeze. His long beard was blown under his chin. "Is that why they call you the mechanical medicine man?"

Scott laughed. "You've been eavesdropping on my technical crew. Great bunch of guys and gals."

"They look up to you, and not just when you're on a ladder."

The clamor of activity was getting louder. Work crews shuffled back and forth with materials, Bold One was forming a scouting and hunting party, Windy and Broderick were setting up a perimeter defense, and Jane was gathering women to forage in the woods for fresh fruits, vegetables, berries, and exotic plants of medicinal value.

Scott stepped aside as one of the technicians clambered up the ladder with a wrench. The totally demolished cones and nodes were being dismantled. The big dent in the undercarriage was the imprint of the missile's nose cone. Surrounding it, the lifting cones and time transfer focusing nodes suffered varying degrees of damage.

"Let's go for a walk." He led Doc beyond the perimeter of the *Ark*. The sun shone down with a warmth that took the bite out of the air. Scott enjoyed the crispness, but was thankful for the long-sleeved shirt. The scent of pine was strong, wafting across the glade with the freshness of a newborn world. Scott swept out his arms to bespeak the surrounding forest. "You know, this all seems too good to be true."

Doc nodded knowingly. "It is easy to be struck by the pristine splendor of the land, by the flush and fragrance of flowers, by the chirping of birds in the trees. After the primeval world of the Cretaceous, the Pleistocene assumes the appearance of utopia. Keep in mind, however, that the presumption of innocence is based on our anthropomorphic concept of the world. Those birds—"

Gaily plumaged swallows flitted through the branches, chirping merrily. Warblers sang out in repetitive song, clung to tree limbs with delicately clawed feet, fed fledglings in their woven nests, or stood by their aeries high in the upper canopy. Squirrels and chipmunks added their high-pitched calls to the strident sounds of insects. The whole was an orchestration of nature supreme.

"Those birds," Doc continued, "do not sing for pleasure, either ours or theirs. The virtue of their song is a human conceit. The wild cacophony you interpret as exhilaration and content is the fight for survival: a signal for danger, the bid for a mate, the mark of territoriality. Underlying the melody is a strain of fear. There is brutality in these woods, there is unseen suffering, there is death and destruction. Everything has a purpose, and everything is not as it seems."

"Come on, Doc. Don't put on such a downer. I'm feeling guilty enough about enjoying the scenery. Don't make it worse."

Doc uttered one of his curt humphs. "I did not mean to spoil your zest, only to break your enchantment. Certainly this world has not yet known the depravity of biblical man, or the civilized cruelty of the twentieth century. But remember that the brutality of survival often exceeds the cultured torment and mental anguish we inflict upon ourselves. Then, too, there is the malignity of dragons."

"Another cheery thought." Scott kicked away the clinging underbrush and climbed onto an angled slab of rock that was partially covered with red cusps of lichen. He perched his hindquarters on the cold stone. "Do you want me to share your melancholy?"

They were slightly higher than the command bubble of the *Ark*. Looking through the clear canopy, Scott detected motion on the bridge, but was too far away to distinguish faces. The saucer rested on its wide landing pylon, balanced by four outriggers. Wary gun crews remained at their stations in the blisters and kept a strict vigil. Beyond, the mountain they had almost become part of dominated the southern horizon. Most of the steep facing lay in shadow: a barren, icy, hostile, but somehow alluring mass of rock.

"Such caveats are merely the signposts of reality." Doc's speech was punctuated by short gasps for breath that did not slow him down in any way. He planted his cane on the granite surface, pivoted around it, and slid to a sitting position with practiced ease. "Let's look on the brighter side. This untarnished world is a cornucopia of delights, with continents to explore, new lands to settle, wildlife to tame, a civilization to build. We are here to witness the dawn of man, undoubtedly the most stimulating time in the history of this planet."

Scott rubbed his hands together quickly. The friction warmed his skin. "That *is* pretty exciting. I've been wondering what I'll say to the first caveman I run into. Probably 'ugh.' Maybe instead of trying to educate Windy, I'll try my tutorial skills on the local population."

"You've done it before with great success. Perhaps you should."

Scott thought for a moment before responding. "Well, I don't know. I don't want to do anything here and now that will upset the apple cart later. I think we should avoid any contact with Cro-Magnons. The Neanderthals don't matter, I suppose, because they're going to die out anyway. But I sure wouldn't want to create a paradox by doing something to stymie the evolution of Homo sapiens. We may wake up some morning and not be here because we accidentally killed one of our ancestors."

Doc tilted his head back and gazed at the faraway summit, some ten thousand feet high. "On the other hand, if we do not eliminate the dragons from this time zone, they may cause our pre-extinction for us."

"The age-old dilemma: is action more desirable than inaction?" Scott pursed his lips. "Sometimes I think we should just forget the whole thing and get on with our lives in the future—that is, the future as described from now. After all, when you think about it, we wouldn't be here if the dragons succeeded in taking over this time zone. I mean, we couldn't have evolved if they wiped out our Pleistocene progenitors. The very fact that we exist proves that the stock we descended from lived through the reign of dragons as well as the snow of the Ice Age." Then, after a moment of dubious introspection, he added, "Doesn't it?"

"I see that you and Rusty are not of the same mind."

Scott snickered. "Let's say that I don't have his confidence in the unalterable flow of time, or the immutability of events. I'm on your side there—or then. Maybe we can't tear the fabric of space-time apart, but suppose we put a nick in it that runs the entire length of the continuum? That's what scares me. I'm willing to admit only that the past implies the future, that perhaps it does not predetermine what we perceive as fol-

low-up events. And I have to admit that because I've experienced its consequences. But this time selection business shatters my comfortable, preconceived notions about what's happened in the past, and how that'll affect what may happen in the future."

Doc drew his knees up to his chin. "The three of us have such different attitudes. I was brought up in the world of dragons, and in full knowledge of their existence. The nonimpermeability of time was forced upon me as observable fact. You, on the other hand, were raised in ignorance of such empirical data, and have been forced to accept abstractions that are foreign to your experience. But, Rusty—"

Doc wrapped his arms around his shins and tucked himself into a tight ball. Zephyrs carried the chill off the mountain slopes and into the fertile valley. Scott imitated Doc's position, then stuck his hands between his legs. Despite Doc's admonitions, the animal sounds did not seem in the least bit ominous.

"Now, that boy grew up in your environment, with no more appreciation of the outside world than that of a mole—uh, no aspersion intended."

"Sure, Doc." In order to keep the draft off his legs, Scott smoothed his trouser legs and held the cuffs closed.

"Yet, he has leapfrogged both of us in grasping the conceptual significance of space and time not as disparate functions of the evolution of the universe, but as simultaneous points of view of equivalent phenomena."

"At least, he thinks he has." Scott rolled his buttocks. The cold from the coarse rock was seeping through the material of his pants. "I don't care what he can prove mathematically, there's got to be a cause and effect relationship between everything that happens in the universe."

"Oh, I don't think Rusty has any argument with that. He allows for the inclusion of both cause and effect, but he believes that a specific effect may not be the consequence of what we may perceive as the cause. In other words, there may be causes of which we are unaware affecting future events. And, if you grant the idea of simultaneity—that is, that more than one event can occur at the same time in the same place—then that lends credence to his theories."

Scott shook his head. "I don't buy that parallel universe concept because it implies that you can cross over from one to the other like changing lanes on a highway. Traveling through time is difficult enough to comprehend, but jumping tracks in the space-time continuum is a bit more than I can handle."

"Because we do not like or understand an idea is not sufficient reason to discard it."

"That's not the problem, Doc. It just doesn't make sense. We've already got an infinity of space and an eternity of time, why complicate the cosmos with another endless variable? We may as well postulate universes of different scales: electrons as planets revolving around atomic suns, and our own universe as nothing more than a microscopic dot in some vaster, greater universe. There has to be a stop to it somewhere."

"Believe me, lad, I sympathize with your grief. But we cannot restrict the possibilities of the celestial sphere because of limitations inherent in the human brain. Don't you think nuclear scientists were more comfortable when they could describe the atom as an electron revolving around a proton, without having to account for scores of subatomic particles and the interaction of nuclear forces? It was mathematics that discounted the simple model of the atom, just as Rusty's mathematics quantifies a universe that is more complicated than the human senses perceive. What bothers me is the indeterminacy of his formulas. They can be read two ways: either as a synchronism of events, relying on the mutual exclusion principle, or as an effect without probable cause. He will read it whichever way he thinks I want to hear it. But I am on to him."

Scott rested his forehead on his knees. He was getting a headache from the intense cerebration. "I don't know why the dragons chose such an inhospitable time zone anyway. They hate the cold. And cold-blooded animals can't survive in the cold. Hey! That's it." His head jerked up with the light of an idea. "Maybe they didn't intend to come here. Maybe it's all an accident."

"Where else could they go?" Doc countered. "Their TTS was anchored in space."

"No, I mean, maybe they didn't intend to come now—to this time zone."

"Dragons never do anything without good reason."

"Dragons can make mistakes, too. They've made a couple of big goofs already. Or, maybe they came to this TZ out of desperation. We had them on the run, they had to escape, and they chose sometime close; sometime when they

wouldn't use too much energy in getting here—now. And maybe later on, without our intervention, they'll meet their end naturally, because they couldn't adapt to the cold."

"And perhaps they used the TTS to bring them to this time zone, with the idea of using a space machine to carry them to a more temperate climate," Doc countered. "Remember that their choices were limited by the crudity of their time transfer technology. But more important than why they chose this TZ, is why they felt the need for a remote storage facility."

Scott shook his head. For the moment the cold was forgotten. "If the crystal had only been a more recent backup . . . "

"That is why we must find out for ourselves. Dragons are not devious. Their thought processes are straightforward; it is just that their minds work in a manner that is alien to our way of thinking. And while I may be confused about space and time and other things, I am wise enough to know that we cannot afford to underestimate the grand design of their scheme. I am certain that the dragons have a purpose that we have not as yet divined. And even if we do not succeed in killing a single dragon, we must at all costs discover that purpose. Only then can we be armed for the future."

CHAPTER 9

"You do not have to go."

Scott threw the combination battery/backpack over his shoulder. Food and supplies were carried in a satchel attached to the top of the laser gun's battery pack and capacitor module. "Yes, I do."

"But, you are needed here—" Jane pleaded.

"The tech crew can handle all the repairs. There are enough spare lifting cones and focusing nodes in the hold to build another ship. And Rusty can take care of any problems that crop up."

"But—"

Scott cut her off. "I *have* to go. I *need* to go. I need to get out there in the wilderness and prove to myself that I can still handle it. The *Ark* will be here when I get back."

Jane was silent for a long time. "Then, you know that I must go with you."

Scott took a deep breath. The air was clean and cold, redolent with the smells of nature. "I know, Honey." He bent down, ruffled her long, straight hair, and kissed the top of her head. "I'm sorry you feel compelled to watch over me."

"It is not—"

He smothered her face against his furry greatcoat. "I know what it is. And I want to have you along. I love you, and your company. I'm just sorry that my stubbornness is forcing you to go on this mission. I'm sorry for placing you in such danger—"

"I have lived my whole life with dragons." Jane pulled back and smiled at him pertly. "It may be that I can offer advice that is borne of experience."

"Did you get that phrase from Doc? Because if he's been brainwash—"

"Did I hear my name in vain?" Doc strode into the staging area with his own greatcoat draped over his arm. All around, men and women prepared for the assault on the dragon fortress, packing warm clothing and checking arms and supplies. "My dear, you cut a handsome figure in that outfit. A black beaver pelt, is it not?"

Jane smiled. "I stitched it myself. Scott's too."

"A smart-looking lad." Doc made a show of donning his own garb. "I rather fancy the glistening auburn coat of a curious and so far unnamed horned rodent, although I would not like to fight one of the creatures for its skin. They grow upward of three feet, you know, and have claws like daggers. Thanks to the Nomads' trapping skills and Helen's expertise as a seamstress, I have a tailor-made garment that is the rage of fashion." He looked askance at Scott. "My boy, you are going to suffocate in that attire until we get out of the lowlands—"

"Doc, I know you're trying to change the subject." Scott struggled out of his greatcoat and bundled it into a ball for packing. "I was only trying it on for size. Now, what kind of stories have you been telling my wife?"

Doc pooh-poohed Scott with a wave of his hands. "I was merely pointing out that a well-rounded army has the advantage over an enemy whose tactics are known and whose strategy is predictable. We are stronger for our diversity of arms and nuance of attack. Primitive as spears and bows and arrows are, the Nomads can use their weapons effectively, and perhaps in cases where our supposedly superior firepower is impractical."

"But what does that have—"

"If y'all pardon the intrusion, the Texas Rangers are pullin' out." Windy paused at the top of the ramp long enough to toss off a salute. "My outfit's havin' a conniption 'cause Broderick rallied his troops ahead o' ours. Got some time to make up."

"I will be tagging along with the supply train." Doc stepped aside as the heavily burdened soldiers tramped out of the *Ark* on their way to war. He turned to Scott, and faked a look of disdain. "It goes against my grain to let others lead the way. All my life I have been in the forefront of the fight against dragons. Now, I am relegated to the rearguard as 'honorary chief brave.' It seems that youth has privileges that rank has not."

"It also has the strength of two good legs." Helen stepped out of the mass of marching men. "And while I understand that both of you need to prove your manhood, you should be mature enough to know that you aren't judged by your physical prowess, but by your strength of character. Dad, at your age, haven't you yet gained that inner security. And Scott, where is that sense of humor of yours?"

"My boy, I think we have been had. Lead me to the house of dragons, but deliver me from women."

Scott said, "I'm just eager to get going. I've felt guilty sitting around for the past week doing nothing but making plans while the rest of the gang's been hunting and trapping and scouting the route."

The last of the Rangers filed down the ramp. Doc's raised voice rang out in the sudden silence. "Planning and forethought are paramount in any campaign, and are equally as important as the work of the foot soldier. With an enemy already entrenched, we must rely on siege tactics rather than hit-and-run guerrilla warfare. Speed is not essential; stealth and stamina are what will win this battle."

"Uh-oh. Now you've got him started." Helen led the way down the ramp. "We'd better get on the trail before we have to listen to the book of proverbs."

Scott hefted his bulky pack and slung it on his back. He jumped up and down a couple of times to settle the weight and adjust the straps. Then he stretched out his right leg and tapped the deck. "I guess I'd better put my best foot forward."

Helen looked back over her shoulder.

"There's the Scott I used to know."

Jane shouldered her own smaller pack and disembarked with the others. Down on the ground she hitched herself to her travois. The plastic frame was jury-rigged from spare parts; wheels built into the trailing poles made it easier to haul through the woods and over the ice. The netting was piled high with tools, clothing, and camping gear. The army carried only a small amount of food, expecting for the most part to live off the land.

Doc doffed his greatcoat and lashed it to the frame of Jane's travois. "My dear, I want to thank you for volunteering your services.'

"Youth has not only its privileges, but its responsibilities."

Doc's jaw dropped. He ogled Jane as if she were a figment of coalescing ectoplasm. When he finally found his voice, his words came out cracked and rasping. "I suppose a mentor should be honored by his student's emulation, but I find it a bit embarrassing."

Scott laughed raucously. "Serves you right."

"Dad, you may have created a soul in your own image."

"Hey, if you guys're finished lolling your tongues, we got a show to get on the road." Sandra stood fiercely, with her knuckles tucked on her hipbones. She wore a knee-length smock that disguised the evidence of pregnancy. The sun striking her black hair made it glisten like the feathers of a starling; her voice was as harsh. "I don't like lagging behind my own platoon. Now let's move it!"

Scott looked at Doc and forced his lower lip to tremble. "She scares me more than the wild animals."

"I believe the commission has gone right to her head. Such is the influence of newly promoted authority."

"Coming, Lieutenant," Scott sing-songed. He traipsed along behind Jane. Doc was by his side. Helen cinched down her harness straps and followed behind with another heavily laden travois.

"Mother, are you sure that's not too much of a load for you?"

Helen shook her head. "I tried it out yesterday. I can handle it. Where's your father?"

"Out in front, as usual. With Bold One. The Nomads are leading the parade, with the Fusiliers and the Rangers spread out behind 'em on parallel tracks—assuming the Rangers catch up. We're bringing up the rear. Early camp,

today. Jane, if you get tired with that rig, let me know so's I can relieve you."

"Thank you, Sandra."

Scott squinted in the golden glow of the sun. From the edge of the forest he glanced back at the *Ark*. The top of the giant saucer was cleverly camouflaged with brush and branches piled so deep that the upper time transfer focusing nodes were visible only upon close inspection. "Where's Rusty? I thought he was out here seeing everyone off—"

As if on cue, the redhead stepped out from behind the trees. He carried a sheaf of vellum in his hands. He peeled one off and handed it to Scott. "I was making sure everyone got a map, in case they became separated. This is the final update. When I reviewed the tapes from the flight recorder I noticed some discrepancies between the printout and what the Nomads drew from their scouting excursions. It has to do with sight angulation. I used a computer simulator to interpolate the actual elevation changes in the terrain—"

"I get the picture, already." Scott tucked the smooth vellum into an outer vest pocket and buttoned the flap. "I'm sure the topography will conform to within a fraction of a percent. Now, listen." Scott wagged a finger at his companion. "You take care of my baby. I want her in tiptop shape when I get back. And if you have any problems, call me."

"The tech crew will take care of it."

"Her. She's a ship, and deserves the respect of her calling."

"It's a machine. It doesn't have a gender—"

"Then why, when you were under the stress of escaping those missiles, did you refer to her by the feminine pronoun?" Scott watched Rusty's discomfiture with pleasure and with a growing smile. "Ah-*ha*. You thought I wasn't paying attention."

"I never—"

"Then play back the audio flight recorder. It's all on crystal."

Rusty deliberated, casting his eyes down at his feet. "All right, I'll take care of—her. But you take care of yourself. All of you. And don't leave us out of the picture. Keep in touch. I want twice-daily reports; more if you encounter anything unusual. Britt will be monitoring your channels at all times. Both of us will be sleeping on the bridge, so one of us will be on watch—"

"She's a nice gal, Rusty. Do you think you

can keep your mind on your work with her around."

Rusty's face turned the color of his hair.

"Stop teasing him," Helen said.

"What do you think, Doc?"

Doc turned the corners of his mouth into the caricature of a smile. "I think we had better get moving before our computer whiz suffers from a downloading fault and before we incur the wrath of an impatient platoon leader."

"You got that right," said Sandra.

Scott took his cue. He waved one last time to the ever-alert gun crew, sitting inside the blisters, and ducked into the cover of Pleistocene foliage. It felt good to be starting on a journey—even if it was a crusade from which not everyone was slated to return.

Time would tell many things.

CHAPTER 10

The gently rolling savanna stretched as far as the eye could see. Dense groves of evergreens alternated with open vistas that were dotted with lone birches and aspens and small stands of elms. Tall oaks dangled lofty branches high above waving fields of rust-colored grain. Rock outcrops were carpeted with lush moss in a kaleidoscope of muted oranges, reds, and greens. Long-stemmed purple flowers grew indiscriminately.

Dominating the foreground was a solitary mammal the size of a small elephant. It used its flattened tusks like twin shovels, rooting through the damp grass along the bank of a clear, shallow stream. It raised its head and grunted every minute or two, as if calling to the yellow sun that hung in the cloudless sky.

In the distance a herd of shaggy musk ox, whose drooping horns made them look like a gaggle of lugubrious women, grazed quietly. They paid no attention to giant birds soaring overhead on wings the size of plywood sheets. Even as one teratornis swooped down and plucked a two-foot-long, needle-nosed rodent from its mound of dirt before the squawking creature could scrabble into the safety of its hole, the musk oxen, oblivious to their surroundings, chewed their food with a dull, vacuous stare. They were too big, and too many, to care about the screech of a bird or the squeal of a rodent.

It was a world that was far from idyllic. Predator and prey waged a constant battle for survival against the forces of nature; predators fought starvation, prey scrounged for nourishment while trying not to become the nourishment of others. The world offered no securities, nor made any guarantees: it bequeathed hunger to the inept, death to the unobservant. Life was fraught with sickness, disease, pain, and suffering.

Death Wind held no illusions. He recognized the perils of the wild. He also understood, in a great, blinding flash of insight, what the world must have been like before there were dragons—or men—to desecrate it.

Not more than a third of the Pleistocene landmass was ice. Most of the Earth was cold, windy, and raw, but so alive. It was also rampant with wildlife that had adapted to prevalent conditions. This time zone was the Age of Mammals and, except for the last stronghold under dragon control, was soon to become the Age of Man.

Death Wind knew this from his history studies. Looking out over the land, he could well understand how mankind could take root here. The Nomad in him saw a world of plenty in which to roam free. The savage inside saw, instead of herds of musk ox or fields of grain, an endless supply of meat and bread. The Cro-Magnons were lucky to have been born in such a time, with so much room for expansion. Little wonder that they were unwilling to share the land with ignorant, backward Neanderthals who lacked the sensitivity to feel the exhilaration of the wild.

With a tingling in his groin, Death Wind also knew that unless he and his companions rid the Earth of dragons, mankind could never develop cultures.

It was a terrible responsibility that only a brave could bear. Even as he thought it, Death Wind knew that he would fight to the death for the near humans of this time zone. Men stuck together despite the barriers of space and time, for that was the code of Nomad tradition.

Thus it was with great sadness that he watched the small band of Neanderthals creeping through the tall grass, stalking the shovel-tusked elephant. Even if they succeeded in bringing down the beast and supplying the tribe with fresh food, they were ultimately doomed to extinction. The history books said it was so, and so it must be.

The amebelodon raised its mighty trunk into the air and trumpeted a baleful warning. The base tone echoed from the hills and lingered in the distance like a returning call. There was a flurry of motion in the reeds, and a cloud of dust that erupted from the ground as if a mine had exploded under the grass. A huge orange blur vaulted through the air toward the startled amebelodon.

The elephant reared on mighty hind legs that were like two hairy pillars. Massive forelegs punched the air crazily. The thunderous trumpet was met with a high-pitched caterwaul. The orange bundle of fur, five times the size of a man, raked the amebelodon's barrel chest with outstretched claws. At the same time, the elephant fell forward so its padded forefeet struck its attacker's long back. Then the orange predator was crushed under the full weight of the elephant.

The shrill cry continued, and the next moment a giant cat slithered from under the trumpeting amebelodon. With lightninglike speed the cat bounded away, but not before its hindquarters were stabbed with long ivory tusks. The cat's body slewed sideways. It was knocked halfway to the ground, but it quickly regained its stance and ran straight away without once looking back.

For the amebelodon the fight was over. The cat's claws had barely penetrated the thick hide of its breast. The ancestral elephant thumped across the savanna to seek more solitary grazing grounds.

The giant cat's speed was so great that in seconds it covered several hundred yards. It skidded to a halt close under Death Wind's rocky perch, and in the midst of the stunned Neanderthals. The cat was so stunned that for a moment it just stood tall, tail flicking, dark eyes observing. Slowly it fell back into a crouch and uttered a hiss that sounded like a broken steam line. It bared its teeth, revealing a pair of long canine teeth that jutted downward like upside-down tusks.

Death Wind knew at once that this was not just an oversize cat, but an ancestor of the saber-toothed tiger.

The Neanderthals posed like cigar-store Indians, apparently frozen in fear. Fist-sized rocks held in limp hands were no defense against the fangs of the great cat, even if the subhumans had the nerve to fling them. The tableau lasted but a moment. Then two things occurred at once. The prehistoric tiger leaped at the nearest Neanderthal, and Death Wind notched his longbow.

Muscular arms bent the still-green wood until the ends nearly touched. The plastic, dragon-made string was as taut as spun steel. The shaft was mated to the bow at the base of the knapped flint. Death Wind led the charge and released the arrow. Bird feathers—real bird feathers—guided the yard-long arrow through the air. The deadly missile caught the cat in midair and buried itself into the brawny shoulder blade.

Fangs aimed at a Neanderthal's throat missed their mark as the tiger's head twisted around and snapped at the sudden cause of agony. The cat's forward momentum did not change. One paw the size of a bushel basket rasped the subhuman's abdomen with telling effect. The claws eviscerated the hapless creature in an instant.

The remaining Neanderthals dropped their rocks and bolted. The enraged cat spun in circles, screeching and biting. By the time it succeeded in breaking the shaft in two, another landed in its midriff. A third soon followed.

Then came the Nomad war whoop as Death Wind leaped off the low precipice. Well-toned legs absorbed the shock as his moccasins struck the soft soil. He dashed forward like a pole-vaulter, leading the charge with the tip of his spear. The tiger struggled to gain its legs. It had time to lean back and hiss only once before the thick steel point slipped beneath its head and entered its heaving breast.

The tiger whirled with uncommon strength, catching Death Wind unawares. The violent reaction knocked him off his feet and sent him tumbling. He hit the ground hard enough to knock the wind out of him. Instinctively he rolled away in order to clear those swiping, taloned paws. When he came up against a mound of dirt he climbed to his feet; he still had not been able to force an inhalation. He whipped out his knife and poised defiantly.

The cat charged him, seeming to ignore the spear that was buried in its heart. The butt of the thick wooden shaft caught Death Wind in the belly and bowled him over. He wrapped his fingers around the spear. Relentlessly, the tiger crawled forward, kicking great clods of earth from under its four paws. Death Wind hung on for his life. His body was lifted and pounded into the ground; he plowed a furrow across the grassy plain as if he had been strapped to the end of a seesaw that was being pushed by a bulldozer. The antediluvian tiger refused to die.

Death Wind felt his strength ebbing. He was losing his grip on the shaft. Still the tiger crawled, reaching out with one paw, digging its claws into the earth, pulling itself forward at the same time it kicked with its hind legs. It did not hiss, it did not screech. It just kept crawling.

As Death Wind's muscles weakened, his arms slowly unbent. The length of the spear was all that kept him and the tiger apart. Slowly they were drawn closer together. The tiger kept crawling, step by painful step, pushing the Nomad's weakening body ahead of it.

Lightning struck Death Wind's calf: a searing, numbing pain leaped the entire length of his leg. He jerked his knee, but his lower leg was pinioned and would not move. Death Wind had made two mistakes: first in attacking a fully grown tiger, then in being rash enough to face the wounded animal in combat.

This time he was lucky. The tiger died.

Two two-inch-long claws were embedded in the muscle of his calf: puncture wounds that would heal with time and proper treatment. If the cat had had the final strength to pull back its foreleg, it would easily have ripped off Death Wind's foot.

The Nomad lay like a corpse for many minutes before he regained the strength to move. Then he folded his body at the waist so he could reach his trapped leg. The tiger paw lay on him like an oversize mop that was armed with spikes. He studied the cat's exposed claws in order to determine the curvature. Then, he eased the sharpened talons out of his leg. It was less painful than he expected.

For five minutes he sat without moving. Although he was battered and bruised and felt a stabbing pain in his ankle, he was not seriously injured. Finally, he rolled over onto his hands and knees, and pushed himself up off the ground. He felt woozy at first and knelt back down on one knee. When the nausea passed he stood up again, slowly.

He stumbled back along the tracks that were gouged in the topsoil. It looked as if a backhoe had dug up the ground. Steel glinted in the sunlight. Death Wind groaned as he stooped to retrieve his knife. At the end of the trail lay the Neanderthal. She was ripped open from breastbone to groin; her intestines and most of her organs lay in a puddle of blood alongside her body. Yet she breathed.

Death Wind crouched by her side. She was big-boned and brawny, and covered with a thick mat of hair. Her arms and legs were long and muscular, her chest broad, her hips wide, her feet large, her toes splayed. Two ponderous mammary glands sported tiny pink nipples that protruded through the thatch.

Her head was much larger than the human head, and contained a brain that was larger than a human brain. But sheer bulk of gray matter was not the sole measure of intelligence. The structure of the brain was more important than its capacity. Neanderthals lacked the essential ingredient that was the quantum difference between racial genetic imprinting and individual learning ability.

Death Wind touched her jugular with extended fingertips. The pulse was faint. He left his hand where it lay as he surveyed the damage done to her body by a single swipe of the giant tiger. Her entrails had not been surgically removed by those monstrous claws, but had been torn to shreds as well; they could not be scooped up, replaced in the body cavity, and stitched in place. Even Doc, the greatest healer Death Wind had ever known, did not have the medicine to save this one.

The Nomad recognized the organs strewn in the bloody froth. The intestines were shredded like confetti, the stomach had disgorged the contents of its last meal, the liver was split in two. And the uterus . . . The heart still pumped, the blood still flowed, and that wet, pulpy sac that was the womb still quivered with life. Even as he looked, with his fingers frozen on the throbbing jugular, tears in the uterus spread the mass apart. A tiny, dark foot kicked through the outer lining, followed by a hand. All at once the sac burst apart and spilled out a nearly grown fetus. The hairless doll kicked a few more times, and then lay still.

Neanderthal eyelids fluttered. Black eyes peered from under protruding brow ridges. The female stared sightlessly at the blue sky. Slowly, painfully, the eyeballs moved in their deep sockets. With gimlet eyes she looked directly at Death Wind. Expressionless, she stared for a long time. After an eternity, her arm struggled up against the awful pull of gravity. Fingers weak from shock touched the Nomad's throat. He felt a sight pressure. The hand dropped as if it had been given a brick to hold, but subhuman eyes held their grip.

Death Wind saw in those silent orbs a prehistoric creature with no hope for the future. Already her unborn child was dead. Her own death was inevitable, and not far behind. Soon, her entire race would follow the path to extinction.

The Nomad understood her feeble gesture. As she watched him, begging for mercy, he pressed down harder on her jugular, spread his fingers until they encircled her hairy throat, tightened his grip. He stopped, but her eyes urged him on. He squeezed delicately, not choking, but embracing her larynx with a love and a strength that he did not know he possessed.

Her primitive anthropoid brain desired release. And in that simple wish was more meaning, more comprehension, more humanity than could possibly exist in the mind of a mere mammal. As primal as she might be, she commanded the faculty to pray for death despite the animal instinct for survival.

At last her eyes closed. Her chest heaved in convulsions as her lungs screamed for air. With tears streaming down his face, Death Wind held her tight. In a few moments her body ceased all movement, her blood no longer flowed, her veins no longer pulsed. Her face, brutal and atavistic by modem standards, assumed an aura of hushed tranquility.

If her kind had the imagination to conjure the hope for life after death, and to invent the concept of God, then the soul of this unnamed creature entered whatever heaven she believed in.

CHAPTER 11

Scott struck chords on the remote toner, using dragon tone talk to transmit his message. "Peg-leg toning the *Ark*. Come in, *Ark*."

Acknowledgment was immediate. "*Ark* here. Britt toning."

Scott strummed again. "Halfway point reached this noon. All well. How's with you?"

The receiver toned in a clean, harplike timbre. "All well. Repairs under way. Forty percent complete. Rusty warming."

"Prosperity."

"Health."

Scott slipped the transmitter into the tanned hide case that was strapped to his backpack.

"What was that all about?" Sandra stirred the pot of soup with a shaved stick. "I know your handle and the sign-off cipher. But what did she mean by 'Rusty warming'? What is she doing, stirring him into a kettle of stew?"

Scott laughed and exchanged winks with his wife. "She's got her hooks into him, but he's putting up a good fight. That's why she didn't come on this safari. She's afraid his fingers will grow roots into his input terminal, and he'll become a talking computer link."

Sandra cocked an eyebrow. "She's got her work cut out for her. If she keeps the chlorophyll out of his diet and the calculus out of his sleep, she might have a chance."

The sun was a dull orange ball that hovered a few degrees above the western horizon. The sky was only partially clear after yesterday's rainstorm. For Scott, the day cooped up under the tarps, keeping dry, had had its advantages: rest, recuperation of sore muscles, and time to share with his wife. Then, the entire People's Expeditionary Force spent the morning in drying out moccasins, clothes, and the furred skins that they used for blankets. But the rushed afternoon, double-timing through heavily forested terrain to reach the caves that had been spotted by Nomad scouts, had tired him even more. The breakneck pace was almost more than he could stand. He propped his footless leg atop the supply stash; as the blood drained out of it by the force of gravity, the pain induced by venous pressure eased off.

Jane dragged the travois farther into the protection of the sandstone overhang. It was loaded with wood that she had collected while the others were setting up camp. She propped the logs and branches against the back wall for drying. When her chores were completed, she pulled two small bundles of fluff out of her pack. Cradling them in her arms, she held them out where Sandra could see them. "Have you seen my new pets?"

"Hey. They're cute. What are they?" Sandra left the stick in the pot and took one of the furry animals. For a moment her upper lip curled. "Uh, they're not Pleistocene rats, are they?"

Jane laughed. "No. They are wolf pups."

"You mean, like one of those pack hounds that attacked us the other day?"

Jane nodded. "The mother was killed. Bold One found the litter nearby. He kept two, and gave two to me."

Sandra puckered her lips at the little critter,

then nuzzled its soft, silky fur against her face. "What're you gonna call 'em?"

"Pete and Repeat if they're boys," said Scott. "Joyce and Rejoice if they're girls."

"Oh, you."

"One is male, the other is female." Jane knelt and let the pup sit in her lap. She ran her hands along its sleek fur.

"Okay. How about Jack and Jill?" Scott offered.

Doc entered the arena carrying a slab of meat the size of a man's torso. "My dear, do not tell me you are going to the wolves?"

Sandra looked up startled. "Pop, where did you get that steak?"

A plastic packing sheet lay by the fireside. Doc blew the dust off the top, then placed the massive hindquarter on the sheer surface. "It is more rightly called venison, I suppose, since it came from a kind of antelope with a great rack of horns. I strongly suspect that it might be the famed Irish elk, although my biological studies of this time period are seriously lacking. Would you mind if I thickened your soup with it?"

"Mind?" yelled Scott. "Try to take it away."

"I rather expected that attitude from you, my boy. To answer your question, Sandra, the Nomads managed to drive three out of a small herd over this very precipice yesterday." He pointed upward, indicating the cliff above the overhang. He took a long-bladed knife out of the sheath that was strapped to his waist, and carved the meat into bite-sized bits. "It was when they climbed down to retrieve the flesh that they discovered this shelter. Instead of bringing the meat to us, they brought us to the meat."

"It's nice and cozy in here, I'll grant you that." Scott stabbed a chunk of meat with a screwdriver that was honed to a point, and shoved it into the blue flame just above the red-hot embers. "With the fields and open plains right out in front, it would make a good permanent camp—if we needed one."

"Yes, the Nomads are of the same mind. They are quite enamored by the profusion of wildlife and the vitality of the soil. They see a land where food is plentiful, and there for the taking; quite different from what they are used to. Besides a boundless supply of animals to hunt, they imagine cultivated grain and rows of vegetables, even orchards of fruit trees."

Slender Petal climbed up the dirt embankment and stopped at the fire pit. She bent over in

order to tear apart a leather bagful of small wild cabbages, and deposit them into the pot of steaming water. Her pitch-black hair was tied in a ponytail and hung down her back as far as her waist. She flashed even, white teeth. "Earth good. Grow much." Like all Nomads, she made her point without saying more than necessary.

Doc grimaced. "Yes, I just conveyed the same sentiment in ten times the wordage. I sometimes get carried away with my rhetoric."

Scott rotated the bite of venison on its makeshift spit. "What you call rhetoric, others call fustian."

"The point was made without such accuracy of definition."

Slender Petal pulled carrots out of her tunic pouch and pointed one at Sandra. "Wolf." She diced the cleaned roots into the pot with deft slashing motions of a slender knife. "Keep?"

"They belong to Jane." Sandra put hers on the ground. It swayed back and forth on wobbly legs. "Aren't they adorable?"

Doc plopped a double handful of meat in the pot, then tossed a slice of raw fat in front of the pup. "If we are going to feed them scraps, we will have to call them dogs."

Jane took a bit of meat and held it out for her pup. "You may keep one if you like, Sandra."

"Really?" Sandra scooped up the critter and held it in front of her face. "I guess if we killed your mama we'll have to take care of you. Little orphans like you won't last long alone in this country." She rubbed it against her cheek. "Jane, thank you. I'd love to have it."

Jane pointed to the travois. "I will carry him."

"Hey, I never knew being pregnant had so many perks. I don't have to carry a pack, or haul a travois, or hunt for food. Maybe I'll make a career out of having babies."

Slender Petal slowly shook her head. She picked up the shaved stick and stirred the brew. "Raise children much work. Break things. Make trouble. Run away. Death Wind bad boy. Never listen." She pointed to the wolf. "Easier to train pup."

"Yeah?" Sandra corralled her puppy. "Tell me more."

"Uh-oh. Wait till I tell Death Wind that his mother's telling baby stories."

"Scott, you keep out of this." Sandra winked at Jane. "We'll talk about it later. In private." She stuck out her tongue at Scott. "Away from prying ears."

Sam and Helen, holding hands, wove a path through the campers to reach Sandra's fire pit. "What's this about prying ears?" Helen wanted to know.

"Mother, Slender Petal's got some delicious tidbits about Death Wind when he was a little boy. She's going to tell me all about him—later. When we get rid of the men."

"Sandra, you're becoming such a gossip."

Sam waved a hand to attract attention. "I hate to interrupt such an important discussion, but would anyone like to hear the news." He waited for a moment, scrutinizing each person's eyes, until he had their attention. "The dragon fortress has been spotted. Right where Rusty said it would be."

Scott forgot the pain in his leg and jumped up. "Wow, that's great. And I just got finished telling Rusty that we were only halfway there."

Sam held up his hands. "Sorry. I didn't mean to give any false impressions. It's still pretty far off. Bold One and Death Wind and some of the other braves saw it from the top of Mount Ararat."

They had named the mountain after Windy's stuttered remark.

Scott remembered the near collision the *Ark* had had with the snowcapped peak. "I've been as close as I want to get to that place. What made them climb to the summit? I thought they were just going to scout around the base."

"You know these Nomads. Sorry, Slender Petal. I guess you do know them. Well, once they got close and saw the ridge in between, they figured if they got high enough it would save them from having to make an actual reconnaissance on foot. You know, sort of seeing the lay of the land from up above?. Well, sure enough, once they got up there they could see the glow of the TTS in the distance. They camped up there overnight. Sounded like pure hell, even with the insulated moccasins and musk ox blankets."

"Did I understand you correctly, Sam?" Doc asked. "They could see the focusing nodes coruscating? As if they were in use?"

"That's what they said. Well, I mean, that's the message they sent back. The runner just got in. The rest of them will meet us on the trail sometime tomorrow."

Doc rubbed his white beard thoughtfully. "That is very strange intelligence, indeed. If, as we supposed, the Pleistocene structure is the last

stronghold of the dragons, when are they transporting to—or from? They have no past, the future is blocked, and they have nothing to gain by selecting another upstream destination when the geological record shows no evidence of dragon incursion."

Sam tilted his head questioningly. "I don't know, Henry. I'm just reporting the facts. Scott, get on the toner and tell Rusty what we've found. Maybe he can search the crystal and pick up something we missed. He told me the dragon menus are difficult to trace because they rely on key words that he might be unfamiliar with."

Scott eased himself down by his pack. "I thought they just used this TTS as a receiving station. But if they're transporting elsewhen, we've got to be careful not to destroy any documentation about their whenabouts. Doc, I apologize. You were right about not coming in with guns blazing and obliterating the place."

"Yes, now more than ever we must proceed with caution."

"Not only that, we've got to be sure not to tip our hand about the ground assault. Granted the dragons may not be expecting us to waltz in among the glaciers, but if they've got observation posts surrounding the fort, we want to make damn sure that if the alarm is given, we're ready to storm the place before they can mobilize."

"I've sent out a fresh runner and told her to get the boys back here on the double. I don't like having my troops spread out like this. Especially since Death Wind came so close to becoming cat food. I've issued orders that there's to be no more solo scouting. But you know that boy. He's got his own head."

Sandra smirked conspiratorially with Slender Petal and Jane. "Yes, so I'm told."

"And his father's just as bad. Between those two, I sometimes wonder if giving instructions does any good. They're going wild out there in the forest, as if they'd just gotten out of jail. Slender Petal, was Bold One always like this?"

Slender Petal nodded but once. "Always."

"Like father, like son," said Sandra.

"Yeah, well, they may be two of the best scouts in the world, but I'd like it a hell of a lot better if they'd follow the routine instead of their noses." Sam ran a hand through his hair and scratched his black beard. "This place can't be taken lightly. It's utterly different from anyplace—or anytime—in our experience. Sure, it's full of wildlife; but most of it's lethal. You've got to watch yourself every step of the way. It isn't like home. We didn't have wild animals to contend with. We never had to worry about anything but dragons, and we knew how to hide from them. But here you've got packs of bloodthirsty wolves, saber-toothed tigers, bears the size of a house. To say nothing of the swarms of smaller types that are constantly nipping at our heels. This is the Age of Mammals, all right—predatory mammals."

Slender Petal sat back on her haunches. "Much challenge."

Sam scowled. "I'm sure that's what the Nomads like the most about it. Well, to each his own. I just want to win this war and not have to fight anymore: with dragons or wild animals."

"Sam, I don't think you're being fair," said Helen. "You're not looking at what this world has to offer, only at how hard you have to work in order to earn its fruits." She gestured toward the savanna in a supplicatory manner. "Compared to this, our world is a barren wasteland. Up till now, the largest mammal I've ever seen is a rabbit—"

"And they're practically overrunning the Holocene forests."

"If we catch a glimpse of a raccoon or a chipmunk—"

"They're not even worth eating."

"—we ooh and ah because so few mammals survived the holocaust. How can you be so calloused in a world so alive, so full of the wonders of nature—the world the way it used to be before the coming of the dragons?"

"Okay, okay." Sam held his hands out in front of him, defensively. "I didn't mean to sound like a pessimist. I'm just saying that this world is a seductive pitfall. You've got to be on your toes all the time."

"Easy for you to say." Scott removed the browned venison from the flame and nibbled the edges.

"We've got to watch out for insects, snakes, and birds of prey. We've got half a dozen people down with fevers from stings and snake bites, one gal nearly lost her head when a teratornis mistook her hair for a nest and tried to fly off with it. Those wolves mauled two men before they were beaten off. Even a herd of herbivorous musk ox charged through the Fusiliers' formation and caused such a rout that they had to drop their packs and run for their lives. We were lucky not to have anyone trampled by those

cloven hooves. Hell, one of the Nomad women was feeding a cardinal out of her palm and the thing pecked her face and almost took her eye out. We've got a dozen casualties, and we haven't even met the enemy yet."

"All of life is a risk," said Doc.

"Henry, this isn't the time for philosophy. We're at war. And I'm wondering if we'll have any soldiers in fighting trim when we reach the battlefront."

Scott swiped several more chunks of meat off Doc's makeshift cutting board, slid the metal point through them, and placed the miniature shish kebab over the fire. "There's a lot to what you say, Sam. Invasion forces are always at the mercy of the elements, the terrain, and the unknown defenses of the enemy. But look at the brighter side. We've been able to live off the land with relatively little expenditure of time and resources. That means light loads, fast travel, and no supply line."

"And don't say that having pregnant women along slowed you down any," Sandra scolded. "We've all kept up the pace and managed the work load, without complaint."

"If it had been up to me, you'd have stayed with the *Ark* until we called for reinforcements," said Sam.

"No way, Daddy. I go where my husband goes. If he wants to walk halfway around the world, I'll follow him."

"An admirable quality that you get from your mother."

Helen nodded. "I seem to recall giving birth to Sandra on the trail. That was how we lived at the time. We were always on the go, trying to keep one move in front of the dragons. We hid in a rock shelter for the night and started out early the next morning with a papoose in a blanket tied to my breast."

"But that was necessity. It was either run or die. This is a planned military campaign, not a family outing."

Helen shrugged. "Conditions may change, perceptions may be different. But women are women, no matter what the age."

Sam flung his hands in the air. "I should know better than to argue with you. Or your daughter."

"Our daughter."

"Our daughter," Sam said grudgingly. "Sometimes I think I should just let the Femme Fatales infiltrate the dragon stronghold and talk their ears off while we read all their crystals."

Scott said, "Lizards don't have auricles—"

"Don't *you* start," Sam cautioned, wagging a finger. "I've got enough trouble on my hands."

"And you may have more trouble—later." Helen put her hands on her shapely hips.

Sam feigned a scowl. "I never thought a general had to fight on so many fronts."

Scott removed the venison from the flame and blew on it to cool it off. "Try being a private."

CHAPTER 12

Bold One and Death Wind ran side by side, like split images of the same subject. Each wore hide jackets and leggings, each slung a bow and quiver of arrows over broad shoulders, each held a spear at the balance point. Their pace was fast, and one that they could maintain for hours.

For the first time in his life, Death Wind felt as free as the wind that blew the hair off his neck. The dragons were a minor nuisance, to be taken care of in due time. But for now he reveled in the thrill of the hunt, in the rush of the chase, in the longing for dominance over this primitive world. He and his tribe were the lords of this planet.

Bold One raised a hand to signal for attention, then bent his wrist and drew back three fingers so he was left pointing. Death Wind saw, and nodded in silent assent.

They separated, each veering to opposite sides.

The ground was purified by a blanket of snow that was clean and white. The crystals crunched under Death Wind's padded moccasins. Lofty evergreens wore a cream-colored blanket that wrapped around each tiny needle, that pressed down on each slender branch; the trees looked like veiled, mourning ladies. The sun was a muted ball that struggled to shine through the overcast.

Death Wind jogged down the lower slopes of Mount Ararat. The pitch was not as severe as it had been at the higher elevations; a series of long, gentle slopes that alternated with flat, level plains. Far ahead a black dot moved, its size indiscernible because of the distance and lack of perspective. It might be a giant bear such as the one they had killed in the forest. Or it might be even larger.

There was no need for communication, for both father and son knew what to do, and knew what the other would do. Death Wind entered a stand of fir trees. The snow was deeper here because the tall sentinels captured it and prevented the wind from blowing it away. Waist-high drifts barred his path. Death Wind skirted the edge of the grove and slogged through snow that was only knee deep.

He slipped wraithlike around the trees, out of sight of the animal that rested unsuspectingly in the frozen savanna. Many minutes later, when he reached a point as close to the creature as he could get without stepping into the open, he uttered a sequence of hoots in imitation of a fat, nocturnal bird that Doc called an owl. A moment later came the twang of a jay: Bold One's response.

Neither Nomad moved. Death Wind observed the shaggy black mound with growing curiosity. If it was a bear, he did not want to disturb it. It had taken a dozen men and women of the Sintu tribe to corral and kill the other one, and in retrospect they felt that good fortune in addition to their native skills prevented death or serious injury in the ensuing skirmish. Yet, they had proved that with only primitive weapons, coordinated effort, and ingenuity born of a lifetime of wilderness experience, they could conquer the beasts that inhabited this vestal, untamed land. Nomads could adapt.

The cold bit through his clothing. After an hour of astute observation, Death Wind used a trick to keep warm that he had learned since penetrating the frigid highlands. Without moving perceptibly or jumping in place, he vibrated his muscles in a controlled shiver. His entire body trembled, yet his clothing disclosed not a hint of movement. Several minutes of enforced muscular friction warmed him measurably.

Still, the sleeping animal lay quiescent.

Bold One took the initiative. He called like a jay, to let Death Wind know that he was moving again. He had rubbed snow into the outer hide of his clothing, and held in front of him a snow-covered bush. Crouched low, he worked his way toward the monstrous, unknown creature. Death Wind held his place; he was upwind, and would surely be detected should he attempt the same tactic.

His father glided across the snowfield with infinite patience. He was a hundred yards away when the black mound shuddered. Death Wind could not distinguish head from tail. The beast was a giant mop of hair, a shaggy boulder caught in an earth tremor. It heaved upward, then settled back down into its crypt of snow.

Death Wind's gaze alternated between beast and bush. Bold One sank into the snow behind the white shrubbery. He lay there for many minutes, until the animal thrust upward again. This time it rose out of the snow like a mythical titan, larger than any living creature that Death Wind had seen in post-Cretaceous times. The huge bulk was covered with thatch that reached the ground.

The thick coat of hair disguised its shape. One end was lower than the other, much like the stance of a bear, but the angle was such that Death Wind could not distinguish its facing direction. Then, after Death Wind thought the beast was already standing, it heaved once more, lifting the bulk of its body on four massive, columnar legs, like a house on stilts.

The animal rotated slowly. The tail waggled on a low-slung rump like a tassel on the end of a stick. The backbone inclined upward like a ski slope to broad, bulbous shoulder blades. The head alone was the size of a small bear. Then came a great, ear-shattering trumpet as a long, thick trunk pointed toward the sky, and the ivory tusks stabbed the air like curved pikes.

The woolly mammoth directed its gaze toward the hidden Nomad. Its large ears flapped, and its entire body swayed from side to side as it lifted first one huge forefoot, then the other. It seemed uncertain, as if its visual acuity were deceiving its olfactory sensitivity; as if what looked like a bush smelled like something it had never before experienced. It trumpeted its discomfort.

The mammoth approached Bold One warily. The Nomad made not a move. Once again the beast trumpeted, as if showing displeasure at uncertain circumstances, or issuing a final warning. Death Wind put his mind into the brain of the pachyderm, striving to think how it would think, to see what it saw, to interpret situations in light of the mammoth's experience, to deduce what its instinctive reactions might be. Balanced for action, Death Wind clutched his spear tightly, knowing full well that the puny weapon was no defense against a creature of such size.

Less than a hundred feet separated the mammoth from the bush. The trumpeting resounded in the still, crisp air like the deep-throated rumble of a landslide. The tusks pointed forward, the trunk held high.

Bold One lunged out from behind the bush. He raised his spear in both hands and let out a war whoop that rang across the countryside. The mammoth hunched back indecisively, trumpeted, leaned forward, trumpeted, leaned back, trumpeted, and poised. If the Nomads knew how to read such behavior, they could have responded accordingly. But they had never before encountered such an animal—had in fact met very few mammals in their Holocene lifetimes, and those were mostly small ones.

Death Wind waited for the turn of events.

Bold One rushed the hesitant pachyderm. The mammoth charged. Bold One skidded to a halt, spun around, and dashed for the protection of the distant fir trees.

Death Wind ran from his own place of hiding, whooping and waving his arms at the distant pachyderm. The beast was amazingly fast and agile for one so huge; it galloped through the deep snow like a black steed racing across a field of grass. It rapidly closed the distance to the bounding Nomad.

To Death Wind, running through snow was like wading through water. He exerted every ounce of energy to reach his father's side. His angled course closed on a vector with the rampaging, madly trumpeting mammoth. He screamed at the top of his lungs. The gargantuan head swung his way, a dark eye the size of his fist glared at him. The mammoth slowed to a halt. Bold One stopped in his tracks and faced the woolly mammoth defiantly. The pachyderm pivoted its great tusks from one Nomad to the other. It was now forced to confront two opponents. The shaggy head swayed from one to the other.

Bold One feigned a lunge. His son followed suit. But Death Wind had no intention of getting any closer than he already was. He was not going to attack, but he could not let the mammoth know that. He merely wanted to hold it at bay until his father was safe. His heart pounding with excitement, Death Wind stared back at the mammoth. Part of him wanted to attack, to prove his manhood, to bring down the greatest mammal he had ever seen. But part of him knew that this was not a challenge for one brave, or even two. To kill such a beast would require stealth, planning, and collaboration. All he wanted for now was to leave in peace.

The mammoth leaned back again on its haunches. It trumpeted like a peal of thunder. Bold One and Death Wind acted aggressively, each whooping and taking a step forward with his spear raised.

The mammoth's charge turned into a rout. It rolled back on its hind legs, executed a low cartwheel, and took off across the plain.

Father and son exchanged startled glances. Then they whooped in delight and chased after the retreating mammoth. On and on they ran, screaming like banshees. The woolly mammoth outdistanced them with ease. But they ran for the sheer exhilaration of running, ran until their legs ached with pain, ran until their lungs gasped for air, ran until they had their fill of adrenaline and were happy to be alive in a land so full of life.

Then they stopped and watched the pachyderm galloping away, watched until it was a small black speck on the horizon, until its shape blended with the dark trees. Without exchanging a single word, they nodded at each other and headed for camp.

Death Wind felt an ecstasy that he had never felt before. He knew that it was a feeling that he must experience again. There would be other days, other mammoths, other hunts. That was the way of the Sintu.

* * *

Rusty was awake behind closed lids, but so groggy that he could not open his eyes. He snuggled deeper into the warmth of the blanket, soaking in the deliciousness of sleep. Partly, too, he did not want to face the world of reality. Slumber land was so cozy. He dreamt of faraway places, of faraway times, of the infinity of space-times that stretched before him like coarse hemp in which each strand split into myriads of branches, and out of each branch grew smaller offshoots, which branched out farther into slender filaments, which themselves consisted of even tinier . . .

He felt a soft touch on his forehead. He dragged his eyes open as if they were creaky barn doors. The suffused glow that filled the bridge was partially blocked by a familiar shape. Rusty forced a smile. "Did I oversleep?"

Britt shook her head. "You not sleep enough."

Rusty smiled more broadly. "I *do* not sleep enough," he corrected. His voice was cracked and weak.

"You *do* not sleep enough."

Rusty pushed himself to a sitting position, tucking the blanket around him as he did so. "That's right, but without the accent on 'do'."

She perched on the edge of the cot like a bird about to fly away. "Breakfast?"

For one crazy, fear-filled moment he was afraid that she would scoot away and leave him alone. As he scrunched up against the bulkhead and pulled his legs under him, he grabbed her hand and held it in a way that he hoped was not obvious. "First let me get the cobwebs out of my eyes."

Britt leaned so close that Rusty could feel her breath upon his face; it reminded him of a warm spring breeze with the scent of flowers in the air. "Pretty eyes. But no cobwebs. I keep spiders off bridge."

Rusty could not stop from laughing. "That's just an expression, Britt. It means I'm still drowsy."

The smile never left her face. "I understand." She picked up a cup from the floor and held it out to him. "Tea?"

He patted her hand to complete the illusion of mere friendship. "Sure. Thank you." His eyes never left hers.

"Message come in. Say 'ice ahead'."

Wearily, Rusty brought his mind into focus. He forced his memory to dump into the buffer of his brain the programs that he was running. "Oh, that's great. They're making good time." He sipped his tea, flung his feet off the pad, slipped into his moccasins, and took two steps to the computer console. He used his free hand to activate the screen. "How are they otherwise?"

"All well."

Rusty nodded, and continued sipping. He studied the equations that were highlighted on the monitor. He was hardly aware of Britt standing by his side. Reading spatiotemporal coordinates required extreme concentration. He had programmed the onboard computer to function on multilevel problems. Since the calculations he had started were still undergoing checking and evaluation, he let the computer do it offscreen. He booted the crystal format and began menu scanning where he had left off late last night.

With a touch of the controls, Britt pulled back the opaque canopy cover. The light that flooded the bridge was not the yellow beam of the sun, but a white scattering that cast no harsh shadows.

"Look, Rusty. It snows."

He cast his eyes upward. Large, flat flakes landed delicately on the clear plastic bubble, existing only a trice before melting into an obscure smear of water.

"I never see before."

Rusty stared at her numbly, part of his mind still on his computer scan. "Then, how do you know what it is?"

"Scott explain. During ori-en-tation. He talk about this world. About con-ditions. He is good teacher."

Rusty cast his eyes back at the screen. He allowed himself to smile. "That he is—among other things." He glanced at Britt for a moment. "He's a good person, a good friend." A dragon symbol caught his attention. He typed instructions on the keyboard that halted the scrolling data, backed to a suspicious entry code, and stabbed the button for expansion. A submenu appeared. Still standing and sipping, he set the new list into motion. "There's got to be an answer here somewhere. Too many things don't add up."

Britt set a fried cake on the counter beside him. Rusty absently picked it up and shoved it into his mouth. He took another sip of tea.

"If I only knew what I was looking for."

CHAPTER 13

For the umpteenth time Scott pulled his stump out of the morass. The cylindrical leg extension continually sank into the soggy soil like a pointed stick into mud.

The rain forest was magnificent in the panoply of life it offered. Giant sequoias towered hundreds of feet above the lush, moss-covered, root-filled ground. The trunks of fallen trees lay like great monarchs throughout the forest, oftentimes larger in diameter than a person's height: a barrier that meant wide detour. Spanish moss hung in huge clots from the lower branches. Vines clung to bark like varicose veins. Mushrooms grew in great profusion, and added their distinct flavor to the evening stew.

Scott saw more species of animals in one hour than he had seen in his whole life. Everything from colorful slugs twice the size of his thumb, to immense Irish elks that ran through the brush with an uncanny knack considering the wide, palmate antlers they carried on their heads. The ground was alive with fox, raccoon, bobcat, hare, hog, and a wide variety of rodents.

"I don't care what you say, those birds sound to me like they're chirping merrily."

Doc chuckled to himself. "Whatever you say, my boy. If that is what you wish to believe."

"But those damn squirrels—" Scott shook a fist in the air. High overhead, fluffy-tailed tree rodents chattered incessantly. "They have to be aiming. I've been hit by three cones this morning, not counting the near misses. Nobody's going to make me believe they're not dropping them intentionally."

Doc was having the same trouble with his cane that Scott was having with his stump: it kept slicing into the soft earth. The makeshift basket of vine wrapped around the end helped quite a bit. "They are merely expressing an aggressive territorial instinct."

"Yeah, well, if we come back this way and I still have power in this thing—" Scott reached behind and rapped his knuckles on the side of the battery pack. "—I can guarantee you that some of those rascals are going to get fried."

"Save your aggression for the dragons," Doc laughed.

"Believe me, right now I've got plenty to spare."

During the course of the afternoon they continually gained elevation. With the level, open savanna now far behind, and the rain forest yielding to fauna that was more adapted to cold weather, the trees became shorter, the brush sparser, the ground rockier. Scott found himself getting out of breath as the climbing became steeper with each step. He paused more often, leaning forward at the waist with hands on his hips, fighting the agony in his legs.

"Rather a tough climb," said Doc with a hint of a gasp. The older man did not carry a pack of any kind, but Scott still found it amazing that his stamina held him in such good stead. "We need the acclimatization. The worst is yet to come."

The newly trodden trail led to the top of a precipice that overlooked the valley below. Scott was enamored by the open vista. He stood on the very edge and gazed in awe; it was as if half the world were laid out beneath his foot. A glacier-fed, crystal-blue pond supplied water to a meandering creek that carved a deep gorge through the forest. Eagles with their wings spread wide rode the air currents with effortless ease. From a lower ledge, a furry I marmot screamed at the human intrusion. Mountain sheep as white as snow bounded along the opposite cliff face.

Jane was suddenly by his side. "We camp ahead."

Scott kissed her hair. "Good. I'm about tuckered out. Doc, are you okay?"

He was breathing a little harder now. Leaning heavily on his cane, he stared at the green, lowland pasture. "These weary bones are fatigued, my boy, and my stomach grumbles without compassion, but I suffer from nothing that a good rest and a grilled steak cannot cure. Lead on, Jane. I believe I detect the lovely fragrance of a campfire."

"I think if you tried Nomad dialogue it would save you a lot of breath."

Doc ran his fingers through his great shock of white hair, pulling out twigs and leaves. "There is undoubted truth in what you say. I shall give it some thought." He admired the view for another few seconds, then continued on his way before he lost his place in line. A Charon gal hauling a travois stopped to let him in front.

When he was out of earshot Scott shook his head. "He just never gives up."

Jane nuzzled her husband. "Neither do you."

They camped that night in the scrub pine; burning logs scented the air with their essence. Blackened pots hung over the fire pits; the boiling water was thickened with chopped herbs, tubers, and vegetables, collected during the day's march. Escaping steam added its aroma to that of the natural forest. Meat sizzled over the open flames.

The powwow began right after dinner, in the light of upheld firebrands.

"The way I see it is this." Sam scraped a spot flat and drew lines in the dirt with a stick. "Here we've got the stronghold, in the same location in terms of geological reference as Charon in the Holocene. The *Ark's* glide path carried us over the mountain range into this valley. A good thing, too, because it puts us out of visual reach from the stronghold. Right in front of us is the western flank of Ararat, which we can cross here." He drew a jagged line that described a switchback trail to the crest of the ridge and back down the other side. He pointed through the trees behind him. "That's just up ahead. Bold One, you want to brief us on that?"

The Nomad spoke in a deep monotone, like a base fiddle with only one string. "Very steep.

Much snow. Wind on top. No game."

There followed a long pause punctuated by the crackling of embers. The warmth radiating from the fires compensated for the cold of night. The flickering, yellow glow tainted serious faces with a touch of jaundice, while casting dark shadows into the blackness beyond. Bold One made no further attempt to elucidate.

"Right. Well, that was pretty brief." Sam doodled with the stick. "Anyway, we've got plenty of provisions: more now than when we started. But it'll be snow and ice from here on: tough slogging, with no chance for hunting or gathering food. The worst part is we'll be out in the open. Now, we've got plenty of skins for protection from the elements, but what I'm worried about is being exposed on these snowfields. It doesn't look like the dragons have any flyers in this era, but we can't be sure. It might be parked in an under-ice hangar."

Helen raised her hand. Sam acknowledged her. "I've been studying the aerial photos taken on the way in. They're a little blurred because of the *Ark's* speed, but they do show a lightening in color that extends throughout the glaciers that surround the stronghold. If you'll look at your maps"—vellum rustled throughout the moonlit clearing—"you'll see a cloverleaf effect around the central structure. Under magnification these teardrop-shaped arms appear to be interconnected by faint lines, as if the dragons have tunneled under the ice."

"Could they be living quarters?" Scott asked.

"If they are, there are an awful lot of dragons holing up inside that glacier." Helen placed the enlargement where everyone could see it. She outlined the curved perimeter with a long fingernail.

"Correlate your maps with the computer image. See how extensive these areas are in comparison with the central core, which I interpret as the reactor and TTS? There's either a fairly large community of slaves, or these are storage facilities."

"Storing what?" asked Sandra.

Helen shrugged. "More time transport equipment. Extra batteries. Arms and munitions. Food. Possibly flyers that are being assembled this very minute."

Scott thought about making the comment that everything in the universe was happening at this very minute, but let it slide. He was not in the mood for levity, even his own. These were serious matters at hand.

"In that case we need to spread out during the approach march." Broderick was a small man who spoke with impeccable diction. He combed his hair short and trimmed his beard to the same length with a scalpel. "We can communicate by radio."

Sam nodded. "Yes, the Sintus will lead the charge and secure a beachhead. The Rangers and Fusiliers will take flanking positions during the crossing. Sandra, can your gals manage the cannon on that ice?"

"We're going to build a sledge for it." Sandra pointed her chin at her mother-in-law. "Slender Petal is in charge because she's done it before. We'll use the reins from the gun carriage like we've been doing. It shouldn't take any more than four of us to haul it across the snowfield. But when we have to take it uphill or down, we're going to need help from a few strapping men."

"Windy, Broderick, pick two men each and detail them to the Fatales. How much time will we need to make snowshoes?"

"One day," said Death Wind.

"Slender Petal, can the sledge be built in a day?"

"Yes."

"Good. Then we'll stay here tomorrow, rest up, and prepare for the trek across the snow. Bold One, have all the scouts returned? I don't want to tip our hand by having them spotted."

Without uttering a word the Nomad tilted his head.

Doc pulled the bear skin tighter over his shoulders. "No doubt the dragons anticipate an attack."

"But they don't know when, how, or from what quarter. I think a sneak ground assault is our best bet."

"Oh, I do not question your decisions concerning methods of attack. Clearly, the dragons are fully prepared to repel an aerial bombing raid. Nor can we afford to have the *Ark* irreparably damaged. It represents our only way out of here and now. I merely want to emphasize—for everyone's benefit—that we must proceed with extreme caution—perhaps even trepidation. We know nothing about the dragons' motivations for establishing a base of operations in this time zone. We have so far surmised that the stronghold is nothing more than an escape mechanism, but there are indications that reasons more pervasive exist."

"Such as?"

Doc squeezed his long beard as one would wring out a damp washcloth. "Such as surface-to-air missiles. When the dragons constructed this stronghold and armed it for defense, I am certain that they did not foresee an attack by one of their own aircraft. There are no political factions within dragon hierarchy, no competitive infrastructure. Yet they showed no compunction against shooting down a flyer obviously of dragon design and manufacture. There was no attempt at communication."

Long branches spread out from the central fire pit like spokes from the hub of a wheel. Doc snapped off the nearly burned-off tip and shoved the branch farther into the flames.

"I see what you're getting at," said Sam. "It's almost as if they were expecting us."

Broderick added, "They knew exactly when, where, and how we'd be coming."

Doc shook his head. "No, the evidence does not warrant such conclusions. I am merely pointing out that the facts do not add up to any known quantity. Which is all the more reason to enter the stronghold clandestinely, to infiltrate rather than to destroy wantonly, to overthrow their leadership. I have a curious feeling about what we may encounter."

"Henry, it's already understood that we're gonna do as little damage as possible—"

Doc interrupted his son-in-law with an upraised palm. "Forgive me, Sam, but I must be more emphatic than that. We cannot allow any destruction of dragon equipment."

"Be reasonable, Henry. There's bound to be a few stray shots—"

"No demolition whatsoever. We must contain laser fire to perimeter sorties."

Sam's jaw dropped. His mouth opened wide enough to swallow an apple whole. "What the hell are we supposed to do? Negotiate? We didn't drag that cannon through hell and tarnation as a conversation piece. Or all these laser guns, either. If we don't blow the bastards off the face of the Earth they'll be here to haunt us for the rest of our racial existence. I understand about not wanting to damage the controls to the reactor; we don't need to learn any more about plate tectonics. And we've gotta know what TZ they're sending to or receiving from, so we can't tamper with the TTS until we trace its activation memory circuits. And, well, I guess we don't want to interrupt power to the central computer. But—"

"Doesn't leave much, does it, Daddy?" Sandra sidled close to her husband. "Pop's right, as always. If we break a single circuit, it may shut down an automatic override or disconnect an important safety valve. The whole place may be sabotaged for self-destruction. Then we'll never know when they're coming or going."

"Hey, whose side are you on, anyway? You never side with your grandfather—or anybody else for that matter."

"I'm on the winning side, Daddy, and so are you." Sandra pulled her fur coat over her legs. The bulky beaver pelt hid her growing pregnancy. "You've been so caught up with planning this operation as a military campaign that you've lost sight of the final objective."

Sam threw his hands into the air. "Now I've heard everything."

In the short silence that followed, glowing embers crackled like scattered rifle shots. Green wood sizzled as sap oozed into the red-hot coals. A meteor streaked across the star-studded sky with soundless splendor. The tranquility of the night was broken only by the caterwauling of a wildcat seeking a mate, and the stridulation of crickets in the trees.

Windy tossed pine needles into the fire as if they were darts. " 'Pears to me she gots the right attitude, Gen'ral. I may be a blimp brain mosta the time, but I gotta 'gree wit' the young lady."

"I need to gain access to their systems program so Rusty can—" Scott started.

Sam held out his hands defensively. "Hold on a minute. Don't everybody gang up on me. I'm not protesting. I just don't quite know what our objective is anymore." Facing Doc, he said, "If you're trying to tell me we've got to tiptoe in there past armed guards without firing a shot, I won't stand for it. We'll lose too many people. Human wave attacks are for the birds—well, you know what I mean. Don't just tell me what I *can't* do, Henry. Tell me what I *can* do."

Doc took his time before answering. He beefed up the fire again and held his hands close to the flickering flames. "Sam, I have no intention of usurping your authority. You are in tactical command of this outfit, and you are doing a fine job of it. My position here is that of advisor."

"Then advise me," Sam said, raising his voice truculently.

Again Doc paused. He waited until the silence screamed to be broken. Then he spoke in his mellifluous, finely wrought baritone. "Rusty and I have given the matter of paradox as thorough an examination as mathematics and philosophy will allow. In the dearth of empirical data we have come to separate conclusions that, while not mutually contradictory, are at best mildly antagonistic. The only thing we agree on is that the ramifications of time travel cannot damage the universe as an entity.

"But," Doc held up an index finger for accentuation. "The delicate balance between cause and effect can be upset the same as a precarious ridge of snow can be turned into an avalanche by the molecular vibration generated by a sharp clap. In a similar manner, dragon technology has disturbed the fabric of local space-time with results that, as you all know, have had far-reaching effects on the continuance of life and on the geology of this planet. Such worldwide changes are the inherent danger of playing with time."

Sam chafed at Doc's lengthy discourse. He ran his hand through his hair and gritted his teeth at the ground.

"The dragons have started something that we must finish. We cannot take an ostrich posture in light of what we know. The dragons, and the horrible avalanche that they have set in motion, must be stopped before humanity is engulfed in a temporal snowball. That is why we are here now. But we must be extremely careful not to trigger events that may cause our own dissolution. We do not want to overexert our leverage and tip the balance of nature.

"Sam, I must caution against the use of power weapons during the assault phase on the dragon stronghold. The cannon and backmounted guns must be withheld. The Nomads can provide cover with bows and arrows while the rest of us go in with spears and knives. Hand-to-paw combat is the only means of attack that will give us the measure of control we need. If we break a link in the chain of events, the human race may end in the Pleistocene instead of originating here."

Sam exhaled so hard that his breath blew aside the flames of the fire in front of him. "Well, why not tie one hand behind my back, too."

"I understand your frustration. I feel it as well. I would prefer to bomb the glacial retreat and let matters fall where they may. But I cannot in good conscience take that chance when we may do irrevocable damage to the continuity of time. The renascence of the world depends upon conquering the dragons not just in this time zone, but throughout eternity in both directions. What we need now is knowledge, not a body count."

"Okay. Okay. I get the point. You make good sense. You always do. But I can't ask these people to attack the dragon stronghold under those restrictions. I want to win this war more than anybody. But there's still the human equation to figure."

"Son, you are learning that the lot of a military commander is a troubled one. Decisions that involve life and death are never easy to make. Unlike the doctor, the soldier has no Hippocratic oath to shape his judgment."

Sam shook his head. "You're a big help."

Helen rubbed his back through the thick hide.

"Sintu agree." Everyone looked up at Bold One's intonation.

"Yeah, an' that goes fer the Rangers, too." Windy tossed a rock into the fire that stirred the embers and caused ashes to fly. "We ain't afeared to face them lizards with our bare hands. Get a stranglehold on 'em, we will."

Broderick spoke with quiet elocution. "The Fusiliers will do what is necessary to win this bloody war, with or without weapons."

"I'll speak for the Femme Fatales," said Sandra. "We'll back you all the way, Daddy, in a subordinate position if necessary. We came here to fight dragons, and if the best way to fight them is to do as Pop says, then that's the way we'll do it."

Sam looked from one to the other, mouth agape. A cheer went up around the fire, followed by the incantation of the Nomad code. Helen leaned hard against her husband's shoulder. Sam worked his jaw, but no sound came out until he cleared his throat. "I guess—I guess I'm not—a very good soldier. I can't order troops into battle with the certainty that not all of them will survive."

Doc said, "If you cannot order them into battle, lead them. My only request is that I want to be by your side when you do."

CHAPTER 14

The snowshoes were a godsend to Scott. The

flotation offered by the curved hickory sticks lashed together at the ends and strung across the middle with interlaced leather strips gave him the best support he had had since leaving the *Ark*. The long wooden tail helped in tracking by keeping the heel aligned with the direction of travel. Unfortunately, it made backing up impossible.

"Hey, Doc, this is great. With these things on my feet I'm finally on equal footing with the rest of the gang."

"I noticed you were having no trouble in keeping up." Doc lumbered along on his own snowshoes with very little difficulty. The snow was piled high in drifts that would have been exhausting to traverse without the Nomad footgear.

"And I can really get a foothold with the wooden spikes digging into the ice."

"Modified crampons. The Nomads know every trick in the book when it comes to outdoor living. I knew they would be indispensable."

The snowfield angled up a gentle slope that was just enough to keep Scott huffing and puffing. He and Doc were at the front of the Femme Fatales. Far to the left Scott saw the last of the First Fusiliers, while to his right a straggler from the Texas Rangers made his way sluggishly over the glistening crust. The Nomads were out of sight over the crest. Great yawning crevasses of unknown depth gouged the plateau like squiggly fingers.

"You know, I just had a crazy thought."

Once again Scott adjusted his snow goggles: the temples made his ears sore. He had started out with a pair of glasses made from laminations of shaded plastic. They fogged up so often from his exhaled breath condensing and freezing on the lenses that he soon switched to the Nomad variety: a thin sheet of bark lashed around the face with treated gut; pinholes poked in front of the eyes limited the amount of light that was allowed to penetrate.

"Not another one."

"Suppose the dragons perfect the time transfer device like Rusty has done: with infinite incremental verniers. Then they'd be able to go anywhen they wanted with exact precision."

"I think 'exact precision' is grammatically redundant, but I understand your meaning."

"Okay, so how about this scenario? Let's suppose this stronghold is a testing station. Now, we know that in the past the dragons built their time transfer structures way out in the boon-docks in case their future experiments backfired on them; they didn't want to blow up the city, or the taxpayers. But suppose they were investigating new principles of space-time, with possible consequences so lethal they didn't want to take a chance on having something go wrong in their own time zone."

"An interesting speculation." Doc stopped at the top of the rise and leaned against the cane that had been converted into a ski pole by the addition of a woven basket with protruding radial sticks. "They establish a subdivision in the Pleistocene so if the experiment goes awry, they forfeit only the laboratory and its contemporary environs."

"Exactly!"

Doc's face clouded over. "But they would still suffer the loss of highly trained personnel: the technicians and scientific team that was managing the project."

"Not if they transferred the high-echelon dragons a short way through time when the actual experiments were conducted. Time is a better safeguard than space, and you don't have to go very far: a few minutes will do."

Doc nodded thoughtfully. "But that presumes their discovery of a more finely tuned incremental transfer control."

"No, I was just using that as an example. They might have something else up their sleeves besides scales. Even with their million-year transfers, they could still time-warp the VIP's into the past or future."

"Which brings us back to why we must access their computer instead of destroying it."

"Not only that, it means we may be walking into a real hot potato."

"Hey, you ain't gonna get any hot potatoes till dinnertime, and then only if we can spare the wood." Sandra stood with her hands on her hips, her bulbous shape lost in the profusion of furs. "How about quitting your jabbering, and picking up the pace a bit."

Scott feigned a scowl and shook his head. "You are one tough lady, Sandra. I don't know how you can chug along like that with such a burden."

"Children are not a burden, they are a blessing."

"Uh-oh. Doc, she's been taking proverbial lessons from you."

Doc cocked a snowy white eyebrow. "I am

beginning to understand how grating that can become to the senses."

"I've been telling you that for millions of years—" The radio crackled, interrupting Scott's train of thought. "Hold on." He slung the backpack off his shoulders and set it upright on the snow; it sank in the soft surface slush that had been melted by the rays of the sun. He pulled the transmitter out of the leather pouch and plucked away at the keyboard. The tones wafted melodiously across the snowfield like the tinkling of ice crystals on a cold winter's morn.

Jane topped the rise and kept walking until she found a level spot on which to park the travois. The runners were greased with animal fat and slid along the glazed surface at the slightest exertion. "We rest?"

Sandra squinted in the glare. The sun turned the snowfield into a mirrorlike sheet. "Let's get everyone onto level ground, over there by that first crevasse. Those guys with the cannon are so far ahead that I can't even see them."

"White make them invisible." Jane reached down and gathered a handful of snow and rubbed it on the back of Sandra's fur coat. The snow did not melt because the body heat did not penetrate the thick hide. The white covering camouflaged the platoon like snow tigers.

Scott toned away on the transmitter.

"Yeah, well, I guess it works. If I can't see them, neither will the dragons when we sneak into their burg. Hey, Scott, that's a pun. Get it? Burg? Berg?"

Listening to Britt's reply on the toner, Scott waved her off. "How come they're only funny when you make 'em? Huhn? Huhn?"

Jane suddenly froze. She removed her home-made goggles and stared ahead with her eyes pinched.

Scott saw the look on her face, turned with the toner still up to his ear, and saw a bright speck of light rising in the sky. "What the hell—" Sandra started.

"I do not like the looks of this," said Doc.

The long stream of light ascended fast at first, then appeared to slow down and diminish in brightness.

Scott was totally disoriented by the glowing apparition. He thought that the Nomads must have fired a flaming arrow into the air, but could not understand how they could have launched it to such a height. "Doc, what kind of signal—" Scott slowly let the still-twanging toner slip away as his hand dropped to his side.

"It rose from far away," Jane offered. "From other side of crest."

"It is difficult to judge size and distance without perspective. It is either a small object close by, or a large object far away. Despite the optical illusion, I would say there is a fair chance that it is a dragon missile headed our way."

The beam exhaust was partially hidden by the nose cone as the missile reached the peak of its trajectory and angled over toward the ground. The blue thrusters were occulted from Scott's point of view the same as the sun during a solar eclipse.

"It's coming right toward us!"

"Run for cover!" Sandra turned and ran back down the slope toward her platoon.

Scott saw the lip of a crevasse directly in front of him. "Doc! Jane! In here!" Without looking to see if they were following his direction, he leaped toward the opening in the snow. The crevasse was barely wider than his shoulders, with the snow built up like a ramp leading down into the darkness. "Come on!"

He jumped down onto a platform that lay four feet below the surface, sinking past his knees into the powdery drift. He lost his balance and plummeted forward. When his chest hit the snow, the edge of the platform broke away like a cornice; he plunged face first onto an ice glaze and slid down in a tumble to the bottom of the crevasse.

Facing up he saw a slender finger of blue sky punctuated by a few sparse clouds, saw Doc's face peer into the corner of the opening, watched him roll over the edge onto the platform, heard the Dopplering whine of the descending missile, saw Jane leap practically on top of Doc, noticed the fine detail in the mesh of her snowshoes as she did an accidental somersault over the venerable doctor and slid feet-first down the slope, saw a blue-purple streak arc across the top of the crevasse, heard the deafening roar of an explosion, felt the concussion that was transmitted to his body through the hard-packed snow, saw a blinding flash of light followed immediately by a pure white sheet being drawn over the opening, felt pain in his ears as a torrent of snow funneled into the crevasse and pressurized the air, screamed, gulped in a hasty breath, felt the stinging cold hit his face, and reveled in the final, utter blackness that dropped over him like a pall.

Silence ensued.

Scott could neither see, nor hear, nor feel, nor breathe. He was in dark limbo: a place where there was neither pleasure nor pain, hope nor heartache, cheer nor sorrow, life nor death. There was only endless continuance, without meaning.

Sometime in another place, in another time, the essence that was Scott felt the urge to take on new life.

His new body needed air. He opened his mouth to draw in the initial breath of the newborn, but found his throat stunned by cold and clogged with snow. He forced himself to cough with whatever air remained in his starving lungs. Out come a clot of ice, and for a moment a narrow passage existed in the center of his throat. He inhaled hard. The sudden pressure collapsed the tunnel. Frigid snow was sucked into his lungs. He choked. He coughed again, gasped, coughed and gasped, coughed and . . .

Something rasped across his face, brushed vehemently over his mouth. Then warm lips pressed against his, and a breath of hot air was forced into his throat. He inhaled instinctively. As soon as he exhaled, another breath was blown into him. It happened again, and again. Then he went into spasms, gagging on chunks of ice. He spit them out and was able to breathe on his own.

"I can't see."

The goggles were suddenly whipped off his head. In the faint glimmer of light he saw Jane's importunate face only inches away from his own. Her blue eyes were undimmed by the gloom.

"You okay?"

Scott coughed a few more times before he could speak again. "Yes. I'm—No. I feel funny." Then he realized where they were, what their predicament was. He struggled for a moment, then screamed, "Doc?"

"Over here, my boy." The doctor sat up dusting white fluff off his parka. When he shook his head, snow flew off his hood. "I am unhurt, but we are in a bit of a bind."

"I—can't—move." Scott strained against invisible bonds. Try as he might he could not move any part of his body. He felt no pain, just a curious paralysis that struck him from the neck down. Shivers of fear coursed along his spine. But if he could feel that . . .

Jane scrabbled at the snow. Scott could feel

her hands beating against his right arm. Then she shoved back on his shoulder, reached down and located his hand, and pulled it up out of the snow. "You are stuck."

In a few moments she had his upper body uncovered. With both hands free, he helped her scoop out the compacted snow. Several blocks of ice lay on his lap, pinning his legs under their combined weight. Together they shoved them aside. Scott arched his back and got his hips clear. His snowshoes acted like anchors; it was quite a while before they managed to dig out the footgear enough for him to roll free.

"Whew." Scott lay gasping from the exertion. Despite the cold of the snow, he was sweating profusely inside his furs. "Does *that* feel good?"

"If you two have succeeded in disinterring each other, I could use a little help in excavation." Doc was buried up to the waist. When he brushed the soft fluff off what Scott thought must be his lap, it became obvious that he was standing upright. His goggles lay askew on his cheeks; he pulled them up onto his broad forehead. "But please be careful. These walls are undoubtedly less than stable. We do not want to cause a cave-in."

It took them five minutes of hard work to extricate Doc from the drift. Then they all lay on the snow-covered floor of the crevasse, breathing hard. The arched ceiling towered more than twenty feet overhead. An eerie, gray glow suffused through the ice cap.

"We were lucky to have rolled away from the entrance," said Doc, after he caught his breath.

"So we can suffer a slow death instead of a fast one."

"Please do not be so negative, my boy."

"Life means hope," said Jane.

"Oh, no. Another convert. Doc, are you giving these gals lessons in platitudes?"

"I like to refer to it as positive fluxion philosophy."

"That's great. But it'll take more than phraseology to get us out of here. I don't know how much air can filter through the snow, but I'll bet we can convert oxygen to carbon dioxide faster than osmosis and natural circulation can replenish it."

"Have no fear. Those topside will soon know exactly where we are." Doc reached into the ample folds of his overlapping furs and pulled out a tin bowl and a soup spoon. When he clanged them together the sound reverberated

throughout the chamber. He beat a staccato tune that was grating to the ears. "We will not be entombed for long."

Ten minutes later a tent pole was thrust down through the ice bridge. Doc altered the beat. Several more poles poked through the thick crust; one pole fell all the way through.

Scott yelled, "Hey, watch out. You almost hit me with that stick."

"If you guys are finished playing hide and seek, we'll widen the hole and drop a rope down to you." Sandra's voice was muffled by several feet of intervening snow. "Or would you rather stay for lunch?"

Scott made two fists and thumped his thighs. "I hate it when she has the upper hand."

CHAPTER 15

Rusty's hair had not been cut in ages; his curly locks had grown to such lengths that they framed his face like a ragged mop. He stood behind his computer console with a mug in one hand and a printout in the other. He placed the vellum sheets on the reader, punched a few function keys, and gazed intently at the monitor as calculations scrolled across the screen.

He absently took a sip of tea, frowned when he rediscovered for the tenth time that the mug was empty, and lowered his arm to the bent elbow position.

Britt appeared by his side with a fresh pot of brew. "More?" She never poured without asking, because more than once she had begun to refill his mug and ended up spilling most of it on the floor because he was so preoccupied that he had no awareness of her presence and walked away after she had tipped the teapot.

He stared at her blankly. Fully five seconds later his hand jerked upward. "Oh. Sure. That would be great."

She filled his cup with the steaming brown liquid. "Do you have time yet?"

"Time? Time for what?"

Britt pointed to the computer screen. "Time to transport?"

Rusty shook his head. "Oh, you mean, have I figured out the short-cut formula for calculating the infinity variable? Well, almost, I think. It's mostly a matter of reducing a temporal asymptote to a real-time figure with enough precision that I can insert coordinates on the time axis in relation to an arbitrary prime."

Raised eyebrows implied perplexity.

"Okay. Remember when I showed you the meridians on the globe, and how one was selected to be the prime meridian from which all others were calculated?"

Britt nodded as she put down the teapot.

"Okay, we call that the space axis. Now, I've done the same thing on the time axis by choosing an instantaneity from which all upstream and downstream determinants can be computed. But right now it takes an epoch and a half— sorry, I'm exaggerating. It's what we call hyperbole. Anyway, it takes a lot of computer time to run through the mathematics program. Once I derive the formula that accounts for all the variables, I'll be able to tell the computer when I want to go, based on an arbitrary prime temporal meridian. It'll make the computations automatically and immediately, relay the data to the time transfer verniers, and we're then."

"You are very smart." Britt smiled. She reached out for Rusty and ran her hand up and down his slender forearm.

Rusty reacted galvanically to the tingles that Britt caused in him. His face turned a shade of red that rivaled the color of his hair. He backed away and took a perfunctory swallow of tea. The brew was still so hot that it burned his lips; he jerked the mug away from his mouth.

"If I were so smart I'd taste the tea before I scalded myself with a mouthful of it." He put the mug on a workspace.

"You hurt?" Britt placed a tender finger on his lip.

Rusty backed away so fast that he slammed his elbow into a stanchion and nearly tripped over the copilot's seat. "No. I'm okay. It's just that—I guess my mind was on the next set of equations to be input." He quickly thought of something to say. "Do you remember the conveyor belt analogy?"

Britt cocked her head and flashed white, even teeth. "Tell me again. I am not your smart."

"Well, you see," Rusty rushed on. "When you calculate temporal distances on a small scale, you don't have to take universal influence into account. At least, not in the proximity of large gravitational bodies, like planets. A mass the size of the Earth forms its own energy well in the space-time continuum. Temporal interaction with the rest of the universe exists to the same degree as gravitational interaction. It's immeas-

urable in the proportions we're dealing with. We can treat the Earth essentially as an isolated quantity. Are you with me so far?"

"I am with you."

"Okay. If we measure the distance between the two of us, and neither of us moves in relation to the ground, we will always be the same distance apart." Rusty put his hands on Britt's shoulders and made sure she did not come closer. Even at that range he could smell the fragrance of her hair. "That is, throughout the brief span of individual human existence. Understand?"

She pursed her lips. "I understand."

Rusty dropped his hands. "But, even though we can't perceive it with our senses, the ground is in motion all the time. The continents move in a process called plate tectonics. You remember that?"

"I remember."

"Well, these plates slide across the molten core of the Earth like leaves on a pond, and they carry us with them. So, if I calculate the distance between Africa and South America, the quantum result is correct for only a short while—geologically speaking—both upstream and down. But you and I are anchored to the same spot by the product of temporal and gravitational interference. We cannot move in the spatial dimension while moving in the temporal dimension."

Britt stepped forward quickly so that her bust brushed up against Rusty's belly. She looked up at him. "Like this?"

With the chair behind him Rusty could not retreat. He held his ground, but sucked in his stomach in order to break body contact. "Exactly," he said, without relaxing his abdominal muscles. "We are carried along as if the surface of the Earth were a giant conveyor belt."

Britt placed her hands on Rusty's sides. "Now comes the part about the iceberg?"

Due to temperature control within the *Ark*, Rusty wore only shorts, T-shirt, and sandals. Goose bumps rose instantly on his skin. "That's right. You *do* remember. If I were floating across the sea on an iceberg, the distance and bearing to land would change constantly on a scale that I could measure. Well, calculating the distance between two points in time is the same thing. It's impossible to get off the temporal conveyor belt; we must move through time—we must flow from one point to another—because that is what gives length to our existence. Or, tautologically, without time flow our bodies could not exist. Any more than our minds can exist without the physical structure of the brain in which to store the sensory inputs that are the essence of our being."

"You are cute when you get flustered."

"So this temporal forward motion has to be taken into account when calculating the time delay to a specific destination, because we're moving all the time, and a calculation that's good for right now would be way off if I initiated the transfer five minutes from now, because of the geometric progression of time, and the further we want to go from our temporal position, the larger the chance is for error, and if we wanted to define a specific arrival time within the span of days, or even minutes, we'd have to perform the calculations way in advance based on a later departure time, but the dragons don't have to worry about this because they have no variable control and every transfer they make is preset according to their original placement on the temporal conveyor belt so they always arrive the same amount of time after the last transfer, thus avoiding a paradox—"

Rusty fell into the seat with a loud whoosh of air.

Britt plopped onto his lap. "I remember all that. Let us talk about something new."

His Adam's apple bobbed like a cork in a creek. "Do we have to?"

Britt nodded seriously. "No more calculations. I learn fast. I think it is time for us to flow on our own."

Rusty gulped. He opened his mouth to protest, but Britt covered his lips with hers.

*   *   *

Gale-force winds whipped across the ridge line, tossing particles of ice into Death Wind's face. The bark goggles protected his eyes, the fur-lined parka hood was pulled down over his forehead, and a scarf was drawn tightly across his mouth.

"There!" shouted Bold One, his voice barely audible over the shrill blasts of wind. He held out one arm and pointed with the four-finger pocket of his mitten.

They had been trudging through deep snow for hours. Death Wind hunched over with the blizzard at his back. In the near-total whiteout he had to blink several times before his eyes cleared; due to the dry air it was difficult to keep his eyes moistened. He squinted, but there was

nothing on which to focus but swirling snow clouds. "No see."

Somewhere up ahead should be the saddle that showed in the aerial photos. They hung back from the edge that could be a cornice; if the unstable snow bridge broke under their feet, they might plummet thousands of feet down the steep, ice-covered rock face.

"Wait." Bold One dropped his arm.

Nothing was visible but white fog. Father and son stood shoulder to shoulder in the freezing air, waiting for a temporary dissipation in the clouds. The spectral aura of the sun faded in and out of existence like a white globe that was dim enough to look at directly. Uneven gusts buffeted Death Wind from all sides, knocking him about. He clung to his father for support.

Bold One thrust out his arm again. "There!"

Death Wind saw a faint purple glimmer in the valley below. The dragon stronghold's time transfer equipment coruscated in the near distance. The sky cleared for a moment, affording a fine view not only of the alien structure in the middle of the glacier, but of the lower levels of the saw-toothed ridge.

One deeply carved notch dipped down to only a few hundred feet above the lateral moraine of the glacier in which the stronghold was situated. Both sides sloped gently enough to make an easy traverse for an army carrying weapons and supplies in shoulder packs and hauling travois.

"Good passage. We check." Bold One led the way down the precipitous ridge tooth. He slammed his feet down hard, gouging big imprints with his snowshoes that compressed the snow into a level platform.

Death Wind followed in his father's tracks. They sideslipped slowly down the mountain, at a pace geared to ensure the stability of each step. The barren higher altitudes soon yielded to snow-capped scrub pine, most of whose limbs and trunks were covered with snow. They made a wide detour around the trees, for the lower branches often concealed hollows that were gouged by the wind and which acted as traps for one unwary enough to get too close.

A large, white rabbit scampered into a snow hole at the Nomads' approach. Death Wind marveled at the proliferation of life even at this altitude and in these severe climatic conditions. Mice were seldom seen, but not rare; their prints abounded. The large pads of mountain lions and bobcats, or some ancestor of theirs, followed the smaller spoor. Glossy black hawks, oblivious to the frigidity of the upper atmosphere, soared on air currents that swept up the mountainside.

Bold One and Death Wind dropped a thousand feet with relative ease. Below the tree line the wind died out. The snow was piled deep on the gentle slope, and even in snowshoes the Nomads sank a foot or two into the soft fluff. With long, sweeping steps they charged through the stunted woods with savage exhilaration.

Great icefalls hung over granite cliffs like frozen tapestries. Death Wind broke off a slender icicle half his height in length, and sucked on it gratefully. The water was tainted with the flavor of surface minerals. He paid it no mind, as long as it coated his splitting lips and quenched his thirst. He did not worry about lowering his body core temperature because under the furs he was overheated by the exertion of travel.

They took a long circular route behind a rocky outcrop, eventually emerging from the miniature forest on a bluff that over-looked the saddle. Now that they had discovered a pass through the mountain range, they could take a more direct route back to where their companions struggled with their burdens over the snowfields.

"There." Death Wind pointed to a speck in the snow that glistened in the light of the sun. He moved to a position where the reflection did not shine directly into his eyes. The silvery glaze took on a dull orange color. "Stay."

Bold One crouched while his son scampered down the deeply piled snow to the base of the saddle. The wind was funneled through the depression by the high walls on either side. The rock was swept bare in spots. Pools of frosted ice collected in the lee of large boulders.

Death Wind slipped his knee-length moccasins out of the snowshoe bindings and dropped down on all fours. Slowly, cautiously, he approached the orange ball. It had recently been buried, but the shifting winds had swept away the covering of snow and created a huge drift a few feet away. It was clearly a manufactured object: a plastic globe whose surface was smooth and unbroken. Wires protruded from opposite sides, angled down into the ice, and disappeared into the snow.

The Nomad made no attempt to touch the ball. His gaze followed the direction of the wires. The prevailing wind ripped at his back,

forcing its way under his furs. Death Wind tucked the parka flap between his legs now that he was not trying to dispose of body heat.

He saw nothing else suspicious. Careful not to dislodge loose rocks or cause vibration of any kind, he backed away from the plastic globe. He waved to his father. A few minutes later they stood together.

Death Wind shook his head in silent communication. Bold One nodded.

As one they turned and took a course that would take them back by the shortest route to the band of warriors. They had discovered something of greater importance than a way across the mountains to the dragon stronghold.

CHAPTER 16

"This stuff smells awful."

Scott shoved another log onto the fire. "Quit complaining, and just think about how nice it'll make you feel the next time we get caught in a blizzard."

"That's hard to do when my body's this close to the fire and my nose is stuck in the fumes." Sandra stirred the malodorous brew in the cooking pot. "We have to eat out of this pot, too, you know."

Scott ladled out a portion of the viscous tallow and poured it into a plastic bowl. He tested the temperature with the tip of his finger. "Just right." He rolled up his sleeves, exposing white skin that was flaking from prolonged exposure to the dry, frigid ice-age conditions. He shivered involuntarily in the draft. "Whatever we don't use will grease the pan for dinner."

Slender Petal cut slivers of bear fat off a thick slab and placed them in the soot-blackened pot. "Inside, outside. Warm."

"Yeah, well, I'm not too keen on wearing this stuff, much less eating it." Sandra wrinkled her nose, and leaned back as far as she could and still keep the spoon moving. "Besides, I've put on too much weight already."

"My dear, you should not be concerned about obesity. It is normal for a woman in your condition to increase her body mass. It is Nature's way of providing extra warmth during gestation."

"Thanks for the vote of confidence, Pop."

"I say that as your doctor, not as your grandfather. It is also natural for people who live in colder climates to retain a higher percentage of body fat, most of it superficial and subcutaneous. Parturition, continued exercise, and a return to milder temperatures will bring about the return to your previous weight." Doc took a handful of fat, opened his fur coat, and rubbed the greasy glob over his midriff. He let out a groan of ecstasy. "Aaahh, once you put it on you will never want to take it off."

"Don't kid yourself." Sandra continued stirring the pot. "Scott, take my mind off this stinky concoction. What's all this talk about pre-elimination. And what's bootstrapping?"

Scott followed Doc's example and coated the rest of his body with grease. "It's another one of my theoretical brainstorms, this one based on the premise that the dragons didn't come to the Ice Age just to freeze their tails off. Everything they do has a perfectly logical reason within the parameters of their cold-blooded, reptilian intellect. Therefore, they chose this time zone with a specific purpose in mind."

Sandra shrugged. "Makes sense."

"With all the time in the world at their disposal, they can't possibly want to live here. Therefore, there must be something strategic about either the place or the time."

"The middle of a glacier doesn't sound very strategic. Not for a creature that's so lethargic in the cold that they can't move a muscle without thinking about it for a day and a half."

"Exactly. So we rule that out—at least on the count of probability. Unless, of course, there's some rationale for desiring arctic conditions. But we have no evidence for such speculation. So, even though we know the gradations of their time transport equipment are not fine enough to be more selective with respect to temporal displacement—that is, allowing them to land between ice ages instead of in the middle of one—why didn't they just go back another million years? The extra energy required to generate that much more time transmittal for what it would gain them in terms of a more suitable climate would appear to be worthwhile in the long run."

Sandra tilted her head and eyed Scott warily. "Okay, you're still making sense. What're your conclusions?"

"Deductions, not conclusions." Scott buttoned his fur coat, wiped greasy hands on his pants legs, and ticked off his fingers. "One, we know the dragons are here now. Two, since their

TTS was observed in use, we surmise they're also somewhen else. Three, there's an overriding motive in everything they do, one that is beneficial to them. Four, their presence in the Pleistocene is not accidental. Five, they have not yet accomplished whatever it is they came here to do—"

"How do we know that?"

"Because they're still here. If they had finished their mission, I bet they'd waste no time in hightailing it to tropical shores." Scott switched hands. "Six, they don't have air or ground transport—because we haven't seen any. They'd come after us in a flyer if they had one available. Seven, if they don't have spatial transport, they don't intend to stay in this time zone and emigrate to warmer weather. From which we deduce eight—that they will use time transport to find a better climate. Which means nine, the stronghold is a temporary advance base that will be abandoned when they accomplish their goal."

"If you don't get to the point soon you'll be taking off your moccasins."

"One of them, anyway. I've never had cold feet before, now it's halfway impossible."

Sandra grimaced. "Okay, the dragons didn't come here for a winter vacation. Then why?"

Scott held out both hands, palms outward and all ten fingers extended, and waved. "To liquidate *us*."

Pinched eyes glanced from Scott to Doc and back to Scott again. "The cold must have pierced your sinuses and frozen your brain. They aren't following us; we came here after them."

Scott wagged an index finger at her. "That's when you're wrong. You're still thinking in a straight line. When you're dealing with time travel the arrangement of events is variable, depending on your point of view. The end may come before the beginning, and the beginning may come after the end."

"Doc, see if he's got a fever. He's having hallucinations."

"If he is, we both are." Doc finished greasing himself, buttoned his coat, crossed his legs, and let himself down onto his fur bedroll by sliding down his cane as if it were a fireman's pole. He tucked the extra material under his buttocks as insulation from the icy floor. "I think you should hear him out. If nothing else, he has an imaginative sense of the macabre."

Scott said, "Is that a vote of confidence, or

castigation?"

"To one who is secure in mind the former is not necessary, and the latter ignorable."

Scott opened his mouth to rebut, then thought better of it. "Right."

The fire roared. Ice melting off the ceiling dripped like slow rain. Slender Petal continued to add chunks of frozen bear fat to the pot.

Sandra stirred the offensive brew. "The only thing that'll be liquidated in the near future is this ice cave. So get back to your story while we still have a roof over our heads. You were somewhere in the middle, between the beginning and the end, and going both ways at once."

On his knees, Scott shuffled closer to the burning logs. "Okay, what do you think about this? Since the dragons failed to kill us off in the future, what better plan could they have than to annihilate us in the past?"

"Huhn?" Sandra did another double take between Scott and Doc. "Scott, we wouldn't even be here if the dragons hadn't come here first. If they were going to lure us into a trap, even a lizard mentality could find a simpler and more creative way of doing it."

"But suppose they came here to slaughter the Cro-Magnons—our direct ancestors—in order to prevent their propagation? And our genesis?"

Sandra's jaw dropped. "Could—could they do that?"

"Why not?"

"Well, because, we exist. That's a fact. They know it, and we know it. You're talking in loops and circles. Where would we have come from if the Cro-Magnons became extinct? I mean, that's proof already that if that is their scheme then it's already failed. You can't escape the truth, even with time travel."

"I'm not talking about escaping the truth. I'm talking about changing it."

"You can't change the truth," Sandra protested, raising her voice in a mild, high-pitched whine. "Truth is what is."

"No. Truth is what we perceive it to be. Suppose, in a straightforward flow of time, the dragons sent here were hatched after the destruction of their Cretaceous ancestors, and were raised without any knowledge of past and future events. They'd have no preconceived notions about the reality of the future, if indeed there is such a thing as a future. Remember that time can be juggled about just like any other physical quantity."

"Don't be ridiculous. You're saying that what we don't perceive, isn't true. That's like saying that what you don't know, can't hurt you. We're not gods. Or cartoon characters, who don't fall until they realize they've walked off the edge of a cliff. Our perceptions can't change reality."

"I'm not saying they can. But maybe our perception of the flow of events is all wrong. Maybe our entire concept of the universe is based solely on the way our senses perceive reality. Like me looking at your back and having no idea how well built you are from the front. My point of view doesn't alter your shape."

Sandra stabbed a finger at him. "It may get you in trouble, though."

Scott remained serious. "If we accept the fact that finite minds cannot fathom an infinite universe, why can't we accept the fact that neither can we comprehend the workings of time within the framework of that universe? Infinity applies to time as well as to space. So what we see of it is limited by our senses. Which means that looked at from a different perspective, time may have variables of which we are unaware—of which we cannot *be* aware. So, when I talk about making changes in events that we think have been established by observation, I'm not suggesting that the events themselves can be changed, only that the continuity of those events can be perceived in other ways. In other words, there's no such thing as predetermination, postdetermination, or any determination. Everything in space and time is relative."

Doc hugged his knees to his chest. "I think you are obfuscating logic with tautology."

"And I think he's talking through his hat." Sandra banged the carved wooden spoon on the edge of the pot, placed it on the ground cloth, and backed away from the smoke. "I confess naivety to relativity, but I damn sure can't believe you can go around warping reality to fit your notions, whether they're preconceived, postconceived, or ill conceived. Maybe you think you can change the world, but sooner or later you're gonna come up against an incontrovertible truth."

Scott said, "If I recognize it when I see it, I'll fight it with polemics."

Doc sighed. "In that case I fear for the truth, because once you and Rusty put your heads together, the fate of the world is at risk."

Scott tilted his head, thinking over Doc's statement. "Right."

"But, I suppose that is the price one pays for leadership."

"I don't care what the price is, I'm not buying it." Sandra pulled her hood over her head because so much water was dripping from the roof of the ice cave that her hair was getting soaked. "But just for the sake of argument, let's say I believe your crazy conjectures. Whether the dragons know it or not, we're here to save the world. And whether they like it or not, we will."

"That's what I like: a positive attitude."

Sandra brushed him off with a wave of her hand. "What I don't get is how the dragons're gonna bump off the Cro-Magnons when nobody can find 'em." She cocked an eyebrow at Scott. "Or have they already exterminated 'em?"

Scott shrugged. "I don't think so. Or should I say, I don't believe it, therefore it's not true."

"Forget the fancy philosophy. Let's stick to visible facts. Without transportation the dragons can't gun down the Cro-Magnons. So whadda they expect 'em to do, commit suicide? Or come running into their paws pleading for execution? For that matter, where the hell *are* the Cro-Magnons? We haven't seen hide nor hair of 'em anywhere, and we passed plenty of cozy caves along the way. They should have been out there in the savanna where the Neanderthals were."

Scott shrugged again. "It's a big world. And they may be shy people. They could have run and hid whenever they saw us coming. But I'm sure they're here, because future anthropology says they have to be."

"Now you are contradicting your own ratiocination," said Doc. "You are joining cause and effect when in the universe you postulate there may be no such connection."

"Here we go again," Sandra scowled. "I wish you two would stop chasing your tails. It's so confusing."

"It is impossible to argue syllogistically about notions that have no foundation in human perception, and that operate beyond the rules of human logic."

"Well, as far as I'm concerned, what you see is what you get. You wanna make anything more out of it, you gotta prove it to me. I'm gonna wait till we get to the stronghold and see what gives before I make up my mind about all this time travel business. But if I see a Cro-Magnon on the way, I'm gonna tell 'im to watch out for crack-brained clods from the future who might think 'im right out of existence."

Scott laughed out loud, his voice echoing off the chamber walls. People huddled by neighboring fires turned at the outburst. Scott shrank into his parka in a sudden surge of self-consciousness. After the baleful stares melted away, he said in a low voice, "If it were that easy, I'd wake up from this dream and leave the dragons in distant memory. Then I'd pull them out of the past whenever I wanted to frighten little children into doing what they're told."

"Legendary legerdemain," said Doc with a grin.

"Whatever you call it, you better not scare my kids with any of your bogeyman stories. Life is scary enough as it is without making up any— DW!" Sandra jumped to her feet at her husband's approach. With him were Bold One, Sam, Helen, and Jane with the two furry pups on leashes. "When'd you get back?"

"I am back."

Sandra threw her arms around him. "Don't start talking in Nomad monosyllables again. Speak English."

"I'm gonna speak some language to both of 'em that you ladies might not wanna hear." The expression on Sam's face was anything but pleasant. "You know what these jokers went and did?"

Helen held firmly on to Sam's arm. "Now, Sam, you'd better curb your tongue and act with decorum."

"I'm gonna act like a general and give these two the dressing down they deserve. I told 'em not to go near the stronghold, just find a path and we would take it from—what am I telling you for?" Sam faced the two Nomads, who nonchalantly crowded close to the fire, hands outstretched over the flames, and stabbed a gloved index finger in the air. "You should have reported to me immediately when you saw the obvious approaches were mined. Suppose you'd gotten blown away? We'd never have known what hap—"

"They found mines?" Scott said incredulously.

Sam turned in frustration at the interruption. "Yes. Land mines. The dragons seeded 'em across all the easiest routes and buried 'em in the snow. Oh, these lizards are smart cookies, I'll give 'em that. They don't miss a trick. But these two—"

"I have done a bit of mine laying myself in the past—or rather, in the future. That is, in my past, but the Earth's future. Although, if we assume that universal synchronicity is a human convenience, I do not know that subjective tense has any communication value."

"Henry, what the hell are you talking about?"

Doc did not bother to stand; he huddled a little closer to the fire and looked up at the confused general. "The mine is a useful weapon in the arsenal of guerrilla warfare. I have slain more than one unsuspecting dragon with just such a device." Casting his gaze upon Bold One, he said, "Were these contact mines, or command detonated?"

Bold One crouched and threw an arm around Slender Petal's shoulder. He drew her close. "Wire from one to another."

"Hmmnn. Trip wires?"

"Insulated," offered Death Wind.

"Then that infers an electrically triggered mechanism. Sam, I fully concur. We have underestimated the dragons once too often in the past. Or was that the future? I guess it depends upon your temporal position relative to the event. In any case, this is a discovery of mammoth proportions. My congratulations to both of you for your perspicacity. The question that naturally arises is whether the mines were sowed as a purely protective measure, or whether the dragons are anticipating an assault."

Sam stood with his mouth agape.

Rubbing his beard thoughtfully, Doc went on, "Either way, prudence must be pursued."

"Henry, you're missing the point entirely—"

"No, Sam, I am missing nothing. These two braves have brought valuable intelligence that will guide us in a more forceful prosecution of the war against dragon domination. For that they should be praised."

"But I told them not to—"

"Sam, Sam, Sam. Hold back your anger." Doc rolled onto his side and pushed himself up to his feet. He leaned heavily against his cane. "Sam, you are doing a fine job of leading this rabble across the Pleistocene wastelands, fraught with the dangers of natural catastrophe and untamed beasts, and filled with the incertitude of reptilian attack from unknown quarters. We have had our casualties along the way: none fatal—"

"And I intend to keep it that way."

"—but none unexpected considering the hostilities that have confronted us. Against that remarkable record there can be no slander.

Nevertheless, you have become intractable. Your rank has altered your sensitivity to purpose."

"I didn't aspire to this commission, I was elected to it. But I took the office in good faith. I was given a duty to perform. And if I'm going to conduct this army in a military manner, I need the cooperation of every volunteer soldier under my command. I expect my orders to be obeyed."

"No one has ever questioned your authority."

"No one answers to it, either. I'm trying to keep this outfit together for mutual protection. I don't want the loss of good people on my head. But when these—scouts—take it upon themselves to exceed their orders—"

"The wise leader never stifles individual initiative."

"—they jeopardize the success of the entire operation, as well as endangering their own lives. I can't plan a campaign of surprise attack if someone is spotted. And we all agreed right at the beginning that this was to be a clandestine operation. When my best men are insubordinate, how is it going to affect the morale of the rest of the troops?"

"Sam, you are taking too strong a stand on administration and losing sight of the objective: to wage war. That means taking chances, it means sometimes yielding control to the soldiers in the field who have a closer view of the battle than you have from the rear, and it also means incurring fatalities: that is the grimmer but truer side of war. Some things cannot be changed."

Doc held his hands out to the two Nomads. "I love these men as my brothers. We have been together through much sorrow and suffering. We have fought shoulder to shoulder. And someday, each of us, in his own way, must die—perhaps for the cause that has banded us together. That is the chance that each soldier takes. He hopes, though, that his death will serve a greater purpose than he could have achieved by living. The swift stroke of mercy is the only justice that a soldier can hope to receive."

Sam, flustered by Doc's fustian, pulled off his mittens and ran his hands through his dark hair. "I know what you're doing, Henry. You're using elocution to cloud the issue."

"Not at all. I am merely adding temperance to your temper."

"That doesn't change the fact that my scouts keep forging ahead and taking chances."

"Henry, that is what scouts are supposed to

do. That is the definition of a scout: one who reconnoiters enemy territory. If the entire company blundered into that minefield, the results would be disastrous."

Sam held up his hands defensively. "I have no problem with that. But they should have turned back immediately and told me what we were up against. Instead, they went out across the glacier by an alternate route and explored ways to the stronghold. And that's where they could have given us away."

Doc looked dumfounded. He threw up his hands. "It had to be done sooner or later."

"But I would like to have had the army in reserve, so we could press forward an attack if they had gotten caught. Losing shock value is one thing, but completely giving up the element of surprise we can't afford to do—not when we don't know what we're up against."

When Doc shook his head, his great white mane waved like a broaching sea. "I still attach more importance to what they found than how they found it." Addressing Bold One, he said, "Did you also discover a way to the stronghold?"

Bold One nodded.

The faint glimmer of a smile touched Doc's lips. "Then there is a way over the ice despite the presence of deep crevasses in the glacier."

Bold One moved his head once to the left and once to the right. "Under."

CHAPTER 17

The alarms in Rusty's dream clanged incessantly. He tried to shut them off, but his dreams were always uncontrollable. The only way to silence the clamor was to wake up. Since he had been up half the night, that option was not the most desirable.

When he moved under the covers he felt a weight across his upper chest, and a warmth that was not all his own. He wanted to return into the delicious pleasure of dreamland, but the loud ringing would not let him. It was not until he opened his eyes that he realized that the alarm was not in his head, but on the bridge.

He flung aside the covers, slipped out from under Britt's arm, and leaped across her to the annunciator control board. He fanned a switch; the awful pealing stopped immediately.

Now fully awake, Rusty activated the inter-com and toned for input. The singsong notes of a harp played a brief message: someone coming. Rusty toned: acknowledged.

Nothing out of the ordinary was visible on the viewscreens. That meant that a sentry on all-night observation post must have relayed the approach call on a remote toner. Rusty opened the bubble shade; bright yellow sunshine flooded the bridge. Britt was standing in the golden rays, unappareled except for a quixotic smile, soaking in the radiant energy like a flower about to bloom.

It was not until he stood watching her for several seconds that Rusty remembered his own state of undress. He turned aside quickly and fumbled in the bedding for his shorts. He slipped his feet into moccasins.

"I'd better go see what it is."

Britt made no effort to cover her body. "I wait at console."

Nervously, Rusty pecked her cheek as a chicken might peck at a kernel of corn. "Bring the reactor power up to full emergency mode."

"Aye, aye, Skipper."

Rusty was totally disarmed by her charming, carefree manner. He managed a smile and winked at her as he pulled a shirt over his head on the way down the ramp. "And get ready for liftoff, just in case."

The lower decks were a flurry of activity as the crew scrambled to general quarters. Rusty ran down the entrance ramp behind a squad of heavy gunners who were hauling a dismounted Gatling gun out of the ship. They headed for a prepared bunker that was left unarmed in case it became imperative to move the *Ark* instead of standing and fighting.

"What is it, Ned?"

"There's a runner coming in. I hit the siren 'cause I didn't know if anyone—or anything—was chasing her. But now I got word she's bringing a message from the front."

Despite the early morning chill, Rusty wiped sweat off his brow. "Whew, I'm glad of that. I just hope it's good news. It's been four days since their last communication."

"Could be mechanical breakdown."

"Four radios, all at the same time?"

"Mountains in between."

"We were picking them up fine till they missed a call." Rusty strode out beyond the undercarriage, into the full light of the sun. He turned and waved at the overhead camera lens.

Britt waved back from the clear plastic bridge canopy. "How long?"

"Perimeter guard picked her up and is escorting her in. They should be here—"

An owl hooted from the tree line at the edge of the grove.

The clatter of weapons melded with the pounding of feet on the trampled grass as back-up troops tumbled into position behind makeshift bulwarks. Slowly, the muffled racket faded until nothing stirred but a few insects that buzzed in the light mist and the livestock in the corrals. Goats, pigs, and large wild birds seemed not to notice the tension in the air.

When the militia was fully mobilized, a guard chirped from the hidden safety of a bunker.

The owl hooted again. Two people stepped through the thick layer of brush: a tall man who looked like a scarecrow with most of his straw plucked out by crows, and a young woman who would have had to wear more than a loincloth and halter top to weigh more than a hundred pounds. The woman's long black, braided hair and reddish skin branded her a Nomad. Her narrow chest heaved slightly from the exertion of her marathon run. Rusty remembered her as Swift Fox.

"Greetings," she said.

"Greetings," Rusty replied.

"Men stick together."

"It is code."

"All are safe."

Rusty felt his entire body go limp. He had not even realized how tense he was. The release from fear that his companions had been massacred filled him with renewed energy, and took from him the awesome responsibility that he had made the wrong decision by sticking to the original plan not to lift ship until he had proof that the invasion force had failed its mission.

"You bring good news, Swift Fox."

The Nomad acknowledged with a faint nod of her head.

A host of questions wanted to roll off Rusty's tongue all at once. He curbed his excitement. With forced resolve he framed his thoughts toward obtaining the most pertinent intelligence first. "Why did Scott stop transmitting?"

"Radio waves bring dragon death from sky."

"What death? I thought you said everyone was okay?"

Swift Fox repeated patiently. "All are safe. Dragon death come on wings of flame, like

spear that burst. But all are safe."

Rusty did not talk down to Swift Fox in simulated Nomad dialect. "You mean, the dragons fired a missile that exploded without killing anyone?"

Swift Fox nodded. "Get to cover."

"What makes you think the radio brought it?"

"Destroy radio after tone talk. Doc say no use again. Bring more."

"Damn!" Rusty ran his hands through curly locks that had long since passed the description of shaggy. "The dragons must have triangulated their position after the first transmission within range of the stronghold."

"Never underestimate a dragon," said Ned. "The problem now is how're we gonna coordinate an attack without fast and firm communication? We can't synchronize timers if we have to wait for days between messages."

Swift Fox replied, "Sam say first objective is to stop dragon sky death. Call when safe."

Rusty pursed his lips. "I don't like it. Negative communication leaves too much chance for error."

"On the other hand, if we go in there with guns blazing we're likely to get blown to pieces as soon as they get a fix on us. And who knows, they may have a ground radar warning network." Ned addressed the Nomad runner. "Swift Fox, how close were they to the stronghold when you left?"

"Two, three days."

"Hell, they could be there already." Turning to Rusty, he said, "Maybe we oughta sneak a little closer with the *Ark*. At least that would shorten the supply line."

"No. Sam said to stay put until he sent further orders."

"And Doc said to use your own initiative."

"He meant if they got into trouble and there was no other way to stop the dragons. He said most definitely not to be influenced by their plight. You know Doc."

"Yeah, but I ain't gonna stand by and let 'em get slaughtered without going in after 'em, no matter what he says."

"And I'm not going to take a chance on losing the *Ark*. She's too valuable." Rusty covered his mouth with his hand and squeezed his lips between his fingers. "She's our only way out of here and now."

"How about if we pull in our sentries so we're ready to fly at a moment's notice?"

"Do it." Rusty faced an external microphone. "Britt, are you getting all this?"

Britt replied on the toner.

"Good. Get the *Ark* shipshape. I'll help out here. Ned, let's get the livestock loaded."

"Want it butchered first?"

"No, we'll keep them fresh."

"How 'bout that pliohippus the Nomads've been training to haul the carts."

Rusty was on his way across the clearing to give orders to the men and women in the bunkers. "Sure, bring the whole herd. Horsepower is something we never have enough of."

* * *

Scott was having a difficult time in picking his way up the boulder-strewn ravine. Rock slabs that had sheared off the vertical walls lay at awkward angles that were impossible to climb, and whose sharpened edges barked his shins more than once.

"You never did explain about bootstrapping," Sandra insisted.

Breathing hard, Scott struggled to keep up with her. Being pregnant and near the end of her term did not slow her down at all. What was worse, the gals hauling the travois were way ahead; they had doubled their loads, left half the travois behind, and put two gals in the traces of the remaining reins. Only the cannon was behind.

"Yes, well, I was interrupted at the height of my revelations."

"So tell me now. You got something better to do?"

Scott's stump slipped on the wet rocks. "All this moss makes it hard to get a foothold."

"Yeah, I know what you mean. I've bounced off my belly more than once. Don't be surprised if I have an early labor."

"That's all we need." Scott leaped across a trickle of water to firmer ground. Beside him a noisy cascade of glacial runoff splashed into the cold air. "You could have stayed behind."

"What? And miss all the fun? Not a chance. Besides, I've got a sling all rigged up. After the kid is born, I'll just carry 'im on my back like the Nomads do. Having babies doesn't mean dropping out of life, you know."

"I know. It's just that this is pretty rough terrain." Scott got down on all fours as he scrambled up the side of a rounded, house-sized boulder. "If Jane were as far into her term as you are, I wouldn't want her to take a chance of losing the baby."

"That's life in the wilderness, Scott. And I have to give you credit. You're doing okay for a guy with one foot."

There was little enthusiasm in Scott's voice. "Thanks."

"No, I mean it. I think you're fantastic." Sandra stopped for a break. She plopped down on a dry slab where the stream bubbled quietly underneath. "You could have stayed with the *Ark* and nobody would have thought you were wimping out."

Scott untied the sleeves of his parka from around his waist, laid the fur out on the rock, and settled down beside her, grateful for the rest. He never would have made it up the rocky creek bed with the heavy laser gun; he was glad it had been disintegrated by the dragon missile. "You know how I am: always trying to prove something to myself."

"You've proved it to me." Sandra took a plastic cup from her knapsack and dipped it in the stream where the current kept it fresh. "I think you're quite a guy."

Scott's scowl turned into a frown. He accepted the cup and took a long draft of the clear, cold water before speaking. "Did Jane put you up to this?"

"Up to what?"

"You know. Feeding my ego. I've heard more kind words from you in the past hour than in all the time I've known you."

Sandra took the cup and scooped another drink of water from the glacier-fed stream. "Are you counting all the way back to the Cretaceous?"

With the lack of physical activity, it did not take long for Scott to feel the numbing chill. He pulled the parka over his shoulders; it was long enough to still pad his seat. "I guess I have been feeling underfoot lately." He tapped his stump on the ground. "I just can't help it."

"Scott, I know how difficult it must be dealing with your—loss. But that doesn't change who you are—or what you've accomplished. Your true self is no different, only your self-image. Let yourself go, and be what you can be with what you have."

"Footloose and fancy free, huhn?"

Sandra stabbed him with a finger. "See, you can joke about it."

"I know. But that's just a front for the pain I'm keeping inside. It's the kind of thing I don't want to talk about because—well, partly because it hurts so much." Scott absently chucked stones in the stream. He watched the splashes that were quickly carried away by the current. "Partly because I'm afraid of imposing sentiment on people who have other things on their minds."

"Scott, we started this venture together—a long time ago, it seems, although the events have yet to happen in the continuity of this world. And I don't understand any of that stuff. But you do; you're brilliant. I know I've been pretty hard on you in the past—and in the future. But I've grown up since then. I'm a different person now. And I love you. Uh, you know what I mean."

Scott patted her thigh in a brotherly fashion. "I know what you mean."

"So, don't shut me out. Whenever you have a problem, I'm here. Whenever you want to talk about something, my time is your time."

"When you have a time machine, your time is everyone's time."

Sandra slapped his leg playfully. "Stop being silly. I'm trying to be serious."

"Sorry. But as long as we're making up, do we get to kiss?"

She slapped him again. "You never let up, do you?"

Scott cocked an eyebrow. "Should I?"

"No. I guess it's part of your charm." She leaned close to give him a smack on the cheek. Scott spun his head quickly and caught the kiss on the lips. Sandra jerked back as if she had been electrocuted. Slowly, her look of astonishment changed to one of amusement. "Okay, you got me that time. But that's the Scott I like to see."

"Want to try it again?"

"Sometimes I wonder whether you're a guerrilla—or a gorilla."

"Just keep in mind that wherever or whenever you are, you're the gorilla my dreams." The clatter of the gun carriage echoed up the ravine. Four men pulled the traces while two women pushed the cannon from behind. Scott pushed himself up off the rock. "Well, I guess it's time to go." He held out his hand. "My lady?"

Sandra allowed herself to be helped up. "You've always got some trick afoot, don't you?"

"Touché. "

They hopped boulders adjacent to the stream;

they angled away from a raging waterfall that spewed droplets in the air that soaked their outer clothing. They scrambled up a steep embankment to an isolated patch of earth on which grew a grove of trees—an island in the middle of the gorge. People who were congregating ahead indicated that they were close to the headwaters.

"You still haven't told me about bootstrapping," Sandra insisted.

Scott walked more slowly, stopping every few steps to catch his breath. "That's because it's more fancy than fact. But I'll lay it on you. Suppose the dragons refined their time travel technique to the point when they could travel short spans—say, on the order of minutes, or seconds. If they played their paw straight, they could create an army of infinite size by looping their soldiers through time."

"Huhn?"

A fine mist hugged the ground, carrying with it a biting cold. Scott snugged his parka around his chest and pulled up his hood.

"Take a sample soldier who's going into battle. Before the attack you send him back through time, say, an hour. Then, he joins his former self on the battlefield. Now you've got two soldiers standing side by side, one who an hour later will go back through time to become the other."

"But I thought you and Rusty said you couldn't meet yourself without causing some kind of cosmic disorder—or dissolution."

"We don't know that, we just can't conceive a cause and effect relationship that would account for it. Anyway, now you take soldier B and send him back through time. He then becomes soldier C. Do it again, and you have soldier D. Eventually you can create an entire army from a solitary soldier."

"No, you can't, because when soldier B goes into the time machine you've lost him into the past. He's no longer around to fight."

"Okay, so you wait until after the battle and send back one of the survivors. Then, you don't let him fight until he duplicates himself a few more times."

"But, if you keep sending them back through time, when do they get to fight?"

"Well, you stretch your time span over a couple days instead of an hour. Then you have them go into combat after they've all been looped."

"But, what if one of them gets killed?"

"That's the beauty of it. They're impossible to kill because all but the last one will have gone through time to create the successive downstream versions. The continued existence of the army is predetermined."

"Now wait a minute. You keep arguing that predestination is a godlike conceit that can't happen in the real world."

"What is real? What you see, or what you get?"

Sandra tilted her head, wincing with one eye. "Didn't I already state my position on that?"

"The circumstances were different. The question in this case is, how many soldiers do you have to fight if a hundred of them are facing you, despite the fact that they're all downstream versions of the same soldier?"

"Well . . ."

"Accordingly, you can kill only one—the last one to go through time. And you still have to face ninety-nine more. If they were smart, they'd put the final version in a safe place where he would be protected. The only way you could destroy the army would be to knock off the soldiers one by one—in the proper order from last to first."

Sandra was silent for a moment. "Oh, yeah? What if you attack from the rear and knock off the original soldier? Then the rest would instantly disappear because he wouldn't be alive to go through the time machine in order to create all the rest."

"Are you sure?"

"Hell, no. I'm not sure about anything anymore."

"Want to give it a try?"

"No!" she whined. "One of me is enough for this world. Besides, I don't think it'd work because the first me would have preknowledge of what was going to happen, because I'd suddenly find myself surrounded by all my subsequent versions—which is a way of preordaining what I was—or am—going to do. Then, if I changed my mind—"

"As women are wont to do."

"—or didn't do it out of spite, I'd really get the world in trouble because my inaction would alter reality."

"You can't alter reality by going through time any more than you can change the world by crossing space. It's all a matter of perception."

They stopped a hundred yards from the base of a thousand-foot-tall cliff of ice. Scott had been so intent on his footing that he failed to look ahead until he stepped into the penumbra.

He looked up and saw blocks of ice the size of buildings lying in a gargantuan jumbled heap.

A torrent of water spewed from the base of the terminal moraine. The icy river charged over a cataract, spinning and thunderous. The people standing at the base of the glacier were dwarfed by the ten-mile-wide flow of ice.

"Scott, you're crazy."

"That, too, is a matter of perception."

CHAPTER 18

"Glaciers do form creeks and rivers, but usually not of such immensity. The normal rise in global temperature would occur slowly—over thousands of years—causing glaciers to shrink by a reduction of accumulating snowfall. Even during the age of overall glacial recession, I doubt that tunnels like this were carved by natural erosion."

Doc stood on the broad bank of solid ice immediately inside the cavern mouth. The glacier's terminal moraine was unstable; constantly calving blocks of ice that weighed many tons. No one stood in its shadow for fear of being crushed. Those approaching the entrance did so hastily.

"But in this case the process of thawing has been aided by the dragons' need to melt out a stronghold. The heat generators are probably a by-product of their nuclear fission reactor plant. Very efficient, really, since the ice undoubtedly helps to cool the core."

"If you're finished admiring dragon techniques and technology, and can shelve your scientific curiosity, we can get on with the final briefing."

"Pardon me, Sam." Doc tore his gaze from the vaulting, icebound grotto, and joined the war council that encircled the general. "It is true that I sometimes tend to babble over imponderables, but in this case I think that my observations will augment those of Bold One and Death Wind. They may have explored a mile or so up this glacial ice cave, but I have explored much further with my mind."

The ceiling arched fifty feet overhead and curved down to the floor with walls that were glazed to a smooth, scintillating finish. The river lay at the bottom of a deep, narrow gorge. The upper level was wide enough on each side for several armies to spread out their cooking fires.

The cave was contoured much like a mushroom, with the river flowing along the base of the stem, and the upper floor pasted to the frilled underside of the umbrella-shaped cap.

Sam gritted his teeth. "Sorry, Henry. You didn't deserve that. I'm just anxious. Small-time skirmishes I've lived with all my life. I'm just not cut out to be a general who is waging all-out war."

"No one is. And you have every right to be jittery. We are facing what is likely to be the biggest skirmish of all time."

Sam inhaled deeply. "Then let's get it over with so I can give up the commission. I just want to be a farmer and grow vegetables. Now, what point were you trying to make?"

"Simply that I am fairly certain that this highway under the glacier will take us unopposed all the way to the dragon stronghold. Apparently, this horizontal plateau was formed when the dragons melted a hollow where their time transport structure first appeared in this time zone. The initial flood of hot water thawed the ice and created this broad, domed cavern. After the major excavation was completed, the continued flow of melt water gouged this deeper, thread-like notch. I suppose it is not a particularly astute observation, but it should put our minds at ease about the viability of our method of infiltration."

Sam cast his eyes down at the frozen floor. "Thanks, Henry. That's important to know."

"I'll say it's important!" shouted Sandra. "Most of our attack plans revolve around what to do if we run up against an ice wall. I say let's take his word for it. If there's anything in our way, we can melt or chop through it. And we got enough rope to bridge the Grand Canyon."

"Okay. Okay." Sam held up his hands, palms outward. "I agree. Let's just take a count of supplies and pick the rear guard."

Scott wolfed down the last of a bison steak as he hitched himself to the reins of Jane's travois. "This is where the pregnant women stay behind." He wiped his mouth on his furred sleeve.

"Wisht I had one ta leave behind." Windy snugged the laser nozzle in its holster and shouldered the battery pack. His face was nearly the same color as his parka, making him practically invisible inside his upraised hood. "I think ma philanderin' days're over. After this I'm gonna settle down permanent like."

Broderick scoffed. "I will believe that when I see it." He formed the First Fusiliers into ranks and counted them off his slate. Windy did the same for the Texas Rangers.

When the outfit was ready to depart, Jane hugged her husband and kissed him longingly. "Take care, Scott. I love you."

"I love you, too, Honey." He cinched the straps across his chest. "You keep that radio handy. As soon as we're in the clear, I'll give you a tone. Then we'll get Rusty to bring the magic carpet and fly you to the front. Okay?"

"Okay."

Scott tightened the leather thongs that held the makeshift crampons to his moccasins. The flat wooden boards armed with sharpened plastic spikes offered perfect traction on the slippery ice. The moccasins' padded soles and uppers not only kept his feet warm, but prevented the stoppage of circulation from the laces.

They kissed again. Scott leaned against the traces, amazed at how easily the plastic runners slid over the smooth ice. It took very little effort. He passed Death Wind and Sandra, who were still locked in a full body embrace. "Hey, cut it out, or you'll melt the ceiling down on top of us."

Sandra stuck out her tongue at him, then went back to hugging Death Wind. They talked softly to each other. Scott crunched ahead to get out of hearing range. The tiniest sound was magnified by the strange acoustical qualities of the ice cave. Helen and Slender Petal trudged together, fifty feet in front of him.

"The dragons will hear us five miles off," Scott whispered as he caught up to Doc. The cave reverberated the crunching of crampons on ice; it sounded like the tearing of a hundred sheets of paper of unending length.

"I doubt that even a supersensitive seismograph can pick up our vibrations. Although they appear to be stationary, glaciers are in a constant state of flow: they are, in fact, extremely slow-moving rivers of ice. The constant crackling of internal stress produces much more sound than we could possibly make."

"Doc, you're always so reassuring. You have an answer for everything."

"One of my finer qualities, my boy. Knowledge is often its own reward, for it soothes the pain of ignorance."

The strange procession advanced along the tubular ice cave like a cabal of witch hunters. Flaming brands, made from stripped branches that were lashed together and dipped in tallow, flickered eerily in the gathering darkness. The crystalline structure of the ice reflected the yellow glow like a magnificent, multifaceted jewel.

"Then you must be the most pain-free person in the world."

Somewhere ahead, an electric beam powered by a battery pack stabbed out with the intensity of an aircraft landing beacon. The laser gun nozzles were removable, and a variety of accessories such as lights, heaters, and power tools were designed to operate off the stored amperage. Each attachment came with its own transformer. The light bounced off the ceiling, swung down into the deep gorge, glinted off the rippling surface of the river, then switched off.

"Perhaps. Although too much knowledge can sometimes be a bane. Take this cavern for example." Doc pointed his cane, with its tip now honed to needle sharpness, in a sweeping arc in front of him. "It has certainly not escaped you that such a cavity cannot have been sculpted overnight. Unaided geological activity would have taken eons, no doubt, to carve such an immensity. And while I indicated the unnatural building process that created this intraglacial boulevard, I did not expound upon the span of time necessary to gouge such a tunnel."

Scott hardly noticed the slight upgrade. "If you're trying to make a point, get to it before the Ice Age is over."

Doc chuckled. His deep-throated titter resonated hollowly in the ice cavern. "Quite right, my boy. Quite right. The gist of the idea is that this twenty-mile-long tube is not a recent development. The dragons must have been here much longer than we heretofore suspected."

"Are you saying that they didn't come here as a last resort, but sometime contemporaneous to their other temporal invasions?"

"Precisely."

The silence was broken only by the crunching of crampons on ice.

"Well, go on."

"Oh, I have no inferences to make. It is merely an interesting observation."

"But, doesn't that bother you? That the construction of the stronghold was—premeditated?"

"As opposed to being precipitated by our actions against them? No, it does not worry me. But it does make me curious as to its original purpose. If not as an escape mechanism, what?"

Scott chewed on that for a while. Neither he nor Doc carried a light. So much illumination was reflected by the floor, walls, and ceiling, from the torches of others, that none was necessary. They trudged along in the wake of the brigade. The foundation of ice was flat and featureless, without dents or moguls.

"I see what you mean. About too much knowledge, that is."

"No matter how many answers you have, there is always another question to lead you on."

"I'm learning that. I'm also beginning to see that the dragons are a lot more devious than I ever gave them credit for, and their machinations more insidious."

"We have underestimated their resourcefulness nearly as often as they have underestimated ours. In the final analysis, it is not he who is better armed who turns the tide of war, but he who is more imaginative."

Scott grimaced in the dark. "If that's the case, I've shown the imagination of a potato. You know, when I think back on everything we've seen and done, I realize that the script for this entire intertemporal war was written in the geological strata, if only we'd known how to interpret the clues. The Great Dying, plate tectonics—inscribed in stone for all to read, if only you have the key. Up till now."

"By 'now' do you mean the Pleistocene, or our placement along the stream of universal events?"

"Anymore, Doc, I don't know what I mean." Scott loosened the shoulder straps and tightened the waist belt, in order to change the stress points and to relieve pinched muscles. He was not comforted by the fact that Jane had hauled the heavy load for weeks without complaint. "But it scares me that, knowing now what I know about the past—the straight-line objective past of the Earth—that I don't recognize anything in the stratigraphic record that gives a clue to which side conquers in Armageddon."

"Evidence is sometimes circumstantial, conspicuous by its absence."

"Meaning?"

"Meaning that a word-for-word rendering does not always offer the best translation. The language of the rocks is as idiomatic as human speech. Call it geological syntax, if you will. By reading what is not written, I have my suspicions about the final turn of events."

"Well, let me have it between the eyes. Both

barrels."

There was a long pause before Doc spoke again. "I think for now—the circuitous, subjective now of my personal life line—I will keep my own council. Predictions are so self-indulgent."

"Come on, Doc. You've never been wrong in your life." Scott danced ahead and tapped his truncated leg on the ice. "Granted, you've got two feet to stick into your mouth instead of one, but that's never stopped you before from speaking your mind. You're self-indulgent to the point of exasperation."

"Thank you, Scott. I suspect I have had that coming for a long time."

"Half a dozen epochs, at least."

Doc paused again, longer. "Let us just say that our very existence presupposes that we are the masters of our own fate."

"You're talking in riddles."

Doc planted his cane in the ice and shoved off against it as if it were a ski pole. His limping gait and rhythmical cane crunching gave the sound of his passage an offbeat three-quarter cadence. "Such is life."

CHAPTER 19

The shock troops camped that night under a crevasse. In the morning, sunbeams stabbed through the opening like golden spears.

Scott awoke well rested despite the difficulties of travel late in the day. The initial tractable, smooth floor had soon given way to cracks and upthrusts that required caution and hard work to traverse. Even so, they had eaten up the miles of rough ice with the staunchness of will with which they tackled the snowfields in the rage of a gale.

Slender Petal crouched by a fire. The cooking pot held stew, and a kettle steamed with hot water. "Hungry?"

It seemed strange to be hundreds of feet beneath the ice and still be able to see the sky. Scott had fallen asleep under a strip of stars that sped across the narrow opening like a parade in review. Now he lay in the reflected light of the sun; it bore no heat other than that felt in the heart. "I'm always hungry."

Slender Petal smiled with her eyes.

Scott thrust aside his fur coverings and spent several minutes in doing calisthenics before dipping his mug into the kettle and drawing out his allotment of tea. The muscular friction of exercise coupled with the hot, spiced liquid gave him a delicious glow of warmth. By the time he was ready for something more solid in his stomach, Bold One and Death Wind were returning from the part of the crevasse that extended below the level of the flood plain.

"Any problem?" Scott asked.

Bold One shook his head.

"Make bridge," Death Wind explained. "Travois."

Scott nodded. He could hear the sounds of hammering. "With all the ice fractures we've been encountering, it's probably a good idea to not bother reassembling the travois, and carry the timber as trestle material."

"My thoughts exactly." Doc sat up in his bedding, wincing as he stretched his arms over his head. "But if we bring our bridges with us, it means that we can no longer send back runners. This will be our last communication with the outside world."

Scott glanced at the cooking fires that were scattered across the ice cave. Most people were already packing their meager belongings for the day's march. He saw Sam calling orders down the crevasse, while Helen played an electric light on the road crew.

As soon as everyone had eaten his fill, the fires were damped and the utensils were loaded. Crossing the fissure required time and cooperation. A path had been hacked in the ice down to a ledge where the logs spanned the bottomless rift. Each person tied a rope around his waist before tramping across the logs; the safety line was belayed from both sides. Crampons jammed into the wood, coupled with the taut ropes, made an otherwise precarious crossing routine. Getting the equipment across took more effort, but was effected by means of the same procedure.

"You know, Doc, suppose this whole thing is a trick?"

"What thing is that?"

Because of the rough terrain and Scott's difficulties with loss of footing, he had been relieved of his towing job. He had nothing to bear but his thoughts. "Well, maybe the dragons deployed those mines in order to steer us into a trap."

"That *is* food for thought." Doc mulled it over in silence. He let Scott pull him up a pressure ridge and help him down the other side. "The possibilities are endless if we want to play intellectual games of who is outsmarting whom."

"That's what worries me. I always wonder if we're one step ahead of them, or one step behind. When you have only one step it becomes a precious commodity."

They passed under another gap in the ceiling. Tortured chips of ice hailed down in the frigid draft. The stark sunlight illuminated the way for hundreds of yards on either side of the opening. Far ahead, Scott saw another open shaft; and beyond that, another. He came to a deep furrow that broiled with water. The troops were taking turns in leaping the gap. A Fusilier stood safety by the jumping-off point, using his battery light to shine the way as each person hopped over the crevice.

Scott stood on his good leg and swung his other back and forth as he prepared for the spring. "I'm about one foot from serious trouble." He vaulted into the air, scissored his legs in midstride, and came down on his real foot. He turned and held out his hand. "Come on, Doc. You can make it."

Doc did not hesitate, but made a limping, running jump that carried him clear across the void and into Scott's waiting arms. Crampons bit deep into the ice, pinioning Doc to the smooth surface like a weighted schmo doll. "These legs have not lost *all* their elasticity."

Scott had to pull Doc's feet out of the ice one at a time. "You never cease to amaze me."

They climbed up the ice embankment and forged ahead.

By midafternoon, Scott was forced to remove his heavy furred parka. "Is it me, or is it getting warm in here?"

"I can feel the temperature changes whenever we pass under a surface vent." Doc unbuttoned his coat and tied it around his waist by the arms. His great shock of white hair billowed above his head. "Do you feel the breeze? A siphon effect is caused by the mass of warm air escaping down the tunnel and out through interstitial flues."

"The river's falling, too," Scott observed. "Or else the channel is broader here. Maybe the hot water has hollowed out a big under-ice grotto."

The cave was also filling with fog. As warm water contacted the cold tunnel walls, evaporation took place on the surface. White streamers of mist rose off the river like dancing wraiths.

"I suggest that we stay away from the edge.

There is likely to be undercutting and collapse."

"Good idea. I'll pass the word along." Scott dashed ahead to a Femme Fatale, a former Charon resident, and gave her the message. He waited for Doc. "Let's veer toward the wall."

Where the ceiling curved down at the cave's edge, dripping ice formations created a fairyland spectacle of stalactites, stalagmites, and joined columns. Several Rangers were exploring the crystalline city; their lights shone through the vertical maze in breath-taking wonder. Icicles sparkled like diamonds. The magic was made more dazzling by the constant wavering of flaming brands and the crisscrossing beams of electric torches.

Scott broke off a shaft of ice as long and as thin as a pencil, and sucked the water off the sharpened tip. "Good." He bit off the end, then chewed the ice like candy. "It must still be below freezing in here."

Doc snapped off a piece of ice and stuck it between his teeth. "Just barely. Only the sheer mass of the floe prevents the glacier from melting away completely. It serves as its own insulation."

"Watch your head, Doc. These things'll pierce your skull like a needle though sackcloth." Heeding his own warning, Scott backed away from the wonderful landscape, breaking off stalagmites with his feet. "And you could impale yourself easily on these ice spears."

Doc scooped a delicate fragment off the floor and held it up in front of his eyes. "Beauty is often deceiving." He tested the point with a gnarled finger. "Such treacherous elegance."

Farther on they came across columns as fat as trees, and as many as a forest. Their ribbed exteriors glimmered with melted wetness. Flat, faceted leaves of ice, each with a pattern as distinctive as that of a snowflake, curled off the trunks of ice like peeling bark. The floor was damp and strewn with puddles.

Moisture-laden air rose from the river gorge, curled along the icy ceiling, and dripped down in a constant drizzle that was driven by the ever-increasing draft. Wind racing along the wave tops whipped the river surface to an icy froth; foam flecked the edge of the plateau.

The floor tilted downward, its surface solid and without fractures or folds. Great ripples, each the size of a humpback whale, were planted permanently in the ice. Torch-bearing troopers in staggered disarray looked like fireflies flitting across a milky, moonlit savanna. In the limited illumination, the frozen cascade could have been a surrealistic impression of the descent into purgatory.

Far, far away, seen dimly through the clinging haze, a glowing purple dot hovered in an indistinct, horizonless void. "Somehow, I expected to see more," said Scott.

"You will," said Doc, and after a pause, he added, "after sunrise."

*   *   *

Dawn was slow in coming.

Not even the Nomads, master scouts that they were, dared venture into the nebulous realm of the dragon stronghold until the visibility cleared. The sun was an amorphous, dull-white globe that drifted in and out of sight as the morning mists burned off. The ethereal landscape glimpsed through the overcast reminded Scott of Charon at nearly full scale.

"I never grasped the size of it from the snapshots." Scott sat on his haunches on a high bluff of ice that overlooked the stronghold; he felt like an eagle in its aerie. "I thought it was nothing more than a way station, or at most a city in miniature. It looks like a well-developed community."

"There is no traffic yet, although it is a bit early in the morning to expect dragons to be up and about." Doc sat on his furs with his legs stretched out before him and his chin resting on his cane. He wore only long-sleeved underclothing. "They must move with extreme sluggishness under these conditions."

"I think it's kind of temperate."

Despite the solid ice underfoot, the atmosphere was warm and muggy. Water ran in rivulets over frozen hummocks to the edge of a sheer precipice, then cascaded several hundred feet into a clear lake.

Death Wind munched on a blackened steak. "We will soon see dragons."

"That is a prediction I acquiesce to," said Doc.

The entire guerrilla company stood on alert, like sports fans in the bleachers of a stadium. They watched and waited.

As the fog lifted, the evanescent purple glow resolved itself into a time transport structure that occupied the center of the hollow. From rim to rim the haze-filled basin measured five miles across. The melt water that formed the central river flowed around the TTS, creating a moat

that was crossed by a twin-span drawbridge on either side.

The stronghold complex was bisected by the rampaging watercourse; each side was a mirror image of the other. There were duplicate nuclear reactor plants, transmission stations, workshops, and living quarters, all intermingled with lush jungle growth, grain fields, and dinosaur pens. Four squat, multilevel tenements, constructed of orange plastic and lined with windows, dominated the hidden sanctuary; they occupied the four diagonal corners, and beyond each lay a yawning hole that tunneled through the base of the continental glacier.

Steam pipes radiated from the generating stations like giant spider webs; the conduits were buried under plastic roadbeds, and were discernible only by the coiling wreaths of vapor that were discharged into the air to fight the severe cold of the natural climate. The hot air that rose to meet the cold caused a chronic layer of condensation that hovered hundreds of feet above the artificial valley; the light drizzle never ceased, nor did the air ever fully clear.

Most of the dragon stronghold was permanently cloaked in a thick, miasmal distillate.

"Here they come!" Scott pointed to the nearest tunnel entrance, practically underneath him.

Wisps of steam intermittently obscured the scene, but during spells of clearing he saw dragon slaves shuffling along the orangetop. They were clothed in loose-fitting, reflective garments that left the limbs and tail exposed. None strayed far from the vapor vents.

"With all this smoke, I don't think we'll see much about how this place operates."

"Do you recognize anything that could be a missile silo?" Doc wanted to know.

"There's too much ground cover. Any of those tall buildings could hide a launching pad."

"Death Wind, you've got the sharpest eyes here. Can you see any signs of defense armament, gun emplacements, guard shacks?"

The Nomad slowly shook his head.

"I don't like it, Doc. It looks too simple, like we could prance right in. It's not like a dragon to go undefended."

"Perhaps they never expected to have enemies in the Pleistocene."

Scott detected the sarcasm in his voice. "You don't believe that."

"No, but it is still a possibility. Although you would think that since they detected our arrival in this time zone, they would have prepared for an eventual attack."

Scott squeezed his lips with greasy fingers. "I still don't like it. No matter how many land mines they've got topside, I'd expect some kind of home guard like they had in the Cretaceous. I'm not about to walk into another ambush."

"I quite agree, my boy. I quite agree." Doc scrounged in his knapsack for a bit of food. "Let us not jump to any conclusions. As Sam prescribed, we will rest here for the day and see what we can see."

Death Wind suddenly sat bolt upright. He cupped a hand over his brow.

"What is it, lad? What do you see?"

The Nomad pointed down at the nearby tunnel entrance. "People."

CHAPTER 20

With ropes and rigging they let themselves down the ice wall.

The huge, hollowed bowl sported impregnable ramparts that stood hundreds of feet high. As the glacier flowed into the steamy area of dragon occupation, it was continually melted away. The resultant river carved a channel through the stronghold and created a cold-water lake at the downstream end that then formed the tunnel that ran under the glacier.

"Okay, let me go." Scott glanced over his shoulder. A hundred feet below him the waves lapped at the irregular shore. He dug his crampons into the ice, leaned out so that his body was perpendicular to the wall, and walked backward with crunching steps as he let his hands slide along the smooth texture of the rope. A safety line that was wrapped around his chest was held by Windy, who himself was tied to an ice anchor; he kept the rope taut, letting go just enough slack to allow Scott to proceed. If Scott lost his grip, the safety line would prevent him from falling more than a couple of feet.

Scott made certain to jam all ten points into the ice before pulling out his other crampon and taking the next downward step. He climbed in the sequence of pull, lower, jam, pull, lower, jam, until he reached the midway plateau where two Fusiliers stood by. He rested a moment, then proceeded the rest of the way to the bottom.

"If we weren't on such an important mission I'd say that was fun." Scott let a Fatale untie the belaying line. He loosened the harness so it could be pulled up for the next climber.

"I thought it was rather exciting myself," said Doc.

A couple dozen men and women were already hard at work at knocking down the travois and reassembling the lumber into rafts. In the gathering darkness, the opposite shore was a mere silhouette of tall trees that grew down to the water's edge. The mist peeling off the sparkling blue water lent a haunting aura to the scene.

"Wow, that's cold." Scott pulled his hand out of the lake and blew on numb fingers. "I thought it would at least be tepid."

Doc took Scott by the sleeve and pulled him away from the rope fall; a Ranger was on his way down the line. "Although it is colder than you would like, it is warmer than you think. You are feeling the difference between air and water temperatures."

"I'll have to put my furs on before I go swimming."

Doc held out a handful of milk-colored grease. "You had better smear on another layer of bear fat, too."

Scott did not hesitate in complying. "I guess thawing this stuff is out of the question."

All the cooking pots were being used to float essential equipment across the lake.

"When we announce our presence with fire it should at least be with laser fire."

"Only kidding." Scott removed his crampons and tossed them aboard a raft. By the time he was greased and dressed, the last of the commandos had descended the ice wall. Scott was sweltering in his thick furs; the atmosphere was thick and humid. "Okay, I'm ready for the big plunge."

Two women were already in the water, holding onto opposite sides of a raft. They floated high on the buoyancy of their furs. Scott slipped into the water and joined them. His furred trousers and parka were pulled close around his skin, the cuffs tied tight with line. The water that leaked through the seams felt like icy fingers kneading raw muscles. The freezing lake was bearable until he stepped into a hole and fell into water up to his neck. His vital organs reacted violently to the cold incursion. He did his best not to scream.

Doc joined him a moment later and quickly swam to the after end of the raft. His parka hood was thrown back; his hair remained dry and bushy, but his beard dipped beneath the surface and came out looking like bleached, wet hemp. He inhaled sharply. "I do hope this is my last scouting mission. These old bones have seen better days."

Windy and Death Wind joined their raft. Windy's dark hair and beard blended with the fringe fur of his hood. "Ain't so good fer us younguns, neither, Doc."

Death Wind made no complaint.

They kicked with their feet under the water. The flotilla scudded across the lake without splashing or churning. The main current that bisected the lake created a mild backwash that propelled them along the bank in a counterclockwise motion that would eventually bring them to the opposite shore.

Scott chilled down quickly; very shortly he wished that he could suffer again the sweating he had only moments before repined. By keeping his arms up on the end of the raft, he prevented water from running down his sleeves. His moccasin was already soaked through from walking through melt puddles; his foot soon became as numb as the prosthesis on his stump. In order to reduce the lowering temperature of his body core, he pulled his chest partway out of the water.

He kicked furiously. His one foot did not add much propulsion, but the exertion reduced the loss of body heat.

Several rafts floated past, each attended by half a dozen bobbing heads that stretched out of the water like a gaggle of geese. Scott heard teeth chattering so loud that they sounded like repeating rifles in concert. He bit his tongue, finding it strange that his body could be so cold and his face so warm; the air that lay on the surface of the lake carried residual heat from the steam vents.

It seemed like hours before he saw the shoreline approaching. Then he realized that he had not even been looking for it. He was concentrating so hard on fighting off the cold that his awareness extended no farther than the physical anguish that hammered at his brain. Through their combined efforts, the six propellers swung the raft around and pointed it toward the icy beach.

Scott was glad that he was behind the raft, because by that time his muscles were too numb to climb up the blunt embankment. The two-foot-high, rounded ice lip was as slippery as silk.

Scott kept kicking as much to keep warm as to keep the raft butted against the shore. Death Wind was unable to climb straight up the bank; he first had to climb onto the raft, then jump to shore. He carried the painter inland and lashed it to an exposed rock.

With the effortless, fluid motion of water moccasins, the two Femme Fatales glided up the side of the raft and onto the ice. Scott gratefully accepted a feminine hand. He kicked hard against the water with his good foot as she yanked on his arms. Once aground, he lay like a beached whale, gasping for air until he had to crawl away to make room for Doc. All along the beachhead, commandos clambered ashore and pulled up their rafts.

Windy climbed out last. He chafed his body to get his circulation going. "Can't recall when I liked anythin' less. I was better off as a prisoner than a free man. I ain't never suffered like this at the paws o' the dragons."

"But the advantage of free will," Doc chattered through clenched teeth, "is that you can choose the method of your suffering."

"Ain't no consolation to a freezin' man."

On hands and knees Scott waddled through the puddles of warm water until he reached bare rock. The heated air washing out from the jungle soon warmed his body. He stood up on the slick ice, carefully made his way back to the raft, and took a load that was handed to him.

He was just putting down the battery pack when a deafening discharge rent the air; he was blinded by a white flash as bright as a thousand suns. He dropped instinctively and clung to the rock like a limpet. The retinal pattern that was burned into his eyes showed the outline of a human figure surrounded by a ball of flame. As the image faded, Scott realized that he had just seen someone incinerated. A moment later he smelled the nauseating odor of burnt flesh.

True to their trade, not a soul made a sound. Half a dozen laser guns were whipped out of holsters, but the Rangers and the Fusiliers held their fire; there was no visible target.

Scott scampered on hands and knees to the smoldering corpse. It was burnt to a crisp. When he pulled back the furred hood, the person's face came away with it. Scott turned and retched.

He felt a hand on his shoulder. "Who is it?" Broderick said in his perfect diction.

Scott fought hard to find his voice. "I can't tell." Out of the corner of his eye he saw someone else sneaking toward the trees. "Get away from there! It's booby-trapped."

The female Nomad froze in her tracks, a drawn bow aimed at the tree line. She glanced at Scott.

"It's electrified."

Doc and Sam, the two resident doctors, knelt by the inert body. Doc perfunctorily slid up a sleeve and felt for a pulse. He shook his head in silence.

Sam peered into the blackened orbs. "Can't tell. We'll have to take a head count. It's a male—"

Something big and heavy thundered out of the trees. In the near darkness Scott saw what looked like a small house on moving pillars. Crisscrossing laser beams blasted its flank in unison. The arrows that arced through the air disintegrated in sheets of flame as they passed through the electrified zone. The hulk in motion stood up on huge hind legs. The air whined with recharging capacitors. Another broadside brought the creature down in concordant flashes of stimulated radiation, illuminating the beast in the bright discharges. It fell with a thud that shook the ground and knocked over a tree.

Doc said, "I believe we have just killed a triceratops."

Scott did his best to put out of mind the still-mocking cadaver that but a moment before had been a living human being. He scuttled toward the danger zone as delineated by scorched rock and the sparks of burning debris, but maintained a safe margin in case the discharge was static: direct current could leap incredible distances. He lay flat on his belly, looking for some indication of the cause of such a violent, all-consuming chemical reaction.

A moment later Doc lay by his side. "Any ideas?"

"I smell oxygen." With his visual purple destroyed by the blast of light, his night vision was gone. It would be a while before his eye produced enough of the chemical for him to see adequately in the dark. He hissed, "Hey, bring me a light."

After a few moments of scuffling, Windy slithered to his side wearing a battery pack with the laser nozzle replaced by a lamp. He switched it on to low power. "Where you want it?"

Scott took the electric torch and stretched out the cable. He played the light along the ground. At the danger line lay a copper tubing punctured

every eighteen inches with venturis. Just inside it a thick, insulated electrical cable extended along the surface; it was only partially covered by dirt and grass. "Doesn't look as if they tried to hide it very well."

"Dinosaurs are not known for keenness of eyesight," said Doc.

"Huhn? What do you mean?"

"I mean that this barrier is more likely intended to keep dinosaurs in, not intruders out. The dragons would not want their livestock falling into the lake and drowning."

"You gotta be right, Doc," Windy said enthusiastically. "Hell, we could yank out these wires and rip apart this tubing lickety-split. Look-a here. It runs right over the rocks."

Scott shone the light on the copper tubing under Windy's hand. He traced the thin conduit to the water's edge, where it dipped through the ice. "There must be a submerged electrolysis unit that's breaking down water into oxygen and hydrogen, then piping the oxygen up here. In addition to aerating the atmosphere inside the glacial dead zone, where there's very little natural circulation, some of it's used to intensify the oxidizing effect of this—force field."

Doc said in admiration, "Customary dragon genius."

"That lizard genius jus' fried one of our men," chafed Windy.

All three backed away from the invisible fence.

Sam shoved a boulder inside the dead man's parka, buttoned the front, and nodded to the attendees. He turned his gaze on Doc. "His name is—his name was Reynolds. One of Broderick's men. He's got a wife back on the *Ark*. What the hell am I supposed to tell her? That I let her husband become a goddamn firebrand? I should have taken the lead. I should have been in front instead of giving orders from the rear."

Helen placed her arms around his shoulders. "No. No recriminations, Sam. It wasn't your fault."

Sam shrugged her off. He paced a few steps, staring futilely as four pallbearers carried Reynolds by the arms and legs to the water's edge. They laid him down on the ice bank.

Broderick knelt by his friend's side. "He was a good man. But at least he died for a worthy cause."

Doc bowed his head to deliver the eulogy. His voice was soft and solemn. "Casualties are a sad fact of war, not a general's shortcoming. While we put our brave warrior to rest we must remember that hearts are never separated, nor does love ever end. His spirit is kept alive by the continuance of thought. Only when the last member of the human race dies will his essence be lost. It is our task to see that his memory is carried on forever. We fight now not just for Reynolds, but for every human soul that ever existed, or ever will exist, in whatever universal plane or temporal zone is occupied by this great gestalt that we call humanity."

Stifling his tears, Broderick shoved the body into the water. The weight of the rock carried it straight to the bottom. "So long, chum. You were a good mate."

The commandos mourned their loss, but were more than ever ready for battle. They could not allow themselves to yield to the emotion of the moment. They had a higher cause than revenge. They were fighting for the survival of the species.

CHAPTER 21

The rafts were unloaded, broken up, and tossed back into the lake. The lumber drifted with the current, to be taken eventually into the under-ice passage up which it had so carefully been dragged. The fur garments followed. They were taking no chances on stashing their clothes only to have them discovered by a dragon perimeter patrol. The commandos donned their packs and weapons.

Another triceratops lumbered out of the forest.

"Don't shoot!" Scott shouted.

The three-horned beast nudged its fallen comrade with the tip of its central horn. The thick, bony plate that protected its neck was laced with copper-tinted wires. As the triceratops neared the buried cable, the wires glowed; the beast immediately backed up.

"Amazing," said Doc. "The animal is wearing a proximity shock device. Do you know what this means?"

"You were right. It's a corral utilizing a sophisticated electronic fence instead of the poured plastic bulkheads that they used at the Outpost."

"Of course I am right, but that is not the point. It means that dinosaurs have the intelligence to

grasp the concept of learned association: in this case, pain with place. It means that they are trainable."

The triceratops stared myopically at the human onlookers. Its thick tail flicked, and its massive hindquarters swung back and forth like a cat about to strike. It let out a low, caterwauling moan.

"That's great, Henry. That's just great." Sam flung his hands in the air. "Let's save the scientific discourses for later. Right now I need to know how to proceed. You're my advisor. Advise."

Doc said simply, "Oh."

Scott was more informative. "As far as I can tell, the fence isn't rigged with a discharge sensor. Even if it was, a dragon watchman couldn't tell whether it was tripped by an intruder or a blundering dinosaur. I think we're undetected. Now, I can probably cut the power leads, but that'd be a dead giveaway. My advice is, instead of taking the triceratops by the horns, walk around."

Sam mulled that over for a moment. "Doc?"

The doctor pursed his lips and tugged on his damp beard. "I quite agree. As long as the dinosaurs are penned in, the coastal route is the best one to follow."

"Okay." Sam pulled a crinkled sketch map out of his pants pocket. The diagrams that he had drawn during daylight observation, at times of temporary clearing, showed the general outline of the stronghold. "If we follow the lake away from the river it'll take us right to the tunnel entrance in the southeast quadrant. We've got to know what those excavations are used for before we assault the stronghold. If they're full of dragons, I don't want them counterattacking from the rear."

The triceratops bleated as it turned and disappeared into the jungle.

"We must watch for other pitfalls," cautioned Doc.

Bold One produced a long spear that he held out in front of him like a lance. "I lead." He strode off without waiting for acknowledgment. Slender Petal marched half a step behind.

Sam opened his mouth to protest, stopped with his jaw down, then clamped his teeth together. "Okay, people, let's go." The commandos followed the shoreline in single file, staying on the rocks just inshore of the overhanging lip of ice. "Don't bunch up."

Despite Sam's admonition, Doc closed ranks with him. "Sam, please accept my apology for becoming momentarily sidetracked."

"Exchanged for mine for being so uptight. It's a big relief not having to prance through a jungle full of dinosaurs. I've had the heebie-jeebies all day long. Now we know why they weren't roaming the streets. And if this fence goes all the way to the highway, we won't have to worry about crossing swords with those oversized horned toads."

As the coolness of the night settled in, the fog, produced by the generated steam mixing with the cold glacial air, slowly evaporated. Heat inversions caused the stars to twinkle. The moisture-laden air was clammy, the wet rocks slippery. More than once Scott's artificial leg skidded across smooth granite.

The jungle was a cacophony of chirps, wheezes, honks, and grunts. Scott found it disconcerting that fifty feet away, dinosaurs as large as bungalows prowled surreptitiously, browsing and grazing. The intangible barrier gave him very little comfort; the safety it offered was an intellectual exercise in belief in the unseen.

"You want weapon?"

Scott practically jumped out of his moccasin at Death Wind's sudden approach. "Whew, I didn't realize how much on edge I was." Scott felt his heart thumping. He placed a hand on his chest and let out a deep breath. "I guess I've got dragons on my mind."

"How foot?"

"Better than your English. Death Wind, your language skills are retrogressing."

The Nomad shrugged. "Not need. All understand."

Scott humphed. He thought about it before saying, "There's some truth to that. The purpose of language is to communicate ideas. I guess as long as you accomplish that, I shouldn't complain. Still, I'd like to see a compromise between your speech patterns and Doc's. Sometimes he's so long-winded that by the time he winds up his narration I've forgotten what the point was."

"He smart. Very deep."

"Oh, I'll give him that. And I'd sure miss his affectations if he changed." Scott paused, lost in thought. "You know, I've missed you on this mission, too. It's not like the old days when we were always together. Now you're out in front and I'm in the rear. It's good to be side by side again."

Death Wind was silent for so long that Scott thought that he must have lost his tongue. Finally, the Nomad tapped the long hair that covered his temple. "You think farther than I see. You have much wisdom."

Scott's impulse was to object. But when he reflected on his friend's remark, he knew that it was not intended to bolster his ego. Nomads did not suffer from egotism, and therefore did not feed the egos of others. Neither did their make-up contain false modesty. Nomad feelings were primitive in the sense of uncomplicated.

"That is my role, just as yours is to scout."

Death Wind had doffed the constricting, long-sleeved garments. He wore only a G-string, moccasins, and a quiver. He unhitched the belt at his waist and handed it to Scott. "Take knife."

Scott reached out automatically before he realized what the Nomad was offering him. "But, your father gave this to, you."

"You need."

As long as Death Wind had been a brave, that knife had left his side only when drawn and held in his hand. If Nomad psychology allowed for sentimentality, this knife would be Death Wind's most prized possession.

Scott swallowed hard and tried not to falter his speech. In imitation Nomad terseness, he said, "Thanks." He tied the belt around his waist and adjusted the sheath so it lay easily against his hip. He rolled his sleeves past his elbows; he had an unobstructed path to the knife, and could draw it quickly and smoothly.

The word to halt was passed from person to person.

"Scott!"

At Sam's beckoning call, Scott dashed to the front of the line where the general crouched with Doc, Helen, Bold One, and Slender Petal.

Sam pointed to a plastic conduit that stretched across their path of travel. Beyond it lay a grove of shrubbery that was too thick to see through. "Check it out, but be careful."

Scott approached the pipe on hands and knees. At three-foot intervals, mushroomlike caps protruded upward; the opposite facing was scooped out. "Get Windy up here," he hissed.

A moment later the Texas Ranger lay by his side. He pulled out the flexible cable and handed the light nozzle to Scott. "Better use low power. Don't know what's on t'other side o' them bushes."

Scott cupped a hand over the light as he played it along the tubing. He inspected one of the caps, then followed the pipe to a plastic junction box. "You hear that?"

"A kinda whirring sound?"

"Yes." Scott snapped a branch off a nearby bush, shortened it to the length of a pencil, placed one end against the box, then tilted and lowered his head until the other end of the stick slid into his ear. The vibration was transmitted through the solid material of the wood, and magnified. "It's an electrical device of some sort: a motor or a contactor."

When he illuminated the top of the box he saw a dragon claw switch, the kind that was inset and that required the sharp point of a talon to actuate. He gave the torch back to Windy. "Hold it like that." He removed his newly acquired knife from its sheath and used the keen steel edge to hone the stick to a fine point.

As he worked the carved needle into the hole, Windy's strong hand clamped down on his own. "Are you sure you wanna do that?"

"No." Scott stared at Windy's wiry beard and cragged features. "But I have to do something."

"Suppose it blows up?"

Scott wriggled his fingers and worked the stick into a position where he could jam it into the switch. The tiny click was followed by a loud snap and a gushing sound. Windy gasped and shuddered; his eyes rolled into his head. Then his face and Scott's were splattered with water that fell in great droplets from the sky.

"Bombs don't have manual detonation switches." Scott pressed the wooden needle into the hole once more, and the rain ceased. He leaned back on his knees, but his hand was still pinioned to the junction box. Gently he pulled Windy upright. He called out over his shoulder, "It's okay. It's just a sprinkler system."

Sam's shoulders dropped half a foot; from twenty feet away Scott heard the sigh of relief. "Thanks, Scott."

"No problem."

Sam pulled out the map again and tilted it so he could read it by starlight. "The road leading into the tunnel should be on the other side of this bush barrier."

The troops ranged along the hedgerow and sought a way through. Slender Petal found a disguised wicket near the water's edge. Scott checked it for booby traps, gave the all-clear sign, and led the way along a narrow path that terminated at the shoulder of a poured-plastic roadbed. The orangetop was faintly illuminated by ground-mounted nightlights.

"Okay, since everything's going according to schedule, we'll stick with our prearranged plan. Helen, you stay here with the Fatales and guard the supplies." Sandra had relinquished control of her platoon to her mother. "The Sintu will scout inward—but I don't want you straying too far. You got that, Bold One? Death Wind? I mean it. I don't want to get spread too thin, and I don't want to show our hand."

Both Nomads nodded wordlessly.

"Henry, Scott, you're with me. And the Rangers, too. Broderick, leave some of the Fusiliers with the Fatales, then take the rest and look for a place to hole up for the day. Any questions?" No one made a sound. "Henry, any advice or observations?"

Doc looked both ways along the road. Hundred-foot-tall trees lined both sides of the plastic passageway; upper branches intermingled to create a leafy parasol. Steam vents along the curb issued thin streams of vapor: a permanent, haunting fog. The street surface glistened with condensation; water ran in rivulets down the grooved edged and into a culvert. Inward lay the urban area of the stronghold; outward was a heavily constructed mole that cut through the solid wall of the glacier.

He winked at Scott. "Not to be long-winded, I would like to say that even though we saw very little activity today, we do not know whether the traffic was typical, how heavily the inner sanctum is garrisoned, or what light we may find at the end of the tunnel. And while I agree that our initial directive is to proceed by stealth, we must not fall prey to subdued belligerence. We came here to fight, and fight we will. If discovered prematurely we must each take the initiative to accomplish our goal despite our losses." Doc paused dramatically, casting his gaze over the surrounding troops. "I bid fond farewell to those I may not see again. But one thing I guarantee—better times are coming."

There were muttered choruses of "Here, here."

"Thanks, Henry," said Sam. "Your words are an inspiration to us all."

As the commandos settled into their assigned positions there was a short period of hugging and handshaking. These people had traveled together through space and time, thousands of miles and a million years, some to die an untimely death on foreign shores: Some would not return to their homeland, or to their hometime. But all would live on in spirit.

"Okay, let's get moving. We don't have long before sunrise."

Steam vents along the top of the mole spewed heat into the air. It was along this very road that, early that morning, they had spotted human slaves hauling covered wagons, like draft animals pulling Conestogas. The swirling mists prevented an accurate count, but Scott was sure that several dozen had been employed in the task. More might be living in the stronghold—or in the hollowed grotto at the end of the tunnel.

The band of guerrillas loped quickly across the exposed mole. The sidewalls were taller than a man, but short enough for a long-necked dragon to see over. The twin rows of nightlights extended straight as a Nomad's arrow as far as the eye could see, into the dark maw of the tunnel, until they converged in the distance through optical illusion.

Scott peered into the tunnel opening. It was like looking into the wrong end of a telescope. "It shouldn't be more than a couple miles long." At the end of the mole a blast of frigid air mixed with the warmed atmosphere of the inner stronghold, forming a fog bank that ascended with the updraft. He rubbed his bare arms. "I don't think we should have thrown away our furs."

Doc studied the towering ice wall. "Glaciers are in constant motion. I wonder how they keep the ice from destroying the tunnel. Certainly a power that moves mountains cannot be stopped by dragonfactured bulkheads."

"Henry, don't even think about going off on a scientific quest."

"Mere speculation, Sam, and idle curiosity. Nothing more."

They stopped at the tunnel entrance. The black maw was a curved arch fifty feet across. The floor lights seemed hardly adequate for a passageway of such mammoth dimensions.

"It's getting colder." Scott reluctantly rolled down his sleeves.

"Hey, looky over here. In the alcove." Windy stepped into a shadowed opening. His voice became distant and muted. "They got a heater in here. And insulated duds."

As Scott neared the doorway he became aware of a suffused red glow that emanated from the ceiling, as if it were on fire. The heat was a welcome relief; his goose bumps subsided. "It's infrared."

The walls were rubbery and resilient, and seemed to absorb sound.

Windy pulled an odd-looking jumpsuit off a wall rack and tried it on for size. "Made for a dragon." The sleeves were padded, the leggings adjustable, and the tail opening as low as the floor. An attached dickie extended from the neck to accommodate the long dragon neck.

"Not exactly tailor-made, but warm as toast." Scott slipped into a jumpsuit and pranced around the dressing room like a June bride. "But if we hack off the bottoms it'll do the job." The racks were triple-tiered, and extended all the way across the back wall. "They'll never miss them."

Everyone donned the one-piece uniforms, made quick, slashing alterations, and stashed the scraps in a waste receptacle. The oversized, padded booties were the hardest things to refit.

"I certainly hope it gets cold enough to warrant such clothing," Doc said.

"It must be here for a reason."

Doc's face was flushed under the infrared lamps, and sweat gushed down his face and forehead. "I must get out of here at once."

Scott followed him into the corridor, glad for once for the cold.

"Doc, this isn't normal ice temperature. The tunnel is being refrigerated."

When the commandos were all together, they continued their march along the under-ice passageway. They advanced in double columns, weapons drawn; Sam and Doc led the way. The bulkhead was constructed of extruded plastic, like so many items of dragon manufacture. Removable panels were spaced at hundred-foot intervals.

"Sam, I think we should have a look behind these doors."

The Gentleman General looked askance. "Henry, this isn't just a trick to study the workings, is it?"

Doc shook his head. "Serendipitously, perhaps, but my main concern is to ensure that the façade does not conceal guns, guard stations, or warning devices."

Sam thought for only a moment. "Okay, but make it snappy."

Scott and Windy removed the panel and set it aside. Windy detached his laser nozzle from the connecting cable, attached the light, and played the beam inside as Doc directed. The glacial ice wall lay exposed; except for a thin veneer of dripping water, it appeared solid. The crawl space was crammed with power lines, plumbing pipes, refrigeration coils, motors, and transformers.

"Ah, I see how it is done." Doc stepped back and let Scott and Windy replace the panel. He nodded to Sam. "It's a mechanical raceway."

The dimly lit corridor was hauntingly quiet; there was no echo effect as one might suspect. To Scott it appeared that the end was no closer now than when they had started. The floor-mounted nightlights stretched out seemingly forever. They marched on warily.

Scott whispered to Doc, "Did you see the alignment of the heat pumps?"

Doc nodded. "The freezer coils create the abnormally low temperature in the tunnel, while the exhaust heat is used to melt the encroaching glacier. The melt water is channeled under the floor. I suspect that if we were to look behind the right side bulkhead we would see nothing but solid ice. The dragons have ingeniously permitted the glacier to flow around the tunnel without going through it."

"You have to give them credit for mechanical marvels." They passed by a nightlight. Doc's whiskered features were momentarily illuminated. "Doc! Your face."

The doctor's skin was chalky; it matched his beard and great mane in whiteness. "You are looking a bit peaked, too. Almost as if—" He halted in midstride and touched his nose with his finger. "That is strange."

"Hey, I can't feel my skin."

"Sam," Doc called out. "The incredible insulating qualities of these wraps prevent us from feeling the extreme cold on exposed flesh. I am afraid that we are suffering from frostbite."

Scott rubbed his face vigorously to restore circulation. "Okay, at each light I want everyone to stop and check the person behind you." He added in aside, "What the hell are the dragons trying to do, add fuel to the Ice Age?"

As the yards dragged on, the cold became more intense. Ice crystals grew on the plastic walls like hoarfrost, and snapped and crunched underfoot. The guerrilla army sounded like a centipede wearing clackers. The walls sparkled kaleidoscopically as rime ice refracted the light through its frozen facets. The air was so dry that Scott had to constantly moisten his lips with his tongue. His breath condensed and froze on the hairs of his upper lip. When he looked over Doc's face at the next light station, the older man's beard was frozen solid.

"Doc, you look like a snowman. Even your eyebrows are covered with frost."

His lashes were so thickly coated with ice that they hung at half-mast. He paid Scott no mind. Under half-opened lids he stared straight ahead. "I believe we are about to get some answers."

The tunnel flared outward like the end of a trumpet, except that the floor remained level. The huge, high-ceilinged dome was filled with vertical glasslike cases, much like the interior of a colossal beehive except that the prism faces were rectangular. A thick growth of frost made the fronts opaque. Each case was eight feet tall and four feet wide, and separated from its neighbors by an airspace that was partially clogged with ice. Long icicles grew out of the junctions where four cases met.

"Unbelievable," Scott muttered.

"But not unanticipated."

"They must be thousands of 'em," breathed Windy. "Millions."

"Times four," added Doc.

The dome was still and silent. The floor lights were brighter and spaced closer together; additional lamps climbed plastic columns that supported the roof of ice. The cases were stacked from floor to ceiling, and placed back to back in long rows with separations every hundred feet.

As far as Scott could see there was no end of them. "It's a giant warehouse."

The rest of the troops bunched in the bottleneck where the leaders had stopped.

"But storing what?" Sam wanted to know.

Scott did not realize that his mouth was agape until he felt the intense cold on his tongue. He clamped his jaw shut and did his best to salivate. "What would they need to freeze—" The awful truth hit him as hard as a block of ice.

"If my suspicions are correct—" Doc approached the first row of cases. The dragon mitts were floppy potholders on his gnarled hands. He wiped his fists across the front of the lowest storage container. Ice tinkled to the floor with the sound of miniature bells.

Scott joined him. He pounded the prism with padded knuckles. "It's solid." He pressed his face close to the glasslike front.

"Careful, my boy. At these temperatures your skin may adhere to the surface."

With his eyes only inches away from the scraped-off surface, Scott saw a clear, unblemished plastic sidewall an inch thick. The case appeared to be full of ice; fine, weblike cracks obscured a dark, brownish shape that loomed overhead.

"There's something in there."

Scott brushed a wide swath as far upward as he could reach. As the frost fell away, he peered at the long, squat form that took shape like a child's connect-the-dots drawing. "Aaagh." He jumped back two steps when he recognized the reptilian face that leered down at him. He had not seen a dragon since—the Cretaceous.

"Just as I thought," said Doc calmly. "Although why—"

"Hey, there's another one in here," shouted Windy.

Sam brushed his sleeve over another casket farther down the aisle. "And here."

Momentarily out of control, the commandos spread into the intersecting corridors. All reports were the same. Frozen lizard corpses were stored everywhere. The ice dome was a dragon mausoleum.

"Doc!" Scott screamed suddenly, his voice echoing in the tomblike silence. "They're not dead, are they? They're frozen. They're alive. They're an army of slaves waiting to be thawed out."

"Alive I am sure. Slaves I doubt. It seems more likely—"

"Doc! Over here!" Windy stood on the other side of the corridor, fiercely wiping frost off a storage case. "We got people!"

Everyone gathered around the platoon leader and helped him to brush off the adjacent cases. It was difficult to see clearly through the maze of tiny cracks. The bodies were naked and upright, and for the most part hairless.

Sam winced at the entombed humans. "Maybe this is what became of the Cro-Mag—"

Scott screamed again. He clamped his hand to his mouth; his eyes bulged. He uttered low, guttural sounds like the cough of a wounded animal that was choking on its own blood. Enough of one female was exposed to show a cadaverous face and a head of long blond hair.

Doc rushed to his side. "My boy, what is it?"

Scott wanted to scream again, but his throat was paralyzed. He desperately wanted to cry. He could only raise his mitted hand and point.

"You look as if you have seen a ghost."

Scott felt himself go weak. The strength left his legs so quickly that he fell back into Doc's arms. Sam rushed to help. Together they eased him down to the frost-covered floor. Scott closed his eyes as his head lolled back on a rubber neck.

Doc pulled up an eyelid and glazed into the dilated pupil.

Scott was aware of his surroundings, but everything was moving in extreme slow motion. He squeezed his eyes shut, then opened them quickly. He glanced up at the figure in the crystal coffin. It was no dream. The girl was really there. She looked so peaceful. She was tall and lean and shapely. Her eyes were closed, as if she were merely taking a short nap.

In a halting, high-pitched voice that was barely a whisper, Scott finally blurted, "She's—my—sister."

CHAPTER 22

Ned appeared breathless at the top of the ramp. "I was out checking the perimeter. I came as fast as I could." Chest heaving, he paused to suck in some air before continuing. "You got a message?"

Rusty shook his head. "Not a tone."

"But Britt said you wanted to prepare the ship for flight. I've got everybody boarding."

"That's right. We're leaving. But we don't have to rush. We can take as long as we want."

Ned used his sleeve to wipe sweat off his forehead. "I don't get it. Where are we going?"

"To the dragon stronghold. We'll be there in no time."

"But the missiles."

Rusty grinned enigmatically. "By the time we get there they won't be able to get us. We'll be out of range."

Ned was breathing easier now. He approached the computer console with his head cocked and an eyebrow raised. He looked at Rusty askance. "Okay, Rusty, take it easy, and let's talk this out. Now, I know you've been under a lot of strain lately—"

Rusty laughed raucously. "I'm not crazy, Ned. You just don't understand what kind of morning I've had." Rusty wiped off his grin and replaced it with a half-serious mien that could not hide the excitement that he felt. "Not only have my infinite-time calculations been resolved into a short-order formula, but I've broken a dragon access code that I didn't even know existed. Ned, I know exactly when the dragons went, and why. And I can go then at a moment's notice."

Ned was still standing glassy-eyed when Britt appeared on the bridge. "Almost ready."

"Good. We'll take off as soon as Ned gives us the okay." Britt sidled past Ned and tucked herself under Rusty's arm. He gave her a peck on the cheek.

Ned's eyes roved from one to the other. "You're serious, aren't you?"

"That's why I'm not in a hurry. It doesn't matter when we leave, we'll get there at the time I choose. I just program the *Ark's* time transfer equipment to launch us through the space-time continuum in accordance with the computer's preset calculations. It's easy when you have a timely formula."

Ned nodded slowly. "Britt, does he have both oars in the water, or are we gonna be rowing around in circles?"

"I cannot follow. I do not have the mathematics. But Rusty knows. I trust him. If he goes through time, I go with him."

The long silence was finally broken by a toned message from below decks. The troops were aboard, the ship was sealed, battle stations were secured. Ned stood by the bridge toner. He hesitated with his fingers on the keyboard.

"I sure hope you know what the hell you're doing." He gave the signal for acknowledgment, then toned for the backup bridge watch to come upramp. The trainees could handle the secondary controls while Rusty, Britt, and Ned piloted the ship. "Because I hate the idea of leaving our friends in a time of need."

Rusty smiled again. "Don't worry. When we finish our future business we'll come back to this exact moment in time. No one will know we were gone."

Britt disentangled herself from Rusty's arms. She checked the reactor readings. Her fingers flew over the control board. The monitor responded to her commands with scrolled data that she read at a glance. "Power up."

The trainees piled onto the bridge. Rusty directed them to their posts. "Okay, midshippeople, this is the real thing." Rusty took his seat in front of the big screen. He typed instructions into the computer. "We may as well get moving. Once I've set the space-time coordinates we'll

have a strict timetable to attend."

"Okay, but I wanna know what's goin' on."

"Let's get off the ground, first. Taking the continuum as a whole, time is objective. But we, limited by finite references within that continuum, must stick to a subjective sequence of events."

Ned sat in the copilot's seat. He stared at the control board and the vast array of annunciator lights. "You're gonna hafta coach me on this, Rusty. Doing simulations isn't the same as flying."

"Sure it is. The only difference is that instead of just lighting up a screen with the correct responses, your input will have a real-time effect on the *Ark*."

"That's what I'm afraid of."

"Don't worry, Ned. I've programmed a computer module to handle the time transfer automatically. Manual control is a thing of the past. Uh, figuratively speaking. You get us there, she'll get us then."

Britt said, "All systems are go, Rusty."

"Let's hit it." The *Ark* lifted smoothly off the ground. When she reached treetop level, Rusty tapped acceleration vernier buttons until she attained horizontal cruising speed. "I want to get out of stronghold radar range before we increase altitude." Rusty relinquished the controls. "Okay, Ned, she's all yours."

Ned licked his lips nervously. His fingers were glued to the keyboard as his eyes flashed from screen to screen.

Rusty lounged in his seat. "Would you like to know when we're going, and why the dragons went then?"

"Well, uh—"

"The dragons' overall survival plan was more complicated than we thought. It was shrewdly conceived, adroitly constructed, and almost perfectly conducted. The dragons' only shortcoming was in their failure to comprehend the interrelationship between space and time: not as disparate quanta, each with its own set of equations, but both together as observable and interchangeable points of reference within the unalterable reality of the spatiotemporal continuum."

"Rusty, I'm trying to concentrate on—"

"Okay. To put it simply, they charged into time travel in the same straightforward manner they would use to attack a tyrannosaur: head on, and with lots of power. Dragons are blind to subtleties and incapable of understanding abstractions. It's not their fault. That's the way the lizard brain functions. Its capacity for creative thought is limited by its physical design.

"To the dragons, time travel was not a discovery: it was an invention; perhaps their crowning technological achievement. And because they did not take the time to understand the ramifications of tampering with the fabric of space-time, it became their downfall. It's like building a skyscraper, then adding ten more stories to the top floor without bothering to determine if the foundations could support the extra weight. Eventually, the structure has to topple."

"Rusty, I—" Ned was paler than Rusty had ever seen him. He handled the controls crudely. The *Ark* groaned with the strain. "Maybe you should—"

"No, you're doing just fine." Rusty did his best to look nonchalant, but he glanced at the monitors whenever Ned was not looking his way. "Anyway, unlike mankind's skyrocketing evolution, the dragons had a history of plodding advance. Most of their Cretaceous city was thousands of years old. They progressed slowly—until they stumbled over the loophole in the time barrier. Their first jump—to a time zone a million years into their own future—proved to be their downfall. When they saw that their civilization no longer existed, they reacted according to the instincts of their kind: ruthlessly, murderously, cold-bloodedly, and, to one who understands dragon psychology, predictably. Without carefully studying the situation, they made immediate plans to ensure racial survival. The way dragons respond to threat is in keeping with the world in which they evolved: they destroy."

"How far do you want to go before—"

"You can start gaining altitude now." Rusty stood and perambulated around the command center. He checked the read-outs at each trainee's console. "Britt, make sure the radarscope is on extreme scale."

"Roger, Rusty. I activated proximity warning sensors."

He ruffled her hair. "Good gal."

Ned looked a little more at ease. "You can't feel the bumps on the simulator module."

"You're doing fine. Take her straight to the top."

Ned applied full power to vertical thrust. The external cameras recorded the purple radiance of the lifting cones.

"Where was I? Oh, yes: the dragons' inability to perceive the intricacies of time travel, the complications of paradox. That's all philosophical conjecture on my part, but the rest is taken right off Jane's engagement crystal: data that was so deeply embedded under menu codes that I didn't know how to retrieve it."

Still pacing the bridge, Rusty soliloquized, "So the dragons rushed future events without adequate forethought. A million years after the end of the Cretaceous, mammals already ruled the Earth: the warm-bloods who'd been around for more than a hundred million years, coexisting with the dinosaurs in a subservient role, needed only to have the thunder lizards taken out of their way so they could expand into niches that were previously denied them. The dragons hadn't developed the death bomb yet, so there was time to explore farther downstream. Lo and behold, they discovered almost at the limit of the power of their transfer equipment a period of glacial advance. Then, it didn't make sense to restart their global rule knowing that down the line an ice age might wipe them out."

Ned relaxed. There was nothing to do now but wait for the *Ark* to reach her ceiling.

"Now comes the real ingenuity. The development of the death bomb gave them the power to purge the Earth of dominant life forms in order to entrench their own. That's what they did to us, in the Holocene. Then they built Charon and the Outpost to sow the seeds that they carried forward from the Cretaceous. Eventually, they would have planted farms on the other continents as well.

"But the upper echelon, the dragon elite, didn't want to live in a barren, inhospitable world—one that would take hundreds of thousands of years to reform into the image of the one they grew up in. They wanted to move immediately into a world that had been created just for them. And that's where the stronghold comes in."

Rusty felt that it was time to unwind. He reversed his course and paced clockwise around the command center. All eyes were upon him, and necks were craned as he walked behind people who hung on his every word. He stared up through the clear plastic bubble into the infinity of space.

"They couldn't go any farther downstream. The Holocene, which began at the end of the Ice Age, represented the time limit of their equipment. They couldn't start their seeding farms one notch back—in the Pleistocene—because none of what they wanted to plant would grow in the oncoming cold." Rusty stabbed a finger into the air. "But they could use the Pleistocene as a leapfrogging post to enable them to travel farther downstream.

"The stronghold is a way station—not a terminal, but a transfer depot for points downstream, beyond the reach of Cretaceous-based equipment. It's from now that they intend to re-populate the future with their own kind.

"In the hierarchy of dragon leaders it was the lower classes that were sent to do the dirty work in the Holocene, to oversee that plants and animals from the hometime were cultivated across the world. The most powerful dragons would enjoy the fruits of the labor by suddenly appearing another million years downstream—at a time when the Earth would be converted completely to Cretaceous conditions."

Rusty returned to his seat. He fingered the time transfer controls. "That is when we are going. And we are going in time to prevent the dragons from reclaiming a world that they once threw away. You only go through this world once: the dragons had their chance, and they muffed it. Now they want to take away ours."

The *Ark* reached her highest attainable altitude. The air outside was too thin for her lifting cones to push her any higher. But that same thinness would let her time transfer circuits send her through the fabric of space-time with a minimum expenditure of energy.

"And I'll be damned if I'm going to let them get away with it."

Rusty pressed the button.

CHAPTER 23

"The dragon hibernation treatment is quite effective, not only in healing wounds and curing sickness, but in arresting, perhaps even reversing, the aging process. It was never used for slaves and soldiers because they could be too easily replaced: from egg to adult they grew with amazing swiftness."

"Doc, that there's nice to know, but—"

"An organism replaces worn-out cells throughout its lifetime. The adult human being contains not a single cell with which he was born: he is completely renewed every decade.

As the original genetic code is passed from cell to cell, seemingly minor imperfections accumulate until the coding sequence becomes unreadable. Later generations of cells no longer function exactly the way they were intended. Eventually, the organism loses its integrity. It's a process that we call aging."

"But what's that got to do with—"

"Dragons did not excel in the biological sciences, but they knew that with proper treatment time heals all wounds. These people—" Doc swept his arms across the plastic facade. Scott's sister stood in quiet repose, like a perfectly sculpted mannequin. "—are not frozen in the strictest sense of the word. Their body temperatures have been significantly lowered, and they lie immobilized in a crystalline structure whose solid state is maintained by refrigeration, but they are actually bathed in an epidermal revivifying fluid that has the capacity to prevent growth and aging while rejuvenating the internal tissues."

Windy snugged the loose-fitting folds of the dragon cold-weather garb close to his chest. "Are you tryin' to say this here's a hospital?"

Doc opened his mouth, cupped his hand over it, then ran his fingers down over his frosted beard. "I was not. But given the evidence of observation, that is as good an explanation as any."

"What I wanna know is, can we wake 'em the hell up?" With stylus and vellum in hand, Sam wrote furiously as people returned from the far corners of the dome with information about its contents. He was tabulating a body count on both dragons and humans; the subtotal had already reached the thousands.

"Undoubtedly. These individuals were hibernated with just that purpose. But as you know, the thawing procedure is a slow one. Remember how long it took us to revive Helen and the others."

"I'm not talking about length of time, but practicality. Helen was submerged in a coagulated gelatin, like a supercooled amniotic fluid, not a semisolid crystal lattice. This smacks of permanency."

Doc shrugged. "The dragons have a remedy for it, no doubt. Perhaps the indissoluble casing is merely physical protection for long-term patients—or prisoners. At least we know why they chose to bury them inside a glacier. The energy requirements necessary to sustain the congealing temperature of the solution is largely supplied by natural ice-age conditions. It is very efficient, when you think about it."

Sam stabbed the stylus point dangerously close to Doc's face. "Henry, I'm tired of you admiring dragon science and technology all the time. Whenever they come up with some new gimmick, you've got nothing but praise for it. Now, why don't you go over there and talk to Scott. Reassure him. Get him out of his funk. The kid's practically as comatose as these—" He looked at the shapely feminine form. "Well, you know what I mean."

"Of course. That is a valuable suggestion." Unruffled, Doc left Sam and Windy to coordinate the explorers and collect data. He ambled to where Scott leaned with his back against a plastic bulkhead, staring at the domed ceiling.

Scott took no notice of Doc's approach. His mitted hands were tucked into the folds of his jumpsuit. Frozen tears clung to his cheeks like opalescent beads. Blond hair framed the stern features of his face. The resemblance between him and his sister was startling, except that Scott's countenance showed life while his sister's was more like that of a painted, porcelain cherub, or a stillborn fetus.

"Rather an unexpected turn of events, I would say."

Scott did not respond.

Doc ran his tongue over lips that were chapped from the cold. "I had a family at one time. A mother and a father, and"—he thought for a few seconds—"and three sisters: Heather, Betsy, and Pam. Pam died when she was still a baby—natural causes. Cute as a button, she was. Heather was killed in a building collapse when we were teenagers. Betsy, the last I knew, was still alive." He paused reflectively. "But that was many years ago. Both parents were killed by dragons—in a flyer attack. I guess that's when I left home; when I went out into the world to fight back. I was full of pain in those days: angry, aggressive, even vengeful. It was a long time before I learned that the pain of violent emotion was more debilitating than the pain of my loved ones' loss."

Shivering from the cold, Doc walked in slow semicircles in front of Scott. "The pain you feel at a time of loss is one that no one else can appreciate. It is a very private pain. The depth of emotional impact is measured by the closeness of a bond that only you can feel. Of course, life goes on; but it never goes on as well.

"You never get over the crying. Years afterward, for some unknown reason, an image will pop up in your mind—and you will experience a silent moment of remorse. Those moments are very important, so you can remember how much you once loved that person, and so you can remember how much you can love. There is no love without pain; and that pain is what makes us human. It is a small price to pay when you consider the alternative."

Scott cleared his throat. He blinked away more tears, unmindful that they froze barely halfway down his cheeks. "Do you mean—" His voice faltered. He choked. He cleared his throat again and uttered in a froglike voice, "Are you saying that you always have these feelings?"

"Yes, I still have the feelings; but after a while the feelings no longer hurt. The pain becomes a dull ache—and I enjoy that ache, because it reminds me of the love that I still harbor within."

Scott cleared his throat again. He looked down at the frost-covered floor, wiped his eyes with padded mitts. "She's still alive."

"I do not suspect otherwise."

"And the others, too: Mom, and Dad, and—" Scott cleared his throat once more. "We can't see them, but they're probably all here."

"It seems like a logical conclusion."

Scott's eyes grappled with Doc's. "Then why are you making this pitch? Why are you being so negative? That isn't like you. What are you trying to tell me?"

Doc inhaled deeply. The air had a bite that singed his lungs. "I was not even aware of an ulterior motive until you pointed it out to me."

The mausoleum was a strange dichotomy of dark shadows and bright, silvery hoarfrost. The nightlights did not flicker; the cold, steady beams knifed through the frigid air like white spears. Mild air currents, set in motion by the heat of living bodies, rising and mixing with the cold air descending, scraped frost off the ceiling; it fell like fine, granular snow, each crystal twisting and rotating, and sparkling in everchanging nuance.

Doc's voice was soft but vibrant, his words cut crisply. "Life is as fragile as the petal of a rose. It can be snuffed out with infinite ease. That is why you must make of life what you can, while you can. Life is too short, and too uncertain, to do otherwise."

He cupped his palms in front of his mouth, exhaled hard, and let the warm air wash over his face. "Scott, I do not want to raise any false hopes. I do not know if I can save them."

Scott inhaled sharply, his eyes reflecting disquietude.

Doc rushed on. "I know I have done it before. I studied the crystal texts and familiarized myself with the procedure. But I know nothing about the unsolidification process that in this case must precede dehibernation. I do not know what effect long-term homeostasis has on resuscitation. Dragon doctors possess tools and training that I do not."

"Doc, you can do anything," Scott said, imploring. "I've seen you in action."

The doctor maintained solemnity. "I am a man, Scott, with all the doubts and frailties that any man has."

"So what am I supposed to do?" Scott exploded. "Forget my family is alive just a few feet away? Make believe they don't exist?"

Doc spoke slowly and carefully. "How did you deal with their deaths before?"

"Well, I—I—I don't know. I just didn't think about it much. It was a part of the past that I wanted to forget, so I put it out of my mind. And I had to stay alive. I even looked forward to seeing the world, and finding out what it was really like. But now—"

"Nothing has changed, Scott, only the perception of your beliefs."

"A lot has changed," he screamed, blue eyes glaring. "Before, I didn't know they were alive; now I do. I can't forget that."

"I am not suggesting that you do. I am merely pointing out that tranquility is a state of mind that you control. It has nothing to do with reality. Once you accept that, you can deal with any disaster, overcome any sorrow. That is how you mitigated the loss of your foot. You have abnormal strength, Scott. Use it.

"We must take over this stronghold, we must gain access to the computer complex. We must go about it in an aggressive but methodical manner. That is the only way to salvation of the souls residing in this Pleistocene purgatory. But I warn you that despite our best efforts, we may fail. You must understand that the dead do not always rise from their graves. Their condition of finality may already be beyond our command.

"The intricacies of this spatiotemporal battle that we are waging are progressing geometrically. I do not care to predict what paradoxes may occur should we tamper too much with the fabric of space-time. I see another broken thread in every complication. If the tear gets too big, we may not be able to stitch it back together."

"Doc, what's that have to do with—with anything?"

Doc shivered, as much from consternation as from the cold. "I am not sure. The dichotomous reality of our predicament is difficult to grasp in straight-line terms. In one river of space-time, the Maccam City residents are deceased; in another they cling tenaciously to unconscious afterlife. Were they ever truly dead? Are they now really alive? What happens if we tip the scales away from preconceived truth?"

"Doc, you're not making any sense."

"There is no sense in time travel, only interpretation of events. You yourself admit that Maccam City was destroyed by a corrosive gas—"

"No, Doc, that's what I *think*. That's my interpretation of what happened. But it's purely subjective and subject to change. Even if I had actually seen them killed, I'd have to believe the later evidence of my own eyes."

"Would you?"

"Well, of course."

Bushy eyebrows, coated with ice, arched into a wrinkled forehead. "Interesting. The question then arises: how did they survive? Or, in another frame of reference, *did* they survive. Perhaps, for some frightful, unfathomable reason, your people are not in stasis; perhaps the dragons collected their corpses for some diabolical experiments—" Doc stopped with his mouth ajar. "Uh, I apologize, Scott. I did not intend to speak so crudely about your loved ones. But I wonder . . ."

"Yes, I wonder, too. And I'm beginning to see what you're getting at. Life is more than a chemical reaction, it's also a state of mind. At least, intelligent life is. Once we add consciousness to the space-time equation, we have to incorporate the relativity principle: reality then depends on the observer's point of view."

"I believe that is the speculation that was coalescing in my mind."

Scott was on a roll. "So, if I perceived them as dead, they *are* dead—that is, in a subjective approach."

"Out of sight, out of mind, out of existence."

"But if I say they are alive, then, in my heart, they are alive."

"The philosophy of solipsism."

"What you really mean, though, is that torment and internal conflict are the results of a conscious decision:"

"Or a subconscious decision. Peace of mind is a mental exercise that takes great effort to control. As long as you keep a memory living inside you, its objective position is independent of perspective."

"But doesn't there have to be an absolute reality, unaffected by the way I think about it?"

"I say yes. Rusty says no. He ascribes to the theory of variability, or subsequent coincidental coexistence. That is why he exhibits such audacity while cavorting through time. He does not believe that anything we do can affect the architecture of the universe. The harmony of the spheres, he insists, cannot be untuned by human intervention. I am skeptical."

"Forget it, Doc. I'm totally confused." Scott shook his head. He held his mitts against his face, melted the frozen saline droplets, and wiped them away. "But, at least I'm not as distraught as I was."

"And that, of course, was the purpose of this conversation." Doc offered Scott a bright smile. "I admit confusion about the overall objectivity of space-time. But I submit that human perception affects its own conduct. You must believe that whether or not your folks are alive, at this time and in this place, you can equivocate your feelings according to chosen subjective precepts. That is the way to equanimity."

Doc placed a loving hand on Scott's shoulder. The warmth that passed between them offset the chill of the room. "We will do our best to bring them back to life. But should we fail to succeed, we can always sustain their lives from within. That is the great and awesome power of human emotion. It is truly infinite and unbounded."

CHAPTER 24

"Run for it! Run for it!"

The Fusilier who ran screaming around the corner fell headlong on the deck. He landed with a thump that was padded by dragon clothing, but the battery pack he wore clattered and scraped across the rime-covered plastic. He slid for twenty feet before his pack crashed into an encapsulated dragon. He made no attempt to draw his weapon.

"Come on! Come on!"

Although her arms swung in wild contortions, the woman rounding the corner maintained her balance. Her laser pistol was still snugged in its holster. "Where's Dan?"

"He's down. I saw him faint like the others."

Scott was galvanized into action. He rushed past Doc, skidded in his haste on the ice, and crashed into Sam and Windy, nearly knocking them down. "What's happening?"

Sam ignored him, other than to use his shoulder to lean against while he regained his equilibrium. He blew retreat on his whistle.

Windy crouched and drew his gun. He stood poised with the nozzle aimed along the darkened corridor. "I don't see nuthin'."

The shrill blast of the whistle brought commandos running and slipping from all sides. Hal, the man who lay on the floor at the far end of the corridor, was helped up by his partner, Lynn. They ran as fast as they could on the frosted deck.

"Why the hell ain't they shootin' at nuthin'?" Windy spat, covering for the runaway pair.

The intersection that Hal and Lynn were retreating from exploded silently with a harsh, white light. Despite the weight of the backpack on her slender frame, Lynn quickly outdistanced her companion. In his panic, Hal's feet kept slipping from under him.

"I still don't see—" Although they were several hundred feet away, Scott expected to discern among the shadows some threat of dragon pursuit. Yet, there was no movement but the scampering duo.

Fifty feet overhead, another white light flashed on. Hal slumped to the deck without a word. Lynn spun around, fell, climbed to her feet using a crystal sarcophagus for support, started to go to his aid, stopped, then turned and ran.

Sam kept tooting his whistle. Most of the men and women under his command were pouring out of side passageways into the main corridor of the huge dome. Those farther afield had not yet appeared.

"Doc!" Scott looked to the doctor for aid.

The older man ambled along the frosty deck. "Without more information—"

Several people joined Lynn in her madcap scramble along the central corridor. Another ceiling globe shed light on the deck and on the frosted prism faces. Lynn screamed. Except for the row of incandescent bulbs that flashed on behind her, Scott saw nothing untoward. If anything was chasing her, it was invisible.

"Get back!" Lynn screamed. "The lights—"

Every gun was drawn. The troops were agitated, but no one knew who or what the enemy was, or how to fight it.

Sam stopped blowing the whistle as the frightened gal skidded to a halt on ice-capped moccasins. "What is it—"

"I don't know," she gasped. "Something—I couldn't see. It just—puts you to sleep. The light—a warning—"

Even as she spoke, another globe burst into full brilliance.

Windy discharged his laser gun at it. The globe was over a hundred feet away, but his aim was true. The bulb blew apart as the searing flash of raw energy drilled a hole through it and destroyed a sizable portion of the ceiling.

"Do not bother killing the messenger," Doc said hastily. "It may be our only indication of impending disaster."

"But what—" Sam started.

"A narcotic gas, I suspect, against which we are defenseless. I suggest a propitious retreat." Doc did not wait to see if his recommendation was being heeded. He turned on his heel and shuffled as fast as he could across the slippery floor. For added support, he pushed his cane across the deck.

Scott made no comment about Doc's choice of words, but followed his lead.

It took two seconds for Sam to blow the signal to charge. A few stragglers who were scurrying to join the group found themselves the only ones remaining in the dome. In complete rout, the erstwhile commandos poured into the tunnel that connected the dome with the melted basin. There were no ranks and files, but a disjointed, shuffling mob.

When Scott had prowled the tunnel on the way into the dome, traction had not been a problem. But in the rush of withdrawal, his plastic stump was a major hindrance. He gained extra support by working his hands along the frosted bulkheads. The ceiling-mounted annunciator lights that popped on behind him lent wings to his foot.

"The lights ain't comin' on no more," shouted Windy.

"Don't slack off," Sam called out. "It could be a ruse."

No one wanted to be last in line. The race

along the tunnel was a controlled sprint in which the competitors struggled to maintain footing as well as placement.

Halfway along the tunnel, with no more globes indicating the presence of gas, and with everyone slowing down from fatigue, Sam managed to gasp, "Got any comments, Henry?"

"None that you care to hear."

Finally, out of sheer exhaustion, the commandos slowed to a fast shuffle.

Sam yelled angrily, "Come on, people, get some distance. You're bunched up like grapes."

With the adrenaline flushed from his body, Scott lagged behind. "Could be a death gas," Sam continued.

"Unlikely." Still catching his breath, Doc spoke in terse terms. "Too much inherent danger—to the home guard—collecting in pockets—before dissipation."

"How do we get our people out of there?" Sam wanted to know. "How can we ever know it's safe?"

The jogging gait was a torturous one for Scott. His stump hit the deck like a pogo stick without a spring. Without muscles to absorb the shock, the pounding of his stump sent painful vibrations up his leg.

"We must capture the stronghold in order to learn its operations."

"Oh, we're gonna do that, all right. I'm missing five people back there, and I intend to get every one of 'em out."

Scott thought briefly about the others who were in the dome, frozen in time. He shook his head in order to clear his mind of such abstractions. He must be strong; he must exercise control. The universe was a crazy, contorted, complicated continuum: a space-time full of interchangeable parts: multidimensional orbits of infinite lengths, crisscrossing like wet strands in a pot full of boiled spaghetti.

From his personal pinpoint perspective, the future fluctuated according to what had occurred in his past. But, as he had learned, the past was as malleable as the future. If past and future events interacted, then neither could claim to be the cause or effect of the other. Conversely, if a change in the past could affect the future, could a change in the future affect the past? The direction of time flow was not an absolute, but a point of view. In the grand picture, all moments of time occurred simultaneously; what he interpreted as flow was how he moved with respect to events: that was what gave life continuity.

Scott shrank mentally. According to Scott's placement along the stream of consciousness, he had already suffered the loss of his family: he had experienced that pain, and recovered from it. They died a million years ago, in his past but in this world's future. That torment was behind him. But if he were to lose Jane . . .

"What was that?"

Lost in reverie, Scott had only a subconscious impression of a flash of light. He squinted. Another beam lanced across the mouth of the tunnel. "It must be a fight—"

"Damn!" Sam gritted his teeth. The whites of his eyes glowed in the dimness of the tunnel. "We must have triggered a sensor—"

"We better hurry." Windy drew his pistol. He made wide sweeping motions with his arms in order to clear the folds of his jumpsuit. "Sounds like things're hot 'n heavy out there."

The crackling of laser guns was clearly audible. Muffled shouts attested to a staunch defense. A commando silhouetted in the predawn light ducked into the dressing room, chased by searing lightning bolts. Scott suddenly realized how exposed their position was in the smooth-walled tunnel. Unless they reached the dressing room before—

A wheeled truck rolled to a halt at the mouth of the tunnel, blocking the entrance. The vehicle carried no guns, but a squad of armed soldiers dismounted behind armored flaps. The Rangers hit the deck as laser beams arced overhead. Scott felt naked without a gun.

"Fire at will!" Sam shouted over the tumult.

The front rank knelt and let loose bolts of lightning at the truck. The armor soaked up the energy like a sponge. Stragglers in the after ranks rose up on their feet to fire over the heads of their comrades. The return fire was slow and methodical and not very accurate. Blobs of hot plastic that were gouged out of the floor spattered the troops with telling effect, almost like the blast of a grenade. Commandos squirmed away from the molten showers like noontime worms on a hot macadam road.

"Get fire superiority on 'em!"

Without cover, the only tactic that would save them was to keep the heads of the enemy where they could not see. The dragons did not show themselves, but poked their guns through portals in the armored flaps, and fired randomly. It was a temporary standoff, with the commandos

at the disadvantage.

Out of the dressing room flew an insulated jumpsuit. It landed in front of the truck almost touching the armor belt. Another jumpsuit sailed in the air completely over the ten-foot-high flaps behind which the dragon soldiers hid. Then came another, this one landing on the roof.

A high-pitched voice shouted, "Flame it."

Several seconds passed before someone got the idea. A grounded trooper fired, cycled, fired again, and caught the padded material with a laser beam. The jumpsuit smoldered in the freezing air, then caught fire. The cold-weather uniforms kept flying out of the cloakroom, laying a blanket of combustibles for the pinned commandos to ignite. Soon smoke and flame hid the truck behind a pall. The soldiers may not have been in danger of burning, but the effect was at least as good as that of a smudge pot.

"Cover me!" Scott leaped to his foot and charged for a wall panel. He was fully exposed. He peered through the black haze for signs of movement while his fingers groped along the darkened bulkhead. He quickly located the exposed latches; in a moment he had the access panel removed. He flung it aside and tumbled into the crawlspace amid a network of cables, conduits, and junction boxes. If he had not been wearing the thick jumpsuit, he would have been gouged by corners and sharp edges.

"Come on!" Scott ordered.

Windy climbed in right behind Scott, then turned and helped Doc over the raised lip. "Get in here, ever'body!"

One by one the commandos charged into the confines of the crawlspace, while others laid down a suppressing fire. One dragon soldier lumbered toward the dressing room; as soon as it left the protection of the armored flaps, it was caught in the combined beams of three laser guns. The dragon's breast and bulbous body were drilled through; it lurched over on its side, legs kicking ineffectually in the air. The jumpsuits kept coming and feeding the blaze.

"Let's flank them," Scott said. He squeezed along the crawl space with his hands in front of him, feeling his way in the dark. A pipe rack served as a highway. He did not pick up his foot and stump, but slid his thick booties along the raceway so as not to lose contact with it. He heard people clattering through the wires behind him.

A light flashed on and cast its beam over his

shoulder. Windy said, "Kin ya see where yer goin'?"

"Hold it a little higher. But don't drop the gun nozzle; if it falls through the grate we'll never find it again." Below the raceway lay several tiers of pipes, open trays of insulated wires, and plastic structural supports. "Shine it straight ahead."

There was not far to go before the tunnel yielded to the bridge across the melt moat. In the stark white beam, Scott saw that the maze of pipes and wires converged through a watertight gland. "End of the line."

From behind Windy, Doc called out, "All this piping must go through the abnormally thick balustrades along the bridge."

"That's great, Doc. Windy, shine the light on the outside wall."

The beam jogged in a crazy arc that ended by illuminating the grate. "Tripped over my own two feet."

There was enough side glow for Scott to see the inside of the latch mechanisms. "Never mind. Screw on the laser nozzle." The crawlspace was not intended to be used as a hallway, and the access panels were not designed to be opened from the inside. "We're going to have to blast our way out."

"How're we gonna see where to shoot onct I take off the light?"

The crawlspace went dark.

Through the plastic bulkhead, Scott heard the muted sounds of battle. "We'll do it by feel."

Doc's voice was crisp and clear. "Be careful, my boy. An arm is not as easily replaced as a leg. Why don't you let me guide the beam."

"I'm ready," Windy announced.

"No chance, Doc. Now, Windy, I've got both hands on the cam locks. Hold onto my right hand, aim the nozzle, memorize the position, and we'll both clear the spot. Then give her the gun."

"Gotcha."

Torches bobbed in the background as the rest of the platoon shuffled along the crawlspace. The distant lights were too fleeting to be of any use.

Scott felt Windy's mitt feel its way over his. Windy squeezed twice, then let go.

Scott withdrew his hand. "All clear."

He was looking right at the spot as the laser beam burst through the cam and blew out the mechanism. He was temporarily blinded.

Windy's mitt covered his other hand, squeezed, and withdrew. "Okay?"

"Go for it."

The lightning bolt struck again. Several tiny drops of molten plastic stung Scott's face. His eyes were still recovering from the first brilliant flash as he leaned back, stood on his good leg, and kicked out with his rigid prosthesis. The panel crashed into the tunnel, and Scott wasted no time in tumbling out after it. He hit the deck in a roll that took him ten feet from the wall.

He was aghast to see the truck backing up, its front in flames. The dragon guards were retreating behind their armor. A hundred feet away the last of the Rangers was chased into the crawl space by stabbing laser beams. One dragon turned slowly, looked at Scott on the floor and Windy climbing out the opening, and swung its gun. The lizard hissed a warning to its comrades in arms.

Doc let out a blast on his whistle that attracted the dragon's attention. Windy got clear just as the dragon soldier fired its weapon. The beam narrowly missed the Ranger, and nearly parted Doc's hair as the electric discharge entered the opening and melted a batch of cables. The high-voltage short circuit exploded into a ball of brilliant white light that burned the insulation off neighboring cables.

"Aaagh," Doc screamed as he fell out of the opening with his back ablaze.

Without thinking about his exposed position, Scott leaped on the elderly doctor and smothered the flames with his own body. When he rolled up onto his knees, smoke was pouring off the front of his jumpsuit. He whipped it off and hurled it at the dragon that had fired at them. By this time the others had turned and were leveling their guns.

Windy scored a direct hit through the brainpan of the nearest. Scott grabbed Doc and pulled him to his feet. Quick action saved them all, for the laser blasts hit where the quick-witted humans had just been. Windy could not roll because of the battery pack on his back, but he scrambled on all fours across the tunnel, drawing off some of the fire.

Scott and Doc rounded the corner of the tunnel entrance just as another series of laser blasts seared the deck at their feet. They huddled on a narrow parapet that led down to the water's edge. The glacier wall at Scott's back was a monstrous barrier of ice that soared upward for hundreds of feet. Long, lancelike icicles dripped down the melting face. Cold air that radiated off the surface mixed with generated heat that pulsed outward from the stronghold.

Scott dared a peek around the edge and was quickly met with half a dozen lightning bolts that burned through the block of ice like hot knives through soft butter. "They're still backing up."

"A rather uncomfortable southern exposure." Doc pulled the folds of his jumpsuit around so he could see the hole that was burned in the seat. Then he removed what was left of the material.

"Right now I'm more concerned about our northern exposure." Scott lay flat and ventured a look into the tunnel. Two more wall panels were kicked out as commandos fought their way out of the crawlspace that was now a raging inferno. They were slightly in front of the slowly backing vehicle, and faced with the flames from the burning jumpsuits that clung to its forward armor belt.

Windy bolted to the opposite bulkhead faster than the dragons could track him. He fired on the fly, recording one body hit, then skidded onto the other parapet. He turned to pick off the dragons whose backs were exposed, but got off only one wild shot before he had to duck the concentrated enfilade from the dragon squad.

Laser blasts fired by the commandos who were back in the tunnel exploded against the side of the truck. Two more dragons went down before the armored flaps were folded back to create a cocoon. The flanking maneuver was only partially successful.

"Doc, we're in trouble." There was no place to hide unless they dived into the water and stayed submerged until the truck passed the short expanse between the tunnel and the bridge. Scott pulled out his only weapon, Death Wind's knife.

"So it would appear."

A dragon detached itself from the truck and waddled straight toward them. The rest kept up their fire at the commandos. Windy got off a shot, but nearly lost his head in the process. One dragon was detailed to watch his position and kept its laser pistol firing at the corner. As its weapon recycled, the gun burnt holes through the rim of ice. Windy was forced back by the onslaught.

Doc's jumpsuit sailed in a perfect arc and wrapped itself around the advancing dragon's gun arm. It pulled the trigger, sending a flaming arc through the material and into the tunnel wall. Scott scuttled out from cover like an angry scorpion and pierced the dragon's abdomen with the knife, cutting edge up; then he gutted the stunned lizard with one swift stroke. Doc broke off a long icicle and charged like a jouster. He ran the ice javelin into the dragon's throat. It died without a hiss.

"Good work, my boy."

Scott was too busy to acknowledge praise. As the dragon hit the deck, he pounced on it, pulled the laser gun's connecting cable over the snakelike neck, and, using the dragon's body as a shield, fired into the remaining squad.

Windy was no longer pinned down. He shot into the exposed ranks with devastating effect. A moment later, commandos dashed through the smoke on both sides of the truck and caught the remaining dragons in a deadly crossfire. In a moment the skirmish was all over.

Scott sheathed his knife as he backed away from the blood and guts that poured out of the eviscerated dragon's abdomen. Doc placed a hand on his shoulder as they surveyed the damage. Windy danced around like an egotistic prizefighter touting his victory. The Rangers ran coughing out of the smoke that was filling the tunnel. Flames licked out of the open access panels as fires fanned by the air current raged out of control within the crawlspace.

Sam appeared with Helen in tow. "Well, you certainly gave us the advantage we needed."

"I was coming to warn you that the jig was up when that truck started chasing after me. Then I was afraid I was bringing you trouble instead of getting you out of it."

Sam gave her a resounding smack on the lips. "Well, you sure showed your spunk. You're the greatest."

Helen returned his kiss. "You always say that when I save your life."

As they stumbled away from the broiling fumes, Doc said wryly, "Excuse me for intruding upon your mutual admiration, but have you noticed the time transport structure?"

Scott glanced toward the center of the stronghold. The focusing nodes coruscated with the brilliance the preceded a transfer. A clap of thunder echoed off the ice walls. The TTS went dark.

Something had been either sent or received. What, and when, only time would tell.

CHAPTER 25

The *Ark* popped into real time over an Earth that was green and verdant.

Ned whistled at the downscreen. "Will you look at that?"

Rusty was too busy working the controls to admire the scenery. He glanced only briefly at the luxuriant forests that could be seen through wisps of stratocumulus. He grunted and continued to run checks on the temporal formulations.

Britt concentrated on piloting the craft. Almost single-handedly she brought down the *Ark* in a slow, controlled descent, without inducing a horizontal spatial vector. She maintained an even keel with the utmost precision by modulating the thrusters. "Dragon station below."

"I hope your timing is good," said Ned.

Rusty leaned back as the computer program ran its course. "The *Ark* is our timekeeper. The purpose of the formula is to get us off the eternal treadmill that the dragons are on. If you look at time as a conveyor belt, and the various dragon installations as packages on that belt, locked in position, then you can understand the difficulties of what we're trying to do. Let's say the packages are exactly ten feet apart. If we know how much thrust is required to jump from one package to another, we can do it repeatedly and without error. But suppose we jump from package A when it's passing point twenty-seven; we don't want to reach package B at point thirty-seven, but at the point when it was first put on the belt."

"And that's what your formulation calculates?"

"Ostensibly. In actuality, I didn't have enough points of reference to make a sound statistical analysis in order to define the temporal constant with perfect accuracy. But the time-displacement data gathered from this transfer will help to refine the computation."

"In other words, we're temporarily uncertain of our whereupon. Or is it whenupon?"

Rusty smiled. "I guess you could say that we know our whence, but not our whenabouts." He placed his hands behind his head. Long red curls framed his face like a disarrayed Raggedy Ann doll. "Until I factor in our temporal drift, if I hit the reversing switch we'll go back to a point as far downstream from when we started as we have flowed in this time zone."

Ned nodded, but he wore a puzzled frown. "I think I getcha. But we can't play temporal yo-yo till the capacitors recharge. How long's that gonna take?"

"The drain on the circuits is the product of the length of time traversed, the mass being transferred, and the amount of matter displaced at timefall. Recharging capacity is a straight-line function of available power, minus continued usage. If we wanted to flit a few years we could do it as soon as the focusing nodes cool. To get back to when we started, twelve hours."

"Coming into range," Britt called out.

Rusty leaned forward to study the downscreen. He set the optics to full magnification. Directly beneath the *Ark* stood the dragons' most future construct: a small time transport facility that was surrounded by a few scattered, prefabricated buildings. There were no outlying defense fortifications, no pillboxes, no visible armed guard, not even a reactor plant. The quarters most likely housed technicians that had been sent ahead to erect the housing for the ITS. This station could not yet transmit; it could only receive.

"Well, we could have gotten here sooner, but it looks like we're in time." Rusty grinned like a Cheshire cat.

"Why not go back a few weeks and pick 'em off as they come out of the past?" Ned wanted to know.

"Well, by that time we could have this place knocked out."

"What do you mean by 'that time'? I thought you said there was no such thing as that time, only this time?"

"You know what I mean."

"Hell, I don't even know what *I* mean." Ned scratched his head. "You keep confusing me with all this time talk. I just figured that if we went back a bit we could blow up the joint when the first dragon stuck its neck through. You know, nip it in the bud."

"Then this place wouldn't be here, now."

"That's right." Ned squinted hard. "Wait a minute, if this place is here now, it means we didn't go back and blow it up earlier."

"According to one theory."

"But suppose I convince you to do it? What then?"

"As much as I debated the point with Doc, I'm not really sure. It's one thing to argue theory, it's quite another to test it out. And when you come right down to it, mathematics is a trick: a human convenience that was developed by human mentality in order to create analogies for a mind that can't imagine the resultant concept. Analytical studies may have no validity in a purely objective universe—assuming there is such a thing. Of course, I'd never admit that to Doc."

Ned shook his head. "It's too much for my poor noggin. If I see it, I'll believe it. You gotta show me."

The proximity alarm went off.

"What the—" Rusty sat bolt upright. He stared at the screens with stunned intensity.

The *Ark* dropped rapidly under Britt's control. "Missile launched."

"Impossible!" In the middle of the downscreen Rusty saw the foundations of the new time transport structure; a few low sheds stood nearby. There were no external silos, and under the flame of the rocket that was fast approaching, he saw no opening to indicate an underground launch pad.

"If you see it, you better believe it," Ned yelled. "It doesn't take math to prove what's in front of your eyes."

"I'm taking over!"

Britt relinquished control to the more experienced pilot. "It is yours."

The *Ark's* altitude was so low that contact with the missile was only moments away. He applied lateral thrust, but knew in his heart that he could not maneuver the *Ark* out of the missile's flight path.

"It's gonna be a close one," muttered Ned.

The bridge toner alerted the gunners of impending disaster. Barrels swiveled on their mounts.

"Where did it—" Rusty tapped for full power. Only radical action was going to save the *Ark* on such short notice. "Hang on to your seats."

He switched off the gyroscope, then withdrew all power from the lifting cones on one side of the vessel and transferred it to the cones on the other side. This pitched the *Ark* into a nearly vertical glide, like a child's top on end, and nearly capsized her. Only deft manipulations kept the saucer from tipping end over end. With the upper thrusters blasting away, the *Ark* dived at a speed that she had never before attained.

The missile's course veered, but not nearly swift enough to compensate for the plummeting flyer. The two machines missed each other by a hairbreadth. The missile arced out of sight on a new trajectory. It crashed in the forest with a dull thud but no explosion.

Rusty fought to get the *Ark* under control before she crashed into the ground at greater than full speed. He reversed the lifting cone power controls, switched the gyroscope into horizontal-seeking mode, waited breathlessly while she leveled out, then applied full power to all the cones. Some of her momentum was transferred into lateral motion. The saucer scorched the treetops as she descended into the upper canopy.

Full thrust finally stopped her downward motion and very slowly began to lift her out of the leaves and branches. The fragile vegetation did no damage to the *Ark's* undercarriage. Rusty began to breathe again. He looked for the first clearing that was big enough to accommodate the saucer's diameter. He made a successful if somewhat shaky landing.

Long afterward, he sat shaking his head in disbelief. "I still don't believe it."

CHAPTER 26

"Time marches on."

"A very profound statement, Henry." Sam led his troops across the bridge at a fast walk. Despite the exigency of the situation, they were still recuperating from the exertion of their two-mile jog out of the tunnel and the fight at the end of it. It did not pay to go into battle completely exhausted. "But which way is it marching?"

"As far as we are concerned, downstream, into the unknown and the unknowable."

"I'm not so sure about that anymore, Doc." Despite the pain in his leg, Scott maintained the pace. The battery pack and laser gun instilled him with confidence and a feeling of power. "I have my doubts about what was, what is, and what will be. All points in time are interrelated, like some cosmic cryptogram. We just don't know how to decipher the temporal enigma."

"Life may be a simple cipher in both meanings of the word."

Windy drawled, "I wisht I knew what you fellas were talkin' 'bout."

"So do I," said Scott.

Helen pointed to a glade on the right side of the road. "We're holed up in there. The forest is honeycombed with animal trails. Watch out for the critters that make them: two-legged dinosaurs like giant turkeys. They run like the devil, but if you get them cornered they'll peck you to pieces." She pointed to her bare thigh; the bronzed flesh was pockmarked. "They have sharp beaks, but fortunately they don't have teeth."

Scott would have walked into the fence had not Helen stopped the procession. The strands were made of clear plastic and stretched from tree to tree to a height of ten feet. Helen took them through a gate that had been made by burning the drawn plastic off tree-mounted pegs. When everyone was inside, she lashed the strands together with sections of vine.

The sun was not yet visible because of the depth of the stronghold inside the glacier, but the sky was brightening. The tall grass in the glade wavered as scuttling creatures dashed away from the approaching warriors. Helen took them to a nook created by dense, overhanging branches. Waiting for them, with weapons drawn, were half a dozen women who were guarding supplies.

"So where's the fighting?" Sam wanted to know.

"There hasn't been any—except for the trouble that you stirred up. Out here it's been quiet as a spring morn, with nothing moving but these damnable insects that the dragons must have brought from the past."

"Hell, I thought we were getting in a major confrontation."

Helen shook her head. "No, that truck must have been a border patrol vehicle. When I saw them coming down the road, I ran across the bridge and hid on the parapet. They didn't know I was there. It wasn't until I saw you in the nightlights, and they started to cross the bridge, that I went to warn you."

"Well, the alarm's given now." Sam looked back at the smoke curling up from the tunnel entrance. "I asked the Nomads not to give us away, and I went ahead and did it myself. Now we're in for it."

"Our hand is certainly tipped," Doc admitted with a wry grin. "What began as a siege has just been promoted to a full-scale invasion. I suggest that while we are experiencing a temporary lull in the fighting, we push our advantage toward the inner stronghold."

"Let's do it. Helen, get your gals together and follow us with all the supplies. We don't know what we'll run into. Windy, send your fastest troops ahead with the message that we're attack-

ing in force. Work out flanking maneuvers with Broderick. And if you can catch up with Bold One tell him to—uh—hell, the jig is up. Just tell him to use his head."

Windy threw off a salute and dropped back to his platoon.

The Femme Fatales within hearing range did not need to have Sam's orders repeated by Helen. Helen said, "What about the cannon?"

Scott thought about the weeks of hard work in dragging the heavy-duty laser cannon through the Pleistocene forests and swamps, across the continental ice fields, through the long glacial tunnel, until it had to be lowered by ropes down the cliff face, loaded on a raft, and paddled across the near-freezing waters of the lake. An incredible amount of energy had gone into getting it this far.

"It may be the only thing that'll knock out those armored trucks."

Sam rubbed his hands over his black beard. "You're right, Scott. Hell, we brought it this far, we're not gonna leave it now. Windy," he called out. "Detail a couple of men to cut a path for the cannon. Helen, can your gals manage to keep hauling it?"

"You try and stop them and you'll have a mutiny on your hands."

Sam gave her a peck on the cheek. "That's the spirit." He raised his voice authoritatively. "Okay, let's move out."

Two women slipped into the traces of the travois with the laser cannon and its battery packs. Others picked up packs of food, fuel, tools, utensils, and miscellaneous supplies. The Rangers struck out through the forest, beating a path through the brush and chasing out the dinosaurian vermin that flocked in hiding.

After thirty minutes the troops made a strip stop. Scott shed his long-sleeved tunic and cut the leggings off his trousers. Tropical conditions seemed unnatural during an ice age and in the middle of a glacier. If the dragons could not land in a time that suited their needs, they converted the environment to suit them.

Death Wind appeared among them as silently as a wraith. "Got message. We still undercover."

Sam stuck out his hand and grappled arms in traditional Nomad style. "Good to see you, Death Wind. Are all your people okay?"

The single, slight tilt of his head was an affirmative nod.

"What about enemy movement?"

"Trucks in road, but dragons stay out of woods."

Sam scowled. "We could snipe them to pieces if they'd fight on our grounds. Okay, what's the layout? How close to stronghold central can we get in the trees?"

"Some pens big dinosaurs, we avoid. Other pens little. Soon we come to end. Buildings. Roads. Much traffic now."

"You know we blew our cover?"

Death Wind nodded. "Dragons not know we are in pens. We wait for orders. Once we leave forest, all is open. No cover."

"Good work, Death Wind. Well, Henry, what's your advice? In twenty-five words or less."

Doc pursed his lips and tugged on his beard. "Quite a task, considering my penchant for verbosity." He paused to collect his thoughts. "Since we have control of this quadrant only, and since the roads between quadrants are now being patrolled, chances are that we cannot successfully execute our original diversionary tactic. Therefore, instead of feinting from opposite sides, I suggest that we make a direct frontal approach with everything we have."

"Take the ball and run right up the middle, huhn? It smacks of the kind of audacity I'd expect from you. But the troops'll be exposed to danger the whole way. And if the dragons've got those shielded vehicles to hide behind, we'll be at a disadvantage. You saw our laser beams bounce off the armor belt."

"If you want a guaranteed victory, I cannot offer it. The only guarantee in war is that of an honorable demise."

Sam sighed. "I don't like to hear that, but ignoring the truth won't make it go away. Okay, let's get on with it. I want everyone massed at the innermost fence, the Rangers at one end, the Fusiliers at the other. The rest of us'll spread out in a line between."

It took an hour to get into position, by which time the dragon border patrol was in full force. Surprisingly, the actual count of enemy soldiers was not as high as was anticipated.

"You know, it makes sense in a crazy kind of way," Scott crouched by the trunk of a magnolia tree and peered through the brush at a patrol truck passing slowly along the inner circle route. His hands sweated in anticipation of the upcoming battle. "This place isn't built like a fort or garrisoned like we'd expect. The dragons couldn't have known in advance that it would have to be defended—not even by wild animals. I don't think we're going to find much resistance."

"I do not want to appear overconfident, but I quite agree with you." Doc knelt with his bad leg stretched out; he balanced himself with his cane. "The stronghold appears to be impregnable because of the sheer ice walls. Once it was cut off from the other time zones, there was no way to bring in reinforcements. These armored trucks are more likely proof against escaped dinosaurs—such as those triceratops."

"Theories later. For now I'm gonna expect the worse." Sam blew a signal on his whistle. "All right, let's go get 'em. First thing we do is take out that truck."

The fence was cut in a dozen places. As the nearly invisible strands fell away, the commandos slipped through and created a battlefront. Two women dragged the laser cannon out of cover and parked it at the edge of the road. The truck slowed; it was in range of the cannon, but the cannon was not in range of the back-carried guns of the soldiers on the truck.

One well-placed shot blew away the grill, and destroyed the motor and the first two axles. A loud hurrah went up from the commando ranks. Sam blew the signal to charge. The entire company flowed out of the trees and onto the road, completely uncontested. They screamed like a tribe of attacking Indians in a Western movie.

Scott felt the thrill of excitement race through his body. His plastic stump whacked against the pavement, but he ignored the pain that it transmitted up his leg. The exhilaration of the charge obliterated all other feelings. This was man primeval: a raw, uncomplicated bundle of nerves, acting instinctively and without forethought; the deeply embedded trait that carried men into battle without fear of death; the unreasoning part of the brain left over from earlier evolutionary beginnings.

The time transport structure stood nearly a mile away, tall and coruscating. Between that and the edge of the forest and dinosaur pens lay low buildings, courtyards, alleys and pathways, and a series of thoroughfares that radiated outward from the TTS like the strands of a spiderweb. The commandos raced toward the center of the stronghold while screaming war cries.

Scott was unable to hop about the plastic barricades like the others, so he stayed on the main road, leading the way for the gun carriers. An armored truck coming straight toward him slowly extended its flaps and deployed marching dragons.

"Come on, let's blast them!" Scott shouted to the cannoneers.

It took but a moment for the women to pivot the travois in a semicircle in order to train the laser nozzle at the truck. The first shot blew off one of the flaps and bowled it over the soldiers that were hiding behind it. Scott whooped as he ran along the roadside bulkhead toward the regrouping dragons. He heard the cannon charger whining, felt a blast of heat, saw the other flap destroyed and another squad of dragons knocked onto their tails.

"Way to go!"

The truck's cargo bay disgorged another squad of soldiers. This was no nighttime patrol, but a fully loaded troop carrier. Laser beams licked the orangetop at Scott's foot; he ducked into an archway that led into a courtyard that was filled with lawn furniture and fleeing slaves. Hand-to-hand combat between Fusiliers and the house's inhabitants was raging unchecked.

Scott dashed up the interior ramp to the top of the roadside bulkhead. From this vantage point he fired down into the slow-moving soldiers. A flight of arrows descended into the melee as a squad of Nomads attacked from the other side of the road. The dragons were cut to pieces in the crossfire. Another blast from the cannon lifted the front of the truck straight into the air; for a moment it hung there like a rearing stallion, the wheels of all ten axles spinning madly. Then it fell forward with a crash and lay still in a cloud of smoke.

Using the bulkhead as a highway, Scott raced alongside the road, vaulting the archways as he passed from courtyard to courtyard. The weight of the battery pack was offset by the flow of adrenaline. Soon he was far ahead of the rest of the troops, deep in enemy-held territory.

Another armored truck turned the corner of an intersection and bore down upon him. The laser cannon was hundreds of yards away, on the other side of the flaming debris of the demolished truck. Scott hunkered down and waited for the troop carrier to pass. He sniped at a reptilian head that stuck above the folded flaps; the lightning bolt arced through the open mouth and out the back of the scaled head.

Scott was chased off the bulkhead by three retaliatory laser beams. He plastered himself to the parapet until the dragons adjusted their sights and fired their needle beams right through the plastic bulkhead. On hands and knees he scrambled out of the line of fire.

He had never felt more alive than after that moment of escape.

The truck halted to take on the single attacker. Scott popped his head over the bulkhead, fired, ducked, and crawled away before the return shots riddled the bulkhead and left it looking like a colander. Try as he might, he could not make a hit once the dragons were aware of his presence; they stayed behind their armor and fired through tiny slits as they adjusted their aim by looking through small transparent ports. As long as the dragons stayed inside, they were impregnable to assault by small-arms fire.

The Nomads beat this technical standoff with primitive weapons that could do one thing that Scott's laser gun could not do: go around corners. They lobbed their arrows high in the air and let them curve into the open cab. Two dragons were transfixed with the deadly plastic tips. A second flight did as much damage. Under the protection of a third volley Death Wind sprang across the open space between the opposite bulkhead and the truck, and flattened himself behind the rear armor beneath the gun ports.

As soon as another flight of arrows thwacked into the cab, he grabbed hold of the top rim, pulled himself up, and stabbed his spear into the nearest head. Then he fell back down and got low.

After another volley pinned the dragons in their truck, he repeated the maneuver with the same effect. One dragon stuck his laser nozzle over the top and fired straight down at the Nomad. The blast dug up orangetop, but Death Wind managed to sidestep the actual beam.

Scott stood up in full view on top of the bulkhead, stretched his arm out straight, and fired an energy beam right through the dragon's snakelike neck. It hissed painfully as it fell back atop one of its comrades. Scott gave Death Wind a thumbs-up. The Nomad returned the sign.

The truck retreated. The Nomad squad launched another volley of arrows into the troop carrier. Death Wind repeated his tactic. Scott sniped whenever he saw scales. Then Death Wind climbed onto the armor flap, straddled it with his legs, and picked off the stunned dragons with eager dispatch. Finally, he dropped inside the cab, slipped behind the driver, and jabbed him through the back with his spear.

Scott rolled off the bulkhead, hung by his hands, and plopped down to the road surface. He climbed up the side of the truck. "Nice going, Death Wind." In a flash he was inside, putting a stranglehold on the driver. "Give me a hand."

Together they dragged the heavy lizard out of the seat. They left it in the cargo compartment with the rest of the bodies.

Scott shrugged out of his battery pack and took over the controls. "Okay, let's turn this baby around and head for the command center. Then we'll give them some of their own medicine."

By now the shouts and shots of combat filled the air on all sides. The commandos were largely avoiding the streets where armored vehicles could hold them at bay. Instead, they dashed through the living quarters raising mayhem, and headed straight for the main objective: ignoring the pawns and going for the king.

While Scott turned and backed up the truck, the Nomad squad boarded, found the hydraulic mechanism that opened the rear armored flaps, and, after removing their precious arrows from the bodies, chucked out the dead and dying dragon soldiers.

"Wait for me," shouted a familiar voice.

Scott slammed the control rod into the neutral position and let the vehicle coast to a stop. "Hop aboard, Doc. This is the express bus to the time transfer station." Scott brought the multi-axled vehicle into a sharp turn by reversing the independent wheels on the left side as the right side wheels were still turning forward. "Just like you said, Doc: right up the middle. Dragon central here we come."

The truck lurched forward. Since the armored control cabin was designed for long-necked dragons, Scott had to stand in order to see out the pilot port. It felt good to have a machine under his control again.

"I must say, my boy, you have not lost any of your driving skills."

"Hey, I've been tooling these things around for sixty million years. Not to shower praise, but if you've driven one dragon vehicle, you can drive them all. They're consistent that way."

"Typical dragon uniformity. It is that predictable psychology that has allowed us to follow their temporal wanderings with such comparative ease."

"Yes, well, let's not start getting overconfident. We've done that too many times in the past—and in the future."

"I quite agree, my boy. I quite agree."

The truck hummed along the street unopposed. The sights and sounds of fighting were far behind. Death Wind stood on a platform with his head over the top of the cab; his long black hair whipped about in the breeze. The other Nomads kept a constant vigil on all sides.

"Doc, this is too easy. I'm getting scared."

"I understand your feelings. I am experiencing some trepidation myself. However, I can find no logical reason not to continue our course of action. Unless they have a cannon of their own, this vehicle is unstoppable."

Death Wind shouted, "There!"

Scott slowed down as the truck approached an intersection. Steam escaping from vents at the base of the roadside bulkhead formed heat waves in the air. Slaves and technicians that were milling in the alleyway appeared to dance sinuously through the inversion layer. Death Wind and the other Nomads ducked quickly, and stayed low inside the cargo compartment, so as not to give away the presence of an invasion force.

"Look at that!" Scott shouted with glee. "They don't even know the stronghold's under attack."

"Let us not assume that those in command are as ignorant. They did not send troops in armored vehicles as an ordinary course of events."

The TTS towered before them like a pulsating blue monolith. Because of focusing node leakage, it did not pay to recharge the capacitor banks unless a transfer was intended.

"Looks like they're getting ready to do something." Scott squinted through the Plexiglas port. "Reinforcements, maybe."

Now that the day was begun, the streets were crowded with dragons that were lumbering to their work stations. Scott slowed and weaved through the unsuspecting dragons.

"Hey, aren't they walking a little faster than normal?"

"Listen to toner," said Death Wind. "It give warning."

"Where's it coming—" Then he saw one.

Mounted on posts at each intersection were tonal repeaters, like loudspeakers that played only dragon message music.

Doc pursed his lips. "Another case of the unexpected. They are already mobilizing their defenses."

The crowds grew thicker. The dragons paid no mind to the troop carrier, apparently unaware that a captured vehicle was invading their inner sanctum. Scott slowed down even more. He did not want to give away their strategy.

"Notice that building on the left," Doc said softly. "The massive array of external piping is characteristic of a chemical factory. And it seems to me that the TTS is taller and slimmer than the others we have encountered: cylindrical as opposed to domelike."

"Terrific, Doc, but let's forget about scientific observations and concentrate on our primary goal. Unless we knock out that missile site we can't call Rusty for backup."

"Uh, quite right, my boy. I suppose that once we are reunited with the *Ark* we will have unlimited time for future studies."

"So let's avoid trouble and look around for a launching pad or an underground silo."

"It would not detract from our objective to first disable the time transporter. At this point that is a more tangible quantity, the results of which are every bit as important."

"Well, at least it would prevent the dragons from launching an attack through time." Scott made quick decision. "Okay, let's go for it."

He accelerated through throngs of dragons that were now showing signs of anxiety: the sluggish pace had picked up, and beady eyes twitched nervously. Toned commands directed workers to emergency stations and tasks that were unclearly defined, as if no battle plan existed for defense of the stronghold.

"This time I think we caught them completely by surprise," said Scott, grinning uncontrollably; his cheeks were about to burst from the strain. "Dragons have been taking up too much of our time, but I think after today their dominion will be timeless."

"I pray that your prophecy is not deterred by that line of defense that is consolidating ahead."

Several dragons wearing brightly colored capes directed a loose band of soldiers into ranks. Laser guns were drawn and aimed.

"Keep your heads down back there," Scott called out. "When Scott's afoot, dragons are in trouble."

The armored truck broke free from the crowd. The roadside bulkhead gave way to open orangetop that surrounded generating equipment, machinery, storage sheds, and mechanical spaces. Scott kept a steady hand on the control rod as the truck ran the gauntlet of bewildered soldiers. The first laser beam struck harmlessly against the side armor. Another blasted the front grill. The reinforced energy-absorbing plastic shields protected the truck and its occupants from small-arms fire.

"Unless they've got bigger guns than that, we're crashing this party like there's no tomorrow."

"I wish you could phrase that somewhat differently," chafed Doc. "That has such an aura of finality about it."

"There!" shouted Death Wind, pointing to the right.

A single-passenger vehicle that was operated by a caped administrator shot out of a motor pool. The dragon's mouth was open in a hiss that was lost in the cacophony of squealing wheels, zapping laser beams, and exploding lightning bolts.

Scott turned in its direction. "Stand by to ram."

The huge truck rolled over the hood of the roofless car, crushing the engine compartment and bringing the smaller vehicle to a grinding halt. The dragon driver was hurled through the windshield and under the truck's rearmost two axle trains; the reptilian head was squashed like soft dough. The truck trundled onward unabated.

None of the Nomads could return a shot, even with the power weapons that were taken from the vanquished dragon soldiers. To stick a head above the upper shield was to have it baked in the heat of deadly crisscrossing laser beams.

"Hang on, people," Scott sang out excitedly. He was so happy to be in the thick of things with Doc and Death Wind that nothing was going to slow him down. "It's going to get rough."

Doc wedged himself into a corner and held tight to a support bar. "You mean rougher."

Dragon soldiers faded back from the path of the rampaging troop carrier. Scott swerved from side to side, running over taloned toes or knocking lizards head over heels. One woman in the cargo compartment lost her grip and bounced off the walls like a billiard ball until another Nomad caught her. Lightning bolts bounced off armor as if they were no more powerful than flashlight beams.

"Way to go, Scott."

Scott did a double take. He stared at Death Wind for so long that the Nomad had to grab the control rod and straighten out the truck. Scott's jaw dropped; he had never heard Death Wind exhibit such emotion. He was speechless.

There were no more soldiers in front of them. Parting shots sizzled through the air, but were easily absorbed by the rear shield. The path to the TTS was clear. The truck sped across the lowered drawbridge. Mist rising off the cold water condensed in the hot air and clung like a shroud; the swirling white cloak had prevented distant observation of the TTS layout.

"What the—" A thick plastic slab rose to a height of twenty feet around the base of the elongated time transport structure. A garage door being swung shut was attended by a host of technicians, effectively sealing off the transfer area. The focusing nodes were wound to full excitement; blue static discharges crackled off the tips as if the entire structure were drooling electricity. Scott found his voice. "Whatever they're sending or receiving must be important."

Doc peered through a forward observation port. "The slab must be five feet thick. And why would they need a revetment—"

"This is no time to ask questions," Scott shouted. "Hang on, I'm going to ram the command center. Whatever that shipment is will be their last."

He hunkered down and braced his real foot against the forward bulkhead. He held on to the throttle with one hand and with the other prepared to meet the shock of collision. Doc put his back to the wall and closed his eyes. Death Wind wrapped his steely fingers around a support bar. He let out a savage scream that was the Nomad war cry. The other Nomads, hanging on to rods in the cargo compartment, whooped in chorus.

"Ready or not, here we come."

The time transport control equipment was housed in an adjoining building with a clear plastic front. Two caped dragons and a pawful of technicians idled around consoles and computer monitors. Those that were not facing the broad picture window turned around and hissed at the oncoming truck. They had time to do nothing more.

The armored grill crashed through the wall of clear plastic with an awful, gut-rending jar. Shards of clear and opaque plastic exploded inward from the force of the collision. The momentum of mass and speed carried the truck right over the nearest computer consoles and their reptilian programmers, and into the farthest, wall-mounted modules.

Scott was slammed against the forward bulkhead hard enough to knock the wind out of him and wrench a shoulder. He saw stars for a moment. When he opened his eyes he saw Death Wind crumpled in front of him; the Nomad shook his head and spit out a clot of blood. Then he looked up at Scott and gave him the thumbs-up.

Scott smiled. He heard a groan in the corner. Doc waved his hands in front of his face to clear the air. Dust and smoke filled the cabin. "Doc, are you okay?" Scott pulled him out of his fetal position and dragged him into the open air of the cargo compartment.

The doctor coughed once or twice as he groped for balance. "I am fine, but I fear that we may have damaged the transporter equipment."

"Damaged it!" Scott screamed. "Doc, we demolished it."

Nomads rose from the dust like a flock of phoenixes. None was hurt.

Doc brushed himself off. "We may have jammed the controls, but it does not look as if we have affected the imminent transfer."

Bits of plastic and chunks of framing tinkled down from the ruined building. Scott peered through the smoke and still-falling debris at the coruscating focusing nodes that were still spitting arcs. "Well, we can fix that." He dragged a laser gun out of the wreckage, slung it over one shoulder, and clambered up the sidewall of the truck.

No living dragons were left in the command center. The crew of technicians that had been shuffling out of the revetment approached warily until they saw Scott emerge from the cargo compartment. Then they hissed, turned tail, and waddled off like mute ducks.

"Come on!" Scott called to his companions. He dropped into the remains of the control room, amid a dozen small fires that had been ignited by electrical shorts. Pipes, wires, plastic parts, and electronic components lay in a heap, their original forms unrecognizable. He waded through the smoldering debris to the central console. Flames licked through the main control panel.

Scott stabbed the crystal eject button and pulled his hand back before his finger got burned. Nothing happened. Either the power was off or the mechanism was jammed. The console was quickly being consumed by fire. Scott pulled out his knife and jabbed the point into the bubbled facing. The hardened material did not yield easily. He pried off chunks of plastic until he exposed the locking gate, then forced the loading cam off its rails. He burnt the hair off his knuckles, but a moment later he held the diamond cube in his hand; the crystal surface was blackened with soot.

"For posterity," Scott said proudly, ignoring the pain of singed flesh.

The Nomads helped Doc down from the truck's high sidewalls. With pinched eyes the doctor gazed at the crystal surface that was blackened with soot. "Is it damaged?"

Scott humphed. "No way. It'd take more than low heat and a layer of graphite to rearrange the molecular lattice or prevent data entry and access." He stuck the data crystal into a pocket and resheathed his knife. "Let's go."

Scott, with singleness of purpose, did not wait for compliance, but kicked open the door with his artificial leg and stepped out into the sunlight. The air was hot, still, and humid. He strode straight for the massive door of the TTS revetment. It was not locked, but a powerful spring kept it closed. Without electricity to the hydraulic system he could not open it alone.

"Give me a hand."

It took all of them yanking on the full-length handle to swing it back enough to slip inside. They entered a huge room that was dimly lit by ceiling globes twenty feet overhead.

"The power's still on. Must have an underfloor feed."

"There should be a locking mechanism—"

"Forget it, Doc. Let it close." Scott wasted no time on trivialities, but strode across the cluttered room to the opposite door. Even inside the thick plastic walls he could hear the whining of the chargers; the focusing nodes were wound up to nearly full excitement. The closure on the inner door was the same. "Hey, I need a hand with this one, too."

Doc ambled along behind, poking and prodding the strange devices, crates of equipment and supplies, and partially assembled machinery. "This must be a storage facility for—"

"I said, forget it." Scott and the Nomads struggled with the other door. "We haven't got much time."

"This is curious." Doc stopped by a wheeled cradle that was covered with a synthetic tarp. He pulled off the covering to reveal a clear cylinder the size of a fifty-five-gallon drum. He stood like a stop-action character about to be animated.

With the Nomads pulling on the handle, the mammoth door opened enough for Scott and Death Wind to get their hands around the fat lip. They opened the door a body width. Heterodyning focusing nodes screamed; blue sparks showered off the inward pointing tips. Death Wind braced his shoulder against the door while Scott squeezed through. "Doc, are you coming?"

Doc was motionless. He stared at Scott with a quixotic expression on his face and a faraway look in his eyes. "I believe we are on the threshold of a great discovery."

"You got that right. Okay, you people stay here and hold the door." Scott stepped into the time transfer chamber. Death Wind was right behind him.

A hundred feet away stood a shimmering purple curtain that rose skyward like a round-topped granary. Surrounding it was the structure on which were mounted the focusing nodes, crackling in the charged atmosphere. The air smelled of ozone.

Scott studied a nearby instrument panel. The gauges indicated that the capacitors were fully charged: the transfer could take place at anytime. He felt the vibration of machinery through his foot and artificial leg: the transmission lines, the charging apparatus, the transformers, all were buried beneath the plastic decking.

"Either it's jammed, or it's set on automatic sequencing." Scott pulled the laser gun out of its holster and fanned it across the board of meters. Perhaps if he destroyed the instrumentation.

"Come quick!"

Scott jolted at Death Wind's faraway shout. The Nomad was no longer standing next to him, but was poised at the edge of the purple curtain. He waved for Scott to join him. Even as he watched, Death Wind stepped through the translucent barrier and disappeared.

"Death Wind!" Scott hobbled awkwardly because of his fake leg and the heavy battery pack that was slung over one shoulder by a single strap. He stopped at the edge of eternity. The static charge made his hair stand on end. He could hardly breathe. Looking up, he saw the yellow crescent of sunlight that circled the open top of the time transport structure. He felt like a microbe at the bottom of a ballpoint pen, between the cartridge and the holder.

The Nomad popped back into reality, grabbed Scott by the shoulder, and yanked him into the dead zone. The noise, the light, the odor, everything was gone: except the vibration. In the middle of the cone, where he expected to see a stack of supplies or a contingent of escaping dragons, was an empty floor that slowly slid apart like the iris diaphragm of a camera.

"What the—"

A bitterly cold mist rose out of the opening. When the floor stopped dilating, it left a circular pit of unplumbed depths. Despite his goose bumps, Scott stepped close to the edge and looked down. Thick, crystalline flakes surged upward past a pointed cone. A sudden explosion was followed by a blast of heat and a blue ring of fire that vaporized the artificial snow. Then the cone ascended, imperceptibly at first, but with slowly increasing speed.

"Get out! Get out!" Scott screamed. His voice was swallowed by the tenuous atmosphere. "Hurry!"

Death Wind needed no urging. He plopped through the curtain into the world of real time.

Scott saw the cone rise up out of the floor, heard the roar of rockets, then passed out of the semireality of impending time travel.

Death Wind shouted as he ran. "Close door!"

Scott was hampered by the off-centered weight of the battery pack. He struggled with the strap as he hobbled across the deck. He did not manage to dislodge it until he reached the door that the Nomads held open for him. He dropped the laser gun and skidded through the opening just as a tongue of flame erupted through the purple curtain and engulfed the staging area. His back was singed.

Then the door was slammed shut, and the missile rose unseen on a pillar of energy into the nebulous reaches of time.

CHAPTER 27

Rusty shoved Britt's hand aside and answered the bridge toner himself. To Ned's all-clear signal, he responded, "Sit rep." Ned's toned situation report was concise. "Victory. Come get us."

Rusty placed his fingertips on the keys again, to ask for clarification, but realized that Ned did not want to get involved in long-range tone talk when he could report verbally in a few minutes. Ned did not understand the anxiety level of those who had remained behind in the *Ark*. He toned simply, "Acknowledged."

Britt powered up the reactor pile. "If anyone was hurt, he would say so."

"Yes, I guess you're right." Still, Rusty did not like negative communication. It often left too much to misinterpretation. He folded his long body into the pilot's seat and ran his fingers over the controls. "Give the all-aboard."

Britt used the intercom toner to pass the message. One by one the various stations responded. The techs in training fidgeted in their seats as they looked to Rusty for guidance. He nodded silently and prepared the ship for takeoff.

The *Ark* lifted as smoothly on her power-beam pylons as if she were being hoisted by a hydraulic ram. At first the downscreen view was blurred: intense heat produced by the lifting cones reflected off the ground, each beam intermingling with those around it. As the ship rose above the reach of her own fire, the blackened, burned-out landing zone stood out amid the lush green foliage of the surrounding forest.

Rusty leveled off the *Ark* at five hundred feet, applied forward momentum, and sat back to watch the scenery as the flyer cruised over a landscape that was pristine in the abundance of life. Herds of cattle and horses grazed on lush plains, seemingly oblivious to the saucer that passed overhead. Tall oaks and taller redwoods cloaked a menagerie of wildlife. The treetops were alive with the song and the color of nesting birds. A fantastic array of ground dwellers moved like a carpet across the brush-covered topsoil. Flowering plants grew in great profusion. The land was alive.

The only scars were those that were left by the *Ark*'s brief touchdown and the recent dragon incursion. Left to its own devices, the Earth would soon obliterate all traces of both.

"Britt, tell the gunners to be on the alert. And watch the scanners and radarscope."

Britt nodded perfunctorily.

The *Ark* thrummed along with effortless ease. Rusty kept a sharp eye on the viewscreens. The sky was clear and blue, the outside temperature comfortable. If there was anything hostile down there, it was well hidden.

The toner sang. Ned reported that he could hear the *Ark* approaching. A few minutes later he toned that he had made visual contact. "LZ cleared."

Rusty slowed the *Ark* to a crawl, and gradually dropped elevation until she slipped over the upper canopy with just enough height to avoid singeing the leaves. As the machine coasted over the dragon advance base, he saw Ned's assault troops indicating a landing zone. The *Ark* hovered directly over the clearing. The remains of two prefabricated sheds hugged the perimeter, and dragon bodies lay scattered about from the recent fight. The solid plastic pad that was the foundation for the time transport structure, whose construction had not yet begun, was a place that Rusty wanted to avoid. He did not want the flyer parked in a spot where an object that was transferred through time might suddenly materialize. The effect on the *Ark* would be as disastrous as the backlash to the sending unit: mathematics proved conclusively that two material objects could not occupy the same space at the same time. Displacing air at one atmospheric pressure required enormous power; in addition, the energy of arrival was dissipated by an expanding shock wave equivalent to an aerial detonation.

Ned toned landing instructions as the *Ark* settled in place. The troops backed away from the tongues of purple flame. Rusty tapped vernier buttons in reverse, gradually diminishing the power to the lifting cones. The *Ark* landed as softly as she had taken off.

"Okay, shut her down," Rusty left the purely mechanical procedures to his crew. "Come on, Britt, let's go check it out."

Outside, Rusty and Britt dashed across the still-smoking grass. Rusty should have been ecstatic over their easy triumph; instead, he was troubled by the very fact Ned found so exciting.

"Your timing was pretty good. The dragons can't have been here more than a few days—a week at most. There was only one leader, two techs, half a dozen soldiers, and a bunch of goons. We made mincemeat out of 'em—it was nothing more than a mopping-up operation."

Rusty surveyed the crude advance base. "Where's the missile silo?"

"Ain't none. What you see is what you got." Ned stuck his hand behind his head and scratched his scalp. "Sure is a puzzler where that thing came from, 'less they had it sitting there on the TTS pad. Believe me, we checked everywhere. There's nothing within a mile of this

place that didn't either grow or was born here. I wouldn't have given the all-clear otherwise."

Rusty strode toward the circular pad. "It looks blackened, and ripply. But why would they have a missile sitting in the middle of their transfer platform?"

"Beats me. But you notice they didn't have any buildings close by, either. They're all way over on the other side of the clearing."

Rusty stopped at the edge of the pad. "Is it solid?"

"Appears that way. Following orders, I didn't let anyone walk on it in case they got caught in a transfer." Rusty nodded silently, observing.

"We found powdered mix in the storage shed. They got bags of it, and an epoxy additive, too. That's how they poured their plastic. And—"

"All right, let's get away from here in case they make another transfer. Even a small mass sent into a nonevacuated medium will cause a sizeable concussion."

"Could be another reason why the sheds are on the other—"

"Ned, let's saddle up and get out of here, *now*. I want to make a slow circuit to look for remote installations. Did you find any electronic equipment or receiver apparatus?"

"Yes, but we destroyed most of it already. Saved some for you to look at, 'cause it didn't look familiar to me. Figured you'd want to check it out yourself. All battery operated. And they got wires running into the woods—booby traps, most likely, or alarms. We can—"

"No, we'll do that later. Right now I want your troops out of here. Until we know for sure where that missile came from, we have no way of knowing whether or not they've established an auxiliary station that can launch a missile from a remote site."

"Hey, I never thought of that. Maybe we should—"

"We're leaving now, Ned. Britt, let's get started."

Rusty left Ned to gather his troops while he and Britt double-timed to the bridge. In short order the *Ark* was airborne. This time he took her straight up to an altitude of five hundred feet. The lateral thrusters were silent. The *Ark* idled in place as Rusty and a host of lookouts scanned the horizon for signs of the enemy.

"We're so close that unless a missile is fired right under us—"

A titanic explosion erupted on the TTS pad.

The flyer rocked violently and was lifted bodily on a column of expanding air. Rusty was pressed down in his seat by the sudden upward acceleration, then thrown to the floor by the *Ark's* wild gyrations.

On the downscreen monitor he saw a bright ball of blue flame spreading outward and upward. In the middle was a dark, cone-shaped object. His shock was so great that several seconds passed before he realized that he was looking at the business end of an approaching missile. The slender projectile rose slowly at first, struggling to break the bonds of gravity. As it gained momentum, it accelerated along a nearly vertical axis toward the hovering *Ark*.

"It's impossible!" Rusty leaped back to his console. His fingers hesitated over the control board. There was no way the lateral thrusters could move the massive bulk of the *Ark* out of the way in time to avoid the deadly missile. Even if the warhead malfunctioned as the last one had, a direct hit would prove fatal: the *Ark* would crash before Rusty could regain control.

Although the equation was simple, his brain burned in turmoil at the decision he had to make: the *Ark* had to move in time if she could not move in space. And Rusty had time for only one quick action.

He slammed his fist on the reversing switch.

CHAPTER 28

When the flames hit the laser gun's battery pack, incineration was immediate. The capacitor exploded against the bulkhead, shattering plastic, cracking the hinge, and partially dislocating the door. Flames licked into the storage room for only a moment. Then there was a tremendous *whap* as the focusing nodes discharged against their target.

All was silent.

The silence went on and on.

After what seemed like eternity, Scott drew in a deep breath of air. It tasted hot and pungent. He had skidded into a stack of pallets; enough empty, lightweight packing cases had fallen on his head to bury him. He struggled out from under the pile of debris. He did not hurt, and did not appear to be injured.

"Hey, is anyone alive?"

Doc lay on the floor with a tarp covering his body like a shroud. When he sat up he looked like a third-rate movie ghost wearing a sheet. He pulled the tarp off his face. "We appear to have survived another bout against the nominally unexpected."

Nomads lay scattered on the floor like discarded dolls. One by one they picked themselves up. Death Wind felt for bumps on his head. "Okay."

Scott dug dust out of his eyes. "Doc, we've solved the missile crisis. All this time, the launching pad was under the transporter. No wonder we couldn't find it."

"I suspected as much, although I did not grasp the full significance of its placement until now."

"Huhn?" On hands and knees Scott shuffled through the loose crates to Doc's side. "You mean you knew? Is that why you wanted to shut down the transporter first?"

Doc stroked his beard. "Let us say that the existence of an underground complex was indicated by the lack of visible evidence to the contrary. Mine was not an eminently inspired idea, merely one of deductive reasoning. Nor should the concept of a subterranean launch site be difficult to grasp for one of your experience."

Scott grimaced. "I guess I've spent so much time putting myself into dragon shoes, and thinking in terms of alien psychology, that I just never thought we'd both go about something the same way. They're always so different."

"It was you who said that all electrons flow alike no matter who drew the wire through which they move."

Scott held up his hands in defense. "But that's not the same. An electron is a product of nature, and thereby inviolable. Technology is a method of form that's developed according to the ideology of the originator."

"According to universal principles."

"Well, yes, but—"

A hand clamped down on Scott's shoulder. "Fight when right. Admit wrong." Death Wind winked at him.

Scott sighed deeply. "Okay. I'm wrong. But I still don't understand why they—Hey, wait a minute." He leaped to his feet and rushed to the jammed inner bulkhead door. He peered through a stress crack into the time transport structure. The focusing nodes were dark and quiet; the shimmering purple curtain was gone. Bright sunlight that streamed down the inside of the tower illuminated the floor; the iris diaphragm was still open. "We've knocked out the recharging circuit, but the missile—Where did it go? When did it go?"

"That is an answer which at the moment eludes me, at least in relation to this particular missile fired at this particular time." Doc rapped his knuckles on the plastic cylinder next to him. "But this explains why the missile that hit the *Ark* did not explode. It was not armed with a warhead—was not, in fact, designed as a weapon of offense against an aerial attack. Together with this rather elongated time transport structure, the dragon missiles acted as the delivery system for the mass euthanasia devices."

Death Wind gently, almost reverently laid his hand on the clear, glassy surface. "Death bomb."

"Yes. And that means that the Pleistocene stronghold must have been the *first* future base to be constructed in the dragon life extension program."

Scott passed the squad of Nomads who were listening attentively. "You mean, the dragons came here—er, now—in the beginning of their temporal campaign rather than later? But why?"

"It all fits neatly into place. Our own time—the Holocene—lay at the limit of dragon time travel due to the inherent engineering design of their transport equipment. When they constructed this stronghold, it was not only with the intention of leapfrogging into a farther future time, but for the purpose of carrying out the practical aspects of their nefarious plan of conquest. Do you remember the distillation plant that we passed on the way in?"

Scott had to think a moment before he vaguely remembered Doc mentioning it. "Sure."

"The dragons undoubtedly figured that the genocide chemical was too dangerous to produce in quantity in their own time zone—an accident could conceivably bring about the Great Dying that they were endeavoring to circumvent. How convenient to manufacture the deadly product now, when a handling mishap would not affect their home world.

"However, there was still the matter of releasing the chemical into the atmosphere above the various continents a million years hence. They did not have sufficiently advanced technology to construct a flying time machine such as the *Ark*, so they did the next best thing—they devised a stationary time portal through which they could launch missiles to carry the bombs to their future destinations."

Scott's jaw dropped to his chest. "Why,

that's—that's ingenious."

"Do not communicate your exuberance to Sam. He does not share our appreciation for the dragon's brilliance of concept."

"But, what about the missile that hit the *Ark*? And those others?"

Doc shrugged. "Dummy missiles without payload, modified for defense after we destroyed their home world. Dragons do not use explosives, thus they had none on hand with which to arm their warheads. I believe it was Rusty who said that a missile does not need to destroy a craft, it merely has to damage it severely enough so it can no longer fly. As you recollect, we did nearly crash."

"So you're saying that these missiles weren't designed to shoot down aircraft, they were leftovers put to another use?"

"Exactly. Once they executed their devastating pogrom against life in our time zone, and planted their seeding farms to cultivate the kind of livestock and vegetation that they wanted for the future, it was easier to drop later death bombs—on continents where they had not yet spread their influence—from flyers that went on exploratory missions. The extra missiles in the stronghold were probably being held in reserve for emergency use. You know the dragon's penchant for triple redundancy."

Scott nodded slowly, lost in thought. Then he remembered his sister. "And the crypts? Are those slaves and dragons in waiting?"

Doc nodded slowly. "Biding their time, so to speak. Remaining in stasis, in youth and good health, until the time is right—or will be right—to repopulate the future world."

"But, why wait? Why not send them right away? I mean, couldn't they colonize one time zone at the same time they were destroying another? After all, they didn't know they weren't going to succeed—"

Scott was cut off by a tremendous explosion that knocked him to the floor. An instant later a secondary shock wave more powerful than the first rocked the very foundations of the time transport structure. Compressed air forced itself into the sealed room through cracks and pinholes in the inner bulkhead; his eardrums felt as if ice picks had been driven through the membranes.

Sealed containers shattered from the concussion. The tinkling of plastic shards was mixed with the crash of collapsing shelves and cabinets. The roar and reverberation was attended by needle-like blasts of air that, restricted by the venturi effect, darted into the room like solid projectiles. The chamber filled with thick, choking dust.

Scott got his knees under his belly, but could not lift his head off the floor. He huddled on the plastic with his hands clamped over his ears, gritting his teeth in pain. When he finally opened his eyes he saw nothing but dirt and debris. Strong hands yanked him up by the shoulders. "I'm—okay. Check—Doc."

Death Wind went to the doctor and pulled him out from under a blanket of clear plastic shards. "Okay?"

Doc's eyes were glazed, and his head moved jerkily as if the joints were locked together. He was speechless.

Scott climbed to his feet still holding his ears. "That ringing—" Then he stopped and stared at the pulverized remains of the death bomb. Fear gripped him like a boa constrictor. "Doc!" He could not stop himself from backing away from the rising fumes—as if he could outdistance the deadly vapor, or by sheer willpower force the genie back into its bottle. He stopped breathing.

Choking and gasping, Doc waved his hands in front of his face. "Only dust my boy. It was emp—" He was taken over by a fit of coughing. The airborne grit threatened to smother him.

Scott staggered against the inner bulkhead; his knees shook uncontrollably. When he twisted around to support himself on the door handle, he saw through the dislodged hinge pin that the time transport structure had collapsed. The staging area was a giant junk heap of splintered plastic sheets, tangled electrical cables, and smashed focusing nodes. "What the—"

Across the dust-filled room, the Nomad squad shoved open the outer bulkhead door. The twang in Scott's ears grew louder and deeper, like the thrumming of a dragon flyer. Death Wind picked up Doc by the waist and carried him outside like a sack of potatoes.

Scott stumbled toward the rectangle of light. Outside, he eagerly sucked in great lungfuls of air. In his peripheral vision he glimpsed a shaft of purple radiance where the yellow globe of the sun should have been. "It's the *Ark*! Where the hell did she come from?"

"Or when," muttered Doc.

There was no mistaking the flyer for any other: the surrounding pincushion of focusing nodes was distinctive.

Scott grimaced. "This is a strange time for her to appear."

The lifting cones glowed weakly, and flashed on and off intermittently. The modified flyer dropped in stages: quickly when the purple beams died out, slowly when they flickered on. The short power surges were all that was preventing her from plummeting straight down on top of the wreckage of the time transport structure.

"She's in trouble!"

The gyroscope appeared to be out of order, causing the *Ark* to wobble like a child's top running down. With a pronounced but fluctuating list, the saucer edged away, hopscotching across the stronghold on short bursts of energy. She dropped dangerously close to the roof of the nuclear reactor containment building and barely scraped over the multistory administrative headquarters on the other side. Her lifting beams melted whatever they touched.

Scott grabbed Doc's free arm. "Come on. Let's go."

Death Wind, supporting the doctor's other arm, nodded wordlessly.

They and the Nomads staggered across the orangetop in the direction of the *Ark*. Dead and dying dragons lay everywhere; most were bleeding from the eyes, ears, and nose. The terrible concussion that was caused by the *Ark* entering the space-time continuum in the presence of a dense atmosphere was fatal to those that were close to the point of rupture, and that were not protected by an airtight barrier.

Everywhere the destructive force of the temporal incursion was evident. Large buildings were disjointed as if they had been picked up and dropped; small sheds and storage facilities lay flattened; exposed machinery was torn from its mounts; external piping systems had burst apart. As much of the stronghold as the eye could see suffered massive devastation.

The *Ark* disappeared from view behind a group of distant barns.

"She's coming down too fast." Scott cringed as he listened for the sounds of a crash. "If she hits too hard—"

Since the only enemy soldiers in sight lay still in death or writhing in pain, the Nomads relaxed their bows. They ran ahead as Scott and Death Wind kept pace with Doc. Both spans of the drawbridge had been knocked into the moat, submerged except for the broad balustrade that doubled as a piping raceway. The squad crossed atop the shattered plastic rail.

"I thank you for the relief, lads, but I believe I am now able to travel unassisted." Doc tapped the plastic road surface with the cane that he had brought through so many travails. "Almost unassisted."

Scott wiped sweat off his brow now that his hands were free. "Is it me, or is it getting hotter around here?"

Death Wind nodded grimly. "Hot."

Doc observed, "The steam is thicker close to the reactor building, perhaps because that is where the heat is generated."

"No, it's—" Scott glanced around at buildings farther away. "It's not just that. There's more steam everywhere. Visibility's down to barely five hundred feet. It wasn't that bad a few minutes ago."

Vapor rising from buried vents condensed into pockets of white fog amid an overall thickening mist. The stronghold's normally clinging humid atmosphere now took on the viscous appearance of a swampy miasma. The hiss of escaping steam became ever more apparent.

Scott had to yell in order to make himself heard. "Let's make a detour to the reactor building and check out the control room. This may be important."

The three of them veered toward the tall structure. The roof was a puddle that drooled off the edges like a cartoon caricature. The plastic melted by the heat from the *Ark's* lifting cones was slowly solidifying into bulbous masses; the walls sagged, then refroze in a permanent outward bulge. They entered the building through an opening whose door had been blown inward off its hinges.

"It appears that damage from the pressure wave was severe," said Doc, barely audible against the screaming clamor.

"I'll say it was. And dissolving the overhead power lines didn't help any, either. This place is a shambles." Superheated steam filled the corridors and seared Scott's lungs. "Forget it. We can't get in there."

Doc faltered in the ovenlike heat. "I cannot—"

"We leave." Death Wind turned Doc around and shoved him toward the doorway.

"Wait a minute," Scott shouted. He was practically blinded by the searing heat in his eyes. He blinked away the tears, but still could not see through the veil of steam. He felt his way along the corridor. "There may be a—"

Alone, he worked his way deeper into the reactor building. He heard Death Wind's muted shout, then the roar of venting gases drowned out all other sounds. He hunched low and maintained contact against the wall with one arm. If he ever became lost in the maze of hallways, he would never find his way out.

He reached an intersection, followed the corner around, and stumbled on. He tried to remember the layout of the many reactor buildings that he had penetrated in the Cretaceous, when he was sabotaging fission piles. Dragons were amazingly consistent in manner and method, taking uniformity of construction to the nth degree. He soon found what he was looking for.

The main control room would be situated close to the reactor core so that duty personnel could be near the manual overrides. Remote auxiliary testing stations were located strategically in order to allow backup crews to monitor such functions as radiation levels, power fluctuations, and coolant activity. These were not regulatory stations, but observation posts.

Dead dragon technicians lay sprawled on the floor or hunched over their consoles. This part of the containment structure was not kept airtight: there was no need to keep negative pressure anywhere except where radiation leaks could occur. The dragons had all died from concussion.

Scott cupped his hands over his eyes in the steam-filled room. The main computer was inoperative, and all the screens were blank. High temperature had fried the solid-state circuitry, and moisture had destroyed the keypads and electronic sensors. He pressed his face close to pressure gauges, thermocouple readouts, and glass-encapsulated dials, studying the mechanical pointers of each. The data he garnered was enough to corroborate what he feared.

He worked his way back to the door, ducked through steam into the corridor, and slammed into a resilient, moving object that knocked him hard against the frame. A mouthful of teeth glared down from a height of eight feet; sharpened talons gripped his shirtfront. Scott gasped as the dragon pulled him up against its scaly chest.

Its breath was hot and fetid. The lower jaw unhinged with snakelike breadth, and the slender tongue darted vibrantly with carnivorous intent. The beady eyes were twin incarnations of hellfire. The neck arched in the shape of a horseshoe as the ugly head reared, then plunged for the kill.

Without thinking, Scott whipped out Death Wind's knife and stabbed upward into the descending throat. The razor-sharp blade slipped through the soft underflesh and into the mouth; only the hilt prevented the tip from reaching the brain. If the caped dragon hissed, it was lost in the cacophony of shrieking steam. The head withdrew into the swirling mist as suddenly as it had appeared, leaving Scott staring at his upraised arm and the bloody knife as if it had all been a fantasy.

Scott kept the knife held out in front of him as he made his way blindly along the corridor wall. His throat burned as if he were swallowing fire. His eyes teared unmercifully. He got down on hands and knees to escape the thickest of the rising steam. At the first intersection he turned and kept sidling along the plastic bulkhead.

The wall bent back at a ninety-degree turn. Panic-stricken, Scott could not remember passing another intersection. He must have made a wrong turn.

A familiar face took form in front of him. "I worry."

Scott closed his eyes in relief when he realized that he was actually outside the building in the midst of escaping steam. "You were going in after me, weren't you?"

Death Wind did not answer, but pulled Scott away from the doorway. The savage led him across the orangetop to a thick plastic barricade. The air was still hot, but not steaming.

"Is the nuclear pile in danger of exploding?" Doc asked calmly.

Scott took several deep breaths before replying. "No way. Dragon reactors have too many built-in safeguards." He placed his hands on his hips, bent at the waist, and continued sucking in air. "But the radiation counters are all off scale. If you think this is hot, an hour from now we'll be glowing in the dark. At this point a meltdown is inevitable."

CHAPTER 29

"Are you sure she's in here?"

"I watched her come down. She hit pretty hard, but I didn't see no explosion."

Scott stared at the triple-canopy jungle on the other side of the severed fence. "Where's everyone else?"

"Bold One and Slender Petal, along with the rest of the Nomads, went in to scout a route. Sam an' Helen're hanging back fer Broderick an' his platoon—they got pinned down by a armored division an' lost a few troops." Windy pointed his laser gun at the trees. "Got some pretty mean critters in there, too. Big things like tanks with clubbed tails. I went in as fer as the pond. That's where I saw them giant turtles— the size o' ships they were, with heads like dormers an' oars fer feet."

"I have no doubt we can avoid water creatures, as well as slow-moving herbivores that are not aggressive by nature. Did you see any triceratops? They are a bit territorial."

"Nary a one. But that don't mean they ain't in there."

Doc bunched his lips. "Dragons mix their livestock less often than you mix metaphors. With a modicum of caution and a show of aggression, I think we can avoid direct confrontation."

Death Wind held up his bow. "Quiet weapons no good. Scare with noise."

"Yes, a near miss with a laser gun can no doubt frighten an entire herd. Well, we cannot do any good out here. Are your men—"

"Whoa, Doc. Here they come now." Scott thrust his finger at a group of people who were emerging ghostlike through wreaths of steam. He waved his arms over his head. "Sam! Over here."

The Gentleman General approached looking more grim than usual. "I'm sure glad to see you fellows. I thought we'd never find you in this mist. What the hell is going on? First the *Ark*, then all this steam."

"Doc thinks the *Ark* made a temporal breakthrough, but why here and now we don't know. The steam's being generated by a runaway reactor."

"Oh, great. That's all we need. Half the Fusiliers are still fumbling around in the fog. And we picked up a bunch of mutes from Charon." Sam jerked a thumb in the direction of the reactor. "Can you shut it down?"

"No more than I can turn off the sun. The radioactive core is melting right through the foundations of the containment building. The steam will stop, though, as soon as the pressure reaches the breaking point. It'll blow sky high." Scott saw the horror on Sam's face. "Not a nuclear explosion. That can't happen. But the steam vessels will burst. The heat's already expanded the turbine casing enough to lock it up, so there's no more electricity being generated."

Sam mulled the information for several seconds. "How long have we got?"

Scott shrugged. "We're out of range as far as shrapnel goes. It's the radiation that'll get us." He shrugged again. "Minutes. Hours. If we get a large enough dose we might live for now and die in a few weeks, or months."

Sam made an instantaneous decision. "Okay, I want everybody out of here. If the *Ark* is in there somewhere"—he jerked a thumb at the jungle—"find it. I'll stay behind."

"I'm not leaving you," Helen said calmly.

"Helen, we don't have time to argue—"

"Then, don't. Daddy, tell him how stubborn I can be."

Doc nodded grimly. "Sam, you—"

The general growled. "Never mind. I know what she's like once she makes up her mind. All right, get going. We've lost a lot of Fusiliers already. I can't abandon the rest. Just mark a good trail."

"A wise move, and a logical one." Doc started off through the parted fence. "Well, the decision is made. Let us act on it."

Windy yelled in his craggy voice, "Okay, troops, saddle up."

Scott said, "As soon as the steam plant blows, things'll start clearing up. If the *Ark* can still fly we'll come looking for you."

As he ducked into the dense brush he heard Sam call after him, "Only if it's safe. Otherwise, save yourselves."

Scott did not answer. The question that was paramount in his mind was: what if the *Ark* can't fly?

Death Wind took the lead, effortlessly following the path of his tribe members. The dense brush close to the fence was more of a sight barrier, and soon yielded to more open areas that were easy to travel. The soil underfoot, all of which must have been transported through time from the Cretaceous, was soft and loamy: a startling recreation of the dragons' home world.

Turkey-sized dinosaurs scuttled everywhere, and smaller cousins clung to the bark of magnolias, dogwoods, palms, and willows. Huge insects flitted about the laurel. In a clearing they spooked an ankylosaur, a squat quadruped that was armed with twin rows of spikes and a clubbed tail, but it scampered off at the first sign of human intrusion. Scott wondered how long it took a forest to reach its present dimensions. Dinosaurs matured quickly, but some of the trees were over a hundred feet tall.

"Ain't gonna find no tyrannosaurs, are we?" Windy asked softly.

"Dragons did not bring predators into the Holocene, so I doubt that they had a need for them now. Just keep making noise. I am sure that most of the inhabitants will run at our approach."

"Didja hafta say 'most'?"

Doc swiped his cane through the dangling vines as if it were a machete. "It pays to be alert."

The steam vents were cleverly covered with grates or thick screens that could bear the weight of the multiton denizens, and were placed near trees where they were less likely to be trod upon. Besides furnishing heat, the rising mists conferred an eerie, preternatural dawn-world appearance to the jungle landscape.

"Have you noticed that there are no rotting logs or dead brush?" Doc tapped the green grass with his cane. "No decomposing vegetation as you would expect to see in a truly ancient jungle."

"I wasn't really paying attention." Scott concentrated on watching for boisterous dinosaurs and swatting gargantuan insects. He turned around to make sure the Rangers were behind him. He could see two or three, depending on the amount of the steam. "Windy, what made you break off the attack?"

"di'n't break it off. We're still attacking. Sam figgered as long as the *Ark's* here an' below missile interception height, we'd regroup an' use her cannons to fight it out. An' with all this steam we can't see nuthin' without radar nohow."

"A logical course of action," Doc said.

"Nuthin' gets by Sam. He's plenty smart even if he don't like generalin'. If this war ever ends, we're gonna 'lect him president."

"I am doubtful that he will be overjoyed at the prospect," Doc said sarcastically. "Perhaps you can persuade him to—"

"Hey! What's that?" Scott held up a hand for silence. The platoon stopped in its tracks. Off in the distance he heard a strident tune that was not the chirp and buzz of birds and bugs. "It's a toner."

"Yeah, but it's behind us," said Windy.

A Ranger pushed through the file of motionless commandos, jabbing a thumb over his shoulder. "It's my radio. I'm getting a call from the *Ark*." He presented his back to his platoon leader.

Windy pulled the transmitter off the radioman's backpack and keyed a reply.

Scott listened intently. His pinched eyebrows gradually relaxed, then a grin broke out on his face, and finally he whooped and whirled like a dervish. "Did you hear that, Doc! The *Ark* is okay, and the Nomads have found her in a clearing due east."

Death Wind looked up at the clinging mist; the sun was completely blotted out. "Follow." He struck out in a new direction.

Doc shrugged his shoulders at Scott. "Always trust a Nomad in matters of woodcraft." He loped along after the young savage.

Bushwhacking through dense shrubbery required strength, stamina, and an inborn sense of direction. Death Wind not only broke trail, but skirted around trees and impenetrable stands of brush in such a circuitous course that to Scott he seemed to be going in circles. Like Doc, though, he had full confidence in the Nomad's orientation skills.

The next time Scott heard a toner it was in front of him. He stopped beating the bush long enough to decipher the message. The *Ark's* external loudtoner was repeating an automatic directional call. A few minutes later he found himself standing on a burned-out sward. When he looked up, he saw through the mist the business end of a lifting cone.

"Hey! Rusty! We're home."

A familiar red head jumped out of the white fog; wiry arms grappled Scott like a long-lost cousin. "I never thought I'd be so happy to see your ugly puss."

Grinning broadly, Scott hugged his companion every bit as hard. "Well, if it isn't Father Time himself. You know you scared the hell out of us when you popped into space like that. When were you coming from?"

"I'll tell you later. Right now we've got to go get Sam and company. His frequency's been keeping up a constant chatter ever since I toned him."

"You know your appearing act knocked out the reactor?"

Rusty nodded. "That's why we've got to hurry. The radiation counter is clicking like an epileptic clam. If we don't get out of here soon, we'll all be French fried. Doc, Death Wind, I didn't mean to ignore you, it's just—"

"Tut, tut, my boy. We all have our priorities. Right now I agree with yours in abandoning this dragon abode. Windy and the Rangers should be—"

He was cut short by a muffled explosion. The ground rumbled, knocking his cane out from under him. He fell against Death Wind.

"That was the steam vessel," Scott said. "Things are going to get real hot real fast."

Windy appeared out of the fog, his eyes bulging. The Texas Rangers crowded in behind him.

"All aboard," Rusty called out. "We've got one more stop to make before, as Sandra would put it, we blow this berg."

* * *

The terminal moraine towered over the lush landscape: a sheer, white cliff face that stretched for miles across the savanna. The continental glacier was still in a stage of advance, as were all the glaciers in the early Pleistocene. But soon it would recede, leaving in its wake huge piles of boulders, carved valleys, long lines of debris, and gouges in the rock. Then, nature would do its best to cover the scars.

Grass would sprout in windblown soil, flowers would open their blossoms to suck in the energy of the sun, brush and shrubbery would thrust their roots into the earth, oaks and redwoods would launch themselves into the sky, and animals in great numbers would reclaim the land.

That was the way of the world; that was the way of life. Nothing could stand in the way of birth.

"Relax, Sandra. Take it easy."

Sandra gritted her teeth. "That's easy for you to say."

Jane wiped sweat off Sandra's brow. "No, it is not easy. I say it because I must."

Sandra managed a smile. "Okay, I'll do the same for you when it's your turn."

Other women who were clustered in the warm, sunlit clearing tended their chores: stirring the cooking pot, stitching clothes, making booties and blankets. Beyond the perimeter of the campsite, one woman gathered wood for the fire, while another hunted rabbits and squirrels with a bow and arrow. On a high bluff within shouting distance, another woman stood guard; she leaned against the shaft of her spear while, eyes cupped for shade, she scanned the horizon for wild carnivores and returning warriors. The only animals in sight were the two pet wolf pups that were gamboling about the clearing.

The pains were coming quicker now, with clocklike regularity. Sandra grimaced as each pang gripped her groin with growing intensity. "You know, I thought I'd be scared, especially without my mother here. But I'm not. I'm not scared at all. It all seems so—so natural. I'm actually looking forward to it."

"That is the way it should be." Jane patted Sandra's forehead with a hot towel. "That is the way it *must* be."

Sandra felt a stab of pain that was worse than any of the others. She squeezed her eyes shut and drew her knees to her breasts. When the wave of pain subsided, she pulled the smock up to her waist. "I think this is it," she said when she could breathe again.

Jane nodded quietly. She pulled a pot of hot water off the fire, redipped the towel, wrung it out over the ground, and crouched at Sandra's feet. "Whenever you are ready."

"Are you sure you know what you're doing?"

"I have helped many times. It was the way we did it—in the barn."

Two other women sat by Sandra's side. They laid their hands gently on Sandra's arms, to comfort her by their touch, to help her through her trial, to share her experience.

The next spasm was stronger. Sandra gripped the two women next to her; she clenched her teeth so she would not cry out. The pain was sharp and severe, but somehow exquisite.

"Okay, this is it."

Jane nodded silently. She soaked a blanket in the hot water, twisted it, and stretched it out on the ground between Sandra's outspread legs.

Sandra tuned out the sounds of the forest; no longer did she hear the birds singing in the branches, the insects droning through the glade, the wind rustling through the needles and leaves. She existed solely within herself. She had only one function at the moment, and that would take her whole attention. She relied on her companions to help and protect her.

She screamed, then choked it off.

"It is okay," Jane said soothingly. "Cry if it helps."

Sandra's world was one of mixed feelings: she hurt so much, but felt so good. "Ooooh."

"You must push. Push hard."

Sandra pushed. The pain was more agonizing than she could have imagined possible. She did her best to ignore it. She pushed harder. The pain came in waves, washing over her body like flames on flesh, or like sandpaper on raw skin. How long the pain went on she could not determine; she lost all track of time. Time, in fact, held no meaning for her: whether this was the Pleistocene or the Cretaceous was immaterial. What was important was that she was here, now, experiencing the renascence of life in a brand new world.

As suddenly as it came, the pain was gone. A luxurious sensation of peace and serenity flushed through Sandra's body: a feeling of rapture that she never knew existed, nor could possibly explain. Tears of happiness welled in her eyes and slowly dripped down her cheeks. Then she heard a wail that was unlike any she had ever heard before. She blinked away the tears, cleared her vision, and looked down at her feet.

Jane cleaned the infant with a warm towel. "A boy."

Sandra swallowed hard, but the lump in her throat would not go away. She reached out for the child. "Let me hold him."

The baby continued to cry. His tiny, doll-like hands were drawn into fists, his face was flaccid and wrinkled and scrunched into a gnomic caricature. He was the most beautiful thing she had ever seen.

When Sandra took him from Jane he was still attached to her by the umbilical cord. She cradled him proudly in her arms.

The Nomad on the hill raced down with her spear upheld. She stopped reverently outside the circle of midwives. "Flyer come."

Sandra smiled in a way only a mother can. She thought of Death Wind, her husband, returning from war. "Boy, will he be surprised."

CHAPTER 30

The sun shone down on the lush primal forest with a brilliance and a warmth that filled the land with yearning. Each green leaf sparkled with the varnished coating of spring, each flower glistened with early-morning dew. The air captured a vitality that was beyond the bounds of reason, and a crispness just enough to taste.

"Scott, I can save them. You know I can."

"I know you *think* you can. And I know that what you propose scares the hell out of me."

Rusty bent his lanky frame. "But they're alive."

"Everyone's alive—somewhere, sometime. But that doesn't mean that they can be resurrected—or should be."

"I don't believe you," Rusty practically screamed. "I can't believe what I'm hearing. You think because you've given them up in your heart that they no longer have a right to live. That's insane. That's so—selfish."

"No, it's not. It's a recognition of reality. I love them as much as you do, but to rip through time on some impossible scheme—"

"It's not impossible. Not anymore. Not after the refinements I've made after the last jump."

Scott could not look his friend in the eye. "Then it's risky. The timing is too tight. If we make even the tiniest mistake we could do irreparable damage to the fabric of space-time. We could wipe ourselves out of existence. We don't know all the ramifications—"

"That's straight-line dragon thinking, Scott. We're not reptiles, we're mammals: with the mental capacity of a brain that's more highly organized, with the ability to imagine concepts that—"

"That's right. Imagine concepts. Just because we can conceive something doesn't make it true."

"But we've got a time machine. We can go whenever we want—to any point in time, with absolute precision."

"That doesn't mean that we can change history. The book has already been written."

"I'm not talking about rewriting the whole book—I just want to edit one chapter."

"Rusty, let it go," Scott pleaded, with arms outstretched. "The past is over. What's done is done. You have no divine right to transform the world to suit your image of how you think it should be."

Rusty's voice was equally as loud. "This isn't a personal vendetta I'm fighting. There are human lives at stake—and not just strangers: your family as well as mine, and everyone we grew up with. For most of our lives they were our entire world. How can you let them die with-out lifting a finger to save them, when you know that you have it in your power to do so?"

"Because I don't *know* that we have that power. I know only that that's what you believe."

Rusty shook his head vehemently. "It's what I can prove mathematically. Figures don't lie."

"But they can mislead. They can give you answers that don't fit reality. Mathematicians proved that bumblebees can't fly because their wingspan couldn't support their body weight; but that didn't knock the bees out of the air."

Rusty chafed. "That's a problem posed by inaccurate data and unwarranted assumptions. With a properly derived constant—"

"Oh, and we're not making any unwarranted assumptions here," Scott said sarcastically. "I suppose if I told you that it took a hundred hours for one man to dig a hole, you'd tell me that a hundred men could dig it in an hour—or a thousand men could dig it in six minutes—or ten thousand in thirty-six seconds. It just isn't practical—"

"All right, I get the point. But I've been through the figures over and over. I've run computer simulations. I've checked the answer forward and backward, upstream and downstream, past and future—"

"Are you sure you didn't start out with the result you wanted, and work your way back to the question?"

Rusty ran his hands through long, curly hair. "You know me better than that. I'm telling you that I can save them."

"But—they—are—dead," Scott enunciated slowly. "I saw them. And even if they weren't then, they are now. You can't bring the dead back to life except in fairy tales. The radioactivity—"

"You think they're dead because you saw them in this time stream. But I didn't. To my consciousness they aren't here now. What you tell me is hearsay; or, at best, circumstantial evidence. It's not proof in the overall picture of space-time."

"Rusty, we're not arguing in a court of law. This isn't a question of perceptions, it's a matter of cold fact."

"Your facts, not mine. I have no direct knowledge of their death, therefore I'm not bound by your preconceived notions of their mortality."

Scott shivered; the cold chill that coursed along his spine was not brought on by a drop in temperature. The implications of Rusty's proposal were too profound for him to visualize. "But you and I are in the same time stream. What's true for me is true for you."

"Is it?"

That short sentence carried enormous portent. Scott's mind swung like a pendulum, caught between what he believed and what he wanted to believe. His heart fluttered. "I sure wish I had your confidence."

Rusty shrugged and offered a half smirk. "I wish I had as much confidence as you think I have."

Scott shook his head. "Don't say that. I'm scared enough already." He could not keep from smiling. He brushed his shaggy blond hair out of his face. "Well, let's go talk it over with the gang."

The campsite filled a clearing that was bounded by brush and tall oak trees. Rock pits surrounded cooking fires that raged with the abundance of wood. Thin streamers of smoke rose into the air and quickly dissipated in the upper winds. People talked and lounged in attitudes of relaxation; this was the first real rest that they had had in weeks.

A powwow was in progress around the central fire. Doc, Jane, Britt, Sam and Helen, Bold One and Slender Petal, Windy, Broderick, Death Wind, Sandra and child, all sat discussing the issue of the day.

"—rather live with mountain gorillas than with mounted guerrillas." Sandra unabashedly suckled the baby on her exposed breast. "I'm tired of war."

"We are all tired of war, my dear. War is not that which one seeks, but that which is thrust upon those who refuse to bend to the will of others."

"And I'm tired of being a general," said Sam. "This is great growing country, even with all the ice. And that, we know, won't be here forever."

Helen intertwined her arm with her husband's. "We're thinking of starting another family."

Sam winked. "Maybe this time we can have one who's not so quarrelsome."

"Daddy!" Sandra screamed so loud that she frightened the baby. He let the nipple slip from his mouth, and wailed. Sandra let her blouse drop over her breast, hugged him close, and rocked him in her arms. To her father, she said, "You'll pay for that."

"I'm sure I will."

Scott joined the repartee by first kissing his wife. He pointed his chin at the infant. "Have you decided on a name yet?"

Sandra cuddled her baby; gradually, he calmed down to a bare whimper. "He's so sweet I wanted to call him Sugar, but DW doesn't think that's manly enough. We haven't been able to agree on anything yet. Would you like to hold him?" She shoved the unnamed baby into Scott's arms.

"Well, uh—" He held out the baby as if he were a sack of wet cloth. "Sure." After a moment the crying grew louder. Scott stood uncomfortably, looking to his wife for advice.

Jane smiled at him. Her belly was just beginning to show. "Get used to it."

Sandra took back the tiny bundle. "You'll make a great father, Scott. You really will. At least you weren't afraid to hold him."

An awkward silence ensued. People stared at the ground, fiddled with their clothing, played with sticks, stirred the fire: anything to avoid eye contact. Finally, Doc said, "I suppose the time for decisions has come."

Rusty said, "We all know when I stand."

"I say it is about time that we started living life instead of fighting it." Broderick doodled in the sand. "And many of the Fusiliers feel the same way. We are fairly well paired off."

Bold One was terse. "No more roam. Good land. Many herds. Hunt."

"We are healthy. We have medicine," Slender Petal said. "We will live long and well."

Death Wind folded his muscular arms across his chest. "We stay."

"And I go with my husband." Sandra put the baby back onto her breast. "Always."

"But don't you understand that it's not over?" Rusty raised his voice but restrained from making accusatory inflection. "You can't cop out as soon as you get what you want. We're all in this together."

"Rusty, not everyone at Charon, or the Outpost, joined this crusade, but we didn't hold it against them," Helen said.

Doc added, "We must each make a decision based on individual needs; short-term personal ambitions are as important as long-term group goals."

"Besides, for what you want to do you don't need an army—just a small reserve corps." Sam stirred the fire with a blackened stick. "And I don't think anyone intends to block you. We all know what's at stake. Challenging the forces of nature with the fate of the world in the balance is a responsibility that we've already accepted. Otherwise we wouldn't be here, now. If you feel honor bound to fight one last battle, I trust your judgment."

"Thanks, Sam, for your vote of confidence. I appreciate your position as much as you appreciate mine. This is just something that I have to do, or I could never live with myself."

Sandra said, "Rusty, I think you'll agree that I can understand the turmoil of your emotions. I've been where you are now. I know how it feels. No matter how it turns out, it's important for your own well being that you do what you think is right. You have to find your destiny. At the same time, we have to find ours."

"Well spoken, my dear. You make me proud to have you for a granddaughter." Doc sat with his good leg bent and his bad leg stretched out. His cane was stuck under his arm so he could lean back against it. "Against such clarity of thought I have nothing additional to add."

"Thank you, Pop, for helping me to become the person I am today. I don't think I've ever told you this before, but you've had a great influence on me. I love you."

"I love you, too, Sandra—both the girl you were and the woman you have become. I just wish—I wish—" Doc cleared his throat. When he continued, his voice trembled ever so slightly. "I wish you all the happiness that this new, dragon-free world has to offer."

Sandra swallowed hard. "Pop, it was you who said that wherever you are is home. Well, we're here, and this is where I've given birth to my son, so I'm for calling it home."

Doc nodded slowly. "And I am sure that you can help to mold this world into what it needs to become."

After a long silence, Helen said, "Daddy."

"Yes, my dear."

"Does that mean that you are—going?"

Doc pursed his lips before answering. "I must. There is still work to be done."

"Isn't that what you said twenty years ago, when your wanderlust took you away from Sam and me?"

"I suppose it is. It has always seemed in my short life that there is so much to do, and so little time in which to do it. Access to a time machine has aggravated that condition;

contradictorily, it does not give one more time, but more opportunities in which to spend one's time. Remember though, Helen, as I go charging into the realm of alternate space-time, that I am removing from your life only my physical presence. The moments of happiness that we have shared will be with us always."

Rusty choked. "Doc, you make it all seem so permanent. When you have a time machine, everything in the universe is temporary."

"And who are we to say what the future may bring? Or the past, for that matter."

"I don' know what'll it bring," drawled Windy. "But I know them two boys have it in 'em to change the world. Hell, I'd follow 'em to the end o' time just to see what they're gonna do with it."

Scott put his arm around Jane's slender shoulders. "Honey, we've got to do what we can. They're our people."

"It is what I expect of you. We must try."

Scott kissed her on the cheek. "Besides, we can come back anytime we want." He glanced at his lifelong companion. "So, partner, when do we leave?"

Pulling Britt close, Rusty said, "No time like the present."

"I do have a request before we go, if we can spare the time." When he had their attention, Doc said, "I would like to bequeath to my great-grandson a name from my own past."

Sandra studied her grandfather's face. After a moment of silence she approached him with arms outthrust. The babe in his swaddling clothes had sucked his fill and fallen asleep. "What's your name, Grandfather?"

"Well, in the many guises of my life I have answered to quite a few appellations, according to the custom of the day and the people with whom I lived. But the name that I was born with I have not used since I was a lad. My parents called me George, after my father, who was named after his father and his father's father. I did not have a son to carry on the tradition, and do not as yet"—he glanced at Sam and Helen—"have a grandson. Therefore, it would give me great honor if your son, my only male descendant at this time, would bear this name." He placed his lips on the infant's forehead.

Twin tears rolled slowly down Sandra's cheeks. Her chest heaved with emotion. "Then his name is George, after the greatest dragon slayer of all time. That's how we'll remember you."

Doc nodded gratefully.

Scott stood straight and tall, crossed the circle to where Death Wind sat cross-legged, and removed his belt and knife. "This belongs in your family. I guess I'd better return it, and thank you for its loan."

Death Wind climbed to his full height. His dark eyes were deep pools of mystery. "We are same family."

"Yes, and always will be." He handed the heirloom to Death Wind. A knife would be much more useful in this world than the one to which Scott was going. "I want you to retain this knife in remembrance of our brotherhood. Use it well."

Death Wind took it solemnly. "I will miss you."

Arm held out in Nomad fashion, Scott said, "I'll miss you, too. But no matter where or when we are, we'll always be together."

Death Wind grasped Scott's forearm, released it, and rested his hands firmly on Scott's shoulders in the Nomad family greeting. Death Wind's face was expressionless, but his voice was an open book. "It is code."

CHAPTER 31

The desert air was hot, the sand hotter. Heat waves shimmered like dancing ghosts. Six pairs of moccasins crunched through the granules in the shadow of an overhanging ledge.

"It must be in here," said Rusty, looking up from the sketch.

When Scott shone his pack-powered light into the cave, a metallic glint reflected the beam. He stepped into the dark interior. "Looks like a stainless steel door behind that pile of debris." He clambered over loose rocks until he reached the shiny surface. "Yes, this is it." He rapped gently. "Anyone home?"

"Scott!" Jane pulled him away from the portal.

Scott spread his arms. "Only teasing."

"Y'all give us away if ya set off the alarms," said Windy.

"No, there are no exterior proximity devices or contact switches. Every rock fall would set them off."

Rusty handed his map to Britt, turned her around, and took a magnetic interrupter out of

her knapsack. "Thanks."

"Besides," said Doc, leaning against his cane. "It is always polite to knock."

Rusty ran the homemade electronic box around the exposed portion of the doorframe. "The frequency is matched and nullified. Okay, Windy. Burn it."

The door had no outer knob, just a raised rectangle opposite the interior handle. "Watch yer eyes." Windy fired his laser gun at the protrusion. The narrow beam drilled a hole through the steel, then exploded as the concentration of energy spread outward from the molecular impact. "Again?"

Scott leaned his shoulder against the heated metal. The door budged ever so slightly. "No, I think I can get it open." He shoved hard several times before the heavy-duty lock yielded to the force. Rusted hinges squeaked. The door moved inward about a foot before it jammed. Continued beating forced it only another six inches. "I guess that'll do."

He had to remove his battery pack before squeezing into the dank, musty chamber. Windy handed the backpack to Scott, then removed his own and passed it inside. One by one the others entered the dark, steel-walled antechamber. Each carried a pocket light.

"Judging from the amount of dust and the lack of footprints, this place does not appear to have been in recent use." Doc's narrow beam showed nothing but emptiness. "As we expected."

Rusty approached the inner door: an airtight hatch that was built like the door to a vault but without a handle of any kind. "We'll have to burn out the locking mechanism before we can pull back the bolts." He ran his magnetic interrupter around the frame. "It's clear." He stepped back and let Windy do his job.

After half a dozen blasts, the massive lock was a molten blob of steel. "That bugger's built ta last."

Scott took a hammer and crowbar out of Jane's knapsack, and went to work on the exposed drive pins. When they were smashed out of the retaining grips, he used the crowbar to pry the rim off the seal. Scott applied all his strength; well-tuned muscles and two feet of iron leverage gradually pushed open the door. Tortured hinges creaked and groaned. "Okay, folks, watch your step."

Scott slipped into a pitch-black space that was

not a room, but the top landing of a stairwell. His powerful pack light illuminated a deep shaft and a circular staircase. He waited until everyone was inside before taking the lead. Hand-held lights bobbed down the metal steps. Rusty clung to the top rail, breathing hard—not because of the stirred-up dust, but because of what he expected to find at the base of the stairs.

"Another door," Scott called out.

Rusty inhaled sharply and slowly made his way down the steps. He did the honors with the magnetic interrupter, neutralizing the interior alarm systems. Then Windy and Scott did their jobs. The vaultlike door was more massive than the previous one, and took twice as much effort to breach with the laser gun.

Scott stepped back after an attempt at prying. "It's no use. Internal positive pressure is keeping it closed. Windy, you're going to have to drill a hole all the way through."

It took ten blasts on the same spot before the laser beam penetrated the thick casting. A rush of air flowed through the hole like a stream of water gushing out of a fire hose nozzle. Scott worked the crowbar into the crevice that was formed by the hatch on the rim, pushed with all his might, and broke the seal. He fell in with the door when the suction let go.

From the base of the stairwell Rusty heard the gentle whirring of motors and the hum of transformers. As the others filed into the mechanical room, he hung back, afraid of what he might see inside. The air rushing past him was stale and carried with it the animal odors of perspiration. He choked, not only from the stench, but from the memories it evoked.

"Come on, Rusty," his companion called.

Rusty forced himself to enter the room. Pumps and compressors made soughing sounds like wind through trees. A single, dim emergency light sent out an eerie yellow glow that was overshadowed by the electric torches that were carried by the six-person team. Britt held Rusty's hand and led him along the narrow aisles, past a familiar-looking computer console, through an open doorway, and down a long corridor to another door. This one had no lock.

Scott turned the knob and walked into an elevator lobby. "Windy, you'd better stay here with Jane and Britt." He punched a few buttons, one of which switched on a bank of fluorescent lights, while another set in motion an electric motor. He shrugged off the battery pack and

dropped it at the head of another stairwell. "We don't want to look like an invasion force."

Doc consulted the timepiece that he wore around his neck. "We had better hurry. We do not have much time."

The elevator doors opened. Scott kissed Jane before entering the cage. "Hold the fort, Honey."

Doc tapped his cane on the still-bobbing floor. "It has been quite a while since I last rode in one of these."

Scott held his prosthesis in the air. "It beats footing it on the stairs. Rusty, come on."

The redhead was frozen in his tracks. He stared at the elevator car as if it were a slab in a morgue. His mouth worked, but no words came out. Britt took matters in hand and shoved him aboard. "You must do this yourself."

Scott stabbed a button and the doors slid shut. He flashed a quick wave at Jane. "Be right back."

The lump in Rusty's throat threatened to strangle him. As the elevator dropped into the depths, he felt like an escaped convict being forced back into solitary confinement after a short reprieve.

Scott pounded him on the back. "It's okay, Rusty. It's okay."

It was all his idea, but now that he was here he was afraid to carry out the mission that he had planned so meticulously. Some of the butterflies in his stomach were the result of the high-speed plummet into the bowels of the earth; most were from a bad case of nerves. He swallowed hard. Before he could protest, the doors slid open. He saw a long, well-lighted corridor whose walls were lined from floor to ceiling with trays of plants. Trailing branches and clusters of leaves billowed outward to form a narrow, junglelike passage. Thirty feet away, a young girl tested the pH of the hydroponic fluid. She looked up, startled.

Scott strode boldly out of the corridor. "Hi. You don't remember me, but—"

The girl dropped the siphon; the hardened plastic apparatus clattered on the floor but did not break. Her jaw fell to a chest that had not yet begun to sprout the buds of puberty.

"I doubt very much that she can." Doc stopped behind Scott. There was not enough room for him to pass. "Good morning, my dear. I am sure this intrusion is rather unexpected—"

The girl found her voice and an emergency alarm at the same time. She pounded a fist on a mushroom wall button, but the siren was not nearly as loud or as startling as her scream. She ducked into a nearby cubicle and slammed the door behind her.

"That should announce us." Doc grabbed Rusty by the tunic and pulled him out of the elevator car. "Let us head for the meeting hall before it gets too crowded. Scott, you know the way."

Since they were in a service corridor they encountered very little traffic. The few heads that popped out of work cubicles stayed out of the way. Fear-struck faces watched the gruff-looking trio in strange garb march confidently along the hallway as if they knew what they were about.

Rusty's mind raced. The familiar surroundings were a blur: a strange phantasmagoria reminiscent of a time and place that no longer existed. He was hardly aware of the flashing red lights or the wailing sirens or the awestruck people who were pouring into the corridor and staring at him with a mixture of fear and astonishment. Mingled with the smell of processed air and human flesh, he thought he detected an odor that he had forgotten existed—that of an apple pie baking in a convection oven. Memories flooded his mind, blotting out all vision of the present. He turned blindly left and right, pulled along by Doc's warm hand as if he were the caboose of a train. Then he was in the meeting hall: little more than an enlarged cubicle that, as a child, he had thought was a huge playroom with boundaries so vast that it tired him to run all the way around it.

"Who—who are you?"

The sirens stopped; the lights ceased flashing. The sudden silence and the staring faces were intimidating. The room was packed with people, and the corridor outside as well. Elected leaders squirmed through the throng of humanity.

"We're—we're—" Scott's voice faltered as erstwhile friends and family crowded around him.

Rusty reacted nervously to the sheer pressure of people. He found it hard to believe that he had once lived in such cramped quarters.

"We are an advance scouting team that has come here to liberate the citizens of Maccam City," Doc said calmly. "The main expeditionary force is waiting outside. We have an aircraft standing by to transport you to safety."

Tingles ran up Rusty's spine as he recognized one man in particular, and the little girl he held in his arms. He could hardly believe what he was seeing—never before did he have to look *down* at his father. His sister Faron scrunched her eyes at Rusty as if he were a giant ogre.

The man who looked up at him made no notice of Rusty, but faced Doc openmouthed. "You're—an outsider."

"I am."

He glanced at Scott, then at Rusty. Stunned eyes took in their bronzed, sun-baked features, muscular bodies, and long hair. "Where—where did you come from?"

"I am an emissary from Washington."

"You mean—headquarters still exists?"

"It did when I left it." Doc glanced at his timepiece. "We have much to discuss, but now is not the time to do it. We must get you out of here immediately."

Caught up in his own emotion, Rusty suddenly realized how enormous a shock this must be for his fellow citizens. They had been buried underground for a hundred years without contact with the outside world—with no knowledge that people other than they still survived. Then a group of oddly dressed warriors descended unannounced into their secret sanctuary and politely invited them to evacuate at once, with no questions asked, and to forsake the only kind of life they had ever known.

Furthermore, he never anticipated that he would go unrecognized. While only hours had passed for the people of Maccam City since they last saw Scott and Rusty, years had passed for the two wandering sons. They had traveled enormous distances in space and time, and had returned to their point of origin both older and wiser. Maturity had changed them in many ways.

"How did you get in here? The doors are sealed, and the intrusion alarm—"

"We demagnified the tocsin code. But that is unimportant. You must vacate these premises at once."

Faron tugged at the thin material of her father's tunic and stared at Rusty with a jaundiced eye. "Daddy, who is that man?"

"Strangers, darling." He looked at Rusty, then at Scott. "Strangers from outside."

Rusty saw Scott's folks surging forward, with their daughter between them. He and Scott stared at each other. Scott's eyes glistened like wet opals. Rusty tried valiantly to hold back his own tears. He came here as a leader, as a savior, as an intrepid conqueror: it would not look good for him to break down and cry. Then he saw his mother . . .

"We have no time to waste. It is imperative that we get back to our aircraft and depart this time zone."

Rusty's father looked at Doc quizzically. "They still use time zones?"

"Uh, yes, but in a different context." Doc referred to his timepiece again. "We have sufficient capacity for all your people in our aircraft, but I am afraid that we do not have time for you to gather your personal belongings."

"This is all so sudden—"

Doc remained the eloquent orator. "I understand your trepidation, but we really must be going. I can explain the urgency of the situation at a later date. Now, if you can start the procession moving we will lead you out of here and into a world of sunshine and fresh air."

Scott's father shouted in glee and slapped Rusty's father on the back. "I told you it was okay to go outside. This is the moment we've been waiting for. Mister, I'm behind you and your buddies all the way. All I've got to do is get my son in the pump room and I am packed."

Doc glanced at Scott. "Yes, well, we have already accounted for those who were working on upper-level maintenance details. Scott and Rusty, I believe they are, and a motor mechanic named Roger."

"I knew it was all right to go outside. I told you so." He let out a cheer that was shared by at least half the crowd. "This is what we've been waiting for all these years."

Those Maccam City dwellers who shared his partisanship needed no further urging. They in turn shouted down the protests of the bewildered opposition. It was perhaps the shortest revolution in human history. With uncommon brevity, citizens who had been cooped up far too long yielded to the victorious faction. The authoritative voice of one of their own turned a shallow tide.

With great fanfare and hubbub they filed out of the meeting room. Those still in shock, or uncertain of the turn of events, were swept along with the overpowering multitude.

"But, what about—" Rusty's father lingered indecisively. "What are we getting into?"

With a faraway look in his eyes, Doc soliloquized. "That is something that no one can predict—perhaps something that we are better off not knowing. The future is ours for the making; we must make of it what we can. And this time we can do it on our own terms. The war is over. Let us hope that mankind has the wisdom to keep it from returning."

CHAPTER 32

Doc, Scott, and Rusty sat down wearily in the *Ark's* bridge. It had been a long day: morning in the Pleistocene, afternoon in the Holocene, evening in a portion of the Holocene a few years later, in time for their own departure from then into the Pleistocene—plus a few minutes as a safety margin so they did not bump into themselves leaving for the final assault in the Ice Age. When time is your handmaiden, the only passage that counts is subjective.

"I can't believe we pulled it off," Scott said. "The window was so short. Getting there after we—that is, our previous selves—left for maintenance duty, but before the dragons arrived to pump the city full of corrosive gas. I had the jitters the whole time."

"Which self's time?" Doc asked. "Your present self, or your past self?"

"Hell, I don't know anymore. Both, I guess. And every one in between. We've come a long way since this whole thing started. Every moment has been either exciting or terrifying."

"How would you classify today's activities?"

"Transmogrifying."

Doc snickered as he leaned back in his seat. "Rusty, my boy, I noticed you had your doubts for a while. When did you lose your confidence in the success of this mission?"

"About a million years from now. When I popped into the future tense to destroy the dragon advance base, what I saw then made me wonder how this venture would ultimately turn out. I admitted the possibility that somewhen we might have interrupted the continuity of the universe and wiped ourselves out of existence for all time. I still wonder what that future may bring."

"Why? Because you saw an endless pristine forest with no signs of civilization or human habitation?"

Rusty grimaced. "Doesn't that seem strange to you?"

"Not at all. A great deal can happen in a million years. Besides, how far afield did you look?"

"I practically closed my eyes. I was afraid of learning too much."

"What? This from the lad who says that prior knowledge has no effect on future events. You should at least be consistent within your own prognoses."

Rusty shrugged. "Call it the Pandora syndrome. I was afraid that if I made too many direct observations of future reality, I wouldn't have the courage or resolve to make interdimensional alterations."

"Too much knowledge can be a curse," Doc agreed.

"If I weren't so scared, and if I really knew all the secrets of the universe, I'd have tried to figure a way to save Roger's life instead of letting him get beamed down by a dragon laser gun. But since I saw it happen in my own time stream, I thought it might do irreparable damage to the overall flow of events."

"But what about me?" Scott fairly shouted. "And Doc? We saw the Maccam City residents frozen in ice. Isn't it the same situation?"

"Who knows. Maybe you and I are in different continua, and what you saw or experienced has no effect on what I saw and experienced. Or maybe you and everyone else—every*thing* else—are only manifestations in this universe: a support system for my own personal continuum. I don't know. I'm confused."

Doc said, "Think how complex today's events would have been should the people who were rescued from the stronghold have been some of your people, instead of former prisoners from Charon."

Scott shuddered. "What does Mr. Math have to say about it?"

"It depends on how you plug in the variables."

Doc said, "Perhaps we could pick up Roger after you saw him. He might only be injured."

Rusty held out his hands. "Doc, as much as I'd like to believe you, and try to save him, I don't want to take a chance on running into myself out there in the desert. I don't know what effect it might have—and I don't want to know. Not until I work over the formulas a few hundred more times."

"We've got a long way to go in understanding the operation of the universe," Scott said. "The book of time is written in an incredibly obscure language that we may never be able to read—or understand. It makes me wonder if we didn't make a mistake that we'll pay for somewhen down the line. I mean, if we're not here in a million years, what happened to us?"

Doc nodded thoughtfully. "When you think how far mankind has evolved in the past million years, when he had wild animals and the Ice Age to contend with, imagine how far and how fast he might progress without predation, and with complete control over his environment. Perhaps a million years hence, he has turned this part of the continent into a vast park, as a monument to dragon folly. Or perhaps he has left Earth altogether for the stars. Or discovered a place in time that is incomprehensible to us. The possibilities are endless. We can, if we choose, return to that future time and seek an explanation."

"No!" shouted Rusty.

"Perhaps we should consider living in two time frames simultaneously. Some of us could stay here to hunt the dragons' dinosaurs to extinction and seed the planet with Pleistocene wildlife, while the rest of us carry out a parallel life in that future kilomillennium."

"No!"

"Tut, tut, now, Rusty. Let us not retreat to straight-line dragon thinking. Was it not you who said that we are mammals, with highly organized brains that can conceptualize quanta that reptilian brains cannot?"

"Maybe I am. And maybe the dragons weren't so far from the truth after all. I don't know. There's a lot that I don't know anymore."

"Ah, the wisdom of maturity is fast taking hold of your impetuous nature. Is it not strange that one can be born all-knowing, yet the older one gets the more ignorant one becomes?"

Rusty scowled.

"Welcome to the establishment, my man."

Scott winced. "You know, Doc, now that you bring it up, there are a few things that I don't know anymore." He dug the soot-covered computer crystal out of his pocket and flipped it in the air like a coin. "We know the dragons didn't establish base camps in other time zones, so we're not likely to find them hiding behind some future temporal curtain. But what about the Pleistocene stronghold? Why wasn't there any evidence of that in man's past?"

"Oh, but there is."

"Huhn?"

"Not physical evidence, perhaps, because the

glacier has wiped it out. Once the heat was turned off, and the glacier continued its flow through the stronghold, every shred of dragon fabrication was ground to bits, separated molecule from molecule, as the many layers of ice moved downstream at unequal speeds. In a few thousand years all signs of their occupation were spread over half a continent as tiny, indecipherable fragments of a long-forgotten puzzle; radiation as well.

"But the dragons themselves were most certainly kept alive in man's history. They have come down to us in many forms: the cockatrice, the basilisk, the snake in the Garden of Eden, the fire-breathing dragon of yore. They are the stuff of legend. The dragons in man's mind will never die; they will live on as the incarnation of all that is evil."

Scott thought for a moment. "But will they live on in the minds of the Cro-Magnons?"

"Since we are descended from the Cro-Magnons, logic dictates that they must."

"But we never saw any Cro-Magnons, or even signs that they existed in the Pleistocene. If they didn't encounter the dragons—Scott rubbed his chin, scratching his fingers on the blond stubble. "The Neanderthals didn't intermarry with . . . "

Doc slowly shook his head. "No, the Neanderthals died out of their own accord because they were unable to adapt to the harsh conditions of the Ice Age. They were on the road to extinction long before our arrival. The presence of our people will have no effect on the Neanderthals' demise: they will neither interbreed with the Neanderthals nor hunt them down and kill them. They are two separate simian branches on the evolutionary tree."

"Then—what's the answer?"

Doc smiled demurely. "Simply that the archaeological record shows only that Cro-Magnon man lived during the Pleistocene Epoch, not how he got then and there, or when and where he came from. If he did not exist in the Pleistocene before our arrival then, I daresay he lives then now."

Rusty fidgeted in his seat. "What you're implying is a paradox."

"The sudden emergence of Cro-Magnon man under those circumstances is a real contradiction," Scott emphasized. "Not just apparent."

"Yes, he is a parent, in a course of events I prefer to call 'prevolution.' I am certain that somewhere—or somewhen—in the mathematical concept of the universe, there exists an equation that correlates the continuity of space and time in such a way as to account for all observable phenomena."

Rusty squeezed one eye shut. "Do you mean that no matter how convoluted the structure of space-time seems to us, there's a viewpoint that sees it in a straight line?"

"Perhaps. Or perhaps we each create a line that in the end merges with all others."

"I still don't follow you," Scott said, bunching his lips. "You're saying that what I see and do may affect me now without affecting you, but that later it will affect us all. But if we all exist together, and we all belong to the same space, the same time, and the same universe, how can reality be anything but purely objective?"

"I cannot say. That is the beauty of subjectivity. It allows for a way out of every situation without delineating the route. There can be a here as well as a there, why not a then as well as a now? Specifically, time can be broken down into a then, a now, and a later—or past, present, and future: yesterday, today, and tomorrow. When space and time are merged into unity, the implication is that there is a here-then, a here-now, and a here-later, as well as a there-then, a there-now, and a there-later. There may even be a here-there, and a now-then. I do not know. I doubt that we will ever know. But one eventuality that we can count on is that we are here, now—and what follows, will follow. Nothing can change that."

Silence pervaded the bridge as if it were the dark side of the Moon. After a seemingly interminable time, Scott cocked an eyebrow. "Are you sure?"

Doc nodded in an exaggerated fashion. "Absolutely."

He glanced from one to the other to make certain that both Scott and Rusty were looking at him.

Then he winked.

Author's Afterword

The Time Dragons trilogy had an inspirational beginning, a curious history, a jagged evolution, and an aborted conclusion. Originally conceived as a single volume standalone, I eventually expanded the story line to the three novels that were published, and beyond. My readers will find that the beginning, the history, and the evolution of the stories make fascinating subjects, and that a description of the proposed conclusion is crucial toward understanding the scale and breadth of the total ideation. Because the collapse of the paperback industry terminated the series midway, a chronicle of those events will enable my readers to understand why the series was aborted before completion.

THE BEGINNING

As I noted in my short story collections, I wrote my first science fiction tale in high school. I didn't know it at the time, but my love of science fiction was responsible for inspiring my eventual career as an author. I was full of original ideas that I wanted to put down on paper. After service in the Army and a decade spent working in construction, I decided to dedicate the rest of my life to creative writing. Quite naturally, my first efforts were works of science fiction.

In 1981, I commenced work on my magnum opus about the war in Vietnam: *Lonely Conflict*. This was a long undertaking that took me five years to complete. The work was emotionally exhausting, based as it was on my personal experiences in combat. In its final draft, the manuscript ran as long as five books of standard length: nearly 400,000 words. While I wrote about the war overseas and its terrible effects on America, I continued to create science fiction devices in my mind, intending to write more stories and novels after I concluded my Vietnam novel.

Two years into the Vietnam book project, I awoke one fine spring Monday morning with a flash of insight that gripped me with such compelling abandon that I pushed aside my notes on *Lonely Conflict*, and immediately started to write an untitled book that I later called *A Time for Dragons*.

I typed furiously for five days. On Friday evening, I departed for a weekend dive trip to Long Island, New York. I could barely contain my thoughts in order to concentrate on exploring the pitch-black interior of the upside down armored cruiser *San Diego*, which sank after striking a German mine in 1918. The dives were risky enough without the distraction of an overactive imagination that continued to work on characters and plot lines as I decompressed.

I returned home late Sunday night. First thing on Monday morning, I picked up the story where I left off Friday afternoon. I typed furiously for two more weeks, and completed the first draft before my Friday evening departure for another dive trip. I was ecstatic with the achievement. The 75,000 words that I wrote in those three weeks comprised the greatest period of productivity in my writing career: before or since.

I have never been a fast or facile writer. Four years later I had another inspiration, and wrote *The Peking Papers* from start to finish in fifty-nine days of continuous writing (not counting a day and a half that I took off for a lecture engagement). The second (and final) draft of *The Peking Papers* ran to 100,000 words. The writing of *A Time for Dragons* and *The Peking Papers* constituted exceptional bursts of energy and creativity that were uncommon for me. Another book that I wrote with furious abandon was *The Lurking: Curse of the Jersey Devil*. I did not write that book with quite the same speed – but more on that in the author's foreword of the reprint edition.

THE HISTORY

I had extensive travel plans scheduled for the 1983 season: under water as well as outdoor activities such as canoeing, hiking, backpacking, and climbing. I was away for most of the summer and part of the autumn. My writing was sporadic. As a result, I did not complete the second draft until six month later: a total writing time of fifteen weeks. I didn't change the story; I merely fleshed out the action and fine-tuned the description.

Other projects and activities occupied my time throughout the winter. After nearly a year, I recommenced work on *Lonely Conflict*. This book occupied my full attention for the next two years.

In the mean time, I purchased a dedicated word processor from Radio Shack: a TRS-80. It was advertised as portable but I called it luggable: it was the size of a sewing machine (for which many people mistook it when it was housed in its plastic case); it weighed twenty-six pounds. The operating system was special to Tandy Radio Shack; the word processing program was called SuperScripsit. I also bought a daisy wheel printer from Radio Shack: a DWP 410.

The capabilities of the TRS-80 were limited. Each time I switched on the unit, I had to load the word processing application from a five-and-a-quarter-inch floppy diskette. The unit's buffer was limited to a page or two of text. If I didn't save my work to a floppy diskette every couple of paragraphs, I was likely to lose it in a memory crash when the RAM became overburdened. Sometimes the text would loop itself: additional text was lost when the program decided to repeat previously written text instead of saving new text. I quickly learned to make frequent backups – not only to one diskette but to several. The floppies had a tendency to go bad for no reason, disallowing me to access the data that were on them.

For the final draft of *Lonely Conflict*, I investigated the possibility of purchasing optical character recognition software. I attended an OCR demonstration in downtown Philly. The reader was the size of a mouse (either the furry kind or the plastic kind). This reader was dragged slowly over each line of text. Attendees were asked to bring typewritten samples in order to ascertain how well the software would read the individual's work. The accuracy of demonstrator's sample was about 75%; mistaken characters had to be corrected or retyped. I got nothing but gibberish from the text that my typewriter produced.

Back at the drawing board, I decided that it was more efficient to retype the entire manuscript on the word processor. This turned out to be advantageous, because it also gave me the opportunity to rewrite the book and produce a final draft. I relegated the typewriter to the job of addressing envelopes. The tapping of keys on the keyboard of the word processor was a lot quieter than the clacking of the typewriter.

As I neared the end of *Lonely Conflict*, I searched for a literary agent to sell the book to a publisher. The agency that I ended up choosing was the Virginia Kidd Literary Agency. Kidd farmed me out to one of her associates, Jane Butler, who specialized in science fiction and who had an interest in Vietnam. The tribulations of *Lonely Conflict* are recounted in the unexpurgated edition of the published version.

Jane loved *A Time for Dragons*. Before submitting it, though, she made a suggestion for improvement. Historically, authors have told a story from one of two perspectives: first person narrative or third person singular. With respect to third person, she explained how the current style in literature leaned away from "author omniscient" toward "means of perception."

In "author omniscient," the story is told from the perspective of an all-knowing narrator who, like a god, looks down on the characters from above. The author sees everything that every character is doing, and so does the reader. The problem with this universal point of view is that there is no one character with whom the reader can associate. The viewpoint bounces from one character to another.

In "means of perception," the story is told from the point of view of a single character. The reader sees only what that character sees, and feels only what that character feels. This enables the reader to identify with the character. The author can change the means of perception from one character to another, but only after a scene transition or in a subsequent chapter.

I immediately understood the emotional impact that this modern technique could have on a discerning reader. I rewrote the book on my word processor. I alternated the means of perception from Scott to Rusty, at first dedicating an entire chapter to each character, then later using scene transitions to make the switch. I used this technique on all my subsequent novels.

The final draft of *A Time for Dragons* occupied five floppy diskettes. Today, computer technology has advanced to the point at which a single compact disk can now hold every book that I have every written. How humbling.

In early 1986, Jane submitted the manuscript to the Berkley/Jove Publishing Group. The science fiction editor was Ginjer Buchanan. She liked the book, and defended it successfully at an in-house editor's meeting. At that time, Berkley/Jove had such a large backlog of manuscripts that the projected publication date was at least two years away. Jane was hoping for more timely publication.

In what must have been an unusual measure in the competitive publishing industry, Jane asked Ginjer for permission to submit the manuscript to Warner Books, which had less of a backlog, in order to get the book in print sooner. Ginjer agreed, while keeping the book in place in the queue at Berkley/Jove. The editor at Warner ultimately declined to accept the book, so it went back to Berkley/Jove.

THE EVOLUTION

A good novel contains four essential elements: plot, character, theme, and setting (not necessarily in that order). A good science fiction novel contains one additional element: an imaginative concept.

To be sure, many science fiction novels lack an imaginative concept. In these so-called "space operas" (soap operas in outer space), rocket ships may take the place of horses, and ray guns may take the place of six-shooters, but the story is the same except that it occurs on another planet instead of in the wild, wild west. Most modern science fiction reads more like "Sex in the City" than *2001: a Space Odyssey*.

Be that as it may, every one of my science fiction stories and novels is driven by an imaginative concept. This concept is the primary plot device: it determines the direction in which the storyline moves, and around which the other four elements revolve. Without this imaginative concept, the tale would not necessarily be without meaning, but it would most definitely be without fulfillment or achievement. An imaginative concept is the element that distinguishes science fiction from a straightforward novel.

The imaginative concept in *A Time for Dragons* is the explanation for the Great Dying at the end of the Cretaceous. The dragon race was indirectly responsible for its own extinction (although Doc facilitated the dragons' demise by sending the death bomb through the time transporter into the past. This is obviously a paradox, but that is what time travel stories are all about.

I completed *Lonely Conflict* in the spring of 1986. With that monumental work of literature off my mind, I could concentrate on other things. I was able to devote time to creating and developing imaginative concepts for future science fiction novels. Now that *A Time for Dragons* was assured of publication, I thought about it some more. It didn't take me long to create several additional imaginative concepts that I could develop into a series of sequels. Mentally I laid out the storylines and character development.

At first I projected a trilogy. Then I created enough imaginative concepts to extend to six books. Although I could let *A Time for Dragons* stand as it was written, I realized that the overall impact of the completed series would be more effective if I dropped a few seemingly incongruous hints in the first book of the series, then recalled and explained them in later books.

In September 1986, I traveled by train to New York City to meet with Ginjer Buchanan in her office at Berkley/Jove. I hinted at the possibility of at least two sequels, if not more. She was receptive to the idea. I told her my idea of making a few minor adjustments to the manuscript. This was easy to do on a word processor. Instead of having to retype the manuscript in its entirety, I could make editorial changes in the relevant chapters on disk, then print a new version. At her request, I wrote a proposal for two sequels that would make a trilogy.

AS EVERY WRITER KNOWS, THE WORST ENEMY OF THE WRITTEN WORD IS AN EDITOR

Ginjer was pleased with the original manuscript with one exception. A month later, she wrote to me to explain her feelings on the matter. "My only problem – and it is one which was shared by the editor at was considering the book at Warners – is with the character of Sandra.

"Sandra just doesn't ring true as a 16-year-old in the society that you've created. Indeed, she doesn't ring true as a 16-year old at all. She is too immature, and not-focused enough. Even these days, teenagers, though they might be half-grown children in woman's bodies, are, by age 16 more interested in separation from their families than being with them. In the sort of society-under-seige [sic] that you're proposed, a girl of Sandra's age would be a *woman*. She would probably been expected to pair off and breed as soon as she was able, and she would be her mother's peer, not her little girl still.

"As we talked about, there are two ways of handling this. You can either simply make her younger – as young as 13, I'd say. I gather that this might interfere with what you have planned for the next couple books, though.

"The other alternative is to make her more mature. Have mention made of the fact that she did have a mate who died. (she doesn't have to be a virgin, does she?) Have her express the fact that her single-minded pre-occupation with getting her mother back is more than a bit obsessive. (Just rescuing her mother isn't going to change anything. In not reconnizing [sic] that, she comes off as more than a bit stupid.)"

In my long association with editors, I've learned that few of them truly understand much about the workings of an article, story, or book. I've also learned that many editors are frustrated writers. Because they lack the ability to write, they try to make alterations in manuscripts in order to make points that *they* want to make: points that reflect their personalities.

I asked Ginjer what courses she took or what educational degree she held that qualified her to be an editor. She replied, "None." She liked science fiction, so she was hired as a first reader. A first reader is the lowest rung on the publishing ladder. Her job is to determine if a manuscript has sufficient merit to pass on to an editorial assistant, who then determines if the manuscript should go up another rung.

Ginjer worked her way up the corporate ladder to editor. This lack of formal training did not instill me with confidence in her ability to judge characters or storylines that she did not comprehend.

She failed to understand one primary essential of fictional characters: they must grow or demonstrate change or development. (This despite the fact that in real life, many people never grow up or change.) She wanted me to make Sandra the epitome of perfection. I soon figured out why. In the Berkley/Jove offices I saw only women. From that, and from contact with other publishing houses, I learned that the publishing industry is run predominantly by women.

Many of these women are steeped with insecurities. These insecure editors identify themselves with the female characters in the books that they edit. They deal with their insecurities by manipulating the female characters so that readers will not perceive them as unflawed or immature, in the mistaken belief that this perception will rub off on them (the editors). This is the same failed perception that can be readily observed in overweight women who go to great lengths to improve their appearance by coiffing their hair, wearing heavy makeup, polishing their nails, and doffing expensive clothes, while ignoring the fact that what they really need to do is to lose some poundage. The imagery is a delusion. A fat woman is still obese no matter how osten-

tatious her attempts at disguise.

I wanted Sandra to possess imperfections so she could overcome them through the series. In the course of our dialogue, I inferred that Ginjer did not truly appreciate or understand the plot, the characters, the theme, or the imaginative concept. She simply liked the story. (The theme is cooperation among individuals to achieve a common goal.) Nor did she raise objections to the initial immaturity and insecurities of the male protagonists, Scott and Rusty.

In order to appease Ginjer, I made a few changes which, while minor in nature, made Sandra's attitudes slightly more mature while allowing her to retain her childish and whimsical irony. For example, I restructured her dialogue so that she admitted her awareness of her obsession with regard to her mother.

I submitted the manuscript with these final changes in December 1986. I also submitted the first six chapters of Dragons 2, and a synopsis of Dragons 2 and 3. The trilogy then lay fallow for the next two years.

The only activity had to do with the titling. Someone in the Berkley/Jove hierarchy felt that having the word dragons in the title might confuse prospective readers, leading them to believe that the book was fantasy instead of science fiction.

In a letter to Ginjer that was dated May 2, 1988, I wrote, "I am also given to understand that *A Time for Dragons* is coming under the gun sights of the title assassinator. I will once again wax long in explaining my point of view in this regard. A title is part of a book. Its purpose is not just to give a name to a collection of words, but to describe in artistic for the meaning of the work. The Dragons trilogy is a complete, cohesive whole a part of which is the titling of the three volumes: *A Time for Dragons*, *Dragons Past*, and *No Future for Dragons*. What is not yet known to anyone but the writer is that the dragons alluded to in the books are in fact the actual dragons of legend and folklore. I have not planned to divulge this fact to the reader until the last page of the last book. At that time, the few remaining soldier dragons, while in pursuit of our heroes, attempt to follow them through time, and are spun through the middle ages by the movement of a vernier control on the time transfer equipment – thus depositing them in the midsts of pre-historic, Biblical, Asiatic, and European times where they are perceived as fire-breathing dragons. Their fire is, of course, the laser guns they carry, but in the minds of the ancients who have no means of un-derstanding or expressing such ideas, the flame and fire mechanism comes down through history as the monsters we have been brought up to believe once existed. The three titles are not just arbitrary assig-nations, but purposefully chosen descrip-tions intended to enhance the meaning of the work as a whole.

"If there is confusion between dragons of modern fantasy fiction and my dinosaur dragons, I suggest that the cover art, cover description, and back cover synopsis be fo-cused toward the premise of science fiction. A title change will not only seduce the de-liberate origination of ideas that melds the juxtaposition of title with each book, but will also destroy the integrity of the work."

To be fair, since no one at Berkley/Jove could have read the unwritten series in its entirety, they could not have known of my grand scheme. Reluctantly, they conceded to my wisdom.

As every experienced author knows, when agreeing to write a book at the spe-cific request of a publishing house, you don't start writing until the contract is signed, sealed, and delivered; and until the advance payment is received. All too often, the powers-that-be renege on their promis-es, and the author is left with a manuscript that he wrote to meet a particular editor's whims. Likely, the tailored manuscript can-not then be sold to another publishing house, whose editors' whims were differ-ent. Months of work may be left in limbo, perhaps forever.

I signed the contracts for Dragons 2 and 3 on August 22, 1988. According to the terms, I had to submit both completed man-uscripts by January 15, 1989. That gave me less than five months in which to write two books (minus the first six chapters of Drag-ons 2). I started work at once.

THE COLLAPSE OF THE PUBLISHING INDUSTRY

At this time, the publishing industry was undergoing a tremendous setback in book sales. Almost since the invention of the printing press – or at the very least, since the advent of newspapers in the early 1800's – the literate person's primary means of education and entertainment was reading. Recreational reading reached its culmination from the late 1800's through the middle 1900's, when hundreds of pulp magazines graced street-side newsstands with garish pictorial covers and mass-pro-duced fiction. The pulps vied for attention along with motion pictures and radio.

Paper shortages during World War Two reduced the amount of reading material that was available to the public. After the war, just as the paper shortages were diminish-ing, a new menace reared its head on the horizon: television. Household leisure time was then split between reading and view-ing. Every hour a person spent watching television was an hour he did not spend reading. Watching television did not require the concentration that it took to read a book. Once a set was purchased, television viewing became essentially free. Television viewing increased at the same rate at which reading decreased. Readership dropped dramatically. Fewer readers equated to fewer books and magazines being pur-chased.

In 1954, the last of the pulp magazines ceased publication. The pulp era became a footnote in history.

The introduction of paperback books saved the publication industry from total collapse. Paperbacks cost less to print than hardback books. Mass production in the form of large print runs helped to further reduce publication costs. An uneasy balance was achieved between printed and broadcast entertainment.

In the 1980's, another entertainment medium took a slice out of the entertainment pie: videotapes. Before, movies could be seen only in theaters. The invention of videotapes and videotape players made these movies available for viewing at home on television. At first, videotapes were prohibitively expensive, and sales were limited. Then the proliferation of videotape rental stores made videotape movies more affordable. As people bought and rented videotapes, there was less money available for the purchase of books, and less leisure time available to read them. This threw the paperback industry into a tailspin.

Book sales plummeted. Whereas formerly a paperback might have a print run of 100,000 copies, now only half that amount might be sold, or less. This tremendous drop in sales had a number of adverse effects on the paperback industry.

There are fixed costs associated with the production of a book: royalties, administrative services, overhead, copy-editing, proofreading, linotyping, promotion, and so on. Whether a thousand copies are printed or ten thousand copies are printed, these costs remain essentially the same. The monetary saving of a mass-market paperback results from printing copies in large quantities.

Much of the cost of printing a book goes into setting up the presses with lead plates or films: a complicated and time-consuming process. Once the presses are rolling, the only additional costs are for paper and press time. It costs only a small fraction more per unit to double a print run. The more units printed, the less the cost per unit. Taken with the fixed costs of over-

head, this means that it costs only slightly more to produce 100,000 copies than it costs to produce 50,000 copies. But the profit from selling 100,000 copies is significantly higher than the profit from selling 50,000 copies.

Ironically, a publisher could make more money by printing 100,000 copies, selling 75,000, and trashing 25,000, than it could by printing 50,000 copies and, when they sold out, setting up the presses to print another 25,000.

As book sales dropped, publishing houses were left with large quantities of extra copies (called remainders). Not only did they have to pay to warehouse the leftovers, but they had to pay federal income tax on inventories. Worse, bookstores returned all unsold copies. This is because bookstores don't actually *buy* books from publishing houses; in essence, they take books on consignment. Bookstores treat books as cash. Whenever their cash flow is low, instead of paying their bills they simply return older books; or, they exchange older books for newer ones. A bookstore is under no obligation to pay for books until they are sold. Why publishing houses permit such an absurd option is beyond my understanding.

In the old days, bookstores used to tear off a paperback's cover and send it to the publisher as proof that the book didn't sell. This was because it cost more to ship books back to the publisher than the books were worth – this because returned books usually could not be resold: either they suffered from handling or shelf wear, or there was no additional market for the books once it was established that they didn't sell in the first place.

In order to avoid paying income tax on inventory, and to reduce warehouse charges, publishing houses sold returns and remainders at ridiculously low prices to outfits that specialized at discounting them to a fraction of their original retail price.

Eventually, publishers accepted the changing times and began to reduce print runs to numbers that they could optimistically expect to sell.

AUTHOR ATTRITION

Many fulltime authors were driven out of the business by the reduction of book sales in the late 1980's and early 1990's, and for a number of reasons.

An author is paid royalties on the number of copies that are sold (not printed). He receives no money on copies that are unsold, returned, trashed, or disposed of to a remainder store. The royalty rate varies, but it is generally around 10% of the retail price for a hardback, and 6% to 8% for a paperback. When print runs were reduced, authors suffered a commensurate loss in pay.

Whereas paperback print runs used to average 100,000 copies, nowadays they often don't exceed 25,000.

Trade paperbacks are taking over much of the book market. A trade paperback is slightly larger than a mass-market paperback, but costs only a wee bit more to produce (the cost of the extra paper – overhead remains the same). Yet trade paperbacks possess an appearance of permanence because they are closer in size to that of a hardback. Mass-market paperbacks have always been perceived as throwaways – much in the way in which magazines are perceived as ephemeral and not worth saving. Publishing houses have used these artificial perceptions to raise the retail price of trade paperbacks beyond the percentage markup of their actual production cost, perhaps by twice as much.

The average print run of a trade paperback is 5,000 to 10,000 copies. An author cannot live on royalties that are generated by such limited editions. Because of this starvation income, only a small number of authors can survive by writing as a fulltime occupation.

If an author obtains a small edge in sales over his competitors, the publishing house then shifts the majority of its promotion budget to that author's books, at the expense of the house's other authors. This unequal promotion can turn an ordinary book into a best seller by having the title reviewed in newspapers and magazines in which the publisher purchases large-size advertisements for that title, and by having the books displayed prominently in bookstores. Other books are disadvantaged by receiving little or no promotion or advertisement, and the books are relegated to areas in the bookstores that are difficult to see.

A book whose cover is displayed prominently at eye level in a large and well-lighted showcase at the entrance of a bookstore, will sell far better than a book that whose spine is shown on the bottom shelf in a dimly-lighted back corner. Most bestsellers achieve that status by hype instead of by quality.

If a publisher sells 100,000 copies of two titles, it doesn't care whether it sells an equal number of each title, or 90,000 copies of one title and 10,000 copies of the other. But it *does* matter to the author whose title sells only 10,000 copies due to lack of promotion and advertising. Publishers and bookstores are becoming more like fast-food restaurants that sell millions of hamburgers but have a menu that is limited to half a dozen choices. What is important to a publisher and bookstore is the volume of sales, not an equal distribution among titles. If they had their way, they would print and sell only one title that every reader would buy and read over and over and over. This treatment of books as hamburgers produces an unhealthy diet.

The turnover of a mass-market paperback is six weeks. At the end of that time, unsold copies are stripped off the shelves and returned to the publisher, in order to make room for new titles that are speeding off the treadmill. If a title's delivery to a bookstore is followed by a spring flood, or by a mid-winter snowstorm and a lingering

cold spell, when readers are unable or unwilling to travel, the publisher does not take
weather into account as a cause for the lack
of sales. The publisher blames the author,
and that author is dropped from the publisher's list.

NO RECOVERY

A Time for Dragons was scheduled for
publication in 1989 – three *years* after its
acceptance. The sequels were scheduled for
publication at succeeding six-month intervals. The contract date for submission of
the manuscripts was determined by the lead
time that was required for copy-editing,
typesetting, proof reading, and so on.

About this time, Berkley/Jove reviewed
its lineup of forthcoming titles, and made
correlations with respect to the increasing
reduction in mass-market paperback sales.
Times were tough and were getting
tougher. Berkley/Jove decided to tighten its
belt. It did this by severely slashing the
number of manuscripts that it accepted, by
not accepting any manuscripts from new
authors, and by canceling contracts where
possible or practicable.

A publishing contract itemizes the obli-
gations of both the publisher and the author,
establishes terms of payment, and specifies
rights such as movie rights and reprint
rights. In essence, the author agrees to produce an acceptable manuscript by a certain
date, and the publisher agrees to print and
distribute the book by a certain date. The
contract is null and void if either party de-
faults.

After both parties sign the contract, the
publisher must pay the negotiated advance
to the author. An advance is a percentage of
anticipated royalties.

The advance is what protects the author
if the publisher fails to perform its duty to
publish the book; or, looked at another way,
the advance forces the publisher to publish
the book by the specified date, else it for-

feits the advance. Without a financial stake
in the project, the publisher could renege
on the contract by simply never publishing
the book, in which case the author could
not earn royalties, and is tied to a contract
that does not permit him to sell the manuscript elsewhere.

By the same token, if the author fails to
produce the manuscript on time, he must
return the advance in full. This is a great incentive to produce the manuscript.

Berkley/Jove was so oversubscribed with
contracts in a failing marketplace that it
started a policy of canceling contracts if the
author was so much as one day late in submitting a manuscript. In cases in which the
advance was small, Berkley/Jove wrote off
the money as an acceptable loss. This was
the sad state of publishing affairs when I
was under the gun to produce two sequels.

I worked every day – including Thanks-
giving, Christmas, and New Years – until I
completed both manuscripts. The day after
I completed Dragons 2, I commenced
Dragons 3 without a breather.

The book market reached a new low
from which it never recovered. People in
the publishing industry were hoping that
the dip was merely a trough in the sine
wave of business profits and loss, and that
sales would recover after the initial glam-
our of videotape rentals wore off. But just
about when a new balance was achieved,
along came the Internet. Almost overnight,
housebound individuals joined forums and
chat groups or simply surfed the 'Net to see
what wonders it contained. So fast did the
Internet consume the world that only one
year transpired between the questions "Do
you have e-mail?" to "What is your e-mail
address?" – the latter assumption being that
everyone had an e-mail address just as
everyone had a phone number (and today, a
cell phone number).

In genuine déjà vu, every minute that a
person spent on the Internet was a minute
that he didn't spend reading. The Internet
was the death knell for the publishing in-

dustry as a profitable business for everyone concerned. Publishing houses stayed alive only by means of massive mergers. Whereas in the 1980's a literary agent could submit a manuscript to dozens of flourishing publishers, today there is only a handful. All the independent paperback companies have been gobbled up by publishing conglomerate. Once a first reader who is fresh from high school rejects a manuscript because she doesn't care for it or its flawed female characters, no subsidiary division within the conglomerate will look at it.

Ironically, there are more books being published annually now than there were twenty years ago. This skewed statistic fails to account for the fact that the majority of books are published by small presses that cater to targeted markets. Except for a few so-called bestsellers, print runs are miniscule. Subject matter has shifted from fiction to nonfiction.

Most authors write only part-time, and earn a living from a real job or two. Hardly any authors can afford to work fulltime at their craft.

Literary agents work on commission, generally receiving 10% of the advance and royalties that are generated by each of her clients. I saw the handwriting on the wall when Jane Butler took a part-time job at a small-town diner in order to make ends meet. Then she started dropping her less productive authors.

This was how the book world ended, not with a bang but with a whimper.

THE ABORTED CONCLUSION

After all my manuscripts were submitted, I had to deal with the proofreading process. This should have been a painless job of correcting minor spelling mistakes and typographical errors. But, as I noted above, the publishing industry is run largely by amateurs – people who are uneducated in their field, but who gravitated to the job by the

lack of qualifications for more exacting work.

I will provide only two examples of the inanities that I had to endure. Ginjer objected to my capitalization of Earth when the word referred to the planet. She held her ground (so to speak) until I explained in sarcastic detail how the name of a planet was a proper noun, such as venus, mars, jupiter, and saturn; and that capitals or upper case letters were used for the names of streets, town, states, provinces, countries, continents, and, larger than all of them, planets; whereas earth with a lower-case "e" referred to Dirt or Soil. These examples got my point across but didn't win any brownie point for correctness.

She misinterpreted Death Wind's age because I gave it in the Indian fashion: in moons instead of years. Moons equate to months, but I had to explain the difference between the synodic month and the sidereal month. The synodic month is the length of time between one full moon and the next full moon: approximately twenty-nine and one-half days. The sidereal month is the length of time that it takes for the Moon to make one complete orbit or revolution around the Earth with respect to the background stars, ending in the same apparent location in which it began: approximately twenty-seven and one-third days. To most observers, the obvious "moon" is the synodic moon.

Once I jumped these proofreading hurdles, the books were cast in ink.

In most trilogies, the first two books leave the reader hanging: ending in the middle of the story with nothing resolved. This kind of trilogy reads more like three parts of single book. I have always thought that this was a cheap way to force readers to buy subsequent books. I designed my books so that the plot devices in each one were resolved at the end of the book, and the story ended with a satisfying conclusion with no loose threads. I began each sequel by introducing new information on which the next plot revolved. For example, it was the diamond engagement pendant that Scott gave to Jane the furnished the plot for Dragons 3. The diamond that Scott recovered at the end of Dragons 3 would have provided information that led to Dragons 4.

Every one of my science fiction stories and novels is based on an imaginative concept. This concept constituted the driving force for the plot. As already noted, the concept in *A Time for Dragons* was the explanation for the cause of the Great Dying at the end of the Cretaceous. The book can be considered as a juvenile because I purposely selected young characters as the primary protagonists; their imperfections were tempered by Doc's mature wisdom. Although I wrote the book for an adolescent audience, it works just as well on the adult level.

The concept in *Dragons Past* was the explanation for the breakup of the hypothetical supercontinent Pangaea to form the continents of Laurasia and Gondwanaland. The casing of the Dragons' fusion reactor was constructed of iridium in order to account for the iridium layer in the worldwide stratum that designates the end of the Cretaceous. I introduced additional characters, and had the original characters become more world-wise as a result of events and experiences. The establishment of sexual bonds moved the story away from adolescent attitudes. My intention was to influence those adolescents who read the first book into growing along with the characters. A subordinate imaginative concept was evolution of mammal stock from the litter of protomammals that Jane saved from death and released before leaving the Cretaceous.

No Future for Dragons was the most sophisticated volume in the trilogy. Read in sequence after the first two volumes, I gradually drew my readers into the intricacies of time paradoxes by means of philosophical and contemplative dialogue between characters who speculated on the possible outcomes of their actions in disturbing the flow of the time stream. This set the stage for the concept that there are forks in the steam, and that one may take a fork that contradicts the course of known or observed events. I demonstrated the concept by introducing complicated loops in time, first in discussion and then in actual conduct.

Two subordinate imaginative concepts were the origination of Homo sapiens, and the domestication of wolves to breed dogs. These helped to increase the complexities of time travel paradoxes. In continuing with my penchant for comic relief, I incorporated a host of punning phrases and clichés.

The astute reader with a scientific background will have noted some inconsistencies with respect to the geological record – or, at least, the way the geological record is presently construed. Geology and astronomy are two scientific disciplines whose fundamental attributes are constantly changing. Unlike other sciences, whose underpinnings can be repeated in a laboratory, geological and astronomical "facts" are based upon the interpretation of observed evidence or phenomena. Interpretation is subjective and open to change. I have seen many changes since I studied geology and astronomy as a teenager, particularly with respect to geological ages and stellar evolution. A great deal that is "known" is actually speculation, some of it unfounded or unsupported by any kind of evidence.

In the context of currently accepted geological interpretations, the Cretaceous ended approximately 65 million years ago (or before present). In *A Time for Dragons*, it ended 60 million years ago. If Pangaea actually existed, it was supposed to have split in two before the Triassic (248 million years ago), not 60 million years ago as in *Dragons Past*. Cro-Magnons were postulated to have evolved in the late Paleolithic, not before the Paleolithic as in *No Future for Dragons*.

These differences between so-called fact

and science fiction were neither casual nor accidental. I knew all these geological time estimates because I was a geology major in college. I was unable to complete my formal education because I was drafted between semesters. Due to my abiding interest in all matters scientific, I continued my studies by reading science books throughout my civilian life.

I intended to account for these geological disparities in the sixth book in the series.

As in the three published volumes, each of the three unwritten books was driven by a unique imaginative concept. I outlined the continuation verbally with Jane and Ginjer. Ginjer did not reject my idea for a series, but she wanted to wait for the sales reports of the trilogy before she committed herself to more sequels.

Jane wanted me to finish the series in five books, because she thought that two additional sequels would be easier to sell than three. I objected on artistic grounds. Each book was driven by a major concept. To finish the series with two additional sequels would upset the balance of the series. Then she wanted me to finish the series in four books. This would mean dividing the fourth book into three sections, each of which would utilize one of the three major concepts. Or, I could ignore the concepts behind Dragons 5 and 6. Again I objected on artistic grounds.

By way of compromise, a fourth contract was generated and dated the same as those for Dragons 2 and 3, but it was not executed. Under Subject Matter Description, Jane wrote: "The follow-up and concluding book in the trilogy that began with *A Time for Dragons*, *Dragons Past*, and *No Future for Dragons* continues the story of the efforts of a small band of humans to wrest control of planet Earth from the grip of reptilian alien invaders – who are revealed to actually be from Earth's past!"

This contract established my intent to produce a fourth book in the Time Dragons series. When the time came to execute the contract, Jane could then pitch the idea to produce three more sequels instead of one.

Dragons 1 and 2 were published in 1989. Dragons 3 was published in 1990. On January 28, 1991, Ginjer sent me a note that read, "The first three *Dragon* books have done reasonably well, so I think a fourth might be a viable idea. Why not send along a proposal *via* Jane and we'll see what we can do."

In my proposal, I enumerated the imaginative concepts in Dragons 1, 2, and 3. "The concept of Dragons 4 is the creation of life on Earth some two billion years ago: life that eventually evolved into dinosaurs and dragons, then mammals, and finally the human beings who, through conflict with the time-vaulting dragons, ultimately became responsible not only for their own creation (as in Dragons 3) but for all creation.

"No new characters are introduced in Dragons 4. The book begins with Scott and Rusty in the present; both are several years older than when we left them in Dragons 3, and both have children. Doc is dead; or rather, he was dying prior to the opening scene in the book, when he was close to revealing some truths he learned by studying dragon crystals, and was 'frozen' in a dragon stasis block because he found that it could have curative powers; however, he does not reveal how it cures. When the time comes for Scott and Rusty to revive him, they decided to visit the past and let Sam unfreeze him, partly because he is a doctor, partly because he has already done the procedure (he unfroze his wife at the end of Dragons 2).

"Scott and Rusty arrive in the past just as the colony there is attacked by dragons, who are seeking to destroy the human race right at its inception so they cannot evolve into the creatures who eventually caused the death of the dragons. Although it is unknown at this point in the book, the dragons have come from the far future – two billion years in the future, a time to which survivors of the previous holocaust have escaped when they realized that they were losing the battle in the Pleistocene. They did this not by making consecutive 60-million-year jumps but by devising a new method of long-range time travel whose method is unknown to the band of humans. The dragons never invented the incremental vernier that Rusty developed, and are still stuck on the million-year time tread. In order to discover when the dragons came from, and to track them through time, they must capture one of the attacking flyers and access its computer.

"Meanwhile, Death Wind is captured during the first attack, as he approaches an area where the forest (indeed, even the land itself) has disappeared, leaving a gaping hole in its place. He is taken into the future, thus forcing Sandra to leave her children in the Pleistocene in order to rescue her husband, along with Scott, Rusty, the newly revived Doc, and others. As an interesting side effect of Doc's stasis, not only is he cured of disease but his limp is repaired and his hair begins to darken as he appears to have become younger, healthier, and stronger.

"After capturing a dragon flyer, Rusty learns how the dragons sent their marauding flyers through time without using space-based stations as they had always done before. The dragons have learned how to punch through time by utilizing the principle of 'every action has an equal but opposite reaction.' Thus, they travel two billion years into the future by transferring an equal mass two billion years into the past – like one player running from first base to second while another runs from second to first. This accounts for the missing forest.

"The humans ride the capture dragon flyer through time, but through an accident of phasing, travel two billion years into the past – although they do not know this when they arrive. They find a barren, lifeless world of rock and unbreathable atmosphere – the Earth primeval. Eventually, Doc figures out their error, and they jump four billion years into the future, right into the center of the newly established dragon city.

"The rest of the action takes place then and there. The band of humans must attack and overthrow the city. During the course of action they discover what Doc has feared all along, that the reason the dragon stasis machine restores health is because distilled essence of life is infused into the stasis process – and that the essence of life comes from living human beings whose consciousnesses have been sucked out of their brains like a vampire sucks its victim's blood; and that the human victims must be alive during the process, and therefore feel their minds being disintegrated, a mental pain more painful than any physical pain, or equivalent to being tied down as minute animals eat a person's body alive cell by cell, until death finally ensues. This explains why, in the beginning of Dragons 1, there were many instances of dragons capturing humans instead of killing them off; and why, in Dragons 3, Scott's and Rusty's people, among others, were found frozen in the Pleistocene – not to be revived simply as slaves for the performance of menial work, but as host consciousnesses for dragon leaders.

"At the end of the final battle, the humans 'dump' all the surviving dragons into the past, where they die, and where their organic tissue gives rise to the creation of life on Earth.

"The action purposely ends two billion years in the future, where all the issues are resolved prior to the humans going back in time to the present in order to rejoin their families. This gives me a lead to begin Dragons 5, should it ever come about. In that case I can have the returning heroes find that their people have been captured by a rogue band of dragons who managed to escape the end of Dragons 4. I have not tried to develop the plot of Dragons 5, only the concept – in which the far future Earth (that is, the actual planet 20 billion years in the future) is transferred into the far past (20 billion years) through the same process described above, and results in the additional mass that triggers the explosion of the Big Bang and begins the formation of the universe."

I deceived Ginjer with the ultimate imaginative concept. I really intended to divulge this information in Dragons 6. The penultimate concept for Dragons 5 was to be sling-shotting the Earth some 5 billion years into the past in order to destabilize the sun enough for it to cough out the planetary system. At the time, I just wanted her to buy the proposal for Dragons 4. I planned to negotiate for Dragons 5 and 6 after 4 was published.

My title for Dragons 4 was *Untimely Dragons*. My title for Dragons 5 was *Timeless Dragons*. I never created a title for Dragons 6.

It was during this time that the publishing industry crashed. As is typical in the industry, Ginjer did not have the courtesy to reply to my proposal. That was her way of saying that she did not intend to accept it.

Jane tried to market the second trilogy to other publishing houses, but none wanted to publish a sequel whose predecessors were controlled by a competitor.

According to the terms of the contracts, if Berkley/Jove let my books go out of print, I had the option of submitting in writing a request that the company reprint them. If the company failed to do so within six months, then upon my notification, the publishing rights reverted automatically to me. I exercised this option in hopes that another publishing house might reprint the original trilogy once the books were free and clear, then give me a contract to produce the other three. This never happened.

FROM BEGINNING TO BEGINNING

Until now, I am the only one who knew that there was a grander design in the saga of the Time Dragons than was apparent to readers of all three published volumes. As far as anyone else knew, I provided a satisfying conclusion and tied up all the loose threads at the conclusion of Dragons 3. Yet I intended to explain the origin of practically everything in the universe. The central character and chief instigator in all these originations was Doc. At the conclusion of Dragons 6, I proposed to make the implication that Doc was equivalent to God the creator – in essence, creating himself as well as the universe and everything within it.

Dragons 1 was a straightforward science fiction novel that concluded with a simple time paradox. The paradoxes kept getting more complex as the series progressed. Despite my proposal for Dragons 4, I planned to withhold until the final volume the revelation that the dragons' actual purpose in capturing human beings (which was part of the premise in Dragons 1) was to extract their biological essence (instead of keeping them as slaves). No one could have guessed this concept or even seen it coming.

I never wrote any sample chapters of the proposed three volumes, but I jotted down notes as ideas popped into my head. These ideas would have fleshed out the storylines. Some notes were snatches of dialogue, some were time-related puns, and some were circular time twists that I hoped to weave into the action sequences so as to provide conceptual food for thought.

For example, the human survivors eventually learn that the dragons sought out and destroyed Maccam City, as well as the Nomads and Sandra's community, because they already knew that the rockets that destroyed their North American outpost must have been launched by a group of outlaw humans. That was why the increased pogrom activities were initiated before the beginning of Dragons 1. The dragons were trying to locate the origin of the rockets.

It was not a flyer from the outpost that destroyed Maccam City, but a flyer from a future time base that had gone back in time before the outpost was destroyed, in order to find and destroy the rocket center at a time previous to the destruction of the outpost – thus effecting prior retribution and ultimately preventing the outpost's destruction. One might ask: in this scenario, why didn't the dragons in the flyer warn the outpost inhabitants that they were soon to be attacked? One answer is that the dragons sincerely believed that they could succeed in destroying (or preceding) the rockets; another is that they feared to create an obvious gap in the time stream.

Rusty figures all this out in a later book and, after saving his people at the end of Dragons 3, he goes after the flyer that destroyed Maccam City. He knows its direction of travel because he and Scott spotted it in Dragons 1. It develops that this must have been the flyer that went through time to save the outpost, but Rusty destroys it before it can accomplish its mission, thus leaving the way open for the five warriors (Doc, Scott, Rusty, Death Wind, and Sandra) to destroy the outpost as they already did in Dragons 1.

In actuality, the increased dragon activity first started twenty years before the commencement of Dragons 1, when Doc departed from Sam and Helen. It was this flyer's peregrinations that compelled Doc to embark on his odyssean search for ways to combat the dragons.

In Dragons 4 or 5, I intended to have the human time travelers dispose of the death bombs that they found in the glacier stronghold (in Dragons 3) by sending them far into the past. This would account for the previous Great Dyings.

In Dragons 5 or 6, I intended to have dragon-operated flyers engage in temporal and aerial combat with human-operated flyers. As they skip through time, some of

them were spotted in 1947 and afterward, accounting for the first and following sightings of flying saucers and unidentified flying objects. (That was why I described the dragon flyers as disk-shaped.) One flyer is destroyed as it emerges from time over uninhabited territory in central Russia in 1908; the atomic blast accounts for the Tunguska event that leveled a sizeable portion of the forest. Another flyer is destroyed over the cities of Sodom and Gomorrah, resulting in their destruction as recounted in Genesis.

I intended to make other biblical references. After landing in ancient Israel and receiving help from local citizens, Doc convinces Scott and Rusty to take one of them for a ride in the flyer. The chosen one is Ezekiel, who later writes in Hebrew a detailed description of his encounter with "angels" and his experiences in flight. He is forced to describe objects and events for which his language does not have words. His story is later incorporated into the *Bible*.

In repairing their flyer, the human warriors leave behind a damaged dragon battery pack and capacitor, whose discharge accidentally kills people at a distance. The inhabitants interpret the laser beam as the wrath of God. This discarded unit comes to be known as the Ark of the Covenant.

I kicked around the idea of having Rusty crucified. He doesn't die on the cross, but either loses consciousness or feigns death after suffering great privation. Three days later, a human-operated flyer rescues him from the cave in which he was interred.

I hoped to explain the biblical account of Adam and Eve by having Scott and Jane go back to a previous time in order to live on their own. A lone dragon scout tracks them down and tricks Jane into bringing Scott out of their hideaway, in the belief that the flyer was being operated by their friends. The dragon is defeated, and comes down through history as the tempting serpent.

I also hoped to explain the biblical account of Noah by having Rusty and Britt and their children gather a bunch of Pleistocene mammals into a flyer, and take them to a new location (in either space or time) in order to start a new colony after the flood that was caused by the melting of the polar ice caps toward the end of the Ice Age.

At Doc's suggestion, Death Wind paints pictures of bison and other mammals on the walls of a cave, thus giving rise to ancient caveman art.

Not to lose the sense of humor, after Doc is defrosted in Dragons 4, he sees an ancestor of the modern horse, and comments, "What equanimity." Everyone cheers in the knowledge that the old Doc is back, because only the Doc they knew and loved would make such a pun. When he asks Scott what they are doing, Scott replies, "We're just killing time." Rusty says, "You're in for the time of your life."

As noted above, I intended to keep the best till last. Although I implied in the beginning of Dragons 1 that the inhabitants of Maccam City were killed by corrosive gas, I disclosed near the end of Dragons 3 that the inhabitants were actually captured and placed in hibernation. Not until the penultimate chapter in Dragons 6 did I plan to reveal the true reason behind the dragons' motive for capturing humans: that the vitalistic essence of the mammalian cerebrum was crucial to providing the curative solution that dragon VIP's needed to heal sickness and restore youth – the path to immortality. The notion of humans as living chemical factories was to be the climax of the series.

The geological anomalies were to be revealed in the final chapter in Dragons 6. After our heroes' temporal peregrinations, Doc speculates that their tampering with the streams of time created branches or offshoots that resulted in multiple timelines whose simultaneous existences were not mutually exclusive. In other words, there was one timeline in which the Cretaceous ended 60 million years ago, one in which it

ended 65 million years ago, and others in which it either ended at different times, or never ended. The same is true of the breakup of Pangaea and the evolution of Cro-Magnon. Thus my intentional inconsistencies with "known" facts are explained.

The last page of Dragons 6 finds Doc returning to his home in Washington only weeks or months after his original departure (decades prior to the beginning of Dragons 1). His treatment in the restorative bath has returned his body to its youthful condition. After traveling back and forth between the extremes of time, and effecting the changes that resulted in ridding his present-day world of the dragons from the past, he can finally allow himself to enjoy the new life that has been bequeathed to him – and which he, as the primary instigator of subsequent events – was largely responsible for creating.

In the last heartfelt scene, Doc is reunited with his wife – and they live happily ever after.

Doc explains to her, "Time is not like a river, as I once believed, but more like an infinite whirlpool: returning again and again to its multiple points of origin."

LOOKING BACKWARD - AND FORWARD

As I've written elsewhere, one of the greatest satisfactions that an author can receive is to have his books read and appreciated by the multitude. The Time Dragons trilogy is my most widely read and appreciated science fiction.

Lynn Adams, a grade school teacher in Wilmington, North Carolina, told me how one of her students was showing an unusually intense interest in his textbook one day – an interest that he had never shown before. She ambled around the room and walked up behind him. When she looked over his shoulder, she saw that hidden inside the pages of the textbook was *A Time for Dragons*. He was so absorbed by his extracurricular activity that he did not hear her approach. Adams refrained from chastising the student, because she was so glad to see that he was showing an interest in reading, even if the book was not part of his study program.

Everyone I've ever met who has read one or more of the Time Dragons books has told me how much he or she loved them. But the aspect of the books that people always praise is the action. No one – not a single person – has ever so much as mentioned the imaginative concepts on which the books were based.

I have always been greatly disappointed by the fact that my imaginative concepts have not been appreciated. Creative ideas are what science fiction is all about. My creative ideas are what I cherish the most about my science fiction. In that regard, I have never found the contentment that I hoped to realize with my writing.

Nonetheless, I have other imaginative concepts rolling around in the back of my mind. I intend to continue to put them down on paper. Perhaps someday, someone will read one of my science fiction stories or books, and say, "What a nifty idea."

I can always hope.

Geological Time Scale

(mya means "million years ago")

Cenozoic Era
(65 mya to present)

Quaternary Period (1.8 mya to present)
 Holocene Epoch(10,000 years ago to present)
 Pleistocene Epoch (1.8 mya to 10,000 years ago)
Tertiary Period (65 to 1.8 mya)
 Pliocene Epoch (5.3 mya to 1.8 mya)
 Miocene Epoch (23.8 mya to 5.3 mya)
 Oligocene Epoch (33.7 mya to 23.8 mya)
 Eocene Epoch (54.8 mya to 33.7 mya)
 Paleocene Epoch (65 mya to 54.8 mya)

Mesozoic Era
(248 mya to 65 mya)

Cretaceous Period (144 mya to 65 mya)
Jurassic Period (206 mya to 144 mya)
Triassic Period (248 mya to 206 mya)

Paleozoic Era
(543 mya to 248 mya)

Permian Period (290 mya to 248 mya)
Carboniferous Period (354 mya to 290 mya)
 Pennsylvanian Epoch (323 mya to 290 mya)
 Mississippian Epoch (354 mya to 323 mya)
Devonian Period (417 mya to 354 mya)
Silurian Period (443 mya to 417 mya)
Ordovician Period (543 mya to 443 mya)
Cambrian Period (543 mya to 490 mya)

Precambrian Time (from the formation of the Earth 4,500 mya to 543 mya)

Nonfiction

The Popular Dive Guide Series
Shipwrecks of Massachusetts: North
Shipwrecks of Massachusetts: South
Shipwrecks of Rhode Island and Connecticut
Shipwrecks of New York
Shipwrecks of New Jersey (1988)
Shipwrecks of New Jersey: North
Shipwrecks of New Jersey: Central
Shipwrecks of New Jersey: South
Shipwrecks of Delaware and Maryland (1990 Edition)
Shipwrecks of Delaware and Maryland (2002 Edition)
Shipwrecks of Virginia
Shipwrecks of North Carolina: from the Diamond Shoals North
Shipwrecks of North Carolina: from Hatteras Inlet South
Shipwrecks of South Carolina and Georgia

Shipwreck and Nautical History
Andrea Doria: Dive to an Era
Deep, Dark, and Dangerous: Adventures and Reflections on the Andrea Doria
Great Lakes Shipwrecks: a Photographic Odyssey
The Fuhrer's U-boats in American Waters
Ironclad Legacy: Battles of the USS Monitor
The Lusitania Controversies: Atrocity of War and a Wreck-Diving History (Book One)
The Lusitania Controversies: Dangerous Descents into Shipwrecks and Law (Book Two)
The Nautical Cyclopedia
Shadow Divers Exposed: the Real Saga of the U-869
Shipwreck Heresies
The Shipwreck Research Handbook
Shipwreck Sagas
Stolen Heritage: the Grand Theft of the Hamilton and Scourge
Track of the Gray Wolf
USS San Diego: the Last Armored Cruiser
Wreck Diving Adventures

Dive Training
Primary Wreck Diving Guide
Advanced Wreck Diving Guide
The Advanced Wreck Diving Handbook
Ultimate Wreck Diving Guide
The Technical Diving Handbook

Videotape and DVD
The Battle for the USS Monitor

Outdoor Nonfiction
Wilderness Canoeing:
     the Adventure and the Art

Fiction

Science Fiction
A Different Universe: Tales of Imagination
A Different Dimension: More Tales of Imagination
A Different Continuum: Early Tales of Imagination
Entropy (a novel of conceptual breakthrough)
A Journey to the Center of the Earth
The Mold
Return to Mars
Silent Autumn
The Time Dragons Trilogy
    A Time for Dragons
    Dragons Past
    No Future for Dragons

Sci-Fi Action/Adventure Novels
Memory Lane
Mind Set
The Peking Papers

Supernatural Horror Novel
The Lurking: Curse of the Jersey Devil

Vietnam Novel
Lonely Conflict

Visit the author's website for availability of titles:
http://www.ggentile.com

www.ingramcontent.com/pod-product-compliance
Lightning Source LLC
Chambersburg PA
CBHW060942030726
47503CB00003B/693